# Caledonian Road

ANDREW O'HAGAN

# Caledonian Road

faber

First published in 2024
by Faber & Faber Limited
The Bindery, 51 Hatton Garden
London ECIN 8HN

Typeset by Typo•glyphix, Burton-on-Trent, DE14 3HE
Printed in the UK by CPI Group (UK) Ltd, Croydon, CR0 4YY

Permissions credits: Emily Dickinson, 'Not Knowing When the Dawn Will
Come' from *Poems by Emily Dickinson: Third Series*, Todd, Mabel Loomis,
ed.; Roberts Brothers 1896; Traditional, 'In And Out The Dusty Bluebells';
Ted Hughes, 'Mayday on Holderness' from *Lupercal*, Faber & Faber Ltd,
1960. Reproduced with permission; John Bayley, introduction from *Pushkin
on Literature*, Aleksandr Sergeevich Pushkin, Tatiana Wolff. Northwestern
University Press, 1986; page xxxvii. Reproduced with permission from Curtis
Brown Group Ltd on behalf of the Estate of John Bayley; Ruth Padel, from
*We Are All from Somewhere Else*, published by Vintage. Copyright © Ruth
Padel 2012, 2020. Reprinted by permission of The Random House Group
Limited; Frank Fraser Darling, *Island Years, Island Farm* by Frank Fraser-
Darling, Little Toller Books, 2016. Acknowledgements and thanks to the
publishers and the descendants of Frank Fraser Darling; Ralph Ellison,
*Shadow and Act*, Vintage International, 1995, Copyright 1953, 1964 by Ralph
Ellison. Acknowledgments and thanks to Random House, Inc. and Professor
John F. Callison, literary executor of the estate of Ralph Ellison.

A CIP record for this book
is available from the British Library

ISBN 978-0-571-38135-7

2 4 6 8 10 9 7 5 3 1

for
Lindsey

'After a certain distance, every step we take in life
we find the ice growing thinner below our feet, and
all around us and behind us we see our contemporaries
going through.'

Robert Louis Stevenson

# Cast of Characters

**Campbell Flynn** – 52, art historian and celebrity academic
**Elizabeth Flynn** – 54, a therapist, wife of Campbell
**Angus Flynn** – their son, a DJ
**Kenzie Flynn** – daughter, a former model
**Jake Hart-Davies** – a 24-year-old actor
**Atticus Tew** – Campbell Flynn's literary agent
**Mirna Ivoš** – Campbell's London-based editor and publisher
**Moira Flynn** – Campbell's sister, 50, QC and MP
**Sir William Byre** – Campbell's best friend, retail tycoon
**Lady Antonia Byre** – William's wife, notorious columnist
**Zak Byre** – William and Antonia's son, environmental activist
**Milo Mangasha** – a student, lives on Caledonian Road
**Ray Kennedy** – Milo's dad – 50, cab driver
**Zemi Mangasha** – Milo's late mother, a teacher
**Mrs Voyles** – 70, the Flynns' sitting tenant
**Candy, Duchess of Kendal** – Elizabeth's sister. Nickname: Nighty
**Anthony, Duke of Kendal** – Candy's husband. Nickname: Snaffles
**Emily, Countess of Paxford** – Elizabeth and Candy's mother, 86
**Travis Babb** – Milo's best friend, drill rapper, aka Ghost 24
**Vicky Gowans** – William Byre's girlfriend, 23
**Ashley-Jo Abbot** – Kenzie Flynn's partner, fashion designer; aka A.J.
**Izzy Pick** – head of the Monastic fashion house
**Liang** – her assistant
**Aleksandr Bykov** – Russian oligarch, approaching 60
**Yuri Bykov** – Aleksandr's 24-year-old son
**Heidi Mae Adkins** – Campbell's American publisher

**Devan Swaby** – aka **Big Pharma**, 22, friend of Milo and Travis

**Lloyds** – real name **Jeremiah Beckford**, friend of Milo and Travis

**Gosia Krupa** – Milo's girlfriend, 25

**Bozydar Krupa** (aka Boz and Bozy) – Gosia's brother, 35

**Mrs Krupa (Cecylia)** – Gosia and Bozydar's Polish mother, 62

**Andrzej Krupa** – Cecylia's husband, died 2001

**Feng** – the alias of a lynchpin human trafficker

**Stefan Popa** – Romanian, fixer and head of security for Yuri Bykov

**Jakub Padanowski** – 28, from Białystok

**Robert** – 22, Jakub's boyfriend

**Mr Hazari (Babar)** – Jakub's landlord in Leicester

**Rupert Chadley** – editor of the *Commentator*

**Nicolas Lantier** – Yuri Bykov's Belgian art dealer, 30

**Lord Scullion of Wrayton** (Paul) – Labour peer, 65

**Lord Haxby of Howden** (Colin) – Tory peer, 43

**Carl Friis** – Danish artist, Lord Haxby's husband

**Tara Hastings** – reporter at the *Commentator*

**Sluggz** – rapper, lives in Deptford, real name **Sebastian Legland**

**Astrid** – Angus Flynn's girlfriend, chutney heiress

**Mr Skene** – the Duke of Kendal's lawyer

**Professor Jennifer Mearns** – Head of English Department, UCL

**Professor Gwenith Parry** – teacher of Life Writing, UCL

**Mrs Frisby** – housemistress at Framlingham College

**Bishop Cree** – from Diss in Norfolk

**Fergus** – wellness assistant at Hinderclay House

**Fatos** – human trafficker

**Gerry O'Dade** – haulage driver, in his 20s

**Charlo Sullivan** – haulage driver, in his 20s

**Aasim** – manager of a Leicester garment factory

**Shah** – Aasim's son

**Sun Zetao** – architect from Beijing

**0044** – gang member, real name **Damon Taylor**

**Cassie Tom** – English supermodel

# BOOK ONE
## Spring

# 1 Piccadilly

Tall and sharp at fifty-two, Campbell Flynn was a tinderbox in a Savile Row suit, a man who believed his childhood was so far behind him that all its threats had vanished. He had secrets and troubles, yet out of the cab window St Paul's was shining on Ludgate Hill and the angels of London were on his side. On reaching Shaftesbury Avenue, he inhaled his own scent, the faded peaches of Mitsouko, and looked up at the buildings. 'A reborn dream,' the marquee said above *Les Misérables*, and he enjoyed the sensation of applause. Oh, the progress of guilt and vanity in the average white liberal of today. Campbell didn't take people half as seriously as they took themselves, which was the first of his huge mistakes, the second being the proof copy he carried that day in his briefcase.

At Piccadilly Circus, he passed under a giant video advertisement, pink-haired Korean boys dancing in the sun, which slid to a second, 'Own the Streets', promoting training shoes. Campbell stared through the glass roof of the cab, thinking of Elizabeth happy in the countryside while he had to deal with the hazards of city life. He liked to believe that what experience had given him was a habit of self-control. The driver's GPS panel said, 'Thursday 20 May 2021. Temperature: 16°C. Bright then showers.'

The cab stopped at Hatchards. His modern biography of Vermeer had been published during lockdown and had given him a profile that stretched far beyond his field. He could remember a few passages from the reviews word for word. 'It is rare in the history of art biography to see a pure enigma so vividly etched out of the darkness,' *The Times* said. 'A work of mesmerising empathy,' the

*Financial Times* called it, 'engaging with the soul of art itself.' His book appeared to its many readers to argue that unknowability is an essential feature of the artistic life, and perhaps all lives. He had also become a little famous among the young on account of a BBC podcast that often went viral, *Civilisation and Its Malcontents*, a deep dive into the era's shallows, and yet the worry he carried with him almost constantly was about money and his failure to be as well-off as he should be.

After signing a mound of his magnum opus, with its debt to reality, improvisation and surmise, he left Hatchards and was walking towards the corner of Fortnum's, when he saw, coming towards him, Yuri Bykov, the son of the crooked Russian businessman Aleksandr Bykov. He had met him several times at social functions, and he was walking with the actor Jake Hart-Davies, a handsome young man he'd seen in magazines and on TV. The actor was taking up a lot of space on the street, or so it seemed, and how it always seems, with people interested in their own privacy.

'Hello, Professor Flynn,' young Bykov said. Elegant, camp, with short, peroxided hair, he introduced the actor and they all shook hands. The pair had just been to the London Library and were carrying books on Shakespeare. 'Bit of a project,' Hart-Davies said. 'We're going down the mineshaft of human experience.'

'How lovely,' Campbell replied. He looked at Bykov. 'I'm amazed you've got time for plays, what with buying up mansions for your old man.'

'You are *hil-ar-i-ous*,' Yuri said, with a swoosh of the hand. Harrow had given him a rattling English accent, but his mind was Russian.

Neither seemed to notice the rain, especially the actor, who was wearing a T-shirt saying 'Redundant' and caressing his own biceps. It stayed with Campbell, that certainty and confidence, and how turned on he was by himself. He was quickly reminded that the Russian knew his son from school. 'Angus, *oh my God*,' the fellow said. 'What a legend. And your daughter, such a beauty!'

'Thank you, I suppose.'

Campbell knew all the stories: how this kid had always wanted to break from his corrupt, Putin-fearing father to form his own circle. One of Campbell's oldest friends was William Byre, a businessman caught up in a worsening financial scandal. Byre's son, Zak, had gone to Oxford with some of this same set. It was a small world and all the tales had come hurrying back down the M40, of partying and experimenting and being hog-whimpering drunk. Not Zak, who was now an intelligent, passionate advocate of Extinction Rebellion, and too much derided by his parents. He said that Yuri had only got into St John's because his father funded a chair in Climate Change Studies. 'If pollution was an Olympic sport,' Campbell remembered Zak saying, 'Aleksandr Bykov would be Usain Bolt. Faster than anybody, Bykov is killing the planet stone dead.'

Yuri was smiling like he owned a few secrets. 'I was at a party in São Paulo where your son was on the decks. *Fantastisch*,' he said.

'Good-oh. He certainly gets around.'

Campbell looked at his watch.

The actor said they were going over to Yuri's place in Albany to dump the books before heading out to lunch at Oswald's on Albemarle Street.

'It was nice to meet you,' Campbell said.

'Let's have a drink one evening,' Jake said.

'Why not,' Campbell replied, taking a last good look at him.

The rain suddenly got heavier. He turned towards his destination and plucked a thought from the petrol-tainted air. He looked back over his shoulder at the young men, and the actor looked back too. There was a sense of serendipity in the exchange and Campbell began to toy with an idea.

It was a point of principle with Atticus, Campbell's agent, that he always had the table in the right-hand corner, Lucian Freud's old table, and Campbell spied him as soon as he walked into the Wolseley.

Atticus smiled and folded away the *New Statesman*. Campbell sat down, placing his briefcase in the corner. 'I would shake your hand,' Atticus said, 'but my wife's still paranoid. She's American.'

'I know,' Campbell said. He could always be free with Atticus and saw it as a benefit of their professional friendship. 'She put gold taps everywhere in that Bloomsbury cottage in Sussex that you bought for too much money.'

'That isn't true,' Atticus said. 'It was Nicky Haslam.'

'I don't believe you. Nicky does dog baskets shaped like Bedouin tents, but he doesn't do Qatari. Have you ordered?'

Atticus Tew was sixty-one and always looked exactly the same. Campbell knew for a fact that he regularly got his highlights done at Jo Hansford in South Audley Street. He had seen him there one day, a lively flotilla of silver rectangles all about his head. Campbell loved Atticus's tycoon-bookworm look – custard cords and plaid shirts from Harvie & Hudson, knitted ties and tweeds, as if he'd recently stepped off the grouse moor. Campbell listened to his agent's familiar run-down of the menu, drinking a syrupy glass of champagne while taking in a few nods and waves from across the room. The digital artist Carl Friis and his husband, Lord Haxby, craned round.

'How's your beautiful Elizabeth?' Atticus asked.

'She's got empty couch syndrome,' Campbell said. 'She misses her clients and says it's all a performance on Zoom.'

It was day three of the reopening. The staff were still wearing masks. Campbell and Atticus always had the same thing, a way to show their basic equality: escargots à la bourguignonne au pastis, steak tartare and fries, a bottle of the Pauillac de Lynch Bages, 2016. Atticus dipped a crust in his wine, he was oblivious like that, and asked what was in Campbell's briefcase. 'You said you had something for me. Or something for the world, Sporty.'

'Let's have our lunch first.'

'Well, I must tell you that essay you wrote in *The Atlantic* has gone around the world six times. "The Art of Contrition". Liberals are feeling uncertain about how to be sorry, about how to be real while feeling a bit guilty. And here you are, calling attention to the self-indulgence of it all.' Atticus pulled a cutting from his pocket. It was an op-ed from the *New York Times* published the day before. '"The writer is a Humanities hero," the columnist says, "a podcast warrior, using art criticism in the way intended by the great Matthew Arnold: to argue about life. He uses his learning to question everything from Adam Smith to vampire novels. Teenagers have cats and capybaras mouthing his words on TikTok." Then he quotes you: "We participate in the systems that oppress people, we thrive on them, and we think that by going on festive marches and tweeting slogans to our like-minded friends we are somehow cleansed. Welcome to the orgy of white contrition."'

Campbell was delighted to hear his own plain speech coming from the mouth of his highly regarded agent. 'Strong stuff,' he said.

'Well, you've got everyone sitting up.'

'My students are, I'll tell you that.' Campbell paused. 'And it's been like that for quite some time. *They're* teaching me.'

'How interesting.'

'Liberal cowardice is as bad as every other sort.'

'Yes of course, Sporty.'

'And I wouldn't cut my conscience to suit the fashion of the times, as the lady said.'

'Just take some time to breathe,' the agent replied. 'You're not quite as untouchable as you think you are, if you don't mind me saying so.'

Campbell lifted his glass and tilted it to his lips.

He sometimes had to ignore Atticus.

'I need to earn more. Lizzie tells me I spend money like a drunken sailor . . .'

'Your wife has only one vice,' said Atticus. 'She forgives you too easily.'

Money: an English mystery seldom unravelled. Campbell and his wife never really spoke about finances; they made a pose of pretending it was all rather silly. When they got married, they bought a small house in Belsize Park, which quintupled in value. Then Elizabeth inherited the country house from her father. She and Campbell kept separate bank accounts, and had a shared one for bills and school fees. It worked well enough. When they decided to move to the grander house in Thornhill Square, they used all the money from Belsize Park plus a private loan secured by Campbell. She was impressed by his talk of book and broadcasting deals, so he never got round to admitting the loan had come from William Byre (she'd never liked him), and that he was paying it back, incrementally, in the hush-hush manner of the gentlemen's club, with interest, in a painfully private way. That was the situation. That, and the fact that he'd stopped paying his taxes. Elizabeth had a small trust, and the money came in from her psychotherapy practice, and from Campbell's work, but it was an odd convention of their marriage, almost sexual in nature, that money was off-limits. It panicked him to think of telling Elizabeth. It was embarrassing, and it blended with a near mortification that Elizabeth retained from childhood. She'd grown up around invisible money. She had no interest in her mother's wealth, and was amused by Campbell's liking for the Countess, but the truth was he looked to his mother-in-law for a future of convenient security.

Atticus always behaved towards his clients as if everything was about to be redeemed. He spoke about offers that had come in. Campbell was half listening and looking over his agent's shoulder into the room's social pattern. Carl Friis, he thought to himself, the artist over there, has to be an international paragon of artistic pre-tension. The young Dane was talking vigorously. One of his hands with all of its rings was hanging off the table. 'You know that man over there,' Campbell interrupted.

'Who?'

'Carl Friis. So-called digital artist.'

Atticus tore off some bread. 'Yes,' he said, 'but I haven't got the first clue what digital art actually is.'

'The work's non-fungible. It means you can't hang it on a wall. You get a token and it goes on the blockchain.'

'The what-chain?'

'Never mind.'

'Sounds like trickery to me,' Atticus said.

Campbell lowered his eyes. 'He wrote an article for the Tate's magazine arguing that the destruction of Charles Rennie Mackintosh's School of Art in Glasgow was a work of art in itself. The *destruction*.'

'That's a terrible thing to say.'

It was strange: Friis was one of the people Campbell had got to know better because the guy meant something to his children. Rule for life: never compete with your children on relevance. For *Artforum*, Campbell had once gone with Friis to a hillside in Switzerland where an artist called Not Vital had built a house that could mechanically sink into the ground. The image remained with Campbell, sitting in the dark, descending into the hill, with Not Vital's smile and Carl Friis's eyes shining out.

'Oh God. He's coming over.'

These people all stride as if they're on a catwalk, Campbell thought. He commanded his face to make a smile. 'I don't like to interrupt,' Friis said, 'but, my friend, your *Atlantic* article blew me away.'

'Well, thank you.'

'We're all looking for a way out of this horror. *Society*, I mean.' Campbell spent a millisecond pondering how 'society' is a word deployed only by people who never meet anybody who isn't the same as them. 'I'm dying to tell you about a show I'm doing this year,' Friis continued. 'It's for the Gagosian and will undermine all beauty. That's the idea. Beauty is dead. Gone. Good riddance to all beauty. *Heaven*, no?'

Campbell felt unusually alive. Outrage does that to a critic.

'So, it will *exist*, your show?' Atticus asked.

Friis's hands were spinning. 'It's gonna be, like, the biggest ever exhibition of damaged art. Like, fire-damaged Impressionists, waterlogged landscape canvases. Totally delightful! I'd love you to write an essay for the catalogue, Professor Flynn. When the time comes. October.'

'Let's see.'

The artist, it seemed, was wearing glitter on his eyelids. He bounced his palms together and went back to his husband, who was on his mobile. Lord Haxby was a supposed hero of the Conservative Party in the North of England.

Campbell couldn't quite achieve a balance in the way he felt: one minute he thought he might keel over with pleasure, the next, the ground was opening up. 'I have a student,' he said, 'who has an instinct for questioning our morality.'

'That's the sole mission now of *every* student,' Atticus said.

'I find him interesting.'

The agent coughed. 'We were talking about money.'

'Oh, yes. Bills.'

'*Harper's* magazine wants a regular column. And Stanford has been on about a series of lectures next year.'

'Maybe. Probably not. I need something new.'

Atticus took out another piece of paper. '*New York* magazine is proposing a contract for more fashion pieces.'

'You know I've got this gig tomorrow. Kenzie got me involved.'

'The fashion house, yes. That man at *T Magazine* and the new person at *Vogue* say the designers love the stories you wrote for them.'

'Atticus, it's not a compliment. These designers have never met anyone who doesn't talk all day about hemlines, accessories and Beyoncé.'

'True, true,' Atticus said. 'It is unusual, your interest in style.'

There was a small percolation of regret. 'My mother liked clothes,' he said. 'She sewed for a living.'

'Bred in the bone,' Atticus said.

Campbell fidgeted.

'Fashion editors think if you write anything longer than a tweet you should be awarded a Nobel Prize.'

'I'm simply passing on the requests, Sporty. You told me your aim is to increase your earnings—'

'That's a must. I'm running a global operation on a freelancer's income.'

'It's not a bad income.'

'Two houses, Attu.'

'True, true.'

'Islington, Suffolk. The bills! The *loans*. You know Angus earns tens of thousands a night, just for being at a party?'

'He's a DJ. That's what they do.'

He liked his kids having worlds of their own and cash that wasn't his. Or maybe the last bit was difficult. Unlike him, they'd had plenty to start off with, all that *drive* behind them, and now they were miles ahead of their father. At these times, money-talk times, he tended to think of his wife's brother-in-law, a rich man and an awful person. Campbell stiffened and looked at Atticus with the affection of years. 'You've met this brother-in-law of mine, haven't you?'

'Yes, of course. His Grace.'

'The Duke of Kendal. A fraud in every respect.'

'I won't argue with you.'

'My sister was supposed to be on a Commons select committee into Russian corruption.'

'How is Moira?'

'Relentless, as ever. She had tabled a few questions in the House. Then she recused herself from the whole business because his name came up.'

'Jeezo. The Duke?'

'Nothing is proved. Just rumours.'

Atticus paused and took a swig. 'I remember him. Tartan trousers. Infernal oaf. Terrible teeth. The wife runs an organic farm.'

'Yes.'

Atticus began to speak of other offers. A documentary for HBO. A couple of after-dinner talks on the Queen Mary 2 from Southampton to New York. 'They could certainly bring in sizeable fees to help with earnings.'

'That's just it – I'm sick of *earnings*.'

Looking towards the entrance, Campbell saw a blue tourist bus, and, ever so privately, noted a kink in perspective, the room seeming suddenly larger and the space a yawning chasm. These occasional spatial problems, the dizziness, a lack of solidity, they were recent new features, here in the empire of his middle age. 'Well, as you know, I've felt the need for a brand-new project.'

'New is good,' his agent said.

'I have to do this thing tomorrow – Monastic, the fashion house. I have to give them a bit of language for their new campaign. Shetland wool and weaving and oil rigs or whatever. Then there's the perfume meeting. They're determined I should come up with the name they put on the bottle.'

'For the scent, yes. That's the money bit.'

'And then I'm clear, right?'

'Nearly. For the product launch next February, they want you to do an interview for American *Vogue* with the English supermodel.'

'Cassie Tom.'

'That one.'

'And then it's the end, Atticus? Over. *Finito*. It was fun and it kept me in touch with the kids, but that's enough now.'

Campbell grazed the briefcase. He ordered two glasses of Calvados. He knew the one: Dupont 1988. He felt odd about bringing out the proof copy. 'I should be writing about Rembrandt and mirrors.'

'Are you sure you don't want your name on it?' Atticus asked. He pointed to the briefcase. 'It's by Anonymous?'

Campbell waited. 'What do you think of it?' he asked. 'As a *genre*.'

'Self-help is not writing, it's healing. Or publicity. And it's bloody lucrative. The *New York Times* had to create a separate bestseller list for these books. I'm reading one at the moment, *The Heroic Stoic*. Marvellous. Makes a ten-act opera out of having a piss.'

'That's what interests me at the moment. You know when such books sell, they never stop. But I'm also interested in it as a kind of art experiment.'

'I get it,' Atticus said. 'You're getting a big cheque. It's for the money' – he counted on one finger – 'and it's an art experiment' – then a second finger – 'and you like the thrill of having a secret.' He lowered his voice. 'You want to have it all ways, Campbell. All authors do. It makes sense.'

Campbell drew the advance proofs out of his briefcase. He fiddled with the corners, flicked a few pages and handed it over.

'The Americans are leading,' Atticus said, taking it. 'They're fixing a cover and say it will be ready when the editor's finished. So, in ten days' time. They're moving fast.'

'Well, I wrote it in six days.'

Atticus looked at the cover of the proofs and read out the new title. '*Why Men Weep in Their Cars*.'

'That's it,' Campbell said.

Atticus had a touch of the venerable English army officer. He didn't wish to control reality, measure it or resist it, but just to see it through to the end. '*The Crisis of Male Identity in the Twenty-first Century*,' he read.

'Mirna likes that subtitle,' Campbell said, 'but the Americans don't think it's very "self-help". They're coming up with something better.'

'Righto.'

Campbell felt a bit uncertain. 'Do you think it's all right?'

He didn't expect Atticus to respond to that. He never let Campbell feel that he either approved or disapproved of what he did.

'Well, I wasn't sure about offering it to Mirna,' he said. 'It's really not her kind of thing. I mean, they're too posh for this, as a house. No offence.'

'None taken. But the truth is they need something commercial.'

'Yes.'

Atticus rolled the Calvados around as if it were mouthwash. He said he wasn't sure about not having an author on the cover. He said he wasn't experienced in this field, but wasn't it better to have a pseudonym or something?

Campbell put both hands on the table. 'Well, I've had an idea. Just today, actually. I know we don't have much time, but what if the publication was fronted by a good-looking actor, someone well known who could play the author?'

'Like, touring it around and doing the TV?'

'Yes. We could coach him. Make him plausible. Give him lines. He'd be the ultimate sensitive bloke and we'd put his name on the cover.'

'Pick the right man and it will sell a zillion copies,' Atticus said.

# 2 Office Hours

He dipped down towards Piccadilly Arcade. He had the time, but he stopped himself from going into Budd to ask about handmade shirts, striding on and pausing at the window of T.M. Lewin in Jermyn Street, as if he were conducting an experiment in parsimony, to match his thoughts. As he sifted through the ties, he knew the truth. Campbell would continue persuading himself that his secret book was a ripe and playful intellectual riposte to the times they were living through, but in fact he'd just needed the money. He lived with his duplicity as if it were an energy. He failed to see the danger in any of it. He had identified a daft and rather current subject with *Why Men Weep in Their Cars*, a subject he had immediately commodified to his own advantage, hoping it would be the huge bestseller that might relieve him.

'Do you have it with a thinner stripe?' he asked the sales assistant in Lewin's before settling on a spotted tie instead.

Thinking about the book had drawn him to young people, and he was now thinking of the possible usefulness of that actor, Jake Hart-Davies. He almost resolved to go round to Oswald's club and put the book proposal to him right away, then he thought better of it and continued towards Haymarket.

It was three o'clock. He sat on a bench in Soho Square to smoke a cigarette, across from the mad statue of Charles II by Caius Cibber. Butterflies chased each other round the top of the statue, a pair of holly blues. He loved London in May, when the long, cold winter suddenly vanished. He took out his phone: thirty-three emails. All boring. He put in his earbuds and clicked one of his mindfulness apps. He had four: Calm, Headspace, Buddhify and ThinkUp. It was all nonsense, but he liked nonsense and wasn't going to abandon it just as he was about to join the ranks of the self-helpful.

*Why Men Weep in Their Cars.* Out in three months.

It was a good title: a money title, Atticus was right.

He chose ThinkUp – 'personalised affirmations and motivations daily' – and listened ten times to a recording of his own voice saying, 'I am grateful for the good in my life.' You could place piano music over it, and it was lovely to feel tranquil sitting on a park bench next to a yew tree at the end of spring. In his mind, there stood an image of the perfect vase of yellow tulips and he dwelled on it, so simple and so fresh. But Campbell knew he would never reach those flowers, and he began to know why. Something in his life was off, and he felt that he was steering gradually towards a precipice. Atticus spoke of that *Atlantic* essay as some sort of cause célèbre and major success, but Campbell knew why he'd written it: because he knew he was a thinker in danger of becoming *thoughtless*. At fifty-two, he knew himself to be a traitor to the class of his youth and a freak to his own moral understanding. You can't live your life being celebrated for beautifully preaching what you will never practise, and this was the certainty that had begun Campbell's trouble. He'd always written rather blithely about goodness, truth and harmony, but hadn't he, in actual fact, travelled far from these things, and had he any choice now but to find his way back? He knew that hypocrites live on by defending their position against outward reality, but that year, that season, Campbell knew that he could no longer get away with it in his own conscience.

A text from his sister appeared on the screen, so he stopped the app and sat up straight. It was a link to a news website. 'A powerful committee of MPs has warned that the government is putting national security at risk by allowing kleptocrats and human rights abusers to use the City of London to launder money they are keen to get out of the reach of the Kremlin.'

He called his sister back. 'I can't talk for long,' Moira said. 'I have to go into the chamber and vote. It's the new Police Bill.'

'What's that all about?'

'Making provision for the police to arrest more people. Tory nightmare.'

'Where are you?'

'Portcullis House. I'm walking. You?'

'I'm heading into the department. Office hours.'

He was always impressed by Moira's command of the moral stratosphere. She'd been like that since she was ten, two years younger than him, commanding the forces of municipal possibility from a high-rise in Glasgow, before going on to join the Labour Party under Neil Kinnock. She continued as a QC, still fighting the odd housing case, but was generally preoccupied at Westminster on behalf of her narrowly held constituency in Ayrshire. She was 'beside herself', she often said, about City corruption, and felt that Campbell's social world, his mixing in high company, was an unfortunate by-product of his otherwise terrific marriage into Elizabeth's aristo family. But Campbell knew she didn't hold it against him: she liked his writing and his jokes, while doubting his politics. He was liberal in a bohemian sense, and she'd given up trying to recruit him, knowing that only the honours committee could attract her brother to the Palace of Westminster. They shared a wealth of Glasgow patter and deep memories – 'too deep for tears', she'd sometimes say. Nobody really understood it, except his sister, and, now and again, Elizabeth, but Campbell was straightforwardly terrified of ever returning to poor conditions. The fact sat very uneasily with his also having an *amateur de luxe* side the size of the Place des Vosges.

'Did you see it? Your brother-in-law is for the high jump if he doesn't watch himself,' Moira said down the phone. 'There's big trouble coming down the pipe.'

'Let it flow, let it flow, let it flow,' Campbell said. 'Elizabeth says he probably had a narcissistic personality disorder in the womb.'

'Very good. Well, his coat's on a shoogly nail. Half the people in London – at those old boys' clubs you like going to, the ones that hate women – had better watch out because the party is over for them.'

'I applaud your excitement,' Campbell said. 'But you know better than I do, Moira. They'll simply move the party to another venue.'

'I hope you're *wrang*,' she said.

She sounded ten years old again.

He loved their relationship, the embedded trust.

'I'm well out of it,' she said. 'Serving on that committee would have been a nightmare. They're also talking about Russian money being hidden in loans to UK retailers.'

His stomach lurched. 'And William?'

'Byre? Mentioned,' Moira said.

He worried about the extent of his old friend's financial mess. And he worried that it all went still further. He could never say so, but anything involving William exposed a raw nerve in Campbell. He felt *involved* in his financial story, because he'd borrowed from him, and he loved him, his student brother in ink and wine. Campbell had begun to wonder if his own values might be tainted.

He changed the subject, reaching for something that might allow him to feel he was floating above things again. 'I saw my agent for lunch. Talked about this new, quick book I've done. Mirna sent me a proof copy and we're whooshing it through.'

'The Rembrandt book?'

'Not yet,' he said. 'Something a bit different. I don't think Mirna's in love with it. An odd one – about the state of men.'

'Holy mackerel,' she said. 'A book about men? So . . . not an art book?'

'Just for fun,' he said. 'Yet it might be the truest thing I've ever written.'

Moira hummed in that way of hers, spelling out her doubts.

'You're like an artist yourself,' she said. 'Artists are always looking for new bits of themselves they can sell.'

He told her he'd bumped into the actor Jake Hart-Davies on Piccadilly. 'He was with that Bykov kid, the one Angus and Kenzie know.'

'Oh, shite,' she said. 'The *company* your children keep!'

Campbell paused for a second.

'Good-looking, Hart-Davies, in that rather too much way. Weren't his rellies all painted by Augustus John?'

'I've seen his face in magazines.'

'He was on that show, *Aethon's Curse*.'

'I really have to go, Campbell.'

'Okay, Moy.'

'Angus was in touch about the plan for your birthday. I'll see you then.'

She always said 'bye' several times in a row before hanging up.

The spring rain was back, a smirr of the oily past.

He headed towards the English Department at University College. He didn't have many duties there, not by normal standards. His course on 'Culture and the Self' had attracted students from everywhere, but he ran it as a series of lectures and didn't do any marking. The department was empty at the best of times, a sort of ghost village, the chief residents remaining inside their offices in a state of fear that they might be asked to teach, or maybe they were filling out grant applications in the hope of having a year off, or sharpening their pitchforks for the next march into town, or revising for the forty-sixth time a draft of an essay on 'George Eliot and Real Estate' for the *Cambridge Quarterly*. Campbell had taken the job because he liked the idea of having lively, candid colleagues, and the opportunity to test his sense of reality against the determinations of twenty-year-olds. And the money didn't hurt. But here he was in this empty corridor. 'Watch it,' a worldly friend of his had told him. 'Professor of Box Sets, or whatever you are. Podcast king. The academics will see you coming and will hate you instantly, Mr *New York Review of Books*. Mr Bestseller about Vermeer. They've got special rifles for shooting high-flying flamingos.'

Campbell picked up his mail and took out his key. He passed a poster for a conference on Christopher Marlowe. Spotting a party in the corridor, he realised it *was* a party: they were discussing Virginia Woolf. He heard the phrase 'secondary grief' and put a hand out towards the wall, his ears suddenly needing to pop. 'Hello, gentle colleagues,' he said, turning sideways. 'Only passing through.'

'Ah, Campbell Flynn. Rare to see one in the wild.'

Some people genuinely draw out the satirical impulse, and nobody in Campbell's life did this more than Jennifer Mearns. Crimson-bobbed, lover of Victorian shoes, blamer of men, head of department: to say Jennifer was a correctness vigilante would be to miss the main thrust of her propagandistic life. She had searched the universe (and the world's archives) for evidence of famous writers making sexist remarks in or around the year 1888. She had lately moved on, and was eating up days, nights, weekends and research grants, completing a book called *Foreign Children*, devoted to the idea that James Barrie, the author of *Peter Pan*, was a blood-thirsty racist and a pederast. So far as anyone could tell, Jennifer had never laughed out loud. She was rumoured to have drunk a single gin and tonic sometime in 1986. Now she was in charge of the Wastepaper Subcommittee, an actual thing, set up to ensure that no one would harbour in their offices any bin-like receptacle. They were banned (wasteful). 'I suppose it would be difficult for a wastepaper bin *not* to be wasteful,' Campbell once said.

'Bad for the environment!' she'd replied, unsmiling.

Campbell hoisted his mail under his arm and prepared for his evisceration. 'You won't be surprised to know,' she said, 'that I found your infamous *Atlantic* essay abhorrent.'

'Naturally,' he said.

'More than that: it was divisive, Professor Flynn.'

It hurt his face, trying to not smile. Behind her, with its perennially open door, was Jennifer's cold, pristine office, a place of sharp edges and gleaming steel, devoid of all trivial encroachments, particularly fabric and paint.

'Your colleagues put work into opposing stereotypes, when it comes to humans of colour, and then for you to make fun, in the crudest terms, of the guilt we feel about the way our institutions have denied and erased these people for hundreds of years. Well. Who are you to cast aspersions on intellectuals recognising important historical wrongs?' Her voice had gone quite high. 'That diatribe you published was, to my mind, ill-written, badly researched, and showed a dreadful lack of supporting evidence, by which I mean footnotes and the like. We have experts in this field, Professor Flynn, yet you choose to publish a screed of unsettling opinion posing as respectable fact.'

'Respectable fact?'

'That's correct. Aren't you ashamed?'

'I am, Jennifer. May I call you Jennifer? I'm deeply and abidingly ashamed for using my brain in such a wholly independent way.'

He walked on. The young lecturer standing next to her had scarcely cracked a smile, which was disappointing. Campbell had a natural regard for him, chiefly based on his authorship of a rather vivid paper, 'Fogles, Tickers, Traps and Prigs: Dickens's Deployment of Street Language in *Oliver Twist*'. But like all modern academics, the young fellow had become an expert on where the power lies. Like Mearns, he knew how to enforce general laws as if they were personal, which is what, among other things, made them such effective police-persons. 'I'm warning you for your own good,' Mearns hurled at Campbell's back as he turned the corner to his office. 'The faculty can't protect you!'

Campbell's office was like a club room designed by Matisse. It had Edwardian tapestries and Bloomsbury lamps sitting on tables from Heal's. The red Melaka rug came from a sale of the belongings of Bunny Roger. The green teapot had been a present in the 1990s from Anne Yeats, daughter of the poet. Next to the window, Campbell had rested an odd collection of teacups, dainty and blue or patterned with flowers, which sat with a stack of red cake plates from Liberty.

The walls were covered in prints by Scottish engravers and photographers of the nineteenth century, along with a small oil painting by David Wilkie. After Professor Mearns's cheerless lair, students were surprised by Campbell's yellow bookshelves and his drinks trolley, from which, in a direct steal from Anthony Blunt, he often served them whisky in crystal tumblers.

He had twenty minutes. He opened letters, all from publishers, festival organisers or haters. He put the professional ones in a tray, chucked the others into his illegal bin, then opened the packages. Two of them were advance copies from art publishers seeking blurbs, and the third and fourth were from AbeBooks: a second-hand copy of *Shadow and Act* by Ralph Ellison and an anthology of African poetry. He placed the art books on a shelf and sat down with the other two. He didn't get far past the dedication page of the Ellison, then laid the books down in his lap and stared at a framed photo. It was of his mother and father, sometime in the late 1950s, wearing light summer clothes, laughing with their heads thrown back. They were with friends on the Isle of Man, and it had always fascinated Campbell, the unknown joy that came from them in the instant that picture was taken.

He took out his phone and tapped an app: Ancestry. He'd been linked the other day to prison documents about a Glasgow ancestor, Francis Flynn, who was tried for beating someone to death with a poker in the Saltmarket. He turned his phone to examine a record from 1875, scrutinising the faded script. Hearing keys jangling, he opened his door and saw Gwenith Parry, the Professor of Life Writing, across the hall. She was his ally. They now and then shared jokes about their colleagues.

'So, what are you writing, Gwen?' he asked.

'I've spent the last few months on this piece,' she said, 'something long and probably fruitless about Zola and Henry James.'

'Stop being so bloody productive.'

'And you?'

He would tell the truth in good time. 'Another deep dive into the nonsense of now,' he said. 'My ruin, I suppose.'

He closed the door and counted to ten. 'Society ought to be taken by four corners like a tablecloth and tossed in the air,' a card on his bookshelf said.

There was a knock and when he opened the door it was Milo Mangasha, his favourite upsetter. As a student, he was more nervous than he appeared, but he could manufacture confidence. He stared a lot, had Irish eyes and brown skin, and a way of resisting every assumption you might make about him. He had come to Campbell for an extra class while he was doing a Computer Science MSc, and submitted jittery, ambitious papers.

'It's my birthday soon. Day they murdered George Floyd,' he said as Campbell offered him a chair.

His earphones were clasped around the neck of his red puffa and Campbell asked what he was listening to. 'You should avoid certain things,' the boy said. 'Say no to algorithmically generated playlists.'

'I've never met one in the flesh.'

'Spotify tells you what to listen to.'

'I see.'

He took his jacket off. 'Do you listen to music, and stuff like that? You got to find your own, Professor. It's not only the words – lyrics, whatever – it's about the attempt to transform musical space, decolonise it.'

'What if you just want to dance?'

'You can dance. Yeah. You married?'

Cocky, Campbell thought, raising an eyebrow.

That May, the young man didn't know much about him yet. He would ask these direct questions, obviously fishing.

Milo made a kissing sound, then looked down. His thumb moved in a flurry over the screen of his iPhone.

'You're defined by what you *reject*, know what I'm saying?'

*Everything* was a question.

23

'This Kenyan guy, KMRU. Defiant. Private, yeah? He records bunches of stones falling down a well and, like, drones over a tin roof. Puts the sounds into his computer and sets it up so cool in your mind like that.'

Some of the things he said, extraordinary comments in passing, had begun to lodge themselves in Campbell's mind. For example: *Obsessing over failings of speech is a cynical distraction from looking at the system of injustice that really controls our lives.* Or: *Virtual selfhood is the freedom you never found.* Something about that phrase, 'virtual selfhood', snagged on Campbell's conscience, and he'd been left wondering about it for weeks.

Campbell turned the kettle on and took his newspaper out of his briefcase, laying it down on the coffee table between them.

'As soon as something terrible happens,' the student flew on again, 'the Left and the Right run to purify themselves, condemning the guilty parties, who are always the parties they *expect* and wish to be guilty. Meanwhile, the systemic problem remains untouched. People will take down a politician any day, it makes them feel alive, but they won't touch the system of oppression that they are part of themselves, know what I'm saying?'

'I think I do,' Campbell said.

He wasn't sure if Milo was really that together, or playing at it.

'It would be sweet,' he said, 'if people got a bit more practical in their politics.'

Campbell liked that notion. 'Yes. Instead of enveloping ourselves in theory we could tackle actual problems, inequalities. Like the pandemic. It exposed unfairness and it dramatised how unfairness works in this country.'

'That's true,' Milo said, and paused. 'Truer than you know.'

To Campbell, he seemed a little shaken. The off-hand mention of Covid had pulled Milo up short and tapped an emotion.

'Are you okay?'

'Nah man, I'm good,' he said, 'but I've seen things.'

Sometimes a young person can give the young person still alive in you a second chance. The boy was working class, like Campbell used to be; the young man wanted to *act* – and Campbell felt it keenly during the office hour, how a fresh association might replenish him and force him to embrace the change that frightened him.

'How come we've ended up with one of the worst death rates in the world and no one's ashamed?' Milo said. 'Prime minister's a clown, yeah? He makes a joke comparing himself to the mayor in *Jaws* and how he's gonna be keeping the beaches open. It's black people dying out there.'

'I don't think the government knows its own people.'

'Something like 40 per cent of people who live in London weren't born here. And they're still acting like it's Rule Britannia.'

'I tried to say that recently, in *The Atlantic*.'

The student smiled, a sort of dangerous, knowing smile, the one he'd flashed once or twice during previous office hours. 'I see you're a hero to yourself. I read that article. You didn't go far enough.'

He was being marked down.

'Your academic friends think it's about the *terminology*. They think if they police the words then the world is gonna be all right.'

'Writers have to apologise for choosing the wrong word.'

'I've never met anyone who gives a fuck about that. What they notice is police corruption, unfairness, hardship. It's about real change.'

Milo stood up to look at the bookshelves and a row of box sets. He always seemed to be showing off in the way he inhabited a space. Campbell glanced at the boy's coursework folders laid on the floor and could see the labelled dividers: 'Cybersecurity', 'Pattern Recognition and Neural Networks', 'Cryptocurrencies'. They were nothing to do with him, were part of Milo's proper course – his assessments were coming up – but Campbell felt he needed a tutorial. He wanted to understand these unfamiliar and intriguing subjects. It could be helpful for an article, or maybe something more personal down the line.

'Feels weird,' Milo said. 'I'm coming to the end of my time at uni, and I feel like . . . I'm only now ready to learn. I want to rip up the rules and walk about in other people's shoes.' He looked down at the carpet, shyly. '*Other people*,' he said with emphasis. Maybe he was a bit more intimidated than he seemed – but he spoke fluently still, reaching for a way to amplify himself. 'When it comes to stories, appropriation doesn't exist,' he said. 'Art exists, and bad art exists, and new thinking exists, and old. Whether it's a black writer looking at a white man or a white playwright hearing black voices, the only thing that matters is how good it is and how fresh.'

'That's a very humane thing to say.'

He flashed his smile. 'Well, it's the Humanities, isn't it?'

He could make a good teacher, Campbell thought.

'I've got an idea,' Milo said.

He wanted to interview Campbell for the university's literary magazine, *Suppose*.

'Sure,' he said, suggesting they meet the following day at the National Gallery in Trafalgar Square. He wrote the time and the room number on a piece of paper and handed it to Milo as he got up from the chair.

'Cool,' the boy said, picking up his folders.

# 3 Thornhill Square

**M**rs Voyles was yearning for a blast of summer warmth. Not that anything of the sort was ever guaranteed in England, but she could hope, and you haven't run out of everything if you still have hope. The ginkgo tree was in full leaf. Green and mysterious, she thought, like a fortnight's tour of China, and she examined it from the bench and thought of all the different aspects the tree had possessed during her forty-four years in the square. It was golden in autumn with a puddle of leaves that glowed in the dark. She liked the gardens best at the end of the day, as it was now, the bushes heavy with sunshine. She remembered spending time in that square with the other dancers when she was young. People knew how to put nice weather to good use then – but that was before everything changed. She could still see the girls in their pink tights as the boys lifted them across the grass.

She knew her rights. That was the phrase that occurred most often to Mrs Voyles, and she said it many times a day, usually when coming up the steps of her basement flat at 68 Thornhill Square, where she was a sitting tenant. She said it again as she crossed the narrow road from the gardens that evening, undoing the chain she'd bought at her own expense, wrapped several times around the wrought-iron gate. There used to be lovely people here. Islington was a different place in those days.

She was on her steps, looking towards the church at the north of the square, when a taxicab came rumbling to a halt and her landlord got out. Thought he was somebody, *Professor* Flynn. Mickey Mouse academic. She could teach him a few things about painting and good books. She had piles of them indoors.

'Good evening, Mrs Voyles,' he said. 'I see you're still consorting with that terrifying chain. Gruesome object. I've offered a thousand times to have a proper lock installed on that gate of yours.'

'It's not my gate, as well you know.'

'Well, I won't argue the point, Mrs Voyles.'

'There's a smell down here.'

'I daresay there is. You won't let anybody in to clean.'

'It's your pipes that's the problem. And there's vermin! The scratching keeps me up half the night, and it's against the rules.'

'As you know, these are old houses, Mrs Voyles. I've made a dozen offers to renovate the basement flat, but you prefer complaining to the council. When I employ the workmen, you chase them away.'

'I know my rights.'

'And I know my responsibilities.'

Mrs Voyles extended her leg behind her. Yes, she'd been a dancer in her youth. She was seventy now, but she was proud still to get up the steps like a young gazelle. Flynn thought he was so different from other landlords, but she'd seen them all come and go, and they were all the same: their big windows, their 'housekeepers'. 'It was terrific round here,' she said, 'before you all came, with your Land Rovers.'

'Excellent, Mrs Voyles,' he said, walking up his own steps. He flicked the petunias in his window box and she knew he did it to splash her. She twisted round to shout at him as he struggled at the door with his keys.

'And don't be assaulting me with fetid water,' she said. 'I'm a protected tenant.'

'Good evening, Mrs Voyles!' he said without turning round, and disappeared between the white pillars.

After an hour he came back into the hall. He always needed to decompress from the fact of her existence. He would never work out why she got under his skin. She was getting on in years, she'd probably suffered some kind of sadness in her life, and here he was, *competing* with her. She was a not very nice neighbour who enjoyed the *Daily Mail*, but on every occasion his defensiveness and his irritation would rise up to meet her. With no effort at all, she could wind him up like a toy robot.

He thought of opening his Calm app, listening to water falling in Yosemite National Park, but resisted. He looked through the peephole and saw the rain was dripping from the trees and hitting the tarmac like sparks. Campbell believed all Londoners had a version of Mrs Voyles somewhere inside them, and perhaps he was fighting with himself when he thought he was sparring with her. One day, he would look back and see that he'd half created her. His wife said he felt motivated, for whatever reason, to construct their tenant as a wicked crone. She wasn't nice, Elizabeth said, but lots of people aren't nice.

He picked up some mail from the doormat and passed a small nude by Duncan Grant, done in ballpoint.

'Alexa – play Miles Davis,' he said to the kitchen dresser.

It played a fast one and he told it to skip.

'"Round Midnight".'

He always knew the time of day from the way the light fell in that long ground-floor room. At daybreak it came through the front window, looking east onto the square, falling on the kitchen table, and in the evening it flooded the floorboards at the other end, the sun standing high over the garden before slipping behind West London. He walked to the back window and looked down at the glowing peonies. By the stove, a pinboard held multiple photographs. Him, Elizabeth, the children. Surfing in Cornwall, dressed for a wedding, hollering over wine bottles under a pergola in Tuscany.

He took down a plate.

Chopped chicken salad.

Next to the olive oil, stuck to a tile, was a note written on a Manolo Blahnik notepad bearing a phrase in Elizabeth's hand, one of the many random messages she left lying around the house. He read it out.

'New perspectives on living through an artificial self.'

Then he heard it: the scratching below. He went out to the hall and could hear it more clearly, the scutter of rodents, a single sharp squeak from under the floorboards.

Back in the kitchen, he closed the door, breathed, opened his laptop, his email and clicked a link.

'Hello, darling,' he said when Elizabeth's face appeared. She was in Suffolk and they had agreed to have supper together on Zoom. He could see the fairy lights around the wood burner. Her lovely face was aged by spectacles on a chain. He was immensely proud of the cottage, a seventeenth-century thatched confection on the edge of Wortham Ling. The beams were scored and marked, the flagstones shiny with use. Elizabeth went there a lot by herself, to write and pootle in the garden, but Campbell loved it too – the long walks by the Waveney, mornings in his garden office.

'Turn that music off, Campbell,' she said.

'Alexa, *stop*.'

'It's funny what a different life you live when I'm not there. You turn the whole house into Greenwich Village in 1958.'

She was brilliantly particular. Nobody else in his life was like that. They'd been together thirty years and knew how to bring out the other's better nature. Having Angus and Kenzie hadn't altered their basic connection, which was to do with having an amused way of viewing the world, and it seldom failed them. They never got bored with each other, he felt, because they never assumed the other wasn't an individual.

'What's that you've got?' he asked.

'It's an omelette and a glass of wine. The old trusty. My sister sent a man over with a basket of mushrooms.' Elizabeth sat in front of a bevelled bookcase in the dining room. He knew the bookcase very well, and had filled it himself, but he hadn't quite noticed before, until seeing it from this angle on Zoom, that every volume shelved there was a biography. He studied it, feeling something. He wondered if it was the *echt* British literary form: the rounded life and its gracious telling.

'She took me all the way to Glyndebourne yesterday. We had a really lovely time. *Kátya Kabanová*, you know – Janáček. Dress rehearsal; invited audience. The story was totally about her, of course. She was in raptures. Poor Candy. She doesn't have it easy over there with You Know Who.'

'*My Extremely Hard Life* by the Duchess of Kendal.'

'Don't be mean, Campbell. She was always a sweet girl who liked the theatre and now she's married to . . .'

'The biggest crook in England,' he said. 'The biggest duke.'

'You can be so unkind sometimes,' she said.

She was like Maarten van Heemskerck's *Portrait of a Woman* (1529), the comprehension in her eyes, the perfect dimple in her chin, the blush. In a little box on the screen, Campbell saw his own blurred face next to hers, the lock of hair, his pale lips. Elizabeth's beauty was as permanent as a work of art, and his own face seemed temporary, a sort of mask.

'She was positively giddy yesterday,' she went on. 'We had drinks at the long bar and then lunch in that ugly room, you know, something Wallop. Ridiculous. That awful man Lord Scullion was there. It's all Anthony's world, not hers.'

'All these worlds are interconnected.'

'Then it was back inside for Act Three, more high drama along the Volga. Lots of sniffles from the Duchess, as you'd expect.'

'The long and delicious dream of social ruin.'

'Stop it, Campbell. We have to be kind about sisters. I always am about Moira.'

'That's because Moira's wonderful, darling. She works night and day for the poor, running from the frozen North to the House of Commons. Keeping the bloody Labour Party in touch with its core values.'

'Mummy always said Candy was marrying beneath her. I mean, up, socially – but beneath her in every other respect.'

'Never wrong, your mother.'

Elizabeth could always *go there*. It was one of the first things he'd noticed about her, back in 1987, when he met her at college, this poised, perfect girl. She had coloured shawls and smoked Gitanes. She had a set of the Complete Freud in her rooms. She had her own friends, her own dates, and she invented a marriage so unlike the one his parents had. Elizabeth acted as if their relationship, and their work as parents, was part of some bigger universe that could endlessly be probed and improved. She knew how to interrogate her feelings from a slight distance, even while having them.

'It's self-involved of me,' she said, 'but it's hard not to think these allegations against my family —'

'And my friends,' he said.

'—that it tells a bad story about oneself.'

'I don't think so,' he said. 'The upper classes have been behaving badly for so long they feel they are upholding tradition by continuing to do so.'

'Okay. But what about William?'

'William's in a different category,' he said. 'He's used money he shouldn't have. He'll fix it.'

'I like the way you make a special dispensation for your friend,' Elizabeth said. 'Your mirror friend. But my sister's husband is damned.'

'Well, it might not come out,' Campbell said. 'But Anthony is a total fool. *Russians.*'

They ate more supper and Elizabeth rattled off a few items about the children before there was a decent lull.

'I gave my book to Atticus today,' Campbell said.

'Oh, Campbell. I still can't believe you're actually looking to publish that. You're stepping into airport wisdom?'

'Not in my own name, obviously.'

'Oh, please.'

He pondered. 'It's not only cynical,' he went on. 'Atticus says I like the secrecy of it. He's right.'

'It's worrying you should enjoy that.'

Somehow, it came back round to William Byre.

'I'm seeing him tomorrow,' he said.

'Where?'

'At the Club.'

'May I offer you a note?' She didn't wait for a reply. Offering notes was one of the rights that came with their marriage. 'You can support him without feeling you have to justify anything he might have done.'

'What do you mean, Elizabeth?'

'There are rumours,' she said. 'It might be more than financial.'

Campbell hesitated. He was invested in his old friend not being as bad as people wanted him to be. 'As you know, I'm not with the vengeful puritans. But I'm not with the baddies, either. People who are paid to think really ought to do a bit of thinking.'

'Yes.'

'They ought to fire up their ambivalence.'

'Hmm. Not sure about that,' she said. 'We'll see.'

She told him that William's son, Zak, was in *Tatler* with his mum. 'Quite interesting, that boy,' she said. 'They don't give him enough credit, his parents, because they're *so* reactionary. Kenzie tells me Zak and his friends are forming a new action group called Insulate Britain.'

'Jolly good,' Campbell said.

'Don't be dismissive. He's a smart kid.'

'I agree. I'm all for young people supergluing themselves to railings. I just wish he'd wash his hair now and then.'

She sniffed. 'Civilisational collapse is quite possible. I think we should pay attention to the Zaks of the world.'

'Meanwhile,' Campbell said, 'his father's up to his neck in it.'

'It's going to be painful, estranging. They're saying he squandered his workers' pensions. God knows where it will end, but you should prepare yourself.'

Before she signed out of Zoom, she told him she'd taken a lot of mail to the country with her. 'There are more letters from the council,' she said, 'about Mrs Voyles.'

'I met her on the doorstep earlier. Moaning about smells and saying she's going to get us prosecuted.'

'Poor woman. She is living in a dungeon. We have to do something, Campbell. All the time it's getting worse.'

'She's living in one of the best squares in North London, Lizzie. The council has been paying her rent for decades. She's abusing her power as a protected tenant. She's got it in for everybody and is a self-pitying opportunist, the worst combination in the world. It's horrible coming home to your own house, eating a meal, going to bed, knowing there's this toxic little shrew down there.'

'Enough,' she said. 'I'll answer these letters. It's not a big deal. She wants a new boiler and she says her windows are leaking.'

'That's five grand right there.'

'Put it out of your mind,' she said. 'She's lonely. The council has assessed her flat and . . . it's our responsibility. They've served us with an improvement notice and we have to persuade her to let us do the work.'

Elizabeth was writing a book on Winnicott. She often tried thoughts out on Campbell when she was writing, but she didn't that evening, telling him to rest. Eventually, when that year had run its course, she would wonder if she hadn't been present enough, hadn't encouraged him to trust in the people who knew him.

After the call, he took the rest of his mail into the bathroom. Next to the sink was a framed letter from 'Oliver Everett, Esq., MVO, Buckingham Palace' to Campbell's late grandmother at Calton Sheltered Housing, thanking her and the other residents for the jumper they'd kindly knitted for Prince William on his first birth-day. The letter was dated July 1983. Elizabeth always laughed at him for reading in the loo: she saw it as a schoolboy habit, probably relating to cigarettes. Having opened the boring mail and set aside a programme from the Royal Society of Literature, Campbell dis-covered a posh envelope embossed in the corner with the emblem of the Gritti Palace in Venice. He recognised immediately the shaky hand of Elizabeth's eighty-six-year-old mother. 'Dearest Campbell,' it said. 'I'm at luncheon, vulgar to say, and have only this minute heard from one of these embassy people that you are to arrive here any second to take part in the literary conference. They scarcely deserve you. We are docked until Saturday 22nd, then it's up the road to Trieste. Come to supper and I will arrange a berth for you to stay overnight. You can fly home from Trieste the next day. If you ignore this I shall be very cross. Love, Emily.'

There was a thump at the front door. He quickly fixed himself and went down the hall.

Mrs Voyles was standing with a furious face. She was holding at arm's length a copy of the *Evening Standard*, supporting a dead rat. The fur on the animal was wet-looking and the smell was instantly apparent. 'This,' she shouted, 'was lying behind my boiler, rotting, I tell you. *Putrefying!*'

'For goodness' sake, would you put it down?'

She was levitating with rage. 'I have an order from the council. You might own this building, Mr Flynn, but you are not above the law.'

'Professor Flynn, actually.'

'I couldn't care less. I know my rights.' There followed a torrent of officialese: 'Food Safety', 'Damp and Mould', 'Electrical Hazards', 'Section 12 of the Housing Act', 'failure to comply'.

'But we're not failing to comply,' Campbell said calmly. He put the dead rat in his window box. 'We are in touch with Islington Council. We've told them we are more than happy to completely renovate your flat.'

'You are . . . you are . . .'

She was lost for words and he almost felt sorry for her.

'No, Mrs Voyles. You were a sitting tenant in the basement when we bought the property. We have tried repeatedly to arrange alternative accommodation for a short period, so our builders can do the work.'

'You want to change the locks.'

'Please calm down. Believe me, it's a delicious prospect, but you are protected by the law and we respect that.'

'You think you're a man because you can talk down to women? You're the big rich man upstairs, are you?'

'Mrs Voyles. I will not be shouted at in the street.'

'Ah, so you own *the street* now, do you?'

He slammed the door in her face.

He went to get another beer. He could hear her television. It throbbed through the floorboards, then the clack of her typewriter, a letter to the prime minister no doubt. He went up to the sitting room and lit a huge candle, a six-wicker, and things grew calm. He looked at the painting above the fireplace: *Boys Playing* by Joan Eardley. The broken tenements, those faces. It was the Glasgow of Alma and Jim, his parents' world, erased but always alive in Campbell's mind. His father had been dead over twenty years, and she'd lasted until 2018, a totem of unhappiness. She watched TV and sewed cushions, while making long-winded complaints about her children, especially Campbell, who dreamed of somehow rescuing her. Dad had been the same: he was always straitened, and his life seemed to close when his children left home. 'Well,' his mum had said to him one doleful Christmas, 'we worked our fingers to the bone to get you and your sister into the right schools, into the right universities. And we paid for it twice.'

'What do you mean, Mum?' he asked.

'We paid the fees. Then we paid by being left behind.'

It hadn't bothered him in the past, but now, over two years after her death, it had begun to bully him: a haunting sense that he had failed his mother and been worn down by her negative estimate, her belief that nothing in their lives had really worked out. He feared that he'd begun to blame his own children, just as he had been blamed. 'Mum and Dad didn't know how to live, poor dears,' his sister had said, 'and we had to make it all up by ourselves.'

He stared at the Glasgow painting, the damage in the children's eyes. In order to have a good life, Campbell thought, you have to fix all of this and make change. The conviction felt unavoidable and pressing to him as he sat with a beer in that beautiful sitting room in Islington, and his thoughts turned again to the woman downstairs. Why was he so upset by her? He knew the answer. All the elements were able to come together in her: his fear of no longer being a man of the people, his money worries, the ghost of his parents' unhappiness. He pushed for this realisation to become a positive, but sitting there, with those children's faces looking down from what was now a notable painting, he felt a dislodgement taking place in himself, and knew that something was going to happen.

# 4 The Young Astronomer

The hall and the stairs, the front room and the kitchen and even the walk-in cupboard of the flat were covered in framed posters, newspaper stories and flyers for past political events. On the wall next to the stairs, two anti-apartheid posters provided a sunburst of clarity and engagement, along with a green tapestry in support of a united Ireland. Dotted between them were postcards of Hebridean islands, which his mother had loved, far-off Scottish places that became dreamscapes to her, represented on the landing by pink sunsets over the Summer Isles.

Milo's bedroom gathered around a mainframe computer. He also had a laptop, sitting open amid a sea of books and T-shirts. He'd stuck handwritten and printed slogans above his desk and along the top of his bed, between various photos. *The Internet is now the central nervous system of our civilisation, and our task, our obligation, is to reverse the unnatural order, and civilise the Internet and improve the world.*

He had a good relationship with his dad; he felt free to experiment and get excited by his own life. But Ray was in charge, even though he was quiet in his ways, the guardian of the family's potential. They lived in that flat in a circle of pain about his late mother, Zemi, and in a state of deferred hope about the future. Since November, Ray had become a more remote person; other than to Milo, he said very little and saw very few. It was his wife who had animated him and now he was holding onto himself. But in that quieter manner, Milo knew his father retained the old strength and the old conviction. He was still the same guy, the same father who gently pushed at the walls surrounding them.

A small picture of Nina Simone hung next to a photograph of his mother, then one of him aged twelve with his best mate, Travis, both wearing Arsenal strips. On a white bedside cabinet sat keys and old phones. He used to do shifts in the phone shop at the King's Cross end of Caledonian Road, and at Agelgil, an Ethiopian restaurant Zemi had liked. But now he worked for himself. He exchanged cryptocurrencies online, having bought fifty Bitcoin in 2015 from money his mother had saved for him. He never touched that base amount. He knew the day would come when it would be his rescue fund.

*There are no laws, only circumstances.*

He'd copied that from one of his girlfriend's college texts and pinned it up.

*It's About Class, Stupid.*

He saw Gosia's face, her perfectly clear complexion. He picked up his phone and rang her, knowing she'd be at the salon.

'Hey, babe,' she said.

'How's the most beautiful woman in Islington?'

'Is that supposed to be a compliment?'

'Sassy,' he said.

She told him she was walking into the storeroom. 'Listen,' she said. 'I was up for hours reading about that guy.'

'What's that?'

'The guy who wrote the article in *The Atlantic*. Your current obsession.'

'Professor Flynn.'

'Yeah. You know he lives in Thornhill Square? Like, five minutes from you?'

'You're joining me in this?' he said.

'I did a lot of looking,' she said. 'It's all on socials and in newspapers and shit. His background. And there's a shocker.'

'What?'

'His oldest friend is that guy who's in the news all the time.'

'Who?'

40

'Sir William Byre. Owns hundreds of shops, and the Angelique clothing line. He's being done for corruption and whatever.'

Milo was silent for a moment.

'They have all these *connections*,' she said.

He'd sensed there was something going on. It was there in that *Atlantic* article. The guilt and the need for a cleanse, a way out.

'So, what's your motivation?' he asked her.

'Oh, just something I heard. Something closer to home. My brother. I'll tell you later.'

He packed his rucksack for the day, taking a phone charger out of his sock drawer and a few books, including *The Life of Vermeer*. With one finger, he took his Moncler jacket off the hook and was out of the flat in two minutes. He went past Paddy Power and the grocer with its heaps of barbecue coals and fresh ginger, and saw Travis coming out past the Cheque & Pawn, parting the traffic on Caledonian Road with his arms, saying 'Chill, chill' to the drivers as he made his way across the road in a tracksuit and old-school Pharrells. He loved covering his face, not only for videos, but he took the bandana off when he saw Milo, as if to show he was smiling.

'I need to keep a barrier between me and the germs, bro,' Travis said. 'But I'm taking it off for you. Allow that.'

'Pandemic's over, man. Hope so anyway.'

They bumped fists. 'Hey, where you been?' Travis said.

'I'm being assessed for my Master's. I'm mad busy, you know.'

Travis looked over his shoulder, plucking a smoke from his waist-band and lighting it with the Zippo already in his hand. Milo knew the stance from childhood, Travis looking left and right like that, always checking for the police. He said he and their friend Big Pharma had just got off the train from Leicester. They'd been up there selling weed. This was Travis Babb, Milo thought: selling drugs, doing crime, but like a brother, always. As Ghost 24, he was turning into one of the best drill artists in London, him and a bunch of rappers called the Cally Active, racking up a crazy number of YouTube views for their songs. He could practically see the swimming pool down the road where they'd spent their childhood summers. He hoped they'd be reminiscing until they were both rusty.

'Listen, I'm gonna be late,' he said. 'Come and eat with me and my old man soon, Travis.'

His friend swayed on the spot, all loose-limbed.

'I'd like that,' he said.

'Yeah?'

'And get up on Sunday to the bando,' Travis said. He was having a birthday party up in the abandoned flats at Copenhagen Fields. As he said this, Travis was jigging, looking at his two phones. The digital ads on the bus stop were turning from one to the next: 'Make Today a Wins Day with a Scratch Card.' Then a Givenchy ad spun round. Then a thing about shopping in New Bond Street.

'I'll try,' Milo said.

It was nearly empty on the bus. Twigs from the roadside trees were flicking off the windows. They passed Housmans, the bookshop where Milo had bought his latest find, a very Zemi-like book called *Policing the Black Man*, which was in his rucksack next to the professor's *Vermeer*. His laptop was in there too. He put his hand in and touched the cold metal. He was devoted to ethical hacking and looking for vulnerabilities, and he always felt focused when his laptop was near. When he was fifteen, Milo had hacked the payment system of an arcade in Leicester Square. He also made advert-free Spotify accounts for his friends and learned how to divert payments being made for local government parking fines into random donations to food banks in North London.

At the top of Trafalgar Square, two long banners read: 'The National Gallery'. When he gave his name, a guard led him up a flight of stairs and they emerged into a long room, where his footfall, the squeak of his trainers, travelled up to the ceiling and its painted angels. In Room 22, the professor was talking into a microphone held by a BBC producer in headphones. Flynn had the look of someone who cared about himself: the expensive-looking haircut, the tailored suit and the fuck-off shoes. To Milo, guys like Flynn were finessing themselves to look superior, but he understood that, and smiled at it. His own friends were much the same and so was his dad, though when he stepped closer the whiff of aftershave coming from the professor was like a whole different thing.

'Astronomy was of course a huge local industry during the Dutch Golden Age,' he was saying, 'and it's no coincidence that the telescope was invented there. Nonconformist Dutch thinking reached everywhere – stargazing was a means of working out who we are in the universe – and if we look closely at Van Deuren's young astronomer, what we see is evidence of great curiosity.'

Flynn walked forward and the interviewer followed him. 'I'd like to show you a portrait in the next room by Isaack Luttichuys,' he said. 'A brand-new acquisition. It's been here a mere four weeks.' Following them to the next room, going against the arrows on the floor, Milo took in the paintings, trying not to see them as something corrupt. He looked at the labels: *Portrait of a Man in his Thirties*, *Self-Portrait aged 24*, *A Family Group in a Landscape*. White man, white family. 'This oil painting,' the professor was saying, 'was accepted by the nation from the estate of the banker George Pinto, in lieu of tax.'

'I bet it was,' Milo said out loud.

'Okay, can we pause?' the interviewer said, looking bothered. 'Sorry, who is this?'

'This is one of my students,' Flynn said. He nodded at Milo in a courtly way and put a finger to his lips. 'I'm afraid you have to shush. Unless you wish us to make a podcast about the evil marriage of art and business.'

Milo shrugged like he was born to shrug.

'I'm up for it.'

'Okay. Rolling . . .' the woman said.

43

'We come away from Rembrandt,' the professor went on, 'that tomb of browns, with the cataclysm of years that is to be found in these portraits, the artist's sense of ruin – and we find this, an altogether brighter palette.'

Flynn went up close, his left leg touching the rope. 'The sitter's . . . sensitive pallor, and Luttichuys's amazing technical work on the lace edging . . . it's truly a marvel. There's a touch of moisture on the child's lip. This is a new religion of particularity, the individuation of one person as distinct from another, and it was to be massively influential on what we understand by the representation of social reality. The first Luttichuys painting to enter a British collection, this has a great deal to tell us about costume and outward gesture and the meaning of personality in a social setting.'

Milo liked the way he changed his voice for the microphone. It was all performance, he reckoned, everywhere you looked.

'In the religious paintings, we see images of eternal life, but in this kind of painting, and in Vermeer, we see brief lives, local and time-limited – though, of course, we have thrust eternity upon them.'

Milo wandered over to him when the recording was over, hitched his rucksack onto his back and smiled. 'Miles Davis said there were only two categories of thinking: the truth and white bullshit.'

'And I'm an admirer of both,' Flynn said, putting out his hand. 'Welcome to the National Gallery.'

'National *bullshit*.'

'Come on, Milo, you can do better than that,' he said. 'You have as much that joins you to the girl in that portrait as joins you to Miles Davis.'

Milo was stung. 'How's that, then? My mother was Ethiopian.'

The professor did a sort of half-turn to the picture.

'This girl has red blood inside her, same as you. And one can *see* that. That's what makes the painting a work of genius. She's a human being, in and of herself. She cares about what she wears, and has a mind of her own, like you.'

'Don't get triggered,' Milo said. 'I'm only talking.'

'Pictures crack,' Flynn replied. 'Like we do.'

They walked into another room.

Milo began to talk about *Suppose*, the UCL literary magazine. He was at odds with the editors. They were all into striking hipster poses.

'So, you're proposing a special issue on Dead White Males?'

'Nah, we're all beyond that. Though I'm not gonna lie, you're pretty dead and all of that.'

'Thanks very much.'

They found a bench. Milo pressed his phone and started a voice memo. 'So, I've got the Professor of Cultural Narrative sitting here—'

'*Narratives*,' Flynn said. 'Plural.'

'Cool,' Milo said. 'So, tell us about this room. What is this room we're sitting in and what does it mean, and all of that?'

'Well, this is Room 19 at the National Gallery, given over to Dutch landscapes. Like any Western gallery, it's a zone of contention, but it's also a centre of learning, conservation, cultural signifiers and human drama.' Milo noticed Flynn wasn't all that old: he had unlined skin and clear, trusting eyes. And a lot of assumed gravitas or whatever. He swept his arm around the room. 'As much as anything, these paintings speak of the economic life of the Netherlands in the seventeenth century; they will tell you about the pride of the middle classes, of relations between men and women, and Church and State. They will show you the artist as a participant in a nation's self-creation.'

'And how did they come to be here?'

'Van Ruisdael's view of Amsterdam is on loan. Others were bought by the gallery in the nineteenth century. But I think you mean something else.'

'Yeah. Stolen. From one culture by another.'

'If you like, yes. The market does that. But I would maintain, from a conservation point of view, but also from a civic one, that it is better that they land here, in a well-maintained gallery open to the public, than in a private home, where so many of the world's masterpieces languish in conditions of pride.'

Milo was pleased with that answer. He could see it as a stand-out quote in *Suppose*, and knew that it would play well. They stood up and walked through to *A Young Woman Standing at a Virginal*, and Milo handed Flynn the phone, so he could open *The Life of Vermeer* and quote something. '"Vermeer is the patron saint of individual merit," you write. "For thousands of years, privilege and power, determined by birth, were the drivers of history. But with this mysterious woman, standing at a musical instrument or reading a letter in the common light of day, we find that it is merit and individual consciousness, the personal power of ordinary people that rules the world. What is this human being thinking about? What in life is behind her? What brought her here? What is this letter? Again, Vermeer catches human differences at the moment of their occurrence, *in situ*. He is human like us and bows to no power beyond the power of the single mind."'

'Human like us?' Milo said. He felt he'd been storing up energy. He wanted to challenge Flynn. 'Do you really believe all of that?'

'More or less.'

Milo looked at his notes. 'It's kind of empty, isn't it? "The personal power of ordinary people." Are you having a laugh?'

Game on, he thought.

'Say more,' Flynn said.

'Not everyone has the "opportunity" to see their potential. Maybe you *wish* it was true, and so do the people who bought your book.'

'I believe in meritocracy.'

'And I believe in Santa Claus.'

'It may be idealistic,' Flynn went on, 'but art is allowed that. Breaking down barriers is not in itself an evil act.'

'It's motivational speak,' Milo said, 'that uses art as a posh prop. I don't hear you talking about the people who can't be in the picture, who are not even likely to see the picture, unless some special magic happens. It's all a fancy delusion. You surf on an idea of equality that simply doesn't exist.'

'That's a bit of an assumption, isn't it? The National Gallery is free to all. You can simply come here and see Vermeer any time you like.'

'You can simply come here?'

'That's right. Seven days a week.'

Milo walked back to the bench and put the book down. 'You have to know it's here, Professor. You have to know how to want it. You have to know where to begin. Social mobility is a fantasy upheld by guilty rich people.'

'That's good,' Flynn said.

'Are you patronising me?'

Milo stared him out.

'No offence, Professor,' he said, 'but I'm betting you've never risked anything in your life, never really set out to *upset anything*.'

'That's—'

'No, you haven't. You wrote that article two months ago. But have you ever jeopardised what you possess or really questioned your success?'

The professor looked at him, surprised. There was something transgressive in the conversation, the tone of it.

Milo took a step back, dialled down the intensity.

'So, why did you become a writer?' he asked.

'To reach people.'

He found himself asking another question, and he felt emotional in that split second. 'Are your parents alive?'

'No.'

'What were they like?'

Flynn seemed to stare into the picture of the young woman at her musical instrument. '*Eident*,' he said. 'It's an old Scots word. My mother was eident. They both kept their heads down. Sewing, in my mother's case.'

'She was a manual worker?'

47

'Perhaps that surprises you,' he said. 'Perhaps you've already made your mind up about everyone you meet.'

Milo tried to balance his words. 'So you believe in, like, decent conditions for workers and things like that?'

'Of course,' the professor said.

There was a silence, but it wasn't uneasy. They stood again in front of the Vermeer. It was cool the way her quiet gaze, her self-sufficiency, seemed like a trick. The professor went back into his art critic mode, talking about the symbols of love. Milo rubbed his head and interrupted.

'The world's changing, Professor Flynn. It's due a complete reset. Meanwhile, you'll spend your life worrying about what a girl in a Vermeer painting sees in a letter she's holding.'

'Or I'll learn to inhabit her stillness. That's a life's work.'

They stood staring at each other. Milo took it all in. 'Just paint. Just a girl. Just a letter,' he said with a shrug.

'Just *life*, if we can only know it. But if life is changing, if the world is resetting, I'm interested. I'm ready.'

Flynn looked at his watch, an old Rolex, Milo thought.

'I have a lunch appointment,' Flynn said.

Downstairs, he told Milo he never socialised with students. 'But I like the quality of the conversation we're having. Perhaps you'd join me for a drink. Tonight?'

'Sure, yeah.'

The professor looked shy, like he was taking a risk. 'That way we can go further into this fascinating stuff.'

Milo nodded.

Flynn suggested somewhere called the Fumoir Bar at Claridge's.

'Where's that?'

'Brook Street. Ten o'clock.'

# 5 The Club

Holbein's *Ambassadors* was in Campbell's mind as he walked to Pall Mall. The sun was above Parliament when he crossed the road and made for the Club. He saw, poking out of a set of railings by the Duke of York Steps, a few ghostly, white dandelion clocks, the seeds blowing off on their little parachutes. He hung his coat as usual on peg 98, on the left-hand side of a portrait of T.S. Eliot. He went for a pee at the gents on the ground floor and admired an Osbert Lancaster drawing hanging above the urinal, before fixing his tie and giving his shoes a quick buff in the polishing machine. Walking back across the hall he stopped at the board to look at the front page of *The Times*. Newspapers and magazines had only recently returned to the Club (the dessert trolley was still out of action). He flipped a few pages. 'Spain Wrestles with Wave of Child Migrants,' a headline read.

In the bar, Campbell ordered a Negroni as Darwin looked down at him, the chief survivalist, tinting the atmosphere of the Club and the day's news with his constant presence, copied from the original by John Collier. There was to be a formal dinner that evening, followed by a talk: 'Our Time in Yemen, or Recollections of a Whitehall Mandarin' by Sir Evelyn Chippault. 'Not my sort of thing,' the lugubrious barman said.

An actor with a voice like John Gielgud's walked across the red carpet with his guest.

'Ghastly man,' the voice said. 'He comes up to me and he says, "I'll never forget your really wonderful Dauphin in *Saint Joan*," and I said, "But, my dear fellow, I've never been in *Saint Joan*!"' The actor's companion laughed and pointed to a dour portrait of Walter Scott, then to one of Matthew Arnold, both former members, hanging above a black mantelpiece that bore a battered copy of *Who's Who*. The actor seemed to reach down into his voice for a remark. 'Poor Arnold,' he said. '"Dover Beach". He poured scorn on us as a nation of shopkeepers . . . "a touch of grossness", he said, in the British.'

Campbell retired to an armchair by the door, getting up to take a copy of *Tatler*. Elizabeth had told him . . . He flicked through it. Here it was: an event at the Bentley showroom in Berkeley Square from before lockdown, a gargoyle-fest, featuring, the caption said, the Baroness Barrington-Ward and Lady Antonia Byre, wife of his lunch companion – he looked at his watch – each of them holding a glass of Taittinger and leaning against the new Bentley model, priced, it said helpfully, at around three hundred thousand. There was also a picture of William and Antonia's son, Zak, not smiling, bed-headed, wearing a T-shirt: 'Just Stop Oil'. It would be Zak's idea of a provocation.

Ten minutes later, Campbell was at the table with William. 'It was a fundraiser for fibro-whatsit,' William said, before telling the waiter to put the wine on a separate bill. 'Zak says he's got it, you know. Auto-immune thing.' This was the way William spoke. Short sentences. He'd been talking like that since Peterhouse. 'The boy's insane. He's like his mother. Sort of desperate. He loves attention.'

'Elizabeth says he's doing amazing work.'

'What, blocking bridges across the Thames? Him and his eco-rabble? They wouldn't know a day's work if it smacked them on the head.'

'Well, you have to hand it to him. They've got it onto the agenda.'

'What have they got on the agenda? Organic carrots?'

'Mass starvation, air pollution, the planet's incineration, societal collapse.'

'Oh, for fuck's sake.'

'Well,' Campbell said, 'maybe he gets his effectiveness from Antonia. She's certainly been whipping the readers of the *Commentator* into a frenzy every Thursday.'

'It's her only skill, spleen.'

'That's not quite fair, William. She's a splendid cook.'

'Isn't that sexist or something? You'll be cancelled for that. You know what Zak calls her? Basic. I mean, *basic*. What a thing to say about your mother.'

'She's hard to work out. She's always angry.'

'*Always*,' William said. 'Always fuming. Wanting gifts and blaming people.'

'It's sad, because, underneath . . . she's a spirited person, Antonia.'

'She's terrified. All her family were like that, embalmed in credit card statements. It's grotesque. Clever people craving watches from Georg Jensen.'

'Let's not talk about her.'

But William went on, as husbands on the cusp of leaving often do.

'Because you can't feed that, Campbell. You can't fill that grief hole.'

They fell silent and looked around at the vastness of the room, as if they had reached a point of clarity. William took up the menu. Looking at him, Campbell saw that he'd always needed William, his bad behaviour as much as his good, to help him define who he was himself.

'Don't go mad on the wine, William.'

William ignored him. He'd been doing so since Cambridge. William was the brag of the pack, then. He'd been a dynamo at Peterhouse, effortless scholar, valiant drinker, king of the Falstaff Club and favourite of the *Salisbury Review* crowd, the Grafton Breakfast Club aesthetes, the right-wing dons. For two years he was a favourite pet of the historian Maurice Cowling. Terrifically funny and perpetually nasty, William ruled the roost, and though Campbell never shared any of his politics, he shared most of his bottles. It was the pinnacle of male vanity, Campbell now supposed, the way each of them held up his friendship with the other as confirmation of his independent spirit.

'The house claret is perfectly good.'

Campbell needed William the way some people need to smoke, or the way others need to gamble or drink to excess. William was one of his risks. His outer limit. We need a friend who embodies the extent of ourselves. William was nothing like Campbell, but essential to his sense of human character. And whatever happened to his friend caused a leak in his own conscience.

William drew his fat hand to the bottom of the wine list, his eburnean hand, white and plump with supremacy. His flesh was his fullest feature.

'Château Montrose,' William said, checking his phone.

He'd always had friends like that: his alter egos. In the Rosemount Flats where he grew up, he'd had them, his lost boys as he thought of them now, those Glasgow mates whose excesses clarified him. Campbell would drift away from them and move on and forget, yet he measured himself against them, and they supplied the contrast he hoped would always remedy his own self-doubt. And the last of those boys was William.

Before he established Angelique, William owed people money, and after he was rich, he owed people money: that, and rule-breaking, were the true constants in his life. From the very start, he knew how to sell. Then it was shops, factories, superstores and malls, asset-stripping, stepping into planes and yachts, losing ground, threatening journalists, succeeding all over again, facing down his critics, being knighted, having a double bypass. It was obvious, even back in the day, that he was destined for humiliation. It was hot-wired into him, much as Campbell's fear of poverty was hot-wired into him, and he accepted it. But where Campbell's love of success was implicit, and deniable, William's was epic; he could only end up in jail or in exile, and both seemed clear possibilities that day.

'I bought you a present, Campbell,' he said. He took it from inside his oversized suit, upsetting his pocket square.

'Fuck off, William. I hate presents.'

'It's nothing ugly.'

'Of course it'll be ugly. It's from Asprey.'

William chuckled and slid the leather box across the table. 'You're a cheeky prick. It cost me a fortune this morning.'

'Of course it did. What poor widow did you rob to buy it?'

'Don't believe what you read in the papers.'

'I don't depend on the papers. I know you, William. You're a thieving, no-good bastard from Walthamstow.'

'Harsh, but fair. Leyton, actually.'

The thing was, William needed friends, people who judged him but didn't care, which was as much as he could hope for at this point. A diamond tie clip was inside the box. 'Jesus, Will,' he said. 'Do I look like Yuri Bykov?'

'Not yet. You lack the plucked eyebrows. And the shoes.'

Campbell smiled and put the box in his pocket. He wrote out their order and gave it to the waiter. The room filled up and people looked over. William defended himself with scowls and by drumming his fingers on the table. His shops were closing and his factories were on their last legs. 'They want £375 million for the pension fund. I'll find it.'

'What's coming next with these allegations?' Campbell asked.

'Oh, they'll find more. They'll find all sorts of things. They'll have me buggering Prince Andrew by the end of the week.'

Campbell watched him intently as he spoke, seeing he was vain enough to imagine his fall wasn't really about him, that it was an indictment on the society that had thrived off the back of him. 'People love it, in this country. It's all the rage,' William said. 'Make millions off somebody and then call him a criminal.'

'And are you a criminal?'

'What do you think, Campbell? I'm everything you are, except I work like a dog and I'm good to my friends and I don't talk shite about painters.'

'But all this money?'

'I gave jobs to a hundred thousand people. I gave them homes, livelihoods. And if I invested anything the wrong way, they'll get it back.'

During the potted shrimps, a man came over from one of the window tables. It was Rupert Chadley, the editor of the *Commentator*, and effectively Antonia's boss. In theory William would want to be civil to him, for the sake of his wife, but his organisation had run multiple stories about William's financial dealings. Based in King's Cross, the *Commentator* was a new online-only Scott Trust venture, sister to the *Guardian* and the *Observer*, and doing brisk business stirring up fury against the world's easiest targets.

'Hello, gents,' Chadley said.

'Piss the fuck off,' William replied.

Campbell noticed Chadley had that problem, common to school-boys and footballers, of not being able to fix his own tie – always askew or the top shirt button undone or the tie a bit too loud for the occasion. 'I loved that amazing essay you wrote on the shame of being white,' Chadley said to Campbell.

'Thanks,' Campbell said, 'but it wasn't about that.'

'It's the new liberalism,' the editor returned. 'Time's up for the old ways of being a good person, that's for sure.'

William burped. 'Is *that* what you've been all these years? A good person? More like a fucking self-protection mob, it seems to me.'

'Hello, William,' Chadley said again. 'Well, I'm not going to kick a man when he's down. Let's leave it at that.'

'Eat my balls,' William said. 'And who's this reprobate you've got writing shit about me? I should sue her to kingdom come.'

'Ah. Tara Hastings. One of our rising reporters. Don't worry, it's all been lawyered.'

'Lawyered, my arse. She's making it all up.'

Chadley turned again to Campbell. He said how good it would be if Campbell wrote a column for them. 'Brave thinking is what we need. Writers willing to call out the big sinners.'

'And how's she doing, that other brave thinker, the current Mrs Byre?' William asked.

Antonia was Chadley's token right-winger. She was callous, bewildering and had made a career out of exasperating people by writing things just to provoke. To Chadley, who Campbell knew was ambitious for a job on the *Daily Mail*, she was a useful fly in the ointment, and to his colleagues on the *Commentator* she was Medusa with a headache and an account at the Delaunay.

'Antonia gets our readers' palms sweaty. Makes them realise the world is larger than our office. She's a daring journalist.'

'She's a sociopath,' William said. 'And you can quote me on that.'

He gulped his wine and looked dolefully at the editor. 'I wonder if your subeditors and your woke warriors know you're paying her one hundred and fifty grand a year.' He turned to Campbell. 'You must have noticed. She's got the whole country in a bate over migrants. She goes on LBC to tell listeners the Indians are stealing our vaccines. The boys at the Department of Trade say the PM gets into a bad mood for the whole day if he finds, over the Shreddies, that Antonia doesn't agree with him. He should try living with her. She's sitting in St John's Wood as we speak, staking her life on opinions she didn't have yesterday. Any minute now she'll be asked to join the Cabinet.'

'She's well qualified,' Campbell said.

'That's right. Being a journalist. And a liar.'

'I wonder if I could ask you for a reaction,' Chadley suddenly said, 'to the suggestion today that criminal charges are being prepared against you, and that your knighthood is about to be rescinded?'

Chadley's trousers were too tight. So was his smile.

'You know what, son . . . why don't you fuck off and die.'

'I'm not your enemy, William,' Chadley said. 'I work with your wife. I simply think you could help shape the narrative.'

'The narrative? Get lost, you despicable wanker. You people have no shame.'

'It's your choice.'

It was one of William's better traits. He had no respect for authority of any sort, no matter who it was. At Chequers, during a dinner hosted by David Cameron, he'd once poured red wine into an urn in the Great Parlour because it was 'filthy', before telling John Major over the roast beef that Major had once said the stupidest thing ever spoken by a British prime minister, which was, given the abundance of options, 'more of a feat than an achievement'. Major smiled that thin smile of his, nodding as if he hadn't heard, but Peregrine Worsthorne, another Peterhouse man and once editor of the *Sunday Telegraph*, asked what the comment was. 'Well,' William said, happy to oblige, 'once upon a time – what, 1993? – our friend here expressed the view that it was time for us all "to understand a bit less and condemn a bit more". The thin end of the wedge, no?'

'I think it quite a sensible position,' the aged Worsthorne said.

'Well, Perry, you're the thickest man in England,' he replied.

William felt journalists were no better than politicians at being moral arbiters. In truth, Campbell thought, having observed William for more than thirty years, only the market and his own ambition were admitted by William to be moral arbiters, though he had a soft spot for children's charities. As for hacks on left-wing websites, William strongly believed they would say anything and degrade anyone in pursuit of their current obsession, to impress their friends or to meet their deadline. That day at the Club, he looked at Chadley with equal contempt for his 'sources' and his awful tie. 'You learned from that wonderful Mr Blair how to impersonate a decent fellow,' he said, 'while issuing abominations of lies. You and your pitchfork rabble. *Shaping the narrative.*'

'I have no idea what you're talking about. We detest Blair on the *Commentator*. I don't know anybody who doesn't.'

'The clue's in the title,' William went on. 'We have the *Guardian*, a sentimental name for a well-meaning tub-thumper. We've got the *Observer*, a respectable opium den for people keeping an eye on things. Now, God help us, it's the *Commentator*, spouting biased opinion and mistaking it for reporting.'

'Says the husband of Antonia Byre!'

'*Exactly*,' William replied.

'*Desine! Absiste!*' Chadley said, showing off his Latin. 'Stop! You're not helping yourself.'

'That's enough, Rupert,' Campbell put in.

The likes of Chadley were Campbell's friends. They held his opinions, up to a point. But none of these friends could handle being challenged, as if anybody who disagreed with them must be insane. Chadley was too old for that nonsense, but he'd clearly got used to it. 'Well, Sir William,' he said with a final flourish of his tight smile. 'Good luck.'

William tucked in his napkin. 'Waiter! Would you kindly remove this man? Is this not a private members' club? This one's looking for quotes.'

Chadley blushed and made a calm-down motion with both hands. 'I'll leave you fellows to it,' he said, turning away. 'Ring me whenever you want to discuss that column, Campbell. We'd be privileged to have you.'

As soon as he was gone, William resumed his fork. 'That pretentious little man hasn't questioned his own prejudices since house martins last nested in Fleet Street.'

'Shush, William,' Campbell said. 'You've surfed on your own prejudices since you were about eighteen years old. It's what the British do. I've got this student now. Unusual. You should hear what he comes out with, amazing in a kid of, I don't know, twenty-odd. "The first rule of prejudice is that it's much bigger than you," he said to me the other week, "and probably involves you as a secret agent."'

'He sounds a hoot,' Byre said. 'Watch your back. More wine?'

William yawned over the Dover sole, then poured again.

He began talking about steel magnates and various royals and heads of digital companies and what they were known to get away with. Campbell wanted to say something about Mrs Voyles, his sitting tenant, but he heard the comment in his own head and thought it too trivial. Despite the friendship, he didn't really reveal himself to William, or air his worries very much. That day he kept to William's problems and made one or two remarks about Angus and Kenzie, children always a currency in any conversation.

'I see them everywhere,' William said. 'They are stars in the glossy magazines and I wish I had their money.'

'So do I,' Campbell said. He didn't want to say any more about money.

William looked at him with a smile, as if he were conducting a professional appraisal. 'You've never been very sharp about finance, have you, Cam?'

'Says you.'

'Yeah. I've been grandiose. But you're frankly a bit *small* about money.'

Campbell felt slightly stunned.

'No, more than that,' William continued. 'Small-minded.'

'If you mean—'

'I don't mean anything,' he said. 'You're not worldly, that's the word. And you get into a mess about very small potatoes. You always did.'

Campbell was going to say more, to address the loan, but William waved his hand. 'Don't worry about it,' he said. 'I'm the one being toppled.'

They sat in silence for a moment.

'How did you get to have such likeable kids?' William went on, to change the subject. 'I mean, Kenzie's as beautiful as Linda Evangelista. And the other one makes a fortune. I should probably hate them, but they're excellent people.'

'It's all their mother.'

'And I've got Zak. Total waste of space. I'll give his mother the credit too. She's a driving force of personal delusion on an international scale.'

'Is that fair, Will? You're the one facing jail, not her.'

'Fuck you very much,' he said. 'I spoiled them. You'll never know what I gave them and they hate me for it. She is driving around in a Mercedes-Benz Roadster. It cost 120k. Zak despises her for it but lives in one of those new apartments on the canal near you that went for seven million. Spent his time at Oxford learning bad manners from the sons of Russian mobsters. Well, I say mobsters – they're actually middle managers, looters and pirates, backed by a few rusty missiles.'

He guzzled more wine and his talk got slacker as he returned to his son.

'You know he blocked Oxford Circus with a huge pink yacht that said "TELL THE TRUTH"?'

'Yes, a while ago. I saw it in the paper.'

'He wants to give all my money away to wind farms and transgenders.'

Campbell thought it was funny until he saw a tear. William had been swallowed up by the problems and sensations of his own life, and for all the bluster he seemed routed at that lunch, battered by the forces he'd unleashed. 'I don't know what's wrong with me,' he said after putting away another glass. 'I'm fucked, I think.'

'Is it the Angelique pension fund? You can't retrieve it?'

'Look,' he said, 'online companies are killing the high street anyway. I had my fun. But it's worse than that. We live in a world of joke money. All the tax evasion and shell companies and offshoring. Standard issue. But I know a guy who negotiated four shopping malls for the Saudi royal family. Riyadh. Jeddah. Other places. He took all the seed money from this Russian and it all fell through. And now the guy's on his own.'

Campbell knew William was talking about himself.

'You all right, Will?'

'He was a hard worker,' he said. 'And they all did well because of him. The wife who'd stopped loving him years ago. The son who hated him. The guy had to borrow from his own businesses. And then it's the *Ten O'Clock News*.'

Campbell tried to turn the conversation. He said he was going to a conference in Venice the next day and had agreed to see Elizabeth's mother.

'The Countess,' William said, almost lovingly. 'Is she still sailing round the world on that time-share cruise ship, whatever it is?'

'*The Globe* – it's called *The Globe*. Quite small, as these things go. Presently tied up in Venice.'

'She's got the right idea. The rest of society is a mudhole. And she's in her floating bubble, reading books, no doubt.'

'Elizabeth calls her my *ur-wife*.'

'I remember her so well. The jolly lunches in Chester Street. Do you recall she had Scruton and me to lunch one time? She spent two hours quoting Shakespeare and telling us we were wrong to support Thatcher.'

'And so you were,' Campbell added.

They went upstairs for coffee. William took a glass of whisky, and they made their way down the room to a small table. 'Make me feel better,' he said. 'Tell me a secret. I bet you haven't had a secret since the dawn of email.'

'What would you say if I told you I was all secrets?'

'I'd say you were being kind.'

'Well, I'll tell you one.' Campbell felt it wouldn't cost much. 'My life has forced me to be more interested in money than you'd believe.'

'That's no secret. Liberals are always interested in money. They care about it and they care about what it brings, but they reserve the right to disdain that impulse in other people.' Campbell laughed. William lowered his voice and rattled the ice in his glass. 'Here's mine. I'm in love with somebody, Campbell,' he said quite suddenly, with the old twinkle. 'They may destroy me but they can't destroy that. There's a young woman.'

'*How* young?'

'It doesn't matter. Don't be a fucking hack. Her name is Vicky and she's Scottish, of which you should approve. We met in the street.'

Campbell raised an eyebrow.

'Not like that, you dick. She's twenty-three.'

'But—'

'It's been going on for a while. I'm trying to be calmer. She needs me. I found a tiny flat for her in Granville Square.'

'Oh, come on, William.'

'No, please. Enough judgment. I want to take care of her. She sees me as I really am, and if I lose my temper with her, she understands.'

'Why are you losing your temper?'

'It's stress. She knows what I'm like and she doesn't judge me for it.'

Campbell heard what he said but chose to ignore it. Uneasily, he looked up at the clock. It said 3.25. He said he had to get to Clerkenwell for a fashion meeting. 'Writing about skirts and perfume and trying to be cool in front of my kids.'

'The last of the impossible tasks.'

All their disasters were in front of them. All their bonds were in the past. That was the secret of their friendship. William drained his glass and they agreed to have dinner soon at the Guinea Grill. They stood up and hugged in the way that men over forty-five tend to do, making a fuss of their hesitation. William beamed like he still had his good name, and he disappeared down the drawing room, under the watchful eyes of the members, and out through the doors to whatever was going to happen next.

# 6 Fashion

Calls with Angus were frenetic. He was always away. Campbell felt the volume of his success, but in every other respect he experienced his son as a not very momentous absence. He would be in a limousine in Florida or a godforsaken helicopter over Shanghai or São Paulo. At a hundred miles an hour, he would be buzzing about some club or an 'awesome' gig, at Ushuaïa or Coachella. Drake was calling, or a movie person or a shit-hot producer in Belgium. 'Call you back, Dad,' he'd say. 'Give me two minutes.' It was always like that: speed, hassles, the rush of demand. The boy from Belsize Park loving his life and wanting other people to love his life too.

'I need to speak to you about something,' Campbell said, in an effort to take control today. 'It's to do with this birthday plan. Your sister rang me—'

'You're going to love it, Dad. She told you Paris won't work—'

'She did—'

'The 6th is a ghost town right now. I'd got rooms and the penthouse at L'Hôtel for 5 July. Bummer. New variant. I think Kenzie is secretly delighted. She always wanted you to have a garden party in the Cotswolds.'

'That'll suit me fine. I'm not into it, Angus. I know you all love an excuse to spaff money in this family and create a fourteen-act opera featuring unicorns and blood diamonds, but it's not a significant birthday.'

'No, Dad. I'm not having it. I'm in charge of this celebration, and you've been stuck in London long enough. I've got plan B.'

'Which is?'

'*Iceland.*'

'Angus, I don't think—'

'It's on the green list. It's arranged.'

'Honestly. I don't want any fuss.'

'You'll be in the Hotel Borg in Reykjavík in five weeks' time. It's gonna be mega. There's only one place in the world to eat curry right now – this Reykjavík place. Trust me.'

'Have you spoken to—'

'Everybody's cool. They'll all be vaccinated, tested, passports, whatevs.'

Campbell was irritated.

'Do you ever sit quietly in the middle of nowhere and think of nothing?'

'Like, yeah,' Angus said. 'I sleep at night.'

'No, you don't. You party.'

'That's true. Okay, man. I've told Mum all the plans, so you don't have to do a thing. Sit back and I'll get all the peeps up to speed, then away we go.'

Only a few more words, thought Campbell.

'I'm grateful for all your exhausting efforts. I've got Venice tomorrow.'

'Laters, Dad.'

He was gone into his miasma of stuff.

Campbell might hear nothing more for months; that was the reality of having Angus for a son. His existence was a matter of present ego and old family albums, where he was a sweet little boy, somebody waiting to happen.

Campbell's Uber crossed Farringdon Road, spring sunshine flooding the car.

In all the obvious ways, he was an unlikely follower of fashion. He was academic, middle-aged and suit-wearing, believing the well-chosen tie to be a signifier of composure, the knot holding him together. His suits were timeless and his shirts were handmade. It suited his temperament, increasingly, to think of himself as a silhouette more than an embodied person. In any event, beginning in the 1990s, it had been a side hustle of his, the whys and wherefores of British fashion, the psychic gymnastics of the young couturiers, Galliano, McQueen. In some way, he felt he had grown up with the story of their rise and falls, and secretly he felt a kinship with their romantic extravagances and their working-class backgrounds. And there was his mother, the Glasgow seamstress. There was a Holy Communion suit in 1975 with a red sash across the front. She had cried while working on it. She would always lick the thread to help it through the needle, and he remembered thinking that his brand-new suit was held together by his mother's tears.

He got out across from Smithfield Market, by an elegant building in Charterhouse Street, next to the Fox & Anchor. This part of Clerkenwell, with its lanes and passages, was redolent of a bustling old London, and many of the shops still bore the shadow of their former names, fading from the brickwork. But it was all vintage everything now. Pints of avocado craft beer. When Monastic, the English fashion house headed by Izzy Pick, was making its move from Mayfair, there was agreement that the studio would find its true home among the old markets and the urchin pavements of Clerkenwell – a destination sought by other multinational fashion labels keen on talking about roots.

Campbell was met in the lobby by Liang, Izzy's assistant. They passed clothes rails and boxes as they went up the stairs and eventually arrived in an open space. At the far end, behind a white desk hemmed in by four large mood boards and a mannequin, was Izzy, talking to herself and biting her nails. 'Oh, Campbell Flynn!' she shouted. 'You're the kindest man.'

'*La belle dame sans merci*,' he said, kissing both cheeks.

'Everything's a disaster. We need your beautiful words.'

Vanity is the necessary occasion, the *ne plus ultra* of the form, and nothing in fashion lies outside vanity. Campbell had met Izzy, and half fallen in love with her manner, one day in 2017, when he was asked by *T Magazine* in New York to profile Monastic for a special issue. The label was in trouble because its founder and presiding genius, a young Irishwoman named Nora Crowe, obsessed with stigmata, had tumbled into madness and was installed in the Bethlem Royal Hospital before being returned to County Clare. Izzy, her long-suffering assistant, had been asked by the French parent company to step in, and this was the state of play when Campbell had arrived that first time. Izzy had her thumb in her mouth and tears coursing down her cheeks, no doubt relating to the fact that she had to produce between six and eight collections a year. He wrote about her as an English genius, a woman sidelined for too long, a scissoring siren, a Boudicca of bias cuts, and such garbage made him, for a stretch, the fashion writer all the designers wanted. Suddenly, he was being offered all manner of commissions, from Karl Lagerfeld to Acid D, the new hip-hop fashion king. Campbell tended to use fine art metaphors and to compare the designers, and their splendid minds, to everybody from Giordano Bruno to Fantin-Latour.

'Oh, darling,' Izzy was saying, 'I'm glad to see you. Only you. Like that Yazoo song, remixed by Tiësto.'

'You're far too kind, Izzy.' He loved her theatricality. 'Kenzie's coming in,' he said to her. 'She wants to see you, and I'm taking her to supper later.'

'Wonderful. Give me a hand, would you? I've run out of *motivation intrinsèque* and I need some help with the wording of this collection.'

'The label's doing well—'

Her pride then awakened and she gently put him down. 'I know that,' she said. 'You can imagine many things, Campbell, but you are not a businessman. Selling products is something I do as easily as breathing.'

'I know my place,' he said, a bit chastened.

She smiled and touched his face.

'We miss Kenzie walking for us. When she was a student in Paris, everything was brighter . . .'

'We remember it well, Izzy. As Hugo said, "To study in Paris is to be born in Paris."'

'How wonderful. I must write it down.' She rushed for a pencil and sighed a few times while making him say it again. Being head designer, Campbell believed, involves pressures no one would believe who hasn't seen it up close. Most of them live on adrenalin and cigarettes, fearing they are nobody, and Izzy was perpetually at the point where creativity meets exhaustion, feeling emotional and hard-pressed.

'So, Izzy. About this perfume—'

They discovered Campbell's cigarette case was empty.

'Liang! Please, Liang, I'm calling you. We are desperate for ciggies! Twenty Marlboro Lights, *prestissimo*!'

When Liang came back with the cigarettes, Izzy mainly gesticulated with them. She walked to the mood boards and began describing the concept of the next show. 'This is a marriage of Shetland wool, of the "bothy" tradition, with fears of racial war,' she said, waving her short black fingernails. 'These are beautiful coats for the warrior-woman. She is fierce yet she is vulnerable. The Monastic woman is ready for change: she shows apocalyptic courage in a world crisis.' She chewed one of her nails. 'We need your words. Oh, please help me with this, Campbell. I can't stand it.'

'Is she cold?' he asked.

'Ah, Campbell. Always, with the perfect question. These clothes are for the woman who has known discomfort—'

'The discomforts of conscience.'

'Yes.'

'But now she has found her skin.'

'Brilliant! She steps into the northern landscape and is clothed for war, for revolution. It is her skin.'

'Okay. I'll send you a page.'

She calmed down and smoked again. 'Do you think we could

persuade Kenzie to walk for me in Paris? Next year will come so soon, the live shows.'

'I think she's stepped back from modelling.'

'Because of Ashley-Jo? They're going out, right?'

'Em, well . . . A.J. is in every sense multiple. I think they're going out with everybody.'

'No, they're a thing, right?'

'A *sort* of a thing – off and on.'

Izzy didn't like A.J. She had the mentor's wariness of the protégé, and A.J. had built up quite a reputation in advance of their first collection.

'Being difficult is one of their talents,' Campbell said. 'And they *hate* categories, including the category of being someone's partner. So, they're having a thing that is not really a thing but is more like a thing impersonating a thing.'

'Got it,' Izzy said.

'You should ask Kenzie. It might do her good to work again.'

'Paris. Maybe Milan.'

He smiled. 'Remember that show we all did together at the Orangerie du Sénat? It was a beautiful moment.'

'Our Pagan Britain series. Ah, yes. And you wrote that wonderful thing. It's in your book, wait . . .' She reached up and took down *The Life of Vermeer*. The page was marked with a hair slide. 'Here,' she said, and read it out. '"Every colour is changed by the colour next to it, a truth in painting as well as society. No life can exist by itself, even in the eyes of God." I mean, is that not *heaven*?'

'You're too kind. That was a lovely show. Kenzie and all the girls in lace-up gladiator boots. And Anna Wintour came in with Baz Luhrmann, and he cared more about the clothes than Nuclear Wintour did.'

'That's right. I was so nervous. It was one of my first big shows without poor Nora. Oh, darling. It was hell. Sometimes you don't know the hell you've been through until it's over. I hope you never have to experience that.'

68

'I was sitting next to Lee Radziwill. The big cone of hair. And afterwards I took her in the limo to that grubby boutique club, Le Perchoir. She insisted on smoking in the car and the driver was furious. Everyone came.'

'It was the best.'

'It's where Kenzie met Ashley-Jo,' Campbell said.

'They had actually met once before, at the *Harper's Bazaar* Women of the Year Awards at Claridge's.'

Campbell remembered. Elizabeth was with him that night – snorting with laughter when the pregnant Model of the Year stood up to collect her award and thanked her unborn child. He'd been a bit intimidated by Ashley-Jo, the sometime lover, who had started the evening off by telling Elizabeth they often dressed to express their feelings about the destruction of the planet.

Izzy was speaking about her new line of trainers. 'Signature Monastic apparel and no mistake!'

'For the Shetland collection?'

'Yes. The common training shoe is all that stands between my woman and her toxic environment.'

Izzy smiled. She liked being ludicrous. Campbell should have hated it here – he wanted out of writing about fashion – but he couldn't help enjoying her mad collision of style and eccentricity and money. It felt real to him, and that in turn felt shameful, when he thought of his mother and the way all of this seemed like a higher and more successful form of something that was very native to him and rather tragic.

At 5 p.m., Izzy chaired a meeting about the new fragrance. Two men were there from the partnering firm, Procter & Gamble, plus two parfumiers from Paris. Campbell hadn't had a single thought about the perfume or what it should be called. Wait, there had been a moment, that morning in the National Gallery, when he'd looked at a painting of flowers and tried to imagine their smell. But he hadn't quite got there yet. They were talking about ylang-ylang, herbs, tuberose and citrus. He gazed down the table as if his thoughts on the subject had been real and ground-breaking. Izzy kept shushing the others to hear what he had to say. 'Did you determine "she" was urban?' he asked.

'She is an urban wanderer. Instinctive. But mysterious,' Izzy said.

'Perhaps *un petit peu* . . . religious,' a Parisian said. 'I mean, ah, she has conviction and she is, how would you say – *spirituelle*.'

Campbell nodded. He always enjoyed occasions when his chutz-pah helped him survive. 'I have some notes for the ad agency,' he said. He took a ludicrously deep breath before speaking. 'She is alone in a boat, on a canal. Behind her we see an industrial landscape and the cross of a church.'

'Yes . . . mmm, yes,' Izzy said.

'Yes,' the others said.

'She floats – we are in black and white. She trails her fingers in the water. She is independent. She is all spirit. Beautiful. She is leaving her body.'

'Yes!'

'Whatever she touches becomes colour. A trail of colour. A blade of grass. Wild flowers pop into life around the banks of the canal. And finally she stands up and looks ahead. Her hair is blowing in the breeze. She is commanding. We see the cross again and the world behind her. She performs miracles. She is moving from the material world. She is a leader, renewed by herself and her potential.'

'That's good, Monsieur Flynn!'

'And she sees the horizon. She wears . . .'

All the way down the conference table they were nodding. He had played them exactly as they wanted to be played.

'Monastic,' he almost whispered. 'She wears *Monastic*.'

Izzy clapped her hands.

'It was there all along,' one of them said.

'Monastic,' Campbell repeated. He tapped his empty pad with a pencil and Izzy came and patted his arm. The meeting was over.

Kenzie was sitting in reception. He hadn't seen her in a fortnight. She looked radiant and young, her brown legs and her huge eyes.

'Oh, my darling Kenzie. What *are* these clothes?' Izzy said as she came out of the stairwell behind him.

'Whistles,' Kenzie replied. 'A bargain.' She kicked back one of her heels. 'Sandals from Mango. I'm not kidding.'

'We must stop with the Little Match Girl look,' Izzy said. 'You know I'll dress you any time you like.'

Ashley-Jo was outside taking a phone call.

Izzy took Kenzie's hands. 'You will walk for me again,' she said, as if raising an especially unresponsive Lazarus. Kenzie failed to commit, using her smile and all her mother's gentle affability.

Ashley-Jo popped in for a minute. That was their whole demeanour. As a former junior of Izzy's, they reserved the right to show utter disdain for their old boss and her whole operation.

'Ah, Izzy-Izzy,' Ashley-Jo said, with air kisses. 'How's the world of corporate suffocation? Got any employees of colour yet?'

'We have several. *Several-issimo.*'

'Good *work*,' they returned. 'When I was here, it was like working for the Foreign Office in the 1950s.'

Campbell smiled at that. He wanted to like A.J. more than he did. They had a style of being that made this hard for anyone who wasn't exactly them, but, on the other hand, they could be terribly funny and they were right about most things. He mustn't overreact to their hatred of small talk and of white men who think they rule the world. But being right, to them, was like having a passport, Campbell said to himself. You can't get anywhere without it. Unless you're right, you don't belong anywhere and all borders are closed. A.J.'s rectitude, their correcting glee, could be enjoyed if one simply relaxed around it, and he had to remember that being with A.J. had helped Kenzie out of a depression.

With Izzy, A.J. was now being brilliantly annoying, claiming that they disdained the separation of collections into menswear and womenswear, saying they aimed, next year, to reclaim khaki from hunting, militarism and colonial exploits. 'The whole concept of *luxury* makes me sick, actually,' they said. The thing now was 'Ebonic structures'. It was about 'the construction of the male', about queerness and 'freedom in the deepest sense'.

Before Campbell left, Izzy's assistant told him he would be sending the finished contract to his agent. 'The only extra thing the company is asking you to do, in connection with the product launch, is a feature for US *Vogue* with Cassie Tom, the supermodel fronting the campaign. She *is* Monastic.'

'Fine,' Campbell said. 'When will that be?'

'Next February, I guess. You'll totally love Cassie. She has style in her DNA. At the moment she's all about Regencycore.'

'Of course,' Campbell said. 'Who isn't?'

Campbell had reserved a table at St John. He told Kenzie it was his shout – it was always his shout and he liked it that way. His chief vanity was that he never wanted to appear to care about money, even while the issue was fomenting a riot in his secret self. What he fancied that evening was old-fashioned bone marrow and quails' eggs. Ashley-Jo was not happy as they sat down.

'But you've got to admit Izzy is like the worst person actually living on the planet right now,' they said, dragging off a double-breasted blazer they'd stitched themselves, revealing a green-and-black jewelled tracksuit underneath. 'A capitalist nightmare. Like a freak of actual nature. Still making weird disco space-gear for Eurosceptic cokeheads.'

'Don't be too harsh on people,' Campbell said. 'It takes all sorts.'

'And *other clichés*,' they responded.

If ambiguity was the spirit of the age, Campbell felt he'd been a dutiful officer in that war, he had given his life to insurgencies and advances, arguing for freedom, outwitting his parents' conformity and using his pen. But it wasn't enough. He'd marched against Section 28, he'd read every book on the fall of empire, was the proud father of a queer daughter, the first into pronoun therapy, yet his destiny, like everybody's, was to fall short, and he knew it would be better if he could see the funny side.

A.J. ordered a dirty Martini. 'I mean, who is she anyway? She makes Oscar Night frocks for racist has-beens.'

'I like her,' Campbell said. 'She's ludicrous and eccentric and she has a kind heart. But a lot of talented people are like that.'

'I like her too,' Kenzie said. 'Certainly, when it comes to the shows, she's one of the best employers I've ever had.'

'Am I having an actual *stroke* over here? *You can't say that.* This woman is like one of the true psychopaths of all time. She told a friend of mine to lose a stone before Fashion Week in New York, and that dude was already like actually bulimic. Oh my God. She destroys people. Basically, if Napoleon was a designer, if he went around with, like, scissors instead of a sword or whatever, he'd be Izzy Pick. She's basically a serial killer. She's like Jeffrey Dahmer. Like a cannibal or whatever. I've known literally a hundred kids who died because of Izzy. I'm totally not making this up.'

Kenzie and Campbell burst out laughing, then A.J. did too.

This relationship won't last, he said to himself, but it was nice to see his daughter smile and the world needed more disrupters.

'You're all sickos,' Ashley-Jo said, tapping in their EarPods.

Maybe Ashley-Jo gnawed at him because their modernity aged him. They flitted in and out of everybody's life as if permanence was a conspiracy supported by old people and their nostalgic governments. Instead of investing in A.J. and making them an emotional pal, he too often felt moved to do the opposite, to behave like his parents. The house of cards inside us becomes shaky when we realise, one day, that we breathe no differently from our parents, and are nervous like them to hold the world steady.

'I'm gonna let you guys talk,' A.J. said. 'Don't think I'm rude. I'm studying the menu and listening to shit.'

He and Kenzie talked about his birthday. He made the usual noises.

She said it was important sometimes to let Angus be the leader. She said she wasn't modelling again and was more interested in quiet activities at Chester Street, where she was living by herself in her grandmother's London townhouse. 'You're seeing Granny?' she said. 'You're so lucky to be going to Venice.'

When she spoke about the house and its garden, Kenzie was a child again, wandering up the path with a pail of mud and an excited face. She went into detail, plans she had for pear trees and a white garden by the old sycamore in Belgravia, like a mini version of the one at Sissinghurst. She'd taken up weaving. She was happy at last.

'I'm sorry,' Kenzie said. 'A.J.'s got social anxiety.'

'What?' A.J. said, looking up and showing their perfect teeth.

Kenzie smiled too and continued with Campbell. She took his hand. It had always been like this between them, secret jokes, nothing mattering.

'You know, your granny was something of an activist in her day.'

'The Countess?'

'Yes. In the 1950s – in America. Apparently, she made a tremendous fuss about the use of elephants in circuses.'

'Seriously?'

A.J. eventually looked up again. 'I'm bored,' they said.

'Good-oh,' replied Campbell. 'Let's have an inter-generational argument.'

They clicked their tongue and made big eyes. In that moment, Campbell decided that if his children's generation could get their sense of humour in order they might turn out to be the friendliest the planet had ever seen. Generation X logic, he assumed. He made a few remarks along those lines, was accused of being patronising, then sat back, sipping his wine, enjoying himself immensely while Kenzie darted looks at him and laughed at the temporary arguments of her temporary partner.

'Look, you won,' A.J. said. 'You won all the money. You won all the houses. You won all the *second* houses. You won all the institutions, okay, Mr Boomerang of Boomtown? You won! And now you have to win all the arguments as well? Would it really kill you to lose just once, and say, "We fucked up the world, so please help us"?'

He sat in the Fumoir Bar at Claridge's with a large Oban. This might be the best bar in the world, he thought, looking up from the deep black gloss of the table and catching a frosted mirror and a vintage photograph of a 1950s lady smoking a cigarette. He recalled a birthday party, his fortieth, in one of the suites upstairs: light tartan carpet, Art Deco, a bash thrown by his sister-in-law, Candy, on a day when she was being the Duchess. Elizabeth had kept it a secret and taken him upstairs after a drink. He could see Candy in a blue floral jumpsuit, commandeering the waiters and playing mistress of all theatricals, while her husband, the frightful Anthony, Duke of Kendal, whom she called Snaffles, stood in the corner, talking to Campbell's literary friends about the Falklands. It still made Campbell cringe now to think of the Duke saying to Mirna Ivoš, Campbell's editor, 'Would it really have been so awful if the Germans had set up shop here?' The Byres had been there that night, glowing from William's new knighthood.

All these men, falling apart. Campbell didn't quite feel himself to be one of them, not yet, but writing the little self-help book had unnerved him. His past was available all of a sudden. He tasted burned grass and Argyll water – the mild whisky, another Scottish hinterland. He'd drunk quite a lot at dinner. He did that more now, punctuated the day with whiskies, a drink he loved but which was able to hurt him, dredging long-distant streams of memory and causing him to black out when he drank too much.

At around ten, Milo appeared. He was wearing a suit. He narrowed his eyes in the dim light of the bar. The teacher was, for a moment, taken aback by how professional his pupil looked. It was a three-piece suit, not the best, but he was so slim it didn't matter. He had the swagger to make almost anything persuasive.

'This place is a riot,' he said, grinning. 'Out in the foyer or what-ever, there's guys in top hats and shit like that.'

'Don't be fooled. It's a Salvation Army hall.'

'I don't think so, my friend.'

It was a sign of Campbell's new confusion, that he was at the same time irritated and pleased with the boy's use of 'my friend'.

'Perhaps it would surprise you, Milo,' he said, 'in your general hurry, but this hotel gave up its kitchens during lockdown to make food for NHS workers. Life is often a bit more complex than we want it to be. You can quote me on that. Maybe it will upset some of the diehards on the university rag.'

'All right, top dog. Let's get to know each other.'

For all his confidence, Milo had a certain uneasiness with the waiters, asking for a Hennessy with ice. But after that, the drinks kept coming and Milo talked about his life – picking up where they'd left off that day, but becoming more personal. He said he had a girlfriend, Gosia, who liked to do ordinary jobs, and hairdressing was in her family.

'But she studied English,' Campbell said.

'Yeah. She's into ecology. She's the smartest person I know,' Milo replied. 'Apart from my mum, who was stolen from us.' Campbell saw it again: the emotion, that little tremor he'd noticed when they were discussing politics yesterday.

They had something in common, the working-class background, the Irish ancestry, perhaps, at several removes in Campbell's case, a natural resistance to rules, a wish to know art. The young man had edges and they often glinted on the blade of his charm. He screwed up his face when Campbell told him his son was a DJ.

'He's a *what did you say*?'

'Let's not talk about it. He doesn't have a single idea in his head.'

As time passed that evening, they went deeper. When Campbell asked him a question about race, he said his main interest was class. He looked around the room at all the businessmen in the mirrors. 'I don't care about rich man's energy. I care about unfairness. You bring with you the concerns of your background.'

'Yes.'

'It's the perpetual mindfuck – *unfairness*, you know?'

Campbell felt he very much did know. He felt unusual that night, having a drink with a student; it felt slightly wrong, not like it would if Milo was a girl, but overloaded with potential for things to get wayward. Milo spoke with no discernible hesitation or self-consciousness, though Campbell wondered then, as he would later, if there wasn't a fear of falling in Milo too, a youthful amateurism at the heart of his mastery, a tincture of pain. And he had a face he used for seriousness. He deployed it now.

'Obsessing over personal failings of speech,' he said, 'is a cynical distraction from looking at the system of injustice that really controls our lives.'

It was a carbon copy of something he had said before, and also of what Campbell himself believed. But he didn't question it and was pleased that the young man was taking the time to get to know him.

'As I said, there's a digital selfhood,' Milo went on, 'and I'm all about that.'

'Don't be too earnest,' Campbell found himself saying. He didn't mention the other half: it's a thing with the young – like A.J. – the urgency for rectitude.

'Time's out for flippancy,' Milo said.

'This book I've written,' Campbell said, feeling suddenly high, 'it's a sort of self-help book. I'm going to let an actor go out as the author. It's a bit daft, when you think about it. He can do the festivals, the TV shows, the meet-the-author events. All that.'

'That's cool,' Milo said. 'It's all about staying anonymous.'

He was *very* earnest. And yet true to something.

Campbell ordered again. He tried to say anonymity was fine but what about the authentic self?

'Eh?'

'What about Henry James?'

'Fuck Henry James. We're all on the Net.'

'But private life makes a person.'

'Maybe in your world,' Milo said.

Campbell didn't say much more of a personal nature that night, but he felt he could have. His student had lots to offer, much of it political and personal at the same moment. He ordered another round. Before midnight, he felt he had to go; he had the flight to Venice in the morning and he hadn't packed. Milo asked if he could stay on in the bar, to watch people and finish his drink. 'Of course,' Campbell said. 'Look, why don't we exchange phone numbers?'

He was stepping over a line. He didn't have a single student's number in his phone. But there was something different here, maybe the beginnings of a mentorship, a political rapport he knew he needed.

'Yeah, man. Good idea.'

Milo took out his phone and did the whole thing in seconds. When Campbell glanced back from the door, he seemed serene, the possible friend in his young suit, drinking his drink, looking at the people in the mirror.

# 7 Rialto

In Venice, the city reflected itself, the medieval brickwork of the Doge's Palace elongating from the quay, and Santa Maria della Salute, over the way, seeming to undulate in the dark water, all these reflections breaking apart when the vaporetto cut across the centre and headed for the stop at San Marco. Campbell could smell the algae and the mossy steps from his balcony high at the front of the Hotel Danieli.

He'd been upgraded because the manager knew of his connection to Condé Nast. He went back inside and sat at the table with his laptop. There was an email from Milo Mangasha, linking to an article in the *Islington Gazette* about the life expectancy of young black men. Underneath it he'd pasted a quote: '"We can't know ourselves until we know people who aren't us, the specifics of their existence. And that effort will be the story of how we lived." Campbell Flynn, *The Life of Vermeer*.'

There was a knock at the door. Breakfast. The masked waiter wheeled a trolley into the room and arranged cutlery and poured tea from a silver pot. Campbell ate some toast, then shifted his laptop onto some large books, so he could Zoom with his agent, who was waiting in London.

'Well, Sporty,' Atticus said, 'I read your little book again in proof and can tell you it's ideal for the current market.'

Atticus never overdid it with the praise.

'How is my British publisher coping with it?'

'Don't worry about Mirna. She loves you. They're leaving most of the decision-making to the Americans. Barricade Books has a track record with this sort of thing.' Campbell expressed a few quiet anxieties – about it not being a serious book, about being unmasked – but Atticus smoothed it all away with an experienced hand. 'A good book is a good book is a good book,' he said, 'and people have been waiting for something like this.'

Campbell could hear seagulls at the window. He heard the sound of a boat's horn too and was keen to get moving. 'The crucial thing, anyhow,' he said, 'is my pseudo-*homme*. You said he'd agreed?'

'Jake Hart-Davies is keen to sign on. He's studying the text and will then get into gear once this Thomas Hardy movie is finished.'

'Yes, *The Return*. He's playing Clym Yeobright.'

Atticus nodded. 'His agent wants 30 per cent royalties on the book.'

'Fine. He will bring a lot to it.'

'You sure?'

'Yes, Attu. He's got the face. The voice. I want *nothing* to do with it.'

'Very good. We'll alter the contracts.'

'This book is a burner,' Campbell said.

'A what?'

'Like a burner phone. Not registered. Not traceable.'

'Hart-Davies sees it as a "synergistic acting experience" – his very words – and is a bit of a soul-searcher, if you know what I mean. I think we can trust him. He keeps talking about "testing the real politics of blame culture". He says *Why Men Weep in Their Cars* could be a really terrific new kind of TV drama, which he'd like to be "showrunner on" – and those, too, are his words.'

By way of an eye-roll, Campbell rolled his entire head. 'God, actors are something. He already believes in it more than I do.'

'It's not a money job to him. He takes every word seriously. I think he's memorised half of them already.'

Atticus clicked a few keys and found an email from Hart-Davies. 'He says here "it goes to the heart of the modern-day conundrum of being male".'

'We shall have to give him a few new words. I mean, a script, before he goes anywhere near a microphone.'

'Par for the course, Sporty. He's an actor.'

'Very good. Make every decision on your own, Attu. Send me the cheques. Lots of them.'

'All right. This should be fun.'

Downstairs, Campbell gave a 50-euro note to the concierge, who promised to have his luggage delivered to the check-in desk which served *The Globe*, docked that day at the western end of the Lagoon. The concierge explained the pandemic precautions that had overtaken the city: the wearing of masks was an ancient ritual now suddenly modernised, and Campbell must adhere. With the pink palace behind him and a tote bag on his shoulder, he walked to the Piazza San Marco, turning to see the golden basilica and its frothing stonework. On one of the bridges, he felt the pull of the open space – that midlife dizziness again. He could trace the moment it had begun: last November, the day he learned from the council that Mrs Voyles 'would accept' £400,000 to give up her protected tenancy. He thought he was having a stroke. At the Royal Free, they gave him a brain scan, said he was okay, and sent him home with his little box of prochlorperazine, a drug for vertigo.

He was early for the talk he was due to give at the Teatro Goldoni, so he found a threadbare trattoria, where he started with a Campari. He took the Ralph Ellison from his bag and flipped to a page he'd marked. Ellison was talking about his mother's job and that she used sometimes to bring home copies of *Vanity Fair* and opera recordings from the houses where she worked. 'You might say my environment was extended by these slender threads into the worlds of white families, whom personally I knew not at all.' Campbell read the passage again, then went on: 'These magazines and recordings and the discarded books my mother brought home to my brother and me spoke to me of a life that was broader and more interesting, although it was not part of my own life.'

After an hour, Campbell got up and went to the theatre, where ladies awaited him in protective masks, ready to spirit him to the green room for English tea. During his talk, he spoke of a work of Bernini's from the Galleria Borghese, *Self-Portrait as a Young Man*. 'We make too much of youth,' Campbell said, 'because we fear it represents the best in us, and what is lost. Maturity is the compensation. In this second picture we see a man of achievement, a deeper soul, but his eyes show he lacks the innocence of a freshly embodied truth.'

The ship was a sleek white liner with two funnels and a single blue stripe from bow to stern, tastefully nautical. In effect, it was a shopping mall fitted out with expensive boutiques – Old Bond Street *en mer* – and Campbell boarded with a slight sense of mortification. He showed his negative test certificate plus evidence of his two jabs. The man at the front desk then offered him his bag from the Danieli, and a glass of Krug. He took it, with its dunked raspberry, and sat on one of the huge, brocaded sofas in the foyer, laying the white roses he'd brought for the Countess on a needlessly large glass coffee table. When he was summoned, Campbell took the elevator to level 11 and followed the feather-patterned carpet that led to the Countess's apartment. A maid answered the door. She gave a short, practised curtsey, which Campbell felt she rather enjoyed, then she took the flowers and walked crisply away like a busy little ghost. Standing in the hall of his mother-in-law's floating palazzo, he looked at his phone and scrolled through his emails.

Looking into the hallway mirror, Campbell had a sudden vision of himself as a boy on the bus to Hutchesons' Grammar School. With his hood up, that boy was playing with a Rubik's Cube, and it was freezing outside, and he was overwhelmed with the certainty that if he could match up all the sides he would be rich and famous.

When he turned round, he saw Emily, Countess of Paxford. She was eighty-six years old and she smiled like a person on whom nothing is lost, with her high white hair and her periwinkle eyes full of wisdom and affection.

'Well,' she said, quite grandly, 'isn't this simply the most regrettable vessel you've ever seen in your life?'

In the suite's drawing room, Campbell was scrutinising a picture he said he couldn't recall having seen before, and he turned to Emily with what seemed like enthusiasm. 'Lorenz Strauch,' he added, with one of his smiles.

'Yes, a present from my father.'

'A sixteenth-century schoolgirl,' he said, 'really quite wonderful, with her interesting ring and her pale face.'

Campbell was such a resourceful, clever man, Emily thought, with all his elegance and talent. 'It's richly interesting that picture,' she said, 'and reminds me, every morning, as I idle about the oceans, that the schoolgirl never dies.' She sat herself down in an iris-patterned armchair, a Georgian table behind her covered in family pictures in silver frames. 'Thank you, my dear,' she said when the maid brought the champagne and poured her a full glass. 'I don't go out much,' she went on, looking to Campbell. 'I went to lunch, the day I wrote to you. But basically I see the maid and no one else.'

The Countess hated small talk: she wanted to say more about her old school, Hengrave Hall in Suffolk.

'It had twenty-one pieces of Flemish glass in the chapel, depicting salvation. Quite excessive, really. The last surviving pre-Reformation glass in England, I believe.'

'That really is something.'

'Well, it was, you see. By the time I arrived, it was run by the Religious of the Assumption, a tribe of nuns obsessed with one's knickers.'

Campbell always laughed in her company. She sipped and shakily deposited her glass on a side table. 'How delicious.' She paused. 'You weren't allowed to wash your hair if you had your period. I'm serious. And, Lord save us – *posture*. The school was eventually run by a terrific pair of ancient lesbians, Miss Seasley and Miss Dodds.

Non-nuns. And the headmistress, Mrs Ferguson, whose young husband had died at the Somme. She was singularly unhappy and Scottish in her tweed skirt and her sweater and pearls.'

'I'm sure it made you the woman you are.'

'It was simply killing. I was always conking out or fainting from hunger – that sort of thing. To this day, even when I'm away from London, I still feel homesick on Sundays. And I still expect fish on Fridays. I tell you, Campbell, Proust would have had a field day. We used to pick rosehips to make syrup, and we made Assumption Tarts with the lay nuns. And my father would come down for exeats, you know, and take me to lunch at a country hotel. There was a particularly disgusting one near Saxmundham. But it never leaves you, this kind of thing. I swear to God, it was singing the school song that kept me going through the agonies of childbirth.'

'I don't believe you.'

'That, and reciting the poems of Herrick.'

Preparing for Campbell that evening, Emily had chosen a beautiful beaded gown. The maid told her the label was gone, but Emily thought it was Louis Féraud, and she hadn't worn it since the 1980s, around the time David died. She'd added a touch of rouge, then a spritz, she called it, of Attar of Roses.

'So, how are my lovely offspring?' she said to Campbell. 'How's darling Elizabeth?'

'She's deep in her work,' he said. 'She's writing a book on Winnicott.'

'Heavens,' Emily said. '*Home Is Where We Start From*. The poor mother always getting it in the neck. Oh, well. Jolly good.'

They spoke about Angus and Kenzie. London. 'One never hears from Angus,' Emily said. 'He only exists with a bang.'

'That's right. He's the visible invisible man.'

'Well,' she said, 'I'm sure he'll turn up when it matters. Perhaps at one's funeral, or something exciting like that.'

Emily said she knew about London because she was regularly on the phone to Kenzie. A beautiful friendship had sprung up between them. Plus Emily read the papers. 'It's fantastically vulgar here,' she said, 'but I happen rather to like it. You know, waking up to see a penguin. That sort of thing.'

'Don't you miss London?'

'Oh, my dear man, please don't ask me banal questions. You have a gift for chasing down sentiment in a voice of utter seriousness.'

'Do I?'

'I'm afraid so. It's a social blemish.'

He was never quite finished, as a person, she felt. It didn't exactly disappoint her, but she saw that it must annoy him.

'One misses all sorts of things,' she said. 'Old age is a catastrophe. But I'm not going to sit around like a dying duck in a rainstorm. I miss bath salts and decent teabags. I miss my Mason Pearson hairbrush. I left it in the bathroom at Chester Street.' She turned round to the prized photograph of her and her father at a picnic spot called Topi Park in Rawalpindi. They'd watched the cricket that day.

She had married David, the late David Wipps-Cooper, Earl of Paxford, at St Margaret's Church, Westminster, in 1962. In those days they called it the parish church of Parliament. She saw herself walking down the aisle in that pretty dress by Norman Hartnell, happy on her father's arm. Her dadda: Captain Harold Eglantine, 'the Egg', a soldier who'd grown to be something in the Indian Civil Service. Going down the aisle at St Margaret's, she'd looked across to the west window and the dashing figure of Sir Walter Raleigh, the sea all about him in the stained glass.

She found Campbell very easy to talk to. They were still docked when the waiters brought supper. It was all on trolleys with silver domes. She realised she was fidgeting around the plates, asking for this and that, but they did often forget things and she wanted Campbell to have a delicious time. She pointed to a Peruvian trout all dressed and garnished, and Campbell broke off a piece, going round the trolley to make sure she had what she wanted. She began to talk about psychotherapists.

'There was a dreadful man called Masud Khan,' she said across the table. She and David had met him, she was sure, through Isaiah Berlin, whom David had known through his friends at All Souls. 'My father-in-law, the previous Earl, had a rather horrid time altogether. Wasn't right in the head, poor man. He had nurses who were unkind to him and he died in a rather grim mental institution in Epsom. So my husband was rather, you know, muddled by all this, and in the 1960s – we'd only been married a few years and the girls were small – he went to see this abominable fellow, Khan.'

'Yes. I think I read about him.'

'A horrific social climber. I mean, the Edmund Hillary of the type. One can hardly conceive of an analyst becoming such an intruder. A show-off, always boasting about his perfectly banal social connections. Princess Margaret, that sort of thing. He wore a riding jacket. He had friends in the theatrical world. An absolute fright of a man, and what damage he did to poor David.'

'We are merchants of hope,' Campbell said, 'writers, therapists. But it sounds like David had an unlucky experience.'

'He was mugged, my dear, by a would-be healer. I daresay you know how to spot such dangerous people, I always thought you could.'

'Maybe I don't,' Campbell said. 'You get attracted to people. Not sexually, I mean new people asking new questions.'

'Or answering the old ones,' she said.

'Yes. I have a student like that.'

He had lovely manners, she thought. God knows where he picked them up, but he had them, coming around the table to fill her glass, finding a cushion for her.

He was silent for a second when he sat back down. 'I've written a secret book,' he said. 'I'm publishing it under an assumed name, in two months or so. It's about men.' He told her about its various chapters. 'On Fatherhood', 'On Money', 'On Ageing', etc. He seemed to hate the idea of letting her know he was trying to make money, so he put the book up on stilts, as he sometimes did with things, making out it was something more. 'It's a kind of literary experiment,' he went on, 'a tease about autobiography and self-help. Not to everyone's taste. I've engaged an actor to pose as me.'

'Oh, really?' she said, chuckling. Sometimes a chuckle was better than a speech for creating an amusing climate.

'Maybe it will offer consolation,' he said. 'Explaining why we're in such a state.' This was evidently something he aimed to convince himself of.

'Naturally,' Emily said. 'Being *toxic* and everything, men are always seeking consolation and whatnot. What fools. Men are the same as men have always been, delightful and infuriating.'

She took a healthy sip of champagne and then drew a cigarette from a purse sitting on the table beside her. 'You'll join me in a gasper?'

'I will,' he said.

She had a novel on the table. *Across the River and into the Trees.* He gestured to it and she blew smoke in its direction. 'The most wonderful title,' she said. 'Isn't it strange that it's often second-rate novels that have first-rate titles?'

'Examples, please.'

'*Hangover Square. Other Voices, Other Rooms.*'

'Very good.'

'And the masterpieces are called things like *War and Peace* or *Ulysses*. I mean, one oughtn't to mind particularly.'

'It's wonderful you're still finding truth in books,' he said.

'A real writer doesn't reveal the truth,' she said. 'He hides it beautifully.'

Emily then excused herself. The maid came to help her and Campbell retired to one of the armchairs to check his phone. He read the same email several times, and was still mulling over it when Emily returned to her chair.

'That's really weird,' he said. 'An email from Elizabeth. She's back at the house in London. She says small amounts of money have been withdrawn from our joint account and donated to certain charities.'

'You mean debit things? I have several.'

'Yes. But we didn't set them up.'

'What sort of charities?'

He looked at his phone and touched the screen. 'Red Card? . . . Apparently it's a charity that uses footballers to oppose racism in schools. An education thing. And StopWatch UK, promoting fair and accountable policing.'

'They sound like perfectly reasonable causes to me.'

'I'm sure,' he said, standing up. He looked with great concentration out the window, then replaced the phone in his pocket. 'Do you like young people, Emily?'

'It's a rather good question,' she said. 'It puts me in mind of a thing that was once said to me at supper, by Doris Lessing, of all people. She was really quite old at the time. I had dinner with her in Camden Town and when I asked her what she feared in old age, she said, "Being overtaken by a young man."'

'Really?'

'Yes. She put it very simply. She said a young person could easily swamp one and there was nothing one could do about it.'

Campbell leaned against the fake fireplace and took a sip from his glass. He looked at the walls, the art, and told her she'd always had exquisite taste.

'Not easy on this sea-going latrine,' she said.

'But I thought you liked it.'

'Oh, I do, my dear,' she said. 'Ugliness has its place.'

She'd sold most of the pictures. Most of everything: the silverware and all those Jacobean antiques that went with David's estate. They all thought she was committing an act of gross exorcism in selling up the manor house, but it was all dead, and she had thought then that her money would eventually go to her two girls.

He came back to sit at the table and Emily asked for gossip. He told her about the Byres and the worsening storm over William's business affairs. He didn't say it, but Campbell was deeply anxious about his old friend: today's news had picked up on the rumours of sexual misconduct, and perhaps William was scuzzier than Campbell had ever admitted. He wasn't sure. He didn't want to be sure. But Elizabeth had always hinted at it.

'I rather liked him,' the Countess said. 'He's as silly as an afternoon at Ascot, but quite amusing in the same way.'

'He used to be. It's all going wrong now.'

'That wife of his, what's her name?'

'Antonia.'

'An absolute stoat of a woman. Horrid, common little opinions.'

He said there was always too much going on in London. 'Elizabeth prefers the country and being near Candy, getting on with her writing.'

'Give me news about Candy and the Duke.'

'Bad loans, I think.'

'But he doesn't need loans.'

'I know. But they all have them, to fund their charity works. They don't want to use their own money but they want to run foundations, so they get it from these Russians who are keen to launder their money in the UK—'

'Mr Putin's so-called friends.'

'Yes. Moira says he's caught up in it.'

'And you think it will all come out eventually?'

'Maybe not,' Campbell said. 'But he's vulnerable. He's an idiot.'

She put down her spoon.

'He is, you know,' she said. 'Rather sordid, actually. All these estates and charities and what have you, and poor Candy gone quite mad with yoga and tea rooms. The man likes polo, what can I say? Such a nasty Argentinian sport. You'd have thought he'd had quite enough of them during the Falklands business.'

'Family,' Campbell said. 'The Duke's in the soup.'

'Oh well,' she said. 'Chickens one day, feathers the next. Don't dwell.'

It was dark outside as the ship began to move. He said it was lovely to be overnighting with her to Trieste. Emily would then continue on to Greece, the north coast of Africa, the east coast of Spain and a week in Monaco. She said she would tell him at breakfast all about her plan to escape England for good.

'Oh, come on, Emily, you'd miss the general fiasco.'

'Not much, I have to say. Though I'll return for Garsington. I do love it there, and this year it's *Eugene Onegin*, I believe.'

Outside, along the Grand Canal, all the lamps were aglow, and Campbell went with her onto the balcony to say farewell to Venice. She took his arm and it was lovely to see the corner of Harry's Bar and all the famous buildings along the quay. Campbell looked again at his phone, that horrid glow lighting up his face.

'Is all well, my dear?' Emily said.

'Oh yes. It's so lovely to be away.'

She didn't turn but decided to say it. 'You take something of a free hand when it comes to self-pity, Campbell. I wouldn't allow it, if I were you.'

She noticed that he bristled. Like many entertaining people, he didn't care for the truth.

'You must handle all your affairs with kid gloves,' she said.

She patted his arm as the ship plunged out into the waters of the Adriatic, and she saw lights glimmering in the distance. She pulled her shawl tighter and tried to remember the names of all the towns over there, the places she had been to and the ones she presumed she would never see again. Campbell's phone lit up in his hand and she could see without her glasses the single word 'Milo'.

# 8 Copenhagen Fields

It was the day of Travis's birthday and he was feeling ripe. He woke up late in the afternoon and took a shower that lasted for twenty minutes. He let the warm water splash over him like it might take off the old skin, and he loved the steam filling the bathroom and clouding up the window and the light bulb. He grabbed a towel and the deodorant by Malin + Goetz that smells of eucalyptus, then he brushed his teeth. Calvins on. The flat was empty so he turned the music up, 'Rise & Prosper' by Ard Adz, before pulling on a black T-shirt: 'Undefeated Athletic Club'. Splatter paint hoodie. Black jeans ripped at the knees and a red varsity jacket. Reeboks. He was good to go. The rain was beating down outside and he opened a beer and toasted himself in a piece of broken mirror that was propped up behind the kitchen taps.

The boys got together on Caledonian Road around five o'clock. A girl from an underground radio station was down in the car park at the bottom of the Copenhagen Fields block. She was holding up a mic. Her Smart car said #blackradio. Travis and the boys were shooting a video for a new track, 'Previous Convictions'. They were pumped. They talked to her afterwards, about the video and what they were trying to say. The director had made a video with the Shakspeare Walk 4X, a gang from Stoke Newington that already had a million views on YouTube and were flying high. Big Pharma had a cousin who lived on the Milton Estate up there, so there was no turf war any more, and the Cally Active, Travis, Lloyds and the boys, were allies with them now. The two gangs had a running war, though, with a few postcodes in South London, mainly Deptford Grove, because of insults in songs and drugs supply. There was beef with gangs in Hoxton and Clapton too.

Travis had his hoodie up and a scarf over his face and he told the radio girl the boys loved King's Cross, but the police kept arresting them.

'It's society that's violent, not the music. They think if you're young and black you're already a criminal.'

He went up the block after it was all done and it was dark outside. Nobody lived on the seventeenth floor; it was derelict, and the wind howled. Brothers would always turn up at the middle flat to smoke and watch films on Travis's laptop. There was no lock on the door, but nobody came in who wasn't with the gang in this way or that. This was Travis's real house, a manky old bando from the 1970s with holes in the windows. Not the flat above the Nisa shop he shared with his mum.

His hands were sticky with Hennessy. They'd been throwing it about for the video and he'd drunk a decent amount from the bottle. Travis loved it: giving the finger to the camera with his friends and all bopping around having a good time. He washed his hands in the kitchen, dried them on his jeans, then drank some water and pulled a crumpled letter out of his pocket and a bag of weed and Rizla. He spread out the letter: Highgate Magistrates, probation for a drugs offence, and a date to appear. He lit it with his Zippo and left it in the sink. He sat in a burst armchair by the front window of the living room, looking back at the St Pancras clock, and beyond that to the Telecom Tower and the West End. He balanced his iPhone on the arm of the chair and blew smoke at the window. Raindrops there. His boys were back out selling weed but would be up for his party soon.

Looking out at London always gave him the feels, because it was looking into his own history and he knew he belonged there. He wasn't sure you could feel patriotic about a city, but it was something like that – his home ground, his people – and on a day like this it was really nice, thinking about that. For Travis it wasn't about nations or wars or England or bullshit: it was North London. The trouble he got into never made him feel alone; it was all part of the active life, he reckoned. The thing that made him sad, sitting on his birthday armchair and looking out, was regret – regret about family he couldn't speak to or girls he didn't see any more, lost friends.

He took out his phone and swiped.

'Remember my birthday party Milo 5.'

They had names like that, back in the day. Travis was TR7 before he was Ghost and Milo was always 5, because one time in the playground at William Ellis he ate five Snickers bars one after the other. Pharma was always Bigs.

No answer to his message.

Maybe that was a song: 'No Answer'.

He thought of the days taking their skateboards up to Cantelowes Park. They were small then and could wander in and out of all the territories, Agar Grove, Camden Road. He'd never been determined about anything in his life like he was about getting good on his board, practising ollies on the pavement for hours instead of going to school or getting involved at home.

He got out his papers and rolled a thicker joint. 'I loves me a big birthday zoot,' he said to the empty room, cackling.

He thought of his mum. She disappeared for weeks at a time from the flat at Ritson House and he wasn't sure where she was now. She kept losing her phone. It was always hard for her and he wasn't able to fathom it.

She told him she couldn't remember his father's name.

*'Travis Babb, has no dad, Travis Babb, Travis Babb.'*

'Fucking losers,' he said.

He sparked up the joint and blew smoke past the naked bulb. He would like to be taking kids to the football pitches – the red ash ones he used to play on with Milo during summer nights when they were young. Mr Panday, their old sports teacher, loved football. Loved cricket, and all sports. That's a life, Travis said to himself, if music goes to shit or the deals don't come through, and he smiled to fill the room. He could see himself riding to the top of the bowl at the skatepark and beating gravity.

Earlier that evening, Milo was on a date with Gosia. They'd gone to see *Fast and Furious 9* at Tottenham Court Road, and laughed all the way through. 'This is stupid shit,' Milo said a dozen times.

'I totally love it, though,' she said. 'Man with deep voice in really fast car.'

Milo spoke into his popcorn box, jutting out his jaw, impersonating Vin Diesel. 'Nobody can speed away from who they really are.'

She giggled in the empty cinema. Gosia was one of life's natural gigglers. He emerged from the popcorn box with bits stuck to his face.

'You're an idiot,' she said, picking the bits off.

Gosia had an unforgettable face, freckled skin with soft rosy lips. She made a fuss of her hair, which was deep brown, like her eyes.

On the way back up Charing Cross Road, she spoke to her mother on the phone. Mrs Krupa was always upset about Gosia's older brother, Bozydar, his bad marriage. 'My mother lives in a Barbra Streisand song,' Gosia said. 'It's all about the power of the struggle and the wholesomeness of the ending.'

'And how does she feel about Black Streisand?' he said, hoisting his rucksack onto his shoulder and making big eyes for a joke.

'Don't even go there.'

He felt that they lived in a love of jokes, but the mood could quickly turn stern, or more interesting, to their minds, with talk of their 'Project'.

He took her to Byron Burger in Covent Garden. She was a child in there, dipping her chips into her milkshake. 'Listen,' Milo said, pulling her back into a conversation. He filled her in on his latest discoveries after hacking into William Byre's company: emails referring to false sets of accounts, texts between board members suggesting hundreds of millions in hived-off pension funds. One email thread hinted at a Metropolitan Police investigation into Angelique's employment of illegal Polish immigrants over a long period, but didn't say anything explicit. He was looking for a way in.

'Some of it's already proof. Some of it will lead to proof,' Milo told her.

For computer-heads, the real ones, it was always about the slow joy of exposure, the game of closing in, subverting from within. Gosia said she had continued to look into his professor's family associations, stuff like that.

'His wife is, like, aristocratic or something?'

Gosia put down her cheeseburger and her face was lit. 'Her sister is married to the Duke of Kendal. He's in the House of Lords . . . He's related to the Queen or whatever. But there's hints in the newspapers that he's involved with Russian money.'

'I'm going there next. All the way in.'

'Nobody can prove it yet and it's all unfolding really slowly but they're saying it involves MPs and businessmen—'

'Including . . .'

'Yep. Sir William Byre. He took loans.'

'So that's, like, two of Flynn's nearest associates.'

'That's all in the public domain,' she said.

She went into a zipped pocket of her rucksack and handed him a USB stick. Milo took it and turned with a big smile to the window and the people passing by. '*Giiiirl.*'

'You can do your hacking magic,' she said. 'I'm just reading. It's fun. Or horrible. And it involves Bozydar.'

'Your brother?'

'Yeah. He's been doing dirty work for those companies.'

'This thing is crazy,' Milo said.

* * *

Lloyds was at the door of the abandoned flat, walking in all business-like, carrying a case of Moët in one arm and shouting down the phone to their friend D-Mok. He ended the call and looked over at Travis. 'Bro's spitting bars in prison. Wants a record deal.'

'Course he does,' Travis said.

'He uploads his videos on Insta.'

Travis flicked ash off the end of his joint. Lloyds began unloading the bottles and stacking them on an old kitchen table in the corner.

Lloyds's real name was Jeremiah. He was all about the lifestyle and the money (that was how he got his name). He liked his music commercial, but what he loved most, Travis knew, was the CEOs, big cigar-smoking dudes like Suge Knight. Lloyds was always moaning there were no high rollers like that in the UK.

'You know what, Lloyds? You're a greedy motherfucker. You think you're in *American Gangster*.'

'Trust me, fam. You're talking to the Den*zel* of NW1.'

Lloyds had his hair in twists all round his head. They were usually jammed under his cap. The room was starting to fill up with the Cally Active now, mainly the ones who'd been jumping around in the video, and most of them were blazed. Travis looked at his friends. Big Pharma arriving wearing a Vuitton jacket. 'Looking fresher than you, man. Trust me.' He'd been to see a promoter down at the Scala. Bigs loved Jamaican pirate radio, dancehall, handling a microphone. His dad was into music too and his cousin in West Norwood was a speed garage MC. That connection meant Pharma always tried to calm the beefs with other gangs down South, like Peckham Boys and the Brixton crews. He wanted to stop it flaring into real violence. That's good, thought Travis. That's cool. Pharma was well known on the Angell Estate because of his family associations. His mother never knew he was called Big Pharma. It would have killed her to think of Devan as a drugs person or gangster.

He had a beautiful voice, warm and high like Frank Ocean's. At the birthday party that night, you could hear him talking over the music. 'Nah, I'm serious. You never forget the stuff you watch when you're young. I'm still trying to work out why Tony Soprano killed Christopher. Shit like that. And the finale! The screen goes black in the diner or whatever and you don't know if Tony gets whacked or what. That's class.'

An hour later, the party was full on happening in a thick bubble of weed smoke. Travis sat in the armchair in his red jacket like the leader of the chat. The thing none of them could ever agree about was football. Big Pharma and Lloyds supported Spurs. Travis was Arsenal all the way, and so was their man Milo, wherever he was. Milo always went on a different path. Loving books. Spending all his time with that beautiful Polish girl whose brother was a dog. The old days with his friend: drinking Smirnoff and breaking into the Wireless Festival in Finsbury Park. Seeing Stormzy young, the whole day as sweet as a day can get. Milo's mother, bless her soul, would make those Ethiopian snacks; she'd put them in zipper bags, had no idea they would be going over the fences or whatever. When the police stopped-and-searched them they found these bags of crushed pastries. They thought it was hash, and Milo gave them a lecture about indigenous foods. Travis didn't seek status then, he had it for free, taking gulps of air and shining with life.

Milo probably wouldn't come. He was floating up like a kite, entering his own atmosphere or whatever. The room was mad with people. He reckoned his friend would be at home, doing his thing on the Net, copying the white man. Travis was sure his old mate didn't even like their music. He had sent him a link to one of the videos, and Milo texted back: 'I'm not cool with black people killing black people, even rapping about it.' He wondered if he knew his girlfriend's brother was the one keeping the Cally boys active, with weed to sell and stuff like that.

'Do you ever see him,' Travis asked him one time, 'your girl's brother?'

'Nah, mate. We don't like each other.'

The boys were making their ruckus when a small white kid called 0044 opened a JD Sports with knives in it. Big knives; machetes. He was showing them off, but was so wrecked he was practically drooling, flailing around. 'That yute is a proper nitty,' Travis said to Big Pharma and Lloyds. 'I'm serious. Look at him. He's always popping on suttin? What's he doing here, bruv?'

'He's friendly, innit,' Pharma said. 'My close peoples and that, some of them in Brixton now, try to look after him. He's young. Mandem likes him. Boy's getting a name, though, in Deptford and whatever. Trapping out in wrong places. Getting on people's patch. Guys in Deptford Grove and Catford Ghetto Boys want to fuckin kill him, bro. He got stabbed up about five times. Ain't shook, though. Kid's off his nut.'

'Forreal?' Travis said. 'Five different times?'

'Yeah, man. Got soaked outside the Lidl in Catford other week.'

'You need to control him, Bigs. We don't want it kicking off. The music's the thing. I don't want any big beef.'

The boy was jumping about and then he fell against the kitchen wall and slid down and was mumbling and swinging his arm. Blades on the table. When he stretched out his leg his trackies rode up at the ankles. 'Check it,' Lloyds said. 'He got a shank down his leg. It's not in a sheath or nothing. Blood on his sock.' The kid was sixteen. Total white boy with floppy hair over one eye and fluff on his chin.

The party was moving onto the balcony and the rain was drumming out there and the music was sweet. London was breathing. Somebody cleared away the JD knife bag and the energy got cooler, and Pharma perched on the edge of the busted armchair with Travis, singing along with a track. It was lyrical warfare, a track by Agar Active about a killing in Kentish Town. Travis held smoke back and when he began to speak the puff came out with his breath. Somebody handed him a rolled-up note.

Eventually, he went into the kitchen and broke into a smile. 'Milo 5! You came, bro!'

He was standing next to the sink with his rucksack, wearing an old Supreme hoodie.

'You're my buddy for time, Trav. I wasn't going to miss your birthday.'

They clasped hands and snapped fingers. Travis put his arm round his neck. 'The bando's rocking, fam.'

Travis chucked him some papers and they went through to the erupted chair. They lit up and floated in and out of the smoke, lighters flaring. Travis put on his ribbing voice and said that his friend was loved up.

'She's a smart woman.'

'I get it, fam. I'm gassed for you, trust. I don't see you enough, still.'

'You're out there, fam,' Milo said with a smile. 'Hiding on YouTube.'

They necked from a champagne bottle and spoke about the time they got kicked out of the Cally Leisure Centre for throwing a bunch of bath bombs they'd stolen from Poundland into the water. Milo was cackling. 'The whole baby pool fizzed up and all the mums were like, "What the . . .".' Travis was in his element, loving and forgiving, back to being the way Milo liked him to be, the sport-loving young sneakerhead, whistling through the gap in his front teeth.

Milo told him he was scoping out one of his professors, that the guy had been involved in the past with Zemi's school. 'Doing charity work, so-called,' Milo said. 'Not that he remembers my mum. He's a smart guy, but we'll see how smart.'

'You talking about this guy who taught you?'

'Yeah. He thinks he's one of the good guys.'

The boys on the balcony came in when the rain got too hard. Lloyds brought more powder and gave it to Travis.

A couple of hours later, things were quieting down. A lot of the crew had left but the hardcore stayed on. Milo probably had books he had to read and the bando was not his thing. But Travis wanted him to stay with them, and said so. His boy reached down by the chair and took a laptop out of his rucksack. They had Wi-Fi in the empty flat, coming from the legit unit upstairs, belonging to an old boozer called Graham, who lived alone and was too scared to complain about the noise. Quickly, Milo had them online.

Big Pharma was high, bopping alone with the music, and he came over to Milo and started agitating for videos, shouting out for Jammer, Vybz Kartel.

Milo's fingers went fast. He checked a password on his phone and started downloading something. 'Hold on,' he said.

'If you can rule a computer you can rob a bank,' Lloyds said.

Travis's gaze wandered again to the window. Red crane lights blinking in the distance. Then lightning. He felt emotional. He had a sudden hash-dream in the middle of the thunder, that he was driving his mother in a great big car or was getting an award and making her proud as fuck all over again. He wanted that, not another weeping mother at the back of a court room.

'I miss your mum,' he said.

Milo glanced from his laptop, but he wasn't able to say anything. It wasn't even a year yet and it was too raw.

On the computer, something was downloading. While they waited, Milo opened a video.

'What's all this?'

Milo put a long finger to his lips. 'From the news,' he said. 'Something my mum was into.' He set the laptop up on a box and let it play.

'Aite, fam,' Lloyds said. 'I'm wit you.'

A newsreader was on the screen.

'Primary school children in the UK have fallen dangerously behind,' the newsreader was saying. 'Parents are worried about a lost generation, and education authorities suggest that migrant children are doing worse than any other group in the country. We sent our home affairs editor, Nathan Eldridge, to Manchester . . .'

'This is what my mother cared about,' Milo said.

Big Pharma leaned into Travis, high but clear-minded. 'Some kids have it rough, you know? That's how our ends got the name. The Cally's named after an orphanage for kids from Scotland or some shit. Didn't we learn that in school?'

'Nah, bruv. I never heard that,' Travis said.

'Yeah. Trust me. It's where mumzy's crib is now.'

Travis saw Milo press his lips together.

Apart from the lighters, the room was dark now. But Milo's concentration and the screen glow was like a beam and they all gathered round. He leaned over the laptop and hit a few more keys. 'You're gonna love this,' he said. 'By the magic of hackerdom – get this . . .'

It was pirate material from *The Last Dance*.

'The Michael Jordan thing!' Lloyds shouted.

'The offcuts. Material they didn't broadcast,' Milo said.

He tapped the keyboard and a basketball court full of players appeared. 'Jheeze!' Travis shouted, then he whooped when Jordan ran, jumped and paused in the air.

# 9 The Brambles

On Sunday 30 May, the meadowsweet was blooming on the banks of the Waveney. Campbell loved the way it frothed into the river. From the kitchen window, he could see the water's gleam as it pooled near Wortham Ling, and a pair of rabbits hopped in the furze and scratched in the sand, their nervous systems somehow connected to the possibility that a human being might be passing up on the road.

It was a week since Campbell had returned from Italy. Next door to the house in Suffolk, their neighbour had an honesty larder in a box by the road – eggs, plants, strawberries – and Campbell went over in his dressing-gown and slippers. When he didn't have coins, he left a fiver, which he knew they considered very London. Coming back, he turned into his front garden and looked up at the cottage. He'd spent thirty-five grand underpinning the fireplaces, with a lot of interference from English Heritage. And now it was the thatch, greening with moss under the wire netting. Birds were nesting along the ridge at the top and the whole thing needed redoing. More money. He went into the kitchen and cracked the eggs and poured them into a pan. Cheese. Chives. Elizabeth had come down late the night before – she hopped on the M11 like it was an escalator. He took up the breakfast and sat on the bed for an hour telling her about Venice and Trieste.

On the pinboard in his garden office, among spurious self-help notes – the sort he scribbled to persuade himself his book wasn't just a quick, shameful attempt to use his own confusions to earn a buck – there were clippings about Dutch art, along with a piece of junk mail from the previous December. Its wording summed up, for him, the Suffolk worldview. 'Once again,' wrote supporters of the local church, 'we are collecting Christmas presents for homeless people in the city of London. There is a particular need for practical gifts for single men, such as toiletries, underwear, socks, etc. Please give new items but nothing containing alcohol.' It made Elizabeth blush, the sense of a raging Babylon just over the horizon, a Hogarthian stew of poor and toothless unfortunates swigging aftershave and lighter fluid. Also on the noticeboard, stuck with a love-heart Post-it, was a picture of Barbara Hepworth's sculpture *Mother and Child*, with a note in Elizabeth's handwriting saying he should buy it for her one day. He didn't like the countryside half as much as she did, but he studied it, the flora and fauna, because studying had always made something noble of his disorientation. He missed King's Cross, everything about it, all its roiling possibilities, which during weekends at the Brambles could sometimes resolve into a quietly depressive *nostalgie du pavé*, unless he was writing something.

A bunch of cornflowers sat in a mug. In the bookcase, his eyes passed over a shelf of poetry, including volumes by the two Roberts, Lowell and Bly. He'd always resisted the idea that poetry was like medicine. He thought about Bly's book from the early 1990s, the one that had urban men beating their chests in the woods or whatever. It really was another world back then, when Campbell was in his twenties. He was now beginning to wonder whether he himself wasn't part of that toxicity they all spoke about. He'd always felt shielded by irony and art's mysteries, but sitting in his cosy hut, it again occurred to Campbell that he was not above it all. Maybe that's the way a crisis gathers force and dimension in a person's life, when anxiety metastasises from one damaged area to another.

He spent an hour or so replying to emails, then sat with his phone. His student messaged to say he should be thinking about the Dark Net and 'alternative economies'. He also offered the opinion that

Campbell's podcast series was 'bullshit' and not worthy of him. Campbell was still smarting from the mystery of the charity donations. But he'd decided not to bring the whole thing up with Milo. It was a process. Maybe it was just the young man's way of telling him to think about inequality. Campbell decided the unmentioned donations could be a way of showing Milo that he trusted his judgment and wished to learn. His new comrade was a disrupter, and rightly so. Campbell had never experienced anything like this with a student. He told Elizabeth the donations were a glitch. He didn't say more.

A couple of hours later, getting up from his chair, he tried to shake himself out. He stretched up and touched the ceiling, then did some press-ups out on the grass, the small of his back saying no and the laughter of the birds chiming in. Reaching across for his phone, he swiped to Calm and found himself for ten minutes among 'Highland Birdsong', enjoying the weird clash of the real birds in his garden with the digital chirps in their unknown glen. It felt rich, like a new form of experience.

He met Elizabeth inside the cottage. She reminded him they were due at Hinderclay that evening for supper with the Duke and Duchess. She disappeared for a moment, and when she came back he was on his phone again, studying some 'hints' from Ancestry, suggesting more names that might have a place in his shady family tree.

'You're always on that,' she said, setting down two glasses of white wine.

'Not that much,' he said.

She'd asked him if he was trying to connect to something. 'These shadow-figures from your Glasgow past. It's interesting to me,' she said, 'that they seem to be preoccupying you in a way that they haven't before.'

'Not everybody's family is established, Elizabeth. Or even known.'

'Okay, don't take it the wrong way.'

He sipped from his glass. 'Not everybody's father and grandmother and great-uncle Dicky were painted in oils.'

'Oh, shush,' she said. 'I'm building a fire. It's weirdly cold for May.'

She had the good therapist's capacity to appreciate the interestingness of things that wouldn't immediately submit to her will. Campbell wasn't sure he had that. On the table, a bunch of mail was spread out, letters Elizabeth had brought up from Thornhill Square.

'There's another letter from Islington Council,' she said, 'and it rather goes beyond belief.'

'Don't tell me . . .' he said.

'I'm afraid so. Mrs Voyles.'

'What is it now?'

Elizabeth flattened the letter on the table. 'She wrote to them about the smell. The vermin. They visited again and came up with a list of hazards. I mean, she does have a case. She's really rather a vulnerable person, darling.'

'What does she want from us?'

'New flooring.' She pushed up her spectacles. 'And perhaps another radiator at the back of her flat. There's no guarantee she'll let the workmen in, obviously.'

'Fucking hateful,' he said. Had he been able to, he might have followed his wife's example, finding the whole thing a bit pathetic. Instead, he took out his phone, dialled the woman's number and hit speaker.

'Is that Mrs Voyles? Yes. Professor Flynn.'

She warbled about being busy and not liking to speak on the phone.

'We're in Suffolk. I have here a letter from the council suggesting various remedies to your flat.'

'It's not my flat,' she said. 'But I have an order from the council to have these hazards attended to. I will not live in a slum. I told them about you shouting at me in the street last week. And slamming the door in my face.'

'We will try again to have the workmen do what is necessary under the law to make the flat habitable.'

'I'd sooner you got on with buying me out.'

'I beg your pardon?'

'Buy me out. Make me that offer.'

Campbell was not a born property owner, he was not a profiteer, and he considered himself to be a liberal intellectual with a large capacity for social justice, but this woman's attitude killed him. 'You are outrageous,' he said to her. 'You have lived in that building for forty years. You have made no contribution to the upkeep of the place and your rent is paid by the council—'

'And I suppose you are in your second house, are you? It being Sunday?'

He was stunned. 'End the call,' Elizabeth said. 'Campbell! We will deal with this through the proper channels.'

'We are peaceful people,' he continued into the phone. 'I do not expect gratitude from you for the work we're doing, but I do expect co-operation. We are in no position to "buy you out". I will seek a legal injunction to have you comply with the upgrades demanded by the council. Repeatedly, we have underlined our commitment—'

'Oh, please!' she said.

'I am sorry for you if you are an unhappy person—'

Mrs Voyles hung up on him. He was stunned all over again. He held out his iPhone, his mouth gaping.

'Crikey,' Elizabeth said, laughing. 'There's a woman who knows her own mind.'

'*Unbelievable.*'

Elizabeth's mirth disappeared when she saw how furious he was. 'Come on, Campbell,' she said, 'you're giving this too much energy.'

He knew his face must be a picture. 'I absolutely fucking loathe her.'

This was a bad policy with Elizabeth. She hated slack talk. 'I don't admire you in this mode. You prize your own feelings over everyone else's, and you are showing a lack of humanity to this woman.'

'Why are you defending her, Elizabeth?'

'She has redeeming features. You choose not to see them. She's quite a cultured person. She used to be in the Royal Ballet. And she's kind to the men laying pipes in the road, bringing them tea and biscuits. You're turning her into something else.'

She'd said it to him before, in a previous row.

'Just watch out,' she said, taking a sip of wine. 'You may be in danger of becoming too fascinating to yourself.'

'Oh, fuck it,' he said. 'I can't see why I'm the bad one.'

'Just remember you're much luckier than she is.'

His phone buzzed in his hand. It was William Byre.

'Are you up at the house? Shit's hit the fan, I'm afraid.'

He turned up at the Brambles an hour and a half later, wild-eyed and scrofulous. He was wearing a double-breasted suit, a bit crumpled, and had flaking skin around his mouth. His grey hair was flattened. Campbell's shirts were too small for William, but he found a big T-shirt and sent him for a wash while he prepared lunch, asking Elizabeth to come down from her study to join them if she possibly could. 'His driver took him to Cambridge,' he said. 'He just wandered around, apparently. I think he's unravelling.'

William didn't touch the food. He asked for a glass of wine and didn't care for the leftovers they were drinking, so Campbell opened a bottle he'd brought back from Italy.

'Well, that's it,' William said. 'The knighthood. The companies – fucking disaster. I knew it was coming. But it suddenly feels real when the hacks turn up at the house.'

'That's nothing new,' Campbell said, trying to sound light. 'You had the hacks *inside* the house already.'

'So, what's happening?' Elizabeth asked.

William rubbed his chin. 'It's gone from whispers to shouting. An increase in volume. And there are new allegations. These women . . .'

'What's Antonia saying?' Elizabeth said.

'She hasn't officially thrown me out. She's playing the long game.'

'Are you ruined?'

'House is fine. We have money abroad. But it's hell. Antonia's a bitch.'

Campbell saw Elizabeth sink back in her chair.

'You know she was an agony aunt who is now paid to give her views about world affairs?' William offered. 'She's professionalised all her neuroses. She takes up the issue of the week, whatever it is, no matter how harmful to her loved ones, and this week it's men who cheat on their wives. She's writing delusional, self-serving nonsense for a tribe of nutters who see no difference between accusations and evidence.'

'So you want all this to be about Antonia?' Elizabeth said.

'I thought you'd already lost the stupid knighthood,' Campbell said, trying to draw the conversation back.

'It was only rumoured before, but now it's actually gone, according to the *Sunday Times*.'

He found the news story and passed the phone to Campbell.

'Let's take a breath,' Elizabeth said. William's face was pink from the razor; his eyes were brimming with tears. 'Campbell tells me you have a new partner.'

He took a swig from his glass. 'Vicky. She's probably the only truly good person I've ever met in my life,' he said.

'She must give you comfort.'

'It's not like that. I don't love like that. Most women are frightened of me.'

Campbell found that disquieting. Bizarre. He kept his eyes down. 'The *Sunday Times*,' he said, trying again to alter course, 'says there's an honours forfeiture committee. Who knew? "The Queen is stripping honours from increasing numbers. The committee sees its function as one of renovating the past."'

'That's rich,' William said. 'They should look in the mirror.'

'Kim Philby, Anthony Blunt, John Profumo, Robert Mugabe.'

'These human beings appear to have something in common,' Elizabeth said. She lifted the plates and then disappeared into the kitchen.

'Thank you *very much*, Lizzie!' William shouted after her.

Campbell wasn't sure why he'd come. Homing instinct, probably. After another glass, he suggested they go for a walk. William was resistant: he said he hadn't gone for a walk since they'd visited the Pyrenees in 1996. He had the wrong shoes, but everything was wrong, so it didn't seem to matter as they walked up the lane, passing the beekeeper's cottage.

William began to talk. He said his money had always been a burden to him, which grated on Campbell. And then, suddenly, an admission. 'The factories are full of illegal workers. Poles and Albanians run by gangs or whatever. And now with Brexit, it's all collapsing.'

'So it's all true?'

'It's . . . business. It's how it's done.'

'You've let everything run out of control, William.'

There was a half-smile on his face. 'Free markets,' William said, breathless, stopping to lean against a tree.

'You all right?' Campbell asked.

'I gather this fucking journalist on the *Commentator* has new information about me too. Nonsense about women, stuff about low wages. She's got a source—'

'That journalist is making quite a name for herself.'

'Tuppence ha'penny website. The fucker's been trying to destroy me.'

They walked through daisies up towards the church. The graveyard was quiet and they saw a fresh trench had been dug by the stone wall. There wasn't much of a breeze, but a cascade of tiny, papery wings blew from the trees above their heads and fell onto the gravestones. Campbell bent down. He picked up one of the samaras and rubbed the seed between his fingers until it popped out. William read a few of the inscriptions and then turned to Campbell as if to announce his latest wheeze. 'What would happen,' he said, 'if I lay down in that hole and you covered me up with earth?'

'Stop talking like that.'

'You get destroyed, Campbell. That's what happens. It's all around you, don't you see? You end up owing everybody your life.'

Campbell shook his head. A blackbird landed on the wall with a caterpillar in its yellow beak. 'We'll survive,' he said.

When they were down near the Ling, William took out his phone to summon his driver back to the house. His hand shook. They made a promise to get together soon and Campbell told him to remember who he was, thinking of the witty and belligerent young man he'd known years ago.

'*Per aspera ad astra*,' William said over the hood of the car, then he climbed inside and was gone.

Campbell liked that hour, upstairs with his wife, getting ready to go out, the flirty burlesque of dressing and combing. It was an important ritual of togetherness and social union, the straightening of ties, the zipping of dresses, the glances in the mirror and the spritzing of scent.

'I love that shirt,' she said. 'It's the perfect light blue.'

'Is the scarf all right? I like to go a bit Ballets Russes for Candy.'

He was wearing a soft brown jacket and a claret-coloured scarf covered in tiny dots, which he'd bought at a Boggi shop in Italy.

If being long-suffering is a high art, then Candy Crofts (née Lady Candida Wipps-Cooper), the Duchess of Kendal, nickname Nighty, could be considered the Caravaggio of the form, achingly baroque against a dark background. At times, with her perma-smile and her art charities and her ceaseless attempts to 'save' the ancestral home, Candy could seem like the liveliest little disaster in England, trying her hardest to be interesting when all around her was vile and inscrutable. When they arrived, she was standing under the porch light of Hinderclay House, wearing a thin dress and ballet pumps, as usual. Elizabeth walked across the pink gravel and they exchanged the usual shrieks and kisses.

Campbell wiggled her ear. Poor Candy had been groomed for this torture. After a modest primary school in the Cotswolds, she was deposited at Cheltenham Ladies' College, before being dropped into a secretarial course in the King's Road. Thus prepped, she met the Duke of Kendal in 1981 at the Warwickshire Hunt Ball in Tysoe Manor. Nowadays, she was associate director of the Thetford Poetry Festival, a trustee of Himalayan Life and ran the organic farm and wellness centre at Hinderclay, as well as being patron of the Gaelic Society in Beauly, Inverness-shire, about five miles from Crofts Castle. 'Elizabeth is different from her sister,' their mother had told him. 'With Candy it was always titles or death. And she's been swimming towards the life raft ever since.'

Walking into the hall, Candy held Elizabeth's hand.

'Did this year's poetry thing come off all right?' Campbell asked her.

'It was divine,' Candy said. 'Completely online. Such fun. We had people Zooming from Peru and all sorts of places.'

'Jeezo. Who'd have thunk it? All for poetry, "the nightlong frenzy of shrews", as Ted Hughes called it.'

'Stop it,' Candy said. 'It was wonderful.' She pondered. 'We loved Ted. You know my godmother was lady-in-waiting to the Queen Mother?'

'I think I did know that.'

'Well . . .'

She handed their coats to a member of staff.

'. . . she told us Her Majesty was utterly in love with Ted. I mean, *passionate*. They used to go fishing together and her heart would throb to smithereens. They had pet names for each other and the whole thing was terribly sweet.'

Standing in the hall, Campbell felt positive: it was one of those bright evenings in the country when everything seems well. The birds were singing as the setting sun struck the mullioned windows, giving hope. Hinderclay had the dusty, resplendent patina of centuries. The Kendals went all the way back to Flodden, and they had the musketry to prove it, gleaming darkly from the walls above the tapestries and busts. In the drawing room, Murillos and Hoppners jostled on the red damask wallpaper, and the multiple sofas were backed with tables crowded with family pictures – no children, alas, but adults choked in uniforms or pearls. A number of people stood in the room, but Campbell walked alone to the drinks table. They always had these tables everywhere, with tins of tonic water and tomato juice stacked up, cheap whiskies and old tumblers. He poured a gin and looked up at a cabinet of books, a full run of Trollopes bound in red leather. At the end, on its own, was a copy of Campbell's *Vermeer*. He surveyed the room and took a deep breath. The Duke had been off his head, Campbell thought, since Candy turned forty-five and Anthony realised their inability to produce an heir meant the dukedom might die with him. Such things can corrupt.

He was all of a sudden beside him, the Duke, dressed in a ridiculous Nehru jacket and white linen trousers above a pair of slippers. 'I have to confess,' he said, 'I still haven't read this book of yours. Too much work, if you ask me.'

'That's idiotic, Tony. I speak as a writer.'

'Of course you do!'

He touched Campbell's arm as they turned towards the others. 'I'm afraid I'm rather depending on you tonight,' the Duke said. 'We've got one or two absolute crashers.' It wasn't really possible to be with Tony without wanting to alter the world. He emitted ghastly opinions from a mouth filled with distressed teeth. Seeing his face and the crimson faces of all his friends, as well as the pinkly depraved ancestors looking from his pictures, made you want to set fire to it all and go home. With a moment's defiance, Campbell paused, not wishing to be led, and looked into a mahogany vitrine, where a collection of ancient coins let him catch his breath. He saw a George III shilling and a 1687 Maundy threepence, as well as an Augustus Caesar denarius, which had existed before the decline and fall of an empire. He stared down and saw his own face in the glass. He was still thinking about William and the disaster now engulfing him. It sent a depth charge into Campbell's system, that he had cloistered himself with badness.

'Have you met my dear friend Colin?' The man in front of him was thin and spoke with a Yorkshire accent.

'Yes, I think I have,' Campbell said, shaking the hand of Lord Haxby, the artist Carl Friis's husband. 'I think you know my children.'

'Aye. Well, my partner does. They're pals. Specially Angus. Carl and he have worked together in the past, I believe.'

'Probably sees more of my son than I do.'

The Duke gestured to the others in the group, introducing Campbell. 'Renowned art historian and penman. My wife's brother-in-law. Forever rattling the cages of the public in the *Spectator* and whatnot.'

'I've never written for the *Spectator*,' Campbell said, nodding to a jolly lady in a long skirt, then to a rather deluxe bishop.

'Mrs Frisby is a housemistress at Framlingham College,' the Duke said. 'A huge friend to Candy in her efforts to place poets into schools. Isn't that right?' The lady was excited and eating a square of smoked salmon. She put her glass of champagne in the crook of her arm and offered a fishy hand to Campbell. 'Bishop Cree is from Diss,' the Duke continued, 'previously of Ipswich. Recently returned from Rome.'

'Thank you, Your Grace,' the bishop said. 'I am honoured and indeed a modicum fearful in meeting you, Professor Flynn. It has been my pleasure to meet many representatives of the artistic world, but a man of your standing, with such controversial views, and indeed important points to make, is, yes . . . an honour.'

'He's rather long-winded, I'm afraid.' The Duke slapped the gentleman's empurpled back and hooted. 'Self-involved, like a tree.'

'That's a rather wonderful scarf,' the bishop said, unperturbed. 'Rather reminds me of the sort of garments once worn, ahem, by my late friend, the Monsignor Brian Brindley. Did you ever have the pleasure?'

'Sadly not,' Campbell said.

'No, no, well,' the bishop continued. 'He was the most terrific dresser, if I may say so. That was most assuredly one of his strong points, I'd say. Most definitely. Red slippers. Grapes hanging off the biretta—'

'Good Lord.'

'He died at his club, poor man, surrounded by his young friends. He was quite the aficionado, you might be interested to know, of the works of Durante Alberti. And an aficionado of young friends, I daresay. Ahem. A private supper, they tell me, a rather fierce sort of gathering altogether, there can be no doubt. Brian's light appears to have expired somewhere between the crab mousse and the *boeuf en daube*.'

Candy had been out showing Elizabeth the yoga studio they'd had built. She was now telling them all how Hinderclay cost a fortune to run, and they'd lost all their revenue during lockdown. They'd had to furlough many of the staff. But now it was all over, she hoped. The tea shop was open again, and tourists were returning. 'We think the crisis has given birth to a better sort of humanity,' Candy said, 'and wellness is the new . . .'

'Religion?' the bishop suggested.

'Well, no. I wouldn't go that far,' she said. 'But spiritual healing is our mission. All the tribal divisions that have separated us for so long and caused such suffering, I believe they can now be addressed in a climate of forgiveness.'

'Here's to that!' Mrs Frisby said. 'Our girls are heading in a similar direction. I'm always using the example of modern Tibet to the girls in our House. I say to them, "Human beings cannot live by exam passes alone." You have to go outside to make a difference. Expand the lungs! Enter into communion . . .'

'Oh, yes,' the bishop said.

'. . . with nature as it presents itself.'

'We have a fire ceremony every Friday to offer gratitude,' Candy said. 'And now that we're fully open, we will return to wild swimming, moon bath rituals, the cacao ceremony and meditation, as well as soul definition.'

'Bloody hell, I'm starving, Nighty,' the Duke said. He had absent-mindedly removed a first edition from the shelf and opened it, Thomas Dyche's *Guide to the English Tongue*, then snapped it shut.

They sat down at a long table, the wood alive with candlelight. It turned out Candy was in discussions with various officials from the Smithsonian Channel to present a new series called *The British Aristocrat's Guide to Life*. As she said this, the Duke spat wine into his napkin and stormed off to the cellar, because it turned out the two magnums of Château Talbot on the table were corked. 'We're also rather busy at the minute,' she continued, 'distributing meals from the café kitchens to local people who are vulnerable.'

'That's the Lord's work,' the bishop said, sitting across from her and vigorously buttering a roll.

'It's my own idea,' she said. 'If we get the TV series off the ground, I aim to start a meditation circle here. It's a new concept: Whole-Self.'

Elizabeth looked over the table at Campbell. He could tell what she was thinking.

He shouldn't make that face.

Self-help, indeed.

Who was he to be so superior, simply because he threw in a few quotes from Philip Roth and Marcus Aurelius?

Campbell listened to some lengthened, sage advice from Mrs Frisby, who wanted him to understand how deeply she felt about China. Several of her girls were taking part in an exchange programme and it was all lovely. On the wall above the wine table, Campbell was pleased to see again a very obviously fake Constable and, below it, a portrait of Otto von Bismarck from about 1890, accompanied by a signed letter, framed beneath, offering good wishes to the Duke of Kendal from the Chancellor of the German Reich. Campbell drank another glass of the Château Talbot 1961, still dodgy, and pushed a piece of gristle across his plate. It was school dinners as usual, except now Candy was on the Lion Diet, so the supper mainly consisted of raw meat and salt. She regularly put up YouTube videos of cooking classes she ran with the fluffy-haired farmboys, and one of these employees was there at the other end of the table, Fergus – the landscaper and 'mindfuckness guru', as Campbell had named him. Fergus had the blondest hair anybody had ever seen. He was broad. I hope he's shagging Candy into the middle of next week, Campbell thought, picking up the dish of Béarnaise sauce, then turning to Lord Haxby, on his left, who'd been waiting to speak.

'Who was that man you were with at the Wolseley?' Haxby asked, with all the forthrightness he mistook for integrity.

'He's my agent.'

'Aye. Drunk-looking.'

Campbell took in the raffish appearance of the peer. 'You don't have much of an appetite for pity, I see.'

'I speak as I find,' Haxby replied. He forked the meat and over-chewed it. 'Carl's gone off to Helsinki. At the docks, there's this warehouse filled with destroyed paintings. Art from all over Europe. He loves it.' They talked about the show Friis was planning and the artist's hope that Campbell might write something for it. He felt goaded by this fortysomething: the amplitude of his self-certainty, his natural boastfulness, the weary way he talked about Parliament and his 'battle with idiots'. Campbell knew that Moira despaired of Haxby and all the 'natural Labour supporters' who'd turned Conservative. A number of them turned invisibly, or at least quietly, but Haxby had crossed the floor, noisily trumpeting his view that socialism was dead in the North.

'You used to work for Lord Scullion,' Campbell said. He had decided to share nothing of his animosity, but to press a nerve.

'I was his researcher in the Blair years, when Paul was a minister.'

'And you still see him?'

'On the regular. He's a Labour peer, as you know, but he gives me advice about fundraising. It's a true, deep friendship.'

'A Labour peer gives a Tory fundraiser advice on how to go about raising funds for the government party, which is not his own?'

'That's right. Things have changed, Professor. We're old friends. And friendship is much stronger than party politics.'

'You deal in fallacies, Lord Haxby. *That's* modern politics.'

'I don't know about that. But fallacies make great projectiles.' He leaned back in his chair in a skittish way, as if to take a long look at his opponent.

'Like a good boy, you've eaten up all your Trump,' Campbell said.

The peer put his hands flat on the table. 'Seems to me you writers are paranoid. You don't take many chances, do you?'

'What do you mean?'

'It's all low stakes with you guys, keeping your nose clean, being fearful, observing the rules. You're in the reassurance game, mate.'

'And what game are you in – *mate*?'

'The "turning things around" game. The "making a difference" game. Taking risks. Knowledge, youth and purpose. You should try it.'

'Wow.'

'You canna be safe all your life,' he said.

Campbell went to the loo: he wanted to google him. Colin Haxby did Modern Languages at Balliol and then worked in public relations for Leeds Council, before becoming Paul Scullion's researcher, and winning the Sunderland by-election in 2005. When first in the Commons he was married to the heiress Serena Chalfont and they had two kids. He left Parliament in 2010 to work as head of communications for Plusgaz, the Russian energy company, travelling between Moscow and London. He was said to be an expert in London property. He was made a life peer in August 2015 and created Lord Haxby of Howden. He had in recent years taken up an executive chairmanship with Chernaya House Group, a natural gas company owned by the Russian oligarch Aleksandr Bykov. In the 'Personal Life' section, all it said was that he'd left his wife in 2018 to enter into a relationship with the artist Carl Friis.

As he washed his hands, Campbell looked up and saw a framed photo of his brother-in-law when he was the young Major Crofts, dated not long before he succeeded to the dukedom, in uniform onboard HMS *Hermes*.

Walking down the corridor, Campbell felt a text buzz in his pocket. Another one from Milo Mangasha. A joke about the police. He sent jokes and sometimes slogans, several in a week.

Campbell grinned and sent back a thumbs-down emoji.

On re-entering the dining room, he saw the Duke was up on his feet and pointing to one of the plinths in the corner. His voice was loud, and he was schooling the bishop in the history of porphyry. 'There's none of this rock left, I'm telling you. They dug up the whole bloody lot and made busts like this.'

'It really is rather ruddy,' Bishop Cree said.

'That's right. The popes used to love it because of the *red*.' The figure of Byron seemed to rock a fraction on the plinth when it was poked. A portrait of William Crofts, the 9th Duke, a rather romantic work by Edward Halliday, was above the fireplace. The late aristo looked down at his son from an elevated balustrade, the rows of medals and the grandeur of his cloak insufficient guard against the indignities of his afterlife. The Duke slumped back into his seat and Candy let go a tiny cough. '*That*,' he said, holding on to the bishop's cuff and pointing to an Allan Ramsay painting of an elderly maid, 'is an old Scottish whore that used to hang in our drawing room at Crofts Castle.'

'In fact,' Campbell immediately said, 'it's a delicate and rather beautiful example of Scottish portraiture at its finest, painted 1740.'

'Napoo for Scots tarts! Reminds me of one who used to work in the kitchens here, brazen as a red plaid shirt—'

'Tony, please,' Candy said, her face flushing.

Campbell returned to his place.

'It's all right, Nighty,' the Duke slurred. His eyes were flaring. 'She had an ill-conditioned mind and a rough tongue.'

'I must say,' intervened Mrs Frisby, all giggly, 'the girls at Windsor House are using the most wicked language at the moment. Heavens. Colourful indeed! And our Chinese students have no idea what precisely they are saying, which is a good thing, thank the Lord. Pardon me, Bishop!'

'Not at all, Mrs Frisby. He is the Lord, after all, and liable to be thanked, for this and that good fortune, or unavoidable trial.'

The Duke ventured with the view that all art is, in a manner of speaking, fake. He said that the Chinese architect he was using for the library wing at Segdoune Grange came highly recommended by one of his friends. But the architect was also a painter who could produce a perfect reproduction of anything you might ask for.

'Sun Zetao,' Lord Haxby said.

'Exactly,' the Duke continued. 'A mysterious figure. No speech. But he can do you a Rubens as fast as look at you. And what's the difference? These Leonardos and so on are so overpainted there's nothing left of the artist anyway.'

Bishop Cree, it transpired, was an antiquarian with a special interest in early manuscripts, an authority on the losses of the Reformation. It appeared he had leaned on the Duke once or twice, when it came to buying papers and ancient coins, and was treated, despite his usefulness at dinners and so on, as a sponge. Rhubarb fool was served, and the conversation turned, as it does, to the question of whether culture is worth defending. 'Somebody sent me a book the other day,' the Duke said, 'about the rape of Worcester Priory. Apparently, there were over six hundred books in the medieval catalogue, and old Henry VIII burned all but six of them. Now, here's a philosophical question: is it not worse, the loss of nearly six hundred priceless volumes, than the loss of another six hundred lives in some Polish forest during the Second World War?'

'Goodness, Your Grace,' the bishop said. 'That's quite a question. I am bound to say that life is sacred – above all, human life.'

'More sacred than these sacred texts?'

'I think so, sir. Yes, I am bound to say so.'

'I disagree,' the Duke said. 'There are many lives. Billions of them. Most of them spent in ignorance and insignificance. But each of these books represented a leap in our civilisation. Their loss is a historical disaster. The lives of most people are not worth a single folio. Who's to say flesh is worth more than parchment?'

'That is grotesque,' Campbell said. 'I thought you found books boring?'

'No, I said *reading* was boring. Not the same thing.'

The bishop wiped his befuddled face with his napkin and put it down. 'There is the spirit, Your Grace. We mustn't overlook—'

'Bishop, you know that is bunk. There is more spirit in a thirteenth-century book by Thomas Aquinas, fifteen by ten inches, held at Salisbury Cathedral, than in the whole population of the county of Essex today.'

'How terrifying,' Elizabeth interrupted. 'People like you used to burn books, now you praise them – as artefacts, or totems. Perhaps, Tony, you should step down from your platform once in a while and read one.'

Fergus from the wellness centre made the gesture with both hands that indicated a head exploding, and the conversation dissipated into pockets. Haxby took the opportunity to return to his mainly one-sided conversation, using words like 'inclusivity' and phrases like 'civic responsibility' while leaving Campbell in no doubt that he was steeped to the bottom of his soul in dirty money and lurid connections. He spoke at length about a ball he was helping to organise at the Natural History Museum, a 'back-to-normal' fundraiser, and he mentioned a number of people who would be in attendance.

'I couldn't help overhearing,' Candy said, leaning on the table. She had space for her hands because she wasn't having pudding. 'I wish you would help *us* fundraise, Colin – we've been absolutely walloped this past year.'

Campbell felt his boats burning.

He sat back and thought of his students, and of one in particular. He recalled the Rich List and how the Duke was down to his last £149 million.

'Candy, you really must stop this nonsense,' he said.

'Campbell – *no*,' Elizabeth said.

'I'm sorry, but this is insufferable. To talk about raising funds for these stupid things, right now, with ordinary people suffering, losing their jobs and . . . minorities in this country taking the brunt. Disgraceful.'

'Things are on the up,' said Lord Haxby. 'You're wrong. We are pulling the true people of this country out of the mire.'

'*True people?*' Campbell said. 'What does that mean? This isn't about real people. You're talking about cartoon Britons. People who you find it useful to invent. You are creating distress. You are causing hatreds. You are blinding people. And you are building a society of gangsters to fund your own delusions.'

'What's that?' the Duke said, as if he'd missed something. 'We should march into Europe and show the bloody lot of them what's what. The bloody truth, if you want my opinion, is that the EU's about as natural as a frankfurter.'

'You should all be ashamed of yourselves,' Campbell said.

'Why are you getting into such a stinking bate?' asked Haxby, looking around the table for support.

'Kleptocrats taking advantage of this country,' Campbell said, turning to the peer with a sharpened sense of outrage. 'I know all about Aleksandr Bykov, who you work for. These are dangerous, amoral men.'

'I think you're confused,' Haxby said.

'Campbell,' Elizabeth said softly.

'And that son of his – Yuri Bykov.'

'They're frightfully strong, actually,' the Duke said. 'Men of business. They get things done and that's not to be sniffed at.'

Haxby smiled. 'You take life too seriously, Professor Flynn. Yuri is a philanthropist. He's a keen young man. He cares about art, like you do, and his father is close to the Russian president. Why not make use of that? He may prove to be a significant asset to this country and you ought to encourage it.'

'You only care about money.'

'And don't you care about money?' Haxby asked.

Campbell fell silent and felt himself staring into the old conker brown of the table.

'Bloody well said!' the Duke intoned.

To change the subject, Candy mentioned that Campbell had only recently been to see her and Elizabeth's mother in Venice.

'Parents,' the bishop said, 'they really are the engine room of family life, the creative wellspring of good family relations and harmonies.'

'And what would *you* know about family?' the Duke said to Bishop Cree.

And that's when it came, the thunderclap to end all thunderclaps, a remark from Fergus – his only remark during the whole dinner – addressed in full innocence to the hapless bishop, who seemed to accept it as a rough spiritual test.

'I knew a priest once,' Fergus said, all clear-eyed with health, 'and after Confession he'd take down our shorts and examine our bums.'

'Good grief,' said Mrs Frisby. 'We can't have *that*!' At which point, Elizabeth started shaking with laughter, and so did Candy.

Campbell sidled off into the corridor again to look at his phone. He didn't care if it was rude. He scrolled through his messages. He felt in charge there, in touch with another self. The library was blue, the windows enormous, and eventually Campbell stared out on the beautiful parkland of darkening oaks.

# 10 Albany

When he wasn't in the country or at their mansion in Holland Park, the Duke was often at his old bachelor set at Albany, Piccadilly. His rooms were halfway down the rope-walk, opposite Admiral FitzRoy's storm barometer, which that day indicated a fair wind. For some time there had been work going on above him, an 'Oedipal struggle', the porter said, between the young playboy Ralph Trench and his father, the decorator Hartley Trench, who had made his name, and his family ill, via a lifetime's association with Sibyl Colefax and the Prince of Wales.

When the son moved into number E.12, it was goodbye faded chintz, goodbye hand-printed wallpapers and pelmets. The flowery curtains, meticulously swagged, fringed and tasselled, were ripped down in a single morning and taken to the Wandsworth dump. Young Trench put a dayglo obelisk in the central room and had the walls emblazoned with murals of Renaissance Florence, before installing four orange pouffes, a Bauhaus desk and an Alhambra-style carpet made specially by his father's rival, Alidad. It was an eternity of banging for the Duke downstairs and the former spycatcher who lived across the way. Then it suddenly concluded, as these things do, at Knight Frank, which placed a price tag of £4 million on the property, despite its being 917 feet square. The advert didn't make it as far as the estate agent's window, because the Duke texted his friend Aleksandr Bykov immediately and he made an offer sufficiently over the asking price, securing it immediately for his son, Yuri, who moved in the week he left Oxford.

Yuri had grown up in Mayfair, and had spent the last few years partying and meeting people, establishing his own world. Today, he had a window open and was playing *Eugene Onegin* in preparation for Garsington. He'd kept the Freudian revenge décor, adding a few elements of his own, mainly pictures: a Warhol *Mao* over the fireplace, a Peter Doig in the hall, a series of Dash Snows opposite the velvet four-poster in the bedroom – the pictures a twenty-first birthday present from his mother, to show her insouciance after the mega divorce settlement. Yuri sat on a lime green sofa, conducting the music. He'd had a few illegal soirées over the last year at Albany, a few coke binges, a giant photoshoot, but now he was settling in to show his father who was the better Londoner.

The great Aleksandr, so loyal, so vain and so immensely rich, now had Cypriot nationality, making him a citizen of Europe. Yuri thought about it: the expensive passport for the Russian state actor, a lover of Tolstoy and a raider of Soviet utilities, eager to mingle with anyone who could secure his investments. All his father wanted was security, the money to thrive in a protected space, and here was London, the best of all laundering-places, the art so easy to buy and the huge properties so abundant. At his height, they were sanitising a billion a month. Yuri had become crucial in finessing his father's way into the art market, introducing him to a new generation of sellers, a new generation of legislators, the London media world, while increasingly showing zero respect for the old man.

Yuri had the habit, common to first-generation English Russians, of taking the high life for granted; the thing he didn't take for granted, but was driven towards like a sniffer dog, was the low life of the United Kingdom. He loved it. He adored its every aspect. Where his father and his friends wanted the imprimatur of Ivy League univer-sities, dinners with princes, a club membership or a gong from the Queen, Yuri wanted, more than anything, the attention of meatheads and drug dealers, hookers and party boys, art-crook impresarios and online pirates. He was born to it, in a way he couldn't quite explain but which gave him a feeling of power.

It had been almost two weeks since his lunch at Oswald's with

Jake Hart-Davies, a man he probably loved, at least for now. He was determined to devote June and July in London to improving himself with opera and drama, all the better to snare the famous young actor and spite his conforming father. Yuri reached above the sofa to the row of Shakespeare. He'd bought the books at Jake's insistence. 'Nobody is a true Englishman who can't quote the Bard,' the actor had said during one of their tutorials, so Yuri spent a fortune on the volumes, an early nineteenth-century set edited by Edmond Malone, which came from Sotheby's. Turning the pages of *King Lear*, Yuri contemplated the vanity of fathers. Before 2020, the old man had been a more regular visitor to London. The lackeys were working hard now, and they were sure that the senior Bykov would soon be free of the parliamentary subcommittee's attention. He was paying Lord Haxby a retainer of $3 million to finesse it all away.

Yuri looked at his watch. He meant to swap it for the Breguet, then changed his mind and fixed his hair. Outside, he passed busts of Byron and Bulwer-Lytton, and he felt slightly pleased, a blush of ownership, as a red bus crossed his vision. He turned onto Piccadilly. Yuri loved how well he knew London. It was his city, his secret. Passing the Ritz he would think of Evelyn Waugh, that brilliant, English, very terrible man, the worst of all fathers, lunching on caviar, grouse and peaches. He pictured those characters in 1939 who sipped and suppered on the brink of war, with fresh and appeasing oysters at Prunier and lunches at the Dorchester.

Arriving at his club, 5 Hertford Street, he went straight to the bar. He was popular at the club, having scored off every expensive bottle on the wine list. He knew the members, especially the Tory politicians, the donors, the hot-trotting Brexit crew, and was always glad to nod to them as they passed up and down the stairs to Loulou's. Somebody called it 'the new smoking room of Downing Street', and Yuri had seen it all: a hypocritical minister canoodling in the corner with a young female relative of the Queen's; a famous footballer getting rowdy with the doorman for failing to supply him with what he 'needed'; a barrister who asked a waitress for a blow job in the lift. (He said he'd pay. She pressed charges.) Yuri adored the heavenly drama. He knew the glossy editors and their pop star friends, and his main art dealer, when over from Belgium, was always mesmerised by the country-house feel of the place, and by the way Yuri, the soul of English discretion, cuddling up to everyone, could pass wraps of cocaine, which had made it past the friction of the new borders, into the sweaty palms of the young political heroes who had done so much to impose them.

'Hello, kiddo,' Lord Scullion said, sitting at the mirrored bar.

'Aha. The Labour Party's last stand,' Yuri said.

'I'd sooner die here than in West Yorkshire.'

'Good decision. What can I get you?'

Scullion tilted his glass to the light and said, 'Only water.' Yuri wondered if there wasn't a better water he might order, a healing glass from the spring at Lourdes, but he pointed to the tap and then ordered himself a Grey Goose. Yuri knew that Scullion was a kind of enemy. 'How's the old man?' he asked him.

It was obvious Scullion was here at the behest of Yuri's father. It was to honour that friendship, that fruitful association that had begun in the 1990s. Scullion had once been a sort of communist, back in his youth, but then so had Aleksandr. They seemed to believe that their early mistakes came from not entirely knowing the ways of the world. In the old days, Scullion would have met Aleksandr Bykov at the Queen's Club in West Kensington to play squash, or they'd smoke cigars together at Ten Trinity Square, but, since the US began to put on political pressure, Aleksandr seldom visited London. Yuri was the contact, and a not very willing or pliable one.

'It might go our way with the American sanctions,' Scullion said. 'There's been a lot of work done.'

'Yes. By Haxby.'

Scullion smiled. 'We've given him strong guidance.'

'The fact is,' Yuri said, enjoying his moment of being principled and strong, 'the Americans will sanction people like my father into the ground, and unless things change, the British will be more *tolerant*. There are, of course, many hysterics in your own party who would prefer us to be drowned in the Black Sea.'

Scullion wiped fluff off his knee. 'Well, some members of my party continue to have an unreconstructed sense of what we are for.'

'And what are you for, Lord Scullion?'

He didn't answer.

'Has it slipped your mind, dear? Well . . .'

Yuri adjusted on his stool.

'You were good at getting money for government projects by promising foreign investors favours from people in high places. And now – after all the ideals, my friend, new Britain and all that – you offer the same investors favours to get money for yourself. It's the oldest story in the book. It's why ordinary people have detested you for over twenty years.'

'Well,' Scullion said, 'we thrived, once upon a time, on a little of the old hopey-changey stuff.'

Scullion seemed supremely unbothered. Everything that could be said of him had already been said, and he had a rhino's skin. Smiling, he waved over to a table of girls from *Harper's Bazaar* and then smoothed his tie. 'You're a bright young man, Yuri,' he said. 'What we've always been in favour of is . . . open trade. Unhindered investment. International understandings that allow for prosperity and growth. That's my mission. My only one. And I would like us to work together to ensure those freedoms.'

'Naturally,' Yuri said. 'It's a comfort to know you'll be looking after our freedoms.'

The former minister sipped his water. He lived at the gym when he wasn't oiling up the world. Life was a litany of gifts and expenses, chairmanships and consultancies, then it was back to the cross trainer, the bid to live forever, the vampire life of knowing the dark and drawing blood. He began talking about his attempt to twist the arm of the Financial Conduct Authority, who were taking a harder line in blocking certain companies from being listed on the London Stock Exchange. 'Post-Brexit, the government wants to present a clean bill of health,' he said, 'maintaining London as a global financial centre. It's all bullshit from them: it was us that made it clean.'

Yuri raised a finger from his glass. 'It's me you're talking to, Paul, not some journalist. Clean? Give me a fucking break.'

Scullion's smile had a small sting in it. The Botox, probably. 'You've always been very charming, Yuri,' he said. 'You enjoy life, and that's an admirable thing. But I'm speaking of something quite serious now. Your father's energy company was listed on the London Stock Exchange nearly five years ago. It was all tickety-boo and no problem. But since the US sanctions—'

'Which are bullshit.'

'Agreed. But they are now threatening to block listings, and future ones, including most of ours—'

Yuri leaned in and flicked the peer's tie. '*The Bykovs*'.'

Scullion nodded. 'Your father's. They want to block them. And if the FCA do that, it essentially ends the free flow of business and threatens London's status as the biggest listing location in Europe. And that's not good.'

'Boohoo,' Yuri said.

Scullion could switch on the dark in his eyes. 'There are other issues,' he said, painstakingly. 'Your old man is concerned.'

Yuri shifted in his seat and knocked back his vodka.

'As you may have seen in the news, certain things are coming to a head, regarding, shall we say, controversial parties with whom we had, or your father had, working relationships. A few of these people were helpfully introduced to him by you.'

'William Byre.'

'I'm talking about several people. We have to limit the damage that a hostile British press can do when it comes to these individuals.'

'Fuck the press. And fuck Byre. He's his own enemy.'

'It has a long way to run. We think the woman on the *Commentator* is being fed stories by people inside Byre's companies. New allegations. Someone inside the system is getting close to our . . . private arrangements. So, in this context, I wish to impress on you that your own activities must be . . . carefully managed.'

'My life's my own, Lord Scullion.'

'They must be pristine.'

'*My* life.'

'Indeed it is, and a young man must . . . be free.' He smiled. 'Aleksandr has his own ways. He has interests inside government, inside the universities, inside huge companies whose developments and investments matter—'

'It's my own investments that matter to me.'

'They are inseparable, son.'

Yuri took a moment to look at Scullion. He wondered how complex the peer's system of denial must be, what he must have to say to himself in order to go on functioning as the person who did what he did. Of course, an instinctive, vain elaboration of realpolitik would probably do the trick for him, dignifying his actions. In the small hours, though, when money and influence can do nothing to help you sleep, how did Scullion comfort himself when faced with the undocumented truth of who he was?

'Your father only wishes to protect you.'

'From what?'

'From mistakes, Yuri. There are people who would enjoy rummaging through your life to find unsavoury friendships.'

'That's a good one. *Unsavoury friendships.*'

The peer pointed out, with the granted authority that was no different from blackmail, that there appeared to be vicious, dangerous extremes in Yuri's life, which might draw 'disastrous attention' from a high level in Moscow, as well as there being 'local entities from whom I also cannot protect you'.

'Nobody knows anything about my life.'

'But the worry is that we are all about to find out. It could be *extremely* damaging. That's your father's worry, and mine too, Yuri.'

'I don't need your protection. I need some of that freedom you spoke about. The freedom you and Mr Blair sold in barrels.'

Scullion hesitated. He had one terrific English trait. It was impressive, the degree to which he was unable to seem insulted. Nobody in Russia was like that, Yuri thought. Feeling insulted was a national sport.

'You must listen to me,' Scullion said. 'The scenery is changing.'

'What is that supposed to mean?'

'Investigations. Information about party funding. Border issues. We have to seal up the rooms, if you know what I mean. Avoid problems. We have fantastic contacts in journalism, and we are in possession of compromising material on many high-ranking individuals in the UK, the most high-ranking, indeed. They want to leave us alone. Yet we must avoid making ourselves an easy target in the British press.'

'Ourselves?' Yuri said. 'You are not a member of my family. In fact, who are you?'

Lord Scullion smirked.

'I'm the best friend you'll ever have,' he said quietly. Hanging out with petty lowlifes, he went on, was a sure path to destruction.

'But I like destruction,' Yuri said. 'I'm helping Carl Friis organise a show of destroyed art, opening during Frieze Art Fair.'

'Good for you. I like Carl. Continue to build your network. But stick to *admiring* art, not selling it.' He lowered his voice even further. 'And give the widest berth to anything to do with . . .'

He coughed lightly into his fist.

'Let me be very specific here – migrants, smugglers, grow-houses or gangs.'

'Suddenly you don't like gangs?'

An audible sigh came from the peer as he straightened up on his bar stool. 'He who digs a pit will fall into it,' he said slowly. He took a fountain pen from his pocket and a plain card, on which he wrote three words. He pushed it across the bar top and then turned away with a certain coldness to take a sip of water. The card said: 'Feng' and 'Nicolas Lantier'. Yuri read the names. The best policy was to say nothing.

'I am on your side,' Scullion said, facing the gantry. 'I am on your side and on the side of your family. You must listen to me.' He pushed his glass forward, climbed down from the stool and left the bar without another word.

At Kitsch in Old Burlington Street, six hours later, Yuri was surrounded by social media tramps and party animals. He'd ordered eight magnums of Cristal at £1,500 each, two bottles of Belvedere at £600, any number of espresso Martinis and Bellinis, and a few bottles of Dom Perignon, brought with sparklers by the new Russian models working the floor. The crowd around Yuri were selfie-obsessed. Long painted nails slashed through the air and plumped lips were stretched back, exposing veneers, as they raised their phones and snapped. Yuri loved it. At one point, the prettiest of the high-cheekboned actors, a Welsh lad who'd appeared in several costume dramas, put a large ice cube in his mouth and passed it to the beautiful man next to him, who then passed it to Yuri, pushing the ice further in and searching with his tongue.

Yuri's head of security was a Romanian guy called Stefan Popa. Broad-shouldered and bald, he kept everything dark, carrying all the information in his silent head until Yuri asked a question, whereupon Stefan would unravel all their business quandaries in thick, choppy English, masticating a frown. He drank only Red Bull and was the sole person ever to have met the mysterious Chinese lynchpin of the migrant operation. While the music pumped and the friends splashed champagne around the sofas, they found a quieter corner to talk about the grow-houses they'd established in South London and plans for other factories in Kent. Stefan reported on the performance of their new point men. He was pleased with the Polish guy in King's Cross. He owned a car wash, could launder cash and was good at handling incoming workers. Some he put in factories, others on the farms. Stefan said this guy Krupa would be useful in Kent. Feng was happy, he told him, and the organisation would expand, bringing in a lot more workers. Yuri couldn't think of 'Feng' without seeing queues across the world, people being slowly moved by the invisible operator.

Jake Hart-Davies arrived with two male models. They spread among the group, lighting each other up, touring their phones. Yuri came back to the banquettes and celebrated Jake's arrival by ordering six more bottles of champagne. The actor was the central energy. People got high from being around his fame. And he couldn't stop flirting with each of them, praising and imitating, before disappearing into his little cloud of wantedness. As if he needed to make himself present in people's minds and then confirm it with his absence. That's why he was such a bad friend: he wished to lend people his aura rather than his ear. Sitting next to Yuri, he didn't flinch when the host pushed up the sleeve of Jake's T-shirt and licked his tattoo, a small turtle over the word 'True'. Looking up, Jake asked Stefan, with a whip of his finger, to get rid of the people who were standing on the other side of the red rope, taking pictures. Stefan grabbed their phones. He made them delete the pictures and then he had the fans ejected. After that, the corner got louder and crazier until, at three o'clock in the morning, Yuri decided to do a speech from *King Lear*, with Jake pretending to guide him.

Eventually, when the music stopped, the table covered in burned-out sparklers and half-empty bottles, Jake spoke lines of his own – or were they his own? – a passage about the trials of masculinity, threaded through with references to art and poetry.

'Wow,' Yuri said, several times. 'I went to a place there. I got the tingles, Mr Hart-Davies. I got hard. *You* did that!'

The bill would be close to £50,000.

Yuri's phone vibrated. Lantier. He was calling from Dakar. He'd that day come in from Johannesburg and, before that, Côte d'Ivoire. Yuri listened. Lantier spoke whispery English with a rather theatrical Belgian inflection. He was talking about paintings he was preparing to sell on, and Yuri absorbed the information while twisting his finger in the tousled hair of the boy sitting next to him. Beauty was everywhere, thought Yuri, licking his lips and seeing himself as a conductor. He loved to think of all this champagne and all this beauty, while the old Russians spun in obsolescence, plotting their military fantasies and getting the West all wrong. Yuri had Shakespeare, handsome boys, endless nights and his own small, dirty businesses, and it thrilled him, head over heels, to learn that several Barnett Newmans were coming into their hands.

# 11 Skunk Hour

Campbell and Elizabeth returned from Suffolk on Monday 31 May, and he found he couldn't work. After the dinner at Hinderclay and his last encounter with William, his mojo, or whatever it was, had somehow been transfigured, or reassigned. And later that week, in a critical moment of life-changing clarity, he called his producer at the BBC and said he wouldn't be renewing his podcast contract. He didn't say it, but on listening to the edit of the upcoming show he felt an overwhelming and entirely new disgust at the self-delighted swagger of his broadcasting voice.

'The one we recorded at the National Gallery, "Dutch Painting and the Autofictional Impulse", will have to be my last,' he said.

'But *Civilisation and Its Malcontents* has become an institution.'

'And I'll end up in one if I don't stop,' he replied.

It did occur to him, as he said this, that hiring an actor to play oneself is exactly what a person who hates his own voice might do.

At 11 a.m. the next day, he was at his gym in Mecklenburgh Square. In a weird way, he was feeling beyond himself. It felt like a sort of freedom.

After speed-walking uphill for an hour, he was lifting a 12kg kettle-bell when he saw William on the television screen.

'Business Tycoon Scandal,' the breaking news banner said.

He could hear the TV when he stood close to it. 'Former knight William Byre is said to be on the cusp of being charged as public prosecutors pursue him over a number of allegations relating to his employees' pension fund and other financial matters. There are also new accusations of sexual misconduct.'

Campbell laid down the weight and stepped closer to the TV screen. 'It is believed that private company emails have been shared with an online newspaper.'

William could be seen coming out of his house in St John's Wood, jostled by photographers, and he looked terrible as he sunk into a waiting Daimler. Lady Byre was closing the door of the house. The item showed her later emerging with a tray of tea. Campbell thought of the girl William had mentioned – Vicky? It was hard to think about William's life and where it was going. His pride was equal to his other vices. Maybe it was wrong to wish him peace, but he did.

There was a message on his phone from Milo.

'*We are who we know.*'

Campbell thought it a decent piece of joshing.

Going up the steps of the Hotel Russell (now called something else, he noticed for the first time), a man was never more streamlined, moisturised, combed and scented, wearing a new bespoke suit by Monastic and a perfect dimple in his Charvet tie. He looked up and thought how settling it was to see aeroplanes over London again. His editor, Mirna, was sitting on the edge of a purple banquette in the cocktail bar, dressed in different greys, the cashmere of her sweater somehow underscoring her self-sufficiency. Mirna was Serbian and had worked in England for years. She had known all the battles. 'Maybe the worst of Covid is over,' Campbell said, 'and we can start again, though I fancy it will never be the same.'

'Absolutely,' she said, crossing her hands. 'Every generation has to feel the threat of annihilation in a mass way, don't you agree?'

He looked at her askance. 'Is this one of your theories, Mirna?'

'It comes around. For my parents, it was the Holocaust. For my generation, it was nuclear war and the threat of the bomb. Then it was AIDS. We only come together as human beings when we realise how eradicable we are.'

'Eradicable? Are we allowed that word?'

'Probably not. Vulnerable. Let's have a Martini.'

They were soon joined by his American publisher, Heidi Mae Adkins. She drank black coffee and refused all the snacks, bringing Campbell up to date on New York – 'where *nothing* is happening' – before launching into the most incisive summary of *Why Men Weep in Their Cars* and then a kind of Gettysburg Address about its assured success. 'I mean, it's been a trying time for us humans, right? And people need an injection of style and a whole lot of guidance at this moment. Seriously,' she said. 'People look at their husbands and their boyfriends and they're like, "What is *happening* to you?", and this book, oh my God, it comes out of nowhere. Like, right away, the whole thing makes *amazing* sense. Wives will buy this book to understand their husbands, children to understand their fathers, and men, listen to me, I've been here, men will buy this book to understand *themselves*. We're going straight into paperback with a huge marketing campaign.'

'I'm worried,' Mirna said. 'We're handing a lot of it over to you because you know this territory. But it's risky. Campbell is a philosopher of art. He writes—'

'Listen to me. The book is a *phenomenon*.'

Heidi Mae used her long Dürer fingers like pincers.

'You have world rights, Mirna, and you brought it to us for a reason: we *are* the self-help industry, and we paid a lot of money. This book will be number one for the next five years. It's the book the market wants. You go to Frankfurt every year and publishers think they're waiting for the next big novel that explains blah blah and whatever, okay?'

'It's just—'

'No, Mirna – listen. I'm from Guthrie, Kentucky. I know what people want and I'm talking about everyday people. What *we* want is a book that will play forever in the airports. Forever on the talk shows. A book that shows what's inside. I'm talking about the real deal. Are you kidding me? Readers want to understand the person lying next to them, the whole goddamn thing – who they are and what went wrong and how to fix it. They want *Why Men Weep in Their Cars*. They'll buy it for their friends, and say, "Oh my God, *you cannot go on with your life without reading this book.*"'

Mirna exuded quiet experience. She had listened with what seemed like a world-class instinct for tolerance. 'Nevertheless,' she said, making the word sound like the inauguration of common sense, 'there are angry men in our societies at present, many millions of them, who wish to blame women —'

'Oh, Mirna,' Heidi Mae said.

'Let me speak. They wish to blame women for what they see as an attack on male privilege. They wish to dignify their misogyny. Campbell has written something . . . useful. But I wouldn't want it to be taken the wrong way.'

'Look, Mirna.' Heidi Mae Adkins from Guthrie, Kentucky, suddenly looked as if she pitied Mirna and all her old, timid instincts from 1962. 'Argument is the oxygen of this marketplace. People want to hear about what's really happening; they want to punch it out, and this book provides a new way of thinking about our times.'

'If done in the wrong way, it's very dangerous.'

'Well, let's do it in the *right* way, Mirna. It ain't for trolls.'

Mirna made a face at Campbell, as if apologising for all she might have done wrong, and he touched her hand.

'Above all,' he said, 'we must keep our sense of humour,' and he chuckled as the American publisher dipped a hand into her Kate Spade bag.

The card was A5 size. It showed a hairless male torso, perfectly defined, young, with a rosette saying 'First' pinned to the skin above the heart and a thin trail of blood running down from the rosette to the abdominal muscles.

*Why Men Weep in Their Cars*
*How to Get Over It and Fix the World*
Jake Hart-Davies

Campbell grinned looking at it. 'We've found our Everyman,' he said. He turned it towards Mirna and she sort of gulped, clearly embarrassed.

'Gosh, that title. It's horrible.'

'Perfect for the current audience,' Heidi Mae said.

'A very *selling* cover,' Mirna went on. 'I worry it's a bit . . . I don't know, Campbell – a bit lower order.'

Campbell felt he needed to underscore the agreement. 'Let's not be snobbish, Mirna,' he said. 'You're a literary publisher, but we offered it to you on the understanding you'd have world rights and go to super-commercial publishers for the rest of the world. That is what we've done and it's working. Good for both of us.'

'Yes, of course,' Mirna said. 'It's only . . . it looks . . . a bit trashy.'

'You won't think it's trashy when it has cash registers ringing across America and you get your slice,' Heidi Mae said, laughing.

Mirna went frosty. 'Cash registers don't ring any more,' she said, her chief editor's punctilio suddenly appearing for the defence. But the truth was Mirna needed a hit. She had a sublime first novel coming and a group biography of English post-war painters: Patrick Caulfield, John Hoyland, Keith Vaughan and Euan Uglow. She'd told Campbell all about it. He put a hand over hers. A bestseller would let her retire with a bit of extra glory. He wanted her permission and he was sure his eyes told her so. But he knew she had travelled a long way from her Nobel Prize-winning Europeans. Campbell intended to put his share into something digital. He was developing a yearning to be inside the new technology.

'It's okay, Mirna. Just this once. The book is an experiment. The whole thing is disruptive, as I see it, a questioning of authorship, and we have this well-known actor preparing to take on the role. So, let's see.'

'In that spirit,' Mirna said, 'the cover does the work.'

He turned to the US publisher. 'You've got flap copy. And what about the back?'

'We'll take care of all that. We propose using a portrait of Hart-Davies, which he wants us to use full-bleed.'

'Sexy?' Campbell asked.

'*Naturellement.*'

Atticus had explained the money: Mirna hadn't paid much but the Americans had come in with $600,000. A third of that would go to the actor.

As they were wrapping up, he told the publishers it was his birthday in just over a month and that his family were taking him to Iceland. He flushed as he said it.

'Iceland?' the American said. 'You guys are nuts.'

'The Hotel Borg. Steam baths. Raw fish. I don't know what else. No doubt, Angus and Kenzie will . . . to tell the truth, I feel a bit bullied by it all. I can't really be fucked with birthdays, but there's no quarantine there.'

He counted them off on his fingers. 'Five weeks,' he said.

'You can always rely on Angus,' Mirna said. 'Too cool for school.' Campbell watched her and could tell she was still brooding about the book.

'Come on, Mirna! This project will be fun.'

'Okay, okay,' she said, joining her hands. 'I'm all for fun. No harm done. So long as it is completely airtight. This is not a book by Campbell Flynn. I repeat: this is not a book by Campbell Flynn. His name does not appear.'

'It's going to be terrific,' Heidi Mae said, twinkling. 'You both know a lot, Professor, but you don't know mass-market publishing. And I'm going to teach you.'

Campbell put out his bottom lip. 'High jinks,' he said.

'Write another one!'

'No, this is an end,' Campbell said.

Heidi Mae left soon after and Mirna took him to lunch. They went to the Savoy for old times' sake, and Mirna spoke winningly about her young authors, about their bold takes on modern life. She had such hopes for them. Then she turned to his plans for the Rembrandt book, saying she loved the way he could bring an artist to life. They made an agreement that self-help is no substitute for self-portraiture. He ruminated. 'But it might have its value,' he said, still reaching, summoning poetry to bolster good sense. 'Those poems of Robert Lowell's, for instance. You could never be sure, or I couldn't, whether he was trying to help himself or simply showing who he was.'

'Both,' Mirna said. 'I'm sure it was both, in his case.'

Campbell nodded. 'I read him again the other day, "Skunk Hour", and it's clear the speaker feels he's losing his mind.'

'Oh, yes.'

'I read it and I thought – that's simple and true, isn't it?'

# 12 Society

On a damp Tuesday morning in early June, Milo's mouth felt as dry as a basket of dust. He was badly hungover, but he pushed on with his tasks. He dropped off a box of books at the primary school where his mum had worked: nature anthologies, bird guides and studies on migration. He wasn't sure how appropriate they'd be for primary school children, but he hoped the school would want them. Standing in the playground before he went inside, he put down the box and took out one of the books – *We Are All from Somewhere Else*. His mum's pencil marks were in it, and he could see her face again, her smile as she read by a lamp in the kitchen. A line was highlighted: 'Home is the journey.'

For the older pupils, Zemi had run special projects – the peace movement, the island birds' frieze in the Year 6 classroom – and she had spent some time leading them in a study of different social groups. Flicking to the back of the book, he could see notes she'd made about Moken sea nomads, Inuits, Bedouins. Several other books in the box focused on the Irish Mincéirí, the Roma, the Yenish. Her favourites, she'd told him, were the tinsmiths and Travellers of the Scottish Highlands. Zemi and Ray were pub philosophers on the subjects of famines and clearances, and his mum said she'd always been enchanted by the word 'Highlands'. It took her back to Ethiopia. 'Home.'

At Charles Booth Primary, where most of the pupils were black kids from the estates, Zemi had shown a lot of courage in questioning middle-class locals, white people from the garden squares of Islington, about their plan to erase inequality. The rich locals wanted the school to be more integrated, more 'cultured' – but to his mother this was a piece of liberal nonsense. She called them the garden-square hypocrites. These people donated to the school, they started a drama club, they arranged gallery visits, paid for a music room, which was all very nice, but only the tiniest number would then send their kids to the school. The ones who did quickly set up a 'gifted programme', special classes that were soon full of white kids with pushy parents, which the Department for Education fastened on to and advertised as a triumph. 'These people don't know who our children *are*,' Zemi had said. 'They know nothing about their needs. They come with their donations and their violins and it's obvious what *they* need – to feel better about themselves while giving their own children advantages.'

Milo could remember the conversations over dinner in their small kitchen. And he could feel it all still happening.

'The whole concept of a "good school" versus a "bad school" is so Thatcherite,' his father had said one evening. 'Disgusting, actually.'

Milo would sit there as a child and listen. He could see it now: the drop-leaf table and three stools, the brightly coloured salad bowls.

'It's immoral to delude yourself that you're doing good, when what you're doing is making yourself *feel* good,' Zemi replied. 'They bend things so that their own kids feel naturally superior, with private tutors or special classes, then they feed the crumbs from those tables to the underprivileged and call it inclusive.'

'And these Gibson Square types with their Euro window stickers think they're in a different universe from the Little Englanders,' Ray added.

'That's right,' Zemi had said. 'But they vote for segregation every time they go private. And they teach their children to expect life to be like that.'

'You have to keep saying it at the meetings, Zemi. Richmond Crescent and Thornhill Square: they live a lie, those families.'

Last night, Milo had been in another zone, the present, but the subject of the garden-square hypocrites had come up again. He and Gosia had gone to an engagement party: one of the girls in the salon was marrying a nice builder called John. They all got drunk on daft cocktails in Camden Town and ended up at a karaoke bar. Milo stunned Gosia by offering a rendition of 'Luv Is Dro'.

'That was word-perfect!' she shouted.

They'd carried on to Koko in Camden High Street, and took a few dabs of MD. They smoked a fly cigarette between them out on the balcony, entangled with each other, loving their time. They felt earnest, which was a thing with them, especially when a little high on a night out, beaming and sharing secret snatches of the project. 'Campbell Flynn, liberal academic,' he said. 'William Byre, corrupt businessman.'

'And you're seeing more and more,' she said, nodding to the music.

'Yes,' he mouthed.

That's when he mentioned the hypocrites, confirming the Flynns were among them. He was about to get deeper into it, but the happy couple appeared with a tray of blue shots. Gosia toasted the company with her shot glass and winked at Milo before knocking it back.

His hangover didn't improve at the British Library. He'd drunk a carton of milk after dropping off the books and still the reading room was pulsing. He stared into the white pillars and tried to think of the tasks he had in front of him. But his mind was elsewhere: it kept returning to Zemi. He went onto the library website and requested something special from the stacks.

Staring at his laptop, focus slowly returned. The known world grew fuzzy around the edges, becoming a sort of wallpaper. He settled down to work. He was beginning to establish himself as a fierce hacker now. A pirate. He had spent all of yesterday afternoon preparing a bespoke security gremlin, a piece of software he'd developed from an old gaming platform. And now this little Trojan was about to enter a network of Her Majesty's government. One man at one desk, he sent out a million marching skeleton keys to unlock a single door.

The Home Office. The main files opened up. Others did not. He'd have to do more work to find the emails surrounding the investigation: but the reports were wrapped in a thin grey blanket of digital material, suddenly clear. He isolated anything relating to the Byre case: illegal workers, financial dealings. He copied these files with a few flicks of his trackpad and then concentrated on the word-search 'Poles' and 'Polish', quickly finding the investigation he'd identified a few nights before – 'Poldark'. The digital papers on his screen were covered in stamps and initials, mainly from the Met Police. They detailed a growing operation, also involving police in the Midlands, Lancashire and Scotland, to locate and overturn mainly London-based gang bosses who were committing offences under the Modern Slavery Act, using employment agencies with links to online traffickers. Milo found transcripts, witness statements, haulage receipts and memos. He found remittance slips for Angelique clothing and logs of telephone calls. Accounts. Photographs. All the ephemera of Byre's world.

You only had to look in the right place.

Before their project had even got off the ground, Gosia would talk about guys sent from her brother's car wash to various garment factories. She'd always known they were being 'run'. But then she'd made the connection to Angelique and William Byre – and that Byre was Professor Flynn's friend. He could still see her newspaper cutting: 'Factory owner Sir William, husband of the notorious right-wing columnist Antonia Byre, is a wine enthusiast and a member of the clubbable London set . . . his Cambridge University days . . . the Scottish art historian Campbell Flynn, whose sister, Moira Flynn, is an MP. He lives in the leafier part of Islington, and is married to Lady Elizabeth . . .'

'My eyes nearly dropped out,' Gosia had said. 'I was looking to understand what my brother was doing, and then I saw *these names*, side by side.'

'My professor. I was triggered when I read that *Atlantic* article,'
Milo had said to Gosia. 'Stuff he was saying. Another fucking hypocrite, you know . . .'

'And now this rabbit hole. Leading God knows where.'

But here was the proof: 'Poldark'.

The police were looking at trafficking. Sweatshops. Embezzlement.
They were feeling for an underground network of hauliers and drug
dealers.

Milo dragged documents into a folder. He injected a further Trojan
into a deeper part of the network, trying to unlock 'Byre', 'Krupa',
'investors'. There was nothing yet on Krupa. Keyword 'investors'
was sending him to the Foreign Office. There was a triple lock on the
bigger network there, but he unzipped the emails in seconds. And
all over that field, happy as crickets on a summer's day, were links
and speculations, testimonies and materials relating to William Byre's
connections to the Russians.

His eyes began to swim.

He needed a break.

He went across to St Pancras International, bought a sandwich,
called Gosia. She told him she'd spent the morning reading a long
article about kelp forests. 'I thought it might help my headache,' she
said. 'Wrong.'

'Here's the world's best aspirin,' he said, and proceeded to tell her
what he'd found.

'Holy fuck.'

'There's a guy they all know,' Milo said. 'His name comes up in
dozens and dozens of these emails. A Labour peer. Paul Scullion.'

He could hear her typing as he spoke. 'Yes,' she said, after a few
moments. 'There's a picture of him standing beside Byre at a fundraiser. Ha. Another with Tony Blair. He's on the board of Chernaya
House Group . . . not sure what that is.'

'Russian energy company. Owned by Aleksandr Bykov. OK. I'm
going back to it.'

He wolfed down the sandwich.

Back in the reading room, he opened a fresh set of windows and started looking for evidence of Lord Scullion. 'Wow,' he said to himself. Lord Scullion was in that Russian company with Lord Haxby. Whose husband was Carl Friis. The Danish artist linked to Professor Flynn. Full circle.

On a roll, he hit another window. And then . . . amateur hour. His battery died.

He plugged in and waited, the spell broken. Suddenly alone. Disconnected. He knew what he needed.

He went up to the issue desk and found the item from the stacks waiting for him.

A dark blue volume from 1993.

*London Review of Books.*

For Milo, it even smelled like her now. He'd taken it out so many times since November. He laid his hands on it. He didn't want to read the article online, with its digital image of the cover and the contents page. This was something so precious, holding the issue itself and knowing it had been in the world with his mother that March, three years before he was born. He turned the pages with a sense of hurt that seemed eternal, that could not be fixed. It made him feel alive with her, though, to see her name on the contents page. He ran his finger under her brief biography in the list of contributors and felt her voice deep down in the actual ink: 'Zemi Mangasha is a student at Goldsmiths. She aims to be a primary school teacher.'

The article was at the back. It sat next to a long review of a book about how history was now at an end.

I came here in 1973 to escape the civil war and the famine in Ethiopia. My parents had been killed and I spoke two words of English: 'hello' and 'goodbye'. I was five years old and the first things I recall seeing in London were continental quilts and tins of soup, as well as buses, toffees, houses with doorbells and garden hedges. After a few days, I met my white foster parents. Mrs Fraser was a Scot who had thick arms and a wonderful heart. She had books, lots of books, bird feeders in the garden, and her husband worked at the Institute of Education. They were both in the CND and they hated racism in all its forms. That August, we went on holiday to the Summer Isles in the West Highlands. It was another world, a new world, even to people who had already crossed too many.

When I was small, I was not aware of the fears about immigration that had been cultivated in Britain. I later heard about the collections that were taken in Catholic schools for the 'Black Babies'. I was one of them, rescued (as they liked to say) by a good society. Mr and Mrs Fraser sent me to the local school in Forest Gate, and I soon learned about the legislation – in 1962, 1968, 1971 and 1981 – devised to drive us back, and to kill the idea that the UK had ever wanted non-whites in the first place, despite its vanity about the Commonwealth. I didn't know how to feel. I was plucked from disaster and taken to England, yet, for many people from overseas, the right to citizenship was truncated by legal limits to do with 'connection' and 'belonging'. Of course, we found our own ways to belong. Our presence didn't unleash rivers of blood, as Enoch Powell had warned, but white prejudice existed in our daily life to make us feel alien. What had been an inclusive, welcoming policy in 1948, was, by 1981 – when I was at secondary school – a policy to keep Britain white. Migration is about change, but I came to adulthood knowing it was the cause of a dreadful fear in Britain that the country might never be the same again. I had learned early in life how to scan people's faces for hostility; but it isn't just faces we need to scan, but governments and their beliefs, such as the one expressed by Mrs Thatcher, when she said, 'There is no such thing as society.' I am studying to be a primary school teacher, and I know, despite my inexperience, that no teacher can afford to believe that.

'*Ema,*' he said quietly in the library.

He closed the volume and sat with his head in his hands, the appetite for research overwhelmed and gone.

After half an hour, his phone buzzed.

Flynn.

'I'm working at home this evening. Could you come over?'

He had taught the professor how to use Signal a week before, at his office in college. Part of his slowly accumulating education at Milo's hands. The professor was still typing.

Second message: 'Who owns the police? I wish to know more. I'll order pizza.'

Third message: 'At home. 68 Thornhill Square. 6 p.m.?'

Milo sent back an upturned thumb emoji. It was time to go further with Flynn. To really *see* him.

He messaged Gosia.

'Going to the professor's house later.'

A fellow student at UCL once asked Milo why he didn't use his computing talent and his 'cultural intelligence' (whatever that was) to become a gaming guru. 'You could make millions at one of the online betting firms,' she said. If he didn't want that he could work for Apple. 'Or you could be a trend forecaster for a major network, if you weren't so political or whatever.'

'But why would I work for evil companies,' he said, 'when I can do my own evil?'

'Slay,' the student said.

Recovering from the library, he stopped at Lam's Internet Café on Caledonian Road to meet the boys. He bought a pork bun and a mango juice and sat in the corner. Drinking the juice, he could still taste the sambuca and tequila and whatever madness was in those shots last night. Travis arrived wearing a pair of Balenciaga shades and a new Armani tracksuit. Lloyds was in tow. Travis fist-bumped Milo. He was all hopped up. Said the Deptford boys were being idiots.

Milo didn't want to know.

'But trust me,' Travis said. 'I'll go to Deptford and fix this. No war.'

He was always the emotional centre of the group: buzzing, beefing, patterning up a plan or writing a song or getting mad. He was a fatherless child who made up for it by fathering everybody else, until he couldn't. Milo could see it, the frustration that his mum was off the rails or out of sight, the fear that the music wouldn't succeed, the outsized wish for reputation in case he might be thought small. But the boy he'd loved was still in there somewhere. He stared back at Milo through the same worried eyes.

Lloyds started talking about getting cuffed the day before when the feds stopped him under the Cally bridge. An ally from Brixton Hit Squad was with him. 'You know him – Money? He and 0044 are tight. You know, that kid who was mashed up at the party. Anyhow, Money was carrying a .22, coming on like Mackey in *The Shield*.'

'Jesus,' Milo said, 'now you're walking up the Cally *carrying*...?'

They sat quiet for a second, scrolling their phones.

'This isn't fucking TV, Lloyds,' Milo said.

'That's wrong, mate,' he replied. 'Everything's TV.' He looked around for approval. 'Hey – you see this thing on the box about a fish nobody's ever seen? Deep under the sea. Lights on them! Swear, it's like outer space down there. Miles down. Predators. You've never seen any uglier fish, bro.'

Milo turned to look at Travis. 'What's he on about, mate? Does he think we didn't see *Finding Nemo*?' And Travis burst out laughing.

Lloyds gave up and turned to more practical matters.

'We're getting this new stuff from Kent. Polish man from York Way—'

'Fucking boring,' Milo said.

'They're killing it on the production,' Lloyds continued. 'We can sell it in South London or anywhere we want.'

Milo put his hands on the table. 'Guns? Drugs. It's compliance, what you're doing. Every time a brother gets killed by a brother – it's compliance. It's expected. It's conditioned, you know what I'm saying? It's *ordained*, man. All this fighting over postcodes is bullshit: the only border that matters is the one in your own mind.' Milo wanted to say more, he wanted to shout. But you can't tell old mates what to do.

'Come on,' Lloyds said. 'That's college talk, bruv.'

'We're living in a police state,' Milo went on, 'and the police love this shit. You're feeding yourself to the enemy. They *love* this *shit*: black men hurting black men; right up their fuckin' street. It's what they want.'

Milo's friends looked at him blankly.

'Police invented the sickness they prosecute. Filing false reports, lying under oath, planting evidence, controlling the streets, kneeling on people's necks. You talk about assault: police invented that stuff, and they get lucky every day because you want to play their game. You talk about Tupac being a gangster. That's where he failed. He was a philosopher. He was the son of a Black Panther. He got lost, bro.'

'Tupac lives.'

'He was twenty-five, Lloyds. He had everything. And you know what his last words were? "I can't breathe," same as George Floyd's.'

'You're wrong,' Lloyds said. 'Tupac's last words were "fuck you".'

An hour later, Milo was in another world.

Thornhill Square was sultry and calm in the spring sunshine. The trees swayed a little in the wind and a young couple passed silently on the pavement, as if the placid evenings and the special houses had been built for them. On the doorstep of number 68, Milo stopped to look at the blue flowers all moist in the window boxes. It was his first time there. He took a deep breath before knocking on the door, turning to look again at the shushing trees and take in the contentment of the garden square.

# 13 Passport

June for Campbell was like a spring holiday from himself, this lively intensification of his friendship with Milo. Since that first evening, when the student came round and they discussed a dozen important topics over pizza, Campbell felt different. Elizabeth happened to be away a lot that season, so he felt free to try on new hats. Something about the young man gave him energy, and he supposed it was a wonderful education for both of them, going to galleries together or drinking at his office in town, gaining a foothold in Milo's world of pressing concerns. They studied reports the student found about educational inequalities in England and comparative health stats. One day, he took Campbell around a housing estate in Tottenham, then followed it up a few days later with an invitation to see a film about the influence of industrial pollution on African famines. Campbell wasn't sure where any of this was going, but that was part of the thrill. Towards the end of the month, Milo messaged him in the middle of the night: 'Are you a good person?'

'Ask my wife,' Campbell replied.

The morning of his birthday, 5 July, Elizabeth was in the kitchen worrying about the Reykjavík trip. She liked a jaunt, but Campbell was impatient with airports at the best of times, and she had a feeling his birthday was going to be tough, based on the way he'd been lately. He put her in mind of some of the children she had treated over the years, the patients troubled by a sense of unachievable selfhood. It occurred to her that he perhaps wanted to be several people at once, none of them much like him. Yet Elizabeth could tolerate and understand periods when her husband's outside preoccupations took him out of her orbit, and she saw it as a condition of their marriage not to make too much of it.

'You seem lonely at the moment,' she'd said to him the night before, when she found him up late in the sitting room.

'I'm not sleeping well, that's all.'

He was watching a Netflix show about a computer heist. The programme had sinister music and graphics full of scrolling numbers.

'You haven't spoken to Angus.'

'Are you his special envoy?' he said.

'Stop it, Campbell. I'm worried about you. Your son has gone to all this trouble for your birthday—'

'It's all about *him*,' he said, staring at the screen. 'He delights in having nothing to do with us except when he can draft us into his carnival of self-worth.'

'That's not fair. You're not being nice to Angus at the moment.'

'Oh, come off it, Lizzie.'

'You've become competitive with him. With everyone. And you're not as much fun to be around as you think. *Just saying.*'

'What an odious, self-congratulatory little phrase,' he said.

'Listen to me,' she said. 'We don't get in each other's way and I'm not about to start, but something is happening to you and it's very obvious that your loyalties are shifting towards new people, away from us. Not only from me, but your entire family. Moira you seem to like talking to, because she's an ally of . . . what? Your childhood?'

'Elizabeth—'

'Kenzie you sit on a pedestal.'

'Please.'

'And Angus, you appear to detest him, while refusing to see how much that feeling is complicated by your identification with him.'

Campbell stared at her.

'I need a breather,' he said. There was a pause. 'I don't mean I want to stop breathing.'

She sat down on the sofa and took his hand.

'I think you're depressed, Campbell. I think the William thing has knocked you for six. It's as if you're desperate for . . . a new sense of decency. You've packaged us all up with the self you're running away from.'

He turned to face her and she saw a vague smile. Not in all the years of their marriage had he seemed to her so distant.

'I just need to think,' he said, squeezing her hand as she stood up. Then he stretched out on the sofa and put a cushion under his head.

Milo rounded the West Library as he walked once again into Thornhill Square.

He glanced at the church behind him and then at the pink blossom hanging over the railings. He hadn't seen her before, but at number 68 an elderly woman was struggling to wrap a length of chain around her gate and fasten it with a padlock. 'You all right there?' he said.

When she turned her face, it was full of dislike.

'What's it to you, sunshine? I've seen you before. I've got nothing down there and I'll be back soon with a new padlock.'

He stood back. 'You mad?'

Her shadow loomed on the path. 'I know all about it,' she said. 'There's been break-ins round here. Lots of them.'

'What the fuck you talking about?' She seemed to enjoy his sudden anger, as if it were her language. He walked up the steps.

'That's right,' she said, 'cursing in the street. Friends of them, are you?'

'Somebody should lock you up, missus.'

'That's right. Say what you like. But keep back from my gate!'

He looked at her. This was England: a mad white person shouting at a passerby as if it were her birthright.

'You want putting away,' he said, ringing the bell.

'Never you mind. I've seen the crime figures.'

With a final clank of the chain, she walked away.

It was Flynn's wife who opened the door. She'd always been out on the previous occasions he'd visited the professor. She introduced herself in that way they do, as if she'd waited her whole life to meet him. She brought him into the kitchen and flicked on the kettle. He explained the difficulty with the rude woman, and she bit her lip. 'Certainly a live one, I'm afraid, Mrs Voyles downstairs. Not a happy bunny.'

'A crazy person, more like.'

'She says terrible things, but I don't imagine she believes them.'

The window gave a good view of the square. Mrs Flynn unhooked mugs and opened cupboards. 'He's upstairs on a Zoom call,' she said. 'He didn't sleep well last night. I'm not sure why he chose today for a boys' meeting.'

'He said he had a job idea, something to do with the British Museum.'

She sighed. Apparently, Campbell hadn't given her any details. 'We're travelling to Iceland this evening,' she said. 'It's his birthday. The trip was organised by our children, so it's a busy day.'

'Cool.'

'You take milk?'

'Yeah. That'd be great.'

'I wouldn't mention the birthday thing to him if I were you,' she said, handing him a mug and pointing to a sofa. 'He's insufferable about birthdays.'

'Is it like a special one or something?'

'No,' she said. 'Fifty-three. But the children adore this sort of thing. They travel a lot and it's pretty much instinctive with them.'

'Reykjavík?'

'Literally two days.' She lowered her voice. 'A few friends. A surprise element.'

'Sweet. Nice thing to do on a Monday night.'

He'd done his research and knew she was a shrink. He'd never had one, but he guessed they took their time, like this. She wasn't afraid of silences and they spent a moment looking at the light coming into the room, the family pictures and the order of everything. Cushions and candles. 'So, you're the famous Milo?' she said, as if she was trying to make conversation.

'Yeah. Milo Mangasha.'

'The favoured student. Unusual first name and surname combination.'

'The first name's Irish, from my dad. He was born in Tipperary. My mother was Ethiopian and came to London in the 1970s. Big feminists, so I got her surname.'

'You're a student at UCL?'

'Yeah. Finishing up now.'

'Campbell tells me you've been having fascinating debates. Are you very keen on art?'

'I did the Computer Science Master's,' he said. 'Wanted to try something else, you know?'

'I do,' she said.

'Cultural Studies. Art.'

He felt she had questions that she wasn't going to ask. It was skills, he thought, to create silences so the other person would have to speak. 'I live nearby. Not far up the road, further up the Cally.'

'You're a local fellow,' she said. He nodded.

'Big place.' He looked up at the ceiling.

'Yes, we're very lucky.'

She wheeled the conversation back to him and asked where he went to school and whether he had siblings. He talked about Charles Booth Primary School and William Ellis and fed her all the basic information. Told her he used to have a part-time job in the phone shop but spent most of his time reading.

She wrapped both her hands around her mug. 'So, a friendship has sprung up between you two,' she said. She said it easily, with a smile, like it didn't really matter, and Milo found he wanted to please her by being natural too.

159

'It's been nice getting to know somebody different,' he said.

'I'm sure it's very valuable.'

He nodded and drank his tea. Milo understood they were a sort of power couple: knew everything, but nothing; had everything, but wanted more. He nodded at what she said, then thought, I'll say this.

'I'm not really sure what my subject is yet. I mean, I know what I studied. But I've always been into different things. I'm not into the same stuff as my friends. My mum and dad taught me to think about things.'

'So, you do have friends your own age?'

'Yeah, for sure. Old friends. Young guys.'

It was like she was pushing him but didn't want to go too far.

'But would you say computing was your main language?'

'No,' he said. 'English is my main language.'

His confidence grew. He could feel it.

'Yes, of course. But is computing the main thing you see yourself doing?'

'I'll do what I *can*,' he said, and wished he hadn't. He had given more than he'd meant to. But then . . .

'You have an unusual mix,' she said. The comment lingered in the air as a thing she shouldn't have said.

'Like I said, my mother was Ethiopian.'

'I didn't mean – *Was?*'

'She died, yeah. Last year.'

He tried to keep the emotion out of his voice, the anger.

The woman nodded sort of professionally. 'I'm very sorry.' There was a silence, during which Milo sipped more tea. 'Charles Booth. Mangasha. Did your mum teach at the school?'

'Yes, for a long time.'

He could see her eyes brightening. 'I think I remember her, a very beautiful woman.'

He didn't add anything.

'I remember her face,' she said. 'She looked like you.'

He tried not to appear too cold as he looked up. 'We are more than our faces,' he said. 'My mum used to say that.'

He'd maybe gone too far.

'Campbell and I got involved with Charles Booth Primary at one time,' she said. 'We organised gallery visits and an art appreciation club.'

Milo was aware he was staring straight at her. Yes, indeed. These were the people his mother had spoken about.

'We got a fair bit of engagement,' she continued. 'Campbell even took them to Tate Britain and stuff like that, showing them the William Blakes.'

'Engagement, yeah. Cool.'

She took up her mug like it now provided a helpful distraction.

'Are you an activist, Milo? Are you very political?'

He considered carefully. 'Not so much,' he said. 'To be honest, I'm what they call a loner, Dr Flynn.'

He shouldn't have said 'doctor'.

They could both hear a noise on the stairs, but she wasn't finished with her questions.

'And you care?' she said. 'You're *careful*?'

'I try to be.'

Flynn arrived. He had round glasses in his hand and was wearing a pair of carpet slippers. 'Ah, the fireside chat!' he said.

'Milo was at Charles Booth,' Elizabeth said, getting up. She immediately looked preoccupied and was signing off. 'Such a sweet school.' She turned to her husband and told him he mustn't be long.

'Wheelie case is packed,' he said.

'There's a car coming at three,' she said, before turning to Milo and being polite in a way that he felt must be very practised with her. 'It was nice to meet you. Good luck.' And then to Flynn *Three o'clock.*'

The professor's study was like a painting. It had a sofa and a table that ran along the back, two lamps and jars of pens. The desk had an antique globe on it and a lot of paper folders. It faced glass doors that led onto a balcony overlooking the garden at the back, towards the shops on Caledonian Road. The garden was full of flowers and his wife was down there, watering the plants. On a bookcase to the side of the desk was a typewriter and Milo saw various piles of books; on top of one of them was a watch and a passport. Professor Flynn was at the other end of the room and Milo drew his finger over the pile of books, W. Bode and C. Hofstede de Groot, *The Complete Work of Rembrandt,* and Christopher White, *Dutch Pictures in the Collection of Her Majesty the Queen.* The professor smiled, carrying a heap of magazines that he dumped on a chair by his desk. 'My fashion stuff,' he said.

'What, in magazines?'

'Yes, I'm afraid so. *Vogue.* The *New York Times's T Magazine.* It's something my children got me into, and it was fun, but—'

'You're not writing for them any more?'

'No. It was a revenue stream. And it got me to new places. But I hope to have replaced both necessities with other things.'

Milo sometimes heard the Scottish in his voice. Like when he said 'both'. He'd noticed the same with his father's Irish accent. But with the professor it was also an accent of the mind, like he was being *particular,* in a Scottish way. Milo's mum had loved impersonating the voices she'd heard on holiday. He sat down in a striped armchair, telling the professor about the lady downstairs, and how obnoxious she'd been to him. 'Mrs Voyles,' Flynn replied. 'The bane of my life.'

He noticed that Flynn's face had flushed. There was genuine irritation and upset at the mention of this woman.

'Who is she, anyway?' Milo said. 'Like, some casual racist?'

'I can see you and I will always get along. Excuse the parliamentary language, but she's a manipulative bitch, though not everybody can see it.'

Milo took in the various sedate pictures on the walls as Flynn began to explain why he had asked him over. 'I didn't mention it before,' he said, 'and I don't know how you're situated. But our conversations have been increasingly interesting and you appear to have a knack for research, especially for the kind of research involving . . . computer work and data.'

'Yep,' Milo said, hands clasped, with his legs stretched out over the rug and his trainers tapping against each other.

'This last while . . . How shall I put it? I've been interested in the question of identities and how they meld in the modern world . . .' He broke off, like he was still working it out. 'And I want to pursue that in a professional way. I need a researcher.'

'Oh, yeah?'

'Specifically, to help me with a big thing I'm preparing for the British Museum. The Autumn Lecture.'

'Right.'

'It's a big deal. I'm calling it "The Human Face in the Digital Age". So, portraiture, the art bit —'

'You've got that down.'

'Quite. But I need your help with the other bit. The digital world. I'm interested in your ideas, Milo – I want to give them voice. I hope it doesn't sound weird, but . . . I'd like to absorb some of your perspective in a public performance.'

'Cool.'

Milo simply nodded while the professor spoke about the job and what it would entail.

On one wall, the professor had framed prints of several Vermeers, all showing their subjects lit from the left. Among them, a card was pinned, embossed with his name – *Campbell Flynn*. It had arrows pointing at the reproductions and bore the pen-written description: 'perspective boxes'. Milo continued to listen. Looking around him, he remembered something his mother liked to say: 'You got to bring the fight to the people where they live.'

'I'll do it,' he answered the professor.

Flynn walked over and they shook hands. 'You are always writing about society,' he said, 'whenever you are writing about art. I believe art criticism is a criticism of life. You've got to put your own selfhood on the line. I've come to believe that.'

'Okay,' Milo said.

'I mean, Elizabeth, my wife – she says it's all . . . retributionist politics nowadays.'

Milo realised: Flynn's wife probably knew about the direct debit payments, and had maybe been feeling out her suspicions downstairs.

'But it doesn't matter,' the professor said. 'Things must change.'

Milo merely nodded, like he had no argument. Then he said, 'Thirty quid an hour.'

Flynn blushed. 'That's fine,' he said.

The professor went out of the room and left Milo on his own. He moved over to inspect a few items on the desk, and then returned to his seat. With quick thumbs, he texted Gosia. 'He's offered me a job. And I picked up something interesting.'

She texted back: a laughing emoji.

Flynn returned, popping a pill into his mouth.

For an older, successful guy, there was something innocent about Flynn, something unmistakeably sad.

'Do *you* take drugs?' Flynn asked.

Milo shrugged. 'I know about them,' he said.

'For this, I'll need you to show me the Dark Net – all of that. I want to know how to access it and understand it.'

'We'll do that,' Milo said. 'Soon as you like.'

The professor went to the drinks trolley and uncorked a bottle of Talisker. As he poured, he explained that his ancestors and Milo's had shared window space, here in London, when prejudice against Irish people and people of colour was advertised by landlords.

'The progress of hatred,' Milo said, drinking the malt to add to his fire.

'I really think we might be about to uncover something good,' Flynn said, nodding his head in a serious way by the fireplace.

'I hope so.'

Milo stood up as if the room now belonged to both of them and he walked to the open glass doors, breathing the rose-scented air. He felt tall in that room, as tall as the professor, who put out his glass and clinked.

'I'd better get moving,' Flynn said. 'This bloody effort to get ready for Heathrow.'

'Many happy returns, by the way.'

'Oh, don't you start. But, thank you.'

Outside, Milo paused to take in the white stucco of the buildings and the high sun over the garden square. There isn't a word for it, the expensive sense of entitlement that dwells in these wide London squares, and it bothered him to think about it, but maybe 'self-possession' is close, two words singing in temporary harmony around a hyphen. He bent down to fix his laces. He'd noticed on his way down the steps that the tenant's padlock was loose, so he walked back to her gate and removed her chain. He crossed into the public gardens and dumped it in a bin on the other side of the square. He was heading to Upper Street to meet Gosia, and the sun shone on his face as he walked into Ripplevale Grove, reaching into one of his jacket pockets to feel the shape of the professor's passport.

# BOOK TWO
## Summer

# 14 Haulage

'There's darkness enough in London to bury nine million people.' This was the thought that occurred to Mrs Krupa more than four weeks earlier as she drank her coffee. She came to Granary Square most days, sitting outside at the café tables, looking past the fountains and across the canal to the tall new buildings of King's Cross. She'd lived here since 1985, but it wasn't really living, she told herself. When Andrzej was alive, it was a proper life. She broke off a piece of Parmesan biscuit and remembered the *Solidarność* graffito: 'The Winter Is Yours, But the Spring Will Be Ours.' It was written on a wall of the medical university in Białystok the year they married. Her mind went back even further: snow and soup, her father's combs lined up on a handkerchief at the side of his bed.

She took out her cigarettes, her Karelia Slims. The boys who came and went from her son's car wash on York Way were kind enough to get her cartons on their travels. Looking out, she could remember the original gasholders, the Victorian yards. She was sixty-two and even her English memories haunted her now. It had started with Andrzej's death: King's Cross changing overnight, becoming metal and glass like the streets you saw in advertisements, and the old sense of security gone. Bozydar and Gosia grew up speaking English, hardly a word of Polish between them.

She knew what she would have: two starters. The pumpkin soup and the beetroot carpaccio and nothing else today. Mrs Krupa had secret worries that she took to cafés and mulled over, with cigarettes. She had hoped for the good life, but she suspected her son was doing things that would shock the priests. The idea made her want to cry as she ordered a sherry.

'Here she is,' she said to the waiter.

Gosia appeared out of daylight, her hair shining.

'Hello, Mama.'

She sat down. 'It's a miracle to think of all the changes, Gosia,' her mother said. 'Sitting here every day, I feel . . . you know . . . *tęsknota*, a little nostalgia.'

'Nothing wrong with that, Mama.'

The waiter brought Gosia a herbal tea. 'It's when you're a Catholic,' Cecylia began, 'you see the suffering.'

'Come on,' Gosia said. 'No gloominess today.'

She was a thoughtful girl. She didn't make good decisions, but she was young. Twenty-five. She had plenty of time to sort herself out and find the right life. She was good with people, a good worker. And an English Literature graduate now. The Islington salon was just for fun and the pleasure of earning something.

Cecylia sipped her sherry and looked up.

There was a boy, of course. Gosia had met him at university. She could have been a doctor or a dentist, they said at her school, Acland Burghley, but Gosia was always going her own way, daydreaming. She wanted a new planet.

'Don't talk about suffering, Mama. You're so blessed.'

'I will be, when you settle down with a good man.'

'I have a good man, and we're not settling down. We're settling *up*!'

'Please, Gosia. *Words*.'

Gosia put down her phone. She looked for a moment very grown up and Cecylia felt newly aware of her. 'People think Milo's so *certain*,' she said, 'but he's only a person who was brought up to question things.'

'And he knows everything, all the answers, I suppose?'

'No, Mama. He just wants to progress.'

Mrs Krupa believed her children had learned from television how to dismiss their mother and how to hide what they were doing. These people like Gosia who would save the planet might think about saving their own families first.

They ordered food and she looked out at the afternoon as if seeking clues from the vanished world.

'You can't be anybody other than who you are,' she said.

'I don't believe that, Mama.'

'You'll find out.'

'I suppose we will. But hope is a lovely thing to share with a man. It's what I studied: the imagination.'

'And what can that do, a pile of books?'

She began talking about Gosia's great-grandparents and what happened to them in the woods at Wólka Okrąglik. Here we were in a new century, in a new millennium, but Cecylia still thought of those atrocities when considering her family.

Gosia put her hand across the table.

Mrs Krupa asked the waiter for another light. 'People don't talk about the Catholics. But they're your people. We have to tell these stories, Gosia. Without the stories there is no life. Two thousand Polish priests, for criticising the regime and helping Jews. Murdered. My grandparents. And do you think that kind of Europe is very far away?'

'I'm not sure,' Gosia replied. 'Nothing is far away.'

After lunch, they walked to Bozydar's car wash. The young men were often Polish, quiet, and they always called her Mrs Krupa – which she liked. She'd speak to them in a friendly way and ignore their glances at Gosia. But there was a special boy. His name was Jakub and he reminded Mrs Krupa of a young Paul Newman, the actor, whose grandparents had been Polish too. And the boy was from her city, Białystok. He had worked there as a gardener. He'd caught Mrs Krupa's attention a few weeks before, with his old-fashioned manners and his blue eyes. He told her that he was twenty-eight years old. She'd begun to promote his interests with her son almost right away, saying he was the sort of good-living young man the family should be helping. Bozydar seemed to prefer the Irish workers who kept to the yards and drove his trucks.

When she and Gosia arrived that day, Bozydar was in the glass office. He looked up and lifted his four-year-old son, Ben, onto the desk so he could see his grandmother. The boy was wearing shorts and had a smile the width of the Branicki Palace Bridge. She came in and kissed him and looked around, sharing her pride. The boy showed her the toy cars he was playing with. Gosia kept her distance, as usual, leaning against one of the desks. She didn't approve of her brother, or the calendars on his walls.

Bozydar was eighteen when his father died, and he took over the builders, then the car wash, later adding the haulage himself. He was now in his thirties, bald and with too much fat on him for a man so short and unkempt. Not like his father. Not groomed like him. But he was interested in money and he lived in one of the posh little painted houses down in Keystone Crescent, an enclave off Caledonian Road. He seemed to be making good profits from the trucks and doing God knows what else.

He came over and ruffled Ben's hair, as he often did, and pecked his mother on the cheek. 'It's mad busy in here today,' he said. 'Companies are moving their stock again big time, all over Europe. We've got every truck out.'

'Still bringing in stolen cigarettes?' Gosia asked.

'What you talking about?' he said.

He looked at her as if she were an uninvited guest.

'And *people*?'

He turned to his mother. 'What's she on about? Coming in here like a muppet and talking garbage in front of the boy?'

Gosia shook her head.

'Still got your black boyfriend?' he asked.

'Stop it!' Cecylia said. 'I want to have a peaceful day.'

Gosia made a kissing face and bent down. 'Come here and give me a hug, Ben. I'm getting back to work now. Big hugs!'

The boy ran over and Gosia wiggled his ears. 'I'll see you at the weekend, Mama – okay?'

'Yes, please. And I want you to put something in your appointment book. Write it down. It's more than a month away, but write down 5 July. The Monday. There's going to be a special Mass for cousin Popiełuszko. You know they're raising his name as a martyr. It's important you both come, to St Andrew Bobola. You could do my hair in the morning, Gosia, and then we'll all go together in the car.'

'That's fine, I've got it,' Gosia said, and waved goodbye.

Bozydar returned to his phone and seemed agitated, as he often did.

'Yeah,' he said, 'Sullivan's coming from Preston first thing in the morning. Tipping a load of chickens in Marlow. That's right. Then over to Holyhead – he's got the details on him already. Yeah. O'Dade as well. Early doors at Purfleet. I gave him the code for the ferry. We'll be down there, yeah. Okay, Stefan.'

Cecylia inspected her grandson's face. Andrzej's eyes. He looked like he'd been here before, the wisdom of that child.

Bozydar was so busy, Cecylia thought, and though he was subject to temptation and could be drawn to the wrong path, he was a decent father to the boy, and she hoped his ex-wife appreciated all the things he did for them.

He took his jacket off the back of a chair and said he was going to the bank in Islington. 'I'll wait here with Ben,' Cecylia told him.

'I'll be back in a bit,' he said, spinning his keys on his finger.

After he'd gone, she took Ben to the toilet and then he played with his toys on the office floor. She decided to step out for a cigarette and looked on Bozydar's desk for a lighter. She pulled open a drawer, then another one. There was no lighter, but something else: more than half a dozen wads of plastic bank cards – NatWest, Santander, Sainsbury's, HSBC – held together with elastic bands, many of the cards in Polish names.

* * *

The next morning at 7 a.m., Bozydar was in Rainham, Essex. His trucks coming from Purfleet would always drop off at a spot by the landfill site on Coldharbour Lane. He was an early-morning person: shit, shower and shave, into the car and firing towards the Blackwall Tunnel before things opened up, just to breathe some fresh air and get his head straight while his phones were quiet. Boz felt a really deep sort of connection to the underworld of M25 service stations and repair shops fringing the Thames, the oily-rag world of budget windscreen shops, tyre warehouses and gearbox specialists, offering cups of tea and diagnostics at the crack of dawn. 'MOT Centre', 'Essexmot': he had spent his thirties in yards and car washes with cranked-up radios, by burger vans flying England flags. He'd stopped that morning to get a coffee from a Moto service station in Thurrock preferred by the Albanians. A few were out of their yokes, bleary-eyed, waiting for texts.

As he often did, Bozydar parked a mile up the road from the land-fill site and went to Riverside Walk to find a bench to sit on. Looking up, he could see the sign for Tilda, the rice producer, and its grey silos, the Thames silver from the shore. Four magpies flew over the bank, the grass was so green, and he puzzled over the concrete hulks that lay half sunk as usual at the edge of the water. He stood up and walked forward to study them, stepping over a squashed Lucozade bottle. The Thames was lapping onto the concrete barges, birds flying up, and it was beautiful to see it again in the empty morning. Somebody had told him the barges were used in the Second World War and then scuttled here, sixteen of them. He was interested in history, but also in making money. Essex was the workshop of the English world nowadays: everything got moving here, everything got oiled. He wanted people to come, and here was what they'd see first, the glittering Thames and London's skyscrapers.

About 8 a.m. he walked back to his car and drove it to the place near the landfill site in Coldharbour Lane, where the truck would stop. Within minutes, Stefan had arrived in his black Audi. Stefan didn't give anything away. Bozydar knew he worked for a well-known young Russian, a rich man's kid. It was Stefan who linked it all up. He knew the invisible man Feng, who they say worked out of a defunct acupuncture place in Gray's Inn Road, masterminding all the payments.

Bozydar's guess was that the young Russian's money was now going into the operation somehow, and maybe they shared the profits. Either way, Stefan was the go-between, subcontracting transport and security to people like Bozydar, who had been looking after the English leg for two years. He had nothing to do with the Far East, Russia, Turkey or France, but he knew the coast of England like the back of his hand.

'Did you pick up coffee?' he asked.

'No coffee. I have this,' Stefan said. He leaned back into his car and took a can of Dragon Slayer from the holder.

'How much energy does a guy need?'

'Always more,' Stefan said.

Sitting in the passenger seat of Stefan's car that morning, minding his own business, was Jakub, the car-wash kid with the movie-star looks. Bozydar's mother had been agitating for the kid to be given more responsibilities, so he was being slowly promoted, drawn into these more lucrative, invisible parts of the business. He stayed in the car while Bozydar and Stefan stood by the side of the road, talking figures and the latest expansion plans.

Bozydar was an entrepreneur; he wanted in on whatever new projects were coming, and Stefan told him they could use as many trucks and drivers as he could get. They were going to be moving more people now. He also wanted him – or his Russian boss wanted him – to expand the distribution side with the weed they were producing. 'He likes how quickly you move,' Stefan said. 'He'd like to meet you. More selling. More money.'

'This Brexit situation is fucking us up,' Bozydar added. 'They can't come in and out of the country like they used to. People like this guy,' he said, nodding to the young man in Stefan's car. 'They came on tourist trips and overstayed. But now when they go back home . . . if they want to return to the UK . . .'

Bozydar started reminiscing about the old way of doing things. Before, they only had to go to Victoria Coach Station. 'Thirty hours by bus. Warsaw and Łódź, Wrocław, Poznań and Berlin. Then Antwerp.'

'We do this,' Stefan said, ending the conversation.

'Thanks for bringing him,' Bozydar said. 'His English is perfect. He can help us translate and get the others settled.'

A grey Corsa arrived. It was driven by one of the Albanians, who never asked any questions. Fatos, no surname: willing to deliver cigarettes, vodka and people. He lived in Birmingham, drove in and out of London and always used a burner phone.

At 8.15 on the dot a red truck came up the road and stopped. The driver jumped down and nodded to the men, stopping for a second to fist-bump Bozydar. 'There was no delays,' the driver said. 'Rolled straight off.'

'Good stuff, Gerry.'

Bozydar turned to Stefan.

'This is Gerry O'Dade, one of my best drivers. Always working. I don't think you've met our man Stefan.'

'No names, okay?' Stefan said.

Jakub got out of the car and approached the others. 'I'm Jakub Padanowski,' he said to no one in particular.

'Jesus,' moaned Stefan.

'We fucking know who you are,' Bozydar said.

'Friendly,' O'Dade said, walking backwards. 'I've twenty pallets of wine in here to deliver to Leighton Buzzard.'

'Okay, let's get them out first,' Bozydar said.

The young Irishman went to the back of his container, while Stefan and Fatos opened all the doors of their cars. Bozydar walked to the container and looked in. It smelled especially bad, this one. He raised a stubby finger and quickly counted ten people sitting on the pallets or standing near the doors. 'Right,' he said, holding up his fingers. '*Three* of you in that car and . . . Fatos, you take *four*.'

They jumped down and sprinted to the cars.

Bozydar ordered the others – two returning Poles he recognised and one Vietnamese guy – to get into the back of his car and told Jakub to sit in front.

'Right. All good?' O'Dade said to Bozydar.

'Make sure you clear out the water bottles and piss bags, Gerry. It stinks.'

'I'll park up and do it at the Moto.'

The truck was soon out of sight. The cars followed, with Bozydar's the last to leave Coldharbour Lane, the magpies and the silver Thames. The vehicles split up at the roundabout to head off in different directions, as they always did.

'Tell the boys Britain's even better since they were last here,' Bozydar said, throwing three bottles of water into the back seat.

'I don't think you need me for that,' Jakub said.

The Vietnamese man was exhausted from the journey. Jakub turned and unscrewed his water for him, and the man nodded repeatedly.

'*Merci*,' he said. 'Thank you. Thank you.'

# 15 Paradise Park

The migrant flat at Paradise Park, north of King's Cross, always smelled of dirty socks and hashish. It was two hours since the men had come in with their knapsacks, the new workers and the returnees. They were taken to the kitchen, where a heap of beer bottles sat on the floor and rubbish overflowed the bin. A young Asian woman with a laptop open on the work surface had made each migrant log in and transfer £10,000 for the journey. She only spoke single words. People always speculated about who she was – Feng's daughter? Feng's niece? – but nobody knew, not even Bozydar. When one of the migrants that morning said he was having trouble remembering his password, Bozydar mentioned the Border Force, using the Vietnamese word for 'police'. The young man then began clicking at the keyboard and in a few minutes had transferred the money.

The living room upstairs was about four metres by three and had a huge flat-screen TV in the corner, the wires from a games console trailing across the soiled carpet to some battered chairs and more empty beer bottles. The screen said 'FIFA 21' above a frozen image of Kylian Mbappé. One of the Poles was having a nap on the sofa, and when he woke up he looked around. 'How many people are living in this house?' he asked.

'We're a bit short of space at the minute,' Bozydar said, 'so all you guys who came in this morning will be sharing. Only for tonight. Many of you are off tomorrow. We had to get the bills settled. There are four more.'

'Fourteen, all together?'

Jakub had been living here for weeks. He'd begun to complain: none of this was what he'd expected.

'Three or four of us in each room?' another Pole asked.

'It will thin out,' Bozydar said, and Jakub translated. 'You've been in the UK before, man. You know the script.'

Bozydar clapped the guy on the shoulder. 'You can handle it. The point is: you're back in London now. These Vietnamese are here for the first time. You'll soon be making a lot of money and be able to afford a flat of your own.'

Eventually, the ten from the container were all in the living room. There weren't enough chairs, so some of them sat on the floor with their backs against the wallpaper. Bozydar went round with a sports bag, asking each man to put his passport, bank cards and mobile phone in the bag. 'This is for security.'

A tall guy raised his voice in Polish.

'He wants to keep his phone,' one of the others said. 'It's new.'

'No chance,' Boz said. 'These phones are traceable. I'm only worried about your safety. You could be deported or put in jail. I will give you a new phone each and we'll begin the process of getting you registered for work in the UK.'

They all dropped their stuff into the bag. One or two didn't have passports, but he didn't search them. 'You can take your chances,' he said. 'But your old phones have a chip in them that could lead the Border Force straight to you.' The bag got heavier.

Jakub was still using the cheap pay-as-you-go phone Bozydar had given him. He wasn't legit, so he depended on Bozydar to pay him his earnings in cash until the bank card he'd been promised arrived.

A buzz went round again, so Bozydar folded his arms until it was finished. 'We've taken risks to get you over here,' he said. 'You've paid for your travel, but the cost to stay here is £3,000, with all your accommodation, your bills, Oyster cards, and everything we're doing to get you working.'

They gave up quickly. They always did. 'We will keep your bank cards until the debt is paid off, and we'll continue to give you your wages every Friday, for your security and to keep you safe from the authorities. That's the deal. You'll find duvets in the cupboards, and I'm never far away if you need help.' He threw a bag of weed down on the table. 'Have a smoke on us,' he said. 'Use the PlayStation.'

Sometimes you have to go through layers to get to a person, and when you arrive they're still not there. That's the way it was with Feng. The man existed in the shadows, and Stefan could contact him but he'd never seen him. Each time, he would drop off the bags of money from the cannabis business and see himself out. The shop was dilapidated, with dusty jars on wonky shelves, diagrams of the human body hanging on yellowed strings by the front door, and plastic flowers bleached on the windowsill. The rumour was that someone known to Feng in England, one of his late wife's brothers maybe, used to deal in Chinese medicine, but the shop was long abandoned, and cobwebs hung between the jars. There was a manky white door inside the shop that led to another floor. Stefan would be buzzed in with the money and he would leave the bag on the middle of the stairs, under a dim, naked bulb.

The lynchpin was never seen entering or leaving the premises in Gray's Inn Road. Perhaps he came and went at night, working upstairs on a computer that nobody ever saw. That was the image Stefan had as he drove down Caledonian Road with another bag in the boot of his car, filled with rolls of money for Feng. He had a headache and was crunching Ibuprofen at the wheel. He suffered from regular migraines and wondered if they came from all the things he knew, or didn't know.

'He doesn't exist. So I mustn't, either,' he said to the windscreen.

Stefan rented a house in Hertfordshire with his Romanian wife. They had no children, and he mainly walked his Pomeranians and painted garden sculptures. He was quietly active in the local community in South Mimms: at the weekend, he cut the grass for his

181

elderly neighbours. 'It's these things that keep a man healthy in his own heart,' he told his wife.

He and the invisible man communicated by burner phones, texts only, and often Stefan would find a piece of paper with a new number waiting for him in the shop, on the steep stairs that led up to a closed door. He'd texted Feng twice this morning already. 'Yuri agrees. More stuff and more producers. Krupa at car wash has the vehicles.' Stefan sensed the lynchpin liked the connection with the Russian. He liked investing other people's money. The second text: 'Yuri will pay for new farms in Kent. You bring the people.'

At Gray's Inn Road he was buzzed inside. He walked across the filthy carpet and laid the bag on the stairs. Reaching for a piece of paper on the middle step, he noticed his own shadow lengthening up the wall.

Bozydar was at King's Cross station that night. He often took these trips round the area after dark, going from cashpoint to cashpoint and withdrawing money with the wad of cards in his pocket, each card bearing a different name and a Post-it note with a PIN. Coming back, passing the fast food joints beside the station, he thought of his sister, Gosia. He'd always known she would end up with a guy like that: someone who would drive their mother mad. They were stuck like glue, the two of them, messing about with books. This Milo was some university kid who swaggered about talking big words, but his friends were nothing but local wastemen. Gosia was an idiot. She could have had a successful hairdressing business but thought she was too good for that.

He ordered a large vodka in the Scottish pub at the beginning of the Cally. He drank it down in one gulp and ordered another right after. His phones lit up every few minutes: issues with workers, transport, dealers and deliveries; questions about travel times, payments, application forms and vehicles. He put the devices face down and drank until closing time, barely turning on his stool or saying a word.

It was Friday, so the place was busy. There was an event on the patio; it was all back to normal in the pubs. He began to think about how – with the scale-up Stefan wanted – business was about to go into orbit. After last orders, he tripped out of the doors, crossed at the lights by the Scala and went in the direction of Argyle Square. He held on to the railings for a minute before going to the Avalon Hotel on the far side. He rapped on the street-level window and was let in by one of the girls, the one called Coco. She had a red scarf draped over a low lamp and a couple of girls left her room as he entered. Although he was drunk, he could smell the crack smoke and saw the pipe, fashioned from a miniature of brandy, the glass still warm.

The next day, he was at the Beeline Employment Agency in Hornsey. Six of the men from Paradise Park had already gone to grow-houses in Ramsgate, and three had started labouring work with a gang of builders at Euston, the gaffer saying he would pay their wages using the bank account details Boz had given him. The Beeline girl said they had more work at the Angelique warehouse.

'Yeah?'

'They need overlockers.'

'I've got someone. He can start today,' Bozydar said. 'Bank details to follow.'

They never asked too many questions.

Jakub Padanowski – maybe his mum was on to something: the firm would need a guy like that as things got bigger, somebody who could run the rest of them. He'd have to get him into the English system of things, place him in a factory for a few months where he could learn how to push the others, how to be a lieutenant. He called Jakub on his burner and told him he had a new job. He could work between London and Leicester, and Boz would see to it that he got £90 a week in his hand. (The real wages were £265.) He'd get a bank card of his own when he'd paid off his debt. Boz could hear it on the phone: Jakub wanting to believe him. It was always the same; they all wanted a life that outshone the truth.

# 16 A Place Like England

Jakub spent the first week of June working in the Angelique warehouse, then it was decided he should go to Leicester to properly learn the overlocking machine. The factory in Leicester was in a place called Spinney Hills. He arrived at two in the morning in an oily van full of cellophane and cardboard boxes. He hadn't seen any of England on the way up. Sometimes, he thought he was doing all this for his boyfriend, for what Robert wanted from life. He missed Robert's warmth and the energy that came from him, and often during those weeks Jakub had a feeling of desperately wanting to go home. He'd begun to wonder if England was anything like the myth he and Robert had bought into, the England of pop stars and footballers. But he was determined not to break the faith.

The Irish driver had parked at the back of an old typewriter factory and then disappeared. When it was morning, Jakub got out, amazed by the squalor of the yard, all the windows covered in sheets or jagged with broken glass. He walked down a road of garment factories and curry shops into Green Lane Road, where everything was waking up and the people looked at him. There were dried chillis hanging over the front doors, for protection and good health, a woman told him.

Phone shops.

Big factory pipes with graffiti around them.

A large mosque with white towers rising from the English terraces.

Jakub looked at a sign next to a fish shop. 'Spitting paan on the street is unhygienic and antisocial. You could be fined £150.'

He bought water from a man at a stall.

Each of the brick houses had a satellite dish.

*Nikhy Garments. Milan Sweets.*

He got a text from Bozydar. 'Block A 3 floor unit 7.'

Jakub walked back to the typewriter building. The van was gone and his bag had been placed against the wall. He picked it up and walked past a row of freshly parked silver Mercedes towards a doorway covered in wire mesh.

A smell of garbage filled the stairwell. The tiles on the floor were broken and covered in grease and the walls seemed to sweat. Jakub's mind, as he climbed the stairs, went back to a place of dirty snow, a tenement in Białystok, then to the excitement he'd felt on the bus when he was coming over to the UK. He walked over filthy rags and burst rubbish bags and froze when he reached the third floor and saw a rat in the corner with what appeared to be a used sanitary towel. The door to his right said, 'Jupiter Fashions', and someone had written on cardboard above it, 'For Angelique Clothing Co'. Beside the door there was a buzzer that said, 'Please Ring Me'. He stepped forward and pulled his bag tight to his shoulder. The rapid tap of the machines.

*Tah-tah-tah. Tah-tah-tah-tah-tah-tah.*

All the way into his head, threading his thoughts.

The factory was a long room filled with women in saris. The strip lights made everything yellow and a fearful heat rose from the pressure irons. The boss was a man called Aasim, who constantly smoked and ranted. They wasted no time. Aasim explained the different elements of the factory, and then got Jakub making boxes. After a few hours, the room was like a factory anywhere in the world, but Jakub was determined to be a worker they remembered.

'Hard work, many orders!' Aasim said, passing up the shop floor.

'I understand,' Jakub said.

'No time left.'

In the afternoon, Aasim showed him the machine. He raised his voice to say the same three things over and over.

'We want clean finish!' 'Neat edge!' 'No raw edge!'

Jakub stared through his shouting.

Most of the women sat at sewing machines. Rows of overlockers and lock-stitchers. Groups at long tables hemming and binding. Next to Jakub, the ironers and then the packers, young boys who averted their eyes. Aasim sat Jakub down at a Singer Pro Speed and asked him if he could work the pedals.

Jakub had used a different machine in London. 'I worked the Jaguar 489,' he said, adjusting the tension and fiddling with the settings.

'Is all ready to go,' Aasim said. 'Same machine. Home machine.'

'Give me time.'

'We need leaders. Boz says you can do it. *Intelligent!*'

Jakub nodded and made a calming motion. He could work all the hours here and pay back what he owed Bozydar. Then, real London. Today, he would master the machine. He walked over to the bench where the cutters had piled the material.

He could hem the vests and shorts at speed, his right pedal lifting the gear to slide the fabric under, and the left one running the stitching device and the blade that cut the edges. The room was hot. There wasn't enough water. The women were all ages, and most of them were Bangladeshi. They looked over at Jakub as he worked and he felt they must be wondering who he was. At 4 p.m., the only elderly man in the packing area brought him a samosa and a cup of very sweet tea. Another man gave him a rolled cigarette, but when he tried to go out onto the fire escape, it was blocked with boxes. He went back to the stairwell and closed his eyes while he smoked and breathed hard. He had a text from Boz telling him there was a room for him at 77 Rolleston Street.

He worked late that night. Someone brought dahl on a paper plate and he drank Pepsi from a plastic bottle. Aasim was at a desk behind piles of garments that were being bagged and tagged – the labels said 'Angelique' – readied for high-street stores and online. Jakub understood that it was subcontract work and they were producing items for this British firm alone. Earlier, he'd turned on the desk lamp over his machine and got an electric shock from it. The women left the factory that evening in groups and other women came to work the night shift, and the noise continued. Jakub walked to the open window to take in the cool air.

As the weeks passed, Jakub began to feel at home in Rolleston Street. He had a room in the attic, and the clean and tidy house was owned by a British-Bangladeshi man and his wife, a million miles from Paradise Park. They lived there with their three daughters. Mr Hazari was in a wheelchair and didn't go out much, but he seemed captivated by people in general and by Jakub in particular. He'd begun to advise the young man. He told him all the places and shops he should avoid around East Park Road, and said if he wanted to drink or to meet girls he should take the 54 bus into the city. Jakub showed him the ends of his fingers: they were raw, and Mr Hazari wrapped them in Band-Aids that he kept in an old British Rail tin.

He never asked Jakub any questions about his work or who was paying his wages. He seemed used to these things and would simply wave his hand in front of his face. He told Jakub the building he was working in had once housed the Imperial Typewriter Company. He said it had been a beautiful factory with offices, was one of the best in the Midlands, but there had been a strike in 1974 because the owners were treating the British-Bangladeshi workers very badly and pushed them too far. He told Jakub they all marched in the street, but in the end the whole place was closed down.

The women at the Jupiter factory worked seventy hours a week. When Jakub asked one of the packers what they were earning, the man timidly held up four fingers. Jakub didn't want to say anything; he was doing just as badly, though they all spoke to him like he was being paid much more than they were. He noticed things. The workers had to put their hand up if they wanted to go to the bathroom, and Aasim often ignored them. They kept getting shocks from the machines. Jakub complained to Boz by text, but Boz said he didn't own the factories, his job was to supply extra labour, and he reminded him this was piecework, that it was the best way to start, to get established, get his UK papers in order. 'I have more Poles working in other factories,' Boz said. 'And Vietnamese. We need supervisors.' He said there were lots of opportunities.

The dodgy lamps in the factory fizzed all night. Aasim's son, Shah, would often cover the night shift, sitting with his feet on the desk, ordering Deliveroo or speaking loudly to his friends on his mobile, or watching porn on the computer while everybody worked.

'Come on, man,' Jakub said one evening. 'These women are religious. Turn the sound off or take it away from the factory floor.'

'Shut your gob,' the son said. 'Get on with your work.' He spat on the floor and threw his cigarette butts into the bin.

Jakub was amazed by the women. They seemed to own themselves and their hardships appeared not to unsettle their happiness. They liked Jakub because he took charge, in a professional way, replacing the bulbs in their lamps and getting new blades for the blunt ones in their machines. He opened the windows and, when the plumbing wasn't working, arrived with bottles filled from the kitchen in Rolleston Street. Mr Hazari didn't mind – he was 'a union man' – and he wrote to Aasim telling him the conditions were inhumane, and to get the taps fixed. Jakub had travelled a long way to end up in that broken building and to walk up that polluted stairwell; he was denationalised, trapped, but somehow determined to work on, to get to the better place in his mind. Every day hundreds of garments left the factory marked up and sealed in boxes. Aasim said he couldn't deny it: Jakub was a tremendous worker. 'A bloody pain in the arse as well.'

As soon as he was proficient on the machine at Leicester, they brought him back for two days to teach the workers at a factory in Bethnal Green. Waiting for a lift back to Leicester one Saturday at the end of June, he bumped into Bozydar's mother at the car wash in York Way.

'I haven't seen you in a while,' she said to him. 'What's been happening to you?' She stroked his cheek and Jakub answered her in Polish. They began talking about Białystok, her favourite subject, Mrs Krupa a little emotional. He knew to never show it, but Jakub found Mrs Krupa's interest in him unsettling; it could help him, but he almost flinched as she touched his face. He was conscious that he wasn't as nice as she thought he was, and it bothered him, feeling fraudulent. She laughed girlishly at the front of the garage while the soap suds trickled from the car being washed.

'So, you're working in the factories?'

'Leicester,' he said. 'For weeks. And sometimes here, like yesterday and today, when there's a big order and some training to do.'

'Don't work too much,' she said in Polish. 'I know about these English hours. We need good Polish boys to make it better here.'

'In London?'

'Everywhere,' she said.

'I worry about the future.'

'You mustn't,' she said. 'Everything will be wonderful.' It was as if she was trying to convince herself that her family was normal. 'My son may sometimes lose his way,' she whispered, 'but with Christ's help, he will rectify his mistakes, I promise you.'

Bozydar appeared from the office with his usual face. He pointed to the truck out on the road and said it was time to leave.

Jakub would sleep on these journeys. The Albanian drivers were silent, but not the Irish. Today it was Gerry.

'I'm tipping you in Leicester.'

'Yes, please.'

'Then I'm off to pick up a load of carrots at Newark, near Nottingham, so it is. I'll be tipping them in Edinburgh, then I'm off down to Cairnryan for the boat home. Go and see the mammy for a wee bit. Boz texts me one job at a time. Sometimes two. He's a wee arsehole, but he keeps me busy.'

Jakub saw a sign for St Albans, then one for Luton. He rubbed his eyes.

'You don't like Bozydar?'

'I'm only messing,' Gerry said. He made comments one after the other, texting while he drove, slugging from an energy drink. 'Have you seen his sister?' Gerry asked. 'She's feckan unbelievable, like. I'm not kidding ye. *Gorgeous.*'

'I didn't meet her.'

'I'm not joking, like. She's a ride.'

There were days like this when Jakub wanted Robert to say the words 'Come home'. That England didn't matter, it was only an idea, a fantasy they'd once had when they were drunk and hopeful and unrealistic. He couldn't bear to tell his boyfriend what it was really like here, and that created a deeper loneliness. Robert hadn't come with him because he was finishing his college course. Jakub felt better as he watched the dark road unfurl, deciding everything would improve once they were together.

With the traffic, it was three hours back to Leicester and Gerry talked most of the time. He said a lot about the haulage part of the business.

'I'm talking really dodgy characters,' Gerry said, yawning. 'Mystery men. They're mad, a lot of them. There's only one of them I've seen giving Boz a right tongue-lashing, like. And that's your man Stefan. Did you meet him?'

'He drove me to do a job for Bozydar.'

'A dark horse,' Gerry said. 'Knows where everything is buried, that one. If these Russians ever lose the run of themselves, Stefan's the only one around here who'll be able to sort it out. He's the fixer, for sure. Boz does the trucking. Runs a few of the cannabis farms, like. He runs the dealers too. He's going all in. But your man Stefan now, he's in charge of supersizing the whole thing and it's serious.'

A lot of the women didn't come back in after the Delta variant arrived. The cases were high in the factory. Mr Hazari said it was a scandal. Bozydar sent up a few more Polish workers that week, but they didn't stay. 'Most of these women are on Universal Credit,' Mr Hazari said. 'And now they're in hospital. They weren't wearing masks. North Evington had the worst virus numbers in the country. These people are sitting next to each other all day, passing garments back and forth.' He put his cup down on the breakfast table. 'In future times,' he said, 'they will look back and say the whole thing was about economics.'

Aasim had started paying Jakub some extra cash on the side. He even paid it during the few days that Jakub was off with the virus. Extra cash came from Bozydar, £40 and sometimes more, because the orders were big and Jakub was meeting them. But he was still being paid terribly, and wasn't afraid to say so.

'This is not what anybody was promised,' he said, 'and these workers don't get any breaks.'

'You're one of them fuckwits,' the boss's son said to him one night, tilting a bottle of beer to his mouth. 'Everyone else can graft and shut it. But you—'

'Why don't you fuck off, Shah,' Jakub said. 'You think we don't know what's going on here? We put up with this shit because we know in time we will get something better.'

The young Muslim came up close to Jakub and poured a drop of beer from the bottle onto his shoes. 'You've always got a chin on,' he said. He stepped closer and splashed him in the chest. 'Reckon you're up to it?'

Jakub tried to turn away, but Shah slapped his face. 'D'you wanna go?'

'I don't want any problems.'

'I'll give you a right pasting, you get me?' Shah said.

Jakub stared at him and then slowly withdrew, returning to his machine. Before turning it on and putting his foot on the pedal he saw a rat crawling under the cutting bench. Shah spat on the floor. 'It never ends until it ends, mate, know what I mean?'

On one of his rare nights off, Jakub went out. All day he'd been thinking of having someone's arms around him. He got the bus into town and found his way to a place with a cabaret. Sitting at the bar, he met a couple. Their accents were strong, but they all drank sambuca together and then went to a nightclub called Helsinki. It was all strobe lights and house beats. He was so pleased to be with these young guys who were familiar with everything and knew everybody, and for a few hours it all faded away, the sad, earnest face of Mrs Krupa, the working conditions, the future he and Robert were supposed to have. It all spun away under a glitter ball and he felt nothing was pressing on him, except these boys, both of whom had begun to kiss him on the dance floor and touch his body. He never regretted it, the hours being selfish and abandoned and sweaty and high on that crystally powder. He went home to the boys' flat, and they fucked each other on the living-room sofa.

But the work seemed to lead nowhere, except to more work. Each shift, he was running up hundreds of garments, hardly stopping for a drink or a chat. Sometimes, while he worked, he saw in his mind the wonderful banks of sweet violets that he and Robert had found in that Japanese garden in Wrocław. The hotter it was in the factory, the more he dreamed of these other places: the deep forest of the National Park of Białowieża, where his parents had taken him as a child. He could still see the tree, a Norway spruce, that stretched up over fifty metres, where the sky was clear and blue.

'It's all right,' he said to himself. 'I love him.'

Early one morning, a sunny day, Jakub came up the stairs with a tray of chai. Light was fighting past the dirty sheets on the windows. He was hoping to drink the tea with the night shift women and laugh with them. He often did that, helping them sweep up the remnants on the floor around their tables, before setting himself up at his own machine. As soon as he entered the factory floor he could smell the smoke. He ran to the desk behind the bales, where Shah was slumped over, fast asleep, a bottle of Jack Daniel's on his desk. Flames were coming out of the bin and had caught a roll of cotton fabric on the shelf. Jakub jumped over the desk and could hear screams behind him as he grabbed the roll of fabric, sending flames into the air as it unfurled and bounced along the floor.

'Jesus Christ!' Shah shouted, suddenly awake. Jakub had thrown the chai at it, then kicked the roll out of the door and smothered the fire in the corridor. It was out, but his hands were burned, the fingertips already worn from the machine, and painful. The corridor was full of smoke. A few minutes later Aasim came running upstairs. 'I'm sorry for you, Jakub. My son is such a fucking waste of time – forgive my language.'

'It's all right, Aasim,' Jakub said, trying to support one hand with the other.

He took two days off. Mr Hazari's youngest girls came back on the second afternoon from the Jameah Girls Academy with a slice of melon for him. He could see their eyes smiling, and he felt blessed to be among them as he thanked them. 'You must be very proud of them, Mr Hazari,' Jakub said.

'Yes, I am. We are lifelong learners, all of us together.'

His hands got better with lukewarm water and aloe vera. It was nothing much. He would still pave his way out of there.

'You are strong in your mind,' Mr Hazari said.

'Maybe,' Jakub said. 'But I was wrong about England.'

Mr Hazari rocked in his wheelchair. 'It's Friday,' he said, a moment later. 'I don't drink. But you like beer?'

'Very much.'

'Then I'll take you somewhere. Stay there.' Mr Hazari wheeled himself back to his bedroom on the ground floor. He returned after ten minutes with a blue suit, a shirt and a tie sitting across his lap. He pointed to Jakub. 'For you. It might be a bit big but it will do well enough for tonight.'

'You want me to wear it?'

'Get washed,' Mr Hazari said. 'Put on the suit. Come back in half an hour.'

Jakub shampooed his hair but he couldn't scrub hard. Mr Hazari's wife came quietly and left a belt over the banister at the top of the stairs, plus a small bottle of perfumed oil. After his shower, he dabbed it on his neck.

'We are new men,' Mr Hazari said. His face was shining as he sat in his suit in the wheelchair, motioning for the front door to be opened. 'We'll get there this year if you push. Round to Nottingham Street and then left.'

The sun was behind the mosque and the old factory buildings appeared suddenly majestic in the golden light of that Friday evening. Jakub noticed a green and bronze enamel badge on Mr Hazari's lapel. When he asked what it was, Mr Hazari leaned over the arm of his wheelchair to show it off. 'National Union of Railwaymen,' Jakub read out loud. 'Solidarity, 1984/85.'

He smiled as he wheeled Mr Hazari over the road.

When they got to the Leicester Railwaymen's Club & Institute, the older man hollered in and two men came down the steps.

'Babar Hazari, for God's sake!'

'Don't swear,' Mr Hazari said. 'And be kind to my young guest.'

In one swift movement, the two men carried the chair up the steps, and they were soon in the main bar of the club.

That night, over several ginger ales and many pints, Mr Hazari told Jakub the story of his life. He had been a junior conductor with British Rail. He loved talking about it, the run from Derby and Leicester to London, Barlow's big train shed at St Pancras. He spoke of the long blue-and-yellow trains that had been the pride of British Rail. 'There is no direct service from Leicester to Leeds any more,' he said, 'but I used to work that line.'

'It's nice you took pride in your work.'

'Real jobs, Mr Padanowski. They still exist.'

He smiled at Jakub as if he approved. 'You look good in your suit. You're a young, handsome man. Don't stay here. That's my advice. Go home to your own people. England is no place for strangers any more.'

'It's stupid, but I always want to win the game,' Jakub said.

Mr Hazari looked at him with hope. That's the way it seemed to Jakub, and that's what would stay with him from that night.

Several men came over from the darts board, a real mixture, Jakub noticed, and they seemed happy and at home in their club. Mr Hazari told them about Jakub's accident and said it was nothing compared with his. They all knew the story of his injury in the Stafford rail crash. 'I was doing the Manchester to Penzance line then,' he said. 'Lovely train. Nine coaches. A buffet car and everything.'

'Farmhouse Grill! Remember that?' one of them said.

The men were friendly and Jakub felt safe in their club, a place for good people; he didn't want it to end. They laughed easily and grabbed him by the shoulder, as if to pull him into their company. As the evening deepened, they brought him into the office and took a picture of him, placing it on a card template and putting it through a laminating machine. 'Here you go,' the chairman said, passing him the card. 'You're official now. You can always say you belong to the Leicester Railwaymen's Club.'

# 17 The Canonisation

Gosia wanted to rush into summer. She wanted flowers, she always did, she wanted bright dresses and perfect novels full of light. She wanted everything with Milo to go further and go faster, and it appeared to do that: the project was growing, the teamwork, the shared belief, and it was almost like dreaming, the way it magnified her happiness.

'The trouble with King's Cross,' her mother said, 'is the people around here. They don't come from anywhere decent, and that's a fact.'

'It's not a fact, Mum, it's your prejudice.'

Gosia came back down the hall of her mum's flat carrying a can of mousse and a plastic diffuser for the hairdryer. 'You're always giving out these facts. But they're not facts, are they? It's just something you want to say.'

'Why would I want to say anything?'

Gosia didn't want a fight. The whole thing about 'incomers' – it was about Milo, though Cecylia was careful never to mention his name. The assault came bit by bit, with comments here and there, with themes that developed over weeks, and her mother, if pulled up on it, would immediately retreat into feeling misunderstood. Yet the relentless nature of her campaigns had formed her children. She had no idea how radical her daughter was becoming and knew equally little of what Bozydar was involved in, and only wanted to deny it all anyway. More than a year ago, there had been a party for Gosia's nephew, Ben, at the Pirate Castle in Camden Town. Bozydar turned up when the party was nearly over. His ex-wife,

Dana, was raging and she laid into him. 'Out selling, were you?' she screamed. 'Running your *boys*? Spliff, coke, whatever? Too busy doing pickups and drop-offs to make it to your own kid's birthday party!'

'I'm paying for it, aren't I?' he'd shouted back.

'You will fucking pay for it,' she said, and threw a glass of wine in his face.

Cecylia had been at the party. When her daughter-in-law threw the wine, Cecylia had picked up her bag and left. She beetled off back down the canal and Gosia had to go after her.

'That woman tells horrible lies,' Cecylia had said, completely rejecting the revelation.

But it wasn't a lie. Boz ran drugs. He imported stolen goods. And it had become clear that he was running illegal workers. Those 'Poldark' papers began to tell the whole story – the primary evidence was all there, ready to be shared, though they didn't mention Boz by name, not yet. Milo had kept digging and had shown her the latest documents, circling the words 'King's Cross', 'car wash', 'likely drug/contraband connections'. Gosia had since reached out to her brother's ex-wife. She knew Dana understood his sordid business better than she let on, and that she kept tabs on him. Gosia's need to understand these connections now felt to her like a need for oxygen. But there was no word from Dana yet, and no guarantee she would play.

Cecylia went on talking in the chair, stuck in her own version of reality while her daughter cut her hair.

'Stay still,' Gosia said. 'I want to trim this before I start drying it.'

Cecylia pursed her lips. 'It's the way they rely on the government to pay them for sitting around.' She glanced at Gosia. 'Students as well. In Poland, you had to work even if you were a student. We all worked.'

'So did we, Mama. And I'm trying to right now!'

She'd started the hairdryer. But her mother was experienced in being ignored and she raised her voice.

'It's always been a problem,' she shouted. 'North London. It used to be the Irish. Doesn't that boyfriend of yours have an Irish father? Yes. Two for the price of one.'

Gosia turned off the dryer. 'Mum,' she said, 'I'm not drying your hair if you carry on like this. And I'm not coming to Shepherd's Bush.'

'I am what I am, Gosia.'

'Okay, Mum.'

She took the round brush and twirled sections of her mother's hair on a medium setting.

'And I know what I know. I'm right about these people.'

Cecylia told everybody she was 'rejected' by her local Polish church in Islington, Our Lady of Częstochowa and St Casimir. For twenty years she'd gone to the 10.30 Mass every day after breakfast at Granary Square, but in 2019 they'd had a dispute over non-Poles coming into the church, and now she went to West London. 'We try to recreate a piece of homeland within the Catholic Church,' one of the missionary sisters in the Islington church had said to her, 'for people who start their life in a new society.'

'I don't know who these people are,' Cecylia had said.

'Souls like you, Mrs Krupa.'

And that was the end of the Islington church.

At St Andrew Bobola in Shepherd's Bush, they attended a service campaigning for the canonisation of Jerzy Popiełuszko, a Solidarity martyr killed by the communists in 1984. Cecylia was proud of her family connection to him: he was her second cousin, and the sense of being close to holiness meant she was happy to give money to the cause. She was all nerves at the Mass, fondling her rosary beads, but she was pleased when Bozydar, dressed in a suit, brought out a roll of £50s and put the money on the collection plate. Gosia looked away. When their mother went to speak to someone about the garden committee, she stood with her brother by the church railings.

'That was nice for her,' he said.

'Well,' Gosia said, 'she loves the drama.'

'Why do you need to be so negative?'

'Because I'm tired of all the lies, Bozy. Years and years of pretending. People doing bad things with a clear conscience.'

He threw down his cigarette butt. 'What the fuck are you talking about, Gosia?'

'The car wash wasn't enough for you,' she said. 'A little side-business in weed dealing wasn't enough. Putting Polish boys into factories, Bozy? Factories run by guys who embezzle money? Guys who run sweatshops?'

'You're so pure, Gosia,' he said. 'Who do you think supplies your boyfriend's mates with the food they're selling?'

'Oh, wake up,' she said. 'I know about that. They're *children*. They're wannabes and you're exploiting them, like you exploit everybody.'

'Fuck you, Gosia. You know nothing.'

He grabbed her chin but she pulled away.

'Just make sure Mum gets home safe,' he said. 'Stuck-up bitch.'

He was early for his meeting in Notting Hill, so after parking up he went into the Churchill Arms in Kensington Church Street. There were strings of Union Jacks and bottles of London Pride behind the bar. A model Spitfire was strung up next to a group of gas masks and cricket bats, surrounding a picture of the wartime prime minister chomping his cigar. Bozydar sipped his beer and checked on his phones where each of his drivers was. O'Dade was in County Louth and had picked up a load from the Eire Bake House. 'Heading to catch the Larne ferry,' he texted back, 'but there's a mix-up over import crap, paperwork wrong.'

'What's the matter?' Bozydar asked when he called him.

'Tariffs,' O'Dade said. 'Turns out there's Canadian wheat in the feckan biscuits. So this breaks the EU rules, can you believe it?'

'So, you can't tip the load?'

'I can tip it, aye. But they might be charged. I'm on my way to the ferry now. It's for the Tesco distribution centre in Bolton.'

Bozydar could hear the traffic.

'But you were held up?'

'Aye. Border checks. They were arguing, so they were.'

Bozydar hung up and changed to his burner. Charlo Sullivan was at Coquelles in France. He texted him with a three-word message: 'Did you lift?'

'I did,' Sullivan got back. 'Fifteen heads.'

Bozydar crossed the road. The restaurant was Clarke's and Stefan had said his boss would be there at one o'clock. He fixed his tie as he walked through the place; very smart, he thought, white tablecloths, a fireplace with a big mirror and lemons on the mantelpiece. A sort of fancy, blond-haired man in a dark suit was already sitting there. He stood up and shook Bozydar's hand and showed his too-perfect teeth.

'Yuri Bykov,' he said.

It was a rush, getting to know this guy. Immediately, Bykov waved his hand and ordered champagne. He pointed to the art on the opposite wall and said he used to know the artist quite well. He was dead now. Bozydar was impressed. 'You're an adventurer, right?' Bykov said. 'Everybody has an intrepid artist inside them.'

He took a radish and dabbed it in sea salt.

'I'm a small businessman.'

'There's nothing small here,' Bykov said. 'Do you know Shakespeare?'

'At school, bits of it—'

'*King Lear.* "Almost too small for sight: the murmuring surge."' He nodded his head as if remembering the lines. '"That on the unnumber'd idle pebbles . . . chafes. I'll look no more . . ."' He drank deep from his glass. 'I love Shakespeare. Every Englishman must. I'm studying the play with a friend of mine.'

'You're learning the lines?'

'As much as I can. Look, I saw they have samphire here.'

Bozydar opened the menu. 'What?'

'A salty green vegetable. It's on that man's plate. I'm sorry, you must forgive me. That's how my mind works. They have it here and Shakespeare has it in the play – "one that gathers samphire, dreadful trade!"'

'Right.'

'I'm starving. How about you?'

Bozydar looked at the menu and felt excited. He had definitely never met anyone like this guy. He behaved as if you could say anything and connect anything.

'I'll have the same as you,' Bozydar said.

'Exmoor caviar with buckwheat blinis?'

'That's fine.'

'Then the foie gras with onion marmalade.' Bykov turned to the waiter and was quite familiar with him. 'What is *bottarga*?'

'It is cured grey mullet roe, sir,' the waiter said.

'Ah, yes. We will have Scottish scallops with asparagus, *agretti*, *bottarga* and lemon. Also—'

He took up the wine list.

'Burgundy, please, the Corton-Charlemagne Grand Cru.'

'That'll be no problem, sir.'

'I wasn't anticipating one,' Bykov replied.

When the waiter was gone, he turned again to Bozydar. '*Agretti*,' he said. 'Not at all dissimilar to samphire, in a way.'

Bozydar shrugged. 'Good. Sure. Yeah.'

'"Make your speed to Dover!"' Bykov said, then looked at him.

Bozydar began to see what was happening. That's what smart people did, they spoke indirectly.

'Yes,' he said. 'We are.'

Bykov seemed pleased. He softly bounced a fist off the back of Bozydar's hand, which was resting on the tablecloth. He spoke again: 'And would you say there was scope for increasing the speed, my liege?'

'My what?'

'Could we do more to Dover?'

Bozydar lowered his voice. 'Via Purfleet, yes. I told Stefan.'

Bykov made a slight cough before tasting the wine. 'Delicious,' he said. The waiter poured and Bykov joined his fingers across his stomach.

'We can definitely do more,' Bozydar said quietly.

'And they will gather samphire,' Bykov said. 'In Kent,' he added. 'They can flounce to the new places and grow—'

'Yes,' Bozydar interrupted. He thought maybe this was how English spies spoke to one another about the Russians, and this guy, with his posh accent and his perfect fingernails and his hair all clipped and gelled, had mastered it. He wasn't sure he'd ever heard the word 'flounce' before.

'I have invested in that,' Bykov said.

'Yes, Stefan told me.'

Bykov met his eye. 'No names,' he said.

'Yup. I get it.'

'And I wish now to have a friend, not a fool—'

'A friend, yes.'

Bykov tilted his glass and kept his eyes on him. 'To help me expand this little empire in all sorts of delicious directions.'

'Yes.'

'A new world, darling.'

'Right.'

The man was weird – very fucking weird – but he liked him. He was talking business in a private way and Bozydar understood. He looked around and saw all the people at their tables in their light, expensive clothes. Above one table hung a painting of a whippet curled up and at peace with itself. Bykov saw him looking.

'I could sell that painting this afternoon for £9 million,' he said.

'Is that what you do?'

'One of the things.' He smiled. 'I aim to do everything.'

'I thought you bought houses.'

The Russian flicked open his napkin and spread it across his knees. 'That's what they wanted me to do,' he said, 'and I did it extremely well. Mansions. Artworks. We buy the best and we buy them all. But life—'

'It's about making something of your own.'

'That's correct, Mr Krupa.'

'They call me Boz.'

The name seemed to delight the Russian.

Men of industry. Men of action. People he was equal to, or would be. This was where Boz belonged. Gosia with her boyfriend. So out of touch. Too young. They knew nothing about people's needs and how to harness them. It was left to Bozydar to make real connections, to do the man's work that kept them all afloat. Who was this Milo? Yet another street kid taking advantage of a good-looking girl from a nice family.

They ordered another bottle. Notting Hill suddenly seemed like a place to blow away the afternoon: it was sunny, everything was clean, the conversation kept flowing and nothing small mattered. Gosia wouldn't know how to hold a glass like this, or how to make anything better. They weren't leaders. They weren't in charge of how things turned out.

'I know how to bring in more soldiers,' Bozydar said with his glass hovering.

'Excellent,' Bykov said, pushing his plate away. 'The time might be coming to think about dividing the kingdom. We have Dover. In fact, we have most of Kent. We have samphire. We have soldiers who can bring it to the people.'

'Yes.'

'And I have my own ambassadors abroad.'

Bozydar didn't know what that meant. He thought he was keeping up, but he didn't get everything his friend was saying.

'Many new ambassadors, who wish to serve here.'

Bozydar asked if he would continue to rely on the invisible man.

'There comes a time,' the young Bykov said, 'when the old men begin to speak a dead language, and they grow aggressive, then they fail.'

Later that afternoon, during her break at work, Gosia went to After Noah. She was good at presents. Milo had wanted an illuminated globe and she knew they had one. They switched it on for her. 'Yay,' she said, when all the countries lit up, pointing to far-off places and specks of land surrounded by clean seas. Walking back down Upper Street, she hated the sound of the traffic, the jostling of people, a van, an ambulance squawking. Outside the King's Head she picked up a copy of the *Evening Standard*. William Byre was on the front page. 'Speaking from his home in St John's Wood, the former Sir William insisted that working practices in his factories complied with European standards. "I've never heard of Operation Poldark and I've never heard of any illegal workers being taken on by the factories that produce Angelique. I've struggled all my career to make sure British standards of production are among the highest in the world."'

Back at the salon, a cut and blow-dry was waiting. Afterwards, she went through to the back office and called her mum, checking she'd made it back from the church in one piece.

'The priest made me talk to these people who are making a documentary,' her mother said. 'They want to know if the Catholic Church is still a place for protest. I told them they'd better ask my daughter, she's the political one.'

'Did you really?'

'*Tylko żartuję.* I'm only having a joke.' She sighed the old sigh.

'I'm glad the day went well.'

'What happened to your brother?'

'He had a lunch meeting, I think. In Notting Hill. I'm glad the ceremony went well and you did your thing for your family.'

'Your family too. And Poland is your country.'

'No, Mama. I haven't found my country yet.'

'Don't break my heart, Gosia.'

There was a pause.

'I worry about your brother.'

'I don't want to talk about him.'

'Oh, Gosia. He's a good man, really.'

An hour later, the salon was finally empty.

Gosia liked that time of the day, when everyone had gone. The cleaner came two days a week, but Gosia would always take the task of wiping the mirrors, getting rid of the day's eyes, the long, worried stares of the customers, making her old self disappear too, as she went round and round with a dry cloth.

Milo texted her. 'Two minutes.'

'Hurry up.'

She wanted to feel they were one person rather than two, each of them fully activated by what the other was doing and saying, entwined in laughter and good times. Idealism played around them like an old song. Daft, really. She knew they couldn't beat them all, but they could avoid being like them, and maybe that would be enough. And if they failed at what they wanted to do and be, Milo said to her, it would be *their* failure to live with, not other people's, and somehow that already felt like an improvement.

She twisted her hair into a bun and then fixed it with a claw grip, before putting on nude lip colour and a swipe of gloss. There was a tap at the window. She unlocked the door to let him in and took his hand to kiss his palm.

'What a day, Milo.'

He sat down in one of the chairs and picked up the evening paper from the seat next to him, reading the headline: 'Byre Scandal Escalates'.

'Yes. I saw. The whole thing's moving up a gear.'

He had started giving all the information he had to the *Commentator*. Slowly, cautiously, anonymously. All the other papers were picking it up from them.

206

'We've nailed it on the slavery stuff,' he said. '"Poldark" was heading straight for Byre.' Milo sat back in the chair. 'There's proof of the other rumours too now. Masses of emails about sexual harassment. Allegations from employees.'

'Are you serious?'

'He's a fucking pig.'

She stroked his face and nodded.

'I hope I'm right about everything,' he said. 'It's big. Someone's life. And . . . other people's soon. You get unsure sometimes.'

He made a shrug, then pulled something from his pocket, throwing it down among the brushes and scissors next to the basin.

It was Campbell Flynn's passport.

'That's what you took?'

'Yeah. We'll see how he replaces it. Reckon he'll make a few calls. Could throw up a few connections. Bit of a laugh too.'

'Disruptive energy,' she said, smiling.

He'd never looked so young. He was her man, but she could trace in the mirror a vulnerability, a little shard of fear.

'They're criminals,' she said. 'And so is my brother. Don't forget that. We'll see it through, then we're leaving.'

# 18 The Burlington Arcade

'There's nothing so common as a coloured bath towel,' Antonia Byre liked to say, 'except mushrooms in Bolognese.' She could be sent into a bad mood by such things, and she once nearly walked out of a reception at Clarence House because the woman sitting next to her said 'woo' when someone opened a bottle of champagne. 'Absolutely beyond vulgar,' Antonia said, devouring the newspapers at her breakfast table in St John's Wood. The years had drawn her mouth into a twist of distaste. 'Nobody in their right mind would ever take a trip with one of those airlines. I mean: Chav Air.' She replaced her teacup. 'They climb aboard and buy Lotto tickets. They eat two paninis and a KitKat before forming an orderly queue for the loo. It's disgusting.'

'You have an insane capacity for disgust,' her son said. He was sitting across from her in a grey prison sweatshirt and boxer shorts. He had arranged his bowl and spoon, placing a napkin and a fat paperback on either side.

'You can talk, Zak,' she said. 'You've spent your entire youth hating leaders who aren't even born yet.'

'I wonder why that is.'

'Don't blame me if people are revolting.'

'And don't blame me if you can't process your own self-disgust.'

Antonia believed that men were either stupid or weak. If they were scared of her anger, they should speak to their therapists. One simply couldn't mess about when there were tough decisions to be made, things to be said, to keep the show on the road. She knew she was hard. She had to be. She was unsentimental. She knew what was right and what was wrong. People didn't like it, but that was tough; one tends to lose a few bodies building the pyramids. She knew the difference between a good and a bad teacher, an idiot doctor and a wise one, fine wine and cheap plonk, and she couldn't help it if people had no taste. She never apologised, never explained, never consulted with others or deferred to their reasoning. 'You can't remember your mistakes or even admit to what you've done,' her husband said, but he was always looking to justify himself.

Zak put down his spoon and looked at her. He clearly didn't recognise how lucky he was to have his chief adversary close to hand, and in this case putting oodles of cash into his account and funding his famous rebellion.

'I always know when it's column-writing day,' Zak said. 'I've known since I was about five. You come downstairs revving yourself up to say awful things about disadvantaged people. Your prejudices hit a new high over the coffee machine and swing into action over the toaster. By the time you pick up the phone to talk to your editor, you're somewhere to the right of General Pinochet.'

'Oh, shush,' she said.

'Or Eva Braun,' he added.

'Braun didn't do anything wrong, except love an insane man, which is a crime women have been punished for since Cleopatra.'

'I see you're already writing,' he said. 'Crack on, then. I want to observe that you and your right-wing sisters only ever invoke feminism in your own defence, never in the defence of women generally. You know fine well you're not being criticised for being female but for your own personal vileness.'

'Aw, Zakky. Did you have too much private education? Did we force too many holidays and too many presents down your throat? Is your penthouse too big? I can see it must be hellish to have only one private cinema.'

'Write your column, Mummy,' he said, 'and stop pretending you're an actual person having an actual conversation about an actual subject. The world really doesn't have a clue what you people are like: you wake up every morning with a headache from lying to yourself. And it gets worse all day. It's actually quite tragic.'

'And what will you be doing today?' she said. 'Barricading a few motorways? Storming Parliament? It must be so exhausting, darling. Like *Germinal*, but with oat milk and hemp slippers.'

'Actually, we're meeting Tory backbenchers. It might annoy you, Mother, but disruption and civil disobedience work. In two years, we have placed the climate emergency permanently on the government agenda. So, fuck you. Councils up and down the country have signed up to action. Schoolchildren are going on strike.'

'Oh, heaven forfend, Zachary. All that, just by sinking a papier-mâché house in the Thames. How clever of you.'

'And you'll all be prosecuted one day,' he said calmly, 'at the climate trials, the Nuremberg of the future. Your denials will seem unforgivable.'

He had come for two nights to 'support his father'. Zak knew there was nothing he could do, but the knives were out, the media was at the door. William was on the other side of the house, in his den, where he often slept. (Antonia called it his 'sulking parlour'.) She had tried several times to make a plan with him, but it wasn't working. 'I'm done,' William said, repeatedly. Of course, she knew that was rubbish, but the gloom persisted and now he was bleating about wanting to start a new life. Antonia thought he should mind himself with that kind of talk.

On that morning, 5 July, she was refusing to accept, despite the evidence, that their marriage was over. Marriage was all about hard work, she felt. They had built this thing together, this double-fronted mansion on Queen's Grove, the house in Chipping Campden, the Casa Sóller on Mallorca – and she'd made them beautiful, choosing every sofa, every picture, every tile – and the businesses too were their life. She knew things that the accountants didn't know: all the stuff that William would sooner forget about himself, the annals of the climb, each of the dirty deals he'd done.

'You can't *afford* for our marriage to be over,' she'd said.

When Yashica, their wonderful housekeeper, passed through the kitchen, Antonia asked her to fetch an ashtray, lighting up one of her Rothmans Blue and blowing smoke across the table at Zak. He unconsciously waved it away and continued reading his book. Smoking was definitely common now, she felt, but it was a hangover from her partying days. At least Antonia didn't like dogs: to love dogs was the most common thing of all, next to grieving. She opened a notepad. Yes. How common: grief. As a former boohoo merchant, or agony aunt, she couldn't say that to her readers, especially not in the *Commentator*, but she could say the Queen was extra admirable for always appearing to grieve in complete silence. She picked up *The Times* and then made another note.

'I've got something you can write,' Zak said, looking up and tilting his book.

'Is it about the poor turtles choking on straws?'

'Be quiet, Mother. Your readers will love it. You can add it to your endless light show of self-value. You could tweet it.'

'Twitter followers are a mixed blessing, Zak. They're not my private army. Most of them hate me.'

'I doubt they're that discerning.'

He flattened his sweatshirt against his chest. He was a reasonable-looking boy, she thought, but no girl would ever love him. Too fussy in the wrong ways. Perpetually working out his pessimism and his anxiety. 'Go on, then,' she said.

'It's from this.'

*The Mill on the Floss.*

'Oh God. Are you reading it because of the flood scene? Is it a global warming novel now?'

'No, I'm reading it for the picture it offers of deluded English minds. Here: from page 275.' He held the book at arm's length. '"There are certain human beings to whom predominance is a law of life" – get that, "a law of life" – "and who can only sustain humiliation so long as they can refuse to believe in it, and, in their own conception, predominate still."'

'Is that about your father?' she asked.

'No,' he said. 'It's you *exactly*.'

Antonia was not – she'd often told her readers – one of those modern mothers who want to distinguish their children, their usually plain, boring children, by appending rare disorders and deficits to them, food allergies and the like, as if it would make them more interesting and more needful of special treatment in the cruel, uniform world. No, Zak had actual auto-immune disorders, and was constantly under siege from his own internal system, his body attacking itself under the misapprehension it was a foreigner. He had travelled from psoriasis and mouth ulcers to coeliac disease, and it had been Antonia's duty, over the years (though she got absolutely no credit for it), to sit with him in a succession of deluxe white rooms in Chelsea, straining for explanations.

'Are you sleeping, Zak? You look tired.'

'I have an increased sensitivity to pain. You know that.'

Among the modern disorders offensive to the opinion columnist, self-pity was number one. Antonia said she couldn't abide pity-dependent propagandists – groups she felt were defined by a constant sense of injury – and in this group she included single mothers, eco-warriors, vegans, cyclists, social workers, BLM activists, Harry and Meghan, Scottish nationalists, Liverpudlians, the so-called trans community and migrants, no matter where they came from. She accepted that each, individually, might have a case, it was simply that she, Antonia Byre, was allergic to the demand that society should organise itself around avoiding the possibility of their ever being insulted. 'These are piss-poor times,' she told her followers, 'when policing your own thoughts so as not to "hurt" people is considered to be the chief goal of morality. It is an offence to liberty and to every value these groups pretend to stand for.' The old hands at the *Commentator*, who were few in number and under siege, argued that she got readers started in the morning, reminding them of what they believed in and why, and also sold subscriptions. The younger editors, who formed what she called the Politburo, threatened every day to resign if she wasn't fired; they organised online petitions against her, and called for her to be cancelled. But Lady Byre sailed on, the best-connected journalist on the *Commentator* and a star performer.

Zak had taken his bowl to the sink. 'Why don't you write your column about how Britain will never be a decent society until public schools are abolished?' he said.

'Aw, Zakky,' she said. 'I've already written that one. *Not.*'

'But it's true.'

'But, darling, it's not, you see. That's the problem. Great societies depend on elites, and you and my pathetic colleagues can't handle it, though they – like you – are perfectly content to be at the centre of an elite themselves. The Left is riddled with hypocrites, that's why it's such fun writing for them. They are puritans about every-body except themselves. Then they wonder why the country races on without them.'

'Maybe this isn't the day to be airing your contempt for people who believe in common decency,' Zak said, 'what with Dad becoming a poster boy for capitalist exploitation, due to running sweatshops and stealing from his staff.'

That stung. Especially the last bit. But she wasn't about to let anybody see, so she picked up her notepad and her mobile. 'Thank you for your contribution, Zak. It's always lovely to know we have you with us.'

She went through to the sitting room, placed her notes on a pile of art books stacked on the ottoman, and called the *Commentator*.

'Morning, Rupert. It's your pet liability.'

Her editor offered a few oblique condolences. He wasn't the slightest bit sorry for her and he carried a similar instinct to that of his colleagues. 'Of course, we discussed at conference the possible backlash for us.'

'Of course. Never knowingly unprepared . . . for the backlash.'

'Come on, Antonia. You're one of us, at least in theory. The allegations against your husband touch on one or two core issues for us.'

'I thought you were a newspaper, Rupe. I thought everything was a core issue for you, not only the ones you're vain about.'

'Would you be ready to write about the position you find yourself in, a first-person account of . . . I don't know, the scandal?'

She'd never met an editor who wasn't a bigot to their own cause.

'No, my friend,' she said. 'I won't be writing that column today. Or any day. My private life is private.'

'That might be hard to pull off.'

'You know, Rupert, unlike most of your columnists, I'm not writing for the other columnists on the paper, or for my friends in Stoke Newington. I genuinely couldn't give a toss what people think of me. I grew up in an era when columnists were admired for their courage and their unpredictability. That was the job. So, if you don't mind, I won't be writing for you today about what a shit my husband is.'

'Antonia—'

'Believe it or not, I wish to protect my family.'

'It's my duty—'

'Yes. It's your duty. You have sound judgment *before* the news. It's also your duty to ignore facts when they don't suit your political purpose, or when they don't flatter the seamless character of your readers' outrage. It's also your duty to take the credit when I win Columnist of the Year five times in a row. And it's your joy that my last book was at number one on the bestseller list for twenty weeks. And it's your obligation, I hope, as editor of the *Commentator*, to stand by women when their husbands are accused of actions for which their wives have no responsibility, and about which there is not yet any proof. Your hatred for my husband gives you a hard-on, Rupert, and I know you'd like me to help you fuck my husband with it, but I'm not entirely sure that would be the best thing to do this morning.'

He was silent for a moment. 'So,' he said, 'I take it that's a bit of a non-starter. *Ego sum victus.* What else do we have?'

She cleared her throat. 'Okay, we could do the ruinous middle classes.' She glanced at her notepad but was speaking off the top of her head. 'As recently as the 1980s, about 80 per cent of the richest people in Britain inherited their wealth, and about 20 per cent earned it. Now the position is reversed. The pushy middle classes have taken over the world, pack all the best restaurants, haunt all the events of the season. They have ghastly, grasping behaviour and their obsession with celebrity is a sort of madness. The aristocracy used to exhibit fundamental British values – discretion, perseverance, understatement – but now it's all aspiration and horrific self-exhibition standing in for distinction.'

'And what's the photo?'

'Meghan Markle.'

'Possible. Anything else?'

She flipped a page in her notepad. 'How about the tyranny of counselling? Too many kids asking temporary questions are being met with permanent answers. In other words, we live in a world almost comatose with advice.'

'I'm not having the trans debate. No way.'

'I could probably avoid that. Or maybe not.' She tapped her pen on her knee and wished she was in the Casa Sóller. She was fed up with the UK. The whole day was already making her sick to her stomach.

William took a shower, and was standing in his underpants and white dress shirt before the mirror. 'You have to lose a bit,' he said, stroking his stomach. He could hear his wife's voice downstairs. She was speaking crisply into her phone and William guessed she must be working. He grabbed his mobile from the sink and made a call.

'Hello, yes,' he said. 'It's William Byre.' The assistant on the other end told him the Duke wasn't available.

'Thenk you say much,' she said, sounding posher than her boss, as all secretaries and notable British actresses used to.

He'd first met the Duke a hundred years ago, in the 1980s, when Campbell took up with Elizabeth. Anthony was very much the Falklands hero back then, full of pomp and salty experience, and in love with Candy. William saw her immediately as the sort who only went for titled men. She didn't want a guy in the rag trade, never in a million years, but she was intelligent. Opening an old French glass cabinet, he took out a bottle of cologne, one of the ones Campbell had given him, Habit Rouge, and he sprayed it around his neck and on his hands before going into the bedroom to find a tie. It was Campbell who had led him to the Duke, and the Duke who had led him to his biggest private investors, the Bykovs. William had thought this would facilitate a triumph, expanding into Saudi Arabia, but it was the beginning of the worst three years of his life.

William also had Campbell to thank for the tailors – the young man at Richard James, off Savile Row. 'You must always know where to find yourself,' Campbell had told him. Sitting on the bed, William decided he would go into town and buy something for Vicky. His frustrations could spill over, as frustrations do, especially with someone you love, and he wanted to make it up to Vicky. He wished she could understand him a little better. Sometimes the girl would be too out of it on those drugs she took; he wanted her to stop all that and join him at his level. That's all he needed, somebody entirely his own, who would go through all this with him and quietly love him. And he needed to get out of the house. So he would go and buy her something nice and take her out to lunch.

He was about to phone his driver when Antonia came up the stairs to his den.

'I've got a splitting headache,' she said. 'It hurts my head just talking to my fucking editor.'

'Are you writing today?' he asked.

'Yes, for what it's worth. I'm sure they'd prefer it if I wrote about anger management in the gentoo penguin.'

She'd always been funny. That had been the baseline of their romance. A certain style was native to her and he'd loved that, but there was now something cruel in Antonia's bravado, a person lost in her hardness and refusal.

'What are you thinking about?' she asked him.

'Us,' he said, 'and all this mess I've made.'

'Nobody died. We can rescue this.' She raked a hand through the ash waves of her hair and he looked round, seeing her lowlights and highlights, thinking of all the trips to salons in Mayfair and the nights out, in happier times. He was full of hope in that moment, but the hope was not for them. It was for a new beginning.

'Nobody died,' he repeated.

She put a hand on his arm. 'Where are you going?'

'I don't think I can do this any more,' he said. 'The properties. The marriage. The negotiations. The companies.'

'Please would you stop, William! And don't be silly. It will blow over. We have lawyers, heaps of them. These problems will go away and the businesses . . . well, we can tidy them up. Your working practices have been no different from anybody else's.'

'But these new stories . . . these women.'

'What,' she said, 'some girl whose bum you patted at a Christmas party in 1994? These people can't be serious.'

'They call it *historic abuse* now.'

'Historic opportunism, more like.'

But then he began to say things he probably shouldn't have said.

His hand was still shaking two hours later, sitting in Ladurée at the top of the Burlington Arcade, drinking coffee and decompressing. What had begun in the bedroom with composure and strategy-speak had gone off the rails at his mention of Vicky. 'I'm afraid I've fallen for her,' he'd said to Antonia, which brought from his wife a grave warning about the ways of young women. He was 'spineless'. He was 'destructive'. Then she changed tack, began throwing things, calling him 'a typical man' and 'a danger to women everywhere'. She slapped his face at the bottom of the stairs and he saw in her eye a gleam of hostility like he'd never seen before. Then she turned away, to think about her column.

He had a friend in New York who always said, 'When in doubt, go skiing.' So William walked down Burlington Arcade spending money, having a shoeshine, killing the time before lunch with small purchases and fresh hopes. He held a bag from Vilebrequin containing new swimming trunks, then he picked up an emerald bracelet for Vicky at Michael Rose, a 1962 Rolex for himself and a cashmere cardigan at N.Peal. He was on the phone to Vicky as he walked down Brook Street, then reserved a suite at Claridge's, ten days or so in residence until he got himself sorted with his lawyers, then he'd go to Mallorca. He took a taxi back to Jermyn Street with the emerald bracelet in his pocket, and stepped into Wiltons, where he saw Vicky sitting nervously at the table and staring at the menu. Her skin was so pale it made her hair and her eyes emphatic, Pre-Raphaelite. She wore a white T-shirt and jeans with a blue velvet biker's jacket, which she idly zipped and unzipped. He sat down and they ordered, but he retreated when his mobile rang and he saw who it was.

'William.'

'Anthony. It's good of you to call back.'

'I'm sorry about all this bother you're having. I'm sure it can't be as bad as all that.'

'I'm rather afraid it is,' William said.

'Well, worse happens at sea. I can confirm that. My wife has just built a yoga studio the size of Kathmandu.'

'All in a good cause, I'm sure.'

'Bloody endless costs, and all sorts of fools coming on and off the estate shaking their beads and whatnot.'

'Yes.'

'She has two young female helpers, though. Lovely. Hot as a pair of firedogs.'

William was never sure how much familiarity to assume with the Duke. They had always rubbed along quite well together – in a distanced way, the same distanced way that the Duke of Kendal appeared to rub along with everyone. He knew they had both fed at the same trough, so far as new investment money went, but that had never been discussed. This would be the first time William had ever tried to engage the Duke in any of his business problems.

'I'll get to the point,' he said.

'Yes, it's all a bit chaotic round here.'

'To get straight to it, Anthony. We're family friends. I'm in a spot, and the heavier trouble – not the nonsense in the papers—'

'All rot, I'm sure.'

'Yes. The bigger thing is to do with Aleksandr Bykov.'

William could feel the freeze through the phone.

'Yes?'

'He was the middleman in a huge deal I was trying to put together with the Saudis for shopping malls in the Middle East—'

'Byre, this is not my thing.'

'Hold on. We must keep it in perspective. You know these people.'

'We should not be having this conversation.'

William stopped. Something flared in him, an old injury. 'I know you have the ear of the Bykovs. They trust you.'

'I scarcely know them.'

He could feel his plea being crushed by grandeur. It didn't happen slowly either, but instantly, and he knew the call would end soon. 'Anthony, my oldest friend is married to your sister-in-law. We have much in common.'

He knew he had overplayed it. 'Byre,' came the reply, 'we have absolutely nothing in common.'

'But I know your foundation took money from these people.'

'Mr Bykov is an occasional visitor to this country. His son is a young entrepreneur. We extend our best wishes to them, nothing more.'

'Your Grace—'

The phone went dead.

William was always preoccupied by the thing that had only just happened, and fearful of the fallout. He knew better than anybody the scale of the debt he was in, the impossibility of paying it back and the nastiness of the people he was dealing with. He returned to the table and was full of a sense of dread as he took Vicky's hand, trying not to notice how she flinched when he moved closer.

'They used tae stick tae the rocks,' Vicky said. She was talking about the oysters in front of her and getting them mixed up with limpets. 'You gave them a shake but they jeest got tighter and clung to the rocks.'

'The what?'

'The rocks,' she said. 'Can ye no' understawn me?'

'Sounded like "roaks",' he said.

He liked her green eyes, framed by the reddest hair he'd ever seen. Violent red, for someone so sweet. 'Near where my mammy lives noo, thur's a place called Saltcoats and we yistae play there,' she said. 'There's like wee castles aw roon the seafront and we yistae play there eftir school.'

They drank English champagne and ate venison pie. He took her hand again, and William didn't care who saw them, or what happened. Maybe he would give it all up and go to live with her in Granville Square. He had plenty of money stowed. He could see the blurred edges around her, the drugged aspect, the jangly hands, the King's Cross side. He would clean her up and he would start again. And even as he said it to her, and to himself, he feared that there was no character left in him, no space for rescue, and that his own long fall should not be undertaken while gripping such a person's hand.

'Ow!' she said, and pulled her hand away. 'You're hurting me, William! Why do you do that when we're jeest having a nice time?'

He didn't know why he did it.

His phone was ringing and he saw that it was Campbell.

'William, it's me. I'm in a wee bit of bother over here.'

'What's happening?'

'My passport,' Campbell said. 'It's disappeared.'

'What do you mean?'

'It was here this morning. We're supposed to be flying to Reykjavík, in, like, two hours. The thing Angus has organised for my birthday. Total fucking disaster. People are flying in from everywhere. Moira's already there.'

'This is an easy one,' William said. 'People lose their passports every day.'

'They want me to wait in a queue at Eccleston Square. There's no time and—'

'Listen. There won't be any queue. I'll call Scullion.'

William felt some essential power returning to him. He tried to smile his way past Vicky's scowl as he spoke to Campbell, and eventually she looked down at her own phone, massaging her hand.

'Lord Scullion?'

'Of course,' William replied, lifting a pudding spoon. 'He'll call the Home Office. He owes me one.'

# 19 Iceland

High above the fields of Northern England, and calm at last, Campbell stared at the new blue passport in his lap and sighed. He ordered a can of beer from the flight attendant and drank it while Elizabeth slept. After a while, he looked out and imagined they were over the Clyde and the high flats north of the river, a bird's-eye view of his childhood home and a memory of his mum and dad. Down there, the Glasgow where Jim and Alma had once gone to a department store in St Enoch Square, and stolen a coat.

Campbell's mother adored the melodrama of it. 'The stealing', as she always referred to this and the other small thefts, was allowed to be the central event in her turmoil, and she loved feeling embroiled in the reasons why it had happened, the conclusions to be drawn. It was actually nothing much, two or three bouts of transgression and resistance in a life of dutiful stasis, but in her unhappy mind it all contributed to the shame kitty. Being mortified gave poor Alma something to be, and so the fur coat was a story. 'That day,' she'd said in old age, 'is the lens through which all the days of my life must be seen. The stealing.' Yet his mother's melodrama had served all their lives to make real pain invisible.

He saw the Icelandic wind before he met it, and the bumpy descent over black ash served only to confirm his downward trajectory. The passport nightmare and the thoughts of Glasgow were met with equal tortures at Keflavík Airport. It turned out Angus had supplied no information about the virus procedures. He had only whooped to his mother, with the aid of emojis and exclamation marks, that the country was open to visitors.

At customs, they had to register with the Icelandic government; they had to apply for QR codes, scrolling with humiliating gratitude through the list of participating countries, and, while he reconfirmed his email for the sixth time, Campbell felt he was being roasted over the flame of his son's terrifying ego. Elizabeth kept having to calm him down. They followed the arrows into a detention centre, where they were met by a battalion of smiling students dressed in Jedi poly-thene robes and sporting hate-visors. One of them put a long stick up Campbell's nose and wiggled it until he cried. She did it in his mouth until he coughed. She told him that he must wait at his hotel until the results came, then pointed them to a taxi rank strewn with buffeted, desperate, unwarranted tourists, waiting to step into taxis that would take them to Reykjavík for 17,000 krona each. And this was *post-Covid*. Birthdays had never done it for Campbell, even at the best of times, and this was the worst: 40 kilometres over a tundra of black volcanic rock, a gleam of something vengeful in the oxidised sky.

It was then that Elizabeth decided to say it. As always, she spoke with a rather interesting carefulness, never judging. 'It's not a big deal,' she said. 'I mean, we have a good marriage. But I do want to ask you – is there a sense in which you've become enmeshed with that young man you've asked to be your researcher?'

'What do you mean?'

'Because I think he stole your passport.'

Campbell didn't need to think. 'Well,' he said, 'it's nothing sexual, if that's what you mean. I don't wave, as you know, many flags for heterosexuality as a social imperative, but I married the person I love.'

'I realise that. I merely wondered if he had a grip on you somehow.'

Campbell glanced at the wide tundra and thought it entirely menacing.

'I'm fascinated by what he can show me,' he said. 'That's all. I only have one life and I won't live it with one arm tied behind my back.'

'I have no wish to interfere,' she said, 'but he's a bloody nuisance, if he thinks pulling a stunt like that is proving anything.'

'I'm being put to the test. And it's quite equal. I believe he's gaining a spot of enlightenment from me too.'

'Interesting choice of word.'

'Oh, Elizabeth.'

'Please be careful,' she said. 'You have more than one life in your life. It makes you who you are, but there are dangers. I feel them.'

'Thanks for the therapy,' he said.

Angus had booked the penthouse suite at Opaque, a glass apartment building in the central tourist district, on Laugavegur. He loved that the apartment was above a Taco Bell – he said it was 'pop art'. He'd told Kenzie that she could stay in one of the suite's four bedrooms. Before leaving London, she'd had Ricky at Salon64 chop her hair and dye it blue. Fortunately, she loved it, standing outside on the balcony and feeling chilled and Nordic. Angus himself was arriving on a private jet. Everything had been pushed back by a night because of their father's passport fiasco. As usual, Kenzie felt the different stories in her family encircling her head and threatening her sense of peace, but it was quiet now, and she looked across the road at the Vietnam Market.

Four p.m. It would begin soon.

Instagram had told her that Angus had announced he would do a private club night in Reykjavík, location not yet disclosed. She was preparing herself for the onslaught of cars, schedule-gurus, last-minute changes and hangers-on. He was bringing 'a few friends' on the flight and she smelled trouble. But she never had any luck containing her brother. It had been this way since Angus was thirteen: the random flexing of his need to be special and exclusive and enjoy extra buzz, no matter what. She loved him, but he had no politics. No thoughtfulness. All he cared about was the incoming thrill or the latest remark.

She'd had supper the night before at Moira's hotel. Kenzie was an auntie's and a granny's girl, quite natural with her family at one remove, and she enjoyed the way Moira basically didn't give a fuck. Her anti-corruption work made her a heroic figure in Kenzie's eyes. She also admired her belief that people must remake themselves, political parties too, when the world they depend on changes around them. 'It seems time,' Moira had said, drinking wine and eating chips, 'to locate the real, progressive heart of our politics.'

'Will voters let you do that?'

'After a spell of voting against their own interests, yes. The Conservatives' field day will come to an end when people at home realise, as they will, that the Britain being fetishised by the Tories doesn't actually exist. It died in the 1980s.'

They'd agreed that the birthday plans were risky. 'Angus lives his life like someone perpetually in a video,' Kenzie said.

'And doesn't pause.'

'Never. And he can't separate between personal glory—'

'And a family thing like this – which your father will *really* hate. When I heard he was doing this DJ set before the dinner—'

'It's all over the Internet.'

'Not the point of an evening like this, Kenzie. Your brother is a sweet boy but he has no brakes and is not careful.'

'He doesn't want to be careful.'

'Exactly. He wants to be the person coming into the room. He wants to be the person paying for everything and leaving first.'

'He's nicer than he seems,' Kenzie said. 'Some people are cursed with that, I guess, but he's not a good match for Dad at the moment.'

She stood on the balcony, playing back the whole conversation in her head. She pressed two keys on her phone.

'Hi, fab Auntie. You still at the Hotel Borg?'

'Yes. Fully dressed. My mascara went funny. I look like Carol Channing.'

'What?'

'Google her. It wasn't the look I was aiming for.'

Kenzie chuckled.

'I spoke to your da,' Moira said. 'He's made an executive decision to have a horrible time, no matter what. I've seen him like this before.'

'It's one of his modes,' Kenzie said.

'Angus doesn't help matters, of course. Why didn't he bring your mum and dad on that ludicrous jet his management hires for him?'

'Because he wants Dad to see his life, not be in it, if you know what I mean. He likes to underscore the difference between them.'

'How tiresome,' Moira said. 'It reveals a real misunderstanding of your father. Campbell can't stand *competing* with his children.'

'I've found out where the restaurant Angus chose is. A very un-Dad place called Bergmál.'

'This is the place we've crossed the ocean for?'

'It means "Echo". It's a chain of worldwide boutique restaurants that aim to contradict local conditions at the level of the taste buds.'

'Did you just make that up?'

'Nope,' Kenzie said. 'Straight from the website. Angus swears it's the *only place* anywhere to eat curry right now.'

'Bloody hell!' Moira said. 'I do wish he'd stop talking like that.'

'Brace yourself. It's only the start.'

She went to the bathroom mirror, opened her purse and touched each cheekbone with a dab of Beauty Flash Balm. She wore a metallic-effect midi dress by Maisie Wilen with a pink faux fur.

Ashley-Jo had come to Reykjavík but was staying at the vegan hotel by the harbour. They were being interviewed by a fashion vlogger and had texted to say they were going straight to Angus's gig. They weren't 'with' Kenzie that night, and the stipulation, semi-comical, was something Kenzie could accept because, really, the relationship was a bit anime. Kenzie liked the adventure: she was capturing gems and tokens, but defending her base. Kissing was nice and sex could be lush, but in some way it all merely reinforced her solitude. A.J. was her difficult half, a person who had never gone to sleep without a phone on their pillow.

Walking towards the venue in high heels, Kenzie could see the water and low clouds over the mountains. It's often unexpected, what can make you feel steady in this life, a stretch of water going nowhere, a billowing cloud from a vape. When she got to the road by the harbour she looked across the ice-cold water and saw a boat called *Pinganes* SF-25, built in Hornafjörður. She took her phone out of her bag and opened Safari, to find where Hornafjörður was. South-east: 'fjord of horns', one of the larger nesting grounds for Arctic terns. She put her head back and blew the smoke out of her lungs, enjoying the pure ether of evaporating knowledge.

A girl with a clipboard checked her name and took her temperature. The 'market' had black curtains all around and was rammed with people. There was a drum kit onstage and shining barrels of Viking Brugghús. Kenzie found the VIP area. Angus was there, Hawaiian shirt and too many bracelets, too big a suntan and too low a grasp of human tolerance. He was smiling with his arm around the neck of a Parisian model called Béatrice, who was 'so amazing'. Angus released his arm when Kenzie came in for a hug. 'You look insane,' he said, then waggled his fingers in the air like he was counting heads: 'This is Béa, who you met, this is Finch, this is A.K., this is Gorgeous George Washington . . .'

'Hey,' she said.

'Hey, hey,' Angus said, lifting two glasses of champagne. 'Who'd have *thunk* it? Man's in Reykjavík!'

'Daddy's in a foul temper,' Kenzie said.

'What's up now?'

'Why didn't you stop off and bring him on the plane?'

'He hates all that,' Angus said, swigging. 'Dad still thinks he's a communist. Can't get into it. The jet's for work.'

'What's this gig all about?'

'A wee thing we slipped in, man,' he said. 'It's cool. You have to get the party on if you come to Iceland, know what I'm saying?'

'Not really, Angus. It's Dad's birthday.'

'Chill, Kenzie. We'll have a sick time. The food at Bergmál is mad. I've booked the whole place out. Like, it only takes forty people max. Only place in the world right now where you should eat Indian food.'

She made a face. 'So you said. Including the whole of India? A country containing 1.4 billion people, Angus?'

'Ah, whatever. Nowhere is anywhere any more, sis.'

Auntie Moira arrived, being taken care of by A.J., who had met her on the way in. Apparently, Moira's name wasn't at the door, so Kenzie went up to Angus's manager and told him, quite fiercely, to make sure their mum and dad were on the list. 'If you were at all smart,' she said, 'you'd send a car round to the hotel to bring them.'

There were hundreds of people in the flea market. They were fused in a mass of bodies and were holding up their phones and pointing to the VIP area, from where Angus occasionally held up his fingers in a peace sign.

'Mummy says Dad's off his head with new projects,' he said to Kenzie. 'He's got Jake Hart-Davies from *Aethon's Curse* involved in a self-help book for men.'

'Wait, *what?*'

'Yep. Arcadius himself, scourge of the Visigoths.'

He looked over her head.

'Dad has hired him to make out he's the guy who wrote the book. The whole thing is meant to be hush-hush. He thinks it's like an art project. Published end of next month. Crazy. Dad's the secret author. But like, everybody knows.'

Moira and A.J. were suddenly there.

'Everybody knows what?' A.J. asked.

'When Angus says "everybody knows",' said Kenzie, 'he means about twenty-five people who live between North London and Mayfair.'

Angus addressed the group as if he were the king of jokes. 'Have you met my young sister?' he said, crooking his arm around her neck and pulling her closer. 'She's totally lit. Brainy *and* beautiful.'

'Don't sound so surprised,' Moira said. 'It happens.' She winked at Kenzie and they all looked over at the corner where Béatrice the model was broadcasting live to her seven million followers about the dregs at the bottom of her cocktail. Or maybe it was TikTok: she posted videos of herself dancing, and sometimes crying.

'Just make tonight about Dad,' Kenzie said.

Campbell's phone pinged in the Hotel Borg at around 6 p.m., telling him he was free to go out. They were still naked and lying on the bed. It was a thing about hotels, new sheets, reminders of stolen nights: they always had sex. They were good at being a couple, Campbell felt, inclined towards each other and awake to each other sexually, though not in any routine or anxious way. They were older now and could easily wait, but when Elizabeth undressed and lay on the bed he was immediately hard. The second time, she was on top of him and scratched his chest and shouted out as she ground down on him, but he didn't come again, and was already building up a head of steam about their son's selfishness. He didn't say anything, but he got up on his elbows and kissed Elizabeth with tenderness, trying to hide his irritation.

Showered, and in a sleek Prada suit, Campbell felt that perhaps he could make a go of the evening and present himself as Elizabeth's squire. She wore a blue vintage floral dress by Tory Burch and smelled of oud as they left the hotel, but searching for the harbour, then this 'fleapit', as Campbell kept calling it, served to reignite his unhappiness. By the time he came to shouting their names to the girl with the clipboard, he felt more rage than the occasion required, as if the uncanny power of northern cities, the fear of what was happening with William in London and his sheer anger at Angus's fuck-you mindset were all descending on him at once.

They squeezed through the crowd in the booming hall.

Campbell had done the fashion shows. He knew about after-parties and roped-off areas and the strange bona fides of complete nobodies, but now he lost all sense of how to navigate such things. With the pulse in the room jumping, he could only feel used, tricked, undermined, ridiculed, and it fused – all of it, completely – with a feeling that his reliable old self was now being eclipsed. He didn't get a drink. He didn't head anywhere. They were jostled while forced to stand in the middle of the room, and then, amid a cross-fading of lasers, Angus appeared on a stage and the crowd went mad. He waved to them and bounced up and down, then the lasers turned green and began to whizz as he jumped behind his DJ deck, the crowd moving as one body towards him.

'Please breathe,' Elizabeth said when they got outside. She went with him to the harbour's edge and they stared at the pink in the sky. They smoked a cigarette and waited but didn't speak; something horrible had happened. There was nothing to say.

After a few minutes Kenzie came out on her own, tried to apologise and walked them back to the Hotel Borg. They stayed in the bar, where Kenzie said everything to bring her father round.

'I want you to listen to me, Kenzie. If I could get on a plane to London right now I would do it, and I would be done with him.'

'I know, Daddy.'

'That boy is a sociopath.'

Campbell was convinced he knew what he was talking about. He felt he had form when it came to recognising the behaviour of unconcealed narcissists. (The concealed sort, such as himself, gave him more trouble. Simple egomaniacs he could identify.) He was once backstage with John Galliano. He'd had lunch with Jared Leto. For thirty minutes he'd stood next to Henry Kissinger at a magazine launch on Liberty Island. He understood the machinations of the male ego with an intimacy that could make him ill. And yet, Campbell also knew, in that hotel bar, that the anxieties recently powering him had suddenly increased. In the cool biosphere of Reykjavík, he knew an emergency was imminent. For two months, in small increments and by even smaller understandings, he had felt it coming.

They managed to speak for an hour about other things. Kenzie's life in Chester Street. Her weaving. She was thinking of helping her teacher write a book about it. She was also attempting to make an inventory of Granny's pictures. The conversation was reasonable and, eventually, after a degree of persuasion, and a call from Moira, Campbell agreed they could go to the restaurant. They got a car there and he was suitably disgusted when he saw Bergmál, a tiny shack of a place with a corrugated tin roof painted Yves Klein blue. Obviously, the place was packed. Angus was standing at a tiny bar surrounded by lit phones. His pupils were giant. His friends were shouting on every side and he barely noticed his family coming in. Campbell saw the paper plates going round, the pretence at no effort, the watery beer and the food which was less than any Indian food on the Caledonian Road. 'Hey, Pops,' Angus said, coming up with a curl of his stupidly tanned arm.

'Happy Birthday, Daddy,' Kenzie said, trying again. He loved her so much and he knew she was sending out an appeal to him with her eyes. 'I understand,' she said. Or did she say it? Maybe he only heard the words inside his head?

He could definitely hear Angus's voice. Like an echo. Like Bergmál. Like nowhere in particular but with a sense of being superior to any true origin. 'The best butter chicken on the planet and this dahl is insane,' his son said. 'After this we're heading to a nightclub and we've got, like, a cake from La Pastisseria in Barcelona.'

'Are you all right, Campbell?' Elizabeth said.

Then it came, the roaring of a single word.

'Noooooooooooooooooo.'

He said it like he'd never said anything before. It was a new sound. It was a moan of exhaustion and fear, like something in a bad dream. He shouted at the top of his lungs and it came out like a foghorn during Mass, a plane rumbling into the sea, a dam bursting over a village when everyone is in the fields. The guests in Bergmál all turned, everyone looking, and the music played on its own.

Astonishment. 'I'm not here,' he shouted. 'I don't want to be here and I'm *not* here.'

Angus looked winded. 'What's fucking wrong with you?' he said.

Kenzie stepped in to put a hand on her brother's arm.

'What *is* this event?' Campbell said, his voice turning calm as he stood looking at the centre of his own failure.

He was sad for a second, thinking of the way Kenzie would feel, but that was soon swallowed up by the sight of the others in the room.

'It's your birthday,' Angus said.

'It's not *my* anything. If it was for me, we'd be sitting in one of the rooms at the Athenaeum, drinking wine. Eating supper. This is not for me. None of it is. The fight to get here, the hassle at the airport, this place, these fucking people. None of it's for me.' He looked around him at all the young faces. 'I mean, you probably don't even want it yourself. Did you even stop to think about that?'

'It's a birthday celebration, that's all.'

'No. That's not all. That's not all, buddy. It's a celebration of you, and so is everything in your life – everything in *ours*. Everything is a showcase in your favour, and you have no genuine enthusiasms, except other people's enthusiasm for you. That's it. The end. That's what you want. And you've dragged your mother and me all this way so that you can show us yet again, tell us loud and clear, then abandon us.'

'Uh, the struggle is real, Dad.'

'Eh?'

'You're out of your fucking mind. Everybody can see it except you. Nothing we do is right.'

He looked at Angus as if everybody was one person, one thing and one force, and nobody was on his side or ever had been.

'You know what, Dad? Fuck you. We're all here, but you can only see yourself.'

'Who are *they*?'

Angus took a step back. 'They're *people*. Friends. Family. They're fucking people, dude, and they made the effort. They're on the planet at the same time as you and they came to wish you a happy birthday. What is there to hate?'

'They don't know me.'

'Oh, give us a break, you thirsty little bitch.'

He stood staring at his only son. This is what it comes to, parenting. You swab their knees and wipe their arses and pay for everything and one day they get to treat you like you're simply another pest in their busy lives. Campbell walked slowly outside and the room's attention shifted back to itself. He lit a cigarette as Moira came out too. She put her arms around him without hesitation and whispered in his ear. He pulled away at first, but she went right after him and took him by the arm.

'Stop being a baby!' she said.

She took his cigarette and told him she had a plan.

'What sort of plan?'

'Dill,' she said. 'Now, sort your face out. Come on. We have a table at Dill, the restaurant up the road with a Michelin star.'

'You booked it?'

'For the three of us, yes. I feared this might happen.'

'You're in the right job, Moira,' Campbell said. 'You know what people want before they know that they want it.'

'I hope so,' she said. 'Get your coat.'

Ashley-Jo came out of the restaurant with a vape. To be fair, they looked sympathetic, but Campbell didn't give them a chance.

'Okay, Zoomer,' he said.

They blew out a ton of smoke. 'Cool it with the micro-aggressions.'

They used the vape for the most part like a conductor's baton.

'Or maxi-aggressions,' they continued. 'It's not everybody that can toss a hand grenade into their own birthday party.'

He turned and walked down the street, his wife and Moira following arm-in-arm. It wasn't dark in the city and it looked like it might never be: all the darkness had gone inside, it seemed to Campbell, and he imagined above his head whole crowds of twittering birds whooshing past each other on the cold air.

When they were sitting in Dill, his sister leaned over and patted his hand. 'Women wipe their tears and go back to work,' she said.

'That's why you're better than us,' he said.

He could always trust Elizabeth to forgive, when it was due. As usual, she seemed more taken than upset by life's dramas. Like a tonic, Moira spoke of Glasgow years ago, then about Universal Credit and about housing, while Elizabeth kept probing her, knowing that real conversation was balm to Campbell.

The waiter brought a miniature glass coffin of onions. Then a vegetable broth and a cracker on a plate with dried wolf fish that looked like fluff.

Both women gaped at the food.

Then the conversation turned to William Byre.

'What will happen to his factories?' Moira asked.

'It's a mystery,' Campbell said. 'Nobody really knows what he owns, or what he runs, or who runs them, or how many investors there are. But he's got money hidden. He and Antonia will always be all right.'

'If she sticks with him,' Moira said.

'Oh, she'll stick with him,' Elizabeth said.

After a while, they brought a dish of pebbles. Three crispy pork and mushroom balls were sitting on top. Campbell was so hungry he wanted to eat the pebbles. The sommelier came and poured a cloudy Riesling.

'His companies sell hundreds of millions of garments,' Campbell said. He felt distant and uneasy at the word 'garments'. It started a train of thought. 'And they must've been made by subcontractors. It's all dark.'

'I never liked him,' Elizabeth said. 'I'm sorry.'

'I spoke to him yesterday,' Campbell said. 'He helped me with my passport.' He paused. 'It was good of him to do that, though I have to say I'm no longer confident that I ever really *knew* William.'

'Perhaps he has met his moment,' Moira said.

'I hope it's not mine too,' Campbell said.

Baked potatoes arrived in three pots, with chervil, fennel seeds and lovage. Then a barley dish came that reminded Moira of Granny Flynn's Scotch broth, which used to stink up a whole street in the Calton area of Glasgow. 'You could stand a spoon up in it.' She raised her glass of wine in her brother's direction. 'Happy Birthday, Campbell.'

'Thank you,' he said, then added, 'this is all very delicious, but is deliciousness the same as satisfaction?'

'There are nineteen courses, darling,' Elizabeth said. 'Satisfaction is a long game.'

He was looking forward to for the roasted reindeer-fat toffee. Maybe life is more enjoyable when you know what's coming. Eventually, as if he'd been waiting to say something of the kind, he looked straight at Moira and put out a hand to Elizabeth, which she took and stroked as his eyes filled with tears. 'Sis,' he said, 'what was wrong with our parents? There was definitely something missing.'

Moira dabbed her mouth and put down her napkin. 'People talk about trauma,' she said, 'but most lives don't involve trauma. They involve good people slowly disappearing from their own lives, and that's what happened to Mum and Dad. It was the opposite of dramatic, but it set up a particular drama for us, because we depended on them at one time for a sense of optimism and progress. That's my view, darling. The pain never goes away. They did everything for their children except allow them to be happy.'

The answer caused the tears to fall.

'Thank you,' Elizabeth said. 'You're a wonderful sister.'

'Mum just pined away in front of the television,' Campbell said, 'and saw the worst in everybody.'

Moira sighed. 'There was a time in the late 1970s when they were both in hospital, do you remember, Campbell?'

'Aye,' he said. 'She was in Ballochmyle and he was in that place outside Dumfries, the Creighton I think it was called.'

'That's right. She had her hysterectomy and he was drying out.'

'And they were never happier!' Campbell observed. 'They both said so, in their separate beds in their separate hospitals, "I want to stay."'

'Isn't that amazing?' Moira said, laughing.

'I spent my pocket money on yellow tulips. I can still see them.'

The following day was an exercise in self-calming. Elizabeth and Moira had gone to a hot spring and a subterranean magma chamber, leaving Campbell to walk off his preoccupations in the blue sunlight, adopting an attitude of quiet survival among the cold provocations. Reykjavík became a zone of neutrality, and he took the place in, the folk houses and the bicycles, the boulders in the gardens and the self-conscious coffee shops. At one point he texted his new research assistant to tell him it was like Paisley, but with more vegans. He wanted to register with Milo that he'd made it to his destination, implying nothing.

Milo sent back a laughing face emoji. Then, as if returning serve, the young man added a facetious, but not unwelcome, line about the Duke of Kendal. 'That brother-in-law of yours holds some dodgy views,' it said.

'He's an idiot,' Campbell messaged back.

'More than he knows.'

Campbell headed uphill to the Hallgrímskirkja, the Lutheran church. It looked like an inverted icicle or a colossal stalagmite with a clock on the front, which said ten to three. 'One ticket?' the lady in the gift shop asked.

'One, yes.'

At the top, he stepped out of the elevator into a room behind the clock face. A phrase of his mother's came into Campbell's head: 'He has more faces than the town clock.' A cold wind was passing through the mechanical parts, and he continued to the outside area, where you could look out over the whole city. He stood on a box looking west and could see, a long way down, a series of Lego houses, mainly blue and yellow, and a tennis court that seemed out of place in the cold haar of the afternoon. How would he survive his worries? The money? Would the Countess help, if the book didn't? Might he inherit enough to cover his taxes, pay off the woman downstairs and return to real writing? After a minute, he took out his phone and saw a famous face, dialling in on Zoom.

Jake Hart-Davies had a way of showing interest that Campbell found to be masterfully shallow: he offered a display of concentration, as opposed to concentration; as they started talking business, he agreed too quickly and seemed to watch himself listening with that cool self-possession that sometimes comes with fame. At one point he suddenly went quiet and seemed lost for a moment in a new set of needs.

'Can I tell you something?' Jake asked.

'Yes, of course.'

Campbell felt a light wind blowing through the clocktower.

'I've never had a better part than the one you've given me. I'm heading back to Dorset to shoot this Hardy film, because I have to. The book will come out, then I'm going on the road for my first ever author tour.'

'Keep your distance from everything,' Campbell said. 'I always have.'

He believed it when he said it.

'The book feels so urgent,' Jake said.

Then he started quoting, gazing at the camera with a sense of complete mastery. It obviously hadn't occurred to him that the excerpt sounded ridiculous in his voice. 'My father had no one to talk to. He was a man who spent his life earning money for others to spend. He groomed his hair with a metal comb and splashed his cheeks with Old Spice. Vanity, like sexuality, like morality, like art, was a foreign concept that left him perplexed. Being a man was unforgivable, and he looked from the centre of his life like Rembrandt looks out from his final self-portrait, already sick and already condemned, observing in silence what he knows about the difficulties of being a man. My father's idea of luxury was to die without any personal belongings, having given himself entirely to the wishes of his family and the demands of his gender. He never swam, he never sang, he never danced and he never cried in front of his children. This is where I begin.'

The 4G connection began to blink in and out.

The actor's face was a mask of tenderness, his blue eyes signalling a willingness to meet the danger of experience on everybody's behalf. Every man's behalf, anyhow. He stroked his handsome jaw and pursed his lips.

'I don't know where any of it came from,' Campbell said.

'It goes straight to the heart. And into the breach of who we are and what is happening in all our relationships.'

'All our relationships,' Campbell repeated, staring out at the faraway pines as the screen broke up and the connection failed.

# 20 The Game

Bozydar's mother made her way round Westfield in Shepherd's Bush like a professional, like somebody, he always said, who really knew how to shop. His job was to pay for everything and push the buggy. Shopping bags were hanging off the handles, and Bozydar put an ice cream in his son's hands as they came off the bottom of the escalator and made for Accessorize. His business was about to explode. People thought Boz was basic, but he could hold his own with a man like Bykov. Only Bykov didn't have to take his mother shopping. Imagine being unreachable, unseen, like Feng – beyond interference.

They went to the Disney shop. Boz was telling his mother that he now had less time for the car wash. 'I'm developing new work.'

'Promote one of the Polish boys again,' she said. 'What about Handsome?'

'He's called Jakub.'

'He reminds me of your father. A quiet person, but a worker, no?'

'A quick learner, I'll say that.'

'Bring him back from Leicester,' she said.

Boz stopped by the *Toy Story* stuff.

'Mum, let me run the business.'

The child's face was covered in ice cream. Mrs Krupa got a small paper napkin from her pocket and wiped him clean.

'Anyway, this factory connection is falling apart,' he continued. 'The guy who owns the company is going down.'

'I don't like these factories,' she said.

'That's what I'm saying. I'm *expanding* —'

'I saw things I don't like. I saw bank cards. Your father always said, we run legitimate businesses. We do car wash. We do construction.'

'It's all under control, Mum.'

'I have prayed and prayed. Don't break my heart.'

'Would you fucking stop it?'

'Don't curse at me. I pray to the saints to watch over you.'

He softened a little and sighed at her. 'I know what I'm doing.'

'We are good people,' she said. 'It pains me to think otherwise.'

'It's all good,' he said. 'Don't worry.'

She stopped and pointed at him with her purse. 'But bring that boy back. He shouldn't be in factories. Nice Catholic boy from Białystok.'

'Don't be weird, Mama.'

Bozydar went down to iSmash to get his screen replaced. While he waited, his second phone rang. It was Stefan. 'We have more "samphire" to sell. The Kent farms are producing. We have to get more of it out to your sellers.'

'These kids in Caledonian Road can do more. And their Brixton friends.'

'Your haulage drivers—'

'My Irish boys.'

'You can find more?'

'We've never missed a connection, Stefan.'

Bozydar pulled a piece of paper from his back pocket. In pencil, he'd written all the co-ordinates, codes and ferry times. 'We've got twenty-four pallets of wine coming again from a factory outside Bruges,' he said. 'Heading to Plymouth.'

'Right. With fifteen *ambassadors*.'

'Yes,' Boz said. 'The boys are on it. We'll be dropping them as usual and you have the times.'

'Tell your drivers the ambassadors need to crowd in the middle of the container when they get to the port, do you hear me? The sensors.'

'They know all that. We always tell them, Stefan. Driver taps, and it's all cool.'

'The border cops are stopping a lot more vehicles.'

'We can handle it.'

On 11 July, one of Mr Hazari's daughters came to the factory. Jakub was sitting at his overlocking machine when she reached his bench. Her father wasn't feeling well and wouldn't be coming to watch the football match with him that night. Jakub clocked off early and walked up Spinney Hill Road to find a pub called the Charny. He called Robert on the way. Jakub began in Polish, but Robert always insisted they spoke to each other in English. Robert had never been to London but he knew the names of Tottenham Court Road, Buckingham Palace, Wembley. He dreamed of the nightclubs. Jakub told him there were plane tracks in the summer sky over Leicester, a clear blue sky. It was a beautiful evening, he said. He knew he'd been suffering in England, but he wanted to overcome it, for Robert's sake. They spoke about the final being played that night – they both loved football, or they loved the players – then Jakub quickly said goodbye when a call came from Bozydar.

He was speaking about the factories. What was the English phrase, beating around the bush, not getting to the point?

'What is it?' Jakub said.

'Listen . . .'

It was as if he was speaking somebody else's words.

'You've done really well up there. And I like the way you've got stuck in to training the people down here in London.'

Jakub leaned against a wall. He watched cars going past, England flags fluttering from the windows.

'But the factories are finished, mate,' Boz continued. 'The owner's fucked. The workers . . . a lot of them are still in debt to me, to be honest. We'll find new work for them. We've got a lot of new businesses, okay?'

'What kind of businesses?'

'You like working with plants, don't you?'

'I'm a gardener. That's what I was doing—'

'Well, we can get some of that for you too. Truth is, we have weed production. We have grow-houses in Kent. New ones. They need on-site management. You get a flat and an allotment outside, know what I mean?'

'Weed?'

'Yes – no questions. We call it "samphire".'

'There's a flat for me?'

'Two bedroom, not far from the sea. With a *big* garden.'

'Okay.'

The tables at the Charny had names on them and the pub was already packed. The barman said it was reservations only, so Jakub made his way back down Green Lane Road, ending up at the Lancaster Arms. There were England flags draped everywhere, and the younger men were Bangladeshi, several of them already singing and pointing at the screen, drinks held high. 'You can stick your twirly pasta up your arse!' the boys were singing. 'You can stick your Lamborghini up your arse!'

They wore England shirts and Fila sandals. The tallest of the Bangladeshi boys looked over at Jakub and asked him if he was Italian. He gave him a thumb when he said he wasn't, and another when he stood up to sing the national anthem. The tallest boy knew all the words and he put his hand over his heart as he sang. When England scored in the second minute the pub went crazy. Jakub stood up to cheer at the television. He looked around him at all the happiness and felt part of it.

'Come on, England!'

'Fuck it, England. Come on!'

In the second half, all the joy fell apart. He thought of Robert and his friends and how all this would seem over there. England was two different countries that night, one warm and hopeful, the country far away, and now this, the energy of the place boiling with hatred and all the hero worship gone to shit. He watched the last of the young black players go up to the penalty spot and he felt the blame in the room.

# 21 Blood Loyalty

Some men dream of oil, its slick, black eminence, and Aleksandr Bykov drowned in a sea of oil every night, an expanse of abysmal calm. As he slept, that ocean could also seem like an immense painting, the bright moon high above him. Aleksandr knew he couldn't be heard, his limbs pawing slowly as he tried with all that was in him to reach the surface. He woke relieved each day with an idea in mind, usually a sentence, often in English, and that morning he blinked open his eyes and said, 'Loyalty is the question and the answer.'

He pressed a button and the curtains opened onto the tall, wet Surrey trees. A work by Jeff Koons hung on the opposite wall, subtitled *Goya The Family of Carlos IV*, a blue mirrored ball embedded in the centre and reflecting back an expanse of oatmeal carpet and Aleksandr himself sitting high on his pillows.

Stepping out onto the balcony, he shook his hair with both hands, driving out the night. He made a judo move and then another, greeting the outdoors. A flock of pigeons scattered from the mansard roof. This is not July weather, he thought: what happened to linen shirts and sports convertibles and glasses of Pimm's? He came back in and rang for tea. His man would place a cup on the marble table and he would take it there after his bath, listening to Radio 4. Aleksandr's English was better than the natives', because language was his thing: he now had an Arabic tutor twice a week. 'I have limited knowledge of physics today,' he once said to the Emir of Qatar, 'but I can asset-strip in fifteen languages.'

'He speaks of the past in Russian,' his former wife had said. 'For the future, he speaks in English, the language of his pride.'

'These people are in debt to me,' he said into his phone, mid-morning. He was sitting at the breakfast table in the white conservatory. Big rubber plants obscured the windows and the rain was falling still. He was talking to one of his fixers in the House of Lords about the closure of his mansion in Washington DC. 'These American banks. These diplomats. These officials – fucking *bureaucrats*. They are in debt to me in ways that you will not fail to understand, Lord Haxby.'

'Indeed,' Haxby said. 'It's ridiculous. But we are working at the very heart of government to have these sanctions removed.'

'It's absurd to be punished for being a friend.'

'A hundred per cent. And that is our submission.'

'Deal with them, please. That's why we pay you. I have been a permanent participant in the World Economic Forum since 2007. I am a member of the International Council at Harvard's Belfer Center for Science and International Affairs. I am on the board of trustees of the Metropolitan Museum of Art. We have donated $30 million in the last year to virus research programmes. And they want to talk to us about stupid real estate transactions, human rights bullshit that means nothing?'

'I completely agree. Aye. It's utter nonsense.'

Aleksandr considered his tea. English people were the best bull-shitters on the planet. They could fall back on a thousand years of bluff and superiority, yet in the real world they were powerless, using words because they had no plans. He had never met an Englishman who wouldn't do anything for a million dollars. 'I want to see these people shamed in the press and opposed by your government.'

'We're on track,' Haxby said.

Lord Scullion arrived. He and Aleksandr never shook hands, but they nodded at each other as they took their seats in the long drawing room.

'You seem tranquil,' Scullion began.

'Not entirely, as you English like to say.'

248

'Really? What's the issue?'

Aleksandr ignored the question. He stared at the artworks opposite them.

'What do you think of that?'

'What?'

'These three paintings.' He pointed and Scullion turned. Taking up the whole space, a metre from a Rodin bronze, was a triptych by Francis Bacon. 'It cost more than $120 million, in a private sale.'

Scullion walked up and put on his glasses.

'It's very ugly, isn't it?' Aleksandr said from the sofa.

'I wouldn't say that,' Scullion replied.

Aleksandr got up and joined him. 'They're about revenge,' he said.

'Really?'

'That's what my son told us. They're all based on the Crucifixion. The Son of God in the middle and the thieves on either side.'

'Yes.'

'Except, this time,' Aleksandr said, 'it's like body parts. You can see the middle one's spine all broken. The third one is based on a pelican. Blood everywhere. And maybe a door at the rear to let the spirits in.'

They didn't look at each other. The tension present in the Bacons seemed to diffuse rather naturally into the space between them.

They returned to the white sofas. Scullion told of his attempts to deploy parliamentary muscle, as he called it, to the task of legitimising Aleksandr's business interests. He told a long story about government necessities, the need to field public anxiety, but he assured him that the people in power understood his contribution.

'Do we *have* the government?' Aleksandr asked.

Scullion hesitated. 'We have influence. That was always our goal, to make London a place where you could have influence.'

'True capitalism begins with the state.'

'That's what we did with our socialism too,' Scullion said, smiling. 'You'll remember, back in the day, Blair was awfully keen.'

'Interesting person. Yearns to be liked, especially by God.'

'We all have our weaknesses, Aleksandr.'

'Yes. I have my son.'

Scullion looked like he wouldn't disagree. It was one of the ways he gained favour, not by suggesting he had no morality, but by implying it was completely flexible. 'Investments have become terribly tangled,' he said. 'I'm sure we'll deal with that when the others arrive.'

'Others?'

'I've asked William Byre to join us for a minute. Merely for us to obtain . . . clarity.'

Aleksandr was lost in the pictures again. 'I think we paid at least $35 million too much for those Bacons.'

'Really? And was Yuri involved?'

'He's been involved in every major purchase, as I told you. Not only here and in the other houses, but for . . . well, my greatest friends.'

'All with this dealer – Nicolas Lantier?'

'Yes. One of Yuri's little monsters. And even for monsters, his are especially greedy and careless. This one . . . Belgian, in a large, open-necked shirt . . . his clients are auction houses, galleries, foundations. And now some of my friends are his clients. My son always played games but now he is mad.'

'Well, I believe he's gone in a little over his head,' Scullion said, 'several times over, perhaps. His relationships with these criminals . . .'

'Lowlifes.'

Scullion told him about the meeting at 5 Hertford Street. He said he had warned Yuri about Lantier and the people trafficker.

'And how did he respond?'

'He has a bee in his bonnet,' Scullion said. 'He wishes to be independent and these are the distorted ways he chooses to show it, by running with the worst kinds of individuals. The drug dealers and so on, all leading to this man Feng . . .'

'Who is this person?'

'He might not exist. It's the name associated with an international crime syndicate, smuggling people across borders.'

'He's nothing, then . . .'

'We don't know. Nobody knows. He, or they, or it, is a sinkhole.'

'My son will die trying,' Aleksandr said suddenly. 'He has no sense of duty or destiny. It is a horrible thing.' He paused for a very long time. 'I put you in charge of *energising* him, Paul.'

'I believe he may still listen. I'm sure he will.'

Aleksandr took a breath to focus on larger concerns.

'My mansion in Georgetown,' he said. 'I want to see it again.'

'There's a pain in the arse in the FBI's Art Crime Team. A fanatic. All he can talk about is laundered money.'

'Well, give him something else to talk about, Scullion. *Give* him something.'

'Like what?'

'I don't know. A Monet.'

Scullion stared at him, a little disbelieving.

'I'm a businessman,' Bykov added. 'So, let's do business.'

Aleksandr beckoned Scullion and they stood up and walked through to the conservatory, where rain drummed against the glass. They discussed other business relating to gas companies and banks, and Aleksandr studied his British henchman as if he were a rather poor painting, wondering what kind of skin regime would cause a man to look so terribly smooth and cold.

During lunch, William Byre arrived in a Rolls-Royce Ghost. Nothing like a condemned man, he walked into the conservatory with his arms swinging.

'Hello, Paul, Mr Bykov,' he said. 'It's bucketing out there.'

'Sit down, Mr Byre,' Aleksandr said, without shaking hands. 'Will you eat?'

'I'll always eat.'

Aleksandr pointed to where he could get a plate. 'Thank you for helping me with my friend's passport,' Byre said to Scullion, as he served himself.

'What's this?' Aleksandr enquired.

'An old friend of mine, art historian. Lost his passport a week ago.'

'It was nothing,' Scullion said. 'A single call.'

The footman brought a glass and Byre poured himself some wine. Aleksandr was revolted by the way he turned the label towards himself.

'Ah. Raveneau Chablis Blanchot,' Byre said approvingly.

Lord Scullion was a master of pace: he never said anything too quickly, having the English habit of niceties, gracious formalities which must be observed, even or especially in a crisis. He had helped Byre, he was friendly to him, but he would not hesitate when the moment came to dispatch him from their sphere of interest.

'Now, old boy,' Scullion said after the peaches. 'When the man comes to the door, he comes for everything.'

'What's that?' Byre said.

'We know these are difficult times for you. We gather there are fresh allegations to do with sexual abuse. The rumour mill says that online hackers are pursuing the matter with gusto. But we profess no interest in that.'

Sir William, the foolish knight, picked up immediately on what Scullion was saying, and the tone in which it was being said.

'Who's "we", Paul?' he said, wiping his mouth.

Aleksandr spoke, putting his knife down.

'Let's say we are the people who own all your assets but find them to be a little light.'

'How light?' Byre asked.

'I think you know, William.'

'Well, let me help our friend,' Aleksandr said. 'Since 2017 you have borrowed $240 million to begin these malls in Saudi Arabia.'

'They have fallen through. There are insurances.'

'No, *you* have fallen through.'

Aleksandr leaned back in his chair. 'You people are not even good at stealing. These funds show in your accounts. You are a thief and we will give you five months from today to repay the money.'

'That's a generous time frame,' Scullion said. 'We take account of your personal difficulties. We understand.'

Again, Byre bristled. He shook his head, turning to Scullion. '*We?* It used to be "we" in the Trades Union Congress, then it was "we" in the party. I never had any truck with that. For a while it was "we" in government, "we" at Number Ten. Who is "we" now? "We" in the City? "We" in the state industries of Russia? "We" in the Bank of Cronies? "We" at this table, Paul? Or "we" in the United Arab Emirates? Which "we" are we?'

These men have no discipline, thought Aleksandr. They don't care about the long-term interests of their friends; there is nothing of the nation in their way of seeking success. No loyalty. Each Brit is an island, and they only play at being international.

'Go now,' Aleksandr said to Byre. 'You'll hear from us.'

'Fuck you,' Byre said, banging the table. 'How dare you dismiss me like a servant.'

'Goodbye,' the Russian said simply. 'And you can take that glass with you.'

Yuri came late, arriving after Byre was gone. Aleksandr was looking out from one of his long Georgian windows, and he watched his son's driver get out with an umbrella bearing the word 'Garsington'. Yuri entered the drawing room wearing a blue velvet jacket and black tie, a pair of slippers with a crown sewn onto their fronts. His blond pompadour was ostentatiously fake.

'You are very late,' Aleksandr said. 'And you look grey.'

'To quote the poet, "I am ashes where once I was fire,"' Yuri said, pulling a silk scarf from around his neck and licking his lips. He gestured at Scullion with a languid hand. 'I see you've brought the dogs inside, Papa.'

Aleksandr considered the problem without a word. He'd provided his son with the makings of an enviable career: an apartment on Piccadilly, the running of a company, a deep fund at his disposal

– but Yuri was a lost boy. Some people are born with one eye and some with a faulty heart, a diseased brain, a curved spine: Yuri was born with a tendency towards self-destruction no matter what he was given.

'You are my son,' Aleksandr said, 'but you are nothing.'

He walked to a drinks table and poured himself a large neat vodka. The glass sparkled when he held it up.

'You are nothing,' he repeated, and sank half the glass in one gulp.

'Nothing will come of nothing,' Yuri replied.

Aleksandr's perfectionism could quickly turn to uncontrollable anger. Hearing this phrase of Yuri's, no doubt another quote, was an insult he couldn't tolerate, as if the boy's expensive English education were being thrown in his face. He rubbed his thumb over the ridged sides of his glass and then threw it violently across the room, missing Yuri by no more than an inch. It smashed against the wall, splashing a small zip painting by Barnett Newman. Lord Scullion stood up. But he was unable to help Yuri, whose father was now on top of him, shouting in Russian with his hands around his throat.

'Papa! Get off me,' he spluttered, pulling away. Aleksandr released him. Yuri used the wall to help himself up, brushing down his tailored trousers. 'This is who you are,' he added. 'A man of violence.'

A splinter had cut Yuri's hand. He held the hand out and smiled as his father stood back. He felt the smear of Yuri's blood worked rather well with *Onement VI* and the Bacons.

'I cannot protect you,' Aleksandr said.

'But, *moy dorogoy papa*, I never wanted you to.'

'Your whole life is an extension of mine. Every minute of every day since you were born has been about my choices, my money, my friends, my influence, my hopes, my houses and my thoughts.' He paused with his tongue against his top teeth. 'My thoughts,' he said again. 'And you are murdering yourself. And you do this by stealing from my friends?'

'What, you *dislike* stealing now?'

'You steal from my oldest friends. Federation people. You choose to go into business with a Belgian crook—'

'You are speaking of my dear Lantier.'

'You had the job of investing funds in London. My funds. My friends' funds. I rewarded you. And now we see you associating with this—'

'Charlatan,' Scullion offered.

'He has embezzled $400 million from my closest friends. Fake valuations, fake pictures . . .'

'Monsieur Lantier is no more than a servant,' Yuri said. 'He does what I tell him. I am a patron of the arts. Lantier makes it easier to do business.'

'You are living in the sewers.'

'Lantier's nobody.'

'He is now,' Aleksandr calmly said. 'And he has fooled you also.'

The Belgian had been in on every deal. The background checks revealed everything. Aleksandr now knew Lantier had overcharged Yuri too, never letting him know exactly how much the paintings were being sold on for, Lantier's company pocketing the difference. And Yuri had allowed this criminal to touch his most powerful friends. There was Maxim, a founder of Gazprom, who had wanted to offshore money to England and bought one of the biggest houses on Kensington Palace Gardens. He wanted art and Yuri had helped him spend hundreds of millions on questionable works by Modigliani and Van Gogh.

'They were exquisite pieces,' Yuri interrupted.

'You were Maxim's representative—'

'Working for *him*,' Scullion stressed.

Aleksandr looked at his only son and tried to communicate the last of his pity for him. He couldn't see the small boy he used to be, the child who climbed on his father's shoulders, and neither did he see his mother's charms or any plan for the future. What Aleksandr saw was a weak and hedonistic foreigner with a taste for betrayal.

Walking to him, he already felt his son was a thing of the past, a lost investment. He took Yuri's dripping hand and wiped the blood down his own cheek.

'Get away from me,' Yuri exclaimed, pulling back.

Aleksandr glared at him, touching his face and tasting the blood. He turned to Scullion. 'There are sixty-eight million men in the whole of Russia,' he said, 'and I must have this one for a son?'

'I'll meet you up in your office,' Scullion replied.

There are ways of closing a door. Aleksandr Bykov was practised in the art, and he left the long sitting room as if all within it would vanish.

# 22 Onegin

Mrs Voyles liked spiders, the wonderful extension in their thin legs, the perilous balance. If she had eight legs, she would unfurl them and pivot from one to the other, as Sir Kenneth MacMillan had asked her to do, driving nimbly and lightly from her powerful thorax, proving herself the soul of musicality. She missed her old friends, the dancers, musicians. People move on and you have to learn to live with it. She looked up from her basement at the morning light. She'd long ago given up on curtains. Old towels did the job, and through the gaps she could see human legs going past in their various forms of shoe.

Eventually, Mrs Voyles got off her sofa and went over to pick up the note from the mat. She'd seen him come down and post it. She needed a new chain for the gate.

68 Thornhill Square
London N1 1BE
18 July 2021

Dear Mrs Voyles,
Can you tell me what's wrong? My wife and I moved into this house over four years ago. We were delighted with the house, felt lucky to have it, and were pleased to see that there was a sitting tenant in the flat downstairs. Our place was big enough for us and we moved in ready to do right by you, as your landlords. But ever since then, you have conspired against us, complained about us to the council, claiming we are keeping you

in a slum, and you have made yourself as obtuse as possible. You said you needed a new cooker, so I bought you one and had it installed. You said your flat was damp. I sent in two builders, who set out a plan for a full damp-proof course to be followed by a renovation. You then wouldn't let them in, nor the gasman, but wrote instead to the council about the 'hazards' in your dwelling place, which you are doing everything to block me having fixed!

I reiterate: we are more than willing to fulfil our obligations to you as a protected tenant, and we wish to meet all standards demanded by Islington Council. But I will not be messed around by you or bullied any further. We have rights, too, and your unpleasant behaviour and manipulation of the truth are not to be tolerated.

Yours sincerely,

Campbell Flynn


His handwriting was much nicer than he was, which was one of the ways they try to hoodwink you. She crumpled it up. No wonder his children never came to see them. She took down a pad of Basildon Bond and sat on her mattress to write to Mr Doyle, the young man at the council. She'd had to shout at him a few times, but he tended to follow up on her letters, unlike others in the past. She wanted Mr Doyle to understand she had received threatening letters from this odious landlord and that rain had come into her dwelling.

She'd made friends with an estate agent in Upper Street. He'd known the area for years. He told her she was well within her rights to assert herself in Thornhill Square. He was always doing these multi-million-pound deals, yet he'd make time for Mrs Voyles. One evening he even came round after work with a bottle of wine. He whistled down to her from the pavement and she came up with two paper cups and they went and sat on a bench in the square. 'I'm not only about the millionaires, Mrs Voyles. You have to look out for the locals, right?' The real people of Islington. She told him the area used to be wonderful for young people.

'These big houses were £38,000 back then. The entire house,' she said.

'And now your flat's worth £500,000. Your *flat*, Mrs Voyles! And that's what that gentleman should pay to get you out.'

'He's no gentleman,' she said.

He filled her cup and gave her a cigarette. 'You could clean up here, Mrs V. You've lived here, what—?'

'Since 1979. The month Thatcher came in.'

'Well, there you go. I've said it. You could walk away with half a million, Mrs V.'

Campbell had shaving foam on his face. He walked across the landing with a towel around his waist and looked down into the square, where Mrs Voyles was sitting on a bench with a man. It was amazing to consider that she might have friends, and he was shocked to see her laugh, and even more shocked to see her puffing on a cigarette. He would never understand how she had come to insinuate herself so completely in his head. His downstairs neighbour didn't resemble a person; increasingly she resembled a sectarian movement or a malignant part of his own conscience, and there she was in broad daylight, a normal person in the company of an everyday young guy in a suit. It occurred to Campbell that maybe he was the problem and the old woman was just an old woman.

The ten days since his return from Reykjavík had been the busiest of the year, spent mainly at his office in UCL with Milo. They were long afternoons, during which Campbell was mentored in the art of the Internet, beginning, at Milo's insistence, with a complete guide to the world of Bitcoin. 'After 2008, and the financial crisis,' the boy had said, 'it was obvious the world's financial institutions were corrupt. Cryptocurrency takes control out of the hands of big business and governments; it's peer to peer.'

'What does that mean?' Campbell asked.

'It means my computer talks to every other computer and guarantees transactions. It's a shared ledger and a beautiful piece of computer science. It's democratic. It can't be controlled by any one group or ideology.'

Milo showed him how to set up a Bitcoin wallet. He sat beside him and helped him type in his information and buy his first coin. Campbell would always remember those hours, steeped in the blue swimming-pool light of his laptop, listening carefully to this new doctrine that seemed like an answer to so many of his anxieties. Milo became part of his outlook during those sessions, and the easy banter and the sense of commitment felt so welcome to Campbell in his tender state of mind.

'The Dark Net,' Milo told him. 'This is where the magic happens.'

Campbell took it all in and was soon down at the office on his own, sometimes at night, following the pathways Milo had shown him, entering the Dark Net via Tor, going down the lanes offered by a marketplace called Empire, where UK connections were good. He was told the encryption was safe and he liked the feeling of anonymity and equality, words Milo had used. He didn't want sex sites and he didn't need a gun part or a private helicopter. Campbell told himself it was more like walking through the perfumed lanes of Dhaka or Tangier in the old days, the fear of getting lost but then finding your way out. And, the same as during his student days in Morocco, he discovered a taste for cannabis and began ordering it. Small parcels came to his office, various bits of contraband.

Elizabeth was in the shower. Campbell wiped his face, put on a white shirt and spent ten minutes fixing his black tie, then he put on the trousers and jacket and sprayed himself with his favourite scent, Mitsouko, before visiting his study and closing the door, taking a moment to check the Bitcoin price. Milo had warned him about how volatile the currency was, day to day, hour to hour, and Campbell hoped he hadn't gone and squandered the advance for that little book.

It had already started to bother him. This was how his moods worked now: swirling up then crashing down, with no sense of how to pilot them. He wouldn't be able to say anything about all this to Elizabeth.

'I have a sense of dread about you,' she said to him one afternoon, after failing to engage him in a discussion about why he was spending so much time at his computer when he said he wasn't writing.

'Don't worry. I'm trying something new.'

But he felt he could be responding to some sort of bad news about himself.

'Is it a money thing? You know we can talk if things are difficult.'

'Things are *perfect*,' he said.

When she asked about the post he was bringing home from the office, he waved his hand at her and said a person deserved his privacy.

'You sound like a teenager.'

Sitting at his desk in black tie, he looked over at an original albumen print of a wynd in the East End of Glasgow. The picture was taken by Thomas Annan a hundred years before Campbell was born, and the print hung by his desk, ensnaring him. The ghostlike figures and the shining puddles made darkness visible. The street kids, these ancestors of his, were inside a fog of chemical processes, wet collodion, silver salts, hyposulphite of soda, which arrested the action of light, the movement of his people in their back alleys, migrants to the present. He opened a drawer, took out weed and papers and rolled a small joint. Rootling for a lighter, he swept aside half a dozen Jiffy bags in which his purchases had been posted, sleeping tablets and other stuff. He sat back in his chair. He was developing a liking for being slightly stoned before anything social. He appreciated the sense of separation it brought, the feeling of warm, continuing remoteness.

He clicked on his email and opened a new one from Atticus Tew. 'Let's talk tomorrow,' it said. 'I know you want to keep schtum on this project, but the self-help publication has run into some trouble. A rising storm, I'm afraid. The actor gave an interview on something called *Vulture* saying his book is "a celebration of masculine truth".

This has been taken as a slur on the MeToo movement and weirdos are coming to his side. He has made it worse by saying men are victims and it's time to fight back.'

Campbell texted Atticus immediately. 'He's making it about men's rights?'

'Yes. Under control. But, fuck.'

So much for Campbell's pretensions about *Why Men Weep* being a postmodern exercise. He had written the book secretly and published it secretly to make money, and now it was potentially hazardous.

He took a deep breath before closing his laptop.

'Oh, well,' he told himself. 'It's all on the Bitcoin now. Or Elizabeth's mother.'

The trees at Garsington were sodden and the park showed many variations of green under the dark clouds. A line of posh cars snaked through the woods, where smiling stewards waved the opera-lovers into the dells and VIP enclosures for parking. Campbell took the umbrella from the driver and Elizabeth stepped under it in her ludicrous sandals. She sometimes liked to amuse the bourgeoisie by going a bit hippy. Campbell knew the way, and they padded down a lane and past the cricket pitch to a platform next to the opera pavilion.

The pre-performance drinks were in a sort of barn at the edge of the field, and when they got there the Duke was doing what he always did on these occasions, making a dick of himself, as Campbell saw it, booming and guffawing his way round the various circles of guests, with the old-fashioned aristocrat's tin-eared notion of party talk, obsessed with social relations but clueless about social ease. Campbell thought of several things that Milo had said about the Duke, and put them to the back of his mind for the evening, along with the question of why his researcher was taking an interest in his relatives.

Candy stood like an emaciated meerkat looking out for an opportunity to enthuse.

'Hello, darling,' Elizabeth said, hugging her. 'What a day. It's blobbing down.'

'We flew from Inverness,' Candy said. 'It was biblical. If it rains any more I fear Crofts Castle might sink into the glen.'

'Heaven *forfend*,' Campbell said.

Candy's eyes grew wide when the evening's conductor came up to them. He wasn't what anyone expected: he was rheumy-eyed and tousled, and had the sniffles, talking like a man in an advertisement for a cold and flu remedy.

It occurred to Campbell that Candy might weigh less than her necklace.

'I'm so thrilled,' she said. 'I have to say, I saw you conduct Debussy and Ravel at the Théâtre des Champs-Élysées.'

'Ah, yes. And Haydn.'

'Exactly. I was in *puddles* of tears.'

'That's very kind of you to say,' the conductor said. 'A sublime evening in Paris.' He looked around at the waterlogged grass, then sneezed. 'Our second horn and the principal cello are stuck on the M40, so we might have to start a bit late.'

The Duke sauntered up with a pathetic joke already gambolling around his mouth. 'Ah, it's *the curse of the Campbells*,' he said to Campbell.

'Why would you say that?' Candy said, spinning round.

'You know, the massacre at Glencoe, that was his lot. Bloodthirsty.'

'Don't be stupid,' Campbell said.

The Duke merely hopped to the next topic. 'Isn't Kenzie bringing the great matriarch along this evening?'

'Emily, yes,' Campbell said. 'From Chester Street.'

'Queer old bird,' the Duke went on. 'Don't know how the Countess can stand going round and round the planet on that frightful boat.'

'She likes it, Tony. She can't stand most of the people on dry land.'

'Well, she hates me, I can tell you that. My wife's mother has hated me from the first minute she met me, but I won't be weeping into my porridge. One gets used to the contempt of people who know nothing of one's duties.'

'Duties?'

'We have eight hundred years of tradition to run, Campbell. You wouldn't know about that. But thankfully, Nighty and I are like hammer and nail.'

'And who's the nail?'

The Duke was impervious. He lowered his head and whispered something unhelpful in the conductor's direction about funding.

Tycoons and business leaders jostled in black tie. Campbell saw Carl Friis across the room and they nodded. There was a fluttering out on the lawn and Yuri Bykov came towards them with a bandaged hand.

'Ah, the Russians are coming!' the Duke said at volume. He spoke as if he were a fount of mighty comedy, introducing Yuri. 'I'm sure you've met Nighty's brother-in-law, the art boffin and podcaster extraordinaire, Professor Campbell Flynn.'

'I have indeed. How are you, sir?'

'Medium cool,' Campbell said. 'How's Shakespeare?'

'On hold at present. My tutor is on location.'

'Yes, Mr Hart-Davies,' Campbell said. 'He has a lot on. An adaptation of *The Return of the Native*, I believe.'

'Thomas Hardy. And I gather you two have also been—'

Campbell winked and put a finger to his lips. '*Entre nous*,' he said. 'Very much a "D-notice" kind of thing.'

'What's this?' the Duke asked.

'Nothing at all,' Campbell said, staring at Yuri over his glass.

'Exciting,' Yuri said. 'I love a spot of espionage.'

'Now, Yuri, my young man,' the Duke said. 'If you and I could have a few words. May I show you round the rose garden? The rain's off.'

Yuri smiled and allowed himself to be drawn away by the arm. Campbell was left with Friis. The artist appeared to live with permanently raised eyebrows. Campbell hadn't noticed before, but Friis's

264

make-up – the chilli-red lipstick, the black eyeshadow – was a guard against access. His face was an electric fence. 'I'm detecting Mitsouko,' the artist said, twiddling the air with his bejewelled fingers.

'You have a nose, as well as everything else.'

'How wonderfully ambiguous,' Friis went on. 'A Guerlain classic, but more often a feminine perfume.'

'I don't go in for all that shite,' Campbell said. 'The world's had quite enough of it. Smell is not gendered, and neither is skin. All that "skincare for men" bullshit – it's nothing but marketing. "Cigarettes for women". "Novels for black people". I'm against it. I'm interested in the steps we should take towards achieving equality.'

'Well said, Professor. In certain quarters you'll be assassinated for saying so. You're ignoring all the racist solutions to racism.'

'Hopefully. I hate tribalism of all sorts, especially the white sort.'

'I think you're perfectly evil.'

Campbell took a decent swig from his glass. 'I'm researching a lot of that stuff at the moment,' he said, 'for a lecture I'm giving.'

'I know all about that!' Friis said. 'The Autumn Lecture at the British Museum. A hot ticket, after that *Atlantic* article.'

'That's nice,' Campbell said. 'How's Lord Haxby of Howden? I made a special effort not to put him on my invitation list.'

'He's in Washington, doing work for his gas company, I think. It's all a mystery, but I do miss the small Northern pig.'

'He is rather porcine, isn't he?'

'Now, now, Professor. We must be kind about my husband.'

Campbell looked over Friis's shoulder and noticed an ice bucket with the Ruinart logo. He smiled and drew it to the artist's attention. 'Here's the perfect sponsor for the show you were telling me about,' he said.

'Huh?' Friis turned around. 'Champagne?'

'Ruin Art,' Campbell said. 'Isn't that your thing?'

'Awesome,' Friis said. 'Now, promise me . . . I'd love you to write that essay for my Gagosian catalogue. Say yes.'

'And will you pay me in mutilated Magrittes?'

He shook his bangles and screwed up his face. 'You're funny.'

That's what they do, the young, thought Campbell. When they hear something funny they say 'that's funny' instead of laughing. Maybe that's what postmodernism was in the end: the naming of emotion, as opposed to having it.

Inside the pavilion, the patrons were too posh to wear masks. The rain was heavy on the roof and it felt like a sort of preamble to the advertised tragedy, nature's timpani. The momentous event was the arrival of Emily, Elizabeth's mother, who was halfway up the stairs on Kenzie's arm; a simple, glittering white frock, a rabbity fur coat and a plain blue mask distinguishing her amid the peacocking nouveau riche in their mad jodhpurs. He reckoned about half of the patrons were Russians: corporate sponsors, All-Star Gala types who had completely changed British opera and ballet with their huge cash donations.

Elizabeth was standing to receive her mother, and Campbell leaned out to pluck the Countess from the crowd of velvet jesters. 'Good evening, darling boy,' she said, offering each of her ancient cheeks to be kissed, before handing Kenzie to her father and shuffling along the row to greet the typically soignée Elizabeth, who Campbell felt all over again in that moment to be too good for him. Of all the mistakes he made that year, he would come to feel that holding her outside his conscience, ignoring her unique value to him, was the only one that he could so easily have avoided.

The Countess asked Kenzie to swap seats. She wanted to sit with Campbell so that he could explain who was who, 'In the story, I mean.'

He turned to her as the orchestra tuned up. Emily was wearing her evening pearls and she twisted a finger around them, like a child innocent of their worth. 'It was in the paper again,' Campbell said. 'San Marco is crumbling into the sea.'

'Aren't we all, my dear?' she said. 'I'm perfectly serious, but you see the funny side. I went to that vulgar shop in Knightsbridge.'

'Harrods.'

'Top floor. One requires ropes and an oxygen mask to ascend to this gold boutique that smells like the markets of Kannauj.'

'The what?'

'The perfume capital of India, you ignoramus. It's simply killing. You go to this counter and you ask for the best face cream they have . . .'

They were applauding the arrival of the conductor.

'. . . And the girl behind the counter, she's dressed as Carmen Miranda. I mean, she has a *basket* of apples on her head. She lifts this tub like a genie's lamp and tells you it's called Crème de la Mer and will cost £240.'

The overture had begun. The hesitant strings. The winds.

'That's hilarious,' Campbell whispered.

'*Killing*, isn't it? These brave robbers.'

The man in front turned round with a semi-amused face. It was Yuri. 'Please, shush,' he said, with a finger raised. '*Pianissimo.*'

'Oh, do go away,' the Countess said.

She was quiet for about forty minutes. Her hand began to move over her stomach during the letter scene as if she was channelling Tatyana's desire. Campbell's mind wandered, and he thought about Milo and the new ways he'd cultivated. It had disturbed his view of his family, past and present, but it had made him alert. He'd been ripe for a disturbance: perhaps everybody was in these times. He mused on it as Tchaikovsky's music soared over the chilly auditorium. 'Most citizens wouldn't thank you for actual freedom,' Milo had said. 'The change they want is always in other people.'

Campbell put his hands over the Countess's, meaning to warm them. At one point, she put on her glasses, which hung around her neck on a chain, and opened the programme, pointing during a waltz to a passage quoted from an old friend of hers, John Bayley: 'Pushkin's sense of the humdrum nature of life, which art must both transform and remain faithful to, never deserts him.' Campbell read the passage and closed the programme. He considered his mother-in-law's life. She seemed frailer than she had only a month before, her breath shorter, her wit truncated. Campbell exerted a little pressure on her hand and she did the same without looking round at him. The scene was coming to an end.

'Ah, male pride,' the Countess said, ready for the interval. 'The poor dears. It's the cause of everything that's wrong with the world.'

They were soon out of the opera pavilion, making their way down the uncovered walkway and heading to their interval supper. He was struck by the swifts skimming the lake. He took the lift to the ground floor with Emily and walked slowly behind the others, down the path to the picnic tents. 'Here you are, Mummy!' Candy said when they got there, taking the Countess's arm and steering her towards a chair.

'Candida, do you have a blanket or an item of that sort?'

'Yes, it's a bit nippy, isn't it?'

'For the knees, you see.'

Candy sprang into action like a mime. Her husband was already tossing picnic baskets open with abandon, plucking out bottles and shouting, 'Where's the corkscrew, for heaven's sake? We all need a bloody drink.'

'It's here, Anthony.' Elizabeth was calmly opening another basket and loading the pies and cheeses onto plates.

'Good job,' the Duke replied. 'After all that long-winded carry-on, everyone's desperate for a drop, don't you think?' Candy brought a blanket and pressed it down with delicacy around her mother's knees.

'There you go,' she said. 'Cosy now.'

'Kenzie, darling,' the Countess said, 'would you be a sweetheart and fetch me an egg of some description?'

'Of course, Granny. Didn't Daddy already?'

Campbell looked at Kenzie and felt cut. Oh, not you as well, he thought. The air felt made up of possible criticisms.

Candles were lit and more food emerged. Proper napkins, and the wine was excellent. Kenzie spent a while telling everybody that Angus might or might not be buying a condominium in Dubai.

'God preserve us,' Campbell said. 'He suffers from the same thing those hacks at *Rolling Stone* used to suffer from, *squalid overboogie*.'

'Let's leave it,' Elizabeth said, smiling. 'We had enough of all that in Iceland.'

Campbell pulled back into himself. In the wake of Reykjavík, he'd felt so isolated, so shaken. He couldn't believe what the debacle said about him and his relationship with his family. He liked friends, but maybe parenting was a nervous condition, a programme of affection and responsibility that he could scarcely live up to. An old family alliance, Angus and him, seemed like a fallacy now, the movie nights with hot chocolate, the sticker albums, the drives up to Harrow to instal him in his rooms, the fist bumps, the giggles. Perhaps Campbell had made himself dislikeable to the whole lot of them. The past's laughter was dull in his ear.

'Anyway, one shouldn't fret,' the Countess said. 'Dubai's an interesting place. It's where money goes to die, and one must laugh.'

'What's funny about Dubai?' the Duke asked.

'You know. The vanity of human wishes. The obliteration of taste. Don't you find it all a tiny bit *hilare*, as they say?'

'I could live in Dubai in a heartbeat,' the Duke said.

'I daresay,' Campbell replied.

The Duke laid out all the items – he had the posh person's love of a picnic – but he didn't sit with them. He was standing at the opening of the tent, greeting people who passed. He smoked a cigar and shook hands, speaking bluffly, but his nervous energy betrayed him. Campbell felt he represented the end of something that was once essential to the English – insouciance. Nobody was insouciant any more. Look at Harry Windsor. Look at that snobbish ultra-disaster Prince Andrew, who must, Campbell said to himself, be the commonest person in England, and he's ninth in line to the throne. Meanwhile, Elizabeth's brother-in-law, the Duke of Kendal, was puffing his obnoxious cigar. 'Roger! How the devil are you? Still messing about at the Foreign Office?' To another: 'Nigel, you dreadful old swine. I was speaking to your father in the Lords only the other day. When're you coming down to see us? Bring that ravishing woman of yours, won't you? We'd be chuffed as cherries.'

The Countess also had a succession of toasts with pâté. She then had a lemon tart and seemed quite content with a glass of champagne. She spoke to her daughters and her granddaughter about an 'important meeting' they ought to have. Elizabeth suggested they have a supper to make up for the eighty-sixth birthday the pandemic had forced them to miss. Candy said they could do it in Suffolk, but the Countess said she hoped never to see *that* county again. 'If I might have it entirely my own way,' she said, 'I'd like to do the supper at Chester Street, in my own house, and I can muster some Indian gentlemen who will cook and wash up.'

'Sounds lovely, Granny.'

She specified Sunday 25 July. 'Is that all right for everyone?' She looked at Elizabeth and Candy, who together made the appropriate nods and confirmations. Campbell watched all this as if it had nothing to do with him.

'It sounds a bit ominous, this meeting,' Candy said.

'You were always the nervous one,' her mother offered. 'I'm sure I don't have to tell you, my dear, life *is* ominous. I refer you to *Eugene Onegin.*'

Secret fears can coalesce in a headache, and it wasn't an ordinary headache, either, but a spluttering boombox of the lower mind, beyond paracetamol. It made Campbell feel instantly nauseous, and was related, he could tell, to a horrifying nuance in the Countess's invitation, her use of the word 'important'. He had given years of devoted attention to her and he knew her language. In that instant, he feared a disappointment, the notion that she might have something terrible up her sleeve.

The Duke brought Yuri Bykov into the tent. He surveyed the mess of plates and baskets and said it all looked quite civilised. 'I'd like you to meet my mother-in-law,' the Duke said. 'Emily, Countess of Paxford.'

'But aren't you the young man who shushed me?' she said.

'Do forgive me,' Yuri said, taking the Countess's hand. 'I had no idea. I get so caught up in these stories. I'm a real buff, I'm afraid.'

He spotted Kenzie and blew her a kiss. 'How's Angus? How's Ashley-Jo?'

'All good,' she said. 'Angus is in Dubai. He met a new woman. English. Turns out she's some sort of condiment heiress. Makes chutney from discarded vegetables and only employs former sex workers, that sort of thing.'

'Holy Christ,' Campbell remarked.

They all ignored him. He had no allies now when it came to Angus.

'My Lady,' began Yuri, 'I think I may be in possession of a little Gainsborough portrait that once belonged to you.'

'Good heavens,' she said. 'You can't mean the portrait of Miss Leask, the violinist of Bath?'

'The very one,' he said. 'I believe it has passed through several hands, but I got hold of it for a friend of mine and it is now in the Hermitage.'

'Oh, I do wish you'd bring it back. I miss her awfully.'

'It was painted about 1769, I believe. Very charming.'

'Well, you have succeeded in making me very depressed, Mr Bykov. One ought never to sell anything. It ought to be a golden rule.'

The Duke drew him away into a separate conversation.

The Countess said she might visit the loo. 'It's nice to take a man's arm,' she said, insisting that Campbell escort her.

'Will you manage in the loo itself?' Candy asked.

'I will. These places are palaces of infirmity.'

Crossing the lawn in the fading light, the Countess commented that she and the swifts had a number of things in common. 'We know our way back,' she said, 'but we are never sure if anywhere is home.'

She wanted the gossip. He told her the man she'd met a minute before, the one who brought up the Gainsborough, was the son of that Russian magnate. 'They're the people Anthony is said to be in debt to.'

'*Really?*'

'Yes. As well as a friend of mine, also in debt.'

'He seems like a parody Englishman,' Emily said.

'That's Harrow. Plus money. Plus Russianness. Plus vanity.'

'How riveting,' she said. 'I've never seen Anthony look so dreadfully oppressed. He's such a disaster, that man. Poor Candy. You know, in all the years, I've never thought that way about Elizabeth; she could be a bit independent here and there, and possibly both, but I never had any worries about her.'

'She's not the sort of person one worries about.'

'Precisely. And she married a mystery, which is always the best thing to do if one wishes to have an interesting time.'

'Do you mean me?'

'Oh yes, my dear. You're full of riddles. That's why you like art so much: you have a tendency towards the hieroglyphic.'

Campbell said nothing. He thought it best.

'I remember when Lizzie first brought you over from Cambridge. She was teaching you how to use a knife and fork.'

'Oh, Emily!'

'I'm only teasing. You arrived with armfuls of daffodils and a bottle of Château Montrose, and I thought, "She'll be happy with him. She already looks like a young woman who has found her match. Look how they laugh."'

She took a firmer hold on his arm and squeezed it. She said the second half was the best part of *Eugene Onegin*. 'Prince Gremin's aria about old age. You get to a point where it's the only thing for the ears.'

'Let's take our time,' he said.

'You were always your own *person*, my dear.'

Her presence was solvent, that was the word that occurred. He could forgive Emily anything and perhaps he had to in order to justify his expectations. Yet the evening had somehow given him a throbbing premonition of things unravelling within Elizabeth's family, and his loyalty and love were drifting. He'd always considered Tony a crook, Candy a victim and the Countess a likeable, eccentric old bird – but, really, wasn't all of this to a very large extent disgraceful and mortifying? Their entitlement bred contempt, and it was as if he'd only just noticed how it accumulated.

Intelligent people can read your thoughts. Or they can read the air in which the thoughts are suspended. 'And what about those charity payments,' she said, 'the ones you mentioned in Venice that were being taken from your account? Did you ever sort that out?'

'It was nothing,' he said. 'Just something I owed.'

'Don't dwell,' she said. It was one of her sayings.

The evening was scented now with burning candles and the rain over the park. 'You're a generous old stick to keep me company,' she added.

Later that night, going back to London, Campbell said the Countess had more luck in a ten-minute stretch than his mother had had in her whole life.

'Is that why you're drawn to her?' Elizabeth asked. 'Her luck?'

He shrugged and stared into the coming dark.

# 23 Underground

Milo was alone in his room. He'd been surfing for hours, and went back to a hack he'd performed weeks earlier into William Byre's various companies. It was easy overcoming their security, it was weak and basic, alarmed for financial phishing but with no strong barrier to company emails. This morning he was homing in on a correspondence about Byre's historic sexual abuse of female staff. A former personal assistant of Byre's had sent a long memo to the police, full of incriminating details about the harassment claims. Milo spotted it using a key he'd established during the earlier hack of the Home Office. It's where he first saw the name 'Vicky Gowans' and learned that Byre was abusing her.

'Bingo,' he said, dragging the files to WeTransfer.

He kept a number of screens open, more of them now relating to the Duke of Kendal. He got up for a mango juice. Back at his screen there were a few Google alerts on 'Summer Isles'. He read through the entries and studied the photographs, then he saw a news item. 'The Eilean Ròin Community Buyout Stalls at £500k.'

> The combined effort of the Scottish Travellers community
> and others, including international nomad groups, in their
> campaign to buy the island of Eilean Ròin in Ross-shire has
> run into trouble after reaching over half a million pounds.
> The campaign, which has the support of wildlife groups and
> online entrepreneurs, has an option agreement with Copeland
> Estates to buy the 3,000-acre site in the Summer Isles as well as
> fourteen residential properties for £2.3 million. The campaign

has today made a renewed call for investors who wish to see the land preserved for what it calls a conservation and community settlement for the Internet age, with welfare and equal rights, racial equality and children's rights to the fore.

A light went on in his head. He went back into a number of online threads and read private material relating to the Duke of Kendal and the Segdoune Estate, and saw money going to the estate account from a shell company on the Isle of Man that was known to belong to the Russian oligarch Aleksandr Bykov. He made a locked file and copied all the Kendal data to it, and then sent it to Gosia. 'Remind me tonight: I've got an idea.'

'Tease,' she messaged back.

'Clue,' he wrote. 'Eilean Ròin Community Buyout.'

He put on a fresh T-shirt and went to check himself in the bathroom mirror. The landing in their flat was a glorious zone of engagement: 'Yup,' he said, looking at a banner pinned to the wall with red letters stitched on a yellow background. 'Take a Risk for Peace Now,' it said, and in smaller letters, 'Women Against the Bomb'. His mother had never explained, but he reckoned she had inherited these banners and posters from her adoptive parents.

The professor was becoming a diligent student. Researching for the big museum lecture, he had taken everything Milo was showing him and gone further. He often heard from Flynn now at odd times of the day and night: he was finding new avenues into the worlds of cryptocurrency. He was doing his own research, reading articles in favour of dissolving the banks and giving back all museum artefacts, and he would text Milo to ask his opinion, like they were proper friends. Milo radicalised him, darkening the contents of Flynn's computer screen until it became like a mirror.

The professor had DMed him on Instagram the previous night. 05.43: 'The lecture might end my career. But it's beginning to feel perfect.'

At all hours, a phrase might emerge for the lecture and Milo would send it.

'The vanity of the ailing British.' 04.26

'Surveillance is a form of portraiture commissioned by the State.' 11.50

Another day . . .

'Self-manufacture is the point of social media. And so are half the statues in the Enlightenment Gallery.' 02.15

Flynn would respond, back and forth. They'd meet on Highbury Fields. They'd have a drink in various pubs and talk about digital profiling. There would be sessions at the office, several at the house, in the study, in the garden.

'Take down the old estate,' Milo had written one night. 'Remember you have an Irish name, Professor, and you owe them nothing.'

Then, a minute later: 'Who owns white suffering? *GOD* does. Society. It's never only left to whites. But black suffering? Each black person themselves is expected to own it. And that's racist.'

Prep and research. Load and point.

He had taken Flynn's passport to show him how disruption works, but also as part of a fishing expedition, to see what the professor would do to resolve it, and who he would call. Milo caught him in the act. He hacked the gov.uk website and saw within moments that the missing passport had been hurriedly replaced after a special request came from a Lord Scullion, via the Home Office.

Flynn was part of it – part what he wished to resist.

It was seven o'clock and the betting shop on Caledonian Road was still open. Milo pushed the door open and found his dad at the back, staring up at the big screen, slip in his hand, absorbing information about the dogs. He was in and out of there all day, having 'a wee flutter'.

'Romford?' Milo said. 'They'll take your money off you and steal your car at the same time, that crew.'

'No danger,' his old man said. 'I'm wise to it, so I am.'

Ray's habits had always played their part in Milo's. He thought about his dad a lot, about all that had happened to him. Milo dissolved newer bits of cryptocurrency whenever they needed it, clearing the bills or whatever, and Ray was happy about that but he wanted to remain his own man too, so he kept up the driving, the betting. Ray had no illusions about money: it was all manipulation of one sort or another, and he was happy to see his son overturn the apple cart. He enjoyed his pint at Kennedy's. But after Zemi everything was tinged with sadness. He sometimes spoke of starting again. 'Old men ought to be explorers,' he said. Since Milo had started seeing Gosia, his father had been reading about the Poles in Europe and America.

'I remember when I met your mother,' he'd said in the kitchen a few months back. 'I fell in love with her but I also fell in love with her struggle. That's how it was. London was difficult then, for both of us, Irish people and black people, trying to make a go of it.'

'And Mamma stood out.'

'Oh God, she did. With her bright dress and *netela*. The smile on her. And brave, your mother. At the school, she got reported to the authorities but she never budged.'

Milo had started laughing. 'What?!' he said.

'Yeah, she once told the schoolchildren that policemen are generally stupid, lustful, treacherous and cannibalistic.'

They both laughed. 'No way, man.'

'Oh, aye. And another time, she got reprimanded because she refused even to acknowledge the work of the writer Charles Kingsley, because of his views on black people and Irish people. She banned that poem by Kipling too.'

'"The White Man's Burden" . . .'

'Exactly. You know what she was like.'

Milo looked up at the screen and saw the dogs being loaded into the traps. His dad was relaxed as the announcer spoke the odds.

'What number?' Milo asked.

Ray held up two fingers. 'Blue coat.'

The bell rang and the orange rabbit came round the outside. Ray barely moved as the dogs ran their half-minute, then he touched the air with his fist. 'How much?' Milo asked, smiling.

'Five to one. Two hundred and fifty.'

Walking back from the bookie's window, he stuck a fifty in Milo's pocket. 'Buy that intelligent woman a glass of wine,' he said.

'Come on, Dad. I don't want that.'

'Take it,' he said. 'It will bloody cost that in Shoreditch.'

When they got to the car, Milo saw that the floor was covered in scrunched-up parking tickets. They were always after him. 'Feck 'em all,' he said, driving down the Cally and going left onto Pentonville Road.

Milo was answering a text. It was from Ashley-Jo. He'd been with the professor, working on the British Museum thing in the garden, when Flynn's daughter came by with her partner. 'I'm A.J.,' they'd said. 'Who are *you*?'

They'd asked for his number that day and had texted him since, always wanting to hang out. Milo thought they'd be useful. He was thinking like a gamer – keep all exploits alive, always have a door open, and A.J. seemed lively.

The blue light of Old Street was strong. 'Your mother always liked it up here,' his dad was saying. 'Brick Lane. Zemi liked the clubs.'

'Clubs? What, like, raves?'

'Before you were born, Milo. No danger. We knew how to use a Saturday night. You better believe it. We were young before you were.'

Milo was staring ahead. 'Dad,' he said, 'why did Zemi stop writing? I found an essay she published when she was younger.'

'Teaching, activism, you. She got too busy. She always said she would get back to writing someday, and I believe she would've.'

They stopped in Great Eastern Street. 'Give me one of your daft hugs, then,' Ray said with a big toothy grin.

'Bring it in.'

'Have a good time, now. Mind yourself.'

Milo knew his father had always been on his side. A special island, always there. Crossing the road, he wished he was staying with him for a few pints. Whatever happened, however the plan played out, they would take the old man with them.

Gosia was standing outside the club with the look that says, 'You're late.' They kissed under her umbrella and she flicked his tongue.

'Rah,' he said.

'I hate everybody except you,' she said.

'Don't say that, babe.'

'I do, though. The customers. My family.'

They stood touching foreheads and he breathed her in. They went for a walk down the street and got a cocktail in a shiny bar.

It was just joy and small talk. He sent her a link to some paintballing place in Brighton. 'I love shit like that,' he said.

'I know that. You're such a baby.'

'Nah. I want us to be the Bonnie and Clyde of paintballing.'

He kissed her shoulder. She filled him in on her day and he made light of everything. They were always rolling, always excited. They got serious when they spoke about the project. It was getting big.

'You're not stressed, babe?' she said.

'Nah. It's not that. It's important. Once in a life. I just hope I'm not dragging you into something . . .'

She watched him go quiet and put a finger to his lips.

'It's *our* thing,' she said.

Walking back up Old Street, he was thinking aloud. 'With Byre, the creepy stuff goes deep,' he said, 'and he's been at it for decades.'

'Everybody knows it now.'

'Yeah,' he said. 'But here's *the proof*. I've got a memo sent to the police by a woman who was his personal assistant for fourteen years.'

'Wow. You sending it to Tara Hastings?'

'I'm pushing her towards it now. Letting her find it.'

'Awesome,' she said.

'It's gonna be the end for him. The memo says he's physically violent towards a girl in her twenties. Calls her his girlfriend. I have her name.'

'Really?'

'Vicky Gowans. Hurts her. Bought her a flat.'

They walked on towards the venue. Pharma had texted Milo to say their names were on the guest list, and there was a clipboard guy outside. But Milo hated all that. He took Gosia by the hand and they just joined the short queue, talking in low voices.

'Other stuff,' he said. 'Flynn's passport. I know how he solved it.'

'What?' she said. 'Your thing worked?'

'Yeah. He took the bait. *Scullion* fixed it.'

'You're kidding me,' she said. '*That guy?*'

Milo shook his head, whispered. 'It took me about two minutes to smash into the passport office network – Scullion fixed it.'

'Fuck.'

'Uh-huh. Flynn draws from the same shit-pool as them.'

'And what next?' she asked.

They were ready to go in. He altered his stance and did his Vin Diesel voice.

'"Justice is coming,"' he said, leaning into her giggles.

The corridors were bathed in neon. The walls sweated and danger roiled in the distant throb of the sound system.

'Clubs are so basic,' Milo said. 'Like caves. If you build a fire and bang together a few jawbones, you've got a rave.'

Gosia laughed and held on to his arm as they passed the cloakroom.

'I'd say the revellers are all pretty hammered,' she said.

It was true. They were off their faces. Milo saw a group of white boys in button-down shirts who were passing pills next to the toilets.

Big Pharma was down on the dance floor, rolling his shoulders and pouting for random cameras. To Milo's eyes he was the king of comedy. He could recall him as a kid in a SpongeBob T-shirt, back in their schooldays, when Pharma was always dishing out nicknames for the teachers and hitting up the kids for spare sweets.

He did a funny spin and pointed straight at Gosia. No matter what he did, Pharma was forever the child making moves.

'What's happening, Bigs?' Milo said.

'I'm having me a good time. Love a club night. Love a battle.'

Milo looked over his head. Champagne corks, sparklers. Phones held up, shooting videos. The Underground was a long room with its own atmosphere. It felt like a place where the rules of rule-breaking were stricter than the rules. Four girls in high heels rushed down the steps to the dance floor, sharp fingers aloft.

Pharma was wearing a giant sweatshirt that said 'Calabasas'.

'What are they on?' Gosia asked. 'It's like this party's been going on for weeks.'

'Since early doors today, baby,' Pharma said. 'You guys are late-comers. You just here for the sing-song or what?'

'I wanted to see my boys,' Milo said.

Pharma bopped his head to the beat. 'That's cool,' he said. 'More than that, bruv: that's *Kool and the Gang*. The Cally boys are Gucci, trust me. Brixton guys too. So, Deptford is fucked.'

It was loud. Grinding. The ceiling dripped.

'Nice. A sing-song ding-dong?'

'Old-school rap battle, bruv. We're all lit. It's just about to kick off up there.'

Milo followed his friend's eyes to the stage. Gosia was right: all the faces seemed blurry and the music was tripping.

'There's purple juice going round,' Pharma explained. 'It's Xanax and tramadol, mixed with Ribena or whatever. The hook is you can die of a heart attack.'

'That's the hook?' Milo said. 'What's the up?'

'Three feet high and rising!' Pharma shouted. 'Me, Myself and I. Cause I'm De-La-Lovin' it in my De La Soul. No, seriously – it feels *nice*. It feels righteous.' He did a few robotic moves while laughing his head off.

Travis stood at the bar with the Cally Active boys. He looked up at them with a kind of leer on his face, a look of remote self-possession, Milo thought, as if he'd arrived at a place outside of himself and could only watch.

'What the fuck,' Milo said. He gestured to the bar. Travis raised his cup, and it was clear he'd been drinking that stuff.

'You need to look after him more,' Milo said.

'What the fuck am I, his daddy?' said Pharma.

Milo shook his head, disappointed. 'Don't be a dick, Devan. You know better than anyone how vulnerable he is.'

Pharma tutted and strode away. Bopping again in seconds. It was as if he understood the deep rhythm of the club and how to travel inside it.

Travis and the crew were called up to the stage. Milo and Gosia walked to the bar for a better view, and he bought two beers.

'Get some shots, babe,' Gosia said.

'Yeah?'

'We need to catch up with this crowd. Double shots.'

'Let's do it!' he said.

Travis was staggering about in front of his crew. 'Shout out Stoke Newington,' he said when he got the mic.

'He's known as Ghost 24, yeah?' Gosia asked Milo.

'Yeah. His, what's it called – his *persona*.'

The backing track was whining onstage. The boys swayed. It was as if they owned some combustible licence, newly sparked.

On the count of three, Milo and Gosia knocked back their tequila shots.

'Listen, yeah,' Travis was saying. 'Shout out to my close peoples from Brixton Hit Squad. Up North for one night only. Free the mandem.'

The boys onstage pulled their scarves over their faces. They bounced and pointed to the ceiling with joints between their fingers.

'Free the brothers!' they shouted.

They filmed themselves on their phones. The people on the

dance floor did too, and the music was all hard cracks and horror movie vibes.

Travis/Ghost 24 leaned in. 'We're shutting it down,' he said. He was juiced up. Unreachable. Working the crowd.

'His flow's amazing,' Milo said, handing Gosia another shot.

'Look,' she said. 'It's poppin' off down there.'

She pointed with her shot glass. The dance floor was swelling. A cloud of hash smoke appeared to rise above it.

'True,' he said. 'It's stewing, man.'

He could see 0044 being jostled down the front.

'See that white boy,' Milo said, 'the blond kid, near the front?'

'Yeah. Yeah. Who is he?'

'Mad bastard. Rolling hard. He's the rando who turned up at the Copenhagen block with a bag of knives.'

'Is that the kind of *fans* they have?' Gosia said.

Milo looked up at the stage. A white strobe light was pulsing overhead. Harsh. Guys jumping in their tracksuits.

'Fans, friends, who knows?' he said.

There was a tap on his arm. When he turned it was Ashley-Jo and two guys in designer beanies. New arrivals.

'Hey, what's up?' Milo said.

It wasn't easy to focus. The boom and the white light together.

'I'm shook,' Ashley-Jo shouted. 'Who's that up there?'

'It's my buddy Travis – Cally Active.'

'And the video behind them. Who shot the video?'

Milo cupped his mouth with one hand. 'They shot it in the car park under a block of flats in Caledonian Road.'

'Where?'

'*Copenhagen Fields!*' Milo shouted back. 'It doesn't matter.'

He paused to gather his thoughts. He didn't really know Ashley-Jo. He made an effort because of who they knew.

The music was like the soundtrack for *Halloween*.

The lights turned blue, and he imagined a cabin deep in the forest.

'It's so cool we stayed in touch,' they said.

Milo tried to do introductions over the sound, the guttering track and the Bedlam of everyone talking and laughing.

'I like your dress,' Gosia shouted.

'It's a tribute to Issey Miyake,' said Ashley-Jo. 'I *adore* pleats.'

It was the Deptford crew's turn onstage. Their main man was a lanky rapper called Sluggz, who had braids sticking out of a red cap. He was surrounded the same way Travis had been, except, up on the screen, they patched in an Instagram live feed of a gang member called 77 from his prison cell at Belmarsh.

'This is amazing,' Ashley-Jo said, turning with wide eyes to their companions. 'Is this guy really performing from a London prison?'

'It's all a prison, to some people,' Milo said, too quietly.

As the Cally Boys returned to the bar, Milo and Gosia moved towards Travis, whose face was pouring with sweat. Milo could smell Ribena. He had known Travis long enough to recognise his limits.

'Give me that,' Milo said, taking the cup from Travis.

'Hey, what?' Travis said.

'Nah, man. Enough.'

'The fuck.'

'Just for now, T.'

He hadn't the power to resist, but Milo saw an expression he knew from when they were children – a look of pure hurt. Like when Arsenal lost.

Out of nowhere, exhausted and high, Travis bent forward and put his head on Milo's shoulder. 'Sorry, cuz,' he mumbled.

Milo stroked his damp hair. 'Let's go somewhere quieter,' he said. 'Get some food into you, man. A decent drink.'

Lloyds was beside them. He knew another club in the West End. Pharma said there was a Jamaican thing on Essex Road.

Looking out, Milo could see a scuffle. The seething on the dance floor pulsed in their direction and he wanted to get Travis out of there.

Ashley-Jo cottoned on to the conversation. 'I know a private club,' they said, 'and it's not far from here. They owe me.'

'Yeah?' Milo said.

'Shoreditch House. I can get us in.'

From the roof-deck, London seemed like a spaced-out gathering of filaments, like Hong Kong or an Internet city. Gosia was looking at the skyscrapers, the nightlife, listening to sirens. It was Saturday 24 July. London had that warm night stillness when the city seems deeply embroiled in itself.

'Lloyds is on his Suge Knight thing,' Milo said. His boy was on a candy-striped sunlounger with a bottle of Krug. The rooftop at Shoreditch House was packed, food was going round and A.J. had ordered a bunch of Manhattans. None of the Cally boys had drunk one before, though Gosia had.

'Look, Ma, I'm dancin',' Travis hollered.

Some of them went into the pool. Pharma was explaining his theory of *The Sopranos* finale to a girl with wild eyelashes. 'Tony and his family are in the diner, the screen goes black. That's the end. People think that means he gets whacked, but no, I think Tony goes on to become the head of the New York family as well, across the river, know what I'm saying?'

'But none of it is real, the story ended,' the girl said.

'That's right. Nothing's real,' Pharma said, bending to kiss her. She wasn't into it but she was nice, the way she pushed him away.

Gosia felt amiable towards Ashley-Jo, who, at one point, high as a kite, came over to talk to her. A.J. wanted to talk about Milo's connection to Professor Flynn. 'It was like a total head-fuck, to be honest,' they said. 'Milo was sitting in the garden with my girlfriend's dad, who's an academic bullshitter.'

'Yeah. Milo went to his lectures at UCL.'

'And that's where you two met?'

'I studied English there,' Gosia said. 'I didn't have Professor Flynn.

I met Milo in a sort of night class. We talked about books. Then we went to the same reading group. We talk every day and he's . . .' she whispered, '*something.*'

Ashley-Jo went right past the joyful moment. 'You were lucky to avoid Professor Flynn. He's totally out there, to be honest. He hates humans who don't kowtow. Thinks he's a podcast-friendly intellectual . . .'

'People are talking about this big lecture he's giving in October.'

Ashley-Jo seemed not to listen, but to ponder what she'd said herself. 'It's probably that I'm insecure because he doesn't seem very impressed by me, or whatever. Plus I'm a designer and they think he's some kind of fashion sage.'

'He's into fashion?'

'Dabbles in everything. A pundit. He's always on telly and mainstream bullshit.'

'He moves in quite a privileged world.'

'All marriage connections,' Ashley-Jo said. 'Or university friends. He, like, grew up in a tower block in Glasgow or something.'

Gosia just smiled, like she knew nothing.

'He hates talking about it, which is unusual because Glaswegians usually *love* giving us all the sad deets.'

'Milo is getting close to him.'

'I'm sad to hear it. He's not as much fun as he seems. He furthers his own ego in that totally male way. Everybody's fooled by him, though? I'm talking publishers and producers and fashion editors. *Ev-ery-body.*'

'I suppose he thinks of himself as being part of the Establishment.'

'Nobody's the Establishment in their own eyes, love.'

The phone in Ashley-Jo's hand buzzed with a text. They said it was Kenzie and that she'd just got home from some huge opera.

'She's into all that?'

'Yeah,' she said. 'She goes without me. It's like a vast, white, heter-onormative nightmare.'

Gosia thought their irises were interesting. Fake, obviously, but blue like the pool. Ashley-Jo resembled the people you see on reality TV shows: they assume they're sympathetic, but they aren't always. She'd had customers like that in the salon.

Travis and Milo had their feet in the pool. Then they put rolled-up striped towels under their heads and lay on the loungers, drinking cognac. Lloyds was going round with a compact mirror of powder. Milo was enjoying his time with Travis and the boys, and he had a bit, and so did Gosia. It made the conversation go even faster, and she spoke to Lloyds about his plans to start a record label. She looked over at all these people dancing and swimming and lounging and thought it was safe. She bummed another cigarette, then went to the smoking loft and stood by herself, looking out at the orange mist and black sky. She couldn't say how long she was there but her thoughts seemed to stretch to fill the space.

Boz was out there somewhere making it all worse.

'It's mad beautiful, innit,' Milo said, suddenly at her side.

She leaned in to kiss him.

'Oh, yeah,' she said, leaning back. 'You told me to remind you. That thing. Your idea, the Community Buyout?'

'The Summer Isles,' he said.

'What about them?'

He scratched his head, shyly. 'I want to go there, babe. I want to start again. And it's your thing.'

'But we should finish *this* first,' she said.

'Yes. It's dangerous, but listen . . . we could tie the two. There's a way.'

'How?'

He paused. His eyes had wonder in them.

'Anthony Crofts,' he said. 'The Duke of Kendal. I think we can take him *down*.'

There was a buzz between them now.

'Why him?' she asked.

Milo took his time. 'Byre is done. He's already going down. And I have a feeling about this other one . . . this aristocrat. He's even deeper into everything. I *feel* it, babe. And I'm finding new intel now.'

'House of Lords and all that,' she said.

'Trust me,' he said. 'I'm figuring it all out. He's on a different level. Let's just allow this William Byre thing to play out, then . . .'

She was nodding. She liked it.

'I think we could use the Duke to get free,' he said. 'It's growing in my mind . . .'

'Like reparations.'

'Exactly. Just like that.'

His phone started buzzing. He nodded and the expression on his face changed. 'What? You're shittin' me,' he said.

'What's the matter?'

'We're coming through,' he said, and pocketed his phone.

'Milo, what's the matter?'

'That was Bigs. He got a call a minute ago. Things went off outside the Underground. Brixton and Deptford. That kid 0044 got acid thrown in his face. He's in the Royal London Hospital.'

# 24 Chester Street

On 25 July, Elizabeth was coming to the end of a rare Sunday session. The young woman was crying, and it was good to hold the silence for a moment. 'Take all the time you need,' Elizabeth said as the patient picked up her tote bag.

'I feel I'm starving him,' the patient said.

Elizabeth walked round her desk. 'There are many kinds of dialogue between a mother and her child. Breastfeeding is only one.'

'The very first one.'

'But perhaps not the last,' Elizabeth said.

When the patient left, she wrote her notes.

Looking over at her window and seeing the Barbican tower blocks in the distance, she recalled a visit to Campbell's mother at Christmas in 1990, when she was still living in the high flats near the motorway and unpicking her knitting. That woman was a profound narcissist. She lived to be served and fussed over and could do nothing for anyone. She always spoke to Elizabeth as if she was the English woman who'd stolen her son and was using him. Alma sat in the dark of her living room, wool in her lap, the television the only light, and there was no welcome for her son and nothing in the fridge. The poor woman was alone, and she took pride in nothing but her devotion to washing and ironing, as if order could be made by steeping cloths overnight in bleachy water.

'She used to like Noël Coward on the radio,' Campbell had told Elizabeth. 'It was her idea of posh. But she lived by her own verbs – *to steep*.'

She was aware of the love she could offer Campbell in comparison.

She could inspire him, and perhaps she might still. The Vermeer project had been her idea, on a holiday with the children at an old farmhouse in the Luberon. They'd been to a fire-jumping festival in the village, and after supper the children went upstairs to watch a DVD. Elizabeth sat on in the kitchen, drinking delicious wine with Campbell and talking about the research she'd been doing into sense memory. This led her to Proust – her French was better than that of anyone he knew – and she began to say that Vermeer's life was invisible.

She could still see it: the half-moon, the moths at the window. And there was her hapless husband – he was always that, mysterious and giving, a nice lover, but propelled by the old family romance to prove himself. She could recall how she had pressed him. He was in the mood for criticism, which he often wasn't, and she had told him he ought to focus on his own gifts and develop his talent rather than finding fault in others. It was a big thing to say, because Campbell was always pleading his own case, and could feel isolated in situations where he should have thrived, something he didn't see. That evening in France, he sniffed the wine in his glass as he returned fire about Proust.

'Swann's essay on Vermeer is a study in invisibility. *View of Delft*, I think, for Proust, possesses all the magic of existence transformed into art. Bergotte dies looking at the patch of yellow wall in the painting and wondering at the miracle of life.'

'Well, there you go,' Elizabeth had said.

'What?'

'The subject you've been looking for. There has never been a Life of Vermeer that does what art and biography must do.'

'Which is?'

'Express the secret drama of the creative self.'

There was a sparkle in his eye. She'd always remember it.

'There are very few materials,' he said. 'Only the pictures themselves. And the history of our wonder at them.'

'Perfect.'

'*The Life of Vermeer*,' he said.

Elizabeth closed the door of her study.

The house was full of their marriage, the imaginative tact that had kept them together. But there was a new thing: the smell of weed. Standing on the stairs, she wondered if he might be in danger from those outside forces. All these new ventures of his into social theory and politics, current affairs and self-help. He'd told her it was research, and she trusted him as a writer, a kind of moral adventurer, wrong half the time. Her mother always said Campbell was as good as a novel, and that was true, for the most part, but the Countess never said who wrote it or how it would end. He had always been interested in being a mirror for other people, or being someone else – a natural response, Elizabeth thought, to his mother's TV – but she had always known he might struggle. She didn't mind the games, or the playing out of his needs in his family life or in his career, but she was concerned now, like never before in their marriage, about what was being unlocked in him.

'Darling,' she said on entering the kitchen. 'You hadn't put family names on the invitation list for the British Museum. I added some. It's completely sold out and I don't want people to end up locked out of the event.'

'Like we nearly were in Iceland,' he said.

'We shan't be talking about that.'

'Fucking crème anglaise,' he said over his shoulder. Elizabeth came and hugged him from behind. A bottle of Grand Marnier was open by the stove. There was also a load of jam she had decanted earlier. She reached around his waist and turned the heat down. 'There,' she said.

'Am I doing it wrong?'

'No,' she said. 'Maybe a bit enthusiastically. It was burning.'

*French Country Kitchen* was open on the bookstand.

She helped him strain the mixture onto a dish of fig leaves, then she set it aside to cool as the radio played the news from Afghanistan.

'End of another war,' he said.

'That fish smell in the hall's become really intense,' she said.

He sighed and felt for his glasses.

'I know. I need to look under the floorboards or something.'

She peeked round at him. 'Did you pay attention to what I said about the Autumn Lecture? Everybody wants to come.'

'They could probably skip it. Spare them a heart attack.'

'Is it going to be very controversial?' she asked, trying to make light of it. 'I'm sure it is, after all this secret work from you and your comrade.'

He pulled away and moved some dishes into the sink. 'Don't patronise me, Lizzie. I've been working non-stop, and it's probably the most honest thing I've ever done.'

'I'm only teasing,' she said.

She walked over and picked up a magazine on the sofa.

Family gatherings. She never liked them. But Campbell loved the Countess and he always cooked something in her honour. It was her 'important' dinner. She would have a brigade of fellows making the supper – up all night, pulverising tamarinds – but she liked to give the impression it was all done with no fuss at all.

'Now on Radio 4, *Open Book* . . .'

Elizabeth put the magazine down and listened. She looked at Campbell once or twice, didn't say a word.

The female presenter's words marched out of the radio.

'Toxic Masculinity. MeToo. The end of manual labour. Erectile dysfunction. Today we discuss the crisis in masculine culture. If that sounds a touch heavy, there's music too, from the young Welsh singer and poet Arwen Pidd. Later, the aboriginal painter Helicopter joins us to discuss his book of interviews about tribal art. But we start with a dash of movie magic. Jake Hart-Davies established his name as a leading actor in the dragon-slaying epic *Aethon's Curse*, which ran for seven seasons on Sky and won a slew of Emmys. He went on to star in several rom-coms before gaining plaudits for guest appearances in the *Spider-Man* series and as a UN envoy in the HBO thriller *Yemen*. His next film, *The Return*, an adaptation of Thomas Hardy's *The Return of the Native* directed by Scottish indie hero Duncan Bawn, is currently filming on location in Dorset. Yet it's the surprise appearance of an unusual and highly opinionated self-help book, *Why Men Weep in Their Cars*, that has this week thrust Hart-Davies into the headlines. It has been described as a "tirade", and his publisher remains tight-lipped about how the book came to them and whether he worked with a ghostwriter. I started by asking Jake Hart-Davies about the timing of his book. Is it a cry from the heart from a sensitive man or an apologia for toxic behaviour?'

The actor's voice was caring and responsible. He took to the question like he scarcely deserved its intelligence. 'We aren't perfect,' he said. 'I would be the first to admit that. Look, I work in an industry that has undervalued people of colour, and women, for far too long. I get that. I really do. But what I'm saying with this book is, "Not all men are the same, right?" No two human beings are the same in this world. So, stop with the blaming, stop with the herding people into one enclosure. Isn't that sexist? Isn't that racist? That's what I'm asking you. Men are being abused and we are hurting right now. Men have a lot to contribute to this debate, but to treat us . . . like animals, like irrational creatures, like we're all part of the same toxic tribe, like we're all rapists or whatever, is not something that . . . that most rational people would agree with, and I mean women too.'

'Sounds to me like "the empire strikes back",' the presenter said.

'Holy fuck,' Campbell said into the kitchen worktop.

'*Why Men Weep in Their Cars* is a tender book. It is a healing book. In my opinion, this thing has gone too far—'

'Alexa, stop,' Campbell said.

Elizabeth looked round at him, a look she'd been rehearsing for years. He shook his head at her as if the best thing was to say nothing at all and wait for things to pass.

She went upstairs to get ready.

Campbell stood at the chopping board, mortified. He couldn't believe what he'd just heard. He should have known better: history was full of idiots who commissioned even bigger idiots to represent them and do their bidding. It was stupid. A thing that had seemed such a wheeze was now radiating danger.

He went outside for ten minutes and took a walk around Thornhill Square, feeling the pressure of the dark trees and smoking another small joint to ease his mind, before the pressing business of the evening at Chester Street.

The Countess had gone all out, in her customary way: there were Indian helpers to take coats, others to offer drinks and a whole crew in the kitchen, where Campbell deposited the crème anglaise beside a silver basin of chopped onions. He and Elizabeth went straight to the dining room, where Emily was in a red club chair by a roaring fire. She said she felt the cold after all these months in sunnier climes. 'England is Arctic, my dear,' she said, accepting kisses and a jar of jam. Like a royal, she immediately handed the gift to the person standing next to her, who happened to be Candy.

Campbell's mood had improved in the car. A little stoned, he felt something momentous was about to occur that evening and he wanted to be at his best. The room was as well appointed as any he'd ever seen in Belgravia. The chandelier wasn't like those in hotels or embassies: the old glass was clouded, a kind of vintage yellow, and the droplets of manganese had grown purple over the years.

The Duke entered with Friday's edition of the *Evening Standard*. He was wearing red cords and a frightful checked jacket, a green tie and a pheasant-portraying handkerchief spewing from his breast pocket. 'Bloody papers used to be on one's side,' he said to a row of candles on the fireplace. There was a red painting by Bhupen Khakhar above the mantelpiece; it depicted an Indian tailor on a chair sewing trousers, with striped shirts all around him and palm trees up in the air. Campbell had always loved the painting. He saw it anew, with the Duke huffing about underneath it. 'I mean, these degenerates, whoever they are. Journalists making up stories about one, it's insufferable.'

'Oh, do shut up, Anthony,' the Countess said. 'Have a whisky.' He wandered over like a wounded bear and kissed her hand, which she frailly withdrew. Seemingly oblivious to her action, she wiped it with a napkin.

'Well, really,' he said. 'What happened to Rothermere? Northcliffe? Both friends of my grandfather, as it happens. These men stood for things, you see – that's when a baron was a somebody. Nowadays, they think gossip is history and history is gossip. Never trust a man with tassels on his shoes, that's my motto.'

Candy handed him a drink, but otherwise ignored him. She was talking to Campbell. 'The plan is to rewild the estate in Inverness-shire.'

'Really?' he said, not interested.

'It's the deer, you see. They scoff everything. It's an absolute horror. One spends the entire time fencing off the glen.'

It never failed to amaze Campbell how Elizabeth's family, and all families of that sort, liked to bait, tease and insult each other as a way of dealing with the fact that they had to be close. They were mired in flippancy. 'You're looking devilish skinny,' the Countess said to Candy at one point. 'Won't you take an olive?'

'Heaven forfend,' the Duke blared. 'An olive!'

'I suppose you're rather above olives,' the Countess said.

'You know, I think I will,' Candy said, as if she were agreeing to dive naked into a swimming pool of cold custard. She plucked one from a glass dish and swallowed it with no apparent pleasure whatsoever.

'*Miss Peristalsis*,' the Countess said. 'One could practically follow the morsel through the whole depressing journey.'

'Mummy. Don't be cruel,' Elizabeth said.

The Countess took a healthy sip. She was wearing an astonishing white dress with fake ostrich feathers on the shoulders. She drew a cigarette from a purse and one of the waiters quickly came with an ashtray. The Duke had been mostly at Albany this summer, while Candy got on with her trees, her eco gin, her thyme-flavoured short-bread and fresh air body treatments. She was part of a new scheme called Some Like It Hut, providing beach holidays in Southwold for poor families who'd been stuck inside due to Covid.

There was a roar from down the hall. Emily appeared not to hear it.

'What the bloody hell was that?' the Duke asked.

'Cricket,' Elizabeth said.

'Have you seen anyone while in London, Emily?' the Duke asked.

'Heavens, no,' she said. 'I never see a soul. I'm here for three minutes. I'm seeing you all to tell you my news, then I'm off.'

Kenzie and Ashley-Jo came in trailing cool evening air and fresh lore from a celebrity charity event at Wimbledon. Campbell wasn't sure if they were now just friends or still something complicatedly more. Kenzie walked over and sat next to him.

'Tennis was *such* fun,' she said.

'Who played?' her mother asked.

'Pop stars and reality TV people,' Ashley-Jo interrupted. 'All in a good cause. Like, raising money for War Child.'

'Lawn tennis,' the Countess said. 'It used to be rather culpably placid. Hitting balls over the net and then going for tea.'

The first course came and Campbell learned from Kenzie that Angus was around. 'We saw him in the enclosure.'

'What, he's here in London?'

'Yeah,' Kenzie said. 'He—'

'He didn't say anything about coming,' Elizabeth broke in. 'He went down to Wimbledon with you?'

'Not with us,' Ashley-Jo said. 'It was a Ralph Lauren thing. They sponsored part of it and there was a lunch and stuff.'

'A lunch,' Campbell repeated.

'He was there with the new girlfriend,' Kenzie said. 'Astrid. Really bright.'

'How jolly. Are they coming here?' the Countess asked.

'She's big in sauce,' Campbell said wickedly.

'What did you say?'

'Sauce. Like HP. Ketchup, you know.'

'Oh, darling, not *sauce*,' the Countess said.

'It's chutneys, actually,' Ashley-Jo said. 'Like VIP condiments.'

'Oh, dear,' the Countess added. 'One really despairs nowadays over the things which may cause a person to be considered Very Important.'

They went back to talking about Wimbledon.

'The hospitality effort was first-rate,' A.J. said. 'Like, a pair of Ralph Lauren sunglasses at every place setting. One gives a bit of dosh. Yuri Bykov was there. He was in the enclosure with these MPs, not all of them Tories.'

'Welcome to modern Britain,' Campbell said, a feeling in his stomach. 'Reality TV tennis, and "not all of them Tories".'

The Countess speared a devilled egg. It wasn't clear she could hear everything that was being said, but she seemed quite content.

'Yuri Bykov was dabbing cocaine off his plate,' Ashley-Jo said, too loudly. 'And talking about Jake Hart-Davies, who's his friend. Someone had played him the recording of Jake giving some stupid interview . . .'

'It was nothing,' Campbell said. 'A load of blather.'

'For goodness' sake,' the Duke said, catching on. 'Mr Bykov is a decent businessman, interested in architecture.'

'He's a bit extreme,' Kenzie said. 'He behaves as if he's part of the 1930s beau monde, quite depraved. He knows people called things like Fruity Robbins. I mean, who in this day and age knows a person called Fruity?'

'That's quite dead in England,' the Duke said. 'The beau monde. It was killed, I'm afraid, by very common Americans, who spoil *everything*.'

Campbell made his way along the hall to the bathroom. In the mirror, his pupils were dilated and he felt as if he'd done something terribly wrong. Sometimes he was taken aback by aspects of his own hypocrisy. He felt he wasn't quite solid, and neither were the taps. The hand towel felt like vapour.

Coming out of the bathroom, he bumped into Angus in the hall, looking unlike himself in a light blue jacket and a striped tie.

'Hey, Pops. You look stressed. Everything all right?'

'Absolutely.'

His son seemed like vapour too – the residuum of an old argument. They hadn't seen each other since Iceland.

With a look of slight embarrassment, Angus introduced him to Astrid, and they did that thing of not knowing whether to hug or shake hands or stand back. He commanded himself to find the young lady charming and felt instantly bad for deciding she wasn't. She didn't help, with her first, wild conversational gambit: 'I gather you're some sort of commentator.' It was okay, he reasoned in the hopeless privacy of his stoical resentment, that he *himself* didn't know who he was, but it was quite insulting that other people shouldn't. Before they reached the table, Campbell realised it was the sort of idea that did him no credit, and Elizabeth – who was increasingly biting her lip – would no doubt have berated him for it.

'Ah,' the Countess cried as they entered the dining room. She waved Angus over for a kiss and merrily chattered out a sonnet. "Being your slave, what should I do but tend, / Upon the hours and times of your desire?"'

'Hey, Granny. What's up?' Angus said as he plonked himself down.

Somebody else did the introductions.

'So tell me, Astrid,' Elizabeth began, making an effort, 'how are you finding our capital city after all your travels?'

'I find London a bit intense,' she said.

Campbell took a moment to absorb the word.

Was life a series of densities, he wondered, that more or less excluded the possibility of one ever feeling natural?

Plates of chicken arrived, fragrant with cardamom.

Angus also started talking about Jake Hart-Davies on the radio. Campbell felt a lurch. He placed both hands on the table and struggled to keep a composed face. The Countess, sitting on his other side, gently placed her left hand over his right one. 'People after the tennis were talking about what he'd said,' Angus continued. 'Some of the celebs. That's the kind of shit they love at those gatherings. The guy's sailing close to the wind, no?'

He wiped his nose with the back of his hand.

'He needs to watch what he's saying,' Ashley-Jo piped in.

'Social media's going mad about it. I listened to it on my phone coming over. Didn't seem that bad. A lot of people say he's, like, speaking up for men.'

Angus looked up at his father. Then he looked at Elizabeth, but nothing came of it and he let it go.

'Of course, you are absolutely right,' the Countess said. 'The world's gone quite mad with self-pity and whatnot.'

Campbell heard the laughter but felt it was miles off.

'I'm really cross with these actors,' Kenzie was saying. 'I can't believe they say stuff like that.'

'Perhaps we shouldn't make such a carnival of people's mistakes,' Elizabeth said.

'Oh, *come on!*' Ashley-Jo replied.

'Discussion itself ought not to be cancellable.'

'Well said, Lizzie,' Candy offered.

'I agree with my wife,' Campbell said. 'I generally do.' When he raised his head A.J. was staring at him.

'You are a middle-aged white man,' they said. 'And that's that.'

'Strange, isn't it,' he replied, 'that so many of you, who are so multiple, insist that the rest of us be only one thing.'

'I'm sorry, Mummy,' Candy said. 'This must be terribly boring for you.'

'No, it's all jolly gripping,' the Countess said. 'I barely understand what they're talking about, but it's always lovely to see some fur flying, isn't it?'

When the pudding came, a pineapple thing that seemed to Campbell as if it had been waiting in the kitchen since 1953, a waiter brought the crème anglaise, and the Countess cooed over it and pronounced it decently lumpy. It was one of her traits to be greedy, most freely and reassuringly so, and she ate the pudding in four gulps, taken between puffs from a cigarette fastened into a holder. Angus insisted on boring everyone with a tin-eared account of a nightclub in Beirut. He had the hidden insecurity of the first-namer – everybody was 'Brad' or 'Pharrell', 'Miuccia' or 'Dua', and he used the same words again and again when talking about his girlfriend. 'She's incredible,' he said.

She was still sitting next to him.

'Amazing and *so* killing it. She's fire, right?'

The Duke suddenly exploded at the other end of the table. 'It's *amazing*. Everything is *amazing*. Dear God, Angus. What are you *talking* about? This life of yours! I promise you, I've seen broader shoulders on a boa constrictor. What's amazing is that you ponce about the globe doing absolutely bugger all, so far as one can tell, and get paid handsomely. A few months on the parade ground would sort you out, my boy. A bit of *formation*. You know, a friend of mine is taking that young Chatto into the Royal Marines. The boy was pissing about, like you, taking his shirt off on social whatsit, appearing at parties and so on. The Queen's great-nephew! Now he's getting it together. About bloody time.'

'Do shut up, Anthony,' the Countess said, again. She tapped the side of a glass with her spoon and after a moment the giggling stopped.

'Hear, hear,' Candy said.

Campbell felt a whirr of excitement. He was always on safe ground with Emily, and she was about to say something significant; he could sense it. Ever since Venice, there had been this idea that she would come home only once more, to put things in order. 'This won't take long,' she said, folding her napkin. 'I'm not standing up. I don't want to be a bore or make a huge speech, but there are things I must say. You will all be sick of me, I shouldn't wonder, but my late husband, David, was punctilious, and I've often felt guilty that I was not more so, with the houses and so on, but there we are. It can't be helped.'

Elizabeth, when he caught her eye, had the best expression in the world. She didn't care about any of it, and she didn't care that others did care, which was the true mark of her character and the proof of her settled nature.

'We came into this house in 1962,' Emily said. 'It was waiting for us, and it has always been a happy place.'

'It has,' Candy said, a bit weepily.

Her mother looked equal to the occasion.

'We were sensible, then,' she said. 'I believe we knew how to be happy. David was practical with the estate. We were joyful when the girls came along, and David was simply wonderful. Adored the girls. Rather good at Christmas and games and so on, all in this room. Giant tree. It all seemed rather far-fetched to me, but I was always delighted I didn't live in a regrettable little building in Hove.'

She flicked a feather away from her neck and drank from her glass.

'Anyway. Poor fish. David died and nothing was ever the same. I sold the other place, the paintings, and put the money into a trust. I live for the most part now on a gruesome boat that everybody despises and we go round the world. It's an obnoxious scheme, I suppose, but it rather bucks one up. And I shall be back there soon.'

She waved to the head waiter and he brought a square parcel.

'What fun,' the Duke said. 'Are we having games?'

'I don't mean to be grim,' she went on, 'but certain things require saying.' She looked at Kenzie and seemed faintly joyful. 'I have cancer. Don't ask me about it because it is too tedious, but I will soon die and that's that.'

'Granny,' Kenzie said.

'No, I *won't* have it,' she replied.

Several of them tried to discuss it, but Emily wouldn't engage. She said it was of no interest and repeated that her illness was terminal. 'But, Mummy,' Candy said, 'there are specialists, and we know of new treatments.'

'Oh, silly,' Emily said. 'There are no cures for the inevitable. We can enjoy ourselves pretending, but the thing is perfectly clear and—'

'But, Mummy, I can't stand it.'

Candy began to weep. There was a brief silence and Emily indicated that she'd have more wine. 'I'd like to talk about my affairs.'

'We needn't do that now, Mummy,' Elizabeth said.

'No, I want to.'

She joined her hands and twisted her wedding ring.

'You shall have this house, Kenzie,' she said. 'I am declaring this now so that there is no fussing later. It's all written down. Chester Street is yours and everything in it.' She looked into the pattern of the tablecloth. 'I hope my girls will understand. They have what they need. And they have it without my assistance, which is even nicer for them. One has to be sensible, here and there, and Kenzie has always loved the garden here.'

Campbell looked over. Kenzie was blushing and yet she was poised in success, a reluctant sort of victor but a very natural one. Elizabeth had taken her hand, and she brought it to her lips and kissed it.

The Countess seemed uncomfortable with the sudden seriousness of this gesture. 'Are you all right, Emily?' Campbell said to her.

'Never better, dear,' she said. And with that she pushed the parcel towards him and asked him to open it. 'Something for you.'

He took apart the string and the wrapping. It was a small and very decent Impressionist work by Gustave Caillebotte. Campbell recognised it as coming from the old manor house, and he breathed steadily as he inspected the labels on the back, seeing an early one from the Galerie Georges Petit and a later one from Christie's in New York. He sat it on the table before him and studied the strokes and the signature under the image, a pair of white kid gloves. There was a gleam to the pearl fastener at the wrist of the top glove, and a beautifully tarnished look. 'This is for you, Campbell,' the Countess said. 'It's one of the last of the half-decent paintings one held onto, and I pass it to you in recognition of your wisdom about art. Not hugely valuable, but there we are.'

'Thank you, Emily.'

He didn't know how to manage his face.

'You've been a friend to me,' she said. She looked through the window onto the road, as if to avert her eyes and avoid the possibility of censure. 'There's such a heavenly feeling of summer this evening. I think of the way you used to speak to me about Vermeer, the view of Delft and so on, the yellow patch.'

'It's all gone,' Campbell said, vacantly.

'Nothing's ever gone, if you like art, I suppose.'

She rambled on about his former subject. She wondered if the Jesuit order had any influence on Vermeer's moralistic outlook.

'It's all there,' he said, 'if you look closely at the paintings.'

A crack had opened in his mind and out of it rose a colony of bats, as if from some urban sinkhole at the base of his life. It did not help that he had suspected something of the kind might occur, but only with the final revelation can one really know the meaning of one's dread. In all the years of his marriage, he had believed that his multiple charms with Elizabeth's mother would one day save them from his pecuniary faults, and although he posed at being above money, he trusted her vast resources would banish the troubles he knew increasingly to surround him.

Looking up, he saw that Elizabeth was pleased for him about the Caillebotte and there was tenderness, but in this area she understood nothing. His face was now composed, but over the next few minutes he experienced a bottomless kind of shame as Emily told her family, most of whom did not care, that she was leaving the money in the trust and all her personal wealth to animal charities. 'There's a rather admirable place in Burford that takes care of dogs,' she said. 'Then there's the elephants, of course.'

'Are you serious?' Angus asked. 'You're leaving tens of millions to elephants? That's quite fucked, actually.'

'I don't believe so,' she said. 'They can set them free, that sort of thing. Maybe in another life one would happily *be* an elephant.'

'Oh, Mummy,' Candy said. 'That's so lovely.'

'It is what it is,' said Ashley-Jo.

Before they left that evening, Emily said she was tired. She smiled a very thin smile at Campbell and he was struck by the cruel pinkness of her eyes. 'I have enough experience to know that you're displeased with me,' she said.

'Don't be silly.'

'You don't admire the little painting?'

He kissed her softly on both cheeks, sensing her powdery scent as he straightened up and let go of her card-playing fingers.

'I think it's adorable,' he said.

When they got home that night, Campbell stood in the hall and detected something awful in the fetid air around him. 'I'll be up in a minute,' he said as Elizabeth mounted the stairs. She turned to him and there was a rather sad look in her eyes – he understood it to be pity, but it might have been love.

'Don't be long, darling,' she said.

'I just need a minute.'

'Is there anything we should talk about, Campbell?'

'No, everything's fine. Go on up.'

He vomited in the downstairs loo. And when he came out with his throat scorched, he went to the store cupboard and found his toolbox. That was what his father had left him, this blue toolbox full of old wooden-handled chisels and hammers. He looked at a tape measure bearing a faded yellow stamp: 'Gibson's of Paisley'. He went sniffing towards the front door, then he bent down. Pulling back the rug, he took one of the larger chisels and got it under a floorboard. He yanked it up. Then another. The smell coming from the cavity was noxious in the extreme. He could see light fixtures and tangled wires and could hear a loud TV programme from below about Egyptian mummies. He was holding his breath as he reached down, and eventually he touched a packet of something. He pulled it out and threw it down on the hall floorboards. It was an open box of rotting fish fingers. He could see movement and realised that the box was full of maggots.

# BOOK THREE
## Autumn

# 25 The Reporter's Art

Tara sat by the window in the canteen, looking down at the canal. It was mid-August and she reckoned it must be nice living on a barge at this time of year. A fleet of young ducks was following their mother through the water. The lunchtime conference was looming and she had to think of something. Listening to Marvin Gaye through her earbuds, she felt reality no longer belonged to reporters, yet Vietnam hadn't belonged to Marvin and neither had inner-city drug abuse, radiation poisoning or God. She tapped her pencil on her notepad and wrote the word 'cathexis', then its definition. 'The concentration of mental energy on one particular person, idea, or object (to an unhealthy degree).' That was certainly the way she'd felt about Rupert Chadley, the Latin-loving editor of the *Commentator*, who was now her boss but used to be her on-off boyfriend. He'd since got married to a woman who was keen on horses.

'Conference in ten.'

She heard his voice and turned. He was with the news editor and someone from *Friday* magazine, getting coffee. She removed her earbuds.

'Hey, Tara – see you upstairs? We need to escalate this Byre thing now. Bring your address book.'

'You mean this?' she said, lifting her phone. 'Duh.'

They'd returned to average banter. It was all you could do. He got to be moral leader and she was the determined, tireless newshound. Tara knew she was good, but she suspected in her deepest self that she lacked empathy. She went after stories that mattered, stories that revealed the wrongs of society, but only she really knew how relentlessly she went after them, and how objectively. Victims and perpetrators, it was all material, and she pursued it with a forensic but chilly application.

She edged onto a sofa in the conference room and looked down at her Smythson diary: annual present from Mum and Dad. They both taught English at Haverstock School and her father loved well-made, crafted things. 'Tara Hastings' was embossed in silver on the front, and she used the back pages for notes. Her parents still lived in Hampstead. She pictured them in their new TV room, watching the Proms with gin and tonics.

'August is silly season,' one of the editors was saying, 'but we happen to have some real stories. We're splashing on the fall of Mazar-i-Sharif.'

'The PM is under pressure to accept an influx of Afghan refugees.' This was David, the lobby correspondent.

'Okay,' Rupert said. 'That won't happen. Talk to Features. We have a source at the Foreign Office who is feeding us data—'

'About the Tory immigration nightmare?'

'Yes. Their massive reluctance to accept foreign nationals.'

'Afghans, anyway,' someone from Obits said.

'There's a report from Humanity United,' the Comment editor added, 'about the threats to Afghan women under the Taliban.'

Staff members shook their heads. There were interventions about photographs and opinion pieces, follow-ups and writers, then the news editor filled everybody in on smaller stories.

'Long-form piece in the mag,' someone said, 'off the back of the empty supermarket shelves, talking about the crisis in haulage, after Brexit and Covid. Big crisis in manufacturing overall. Brilliant story.'

Tara was watching the room to see if there was space for a larger conversation about the reported pieces she'd like to do. One of the paper's star columnists, Ed Carr, who boasted he wasn't a journalist but an activist, said the *Commentator* should be taking a stronger stand against the cost-of-living crisis. 'Furthermore to that,' he said, 'we should be doing more on the fallout from the incel outrage in Plymouth.'

'We are doing more,' Comment said. 'We have two pieces, including an essay by a leading author asking why it isn't considered terrorism.'

'That brings us to a difficult issue for the paper,' Rupert said. 'And I don't want any leaking from this room, okay? Not a word.' He used his outspread hands to silence the various moral authorities who tended to judge him weak. 'Quiet, please. Now, as usual, Antonia Byre will be submitting her column —'

The activists hissed. One of them actually said, 'Fascist.'

'Stop that,' Rupert said. 'Lifting off from Plymouth, she intends to write about mothers being blamed for everything.'

'Isn't she actually in favour of mass shootings?' someone asked.

There was laughter. 'On this occasion, no. She feels the shooter's hatred of women is crowned by his hatred of his own mother. She argues that this is the fault of psychoanalysis and more modern therapy. She makes the case —'

'Fucking hell,' the activist said. 'I don't suppose she offers an analysis of sexism within the family or argues for better conditions —'

'You know what to expect, Ed.'

'She's a total disgrace to this paper. A monstrosity. There's a petition to get her out – and you give her a microphone.'

'The readers like it. She's something different.'

'Yes, so is Hibatullah Akhundzada, Commander of the Faithful in Afghanistan.'

There was more laughter, and Ed Carr sat back, obviously delighted. He'd grown hot on a short career of pyrrhic victories.

Tara decided to say something. 'Wait, what? So she's a leader of the Taliban because she doesn't happen to agree with you, Edward?'

'Get a grip,' he said.

'This is a newspaper,' Tara continued, 'not the bulletin of your mates from Islington North. We go out and see what's there. We *report*.'

313

He waved her away. 'I respect you as a woman,' he said.

She crossed her legs and leaned forward.

'Why don't you fuck right off,' she said. 'I'm not asking to be respected "as a woman". I speak as a journalist. It's a profession.'

'So they say,' he replied.

Tara realised she hated him. He was patronising as fuck and had mobilised his own prejudices by posing as a liberator. She recalled doing an event for students with him at City University when he decried the readers of other papers.

'I think Tara comes from a different world from me,' he'd said, ramping up his accent. 'Her great-great-grandfather was Thomas Hastings, the 1st Viscount Cockburn.'

'Are you *serious*?' she had asked. 'You want to beat me up for having an obscure and moderately posh Victorian forebear?'

She remembered the chairman tried to intervene.

'Nah, nah – the thing is, right . . .' Edward butted in, 'the *Commentator* is not the kind of media outlet Tara Hastings would like it to be. We founded it online to give voice to sections of society that aren't being represented by the mainstream media, including by our sister papers, which aren't fully committed.'

'You want to make readers feel proud of their opinions rather than make them question their facts,' she'd said.

She was back in the room. Rupert was leading.

'I've heard all the rants before,' he said. 'We're running Antonia's column, but we'd like something to balance it on the page.'

'We'll talk about it later,' the Comment editor said to Edward.

'Our problem is Antonia's husband,' Rupert said. 'We've run all Tara's brilliant pieces about him, and he's now in serious trouble. Other papers have been following up on our scoops and it's been very good for us. But Tara is still receiving material from her sources, and we're getting very close to proving the allegations of sexual abuse.'

A low whistle went round the conference room.

'It's awkward, but we must press on. William Byre is now in Spain. He is wanted here for questioning relating to slave labour and financial corruption. The *Mail* is going bananas. We can't sit on the news obviously, but maybe—'

Ed Carr raised his voice. 'Am I losing my mind or what? How can she still be writing her column? You're kidding, aren't you?'

Tara was aware her eyes must be blazing. She wondered if her colleagues really did prefer the world as a toxic echo chamber.

'Why don't we fire her?' he went on.

'Eh, because we don't automatically blame the woman?' Tara said. 'Maybe that's part of what she wants to write about? We hold fire, until we know what the story is. I know that disappoints you, Edward. I know it really fucks you up that you can't immediately get into your firework display of execration.'

'Wow, "execration",' he said, to more laughter.

'Your orgy of cancelling.'

'Wow, "orgy",' he said.

'Okay, okay, *tranquillitas*,' Rupert said. 'This is an editorial conference, not the junior common room, and we need to make a plan—'

'I know what you're going to ask,' Tara said blankly.

Rupert continued. He had a habit of bending back each of his fingers as he counted things off. 'These sources have been brilliant. We've set out the allegations about his pension swindling. We've pointed to fraud. We've established that his companies may be using illegal migrant workers run by gangs. We're beginning to consider his possible links to questionable Russian businessmen. And now—'

'Here's the money shot,' Ed said.

'There are sex allegations against him.' Rupert folded his arms. 'We've got sources and women are coming forward.'

'And you'd like me to talk to them,' Tara said.

'Before other media gets to them. And perhaps there's mileage in looking at the effect this is having on Byre's family.'

'Oh, boohoo!' Ed said.

Tara ignored him and stared at the editor. 'Because I know his son?'

'Of course you do,' Ed said.

She turned her head. 'Zak's a friend of mine from Oxford. Plus he's one of the most talented rebels in the country. He's been making brilliant arguments for decarbonisation. Really, I thought he'd be a friend of yours, Ed. Or don't you have any friends?'

'Not ones from families like that,' he said.

Tara went back to her corner of the newsroom. She had a row of journalism books on her desk, propped up at one end by a trophy from the *Press Gazette*. She stared at her computer, then out at King's Cross and the former gasworks. Some day, all this blaming would be recuperated into more meaningful forms of change, but by then the *Commentator* would be gone. Still, she hoped that a long-form piece of reporting might arise from the Byre scandal. She had an inkling: she always did with terrific stories. Her source had been giving her inside material, but the next few steps would be her own. She'd made nothing of it in her reporting so far, but yes, she knew Byre's son, Zak. He didn't like his dad. He'd told her once that his old man was determined to destroy the planet. She pulled up Zachary Byre's Instagram: 'Activist. Writer. Academic.'

Seven hundred and eighty-six posts. 230k followers. 587 following.

His latest post featured a bird against an Extinction Rebellion symbol. 'The Science Is Clear, Our Future Is Not,' it said in black letters. Underneath, a message: 'From wildfires to heatwaves, droughts to rising sea levels, the symptoms of our inaction will only worsen. #needtoactnow #extinctionrebellion #climatecrisis.' Further back, there were photographs from many of the actions he'd helped organise, famous ones, where paint was thrown at statues or Tube trains were mobbed. She liked his face, the dedication and intelligence that seemed to shine from it, and she liked the touches of humour he brought to the seriousness of what he did. 'Milkfed' it said across his chest in one picture, where he and a crowd of breastfeeding mothers blockaded Google's offices.

She'd asked him for quotes in the past, before she started writing about his father. She found an email he'd sent her a couple of years before, when he first became known as a climate-change activist and she was covering one of the big marches. 'My whole upbringing was a lie,' it said. 'We have no future. We are going to collapse. It is coming towards us, the catastrophe our parents made for us and now pretend isn't real. Civil disobedience is the only choice we have as rational creatures.'

She searched Zak on Twitter, finding adverts he'd posted for webinars on 'Class Privilege and Activism', 'Resource Generation' – 'Stop hiding your privilege and use it for social revolution' – and posters for an English action group called Meritocracy Lies. Tara took notes and followed all the links.

Back in her email again there were two messages from her source.

'William Byre bought a flat in Granville Square for a 23-year-old woman called Victoria Gowans. Eyes on deeds, messages, etc. Attached.'

'Byre = friend of the Bykov crew. Look at money from offshore accounts to Saudi contractors for shopping malls.'

Weeks before, she'd seen emails from women who had worked for Byre, attesting to his groping and acts of violence. She'd also seen a much more powerful memo from a former personal assistant of Byre's who was sexually harassed by him, and who separately alleged he had bought a flat for a vulnerable young Scottish woman named Gowans, who was also abused by him and coerced into keeping silent.

All from freshislands@outlook.com.

She knew how to peg out a story, how to master the facts, how to research the geography and the public records before pursuing the unknowns. She spent an hour cutting and pasting a few more entries from *Who's Who* and rummaging through old Cambridge magazines, looking for Byre and his generation. She added to her list of his colleagues, business associates, friends and employees. Eventually, she wanted to write something deeper and longer than her news stories, something that might explore the culture of permission around a man who could harass women in public and hit them in private.

'Hey, Zak. It's Tara Hastings. Urgent, I guess. Can you call me back?'

He got back to her within thirty seconds.

'You calling about Dad?'

'Yeah,' she said. 'The paper's going to the next level.' She said her thing, telling him she'd reported on it with honesty and no bias. This latest stuff, his treatment of women, was something she was determined to cover, but fairly.

'Look, Tars,' he said. 'His behaviour has gone far enough. He's a total fucking dinosaur stalking the earth before the Ice Age, know what I mean?'

She didn't, but she said yes. She pressed her Call Recorder app. 'I'm now recording this conversation, but I won't use any of your words directly if you don't—'

'Use it all, babe. I'm not covering for him any more.'

'Really?'

'Time really is up,' he said, 'and I need to bear honest witness to this shit, or else be part of it. My mother and father don't see any value in what I'm doing with my life, so what's to be gained by giving my protection to them rather than these women?'

'It's a big moment, Zak.'

'What can I tell you?'

He said he didn't know much about the Russian debts. 'But the women . . . the women he's been messing around for years . . .'

'Slow down, Zak. Can we meet?'

'I think you should talk to one person in particular. She was, like, his most recent girlfriend. Claimed to love her and all that, but he abused her. I've got her number. Go onto Signal – I'll message you.'

'What's her name?'

'Vicky Gowans. She wrote to me.'

'She wrote to you?'

'Yeah, yesterday. She says he totally mugged her off. I don't know if she'll speak to you, but other girls are coming forward.'

'No, I'd like to speak to *that* girl.'

They made a plan for that evening, then he hung up. She went onto Signal and after ten minutes, he sent her a message. 'This is the girl's number,' he wrote. 'I spoke to her. She's coming to my place tonight at 7 p.m. So you don't have to call her. Come to mine. Penthouse Apartment 103, GH11, Gasholder Park. Off Stable Street.' In Zak's very productive way, he then sent a further three messages. 'Concierge will show you up.' 'Don't bring anything.' 'You've not been here. It's jokes. Don't judge me, okay?'

He's arrived at his moment, Tara thought. Even his distrust of the media was suspended now by his determination to make a difference. For all the roadblocks and arrests, the deeper, painful rebellion, she felt, lay in his unwillingness to let the old story continue. She made her notes with the thought that it was his own house this time that he was sinking into the Thames.

Charlo Sullivan and Gerry O'Dade were often at opposite sides of the North Sea, but, that beautiful summer's day, both of them had parked at a truck stop on the M25. Gerry was walking to the table with a tray from Burger King; he was all about the food voucher that came with the parking at Moto Services. 'It's not amazing value, like,' he said to Charlo as he sat down, 'but nobody's going to argue with a free burger for your thirty-five quid. Parking's always a cunt.' This was their usual meeting point, the roadside services in Thurrock, and they'd both been there overnight. Charlo had tipped a load from France at one in the morning, down by the landfill site, then he'd mucked out, but his container was still packed with biscuits, twenty-odd pallets of Crimble's, which he would unhook after breakfast for Gerry to take to Reading.

'Bout ye?' Charlo said back.

Gerry leaned over and turned his friend's tray. 'What the fuck, Charlo? *Nutty Super Wholefood Salad?*'

'I have to stop eating shite, man. It's, like, every day last week. Subway. McDonald's. TGI Friday and all that bollix. *Baguettes.* Six *croque-monsieurs.* About twenty cans of Red Bull and a feckan shit-ton of cheese.' He took a swig from a bottle of M&S Blackberry and Elderflower Pressé.

'Get wired in, Charlo. Yer a fat bastard.'

'Fuckit, Gerry. I'm twenty-six. Telling ye. Two stone by Christmas. Three stone by next summer. I want to fit into my new watch.'

'La, you'll be like Tom Holland at the finish.'

'Fuck off, mate.'

They never knew each other before haulage, but had grown up near to the town of Lurgan in County Armagh. Both of their old men were farmers, though Gerry's got into driving trucks in the 2000s. That was his childhood, and Charlo's too, he later found out: driving tractors at thirteen, the school jumper covered in sawdust and chicken blood and the wellies steeped in diesel and cow shite. You got all the stories about the Provos and the Troubles, and the other ones on Charlo's side: the border songs, the border fears, the border slayings and the love of contraband. Back then, there was always stuff coming over, something to buy or sell in the pub, and now the boys did it all through texting and Facebook, and living it large across Europe for Bozydar. They still had their old pals back in Lurgan and Lisburn and Craigavon, the boys still working on the farms or up in the factories, but the likes of Gerry and the bold Charlo were driving the fancy cars and had all the gear from France, and the girls back home liked all that.

'I'm leaving this soon,' Gerry said. He sucked through a straw. 'I'll give it to next Easter, then I'm done. I'll take the money. I'd rather have a wee driving job back home and can watch films at night, know what I mean?'

'Sure, you can get a job anywhere now.'

'They're getting fifty-six thousand a year, Charlo. The super-markets, I'm telling you, they're gagging for hauliers.'

'I know,' Charlo said. 'I'm after turning down a job at Goggins. I don't know what they're paying but it'll be high, so it will. I'm not ready to stop this yet. A few more of these crossings.' He signalled with his bottle to the car park.

People were coming into the service station with their kids. Dads in shorts and young ones with plastic buckets and spades.

Charlo lowered his voice.

'Boz and Stefan are doing more migrants. "Ambassadors." Bigger numbers. There's going to be decent money in it.'

'Not for me,' Gerry said. 'Vodka and fegs is fine, but this is a head-fuck. More stops – the guards arresting the drivers.'

Charlo ignored this and stared at his breakfast salad. He was a risk-taker – but the salad was too much and he went off for a bacon roll. When he returned, he squeezed the top of the roll hard and then took a bite, talking at the same time. 'How much do you know about the Chinese man?' he said.

Gerry pondered. 'Just the name. The ambassadors all ask about him, as if he's a place on the map. Businesses everywhere, I reckon, earning millions.'

'So long as I get me money.'

'Ah, you're full of brains, Charlo.'

Charlo made a go for Gerry's fries and got his arm punched.

'Come on, man. I'm a growing lad.'

'You're a feckin animal. What time's your Rotterdam crossing?'

'Check-in at 4.30,' said Charlo. He looked at his second phone. 'Yeah. Boz's sent me the code for the ticket. So I've got a full day of Netflix in the yoke. I think I might go "fuck it", like – sausage roll from Greggs, a bag of Krispy Kremes and rewatch season two of *Peaky Blinders*. Where's the danger in that?'

# 26 Gasholder Park

Vicky kept the box but sold the bracelet. She had never seen a green like it. 'There's a place in Belize,' William had said to her, 'where the water's green like your eyes, like these emeralds, and I'm going to take you there one day.'

'Aye, right,' she said to herself.

He was going to move in with her.

They were going to hide from the world.

He hadn't contacted her for five weeks and all the trees in the square had turned lovely. She'd expected to buy a suitcase for the first time and fill it with summer tops, to go to Spain with him.

She thought of the way he'd held her hand and began to crush it. That was the way with him, then he disappeared.

She sat on the sofa looking into Granville Square, wearing the jersey saying '1977' he'd bought her in that shop in Marylebone. She liked to watch the kids playing on the swings and feeling feart for them if it went too high.

He was going to sell what was left of the businesses.

Nobody would find them.

Five weeks. Unanswered calls. Just ghosted her. She'd been going to Finsbury Library and using one of their computers to read every story about him, falling asleep at the desk sometimes.

She'd been dreaming about her mum ever since. She hadn't seen her in eighteen months, but she thought of her up there in Ayrshire, at the top end of Stevenston, walking down from the Hayocks and along Keir Hardie Road on her way to work. There was a ruin she'd played in up there when she was wee: Kerelaw Castle, hidden in the trees, next to a burn. That's where she'd had her first drink and her first snog and her first everything. Her mum told her one night, when they were having a heart-to-heart, that there used to be a borstal in the field on the other side of the burn. The boys in the school would sometimes escape at night, and she hung about with one. That was Vicky's father. Later, there was a scandal at the school, and they tore it down, her mum said, when Vicky was about eight.

She never saw him again. The boy's name was Sean.

Vicky shook as she sat smoking on the sofa. She was on gab-apentin for the shaking and propranolol for anxiety. Then they gave her Seroquel for insomnia, though she still took a few wee hits of heroin, to keep her steady. Vicky looked at her phone again and read the son's message for the umpteenth time.

'It would be lovely to meet with you tonight. Sorry about everything. I guess we've all been let down by Sir William Byre.'

Walking down King's Cross Road, she noticed every stranger. She crossed by the Scala and went up Caledonian Road. In the three years she'd been in London, Vicky had never been to anybody's house. That's a lie. She went to a party in a squat in Camden once and the place was trashed – but she'd never stayed overnight, except in a hotel or a hostel, and she'd never gone to any of those plays that were advertised on the sides of buses, a random thought that made her feel like a failure. Walking down to the canal, she saw a group of older boys sitting on a bench with their bikes lying around them. One of the guys was wearing a flash jacket and he puffed on a joint and stared at her as she passed.

'Y'awright?' she said.

She wasn't afraid of boys.

'Yeah, man.'

As she walked by the barges she heard the same guy's voice behind her. 'Did you see her eyes, man? They were like so green, for real.'

She came up at Coal Drops Yard and started looking for signs. She could see the gasholders and walked round until she reached GH11.

The man sitting at the desk got up and opened the door. 'I'm meant to be here,' she said. 'I'm supposed to be meeting Zachary Byre.'

'Mr Byre,' the man said.

'Like, on the top floor.'

'Of course, madam. May I have your name?'

'Vicky Gowans,' she said.

He went back to the desk and looked at a book, then he picked up a telephone and it seemed like he got the okay. 'Let me show you the lift.'

There was a pot of umbrellas, then a marble staircase, and the lifts were all mirrors. He pressed a button and told her to walk round the rotunda and press doorbell 103. She was nervous going up and considered coming back down, running to King's Cross, forgetting she ever wrote to this guy, or ever met his father. In the lift mirrors, she saw she was crying and she wanted something badly – something more than thoughts, something brown that would bubble on a spoon, and Jesus it was all so hard.

Tara Hastings had come straight from her office. She pressed the doorbell at 103.

'Hello, you,' Zak said, as he opened the door. 'How's the culture wars?'

'I dunno, Zak.' Stepping in, she accepted a peck on both cheeks. 'It's summertime. I think the culture war is being run from the Gunton Arms in Norfolk and from the Fowey Harbour Hotel in Cornwall.'

'Take your coat off,' he said, 'and have a drink.'

His place was beyond: a Bauhaus lair in the Kasbah, all modernist rugs and geometric paintings, none of which, Tara knew, would have been chosen by Zak. (She later learned that you got £800,000 off the price if you decided to take it *sans* decor.) But she knew her stuff. A handmade light feature from Atelier Schroeter, a kind of Alexander Calder, which set the tone for the whole apartment, was hanging above the bronze internal stairs. From there it was Dubai-chic-by-numbers: the Paul Smith rugs and the African masks and the cow-hide chairs from Timothy Oulton, standing to bleak social attention around an oak dining table. McQueenishly, there were brass moths on the pendant lights, and piles of oversized books on marble tables – *Louis Vuitton*, *Brassaï*, *Agnes Martin*. Tara wondered what it would be like to step into a lifestyle where nothing was yours. She peered past the potted plants to see a stainless steel kitchen. 'Good Lord,' she said.

'It's ridiculous,' he said.

'If I didn't know you better, Zak, I'd say you were one of those who are into yacht-based radicalism.'

'Give me a fucking break,' he said.

The shutters were open. King's Cross seemed like a backcloth. The coppery lighting and the interior decor made everything distant. 'Upstairs, above the bedrooms, there's a roof terrace where you can see London forever.'

'And downstairs?'

'Conference rooms. Sauna.'

He poured her a glass of wine. He said he was using the penthouse as a sort of headquarters for the new insulation movement, then he'd flog it. It was good for meetings. He said some contradictions take longer than others to iron out.

He looked tired and overworked. He shone with a kind of moral vitality, while seeming like he might need a wash.

She did a 'whatevs' shrug.

'We'd better . . .'

He pointed in the direction of the sitting room. 'She arrived a while ago and we're sitting through here.'

The young woman was on a grey sofa with too many cushions, awkwardly holding a glass. The hellos were easy. Tara thought she had the most beautiful face, her expression irked, like an angel expelled into a world of borrowed, expensive light.

Her hand was shaking and she put down the glass. Zak came in and sat on a metal chair with black-and-white images of old King's Cross behind him.

'I'm really sorry,' Vicky said to Zak, 'for your family and everything . . .'

'None of this is your fault,' Tara said.

'Totally not,' Zak added.

He was sweet to her, and – through a sort of good manners – appeared to shoulder some of the guilt and responsibility for his father's actions. He was awkward, though. Zak's mind worked in global terms, and there was something so small and solitary about the young woman in his sitting room, something so bitten and shy, that he seemed to struggle to fit her into his comprehension of the scale of human wrongs. He spoke kindly and with a sense of culpability, as if all people, all men anyway, must accept their part in messing up the world, and he wanted to apologise from a seat of tranquil reason. 'From what you told me, it sounds like you were coerced by my father into having a relationship.'

'Well. I really liked him.'

'What he's done is shameful,' Zak said.

Tara intervened. 'Zak. Let's take our time.'

'He would hit me, then buy me stuff,' the girl said. 'But I think I wanted somebody to hit me. I feel daft saying that, but it's true.'

Zak became quiet for a moment. Tara sensed these details sent shock-waves into personal places he'd never talked about or really known.

Vicky began to speak about her time in London, coming down with nothing and feeling independent and then feeling trapped. She said that she should have been grateful to meet a man like him, who was really nice to her sometimes and told her he loved her, and that him getting angry now and again wasn't the worst thing.

'I need you to understand . . . I'm a journalist. You can tell me whatever you like, and I don't have to use your name.'

At such moments, Tara always felt a little high on adrenalin. She could hear the beginnings of a big scoop in what Vicky was saying, and her wish to protect the source was already under siege from her reporter's instincts. 'I would like to record this conversation, if you don't mind. I won't use it until we agree.'

'That's no bother,' Vicky said.

Tara knew how to unravel people. It was a slow, shameless task, especially with Zak in the room and all his moral expansiveness. It became clear that Byre had abandoned Vicky Gowans after mistreating her, and the young woman didn't know what to do with herself, except to contact his family. As she spoke, Tara scribbled in her notebook with a fixed smile. 'Green eyes. Sore lip. Blue chipped nail polish.' She knew there was something merciless in her noticing – focusing on the detail, the story, when what the woman so obviously needed was a hug and a decent meal, a friend. At one point, Zak went out of the room and returned with a bottle of Don Julio tequila.

'No, Zak,' Tara said. 'No more booze. Vicky is talking about important things. I don't want the interview to be blurred by alcohol.'

Vicky asked Zak a question about his work. They'd clearly been talking about it before Tara arrived, and Tara could see, as he spoke, how tender he was about it, and how proficient he must be as a campaigner. 'It's the future of humanity,' he said, as if giving Vicky time to gather herself for the main part of the interview. 'I'm happy to go to jail for it, because that's where true dissidents should be, to promote the cause.'

'Is it really that bad?' Vicky asked.

He tightened his lips and showed his dimples. He couldn't help being serious and hurt. 'Millions of people will die in the next two generations,' he said. 'The killing of the planet's poorest people, burned off the map or drowned. And to think we should avoid the seriousness of that fact to protect a few elites, a few reputations, is unreal. My family is literally insupportable, and what they care about, profits and social standing, will come to seem nothing. There is only one story today and we should all be in rebellion.'

'He's really clever,' Vicky said, looking at Tara.

She was holding her hand to stop it from shaking. 'You're so nice. And it's hard to talk about your dad with you here. My mammy would pure kill me if she knew anything about all of this that I did. She's a really nice person. She didnae bring me up to take anything off of people, so she didnae.'

'I'm going to leave you with Tara,' Zak said. 'You'll be safe with her. I'll be down at Coal Drops Yard if you want me.'

'Thank you, Zak,' Tara said.

He opened the window and turned the lights down as he left the room.

In the brown light, Vicky told her story. Byre forced her to have sex with him when she didn't want to and had told him so. He refused condoms. He hit her when he was frustrated with work problems and once he knocked her head against a door. She said it was probably because she wasn't clever enough and wasn't up to his standards. With bitten fingers, she tucked her red hair behind her ears. It was obvious the young woman was using drugs. Tara could see how vulnerable the victim was, and recognised, in those little surrenders of pain to the greater good, that the exposure might harm her, and leave her even more isolated than before. Yet Tara was on a mission of her own, and hearing the worst about this man she'd pursued for the last two years, she circled phrases in her posh notebook – 'he bit my arm', 'he bought the flat' – while the tears brimmed in Vicky's eyes.

Nowadays, in August, William preferred the clear water at Cala Deià, the smooth boulders underwater and the sense that the sky belonged to him. After his swim, he always took lunch at La Residencia, loving the drive back to Port de Sóller. He owned a Moorish villa with red arches and furnishings that had been sourced once upon a time by Christopher Gibbs. He loved the feel of the cool tiles under his warmed feet. He hadn't responded to calls from the journalist on the *Commentator* saying she was about to run a new story. He knew what it was and he ignored it. Idiotic, like so many of the stories about him. But here, twelve hours later, was a text from Antonia: he was a national pariah, and it was over. For the first time ever, it seemed, she found herself in agreement with her colleagues.

He texted her immediately from the veranda. He wasn't ready for her voice. 'Was it that little bitch that wrote it? That friend of Zak's?'

No reply.

'Outrageous CRAP. She's saying I raped her?'

Nothing.

'What should I do?' he texted, with a shrug emoji.

'Em, go fuck yourself?' she replied immediately.

'Don't be like this. She was just a girl.'

He could see she was typing.

There were no more words from her. She simply sent a link to the infamous legal firm of Payne Hicks Beach LLP.

He was in debt to his own companies, and to the Russians, but the divorce lawyers: a whole new ballgame.

'I can close any deal,' he said to himself.

Llorenç and Carla, his Spanish helpers, began packing his bags.

His PA in London summoned the jet.

From a white sofa in the sunroom, he stared out, smoking a cigar. He thought of Vicky's eyes, her youth. Maybe he'd got her wrong. She had problems, and perhaps he shouldn't have given her so much so quickly. People can be unbalanced by having too much. Perhaps he'd been rough and that was unfortunate, but he had, he told himself, cared about her. He watched the cigar smoke rise into the white drapes, the sun revolving. It was quite boring the way people insist on becoming hysterical.

Descending into Northolt that afternoon, he folded his copy of the *FT* and stirred the last of his Negroni. The steward took his glass and asked him to fasten his seatbelt.

'Mercedes on arrival where to?' a text from his assistant said.

The person William thought of was Campbell – he often did at times like this. His friend had a good ear and was intelligent but not judgmental. Campbell's failings were obvious: he was needy for approval, he had no instinct for power, none at all, and he had what William called the mentality of the small borrower. Yet, all his life, whenever William felt nobody would talk to him and he had nowhere to go, he went to Campbell Flynn. So he texted to say he was flying back to the UK and needed to see him.

When they landed, he had to take a flow test and wait. Eventually, there was a cold reply from Campbell. It didn't have any of his usual salutations. It said William needed a lawyer and should go directly to see Moira.

'Your sister Moira?'

'That's right,' Campbell texted back. 'Doughty Street Chambers.'

Moira was flicking through the newspapers that were spread out on her desk. A colleague came in to ask for advice on a forthcoming deposition in Florida, and then one of the clerks wanted her to sign somebody's leaving card. After that, she picked up her phone and took a call from her brother.

'Have you seen it?' he said.

'On the *Commentator* website, yes.'

He was quiet for a moment. Campbell was always quiet when he had too much to say, and she knew instantly that he was struggling.

'He raped that young woman. Paid her off. It's breaking my mind, Moira.'

'Take your time. It's a shock.'

'What would you do if your best friend did that? Somebody you'd made excuses for and defended . . . somebody—'

'Don't fret, Campbell.'

He sounded almost tranquilised. 'I've always known he was . . . brutal and . . . I passed over it . . .'

'No. You had faith in him. It was misplaced.'

His voice went very small, and she could recall hearing him like that only once before, the day their father died.

'I am not *that guy*,' he said.

'Of course you're not.'

She could hear the change, a crisis completed, and after that day, she would feel he was never really the same Campbell again.

'I can't be sure I've ever really known anybody in my life,' he said.

'You mustn't read it like that.'

'I have to go,' Campbell said. 'My research assistant is here and we're working today.'

She had lunch at her desk. She had housing business to attend to, and just before 2.30, there was a knock at her door.

'I'm sorry to barge in,' her clerk said. 'But there's a man in reception. It's *him*.'

'Who?'

'William Byre!'

Moira made a quick internal call, then she gave instructions to her clerk. 'Show him up,' she said.

She had a flashback to her first memories of him. Byre and her brother had been the odd couple at Cambridge, Campbell darting and quicksilver, publishing reviews in the *TLS* and running supper clubs, while William played the part of the right-wing thug, sucking up to Roger Scruton, quoting Thatcher. He had been coarse, exploitative, capable of advertising emotions he didn't actually feel, and already an ace at objectifying women.

'Hello, the Right Honourable Moira Flynn MP, QC.'

He walked into the room with his hands open.

'Do not sit down,' she said.

'Your brother texted me. He said I should come in to see you.'

'*Campbell?*'

She tried to work it out on the spot. She didn't believe it.

'I need a lawyer. I'm not guilty,' he said.

'Please don't say any more.'

'But Campbell said—'

'I have no idea . . . I don't do these kinds of cases.'

He sat down in a chair. It was clear that he didn't believe her.

'It is not appropriate for you to be here,' she said.

She picked up her mobile, went into recent calls and pressed Campbell's name. 'He's here,' she said when he answered. 'At my office.'

'Who?'

'*William.* He says you sent him to me.'

'Why in the name of fuck would I do that?'

'What's he playing at?' she said, turning to her visitor. 'He says you texted him.'

Campbell paused for a good long time. 'It wasn't me,' he said.

Moira stared into William Byre's face.

She told her brother she'd call him back.

'And you think Campbell is so innocent,' Byre said, as she lowered her mobile. 'So clean. He should consider the truth before sending me to talk to you.'

She was trying to think.

'My brother's world is his own.'

'And who do you think helped him into that world, Moira?'

She sat down and folded her hands on her desk. The man was repulsive – the kind of person who was accustomed to his fury leading to action.

'Nonsense,' she said. 'Elizabeth has money. Her family —'

'He's ever so proud. You hardly know your own brother. Nobody knows him. You have no idea how much debt he has. *Personal* debt.'

'Please stop talking.'

She never imagined he'd taken money from Byre. Everything Campbell touched turned to gold, didn't it?

'He always had talent,' Byre was saying from the armchair, 'but I helped Campbell become the man he is today.'

Moira walked to her door and calmly opened it. She was relieved that several of her colleagues had gathered on the other side.

'Don't be ridiculous,' Byre said, abruptly standing up. Moira saw the rage in his eyes as she left her office and locked him in, ready for the police.

# 27 The Convergence of the Twain

It was while filming the final episode of *Aethon's Curse*, 'Dance of the Blades', that Jake Hart-Davies realised he was too big for acting. He was in Belfast Harbour Studios at the time, preparing to wrestle with a giant prehistoric frog called Beelzebufo, when he remembered that he had been born to play Hamlet or to write an era-defining novel. Instead, the make-up and costume girls were coating him in supernatural gunk, plucking his eyebrows, padding out his crotch and blow-drying the fur around his hood.

The disaffection remained in the middle of August, yet he still had hopes as an actor. Now he was down in Dorset, on the edge of a steep incline of enhanced trees and painted gorse, with high water cannons spraying the scene to indicate a deluge. 'This could be my last,' Jake said to himself as he nudged past extras to get to his trailer. Yet he couldn't resist investing heavily in the part he was playing, the titular character in a new adaptation of Thomas Hardy's *The Return of the Native*. Like Hardy's Clym Yeobright, he had returned from Paris, from everything, to blind himself with reading, and he was set to become a labouring man in touch with the pagan land. Closing the trailer door at his back, undoing his Victorian silk tie and bending down to choose one of his herbal teas, the actor, now author, said one of his lines: 'I will invade some region of singularity, good or bad.' And with that he leaned over for his phone and removed his Victorian spectacles. His eyes focused on a line of books above the sofa, three of them works by Campbell Flynn.

Things had kicked off at a Bournemouth hotel last night. Jake had a 5 a.m. call, but a number of the other cast members and crew had decided to destroy the bar until midnight, before taking it up to one of the rooms. The ringleader, as always, was Archie Todd, the coke-head son of a well-known chef, who had gone into acting after being in a TV boy band. Archie was last seen ordering six espresso Martinis to his room at 4 a.m. He tried to climb down a drainpipe to get away from a producer, and by the time his car came to take him to the set, he was barricaded in another room, drinking the minibar and crying on the phone to his mum. Trouble was, the bosses from Netflix were due to visit the next day to see how the production was going. Jake said to the first assistant director, mid-morning, that despite all the Druid energy floating about, this was perhaps not the best day to go full Glasto. Archie by then had his therapist on the phone and the actress playing Eustacia was having issues with her back, plus a few of the farmhands were talking about union rules.

'I'm not interested,' Jake was saying on the phone. 'I have lines to learn. I have to get my head into the space, man. It's fucking stupid.'

The Scottish actor on the other end of the line was passing on the message that Archie had now been persuaded to return to the set. There was a hitch, though. Archie felt vulnerable, he was sick as a dog, he wasn't ready to play the part of the Wessex reddleman, but said that he could cope if an AA meeting could be convened behind the catering truck. 'Listen,' the Scottish actor said to Jake, 'I've got the Big Book here. The Netflix guys are on their way. We've pumped a load of Valium into the wee man. He promises he can shoot this afternoon if we can get a meeting organised. Will you chair it?'

'This is madness,' Jake said. It wasn't that it was comical-tragical, tragical-comical, it was psycho-mystical, it was auto-fictional. He'd sooner be running for office.

'I know, buddy,' the Scots actor said. 'He's a wee shite, so he is.'

'I'm done with this crap,' Jake said. 'I've been standing in a field all morning waiting for Josey to deal with her ghost lumbago. And Dash is crying in his trailer because he spent last night fucking a farmboy, despite loving his wife.'

'I know. It's totally nuts.'

'Yesterday, we lost the afternoon because a bunch of loons at Gaunts Park were clay-pigeon shooting and wouldn't stop.'

'Well, it is hard to film when there's a lot of noise.'

'Oh shut up, Kevin. I'm here in my trailer. I'm learning my lines. I'm doing some interviews for the radio. I'll be ready to shoot a scene when somebody comes to get me and tells me there's a fucking actor in this fucking madhouse who can work. If nobody comes by four o'clock, I'm fucking off back to London. Fuck Thomas Hardy. Fuck the director. Fuck Archie Todd and fuck fucking Netflix.'

His publicist had left a folder on top of the draining board; it was full of printed-out requests to do with his self-help book, *Why Men Weep in Their Cars*. The *Spectator* was asking him if he'd like to write a column. *The Weekend Politics Show* was currently on holiday, the email said, but it would consider coming back to do a one-off special looking at the possible 'myth' of male toxicity. There were messages from Sky Documentaries, from the Royal Television Society about a lecture, from a writer at *New York* magazine suggesting an interview, and from Oprah. The requests from radio talk shows were on a separate list, many from libertarian shock jocks, or from right-wing broadcasters, Sean Hannity, Dan Bongino, Dana Loesch, inviting the actor to 'defend guys' against the 'fake accusations' of the moment.

He did two interviews at around lunchtime. He was definitely growing in confidence and perhaps in stridency; he could use the book, and his own knowledge of art and human behaviour, to say something brand new. 'If you look at BLM,' he said to Chad Benson on Radio America, 'you see male decency. You see leadership. Undermining male role models has not been good for families in America. If you look at *King Lear*, it's not *King Leanne*, okay? Shakespeare understood that there was a universal pressure on men to lead the pack and to fulfil the obligations of nature.'

'The obligations of nature?'

'Sure! I'm not afraid to say it. People can drag men down if they want, but *Why Men Weep in Their Cars*, yeah, it says you can go too far. You want to think about who the real enemies are before you start flying into buildings.'

Every time he spoke, the quotes went viral. He'd seen a parody of himself on TikTok, saying terrible things in a steady actor's voice: 'The poet William Shakespeare was clearly of the view that women were essentially evil.' He couldn't understand it. He was only saying what he believed to be true and what everybody said in private. By mid-afternoon, the unit publicist was getting fewer calls about Archie Todd than about Jake's latest remarks. Was he really saying that men were born to rule and women were born to be ruled? Was he saying terrorists should find better targets?

'Holy fuck, man,' his manager texted him. 'Did you just compare women who call out rapists to the hijackers on 9/11?'

Jake called him back.

'What the actual fuck, dude?' Dylan said.

'Don't you start. It's all a load of bollocks. All I said is that leadership's a thing and people should consider—'

'I know what you said, man.'

'Are you seriously giving me grief about a stupid thing on talk radio?'

'The whole world is giving you grief, dude. Toxic male behaviour is not justifiable.'

'I never said that.'

This was just another moment's hysteria, Jake told himself, that was all.

'Okay,' Dylan said, demonstrating his grasp of the new reality. 'If we handle it right, all this can be turned to our advantage.'

When Jake had fucked up at the Globes, saying something insensitive about how their filming in Africa was a gift to the Africans, it was Dylan who had taken on the challenge of clearing it up. He insisted that BAFTA hire an interviewer of colour as the chair for its platform event with Jake, and he told *Esquire* to find a black photographer for its cover story. Dylan knew how to fight your corner: actors' rights are human rights too.

Jake made a few non-apologetic remarks and then hung up.

The thinking had made him hungry. He got a bowl of noodles from the catering van and brought it back to his trailer. Campbell Flynn called several times and Jake declined the calls – about six in all. His mentor, the real author: he couldn't face the fuss Campbell was likely to make. After eating, he fell asleep, thinking about the wonder he might have created, the debate he'd stirred up.

In the mirror that night, getting ready for the shoot, he realised he was a bold man in everything he did. Whatever he said about giving up acting – and he changed his mind constantly – he was focused on the job in front of him, and he had decided to go a bit Method on this one. Definitely the right thing, he said. It's not enough to learn your lines and figure out the part and then play it. He wasn't merely another pretty boy with a good jawline and sensitive eyes. No, he would *suffer*. It was next level. He would eat and breathe as Clym Yeobright.

'I want to go over a few lines with you,' Duncan Bawn had said, at the end of the first day's shooting. 'A few notes about tomorrow. Jump in the car.'

He knew the director doubted Jake had the chops.

'I can't do that,' Clym said. 'We can take the horses. There's a farm cart here.'

'I'm not going in that! I'm in a hurry, man. Okay, I'll call you on your mobile.'

'I don't know what that is,' Clym replied.

Bawn was puzzled. 'But you've been on the phone. You've been doing interviews for this book, Jake. You've been on your laptop.'

'Not today,' he said. 'Today, I'm in the nineteenth century.'

'Try acting.'

'Please don't question my process,' the actor replied.

He'd taken a note from Hardy's novel that he hoped would nourish his portrayal in tonight's scene. He looked it up again on his phone before being called. There was still a lot of action around his phone that night, a lot of 'incoming', as he called it. His attempts to ignore the device's existence, for Method reasons, had long since failed. But he kept his focus tonight. Not that he cared if he wasn't consistent – he cared that he obeyed the right feeling.

A second assistant director came to collect him. They walked past a grid of vans and monitors to reach a snow-covered cottage. None of it was real, but it was vastly familiar, in a heritage England kind of way, and the yard was full of crew shouting orders. Light reflectors hung at different angles over a festive table, with actors standing around in costume. There was a certain fidget in the air, and they were looking at him, the collection of mummers and furze-gatherers, and sundry RADA graduates in large bonnets, plumes and ribbons. Candles were being lit and live sheep were being herded, fake snow blasting in front of a wind machine. Jake looked down at the second assistant's script.

'EXT. MRS YEOBRIGHT'S HOUSE. NIGHT.'

He suspected the director had moved it outside – who would have supper outside in December? – to make more of the 'shot on location' mania, the moon and the stars and the hoots of the owls and so on. It would add to the pagan spirit, the rustic fuss, to have horses visibly panting in the dark. The scene was important because it was his character's first meeting with the film's heroine, Eustacia Vye. He looked up from the script. 'I have an odd opinion,' he said as Clym Yeobright, 'and should like to ask you a question. Are you a woman – or am I wrong?' He tried it again. 'Are you a *woman*?' 'Are *you* a woman?'

Eustacia would be dressed as a boy, one of the mummers. 'Think *ambiguity*,' Jake said to himself as he studied the script.

He tried it a few more ways. He thought of his sister. He thought of an old teddy. After a few minutes' rehearsal, Duncan, the fêted, bearded hipster who once chastised the British film industry for its love of heritage film-making, approached Jake looking glum. 'Look, maestro, we have a problem.'

'What?'

'Josey, our leading lady, Eustacia fucking Vye.'

'What about her? Where is she?'

'She won't come out of her trailer. She says she won't work with you. Her agent's on the phone. She's threatening to walk.'

'What in the name of Christ are you talking about, Duncan?'

The director turned to the gaffer. 'Shut the lights down,' he said.

The volume of talk on the set had increased and Jake suddenly saw it was real. This was actually happening. The snow stopped.

The guy playing the reddleman, the now penitent, sober Archie Todd, came over and put his hand on Jake's shoulder.

'I'm sorry, mate,' Todd said.

Jake turned to him. Todd's face and hands were covered in red make-up and he was wearing red clothes from head to foot. His eyes peeped out and to Jake there was now something extremely demonic about the set.

Jake looked straight at the director. 'Duncan, is this a fucking joke?'

'No, man. What you said – you fucked it. You can't say that kinda thing. The radio interviews: you can't fucking say that. The shit has hit every fan in the world, and the execs are up the hill with a bunch of lawyers.'

The next day, Jake Hart-Davies was fired from *The Return*.

At the house in Thornhill Square, the smell of rotting fish fingers in the hall had been dispelled by a fortnight of Diptyque candles. Elizabeth had also brought in two pots of lavender from outside. Yet Campbell swore that he could still smell fish, and was forever spraying the hall with air freshener and saying the episode made him queasy. He had sunk low in his own view of himself since the Byre arrest. 'Disgraced Businessman Sexually Abuses Girl 30 Years

His Junior,' it had said on the front page of one of the tabloids. William was on remand in Belmarsh, having refused to surrender his passport, or admit to anything. It couldn't be true, could it, that William had raped a woman and then bought her off with a flat? The whole thing had left Campbell disconsolate in a part of himself that nobody could see. Slowly, a panic of contrition began to show in many of his actions and relationships, not least when it came to the subject of that secret book.

In his study he prepared to join a Zoom meeting with his publisher, Mirna Ivoš. She was in a melancholy frame of mind, which wasn't unusual, with a layer of sheer horror at what was happening. He knew that he had harmed his beloved Mirna and done damage to the house's reputation. It was yet more timber to the fire. But he tried to hold to the initial reason for writing the book, to make up for a growing shortfall in his finances. He tried pathetically to push that back into play. 'It's doing extremely well,' he said. 'And we could always be doing with a book doing well.'

'It depends on what we mean by "well".'

'It's selling. Despite or maybe *because* of all this . . . noise.'

She sighed in full Serbian. 'It has found a vulgar audience, Campbell. The book has some merits, if you understand irony and like examples, but it is being read as a kind of riposte to the age of equality.'

'The book is actually an admission of guilt.'

Her voice went quiet. 'Not as he is presenting it. He has decided to turn the whole thing into a celebration of male dominance.'

'I know.'

'It's a scandal,' she said. 'A huge scandal. Especially in the US. Even the cover has proved controversial.'

I am well protected, Campbell thought. He could say that. He had his surrogate. But at the same time he began to wonder if all his 'selves' weren't liabilities.

'You are hidden,' she said, as if hearing him.

Out of the blue, perhaps to advertise that his comeuppance was at hand, he told her that his wife was not the rich person people often imagined she was. Her father had left her the cottage in Suffolk and a small trust, and that was it, along with her earnings. Her mother, Emily, had recently left her fortune to the earth's plumpest elephants.

'You were depending on this, Campbell?'

'I think I was,' he said.

Mirna appeared to hesitate. 'You are a good writer,' she said, 'but the world has been too much with you, Campbell.'

'I know that.'

'You must return to your talent. It is your only resource.'

'I really don't know if I can,' he said.

She spoke about the Rembrandt book and about the Autumn Lecture. 'I have my invitation,' she said, 'and very handsome it is too.'

'I'm putting a lot into it,' he said.

'Well, good. It's much more your thing. The anticipation is what I would expect, for one who has divined some of creativity's secrets.'

It occurred to him that Mirna had always been like a mother, the birth mother of his adulthood, and he could tell her anything. But she would judge him too. It was her job to judge. 'I have written an opening to the Rembrandt,' he said, picking up a pad from his desk. 'A face is a machine for exteriorising subjectivity, for showing and concealing the mind's construction. Most painters of self-portraits say, "Here I am," but Rembrandt paints with a hand of fire. He is a witness to human souls, a sublime explicator of the life inside, and he looks from the mysterious centre of these works to ask another question: "Who are you?"'

'This is a book you were *born* to write,' she said.

When she vanished from the screen, her spirit stayed. She somehow made him better than he was, with her standards. He had started the self-help book as a quick fix, up late and half pissed, and now it threatened to expose him. Already, he worried, Jake may have accidentally highlighted some hidden truth in it, some innate, unconscious ugliness, a thing unsurrenderable by the likes of him and William Byre.

*William.* If feeling implicated can be experienced as a form of pain, then Campbell was in agony.

He went on Twitter, exhausted now, and searched the actor's name, his eyes staring unblinkingly at the computer screen.

'He's toast this time. #rapeadvocate'

'WT actual F! @JakeHDavies thinks men are supreme! What a complete moron!!! #goodbyeArcadius #aethonscurse'

Campbell tried phoning him again. He went downstairs and his breathing was so heavy he wondered if he should call Elizabeth. Standing in the hall, he heard Mrs Voyles's television blaring through the floorboards and crouched down, holding his knees, experiencing a terrible bout of vertigo there in the lavender-scented hall. For an instant, he imagined every door being knocked at once, and all the screens of all his devices scrolling with data as William Byre went down to a squalid cell at Belmarsh and Jake Hart-Davies became a stupid hologram of every man's quest for visibility. Campbell knew they were all part of himself, part of what he had made of himself – and so, somehow, was Milo Mangasha.

# 28 SE8

They stared into the brown water of the canal. Pharma got up. 'Look at these bubbles, fam.' A bird broke the surface. 'That was a duck, for real.'

'That ain't no duck, that's a moorhen, you doughnut,' Travis said. 'It's totally black, bruv, and it's got a white face, innit. Check it.'

'Shut up, bruv!'

'Don't lie, fam, look at it – white face, like Milo!'

'Raaah, allow it, that's cold,' Pharma said, chuckling.

He took back the zoot and puffed it. 'Nah. Don't joke. Milo is sound. He's educated, innit. White boys don't own that.'

Travis was still staring into the water. 'Remember when his mum did that whole display at school about birds?'

'Yeah. Yeah.'

Lloyds came rolling down on his bike. He was sweating. 'It's 0044, man.'

'What?' Pharma said, worried.

'He's dead up, man. They killed him. He was down Kennington looking for revenge for the acid burns, and he got licked down. Deptford Cartel.'

'Nah. You serious?'

'They're saying it was Sluggz. The Deptford boy from the Underground. Did it on his own. Kid was jumped at the skate park down there.'

Travis bolted. He bombed on his bike up to Copenhagen Fields, diving into the Lycamobile for a packet of Amber Leaf and a bottle of Courvoisier. He climbed the stairs and pushed open the door of the

345

abandoned flat. It was full of empty bottles. He sat against the wall and drank. He didn't want to face any of it, didn't want to live like this – though he felt fitted up for it, like he couldn't get away from who he was.

For a few years, Travis had imagined his father was a six foot one Cameroonian midfielder called Alex Song. He made well over a hundred appearances for Arsenal and scored seven goals, all of them cheered by Travis louder than any other goal. Shirt number eight, Alexandre Dimitri Song Billong, who lost his own father at the age of three, strode the field in 2009, awaking in Travis an idea of rescue he could never speak about. Inside his body, in the privacy of his ten-year-old self and the ten-year-old self that never dies, Travis could believe that Alex Song was coming to make everything all right. It never happened, and Travis ripped all the posters off his wall in 2012 when Song went to Barcelona.

Fitted up: wasn't that the story? Travis believed that every teacher he ever had and every girl he ever met didn't believe in him the way they might believe in someone else. His friends were all he had, and his friends' rivalries were his, and he wanted money to do what nothing else could do: make him untouchable and high above. He didn't want to fight people, but he wanted to win, and the killing of 0044 was a challenge he had known was coming, like a creature through the forest in the middle of a bad dream. But still it left him short of breath, to know that the game he didn't want was on. He had hoped for a career, a following, a recording deal, but none of that would come if his reputation died.

He slugged from the bottle and banged the wall behind him with his elbow.

He wanted to talk it out, calm it down, move on. But keep his rep. Sitting there, he began drumming out a pattern on his knees. He was thinking about some answers, a rhyme to still the mind.

'*Blaze Boy*,' he said, thinking of 0044, and himself.

He was halfway down the bottle when Milo turned up, standing in the doorway in a white T-shirt, looking good. He carried a plastic bag. 'You're fresh out the box, brother,' Travis said from the floor, tapping his knee.

Milo put his bag down and walked over. He took the draw and began to skin up on the floor beside Travis, their backs to the wall and graffiti all around them. 'You been having a party by yourself, T?'

'Trust me,' he said.

Milo was lit that day and he told a good story about a trick he'd played on some business guy who'd been in the news. *Byre. Mire.* The guy was some bigwig friend of this professor, the one he'd been shaking down. Milo hacked the professor's texts. Sent this Byre/Mire to a lawyer's office, where he knew he'd be arrested.

'Skills,' Travis said. 'That's *sick*. You're turning the world around.'

He could feel the cognac roaring in his head, making him smile. 'You're gonna leave, aren't you?' he said. 'Leave London one day soon, you and Gosia.' He gave a little speech about how Milo didn't need his friends any more, because he was loved up and he had his big projects and was crazy-busy.

He dropped his head between his knees, where the bottle was. His mind went back in time again.

'Cally Boys Win Five Medals in Inter-Schools Swimming Gala.'

He spread his hands, marking out the headline.

'Good times, man,' Milo said. 'You were the sports king.'

Travis told him the 0044 news.

'What,' Milo said, furious. 'They killed him? This kinda thing is fucking *old*.'

'The kid was close to Bigs.'

Milo stalked around the room. 'So, it all blows up? All gets bigger? Boys who don't even know each other get dipped, because of some stupid feud.'

'I know.'

'All because of what, Travis?'

Travis pulled his head back and squeezed his eyes shut. 'I don't want any of this,' he said. 'The thing I want is my music. It's not my thing, bruv.'

'Just don't do anything. Leave it.'

There was a long silence.

Eventually, Milo got up and took a box out of the bag.

'I'm late with it,' he said. 'It's your birthday present.' Travis sat up straight. 'Remember the last time we were in here, watching the basketball thing?'

'Yeah, yeah, yeah. The party—'

'All watching Michael Jordan.'

'Yeah, yeah.'

Milo opened the box and took out a pair of trainers. 'Air Jordan,' he said. 'Max Aura 3. Special edition. Happy birthday, man.'

Travis swayed and took the shoes. He held one in each hand. Black on the front and red inside the shoe, a flash on the base. Size 11. He started laughing and it made him feel sober for a second, the brand-new smell of the trainers and the fact that nobody else was going to have them yet. 'Ah, man,' he said. As he stood up and kicked off his old Reebok Classics he could feel himself swaying. He pulled up a leg of his trackies to put on the Jordans. A short knife nearly popped out.

Milo didn't want to spoil the moment, so he let it go.

'Max Aura 3s,' Travis whispered. '*Limited.*'


Gosia was into proper cooking. She would get ingredients Milo had never heard of, spices and herbs from the Middle East, like za'atar. A chicken dish for Gosia could be a whole statement about not conforming to national stereotypes. When Milo arrived at her flat in Judd Street that evening, back from giving Travis his present, he found her baking something. After he took his jacket off, she dabbed his tongue with the spice and then he pulled her top over her head and lifted her onto the kitchen table. He swept the flour off the table and unzipped himself. She gasped when he pushed into her. He loved the way she whispered his name and gently bit his neck.

The table was back to normal an hour later, and they sat on opposite benches with bowls of pickles and flatbreads between them and chicken shawarma, both of them discussing what they still needed to find out, now that Byre was in jail. 'Your brother's involved in new grow-houses in Kent,' he said. 'I know that from my mates. But I'm beginning to draw a blank on the Byre and Bozydar world, the wider circle. Byre – Russians. Duke – Russians. But there's a missing link in there relating to Bozydar. A rogue element.'

'It will come,' Gosia said.

'I want to keep the stories rolling,' he said.

'Do you think she'll go on being reliable, this reporter?'

'I think so. She's getting it out there, bit by bit.'

He looked at Gosia's little fireplace filled with candles, and on the mantelpiece he saw the invitation card he'd put there for his boss's lecture in October. He pointed. 'That's going to blow the roof off the British Museum.'

'Is it wild stuff?' she asked.

'Simpler than that,' he said. 'It's the truth.'

Gosia opened another bottle of wine.

'*Anyway*, the positive news,' he continued, 'is the brand-new intel that I'm finding on the Duke.'

'Tell me.'

Milo turned with a smile on his face. 'Video material. Unbelievable material.'

'What like?'

'Like . . . fascist rants and—'

'*What?*'

'Yeah. He hung out with these army veterans and they pass these images around in private chat rooms. It's nuts.'

'You've got to be kidding.'

'I know.'

'And you can use it?'

'When the time is right,' Milo said. 'I'm harvesting it. Need to polish it a bit.'

She hung back, astonished, then burst out laughing.

'It's like an experiment in justice.'

'Totally,' he said. 'I'm just not there yet. But, yeah. And it's all connected . . .'

She could tell she'd lost him for a moment. This would happen sometimes when they spoke about the plan: thoughts of his mother, she guessed. It felt like Zemi was behind it all, his inspiration. But would she have approved of the risks, the dangers?

'I feel everybody's a journalist now,' Gosia said, to fill the silence. 'Citizen hacks. Or hacker citizens. It's up to ordinary people.'

They went to her pink sofa and opened Netflix. They couldn't decide what to watch so they watched two minutes of everything.

The next day was a scorcher. The junior in the salon arrived wearing a sarong and a bikini top, and then ran out, mid-morning, to buy a fan from Ryman's. An hour later, she went out again to buy iced coffees. At 2.30, Gosia was washing her hands at the storeroom sink when an unexpected name came up on her phone. For a second, she was too nervous to answer it.

'Hello, Dana,' she said, quickly drying her hands.

'I got your message.'

Her brother's ex-wife always got right to the point. It wasn't that Dana was unfriendly, she just didn't waste time. There was little point asking why it had taken her so long to respond.

'Maybe we should meet for a drink or something.'

'I'd like that,' Gosia said. They made a plan for six o'clock.

Bozydar and Dana had never been a good couple. The wedding reception, Cecylia liked to say repeatedly, had lasted longer than the marriage. They were unsuited to an almost comical degree, and Dana brought to the union a healthy East European intolerance of sentiment and prevarication. They separated very soon after she became pregnant with Ben and the custody battle had felt like a car-crash honeymoon. Gosia had been sad for the kid, but not too sad – she always knew Dana would rock as a mother.

'You look happy,' Dana said. 'Are you?'

That was her opener.

Gosia answered with a smile. 'Never thought I would be,' she said.

'I always knew *I* would be,' Dana said. 'Soon as I got rid of a few people. Like my parents. Like your brother.'

Gosia giggled at that. She loved women who spoke their minds. It was the reason she kept working at the salon. Friends.

They were in the garden at the Drapers Arms, one of those Islington pubs where they serve craft beers and heirloom tomatoes. Dana whipped through a series of hilarious events including or starring Ben. Then she went to the bar for two more glasses of Pinot Grigio and was talking again before she sat down.

'Listen . . .' she said.

She'd lowered her voice. That was unlike her.

'I just think you should know stuff that's happening with your brother.'

'Go on.'

'I don't know how much you know, but he was doing stuff for that businessman who got arrested the other day. The pensions guy. Migrant workers.'

'Yeah, I saw that in the papers.'

'Well, there's much more than that. He's been coming to Kentish Town, to the house, drunk like a pig. Late at night. You know he uses prostitutes?'

'Dana, there are things I don't want to know—'

'Well, I'm telling you. He comes round. Ben is asleep. I let him in a few times to stop the noise in the street. He tells me all this stuff. Have you heard of this guy Yuri Bykov?'

'Who?'

'Russian art dealer.'

Gosia shook her head and sipped her wine.

'Son of a big Russian.'

'You mean Aleksandr Bykov?'

'Yes – his *son*. A madman. Like a playboy and all over the place. A big shot. The guy's a fucking lowlife. He takes Boz to lunch. Boz says it's now his big connection. It's changing everything. You know, drunk talk.'

'They go to *lunch*?'

Gosia's mind was racing.

'The guy is at war with his father. Boz is all in. Up to his eyes in it.'

'They're working together?'

Dana was whispering now with her head close to Gosia's.

'They're doing it all in partnership now, but *much* bigger,' she said. 'Running these dope farms. The old business was drying up, so now he has new ones, using these migrants. Big money, he says.'

'Tell me his name again.'

'Yuri Bykov. He is totally turning Boz's head. Actors. Models. Not that he had much of a head to turn, but, you know . . .'

Gosia felt the penny drop a long way. *The rogue element.*

She leaned in. 'And my brother speaks about all this to you?'

'A few times, yes. Drunk. Tells me he still loves me. Tells me he's equal to these Russians and one day he's going to buy a yacht. A jet. Boz now wants to run businesses all the way to East Asia. He wants to be a mystery guy.'

Gosia was turning the new information over in her mind. It was something she hadn't fathomed before: Yuri was *the son*.

'Boz gets all fucked up – crying, saying he will give us a lot more money each month. I'm not taking him back. The whole thing makes me feel sick. Sorry.'

Gosia continued to sit quietly as Dana lit one of her long cigarettes.

'Why are you telling me all this, Dana?'

'I know you're different from him,' she said. She blew smoke down at the stone tiles. 'I'm telling you because I want to live a decent life. I am a mother. I work hard. I am not one of his prostitutes.'

They sat in the truth of that for a moment.

'Has he mentioned an Englishman to you, a man called Anthony Crofts, the Duke of Kendal?'

'No,' Dana said, narrowing her eyes against the smoke. 'Never heard of him. I'm talking about *gangsters*. Boz works for them now. It's a different world. It's not like England at all – is it?'

Four days after he saw Milo at the bando, Travis and Big Pharma were stopped while driving down Eltham High Street. They were in a car with suspicious licence plates and the Kent police were on to them. They got arrested because Travis had panicked and dropped a knife out of the passenger-seat window. Police questioned them by the road and then took them in handcuffs to the police station at Gravesend, but they got out quickly and caught the overground to King's Cross.

Travis's mum was back in the flat at Ritson House. She'd been in Southend, doing whatever. Travis didn't want to know. She had new scabs on her face and was curled up on her bed with a sore stomach and she was vomiting. She looked yellow and he took her that night to the emergency NHS surgery near Fitzroy Square, his mum holding a can of Fanta and nodding off in the waiting room. It turned out she had hepatitis B. They'd refer her for blood tests and a liver scan. It was only a prescription for now. Travis got the medicine from the 24-hour pharmacy then took her home.

'Settle in there,' he said to her, when he put her to bed. He'd borrowed a clean sheet and a pillow from the woman upstairs. He sat at the bottom of his mum's bed that night and watched her wriggle inside her body. When she fell asleep he played on his phone, using a keyboard app to pattern up a couple of songs. The first one was based on a melody he heard one time with his mum at a music festival on Wanstead Flats. He listened to it, a soft folk song by Simon and Garfunkel, and it always reminded him of her, the guitar, the way they did the harmony. He looked out as the words passed between him and his sleeping mother, the guitar fixing the air. Eventually, he fell asleep sitting on the floor with his head on the bed, and he dreamed he was kicking a football through long grass and someone was calling his name. He felt bleached by the street light. He looked after her for five nights.

And so it came to 25 August. Travis had finished a song about 0044 and the Cally Active recorded the video in Paradise Park. It was Lloyds's call. In his CEO mode, he wanted to take advantage of the beef and big it all up for commerce. Travis wore an Alexander McQueen skull-pattern scarf over his face, singing the words while the sun sank behind St Pancras. He was drunk on Hennessy. They all were. Spilling it in the park, jumping for the camera.

They had a barbecue meet-up after the video shoot: all the Cally boys and youngers from Agar Grove were there that night, puffing heavy and swapping gang stories. Travis would remember two things about that August night and the way it panned out: the strength of the weed they were smoking and the way the day became, like, total red sky in the evening. Nights like that would always remind him of his youth. Sweet nights. The darkness held back in that calm summer way and all the boys out on the estate. By midnight, when they were hanging out by the swings, Lloyds was getting texts from his brother Money in Brixton about another flare-up with Deptford. Sluggz had been mouthing off on socials about 0044, dissing him and saying he was a dead pussy, cussing Brixton and the Cally boys.

Sitting on a swing, Lloyds said Money planned to fuck Sluggz up, but Lloyds wanted to calm it down. 'I barely knew 0044,' Travis was saying through a cloud of weed smoke. 'But the kid was good peoples. These fuckers are disrespecting us, big time.'

'Yeah, yeah,' Pharma said.

'Never mind,' Lloyds threw in. 'They're just idiots, fam.'

Travis felt he was getting somewhere with his music, the new songs were good, the emotion was coming into it; he was connecting to himself. He wasn't interested in beefs. He wanted the other kind of respect – he wanted freedom. Not the violence.

Lloyds told them that some of the Brixton boys wanted to go down to Deptford and sort it out, to meet with the Cartel and end it. That sounded good, Travis said.

'The Brixton crew are angrier than that,' Lloyds said.

'Well, let's go and calm them. We can help put this beef to bed,' Travis said. 'If we go down there and talk to them, get rid of it, yeah?'

By about half midnight, they had the address: 'Garvey House, Bronze Street, SE8.'

'That's their turf, right down in Deptford,' Lloyds said.

'It's all good. Let's glide,' Travis said. 'Calm this thing.'

Big Pharma had his uncle's car. All the way down, he played one song on repeat, 'Flowers & the Snow' by Fredo.

# 29 September

His father was concerned with the pride of forty Russian men. To a lesser extent, he was also attentive to the pride of about five men in the Middle East. These obsessions, according to his son, Yuri, dominated Aleksandr Bykov's life, and kept him well supplied with fear. His own power and his own assets might be foreshortened at any moment, and that kept him lively. Loyalty was the only principle in business that made any sense to Aleksandr, the reason, Yuri believed, he reacted so badly to Yuri's independence.

That week, the old man was in St Petersburg with Lord Scullion of Wrayton, both of them guests of the International Economic Forum. Apparently, they had spent the morning walking round the Hermitage, looking for examples of Dutch fakes. Monsieur Lantier, a mere butler, was now fighting for his life at the university hospital in Switzerland, having suffered multiple strokes, which began after he accepted a glass of champagne at a party in Gstaad.

After the glass-throwing incident, Yuri was finished with his father. But he wasn't above sending him the occasional incendiary text. 'They say Lantier was given thallium,' he wrote. 'If he has been poisoned by your friends, this is a disaster.'

'You're the only poison I know,' Aleksandr replied. 'And the only disaster. Don't bother me with your ridiculous theories.'

From the boardroom on Bankside, Yuri saw a pair of swans. There really is something rather overdone about swans, not only in the Pavlova sense, but in their over-feathered, camp, gliding manner. He was already looking forward to Lucerne the following weekend, where he would hear the Berlin Philharmonic. He could drive to see

Nicolas – two and a half hours, Yuri's assistant had told him. Looking up, he saw the tall building at 22 Bishopsgate, then the Cheesegrater, the Scalpel, the Walkie-Talkie, all rising from old London on the other side of Southwark Bridge. He had grown up learning their names, studying the map of the city and dining at the new clubs and hotels as soon as they opened. The Ned. Home House. He had wanted so much to master London and fill it with secrets and investments. Checking his phone he saw brown paintings from the Hermitage, photographed by his clueless father, including a very good 'Old Man with Spectacles', the figure so masterfully resembling a Rembrandt.

Yuri's finance director (Eton and Balliol) was talking to him about investing in other parts of London. Housing in Catford, that sort of thing. Yuri was only half listening, humming a tune. It was like opera, out there in the dark, small places of London, a Puccini world of decadent boys who would die for love; of fights, suicides and patois. Very few people really know how to manipulate a city.

The finance director was looking at him. 'Yuri, are you all right?'

'The street corner shit is over,' he said. 'Time to go big.'

'Excuse me?'

Yuri gathered himself and wiped his mouth with his pocket square. 'I'm sorry, I . . . what were we talking about then?'

'We were introducing a new development in Holland Park.'

'Yes, indeed.'

'We can take it out of the Cyprus fund.'

'Yes, do that,' he said.

'And what about the loans to William Byre? We have the option of taking the majority of his solid assets, the factories and so on . . .'

'It's all junk,' Yuri said. 'I'll leave that to my father.'

He stood up and left the boardroom. He walked along to his office and looked down at the river again to see that the swans had gone.

An hour later, a call came through to say Nicolas Lantier had died. 'He was terribly young,' the friend from the Gagosian said. 'Do you think they got to him?'

A sort of disdain flooded Yuri.

'I think he killed himself,' he said.

'But they're saying he wildly inflated the prices. You must know—'

'The problem with Nicky is he drank too much,' Yuri interrupted. 'He stayed up too late. I think that's his story, poor man.'

Moira Flynn was staring at the carpet in Committee Room 15 at the Palace of Westminster, on her first day back after the summer recess. She was a fan of Commons lore, and she knew the place like she knew the pattern in that carpet, a Gothic fantasia to beat all reality. She was one of only two Labour MPs in Scotland, representing West Ayrshire, and she worried, on any given day, whether she was in the right party or the right country. She spent the week in London and the weekends at her house in Wemyss Bay, where she lived alone. She had once been married but they didn't have children and she was generally too busy for regrets. As the Foreign Affairs Select Committee proceeded (Moira was auditing it, having recused herself from serving), she put a mint imperial in her mouth and considered the matter before her with a clear mind. Campbell always said Parliament was like the famous portraits of it by Monet – all lilac and yellow-coloured smog. But she fought to retain the principle that power could be held to account. Someone said of Charles Parnell that he allowed his political conscience, like a loose anchor, to be dragged away, and Moira was determined not to let that happen to her. She would pursue corruption where she found it and would defend women, that was it.

'We have heard evidence,' the chair was saying, 'which suggests the Sanctions and Anti-Money Laundering Act might not have gone far enough. The freezing of funds or economic resources owned, held or controlled by designated persons – whom some of the witnesses to this committee have called "ultra-connected bad actors" – has not yet had the desired effect, and it is alleged that Russian corruption remains at a high level in the business and commercial life of this country. Excluded persons are reinstated, given sinecures at universities and, might it be added, a small number have been given seats in our House of Lords, the net effect of which has been to undermine attempts to cleanse the system. We've heard from witnesses who speak of a "London laundromat" involving billions of dollars of dirty Russian money, much of it processed by UK high-street banks, flowing through hub companies that are registered at Companies House. One of these companies reported profits of £1 and was later found to have over $12 billion going through it.'

'If I may,' a member said. He was the Labour MP for Salford and Eccles, a young Corbynite who couldn't believe the country was still like this. 'The draft report is clear on the matter of this modern kleptocracy, yet the newspapers in this country have been slow to expose the extent to which it involves legitimate British businesses, British institutions and individuals of high rank and visibility.'

'Indeed. Yet I would remind the select committee that it is not our responsibility to produce material for the press but to investigate matters and report them to the Liaison Committee and ultimately to Parliament. I believe honourable members have taken it upon themselves to report certain findings to the Financial Conduct Authority, to Her Majesty's Revenue and Customs, and other bodies.'

The chair looked directly at Moira. She didn't flinch. She was an expert, here and there, at lining up her thoughts without disclosing them; she saw how action, in the parliamentary world, depended on the gentle promulgation of moral threat, and she did this expertly, with no bells or whistles to accompany her best efforts.

'We have a duty,' another MP said, 'to address the issue when Members of both Houses are accepting money and positions from these people, including ministers—'

'Sorry – forgive me,' the chair said. 'I must prevent you from making individual accusations. It is not our function. I know you are merely alluding to facts, but we must be careful not to impugn . . . that's to say, if you wish to submit written evidence on this particular issue we can perhaps—'

'It is an open secret in this society that oligarchs are able—'

'The individuals who may have benefited, to whom you refer, have no ability to reply in this forum, therefore I will not have them listed here.'

'London has become the world capital of diseased finance,' the member continued. 'We are the hub of the largest network of secret jurisdictions, and British tax havens are central to the movement of illicit funds around the globe.'

'Our recommendations are firm in that regard.'

'I certainly hope so, sir. Thank you.'

'What we know,' an SNP member said, 'is that there are presently a quarter of a million properties in the UK owned by overseas companies, with chains of shell companies hiding the true owners and their influence on British life. Though the present government is still slow, suspiciously slow, to stop this accumulation, or to expose the true owners of these properties, or of the £1.5 billion of British land owned by Russians, we have asked again and again that Unexplained Wealth Orders be expanded.'

'So long as we don't name individuals.'

'But we *should* name them,' the SNP man said. 'That is the point.'

It was all as Moira predicted, yet it only hinted at the kind of relationships she knew to be plaited into her brother's life. She took out her pen and wrote a number of notes and names on her copy of the draft report. She folded the document and placed it at the front of her tote bag. She sat back and clasped her hands. After William Byre had been arrested at her office, she'd received an anonymous text. 'It's all about the Duke now. Trust me,' it said, and from that point on she believed her brother and his family were being hacked. In her mind, it was all part of his complicated life.

She could see Campbell at a young age. He must have been six, but already he had the bearing of a person who wished to aim higher. She recalled that he'd once found a book of cloakroom tickets in the bin cupboard under the Rosemount Flats and started selling them for two pence each in the school playground, saying that David Bowie was going to give a concert at Alexandra Parade Primary School. He had such conviction saying it – describing the band and the tour bus and the set, and his own role as promoter – that all the kids believed him and parted with their coins, and Campbell seemed to grow on the spot. A teacher eventually found out about it and he paid back all the money, but he remained aloof, as if he'd only been testing people's capacity for make-believe.

Moira walked along the committee corridor and down the stairs, then threaded through to the Central Lobby. In normal times, she wouldn't have agreed to meet a journalist in the lobby – too many eyes, all of them knowing, the friendly guys from *Newsnight* and the busy correspondents with whispers and iPads. She saw the woman from the *Commentator* sitting on one of the green benches next to the post office.

'I'm Tara Hastings,' the woman said, shaking Moira's hand.

'I know all about you. I've been reading your stuff. I'm not one for blowing smoke up people's bums, but you're the best writer they have.'

'That's really kind. Thank you. It's not easy over there at the minute. Hard to do your job sometimes.'

'Well, you certainly did it with William Byre, especially that last big piece. Getting the young woman to speak—'

'She's quite vulnerable. I worry about her.'

'Yes, I'm sure,' Moira said. 'We're completely off the record, okay?'

'Yes, of course.'

'You can quote me as an anonymous source.'

'Cool. We're friends meeting for tea.'

Moira led the way. They walked through corridors of dark book-cases. Tara realised she still got lost in this place.

'Byre was always a man's man,' Moira said, 'you know, dining clubs, all that kind of thing. I'm talking about Cambridge. He was there with my brother and they used to come and visit me at Durham.'

They walked towards the terrace. Eventually, they burst into the light which was beating over the river to St Thomas' Hospital.

'Beautiful day,' Tara said, as they sat down at one of the tables.

'A beautiful day for betrayal.'

'Is that how you see this?'

'No, not really,' Moira said. 'Byre is awaiting trial on embezzlement charges, and before long I'm sure he will be charged with the other things . . . you revealed.' Moira felt she was pondering something too deep for statements or tears. They ordered Earl Grey. She took a breath. 'My brother makes his own mistakes, but he's nothing like William Byre.' She paused and looked at the Thames. 'It's funny how we protect men from themselves and from their associations.'

'Yes,' Tara said. She looked at her phone, then put it back in her pocket. 'I think the hackers are onto Byre,' she went on. 'I'm getting facts, figures, private correspondence, text messages, hundreds of private emails. New material all the time.'

'Really?'

'Yes,' Tara said. 'My biggest source is now feeding me information about him and these Russians.'

'Right. Well—'

'It was the source who suggested I speak to you.'

Moira had no idea who that could be. Maybe someone on the committee? One of Byre's employees, perhaps, but how would they know about her? 'People must really hate William Byre,' she said.

'The times we're living through . . . Vicky Gowans can become a poster girl for something women are no longer willing to tolerate.'

'The news of that young woman devastated my brother. He's ill over it.'

Tara slightly raised her head at that.

Moira wiped her nose with a tissue. 'I want this to be on deep background. It's not merely about William Byre and his world, but about my brother's . . . wider family.'

'Don't worry,' Tara said. 'I understand your position.'

'There are several strands,' Moira said. 'You've established the first ones – financial corruption, migrant labour and the women – and there will be lots more to come on those, I'm certain. But the new—'

'Can I take notes, to help me with the facts?'

'Too suspicious here. Let's talk first. I'll hand you documents.'

The tea arrived and Tara took charge of it. Moira reckoned she had the patience of the careful journalist, the way she stirred the cups and stayed quiet.

Moira unfolded her sense of the former Sir William Byre's connection to the Bykov family. She said there was a group of institutions and a number of individuals in the Lords – she looked over her shoulder, as if the chamber might be listening – who had been caught up in possibly corrupt practices and economic relationships involving the sanctioned Russians, and she said it had been covered up by ministers and by a negligent press. 'We are a nation that turns a blind eye.'

'It's very big, all of this,' Tara said. 'My sources are telling me Byre is in hock to Aleksandr Bykov and his companies for something in the region of £200 million.'

'I can't confirm the exact amount, but yes.'

They discussed it further: the mysterious power of Aleksandr Bykov and his family to reach into different parts of British life. 'And that's where it again becomes difficult for me,' Moira said. 'My nephew and niece are friends of his son, Yuri.'

'I know,' Tara said. She shook her head as if nothing could be helped. 'I know him too. He was the year below me at Oxford.'

'Then you feel my pain, Tara. This is . . .'

'Society,' she said, with a disbelieving laugh. 'Zachary Byre is also an acquaintance of mine . . .'

'Are you serious?'

'He helped me.'

'Holy moly,' said Moira. 'Then you're in deep – like me.'

'The whole country's in deep.'

'That's true.' Moira hesitated. 'We must call it out. That's what zero tolerance means. We can't bend just because the offenders are in our contacts. And it's not only William and his world,' Moira said. 'There's more.'

Tara leaned back in her chair.

Suddenly, Moira was nervous. All confidence in her motives froze.

'I want to do this for the sake of decency,' she said. 'Because the world will never be right until these people are named.'

'This is not the Byres?'

'No,' she said. 'It's the Duke and Duchess of Kendal.'

Tara's face showed no surprise. It was as if she already knew, and had come here, as any good reporter would have done, in search of a second source and extra backbone for a story she maybe already had. Moira reached down into her bag and took out the report. 'I have written notes on this draft,' she said quietly, pushing the document across the table. 'It will be clear to you what is implied. I am leaking you the draft findings of the select committee. You will see for yourself. It will provide you with a map of the Duke of Kendal's world. I've added details where the committee could not.'

'Thank you,' Tara said.

She was young when she looked at you straight.

'You understand the situation?' Moira said. 'This document is classified at the moment. For receiving it, you could be excluded from the precincts. Your lobby pass could be removed, and I could end up being suspended by the House. These are unauthorised disclosures, and I am bound by faith—'

'So am I,' Tara told her. 'And I would happily go to jail before naming you.'

She trusted the reporter: they shared similar regrets and, possibly, values. Moira said she wasn't sure her party knew what it was for any more. 'I used to know which part of the nation's struggle we represented,' she said.

'Working people. Decency and fairness.'

'That's right. But what if working people stop voting for that?'

They finished their tea and went over to Moira's office in Portcullis House. Walking along the Commons Library Corridor, they talked about Antonia Byre. She had written a column in the *Commentator* that day disowning her husband and offering her own story as a victim of marital abuse and male bullying.

'I'm not in the game of doubting women who've been abused,' Moira said, 'but she's a piece of work, that one.'

'Tell me about it,' Tara said. 'Her marital abuse story has gone viral.'

In the office, Moira found a collection of papers she'd gathered on the Russian stuff, papers she'd slightly suppressed over the last year, to do with the funding of the Duke's Georgian pile in Scotland. She gave Tara the originals, glad to be rid of them.

For a moment, Moira was distracted by a pigeon at the window. Then her eyes fell on a few framed photographs of her and Campbell with their parents. An invitation to his forthcoming Autumn Lecture was propped against one of the frames. 'I'm trying as hard as possible to remain . . .'

'What?'

Moira pondered. 'My own person,' she said eventually. 'I always thought I *was*, to tell you the truth. But everything's . . .'

Tara waited. She was good at waiting.

'Connections.'

Tara nodded. 'Vicky Gowans,' she said eventually. 'She's young and now she's *out there*, partly because of me. We bring the attention. We get the awards. But sometimes you feel broken for the people you write about.'

Moira regarded her, as if in a fresh light. 'Reporters don't often say that. They behave as if they already parked their feelings back at the office.'

'We've wrapped our defensiveness into our act,' Tara said. 'But the truth is, I don't really think I helped that girl.'

'I think you tried to,' Moira said, and left it at that.

The reporter began to put on her jacket. 'You know she grew up in your part of the world? Her mother still lives there.'

Moira shook her head slowly. 'It galvanised me, reading what you wrote.'

'He pretended he loved her, pinned her down when she said no, when she was crying.'

'It's unspeakable,' Moira said. 'It's why my brother can't get over it. It's not only a question of what William had in *him*, but of what we had in *us*, all these years, by tolerating him, finding him funny and whatever else.'

It was silent after Tara said goodbye and closed the door behind her. Moira realised she was at peace with the decision she'd made. Walking to the window, her eyes returned to the Thames, thinking of Campbell's hopes in the days of their childhood. There was something dreamlike about the river, those passing swans.

# 30 Familial

Nearly a month had passed since Hart-Davies's disastrous interviews and *Why Men Weep in Their Cars* had been removed from bookshops. The publisher had cancelled distribution and warehoused the remaining stock. Campbell received a call from the managing director of his British publisher, Mirna's boss, who told him he was a valuable author and important to the firm. He said the withdrawal of the book was a preliminary measure, until 'some sort of sanity is resumed'. At first, Campbell couldn't tell anyone, not even Elizabeth, who had always disliked the project. She was in Suffolk with her sister and their mother; they'd intended to go to the Chatsworth Country Fair but it was cancelled because of a sudden flood, so they were struggling along at a poetry and cake-making fandango called September at Snape Maltings.

'Mummy is in full rebellion,' Elizabeth said on the phone. 'She's not feeling at all well and can't stand another minute of the Marchioness of Eye. Candy insisted on bringing the whole group of us along to this dreadful flan-making contest.'

'Are you in a tent?'

'We're in the corner of a marquee. It's pissing with rain. Candy seems to know every vicar and every minor poet in the county. And this ridiculous old stoat of a marchioness won't stop pulling rank on Mummy.'

'Oh no.'

'Who much prefers the company of men. As you know.'

'Oh God, she must be reeling,' Campbell said. 'Can't you take her to the Brambles and make her a nice lunch?'

'She doesn't want to be in England. She's hankering to return to that awful ship, but we have to stick with Candy. She's clinging on—'

'Who, your mother or Candy?'

'Both, really.' She halted. 'Somebody's about to give a lecture on ginger cake and Christianity. I'm only half making that up. It's all such epic balls. There are food banks in Ipswich they could be attending to.'

'I miss you, darling.'

'The fields are beginning to change up here,' Elizabeth said casually. '*Embrowning*, as your friend Thomas Hardy would say.'

He didn't want to go into it: Thomas Hardy, Jake Hart-Davies.

'There's such a lovely pre-autumn feel. The colours. A special glow . . .'

As she spoke, he knew he'd told Elizabeth far too little recently of his miscalculations. She was the most intelligent person he knew and he couldn't bear to spoil himself in her eyes, to confirm her doubts. She used to say he was 'performative': he worked for commendation and for the high that came with applause, and that was true in his roles as father and husband too. He had earned and borrowed money for their small family and he couldn't bear to fall short. Whatever else, he hadn't married for money, and professional success was the glory of his soul, a view that he knew to be weak. He never let anyone see that he was only as good as his next big payment, and, although Elizabeth wouldn't have minded, he would have minded telling her: the barrier was ridiculous, but impossible to pass.

'Not much news from here,' he said. 'More letters from the council. Our sitting tenant needs new outside steps and a gas oven. With any luck she'll put her head in it.'

'Campbell! You're becoming incredibly cruel.'

'Sorry, not sorry. Anyway, the drama continues. Some estate agent friend of hers wants to speak on the phone.'

'Oh God.'

'Exactly.'

She changed the subject. 'Are you working at your desk today?'

'No. I'm having lunch at the Delaunay with Antonia Byre.'

'Darling, that's too much. Do you *have* to?'

'She is my oldest friend's wife. And he's in jail.'

'Well, *courage*,' she said in French. 'I'd better go. Mummy's looking furious.'

Elizabeth. She'd been present at all the significant tests of human frailty, the decline and fall of everything. It amused him to think so. His wife was funnier than everyone else because she understood the inevitability of crisis. She had been there at the Fall of Rome and at the Great Fire of London, she'd witnessed the devastation of the Inca, the First World War, the scramble for Africa, the poll tax. *Nothing* fazed her. 'I'll never bore you,' he'd promised her when they were young, but now he saw he'd done worse: he'd hidden from her, and all her worked-for knowledge and laughter couldn't quite reach him. At their wedding, she wrote her own vows, and he could still remember them: 'I promise always to have a higher opinion of you than *you* have of yourself,' she'd said at Chelsea Town Hall. 'And I promise to forgive you whenever you seem to love me less.'

He hadn't seen Milo Mangasha since last week, when they'd met at the Lincoln pub to look over final notes for the British Museum lecture. Milo had found fascinating statistics about self-creation on the Internet – 'There are one and a half billion fake accounts on Facebook, that's people presenting as other people' – and the links had led Campbell into a fresh wonderland of interrogation. The lecture was going to be dynamite, at least in his mind, or their minds, which was all that mattered. 'I'm guessing your task is to question "civilisation" in one of its central hubs,' Milo said to him in the pub that day. 'Your lecture should not be a display of complicity, as these things usually are, but a protest song.'

Campbell had hesitated, but he ventured forth.

'I have to ask you something,' he said. 'It's to do with all this computer stuff. Have you by any chance copied my address book, or maybe cloned my phone? Someone has been sending messages to my family and friends. I don't especially mind. I'm interested.'

Milo did that kissing sound and made a face, as if asking, 'What?'

'It doesn't matter,' Campbell went on. 'I know how agitation works. I'm gripped by the procedures.'

'*The procedures?* I'm not a policeman.'

'It's just, your thing is computers.'

Milo got up a smile. 'All right, *Campbell Essendine Flynn.*'

'You know my middle name.'

The smile broadened, like everything was cool.

'My mother was into Noël Coward,' Campbell said. 'It was a world away from her own and that's the kind of thing she liked.'

'Essendine,' Milo said.

'It's from one of his plays, I think.'

'You know it's an anagram of "neediness"?'

Nobody in Campbell's adult life had ever noticed. Not even Elizabeth. It was trivial, but Campbell told himself it was a powerful signal, the young man working it out.

'I'm a decoder,' Milo said, 'and getting better.'

They drank their beers and the conversation floated to another favourite subject – Bitcoin.

'The price is down at the moment,' Campbell said.

'It'll come back up,' Milo replied. He rehearsed his usual position, saying cryptocurrency freed people from the exploitation of banks and governments, and that a change in capitalism was a change in existence.

'Isn't is just about remaking the economy?'

'Nah, man,' Milo said. 'It's about leaving it. Each family is its own nation. I would like to get a few families into one beautiful space and make a federation.'

He could bend from deadly seriousness to open flippancy like nobody Campbell had ever met. He supposed Milo was typical of his generation in some ways – the way he drank, for instance, not observing rounds, accepting drinks and dispatching them as if he didn't like the taste – and that day he did his thing of blurting out thoughts then retreating into silences. He ignored the possibility of embarrassment over Campbell's hacking questions, just finessed it into crypto mentoring.

'That Bitcoin wallet, make the password *strong*,' Milo said. 'You'll need to use your twelve-word sequence. That's the key to accessing your currency.'

'Don't worry. I've written that down in a special place.'

'You're like all older people,' Milo said. 'No security awareness.'

For his dreaded lunch with Antonia Byre, Campbell had opted to walk down to Aldwych. He often walked into town, but he didn't feel well, in mind or body. He'd tried to carry on very gingerly, and then, by a railing next to Lincoln's Inn Fields, he had to bend down and throw up. It wasn't the first time. Accumulating pressure. He walked into the garden square and looked for a bench. Sitting there, he scrolled through his phone. He thought if he had someone to laugh with, in his old way, or even to talk to, without its being someone he felt he must be letting down, it might help. He stopped at Gwen Parry, the excellent Professor of Life Writing at University College, his only friend in the department. She worked on Henry James and on polishing her put-downs of their colleagues.

'Hello, stranger,' Gwen said on answering.

'Perspicacious as usual, Gwen. I'm a stranger even to myself.'

'Well, that's how we *live*, dear. You know that.'

Campbell had received warnings that the cold front from his colleagues was set to become a nuclear winter.

'I can't last,' Campbell said. 'They hate what I write.'

'No, they hate that you have *readers*. They hate that you have a point of view that isn't a photocopy of theirs, and that you were parachuted into the department without a PhD. They hate that you say unmanageable things.'

'Thank you, Gwen. But what about you?'

'They think I'm a sacred old lesbian who likes cats. I'm safe.'

They both laughed, and when it petered out there was a silence, the silence that magnifies simplicity.

'You know what I have, Gwen?'

'You're going to tell me.'

'A separation anxiety from my true self.'

For a moment, she hummed into the phone. 'Well, dear,' she said. 'You're a Romantic. You believe in alienation and beauty and truth, like Keats. You believe in the persistence of childhood. But please retain your sense of humour.'

'I don't know what's happening.'

'Society is always devising new ways for sending clever people off their heads.'

'What about unclever people?'

'Well, yes, dear. They have their troubles too.'

He liked Gwen so much. She didn't try to please. She really didn't require any of the septic rewards, big money, status.

'I think I'm losing it.'

He meant it.

'Please be careful,' she said, suddenly softer. 'Try to step back, artfully.' She paused. 'One must retreat to the life one can live, dear.'

'I thought I had. I was wrong.'

She had a way of making things retrievable. That was Gwen's style: she saw in literature and in life a programme of failing better.

'I think some people have it in for me.'

'Maybe they do,' she said. 'But you're thinking too much. Anita Brookner once said the Romantic likes to reason in unbearable situations.'

'Is that me?' he asked.

374

'It's one of you,' she said. 'I'm not going to flatter you, Campbell. You're a weak and susceptible person, but one I happen to like.'

'I feel like Prometheus. A vulture feeds on my heart.'

'Come on, Campbell. You're simply a middle-aged man.'

'Exactly.'

Somehow he got to the Delaunay early and ordered a Gibson Martini. He saw on his phone that Jake Hart-Davies had entered rehab in Arizona. According to the sidebar of shame, he was planning his next move. It was actually looking okay for the actor. He was making all the right apologetic moves, buffing up on 'gratitude', learning to listen etc., and his spell in the desert was playing fairly well for him. It said he did yoga in a many-windowed gazebo that overlooked the Apache-Sitgreaves National Forests, 'reorganising his reality'. Meanwhile, according to news reports, *The Return* was back on location, a different though fairly identical public-school boy having been hired to play the part of the idealist from Hardy's novel. It was odd for Campbell to watch all this, the 'author' of his self-help book drowning and being saved in public, while he could only experience the shame in silence.

He looked around the room at the *fin de siècle* splendour of it all. Chasing his cocktail with fizzy water, it occurred to Campbell how typical it was of Elizabeth to say nothing about the Hart-Davies debacle despite knowing what had happened, to let it play out quietly and that way to dilute, within the family, the drama of his error. With a single crunch, he bit down on the pickled onion and let the truth sink in: his loved ones knew he was suffering a crisis, around which they conspired to tread carefully.

Antonia had booked under 'Lady Byre'. He had refrained from rolling his eyes as the maître d' led him to the table, but he felt discomfited. Why had he agreed to meet her after that drivel she wrote in the paper? It was a horribly disingenuous, post-millennial hoax, every syllable of that column about her victimhood, and now he would have to sit through lunch with her as she enumerated her sizeable injuries. She strode through the restaurant fifteen minutes late, and landed in her seat, light as a feather from a broken wing, her eyes full of distrust as she unspooled her pashmina. Her face was a mask of impunity, but it reddened when he failed to stand up and kiss her cheek. 'I suppose you've decided I'm one of the world's terrible people,' she said, summoning a waiter with a freed hand.

'I haven't decided anything, Antonia. Fate decides these things. Or the *Daily Mail* – I've never been able to tell the difference in this country.'

'Good-oh,' she said. 'Best to start on a high plain. But I need a drink first. I'm ordering a bottle of that nice Chablis they have here.'

She spoke about the difficulties of her life in St John's Wood: the hassles of being so discriminating and so right when everyone else was so stupid.

Campbell decided to go on the offensive. You can't school a person like Antonia Byre but you can modify your connivance with them, he thought. 'One of the few things I've learned,' he began, 'is that the delinquency caused by affluence is by far the worst sort. At school, we were taught that poverty caused delinquency, but in fact it isn't the person who steals a half bottle of vodka from Tesco who destroys society, it's all those rich people who dedicate their lives to tax avoidance . . .'

He dried for a second, and slugged the last of his Gibson.

'. . . Or who drive horribly huge cars, or who celebrate their prejudices and underpay people, the ravenous, delusional, entitled rich, who fuck the world every day and drag people down and create the hatred that corrupts our politics.'

'Should I give you a standing ovation?'

That was the ice broken.

At first glance, everything on the menu had either to do with beetroot or parsnips. She ordered a whites-only omelette and Campbell had steak tartare. When she spoke about the people they both knew, poor unfortunates who failed to make the grade, she spoke with the infallibility of a pontiff. Antonia had no time for doubts, regrets, second thoughts, apologies, sensitivities, or the truth. He might have been delusional, but Campbell thought of himself as a feminist. Antonia resembled nobody of any gender. Her disordered passions set her up in a place of her own, where malice was always available and where personal opinion was her passport. Even before her husband became the worst man ever, Antonia was a special being.

'And how is Zak coping?' he ventured.

'Zak is a fantasist, I'm afraid.'

'Excuse me?'

'He's a giant baby, Campbell. He wants to take down his mummy and daddy for giving him too many treats.'

'It can't be easy for him.'

'Like most pacifists, he's unbelievably aggressive. He wants to blame his mother for the state of the planet. He's a dud, I'm afraid. It's the only thing his father and I currently agree on – our son's a complete waste of space.'

'Your only son.'

'A lazy victim, like the rest, and bogus too. You know he was leaving his seven million quid apartment most days last year to hang out in that filthy hole under Euston Square? The HS2 thing? Then he'll drive out to Buckinghamshire in his hybrid car, poor bloody sod, to be with all those Extinction reprobates. That's his level.'

'You mischaracterise him.'

'Have they got to you as well? *The Arctic will melt. The human race will be over.* They're all hysterics.'

'Zak is making a name for himself. He wrote a fine essay in the *New Statesman*. There's something persuasive about him.'

'He's a loser, just like his father.'

Campbell was amazed that such a bright person could berate her own child, insult his essence, without feeling that it insulted her too. But he knew Antonia was violent at the centre of her damage and would dismantle anything in her path before she'd allow it to bother

her conscience. 'I can see you happily judging me at the bottom of your glass there, Campbell.'

'Oh, don't spoil my fun, Antonia.'

'But I do wonder if you judge my husband the same way. You know, the rapist, the serial abuser, the embezzler.'

'Listen,' he said, 'I will sit through anything. I'll go with you to the bottom of the deepest quagmire, but please don't exonerate yourself so cheaply. It's beneath contempt. And beyond belief. What you wrote in that column today, about always having been the victim of male abuse, male ego, is . . . well—'

'The truth?' she said. 'Isn't that the word? Although I don't expect one man who's built his life on lies to denounce another. That's what women have got used to, for centuries, for millennia, the conspiracy of male lies, all set out and sealed and secured so as to protect themselves. While we—'

'Ah,' he said. 'The all-powerful "we". How suddenly useful. Yet it may frighten you to learn that I'm against male lies too.'

'Really?' she said. 'And yet, so threatened by women's voices.'

'Oh stop it. Honestly. You give yourself such credit.'

A young American woman approached the table and apologised for interrupting. She told Campbell she was about to start at UCL and was checking into her accommodation with her parents. He looked over to the other side and saw a man in a business suit next to his proud blonde wife, tense and tickled by their child's social courage. The girl said she was down for his Cultural Narrative course.

'Narratives,' he said. 'Plural.'

'Yeah, totally,' she said. 'I'm so hyped for it. My mom got me your book on Vermeer for my birthday. I haven't read it yet, but we were in Berlin and saw two of the paintings. Anyway, I recognised you and wanted to say hello.'

'Thank you. Good luck settling in.'

As the student walked off, he waved at the parents and felt he'd done his duty.

'Narratives, *plural*,' Antonia said.

He sighed and waited before taking a gulp of wine.

'So, are you in charge of destroying him now?' he said eventually.

'No, Campbell. He's done that job pretty well by himself. I'll be the one saving him. Watch this space.'

'Why should I? I can read your column. Isn't that where you act out all your fantasies of confession and martyrdom?'

He wanted to leave right then. She'd surveyed the scene of wreckage, grabbed a plausible life raft, tossed everybody else overboard and paddled like crazy. 'Do you seriously think it's my fault that my husband decided to go out and sexually abuse a twenty-three-year-old junkie?'

'No,' Campbell said, 'that's on him. Entirely. And I'm horrified. But everything else is on both of you, and your joy in renouncing the complicated life you built with William, the pact you had, is both repulsive and criminal.'

She took out her vape and had a puff.

'There speaks the old-fashioned liberal,' she said. She leaned in and almost whispered. 'I have slept with the man for decades. I know what he's like in bed. I know what he does.'

Campbell was staggered. He'd never thought about it that way.

'It's amazing what the discerning critic can sometimes fail to see,' she added.

'You don't speak for women, Antonia. You don't even speak for yourself, because there is no self. I knew you when you were quite funny, quite stylish—'

'And quite loyal?' she suggested.

'Give me a break,' he said. 'My split with William is more genuine than yours will ever be.'

He swallowed hard. Another part of him was gone. He looked into the bright glass above the far tables and hoped for escape. One's values are never one's values any more, he thought. They are somebody else's issues, and what he wanted then was to flee from

379

the restaurant and its hubbub of doubt and accusation, to walk through London in the cold light of the departed summer and feel free again.

Leaves were already falling that day at St Andrew Bobola. Mrs Krupa had poured money into the place, or so it seemed to Jakub, who'd been back from Leicester since mid-August and was doing gardening work at the church, and being paid more than he'd ever made in the factories. He knew she was behind it and it made him uneasy. He was off to Kent later today.

'They like me here,' she said, in Polish, sitting on a bench. '*W naszej rodzinie mamy świętego.* We have a saint in our family.'

She always gave an English translation. Jakub had asked her to do that: it improved his English, and also, he felt, it pleased Bozydar, who didn't know Polish and didn't like his mother having secret conversations with him.

'Jerzy's not a saint yet, Mama,' Bozydar said.

He was plodding about the garden with a pair of phones. He wanted to get going and seemed agitated. He'd twice told Jakub they ought to be off, but Mrs Krupa wasn't having it.

'This is a good place you are going?' she asked. The question was directed towards Jakub, but it was meant for Bozydar, who answered, saying it was a lovely house by the sea and a real step up for her young friend.

'We look after our own,' she said.

Jakub winced again – like when she spoke of the lovely girl he was bound to meet in Kent. He went along with it. It had been a private disaster, coming to England, but he was determined to make it work. He still felt the force of Robert's hopes for the future whenever he was riven with doubts.

'Right, Mum, that's enough now. We're off,' Bozydar said.

Jakub tied a bin bag of swept-up leaves and threw it in the skip. He got his backpack and said goodbye to the warden inside the church.

Mrs Krupa came up to him as Bozydar turned away; she crushed £100 into his hand. 'You will call me on the telephone and let me know how it is all going in your work,' she said.

'Thank you,' he said.

She put a string of rosary beads in the top pocket of his jacket. 'Work hard,' she said. 'Then you can bring your brother over.'

'*Tak.*'

Bozydar waited by the church gate.

'My son is not as bad as he seems. He has none of his father's wisdom, but he is a worker. He will improve. I see him doing it already and it gives me hope. We can be good people.'

'Goodbye, Mrs Krupa.'

She could see things and unsee them; she could express truths she knew to be untrue, and dim her pain with false remedies. She had to unknow her son in order to deal with him and had to unimagine her daughter's future so that she could bear it. Standing before him, her expression set against reality, he recognised a person who had been hiding for years from her emotional life.

'Please call me Cecylia,' she said. 'I'm Cecylia from Białystok. And I will see you soon.'

'Yes,' he said.

'*Nie jestem taka stara, na jaką wyglądam.* I'm not as old as I look.'

Oh God. He didn't want to hear this.

Gerry O'Dade drove him down. 'The thing I'm saying to you about the A2,' he said as they trundled along, 'is it's all shopping centres. You've got your Bluewater, you've got your Hempstead Valley, okay?' Bozydar was in the front passenger seat, looking out the window. He didn't talk. The new job was in a village towards a place called Seasalter, and Gerry talked about the marshes there, saying the ground was sodden from the Thames estuary. 'It gets misty,' he said, 'like, coming in on the ferry at night, passing Sheerness and Allhallows, coming up the Thames, like, you see all the mist right over the marshes.'

It was a row of houses, ordinary newbuilds with fenced allotments out front and then a mile of grassland. Gerry jumped down
and shook hands with an Albanian guy who was loading bags into
a car. Jakub was sure he had seen the man hanging around the car
wash in King's Cross. They didn't speak. Bozydar was already
walking up the path of one of the houses. 'We own all of these,' he
said. 'Farms. We grow our own special samphire here, and it's better
than anybody else's.' He turned and pointed. 'You see, you'll have a
few of these allotments, you can do your gardening. But this is your
work, you understand? You're going to supervise all the foreigners
in here, yeah?'

Jakub followed him up the path. Bozydar pointed to a two-storey
house painted white. 'You live there. These places cost thousands to
rent, okay? For you, it's free. You work hard, you get money in your
account, then you get your bank card, it's yours. In time, you get
your passport, yeah? And don't talk to anybody about it. You don't
talk to your family about it. You say nothing to Mrs Krupa. Or you'll
lose your job. She knows you are a gardener here in Kent. That's all
she wants to know. You've got a friend there, okay, but don't make
any trouble for me.'

Jakub could feel the breeze; he imagined he tasted salt. Bozydar
was swapping the SIM cards between his phones as they stepped
inside the first house. 'They don't speak English,' he said, passing a
group of young workers. 'They're Vietnamese.' They went through
the rooms and Jakub saw the plants inside. The windows were
blacked out and there was reflective material around the walls, lights
up high, airflow units in the corners and ducting around the walls.
The plants were sunk in troughs: no soil, but a reservoir of fluid and
bottles of chemicals around the edges. He saw 'Nitrogen' on a can-
ister and 'Potassium' on the label of a large vat in the corner. There
was a crawling heat. Upstairs, the rooms were decked out in a simple
way, and there was a bathroom, a single sofa, a microwave oven. The
Vietnamese were bent over the plants.

'They have sixteen to twenty hours' sun,' Bozydar said, 'and four to eight hours dark. That's how it works. Stefan will explain when he comes.'

Gerry said all the houses were the same. But there was a different atmosphere in the second one they went into, a ghostly place filled with plants but no people, except a young Chinese woman who was playing chess in the kitchen with a silent Vietnamese boy. She moved her pieces with a penknife. She looked up at them when they came into the kitchen, and Bozydar told her that Jakub was going to be the new supervisor and had worked in the factories before.

'Okay,' the woman said.

Bozydar tapped her on the shoulder. 'Stefan is here to take you back to London after you see the new place in Ramsgate.'

She looked up, then down. She knocked over the chess king with her penknife, then put the game away.

The house at the end was like a family home, except the living room was full of plants and equipment. There were two good bedrooms upstairs. Jakub was pleased with them and he stored his backpack in the larger room overlooking the allotments. Gerry came in and bounced down on the bed as if trying it out. 'It's not the Shelbourne Hotel,' he said, 'but a feck of a lot better than half the gaffs they run down here.'

'It's dangerous, yes?' Jakub said.

'It's organised crime, my friend.' He said it with a laugh. 'But if you keep your nose clean you'll make a few pound. That's all you want. See this watch?' He held his wrist up and pointed to the blue face. 'Three grand. You'll make money, okay? Get the work done that he asks you to do and you'll have no bother. None of these grow-houses lasts more than eight months. You'll move on, so you will.'

'It's not what I came for,' Jakub said.

'Don't worry, lad.'

'But I can grow vegetables?'

'You can do what you want. They've put all their eggs into this.

They've got an old bingo hall in Ramsgate with dozens of people working there. It's big business nowadays. They've got packaging sorted and they've got us doing haulage. Lads coming in from London to sell the gear and all that. It's all connected. You've got a nice set-up here, Jakub. Keep your nose clean.'

# 31 The Sitting Tenant

There are more estate agents in Upper Street than anywhere in England. Campbell felt certain of the fact as he crossed the street about a week later. He was still reeling from a conversation he'd had on the phone the day before with the man from Foxtons, who in some mad way 'represented' Mrs Voyles. 'Let's face it, she is not living in conditions that any of us would choose to live in,' the estate agent had said.

'We have done everything. Offered everything.'

'It's about fairness and doing the right thing for the community,' he'd added, before saying she would accept half a million. Sylvia Voyles would be out of their hair and she would move away, back to Wales most probably, and the Flynns could draw a line under this awkward business.

'First off,' Campbell said, 'I don't believe in public housing stock being turned into ready cash. Mrs Voyles has the right to remain. She has a right to ask for improvements but she is currently preventing us from making them. And that's because she doesn't really want them. She lives in a pigsty because she made it a pigsty, and she maintains it that way because she wants a big chunk of free money, despite never having contributed to a mortgage or invested in the property in any way. Her position is grotesque, and now she's upping her demand from a year ago by a hundred grand? It is a parody of the greed you seem happy to criticise, in those rare moments when you're not punting six-million-quid houses and talking of a "buoyant market".'

'I could perhaps persuade her to go down a bit.'

Campbell didn't have the money. The conversation ended pretty quickly once he'd shared that news.

Now it was Islington Council. The meeting was organised by Campbell following the letter they sent ordering that her flat's 'hazards' be dealt with, and he carried with him a second missive, scrappily written and torn from a reporter's notebook, received through the letterbox that afternoon and signed by a man from the local paper. It appeared that the estate agent had lost no time in contacting his client with the bad news, for she had immediately called the journalist to give him 'a disturbing story'. Campbell went into the town hall and waited the obligatory twenty minutes, before a young female housing officer came and led him upstairs to a 'break-out area' encased in glass. Campbell began the meeting by reading out the scribbled note from Woodward and Bernstein.

Dear Mr Flynn,

I work for the Islington Gazette and I have been contacted by Sylvia Voyles of 68a Thornhill Square with a disturbing story about a notice of improvement issued by Islington Council.

Mrs Voyles is a very nice lady. She tells me she has been waiting 19 years for 3 different landlords to carry out the works.

We will be running an article on this in this week's paper.

As her current landlord I wanted to ask you about this and why the works have not yet begun.

I would appreciate the opportunity to discuss this with you ASAP.

'Can you tell me,' Campbell asked, laying it on a coffee table, 'in what sense this is not harassment?'

'I can't take sides,' the housing officer said. 'The notice of improvement was issued to you and the tenant reports that the work has not been done.'

'She won't let us do it.'

'That's all I can say. You have ninety days to fix her flat.'

'But you're not understanding the situation. The woman is insane. She will not allow our workmen to fix the problems you have identified.'

'She is a protected tenant.'

Campbell folded his arms. 'May I ask you, Daisy, are you interested in solving this or are you happy being in a short story by Franz Kafka?'

The young woman touched her name badge. 'Listen. I was sent over to that woman's flat the other day, okay? She told me to fuck off five times, and that was her trying to get me *onside*. We have a file of letters from Mrs Voyles going back twenty-five years. I'm talking 1996. The year before I was born! The file is *this thick*. And the complaints have always been the same. She's a poor soul. She's not the only one. The lady is angry and she always will be angry and that's all I can tell you.'

'Jesus Christ.'

She blew her fringe out of her eyes. 'If you quote me on that, I'll lose my job.'

'I know the rules,' Campbell said.

She shrugged. 'But – and this is a big but – you're possibly being too aggressive with her, and that's not good, either. Nobody gets a prize.'

'She torments me.'

'She's sort of famous in here. She used to run a youth club, believe it or not, in Battle Bridge Road, in the community hall. One of our officers who used to live down there remembers her. She used to give dance classes for the kids. It's easy to forget that people weren't always the way they are now.'

Campbell felt chastened. But he just couldn't think of Mrs Voyles that way. It had gone too far. Her reality was no longer available to him.

There wasn't any break-out tea. Daisy brought him a paper cup of water. She said she had read him in the *Guardian* a few times over the years.

'I really wish I could help you more,' she said, tidying her papers away.

'She wants me to buy her out.'

'That's usually how it ends. But they're protected for a reason. There's plenty of unscrupulous landlords.'

After the meeting, he walked towards Islington Green. It was five o'clock. He texted Elizabeth to say he'd meet her at 7.15. They had tickets to a concert of Restoration music in King's Cross. At St Mary's Church, on Upper Street, he stopped, and just at that moment, he looked across the road and saw Milo Mangasha inside a hairdresser's, sitting in a barber's chair by the window. A girl was behind him, laughing into the mirror and stroking his shoulders. Campbell knew it must be Gosia, his girlfriend. It was an odd sensation looking at them and not being seen, as if their real-life privacy was a denial of their fictional life in Campbell's mind. He had enjoyed the concept of Milo as a helpmeet and a reality instructor, but it had never fully occurred to him that the young man might have worlds of his own, which could involve sitting in a shop window with a beautiful young woman. He took out his phone and called him. It was a lesson in absence, and it somehow added to a sense of quickening crisis, as he watched Milo glance at the screen and return the device unanswered to his pocket. Campbell felt a stab of hurt – and a second reflex: he needed somehow to improve their connection.

He was too early for the concert, so he went to St Pancras Station and took a seat at the champagne bar, ordering a large Islay single malt. Nice to see in the autumn with whisky, he thought. Phone out again, he swiped to Ancestry, his new Candy Crush. He spent a few minutes saving old documents, scrutinising addresses on death certificates, the next little increment in the deep history of his family. All these Flynns, Dunns, Flannigans, Morans, Dochertys and Rileys.

'Pauper', 'Journeyman', 'signed with his mark', 'died in the Glasgow Poorhouse'. He tasted the whisky, looking at the death certificate of an Ayrshire relative who had died of cirrhosis. For the first time in history, an entire genetic narrative could be summoned in a flash, and the task, Campbell knew, was to avoid the technology's seeming ability to name your essence. He looked into the glass and thought of lochs, and of drunk uncles who used to visit his parents in Glasgow. He stared at the glowing amber and understood that if he drank eight of these his mind would go blank.

But an hour later, he was sitting in the blue dark with Elizabeth, holding her hand as the countertenor summoned Purcell's 'Fairest Isle'. There, in a cultured sarcophagus of blonde wood and gentle coughs, he could excel in his own way, joining his agreed nature to a programme of splendid music followed by supper. '*Cupid from his fav'rite nation, care and envy will remove; Jealousy, that poisons passion, and despair, that dies for love.*' The music soared over the rows and Campbell imagined it going out the door and up the escalator into York Way, snaking down Regent's Canal to Caledonian Road.

They were passing a bottle of beer and kissing by the petrol station, Milo saying that the stuff he had hacked out of William Byre's company the week before – showing the scale of his debt to this Russian oligarch Aleksandr Bykov – had now been confirmed by the journalist on the *Commentator* with a second source.

'Wait, what?' Gosia said. 'Who's she talking to?'

He enjoyed saying it: '*Professor Flynn's sister.*'

'You serious?'

'Yep,' he said. 'She emailed my anonymous address to say she needed another source on the Russians, and I said Flynn's sister was close to the committee.'

'Fuck, I love this,' Gosia said.

'And I *felt* it about Kendal,' Milo said, 'as soon as you started telling me about him and who he was.'

Gosia was still preening from the meeting with Dana. She'd gone straight to Milo from the Drapers Arms and told him all about the son, Yuri. 'Wheels inside wheels,' he'd said. 'I've heard his name. He knows Flynn's children.'

'There's a corrupt ecosystem,' she said. 'And it's right here. It's in everybody's street in a different way, waiting to be exposed.'

'Everybody's Sherlock on the Internet,' he said. 'Fingerprints everywhere if you know how to dust for them.'

'Jesus. It's exciting. Frightening.'

He paused. 'The big thing now is the Duke. It goes beyond Flynn and the businessman. It's his *family* now. It's *all* their families now.'

'And to think this all started with me trying to understand what my brother was up to. And you trying to understand your professor.'

'It was a relationship,' Milo said. 'Ours. And *theirs*.'

'But maybe we should leave it now,' Gosia said. 'It's gone far enough.'

Milo took both her hands. 'Nah, I can't let this feeling go. It's happening now. I can take all this stuff and fuck them at the very top.'

That night, they enjoyed it all to the full. The thrill. Milo said he loved diverting money to the charity phone lines. He was getting really good at breaking into accounts and setting up bugs like that. 'Such a buzz.'

'Me too!' she said. 'Sometimes I can't sleep.'

As they walked further on, his phone rang. Milo could see it was Travis. He hadn't spoken to him for weeks. Milo had been down so deep with the new stuff he was working on. On the phone, he couldn't hear what he was saying. It was all traffic. Milo handed his beer to Gosia. He called back and could just about hear him, badly stressed. 'Listen,' Travis said. 'There's a situation, I can't go to my mum's.'

'What's wrong?'

'Police are looking for me, innit. To do with that thing in Deptford.'

'What thing?'

'Sluggz got licked down, cuz.'

'What, you serious?' Milo asked.

He felt a lurch. He knew where this was going.

'They're saying I was part of the group that killed him. I swear, I didn't touch him. Know what I'm saying? I wanted to fix it.'

'Where are you now?'

'Jumped off the Tube at Euston. I think they're following me.'

Milo was calculating. 'Listen. Meet me at Copenhagen Fields.'

'At the bando, yeah?'

'Safer there,' Milo said. 'Cut through Somers Town.'

'Cool. Cool,' he said. 'Just you, yeah?'

'Give me ten minutes.'

When he got to the block, Milo took the stairs. He didn't trust lifts.

Ten thousand sodium lamps out there; he could see them from each landing, the lights on the roads, the reds on top of the cranes.

He pushed the door at number 73. It was open but dark inside, and it was only when he saw the spark of a lighter that he knew Travis was there.

'What you doing hiding in the fucking corner, man?'

'There's no place like home, bro.'

There was something in his voice. Trying to front it out, Milo reckoned. But you could hear the fear. Travis was bunning a zoot, paranoid. He'd been moving all day, getting messages about arrests, dumping his burners. Milo took the SIM card out of Travis's iPhone and placed it on his tongue.

'Body of Christ,' he said. 'Amen.'

He went to the balcony and chucked the phone into the trees.

A helicopter was out. It was loud and Milo could see the search-light darting over the rooftops. 'Is that them?'

'Fuck knows,' Travis said. 'They've been building their case for over two weeks. Getting closer to me, but I didn't do nothing.'

'Tell me what happened.'

'That guy Sluggz is dead. He got slashed in an alley in Deptford. Swear down, man, we only went there to speak to them.'

Travis said a few of the Brixton guys chased him down. Travis had hung back. 'Lloyds and Big Pharma too. They were at the car.'

'Okay, okay. Slow down. Where's your knife?'

'I dashed it in a skip down there.'

'At the scene?'

'No, by the flats we were at.'

Milo's stomach went again, lurching through the years.

'Swear you didn't use it.'

'Totally. I didn't touch nobody. It was just a meet. It was gonna be sorted. Then it all went nuts. But I was standing back.'

'Were you, though?'

'Swear down. How come they know I was there?' he said. 'I was wearing the hoodie, a balaclava. WhatsApp's saying they're talking group enterprise and shit. Feds looking for this Male 4.'

'Male 4?'

'Standing by the lane, knife out.'

'You were holding a knife?'

'Yeah. *Holding* it. Like, in case.'

Milo could see how it would all play out now – and at that moment a radio crackled and feet stomped on the walkway. Travis stood up. 'I didn't do nothin',' he said, as the door burst open and several officers rushed in.

'Get down. Get the fuck down!'

Someone pointed a torch and a weapon at Milo and screamed for his name.

'Milo Mangasha,' he said plainly. 'I'm a friend of this man.' The officer yelled at him to shut the fuck up, grabbed Milo's ID card and radioed in his name. He walked him into the hall as the other feds held Travis in the corner.

'Negative,' the officer said after less than a minute. 'Stand back,' he ordered Milo. 'Keep out of the fucking way.'

They patted both of them down.

'No mobile?' the fed said to Travis, who shrugged.

A policewoman came into the room.

'Are you Travis Babb?' she said, looking at Travis.

'I didn't do shit,' he said.

'Can you confirm your name?'

She stepped closer to Travis and stared into his eyes. The cop smiled as she took out her phone, stepped back and photographed what he was wearing.

'You're nicked, young man.'

Milo and Travis stood apart.

'You've been identified via CCTV as being involved in a homicide in Deptford in the early hours of 26 August. You are therefore under arrest for suspicion of being party to the murder of Sebastian Legland on that date.' She then read Travis his rights, and Travis swallowed, as if all his realisations were coming to him at once. 'Okay,' the officer said. 'Your arrest is pursuant to a prompt and effective investigation, to prevent further harm and to assist with further searches. Do you understand?'

Travis sucked his teeth and looked away. An officer was speaking into a radio about transport. Torchlight darted about the walls, highlighting the graffiti, and Milo and Travis stared at each other as more of the years fell away.

# 32 The British Museum

Campbell was pretty much out of circulation for the next fortnight. He polished his lecture with Milo's help and saw hardly anybody else. October arrived as a dirty sky. It was suddenly cold, and the leaves on the ginkgo tree turned yellow and began to fall, creating a drove of autumnal evidence at the centre of Thornhill Square. The evening of the lecture, Campbell's printer was out of ink, so he printed his pages in Elizabeth's office. Everything was tidy on her desk: the pencil cases, a paperback copy of *Moby-Dick*. He stopped for a moment when he saw a Post-it note next to her laptop: 'A loss of self in him is met with no corresponding loss of affection in me, which raises a question about love.'

He turned, his eyes drawn to the pattern in the rug. The swirls seemed to multiply and for a second it seemed as if there was no floor.

'It's me,' he said quietly. 'It's my fault.'

After dressing, he went to the landing and drew a scarf off the banister, a silk number that enhanced his suit. His mind was teeming with verbal events, things he might say or add or emphasise or delete, and he went downstairs to fetch a raincoat with a sense that all destinies must in good time collide.

He read a few texts in the car. The first was from Kenzie: 'Granny can't make it. She feels quite poorly.' The second was from Elizabeth, saying she was leaving her analyst's in Primrose Hill and getting a taxi. She'd meet him at the Museum Tavern. 'Hello, Professor Flynn,' a longer one said. It was from the journalist Tara Hastings. 'Further to my email, the culture editor wants to go with the City Life piece sooner than I thought. Could you cope with an interview mid-morning tomorrow?' Campbell puffed his cheeks. He'd read her stories about William, and he didn't trust her motives. But best to see her and get it over with. Don't fuss. Act normal. Seeing journalists for puff pieces: just an aspect of fame maintenance.

An hour later, he was in the green room, pacing with the printed script in his hand and warming up his voice. 'I'm heading to the reception,' Elizabeth said, picking a piece of lint from his shoulder and kissing his cheek. 'I'm at a table with Candy and the Duke.' She smiled and her smile helped him.

'How was your shrink?' he said out of nowhere.

'Refreshingly banal,' she replied.

The exhibitions and programmes curator, who was half Dutch, said he was totally devoted to the mysteries of Vermeer. He clearly expected Campbell's lecture to be a quiet but vivid disquisition on Dutch portraiture and modern tech. 'The Human Face in the Digital Age', it said across the top of his script, with a pasted-in picture, a kind of good-luck charm, of an Elizabethan gold groat. Campbell accepted a glass of water and spent a few minutes thinking about the shape of the Enlightenment Gallery, going over it in his mind. He felt apart from his own body tonight, and his sense of solidity seemed to have shifted. He was at the centre of the building, at the centre of a drama, and he recalled the same separation in the high flats of Glasgow, waiting for his mother to return from work and feeling magically disconnected. He gained strength from the notion he could pour anything out of himself, because he was a vessel, filled with the energy of other people.

Walking across the Great Court, he could hear the voices, a tremendous gathering of London's top men and women, these susurrating guests, legislators, academics and lawyers. He knew his sister would be there. Thank God, he said to himself. There is nowhere that isn't a bit better for having Moira nearby. He stood at the door as the curator went ahead and a person with an earpiece held him back with two fingers. Then it happened: the swoosh of uncertainty, the late appearance of abject fear, a few staticky pops on the distant microphone, the curator's booming voice and a nod from the stage manager.

The podium was below a second-century BC statue of Hermes. Campbell saw the winged sandals as he went up the steps, the applause relenting as he placed his pages on the lectern and surveyed the Enlightenment Gallery. 'We are here,' he began, 'in one of the Western world's most beautiful rooms.' He took in all the glittering, candle-lit tables, the well-known faces, the dark cabinets and ancient statuary around them. 'It was founded in the early nineteenth century to reflect British collectors' understanding of the ancient world. Towards Room 2, we see Nature, followed by the Birth of Archaeology, Art and Civilisation. To my immediate right, we see Ancient Scripts, followed by materials of Religion and Ritual, and, towards the East stairs, Trade and Discovery. The room is the oldest in the museum, housing, at one time, the library of King George III as well as the collection of Sir Hans Sloane, and it was these, when joined together with several other libraries and a number of discrete collections, that became the basis for the British Museum, established by an Act of Parliament in 1753 and renowned all over the globe.'

Milo was a refracting light at the centre of the audience. Dressed in his suit, he seemed to be the youngest person in the room, sitting behind a flickering candle and in front of a cabinet displaying English helmets from the thirteenth century. In that instant, Campbell saw Milo as a perverse young radical among the British Establishment. He sat there embodying all the questions it hadn't asked. As Campbell spoke, he took in the smiling men in bow ties and the ladies in frocks, as well as Grayson Perry, wearing a dress so pink it appeared to blush at itself. The guests were enclosed, in that part of the room, by volumes of the *Mémoires d'un homme d'état* and by *Religion in England*, adjacent to corals and nautilus shells, to quartz from India and jasper from Russia. Stuffed orioles and starlings jostled in the dark around them, and there was the provocative languor of Praxiteles's satyr, carved in stone 360 years before the birth of Christ.

'In Hermes, above me, we observe the living face of vigorous youth, a messenger of daily truths, aghast, we might think, at the indecencies of man. He is full-lipped, strong-chinned, deep-eyed, powerfully nosed, and for millennia we have admired him and found ourselves confounded by his mysterious face. Is it the expression of a living soul? And what does it tell us about the world he looked upon?' Campbell pointed at the *Rondanini Faun* to his left, and then across to the statue of Venus and her 'simple, manly' face. 'Removed from Campo Iemini in 1794,' he went on, 'it compares badly with another in this museum, a Proconnesian marble statue of Venus taken by the Scottish excavator – and poor portrait artist – Gavin Hamilton in 1775, from the ruins of the baths erected by Claudius at Ostia. Almost seven feet high, she is known as the Townley Venus and was smuggled here after tense negotiations.' Campbell detected a bristling from the director's table.

He continued to the next page.

'I would argue that Venus's face is a synecdoche, if you'll allow me such a word, for the vacantly unknowable faces of power and desire in the Internet age. She is not definitely Venus. She may be Ariadne. She was not definitely found at Ostia. She is adapted from a lost Greek original. She has one eighteenth-century arm, is strangely posed and is, by any measure, an outrageous fabrication, a work of composition in which the museum has played a creative part. If she has a mind, it is the mind of us all, composing ourselves to meet requirements and occasions. Her cracks are our cracks, her lies our lies, and her face a telling fiction as powerful as the fictions in Vermeer.'

He called the museum 'Fagin's Lair'. A fence's paradise. He said we had spent centuries composing a myth of our island story and furnishing it with international swag, which we offered to 'preserve' or 'look after for humanity'. A lack of transparency made the work of the museum no better, and less honest, than the machinations of Bitcoin, and he spoke of the Internet as being like Caliban looking in the mirror.

There it was, he thought. There it is. The first frown on the face of a Tory politician with friends in Russian banking. The first dowager's tut. A certain stiffening in their social postures. They twisted the stems of their wine glasses as the quietness got quieter, the lights hotter, the disaffection beginning to blossom.

He spent the next fifteen minutes talking about the *Piranesi Vase*, which dominated the centre of the room – 'a junk heap of ancient parts, a grotesque, hybrid beast of plundered items, a *glaistig*, a Krampus, owing nothing to science, aesthetic design or justice as it takes its place in the British Museum.'

'That's the point of a museum!' someone shouted.

Campbell couldn't see the person but he caught sight of Elizabeth, listening. My dear Elizabeth, he thought, his mind speaking over himself. He needed her most at the very point where he had made her unavailable. He wondered if he'd lost her, if whatever journey he was on was too big for the marriage of true minds, and he thought of Freud for a second, surrounded in his Hampstead room with his ancient icons. The Duke was sitting beside her, smiling like the satyr and nodding as if the whole thing was a jolly ruckus.

'In Edmund Arwaker's *Truth in Fiction*,' Campbell went on, 'a satire published in England in 1708, we discover a country full of plunder, full of bad money, yet it plumes on the "authenticity" of the objects it steals. Arwaker shows us a job lot of Mercurys, a hatful of Hermeses, and sees them for what they are: plaster bric-à-brac snapped from their native pedestals to furnish the vanity of the ailing British.'

'Shame!' someone shouted.

He looked up from his pages and smiled. 'Perhaps Caliban recognised that too,' he said, 'though the shame of his captors is better earned.'

A few laughs rose from the floor. He felt modern and agile as he surged ahead and his sentences grew elaborate. Half of them were ad-libbed; some were stolen. He now detailed the digital life, the online forging and losing of identities, surveillance, CCTV, the manipulations of self, the rise of avatars and proxies. 'We begin to see the end of privacy, the end of what Henry James called "the sovereignty of private consciousness in the conduct of human affairs". The misinformation that underpins wars will no longer be sustainable; the financial arrangements, the everyday enslavements, the corporate lies, will be denied their secret oxygen. As we survey these stone faces in the British Museum, these classical distortions and all that they conceal, we may begin, in the spirit of genuine inquiry, to replace their beautiful lies with a seeding of truth.'

He told himself to breathe.

'We are a nation of thieves and coffee drinkers,' he said. 'We plunder, therefore we are. To return to my seventeenth-century friend Mr Edmund Arwaker, in his *Fable XXIX: The Coffee-House: Or, A Man's Credit, is his Cash*, we find that news of a British victory is disbelieved, when recounted by a lowly soldier, but taken as gospel when offered by a powdered fop, who comes in with his golden snuffbox and his news from Court. Our institutions are all like that: distinguished foppery and fake baubles. Our museums say nothing about the digital reality in which every day we lose ourselves and become free. The museum itself belongs in a museum, and is as dead as the golden snuffbox. Incidentally, Mr Arwaker, my source, was drawing on Aesop, whom we admire as a moral authority while failing to acknowledge, as we should, that he was an African slave.'

'Not true!' someone shouted.

'Imperialism, ladies and gentlemen, is not a thing to be apologised for, or merely admitted,' he continued. 'It is a process of criminality to be rendered obsolete, as each block of stone in this building, and all the ore it contains, is returned to its place of origin and we learn to live with the emptiness. For this room, the most beautiful room in the Western world, is but a paper lantern: it is a room of fantasy, and we populate it and celebrate our nation's criminality at a ruinous cost to our modernity. When we occupy the emptiness, and fill it with the sound of ethical reason, we will have entered the digital age, ready to make our own compositions in the unacknowledged free spaces of the Net, where we may change our language, surrender our treasure and find the future.'

He pointed to the face of the *Townley Discobolus*, to his right.

'A Roman confection of the second century,' he said, 'copied from the Greek original by Myron. But the head on this statue is an imposter.'

He saw his researcher again, a finger on his chin.

'The only significant heads in English art appear on our coins. We have in front of us the coin cabinet of King George III. Yet these coins too are now tokens of a failed world. They describe a relationship between possession and value, between currency and guarantee, that has been obliterated in the dawning era of crypto-currency. In the future, a currency's value will be agreed, and will be confirmed, by our mutual acceptance of the fact online, without reference to governments or their banks. This cabinet, containing the loose change of history, the shrapnel of civilisation, is a symbol to me of all that is coming to an end. We might admire Sir Hans Sloane, physician, collector and slave owner, but at what point in the history of our liberal tolerance do we say, "Enough"? Sloane was a eugenicist who collected specimens relating to skin colour and chained up his slaves. He spoke of Africa as "the Benighted continent", and this is our museum, our rusted currency and our corruption. At the end of the Enlightenment Gallery, we find the sitting Egyptian figure of Sekhmet, in dark granodiorite, the lion-headed goddess of healing. Smuggled from the Temple of Mut at Karnak by the British proconsul Henry Salt in 1790, she is the sitting tenant of the British Museum, a bogus symbol of civilisation. She presides over this sham, this artful attempt at healing, but any one of us who is hopeful for the arrival of true self-healing in our time may feel perturbed by her presence here and by her malevolent smile.'

When he finished, he stared at Milo. He knew the young man

believed all of these institutions would be brought down in the end. Campbell folded the speech and stepped down to a smattering of applause. He felt he had never in his life been so dignified as he came down the stairs with all eyes on him and the muttering already emphatic. He departed the gallery unaccompanied and made his way to the green room to pick up his coat and scarf. He didn't want to speak, he didn't want dinner, and he left the building quickly. Stepping into Great Russell Street, he felt a rush of clear air mingled with the smell of roasting chestnuts, and he gave £50 to a homeless man, feeling in that second that he understood and was at one with all the exploited people of the metropolis.

Elizabeth had to endure three courses that night. She was normally fine at such events, faculty dinners, but her table was unbearable. The neurotic element was loudly represented by Dame Cordelia Harris, an Australian sculptor who was devoted to telling people off and bossing facts about to suit her prejudices. She spent the smoked salmon going on about Campbell's 'incorrigible wokeness'. His place sat empty the rest of the evening.

'I thought it was jolly plucky!' the Duke said.

'Absolutely!' Candy piped. 'I'd never thought about it before, arms and legs from all over the place. Heads turning up, and so on.'

'It's ridiculous,' Dame Cordelia said. 'This is a bloody *museum*. Civilisation is the whole point of the place. You fill it with stuff. You look after it, you keep it at the right temperature and all that jazz, you clean it. The people who think they own it would have let it crumble into dust years ago, and that's a fact.'

'It's not a fact,' said Atticus Tew, Campbell's agent. 'It's your *opinion*, and a rather reactionary one at that. The man's trying to say something new.'

'The whole lecture was bodgie.'

'I beg your pardon?' said Atticus.

'Garbage. Politically correct garbage. *Professor Campbell Flynn!*

I've had it up to here with self-intoxicated men.'

Candy began talking about a new arts festival she was setting up at their estate in Suffolk. 'Healing. Literature. Food.'

Elizabeth's worries about Campbell were confirmed by the way he had disappeared, and she felt dismayed by the lecture, the clearly borrowed concepts, the echoes about money and digital freedom. Staring across the table, she realised he'd been talking about his own financial affairs, his loss of faith in money. For a while, she'd suspected he hadn't been paying his tax or VAT. She hadn't applied herself to it. She'd scarcely ever brought it up: he was so menacingly private about that sort of thing. It made her more than anxious, every time an invoice was paid, that it might only add to the mountain he owed, but he forbade her from ever mentioning anything about it to her sister or getting loans for him. He withdrew if one tried to speak of it. He always said he would burrow his own way out of it, and it pleased him to think he could do it with his own talent. That's why he'd written that awful self-help book.

Elizabeth straightened her napkin. How can a person who believes in public services not pay his taxes? She'd always felt he was a fairly moral man. But money was like his parents: he wouldn't talk about it until it overwhelmed him, and, even then, it was a well-woven veil that he simply took steps to arrange in a new way. That boy at the next table, his researcher, the one with the sticky fingers and the precocious mind, was allegedly helping Campbell, but Elizabeth knew he was dominating him somehow. She could scarcely believe the ease with which he had come into their lives. 'I'm being put to the test,' Campbell had said to her during that agonised afternoon over the passport, the day before they flew to Iceland, and he very much wanted it, the trial, the exposure to truths and possibilities he'd previously ignored. That's all the boy was. And now her husband had made his magical exit and left her with a trail of smoke and the glint of mirrors.

# 33 The Avalon Hotel

When she thought about Halloween, Vicky could taste toffee apples and tangerines, and she saw weans in raggedy costumes, plus her mammy's ginger hair, like the sparky bonfires on the seafront at Saltcoats. You don't forget the smell of October and all the guisers swinging their plastic bags as they go from door to door. It was turnips they used in Ayrshire not pumpkins. Vicky turned the whole thing over in her mind as she went up a side street in King's Cross, shivering, inspecting the pavement cracks. It's so easy to get lonely in a big place and it made her homesick, knowing London wasn't working. She was just another of those people who got thrown away.

She stopped at the Avalon Hotel in Argyle Square. She tapped the window on the right-hand side, and it only took a second for the curtain to move and then for somebody to come down the hall and open the door. Coco, Colleen. Thing is, she couldn't remember their names and she was jangling because she needed something right away. It was weird: you got a burst of feeling so total and so nice, then you needed it again. The girl let her in and they turned into the bedroom right by the front door. The room was scabby. Full of smoke and spilled drink and rubbish on the floor and tangled blankets. It was dark, apart from an orange lamp lying on its side, and she put out her hand to the guy.

'Fifteen?' he goes. 'Bitch, you owe me forty.'

She handed him a watch. 'Fifteen and this is plenty, okay?'

He turned to the cabinet, handed her two rocks. The girl on the bed was slavering on the pillow, eyes all over the place.

Vicky crouched against the bedroom wall. She took out her pipe and put the rocks in – the mesh was bent, she held it in place – and got the lighter under it and sucked in all the smoke and that was her: she felt brand new, the smoke curling, like somebody found you and liked you and kept their promise.

'What's the matter?' the girl on the bed said.

Coco, or Colleen.

She saw her mammy in the pool at Auchenharvie, shouting, 'Victoria, swim to me! Swim to me, darling.' She put her head back and saw all the fires in Ayrshire.

She didn't know how long she was there. She hugged herself in the corner, then she took off her shoe and found two £10 notes in it. 'I stashed it there,' she said out loud, and went over to the guy on the bed.

'Get fucking lost,' he said.

'Naw, I've got the money,' she said. 'A coupla rocks.'

The word reminded her of William in that restaurant they went to. 'Sounded like "roaks",' he'd said.

The guy on the bed had a needle in his arm.

'Sort her out, will ya?' he said to the woman beside him.

'There's only brown,' the woman said. 'That's all there is, darling. Lovely gear and look at him if you don't believe me.'


Tara was glad she'd worn gloves the next morning. Pigeons were flying about the road and the lady in Thornhill Square was being difficult.

'From the what did you say?'

'The *Commentator*. It's an online newspaper.'

'Never heard of it,' the lady said, her breath rising above the iron gate. 'You know the *Islington Gazette*? The man there is one of the better journalists. Most of them are useless. Journalists, I mean. He's from Cardiff and he knows a scandal when he sees one.'

'I'm sorry, do you live with Professor Flynn?'

'I was here before him. I happen to live downstairs. And that man is a charlatan, a slum landlord. Ask him!'

'I beg your pardon?'

'He doesn't know anything about art. A charlatan, I tell you. Tries to pass himself off as a kind of—'

Tara, in an act of swift mental unkindness, had already put the neighbour down as one of those housing nutters you find in London, but the lady's criticism of her subject had nonetheless interested her. Tara had spent the walk over wondering how deep a hypocrite Campbell Flynn might be. Suddenly, the front door opened and he was there, at the top of the steps.

'Ah,' he said.

'I'm Tara Hastings.'

'Oh, yes,' he said. 'Do come in.'

Tara couldn't make out what the lady was saying as she passed into the house and Professor Flynn closed the door.

'I do apologise,' he said. 'I'm afraid we have the nightmare of all nightmares living in the flat below us. She wants to be a property tycoon and finds herself in the frustrating position of being a sitting tenant. Tea?'

His Scottish accent was more pronounced than it was on his broadcasts. When he moved his phone off the ottoman, the screen lit up and she saw the logo of a mindfulness app she'd heard about. Buddhify.

'I've brought cakes,' she said. 'They have these stalls outside the station. You know, flourless chocolate tart and that sort of thing.'

'Excellent.' He took the bag. 'The new King's Cross. In the old days, it was a greasy spoon jammed with sex workers.'

'I bet they weren't called that.'

'No, they weren't,' he said.

Family pictures. A paper geranium. She'd grown up in Hampstead and knew exactly how these houses were done. A kind of sub-Bloomsbury ecology of painted lamps and English ceramics and honeyed wood. 'I don't know if you've seen this regular feature we have,' she said, as he poured the kettle. 'City Life? It's in the culture bit. A celebrity talks about their favourite place. Not my usual fare, but your name came up at conference and I offered to do it. I thought it would be a good excuse to meet you.'

'I'm flattered,' he said.

He put the tray down. People like the Flynns cared about teapots. The side plates featured designs by Eric Ravilious. Flynn looked okay for his age. Taller than his famous son and with sharper edges, a crisp blue shirt, a blazer with jeans. She often wrote things like that in her notepad during interviews, when the subject imagined she was capturing their words of wisdom. Reporters have to be good actors. On assignment, you take every role in the courthouse – judge, jury, counsel, witness, stenographer – with a sense of being above specific responsibilities. Tara wasn't proud of it, but she had a gift for keeping emotion out of her tasks.

'So, you know this area pretty well?' she asked.

He sat back on the sofa and wiped crumbs from his fingers.

'This is my second time living here,' he said. 'I lived behind the station in my early twenties. It was an old, cobbled street.'

'Right down from my office, where Granary Square is now.'

'The gasholders really were gasholders then.'

'And you rented a flat?'

'Yes. King's Cross was a different world back then,' he said, 'an apex of Victorian life – the two train stations, the gasholders, Regent's Canal, tenements.'

'A kind of seedy backwater.'

'It was before the Eurostar. Centre of London now. There's Google's massive new offices being built. They're planning to have sage and gooseberry on the roof, and there will be an Olympic-sized running track. Plus Facebook is building new London headquarters on the other side of the canal. Expedia is there.'

'What would you say is characteristic about it?'

'With King's Cross, it's the urban fix. It's the online capital of Europe, a vanishable space that is also pretty solid and metallic, which seems, to my mind, entirely consistent with the Victorian past. It has always been a communications hub where people come and go – they arrive and they depart, here and not here, and it seems engraved into the landscape of the place, the idea that nothing is permanent and people disappear and we're all living in a grand state of ephemerality.'

He'd written the article for her.

'Plus,' he said, 'it was always a zone of desire. A lot of that might now be underground, but the puzzle remains, why somewhere so prosperous is so . . .'

'Poor,' she said. 'Unequal.'

'That's right.'

'That's very *Commentator*,' she said. 'Thank you.'

'You have what you need?'

'More than enough. We have a photograph from your publisher. Could you also email us one of you from that time?'

'There's one of me on the roof of Stanley Buildings,' he said. 'My wife always said I looked like a boy off the train from Scotland.'

'Cambridge, more like.'

She was relaxed now, so she resorted to an old journalistic trick: first get what you want and then get what you really want. She felt him out on his background. He was a scholarship boy from Glasgow, she said, but he'd never spoken about his parents, never explained his formative years in any of these essays he'd written. He nodded as she spoke and displayed a well-managed reserve. 'I've heard it said that you erased your background at a young age, that you hardly saw your parents, who were working-class people, is that correct?'

'I saw my parents,' he said. 'I'm not sure that they saw me.'

He nodded like the personal part of the conversation was over, but she continued to inspect him. She couldn't say what it was, but Flynn intrigued her. He seemed to be a cipher in other people's wrongdoing.

'There are a few topics I'd like to speak to you about off the record,' she said.

He pursed his lips. There was something aloof about him now as he poured another cup and smiled. 'What kind of topics?'

'Can I level with you?'

'Please do.'

Tara looked around as if to check they were alone.

'It's entirely private here,' he said. 'My wife has gone to our house in Suffolk. We had a rather busy time of it last night at the British Museum.'

'Busy? Social media was delighted,' Tara said.

He shook his head and frowned, like it meant nothing. He had the kind of defensiveness that can appear steely, but probably isn't.

'I heard rumours that you might have ghostwritten that book *Why Men Weep in Their Cars*?'

'Rumours?'

'All over the place.'

'No,' he said. 'I met the author at the Serpentine party a few summers ago. I don't know him very well. He's a bright young man.'

'You didn't help him?'

'Jake is an actor, and he asked me for a few words of direction. I can't remember what I said to him but I doubt it was of any use. I think there is a new appetite for explanations of how to be, and of why we are.'

'That could almost be a quote from the book.'

'I write about art.' He drank from his cup. 'I've been working steadily on a book about Rembrandt and I write occasional essays. The book—'

'It has this cult following now. Hart-Davies presented it as a manifesto of self-justification for abusive men.'

'That's rather up to him.'

She looked at him and wasn't sure what to say. He was interesting but hidden. So unlike his sister, who was frank and available.

'I wish I could be more helpful,' he said. 'I have a rather wide circle of friends. And I have a passion for contemporary change.'

She scrutinised him when he said that. It was such a weird thing to say. But she noticed that he seemed to grow in stature during this part of their conversation, as if denial gave him a kind of energy.

'I want to ask you about another friend.'

'By all means,' he said.

'William Byre. Zachary's father. I've been working on a new angle, an investigation into his connections to foreign money.'

He now gave her a clear look of distrust. 'I must insist that you turn your tape recorder off.'

'Yes, of course.'

'This conversation is off the record.'

'I want to ask you—'

'Is that the reason you came here today?' he asked.

'It was 50 per cent of the reason.'

He seemed to accept that. 'Well, I don't think I can be of any help with that, even off the record.'

'But did you know of his Russian connections? Did you have any financial interactions with him over the years of your friendship?'

The look in his eye became almost sad. 'You know, Tara, you might be too young to understand this, but old friendship is a thing. The person you're speaking about was someone I first knew when I was eighteen years old. I loved him. He is now in prison awaiting trial for serious fraud. I am as shocked as anyone else that he finds himself in this position.'

'And does it surprise you that he could be accused of rape?'

'It horrifies me.'

'It doesn't seem to surprise his wife.'

He stroked a cushion and shook his head.

'I have nothing to say about that,' he said.

'I have spent time with Victoria Gowans. I wrote—'

'I find it hard to get over,' Flynn said suddenly, and his voice trembled.

'Is that true, sir – or do you have it both ways?'

Questioning people's motives is often a way of revealing your own. She knew that. She was too intelligent to ignore how she might be implicated in some of what she wrote about. It was obvious to her now, and she felt embarrassed as she switched on her recorder again. 'I am now recording,' she said, 'and I wish to ask you, Campbell Flynn – have you or your family ever been connected to money coming from offshore companies?'

'I think you should leave.'

'Did William Byre ever reveal to you his collaboration with Middle Eastern and Russian lenders?'

He stood up and gently replaced his teacup. The tray was now a scene of failed civility.

'Miss, I ask you politely, please leave my house.'

She stood up, her recorder still in her hand. 'Is it true that your wife's brother-in-law, the Duke of Kendal, received payments from Aleksandr Bykov for the renovation of a Georgian mansion in the Scottish Highlands?'

He seemed so distant from her questions – as if he was mortified for her, at her cheek in turning a small arts feature into a doorstepping opportunity – yet his calm eyes and his courtly manners might have concealed a degree of panic. He did say one thing, by the door, that caught her very much by surprise. She struggled later to write it down. 'I think if you accept your own mistakes – try to see them, own them – then you are well placed to make your life into something. That's all I'm saying. I was taught that by a pupil of mine.' There was something serene in his face as he said that. He seemed vividly absent, there but not there, a man without consequences, as if the assertions she'd made were somehow unreal, matters of interpretation quite unrelated to Campbell Flynn.

# 34 Britannia Street

Later that week, Frieze Art Fair in Regent's Park was all about the clothes. It was full of old ladies in skinny black jeans with zips for pockets, young men in baggy Chinese peasant trousers and striped T-shirts, dealers wearing bespoke suits, pocket squares and thin knitted ties. It was the same every year, but with fashion developments. The three hundred or so international galleries had a booth each, and Angus walked through them with Astrid. She was *awesome*, he thought, and they'd had a crazy summer in Dubai.

'Hey, babe, look at this,' she said.

It was like an LED display of rolling data. Three and a half metres long with information speeding past on the screen. 'I love it,' she said. 'It's so empowering to be in the flow of the figures. It's like society *bleeding*.'

'Amazing,' he said. 'Like, totally amazing.'

She grabbed his hand with both of hers. 'It really gets inside you. Like NASDAQ running riot in your mind and shouting, "Be ethical."'

Angus stepped forward. 'You see all that?'

'God, yeah. In a heartbeat, babe. Don't you?'

Angus hated being asked for his views. His parents were always interpreting everything. Nobody having a good time has to ask how.

They were standing in the booth belonging to the Taro Nasu Gallery of Tokyo, looking at artworks 'influenced by the digital nightmare'.

'I could have that in the conference room at Honest Chutney,' she said. 'Ask her how much it is, Angus.'

He came back and told her it was over a million.

'Dollars or euros?'

He went back to the girl. 'Dollars, she said.'

They'd already bought a couple of trial proofs by Ed Ruscha. 'A bunch of gas stations,' Astrid had said to him. 'I mean, there's nothing so empty as an empty gas station in Nebraska, right?'

'But could you wake up to it?' Angus asked.

'To Standard Oil? Honey, we all do.'

She was the brightest woman he'd ever been with. He told Kenzie and she said they should settle down and get an apartment or something. But he thought living in hotels was the more 'him' thing to do right now.

Galleries all over London were holding events under Frieze's auspices, and Angus was keen to go over to King's Cross, where he was booked to DJ at the after-party for Carl Friis's show of destroyed art. But they stayed at the Fair in Regent's Park for a while longer.

Stepping into the VIP lounge, they saw Yuri Bykov. 'You missed your father,' he said.

'But he's coming later to Carl's party, right?'

'I believe so,' Yuri said, passing each of them a glass of champagne. 'He wrote something for the catalogue, so I'm sure he's coming.'

The room was abuzz with entitlement. 'How's your friend, the actor?' Angus asked, hoping to bury his reasons for asking.

'Jake? Still on retreat,' Yuri said.

'What, like a cleanse?' Astrid asked.

'More like a spiritual renovation,' Yuri said. 'They lock them up in Arizona and strip their mental wallpaper of all its pattern.'

'Sounds proper,' Angus said.

'Not my cup of lapsang, either,' Yuri said. 'He's been in a mess about the whole thing. You know he lost the film?'

'He did say some mad shit, though.'

Yuri laughed. 'He's quite gaga and quite evil. Poor Jake. Hellishly good-looking, all the same.'

'Right.'

'I do miss him for Shakespeare. I hope he hurries back.'

'Good luck with that,' Angus said. 'He's probably better off with Shakespeare, more likely to stick to the script.'

Yuri downed his glass and took another off a tray.

'Does your father speak about it?' he asked.

Angus looked Yuri right in the eye. 'We all know about dads,' he said. Then, after a pause and a sip of champagne: 'My father literally hasn't said a word about it. It's like the whole thing happened to somebody else.'

'And you and your sister don't know Jake?'

'No. We watched *Aethon's Curse*. But all this stuff with my dad—'

'I know Jake wants to talk to you about it sometime,' Yuri said.

The guy behind them was talking about Robert Rauschenberg, saying too many works sold at Frieze were obvious fakes. Angus felt authenticity was overvalued, and people should chill out: 'If they like a thing, they like it.' He loved the way the art world was now populated with ex-bankers, a second career for guys from Goldman who'd made too much money. He liked their vibe and he liked what the switch had done to their hair.

On the other side of the park, at Frieze Masters, one of the gallerists jumped up from his chair when he saw Campbell Flynn coming towards his booth. He wanted to show him a bad painting by Laurits Andersen Ring called *Homework*, and then another one, *Evening Thoughts* by Carl Holsøe, also badly painted. Campbell was rather struck by the latter: it showed a man in front of a mirror by a window with the darkness outside. 'Isn't it odd,' the gallerist said, 'how a bad painter will often bring the narrative delights that a good painter misses?'

'It's the marriage of art and melodrama,' Campbell said. 'As in Balzac. As in Magritte. He's not a bad painter, but one who isn't afraid to manage suspense. Too many artists behave as if the only feeling that matters is their own.'

415

They enjoyed further conversation on the topic, and two glasses of champagne, before repairing to the marquee's big restaurant, Folie. They bumped into a curator from the Getty in Los Angeles, who immediately engaged Campbell in discussion about a possible show of Rembrandt drawings. 'Oh boy, did you upset our friends at the British Museum,' the curator said. 'When was that?'

'A few days ago. It needed saying.'

'Well, it sure put the *cattus* among the *columbae*. Apparently, the BM was getting calls from diplomats. The Lithuanian ambassador starts demanding the museum send back all his country's treasures, and they say, "What treasures?" The guy is shouting that they must have miscatalogued them under "Poland". All nonsense, of course. In the end, the BM admitted they had a decorated Lithuanian egg from about 1960 in the stores.'

There was a buzzing inside Campbell – he wondered if it might be worsened by the statins he was taking, along with the more powerful painkillers he'd got off the Internet, and all the alcohol. Since the Autumn Lecture, his trips down the dark digital alleyways hadn't stopped. In fact it had all accelerated. And he was seeing just as much of Milo. Their shared vision felt real to him now. He'd got Milo to help him with the writing of the catalogue copy for Carl Friis's destroyed art show, opening that night. In fact, Milo had channelled Campbell's voice and written the piece himself. Everything was a team effort, and Campbell realised, without saying it to anyone, that Milo's voice had taken root in some new and necessary part of his conscience, and the boy was in the process of replacing most of the people at the centre of his life. This didn't feel sensible to Campbell, but it didn't feel wrong.

At Folie, he was soon joined by more dealers and art patrons. The gallerists wore no socks with their moccasins. One of them spent £500 on a bottle of Dom Ruinart Rosé 2004; another spent £800 on a Meursault 'Clos des Ambres'. Crudités, tapenade and anchoïade, prosciutto and cayenne nuts and olives were placed around the bar, and the drink flowed and flowed. Campbell began retreating into himself as the laughter got louder. 'You should come with us,' Wayne from the Getty was saying. 'There's a dinner tonight at Silvia Pole de Menezes's.'

'The woman who owns all the Modiglianis?'

'Yes. Divorced from the sultan.'

'Mad settlement,' said the guy from Hauser & Wirth. 'Like $740 million. She's now hoarding Bourgeois and Soutine.'

'She'd be thrilled if you came,' Wayne said.

Campbell made one of his instant frowns. 'I can't,' he said. 'I've got to be at the Gagosian in King's Cross for the Friis opening. He's a friend.'

'That show sounds interesting. There was a talk in the Masters series about it, "A History of Damaged Art".'

The Hauser guy was accompanied by a Chinese woman in a poncho. 'I am a fan of your Vermeer book,' she said.

'Thank you so much.' He was feeling very drunk. The woman was talking about the problem of light. In that inebriated, confident way, he was frothing with things to say, but he became indignant when he realised she was advocating a show of the fake Vermeers by Han van Meegeren.

'I wouldn't want to have any part of that,' he said.

'Why not?' the woman said. Her English was weirdly perfect, like she'd gone to a finishing school. 'It asks all the right questions.'

'But the paintings are ghastly.'

'It hardly matters. The fraudster was fascinating. *He* was the work, actually. And that is a very modern show, I think.'

'That kind of thing should be banned. I hate fakery.'

She pouted, as if in quick astonishment. 'Well,' she said, 'that's frightfully old-fashioned of you, Professor Flynn.'

He gulped down the acidic white wine.

The woman had a look of chagrined, sudden bravery. Now that they'd disagreed, she dunked all caution in an ice bucket. 'Your lecture at the British Museum wasn't as radical as you think,' she said. 'Fashionable nonsense, quite honestly.'

'How charming of you to say so.'

'We say what we mean in China.'

'I doubt that very much,' he said.

Wayne was leaving. 'Keep up the anarchy, Professor Flynn. It's been really swell seeing you.'

Tripping his way around Frieze Masters, he noticed a piece of neon from the studio of Tracey Emin. It reminded him of the time he went to the new Saatchi Gallery with Elizabeth and they saw *My Bed*, Emin's smeared, crumpled bed surrounded by debris. The artwork had agitated Campbell. He couldn't work out why, until Elizabeth asked him, crossing Westminster Bridge after the show, if he'd felt safe in his bed as a child, and he told her that he was sometimes physically removed from it by his dad when his parents had argued, and put in bed with his mother. Elizabeth could purify his mind about the art scene. She took none of its self-importance for granted, and felt it was a sort of safe space in which damaged people could act out their damage, creating order.

He went on a drunken excursion through the various booths, hoping to bum a cigarette and maybe buy something small. Down by the entrance, he dipped into the Sam Fogg gallery. Amid the glare of the sprawling Masters tent, this booth was deliberately dim and sepulchral. *A Votive, or Memento Mori Panel with a Shrouded Corpse Resting on a Skull*, the title said. 'Flemish School, 1520–30'. He had seen his own father dead like that in a hospital morgue in Glasgow. No skull to rest on, no warring angels, but the same face and hands. A heart attack at work. He'd been doing the night shift, driving a minicab to support the family. He drank too much.

The dealer at Sam Fogg quoted a high price.

Campbell leaned in to see it better. Above the corpse, the Latin inscription translated as 'And you will live in your father's house forever.'

'It's so beautiful,' the dealer said.

'And so terrible,' Campbell said. 'I mean, full of terror.'

He felt light-headed as he walked to the next booth. Too much wine and too much memory, or too much perspective, or too little. As he entered he instantly heard Carl Friis.

'*Professor!*' he shouted. 'We were just talking about your essay.'

'Oh, goody. Which one?'

'The one for my catalogue, silly!' He closed his eyes to reveal lids of black glitter. 'I mean, *beyond*, as a piece of brilliance. Totally beyond.'

'It's not mine,' Campbell said. 'It was written by one of my students. A young Irish-Ethiopian with a taste for destruction.'

'You *see!*' Friis said. 'The instinct! A brilliant act of deferral! Only he could think of it, to get the student to translate him.'

'Not a translator,' Campbell said, walking round a block of resin by Rachel Whiteread and lifting a drink off a tray. 'He's an original.'

'Huh! Darling, we're *all* original. Which is to say, no one is! We have to leave soon for my own grand party. Showtime!'

'I'll see you in King's Cross,' Campbell said.

'Isn't he *heaven*?' Friis said to his hangers-on.

Campbell circumnavigated a Henry Moore and then stood before a work by Damien Hirst, a Perspex cabinet full of cigarette butts, rows and rows of them, a good few bearing lipstick. He stared far into the curious object. For that moment, it seemed to Campbell that his whole story was there, all the years and all the nights, all the conversations and the clubs and all the efforts.

'Damien and I have a basic interest in ash,' Friis said at his back. 'I think civilisation has shown us that waste is our deepest legacy.'

Campbell smiled at him. Such a fucking fool.

'Okay,' he said, and he was out again into the strained amity of the Fair, scraping past a plethora of Hammershøis and a mobile of Alexander Calder's, which slowly spun in the chill, inauthentic air. He passed wall after wall of offcuts, printer's proofs, cartoons, working models and doodles. Stores and wastepaper baskets all over the world had been raided and their contents hastily framed.

'Richter is really at his most awesome in watercolour,' he heard a visitor gush.

'He's so cute, Hockney. Really cute. I mean the work,' another said.

His vision felt slightly fractured. It was as if his sense of depth was compromised and nothing felt very exactly there.

His mind went back.

'In bed with your mother,' Elizabeth had said, 'you didn't develop love, you developed shame, perhaps, and a rage for order.'

'You think that?' he said.

'It's only a possibility, darling. Your parents fostered aggression. Competition. A sort of death instinct, I guess. You were burdened with impulses that didn't make sense, and still don't, which is why Emin's bed upset you.'

Campbell came to a stop. His eyes travelled a short distance to a white cabinet standing in one of the booths. It had butterflies on it, while around him patrons shuttled past with their manic interpretations. It was a different world. The stained glass on the small cabinet and the mother-of-pearly inlay, it was everything, a piece of furniture made by Wylie & Lochhead in 1901. 'The design is Ernest Archibald Taylor's,' the girl inside the booth told him. She was French and her words came as light as the object.

'It was made in Glasgow,' he said.

'Yes, you know it?'

'I saw a photograph of it once, in the Hunterian Museum. You know, I don't think there are two of these cabinets in existence.'

'No, I don't think so too,' she said. 'We are thinking the paint is original. We made what you call it . . . a *matière colorante* . . . a pigment test.'

'Yes.'

'And it's true. The original paint.'

He walked around it and touched the tiny pewter key.

'What does it cost?' he said. She disappeared for a second. And when she was gone he held the key firmly, then turned it.

Tara often stayed late in the office, writing a piece or getting ready for a party. She didn't have kids to pick up or make tea for, which was fine with her. Her parents failed to understand why she couldn't meet a nice boy and have children. 'I'm not interested in that,' she was saying. 'I'm interested in being the best writer on the paper. And that means working like a packhorse, all hours.'

'You think I don't want the best for you, Tara?'

'I know you do, Mummy.'

'But you have to eat. Come and eat with us.'

'Not tonight. I've got to go to a party. It's work.'

'You're living off white wine and peanuts. We still worry about you, darling. It's easier when your children are younger: back then it was all ponies and insects. You were such a one for nature books and the animal kingdom, Tara.'

'Goodnight, Mummy.'

She ended the call and opened the office window. There was a smell of wet ferns and decaying moss coming up from the canal. She looked over at the gasholders. She picked up her phone again and redialled the number for Vicky Gowans, who had gone to ground. It went to voicemail once more.

She reached into her desk drawer and took out a red notebook. She'd been a stationery-lover since her first year at Camden School for Girls. Her friends wanted Gucci skirts or balayage from Hershesons in Berners Street, but Tara's craving was for Moleskine products and pencil cases from Paperchase. (She asked for a Montblanc for her eighteenth birthday.) Opening the notebook, she saw her pages of facts about Yuri Bykov, quotes from friends, references to deals done or paintings bought or connections implied. She'd written, 'Christie's contact?' In the margin next to some facts about the Duke of Kendal, she'd written, 'Albany?' A lot of it was still supplied by freshislands@outlook.com. So far, every lead had proved accurate. She had gone back and forth with him or her, and they were directing her to some extent, but everything could be substantiated. In her notepad, she had circled the name 'Feng' and had made notes around it, including 'Migrant workers?' At the bottom of another page, after information about Russian magnates and money-laundering accusations and details from her source in Parliament, she'd drawn a long arrow to 'Yuri' and put in brackets, 'cannabis production? Surely not.' Then, 'Duke – historic buildings/laundering. "For the nation"?' The notes were still too disconnected and too random. There was so much of it, and still too much without a secondary source. She needed to put some of the allegations to the people concerned.

So many of the boys she'd known at university, or known about, were always giving parties, and each of them existed at variance with his father. Yuri was the classic, though: the whole Waugh-on-acid vibe of the guy, the spendy-ness. She never trusted that world; they were too right-wing for Tara Hastings of the Labour Club. But Yuri was at least funny the few times she'd met him. He repeated the same stories, in that lethargic manner of his, but everybody lapped them up as if he was simply too camp to be dangerous. She remembered, one time at Wadham, him speaking about parties at Naworth Castle involving government dignitaries. 'The Nights of a Hundred Tsars,' he called them, and she was almost impressed. Campbell Flynn was probably the sort of person Yuri wanted on his side.

There were photographers outside the Gagosian in Britannia Street. She gave her name to the suits with the clipboards – the Insecurity Detail, she liked to call them – and walked inside and across the concrete floor to get a drink. The first person she saw was Bo Spencer, fashion scribe and gossip, surrounded by models. Tara nicknamed him Trauma Capote. He was a sensational tittle-tattle, fun and safely gay, always good for a ciggie or a late-night huddle in a cubicle, if you liked that sort of thing, which models always do. 'Hello, sweetie,' he said, leaning over and *phutting* the air around each of her ears.

'Hi, Bo,' she said. 'What's new in your cruel world?'

The last time she saw him, he told her he'd been sitting next to one of the young royals at a Rolex party thrown by Chinese *Vogue* at Sartoria. 'He said they all *detest* Prince Andrew. They call him the Nonce.'

'In California?' Tara had asked.

'Ev-er-y-where,' he said. 'Except Frogmore Cottage. And *not* when Brenda's around – that's what they call the Boss.'

'Quite funny that – Brenda.'

'Well, she *adores* the Nonce. You can't blame her, really. He was the only one of them that wasn't pig-ugly from birth. Then *Epstein*. I have to say, though, Jeffrey was always very lovely to me. His dinners were the crème-de-la-hoot.'

In the gallery, Bo's cheeks were pink with mischief. 'Oh my days,' he said. 'You would *not* believe what I'm about to tell you.'

That was his standard opener.

He told a horrible story about a media mogul betting against Pfizer.

'Bo, you're not intending to print that, are you?'

'Don't be crazy, baby. I don't print anything I know. I only print shit. I have the best sources in the world – can you guess why? Because I never print what they say.'

Tara blew him a kiss and let him go. An actress from *The Crown* appeared and he moved in on her, narrowing his face for a selfie.

Tara had attended a previous opening of Friis's in 2019, *Material Wealth*, a series of 'sculptures' of fiat currencies – stalagmites of feathers, then shells, cocoa beans, then tin ingots, Dutch guilders, pound notes and euros – each pile charred and glued. She looked over and spotted Angus Flynn, resplendent in a silver puffa jacket, earphones and the whitest sneakers she'd ever seen. He was standing with Yuri Bykov in front of a hideously sun-damaged Manet. Walking towards them she felt nervous.

'Hey, Mr DJ,' she said.

'*Whatdafuck*. It's Hastings!'

'Can't deny it. We doing this?' She put out her hand.

'We totes are,' he said, kissing then hugging her.

'Hey,' Yuri said, holding back.

'What's the deal?' she said to him, casting around. 'You're throwing this big party for Hans Christian Duchamp over there—'

'It's a terrible bore,' Yuri said. 'I'd prefer to be having sex on a rubber mat with four policemen and a bowl of caviar, but what can a boy do?'

She laughed.

'You can quote me on that,' he added. 'Isn't Carl wonderful? And these artworks are certainly the Best Thing Ever.' They all turned and looked at *Chez Tortoni* behind them, a fried platter of flaking paint. You could almost make out a top hat and a man's hand and the base of a wine glass.

'It's everything,' Angus said. 'I love it so much.'

Yuri smiled. She knew he was about to say something. 'That was quite a number you did on William Byre,' he said. 'Fraud then sexual abuse. What's next?'

'He's a scumbag, as you know.'

'There's a lot of them around.'

'I won't argue.'

As a rule, she couldn't keep her powder dry. She felt like turning her recorder on and interviewing him right there.

'Quite a scalp for your little website,' he said. 'I thought you were set up for comment, for argument. What's all this *reporting*?'

'I suppose facts are just too interesting,' she said. 'I'm not pursuing scalps, by the way. A woman was raped.'

'Rape is not cool,' Angus said.

Tara ignored him. She focused on Bykov and wondered if there was anything to be gained.

'I'd like to sit down with you sometime,' she said.

He reached into his breast pocket and gave her a card. 'That would be fun. There's lots of cool things happening. Call my office.'

She looked at the card. 'You're at Bankside.'

'Most days,' he said, turning away, she thought, with a prime sense of owning the world and fearing nothing in it.

'Stick around,' Angus said. 'You look hot, by the way.'

The party was busy, like filthy litter on a windy day, spinning in circles and ready to lift off. The camera flashes outside created a strobe effect in the room, passing through the frosted glass. Tara was strolling with her glass and speaking to the occasional fellow hack who seemed lost in the solar system of it all.

'You know Jack Smout?' the fashion guy from the *FT* asked her.

'Yeah, the TikTok starlet. Mad blue eyes.'

'Coloured contacts. He's here. He's got a gazillion followers. Mainly self-harmers. He's in the corner, Instagramming the dead pictures.'

'Excellent,' Tara said. 'The culture has come full circle.'

'He told me he saw Jake Hart-Davies in New York. He said he'd split my head open if I put it in the Diary. But, apparently, Hart-Davies is a changed man, and now so pure he's like a hologram of the Virgin Mary.'

'Really? What was the therapy?'

'He's gone deep with his colon therapist. You know how it is. They have, like, a colon person, a sober coach, a nutritionist.'

'Excellent,' Tara said again.

'And he's writing a book.'

'Obviously. Because that went so well the last time.'

Tara said nothing more. You have to be careful with news. She'd pissed more stories away at parties than she'd had deep-tissue massages. She did a non-verbal goodbye to her *FT* friend and walked back to the artworks, where Friis was holding court. She took out a notepad and wrote down a few lines of what he was saying, but mainly she wrote down what the guests were wearing and scribbled a few ideas about Yuri the party-giver. How he was standing. Who he was standing next to. At that moment, only a few yards away, he was offering a reluctant boy-hug to a man who looked entirely out of place. Middle-aged, bloodshot eyes, a military bearing that seemed to go with his dry appearance. The Duke of Kendal. She wrote a word in the margin: 'Confirmation?'

'"We could've begun with the Sack of Athens,"' Friis was saying, '"but the British Museum got there first." I'm quoting from the essay in our delicious catalogue, written by my friend Professor Campbell Flynn, with help from his assistant, Milo Mangasha. "All art is theft and all art is lost art," the essay continues.' Friis stretched out his arms and then placed both hands on his heart. 'From the Fourth Crusade to the Doge's Palace fire of 1577, from the loss of Michelangelo's *Cupid* in the Palace of Whitehall fire in 1698 to the Battle of Monte Cassino in 1944, we have lived with the fact that great art is much like the humans who adore it. It dies, it is consumed by flames, it is flooded, it is stolen, it is melted, it is bleached and buried, it falls apart. And destruction has become the hallmark of our combative age: the spirit of art. Like all *value*, art is constantly on the brink of being obliterated or rendered meaningless.'

Tara's shorthand skipped and looped over the page.

'You will find a stone plinth from Palmyra. It is beautifully pocked and splintered, from recent grenade attacks. We bought it in Syria on the black market, as we did with the piece behind me, a battered fragment of Alexander Calder's *Bent Propeller*, which was destroyed at the base of the Twin Towers on 9/11. It was a stunning piece once, and is now an iconic cornerstone of this show.'

Tara went to have a look. She bent down. It was a brown and rusted piece of metal with a shadow of red paint.

'Beside it,' Friis said, 'there are four pieces of Rodin from Cantor Fitzgerald. These sculptures were on the 105th floor of the North Tower. The pieces exhibited here include a broken-off plaster ear and five inches of plaster rope. These were sold on the Dark Net, along with a hand from *The Thinker*, found in Zuccotti Park.'

'It is history,' one of the spectators said.

'Art is always history,' Friis replied. 'The implosion of time by spectacular means.'

Tara got the giggles and hid it with a cough.

Friis was opening up about a pulverised fresco from the Uffizi car bombing. It was a small coagulation of lapis rubble, and Tara saw it as she walked away, taking herself as far as the fire exit on the other side of the gallery. She caught sight of a water-damaged Cindy Sherman which stood under a ghostly light, then she saw Zak Byre a few feet away, standing alone. 'Hello, Zak,' she said, leaning over.

'Hello, Tara. Well, this is weird, isn't it?'

'How you doing?'

He was wearing a dirty tuxedo and a red-and-blue T-shirt that said 'Insulate Britain'. She liked Zak, and wanted to find him inexplicable. But wasn't he, for all his virtue, merely a poor kid who wasn't poor, a lost soul wrapped in cashmere? Didn't he want to transform the world because he couldn't transform himself?

'I'm good,' he said, 'considering, you know, global incineration, while we walk around looking at a few ravaged pictures.'

'I thought they'd be up your street!'

'I suppose so,' he said, looking round. 'Anxiety, ruin. It's a good thing I'm charming as all fuck and have an amazing sense of humour.'

She laughed, and he did too.

'We've got some good things coming up,' he said. 'Epic disruptions. Plus we're getting the ball moving with ministers. Long way to go. I don't have the perfect surname at the moment to, you know, fire up the moral engines, but it's cool.'

'How is all *that*?' she said.

'My father? You tell me, Tara.'

She thanked him without saying it out loud. A mime with the tongue and the lips. He did the same back, flirtatiously.

'The old man's in prison,' he said.

'Not for long, maybe. And only because he wouldn't meet bail conditions.' She paused. 'I didn't expect it to go so big.'

He leaned in. 'Let's keep it big,' he said. 'And then go bigger.'

'You should write a book, Zak.'

He twinkled and seemed lost for a second in all his possibilities. She knew it couldn't have been easy for him.

'I suppose they'll let him off. Men like him always get off,' he said.

'Keep doing what you're doing,' she said.

Surrounded by torn canvases and bleakness, in those few minutes he'd really improved in her eyes. He was one of those people who grow in stature along with the importance of their cause, and maybe her doubts about him were just anxieties about the climate. If he and his friends were right, it would one day eclipse all other subjects, and Tara, like everyone else she knew, would have to ask herself if she had done enough in the war.

They were joined by two of his friends, a crusty-looking pair, who gave the opinion that the whole show was a dissertation on money.

'Possibly,' Tara said, nodding at Zak, who shrugged.

'Quite inspiring, though,' he said. 'Makes you want to work for something permanent.' He looked smilingly at Tara, then melted into the crowd.

*Sir Thomas More and Family* by Holbein. It was burned completely black, apart from a small right-hand corner, where a dog's eyes appeared. Tara approached. The label mentioned the 1752 fire at Kremsier Castle. Further along: *Time Saving Truth from Envy and Discord* (1638) by Nicolas Poussin, now a morass of streaks and gashes, scarcely any evidence of painting at all except at the top, around a god's face, but with lichen and mould festooning the whole expanse of the canvas.

'Beautifully ugly,' someone said.

When Tara turned round, Campbell Flynn was there. 'Poussin was Anthony Blunt's first love,' he said to her, a little fresh-seeming. 'You know who I'm talking about – Blunt? The art historian. The traitor. Perhaps you're too young.'

'I'm surprised we're still on speaks,' she said.

He pointed at the ruined masterpiece with his glass. 'He loved Poussin for being the singular painter-philosopher, for having a masterfully joined-up view of ethics.' He tilted his head. 'Do you have a masterfully joined-up view of ethics, Tara?'

She smiled at him and somehow made it clear to herself and hopefully to him that she intended no harm.

'And now look at the philosopher,' he went on, gesturing again at the canvas. 'His whole design has been overtaken by the designs of brute nature.'

'I didn't think people still referenced Anthony Blunt,' she said.

He took a bottle of champagne from a passing tray and filled her glass. He was drunk or out of it in some way. 'He was a Stoic,' he said.

'And are you?'

That same hostility flashed in his eye. 'It is what it is,' he said. 'Unfortunately, I'm not as interesting as many would like to believe.'

'Your name keeps coming up,' she said.

He was miles away. She reckoned he wouldn't have approached her sober.

'I think your son's about to start his DJ set.'

He kept staring at the mangled Poussin.

'Priapus is actually the god of gardens,' he said. 'And gardens decay. It's upsetting to think of Nicolas Poussin's sublime depictions of nature themselves turning into a corrupted garden. Yet here he is. And here we are!'

He burst out laughing.

A young man appeared by his side. He was wearing a suit with trainers and seemed well in charge of his own good looks.

'This is Milo Mangasha,' Flynn said. 'One of my students, now a graduate. He's been helping me with a few projects.'

'You're a writer on art?' she asked, shaking his hand.

'Nah, man. He's the art king.'

'He works for me,' Flynn said.

The boy was shifting from foot to foot. 'He's not my boss. We're co-workers.' He turned to Campbell. 'Had a few drinks, yeah?'

Campbell appeared to flinch.

Tara looked away and tapped the rim of her glass, waiting for the awkwardness to dissipate.

'This party is stupid,' Mangasha said.

'Watch what you're saying to her,' Flynn replied. 'She's a journalist and she does a good line in conspiracy theories.'

The young man cracked his knuckles. 'This place is a zoo,' he said.

He had a way of looking at you like he knew you already.

Flynn was unsteady now, craning his neck to see who was arriving. She knew they had unfinished business. 'Well, it's a shocking show,' she said, to make conversation.

'Nah, it's mere entertainment,' he said.

'I don't think you believe that, Professor Flynn.'

She stood back as another group joined them. They were young – Tara had seen them in other places; Kenzie's maybe-partner, she thought.

'Hello, Milo,' the maybe-partner said.

'Ah,' Flynn interjected. 'It's Their Majesty – A.J.'

Milo and A.J. bumped fists.

'What, you know each other?' Flynn said to his assistant.

'Well, yeah,' A.J. said. 'We met at *your house*, remember? In the garden? And we kept in touch after that. People do.'

The professor was a bit frozen. 'I have trouble allowing that the different parts of my life might have lives of their own,' he said.

'I know the feeling,' A.J. said. 'But it's nice to be at your abomination party.'

Tara sensed Flynn was very much not enjoying himself now. He had the drunk's aloneness. He watched the group in front of him and

430

seemed to forget Tara was there, watching him. He narrowed his eyes and emptied his glass down his throat.

'It's good to see you, A.J.,' he said. 'We need a sting of *reality* in here.'

'Are you patronising me, Professor?'

'I think I'll bounce, yeah,' Milo said, ready to leave.

A.J. was excitedly waving a hand in the air. 'Look. Brace yourselves. Uncle Tony and Aunt Candy are coming over.'

They meant the Duke and Duchess of Kendal.

'We call them Nighty and Snaffles,' Campbell said. 'Those are their names for each other. Like a pair of cut-throats in a Restoration comedy.'

Tara looked at Flynn, who stared back.

'Definite confirmation,' she wrote in her notebook.

The Kendals were still with Yuri Bykov, and their entourage now included a rival newspaper editor and Lord Haxby, the Tory peer, along with a man from the Serpentine Gallery and the Chinese architect Sun Zetao. Tara saw them coming. They were supremely out of place, and she was surprised at them all flaunting these associations. She wasn't ready to confront the Duke with her allegations, though – not yet. Flynn's eyes were glassy and they slid away when she said goodbye.

In Britannia Street, Tara took out her phone. Still nothing from Vicky Gowans. All her recent texts to the girl remained unread. She checked her address in her contacts and decided to walk up to Granville Square. She could then catch the bus back on Rosebery Avenue, the number 38. After a few minutes she was walking along Wharton Street and the lamplight was falling citrine on the pavement; a sort of drabness oozed out of the October night. All mashed in with the leaves at the base of the dark railings she walked past was a sodden copy of the *Guardian*, its headline: 'Mystery of Who Owns Britain'.

At 37 Granville Square she pressed the buzzer. Silver box: four flats. There was no answer and she looked again at her phone, calling Vicky's number. Standing back on the path she could see the sitting room light was on. She buzzed again and then a sash window was raised on the ground floor. 'You looking for Vicky?'

'Victoria Gowans, yes. I've been calling her.'

The woman seemed nice. 'She's not answering her phone, love. I've been ringing her for two days and I rattled her letterbox as well. I knocked on the door, but she doesn't answer. Her light's on an' all.'

'That's what I thought. Second floor, isn't it?'

'Been on for days, love. Always is. All through the night.'

Tara came in and they had a discussion in the hall. It was decided the best thing would be to fetch a key from the man at the top. He was a good person, the downstairs neighbour was saying as they climbed the stairs. 'Fred makes soup when she's poorly. Always looking out for people. He's a bachelor. Makes lovely soup.'

'That's neighbourly.'

Fred was at home, but it took him ages to find the key. He wouldn't give up, and Tara stood with the woman in the hall, chatting about changes to the area. She said she was sure Tara's office used to be a train station, King's Cross York Road. Her brother used to catch the train from there to Winchmore Hill.

At last, the key was found. Tara knocked on Vicky's door again. There was a noise inside the flat. 'Vicky,' she shouted. 'Are you OK?'

The woman from downstairs was shaking her head.

'Just want to make sure you're all right, love.'

Tara used the key and opened the door. As soon as she was inside, she knew. She could hear the television and feel the heat. She walked straight into the sitting room, a beautiful square room with big windows and a yellow sofa, and there, stretched out in front of a three-bar electric fire, was Vicky's body, needle in arm. The neighbour cried out and ran downstairs to phone the police. But Tara stepped towards the dead woman and leaned down, stroking her face, moving her red hair away from her eyes.

# BOOK FOUR
## Winter

# 35 Windsor

'**S**naffles, darling. You mustn't look at the camera.'

To the Duke, the whole thing was irritating. If Nighty wanted all this bloody television nonsense, she couldn't be stopped, but he didn't see why he had to be dragged into the middle of it and instructed how to speak. He was standing under the portrait of the 1st Duke of Kendal that hung above the fireplace, the fire lighting both their faces, which were remarkably similar, it was often said. The crackling logs began to make a nuisance of themselves for the American sound man.

'Darling, I can't stand here for long. I'm frightfully busy, if you hadn't noticed, and the estate office is on the telephone.'

'Okay, running up,' the director said. 'When you're ready.'

'Here we stand in the great hall,' the Duke said, like there was a bad taste in his mouth. 'The original Crofts Castle was built on this spot, in Inverness-shire, more or less, in the thirteenth century, and destroyed by Oliver Cromwell during his invasion of Scotland. The 1st Duke, whom we can see above me – a portrait by one of the Netherlandish painters – went by a few different names. James Kendal was one of them, and sometimes Crofts. They say he was one of the bastard sons of Charles II. Can one say "bastard"?'

'*Yes*,' Candy said. (Her accent was posher than his.) 'As long as you're referring to a child born out of wedlock, as opposed to the other sort.'

They had come from England the day before. Candy had been doing something stultifying at the Cliveden literary soirée, then she went with her Suffolk yoga-boy to speak in Aberystwyth, at a celebration of the International Sheep Dog Society, before she returned to what was often called the 'family home' in Holland Park, where she spent the night alone. The Duke met her there that morning, coming directly in a chauffeur-driven car from his set at Albany, where he had idled for the second half of the week in the company of several female escorts. They were splendid girls, he noted, only a few words of English between them, but they kept him happy while his wife was off in search of an education. At Albany, he hadn't seen much of the helpful young Bykov, though he saw him the other day at that frightful art party.

After the filming, the Duke got into charity mode. 'Let's go and do a spot of fundraising,' he would say to the staff who worked in the estate office. 'These old buildings won't maintain themselves!' On one of the desks in the outer office were paper plates containing chocolate eyeballs and fingers left over from Halloween. He was undoing the foil on an eyeball as he walked into his office. Before getting to business, one of the secretaries, as he still called them, wanted to show him a bill. All morning they'd been trying to get him to talk about this bloody phone bill. 'What's the matter with it?' the Duke asked, plucking the thing from her hand and putting on his glasses.

'Well, the bill is £26,000 higher than usual.'

'Good God,' he said. 'Is that a joke?'

'The seven telephone lines at Crofts have apparently been used to make hundreds of calls on the weekends and at night, to various charity helplines that take a donation for every call.'

'And have we been making these calls?'

'No. We're talking 26k worth of calls—'

'What charities? We *are* a charity!'

She unfolded a separate piece of paper. The listed charities were all to do with women's groups or Travellers.

'This is madness,' he said. 'We won't pay it.'

'I've spoken to the police in Edinburgh. They say we will have to pay it. They also said we may have been subject to something called PBX hacking, where our phone lines have been directed to call these numbers and make donations.'

'And can't they stop it?'

'They've got our details. But no, they say it's our responsibility to take the correct security measures to avoid this sort of cyberattack.'

This only worsened the Duke's mood. It was an army thing: he hated not being amply equipped and defended. Another of the office staff came with the news that a journalist had rung several times.

'I'm not interested in talking to reporters,' he said.

'She sounds quite serious—'

But he wouldn't let her finish.

'They're never serious.'

When he went into his own office next to the boot room, he was soon joined by his lead man Fionn, holding a fishing rod. Fionn was a landscaper from Kilmorack whom the Duke had appointed as his heritage manager.

'Yuri Bykov has been on the phone this morning.'

'Are we moving forward?' the Duke said.

'You met the architect—'

'The Chinese man?'

'Yes, his name is Sun Zetao.'

'I met him the other night in London.'

'Well, they're flying into Dalcross this afternoon.'

'*Today*? Are you serious?'

'Aye, that's what he said. He was in Paris last night for an opera event and they're flying direct from there in a Citation XL.'

'What on earth is that, Fionn?'

'It's a jet, sir. An eight-seater.'

'To look at the Grange? He'll have to be quick. The Duchess and I are travelling south again tomorrow, for the polo event at Windsor.'

'Yes. It's in the diary.'

'Is Bykov expecting to stay with us?'

'No, sir,' Fionn said. 'They're off again tomorrow but are putting up at Docherty House, the haulier's estate.'

'Right.'

The Duke paused to regain his composure.

'What time?' he asked Fionn.

'I've asked Shona to organise tea up at the house at four o'clock.'

He couldn't believe how quickly these Russians worked. When they wanted business, they got things done overnight, and Yuri was even faster. His father had been careful, investing money in various projects, huge sums, but quite subtle in exchanging it for invitations and influence, or honours, in good time. The Duke had never hesitated to mention his name to palace officials or government people; Aleksandr Bykov was a personage – until the recent American sanctions. In previous years, he was welcome at state dinners, a top-flight donor. The present difficulties were merely a bore and, in the Duke's experience, such problems tended to go away eventually. You can't harpoon the whale without sailing alongside, he always said to his platoon. This country might be overrun by the wrong sort but *these* people were men of business.

He set out at 3.25 for Segdoune Grange, a Georgian masterpiece near the Aigas Dam, and his pet project. This was life to Tony, trundling in a Land Rover over the dirt tracks of the estate. It reminded him of being young and outdoors, the smell of diesel, doing his best for his country, knowing the freedom of open space. When he considered who he was, he didn't think of Crofts Castle or Suffolk; he didn't picture Albany or the villa in Spain. He thought of Segdoune. When he walked the corridors, when he took his place in the famous dining room or slept in a Jacobean bed, he felt himself to be the person he was really meant to be, a man who cared about history. He'd never forgiven his wife's brother-in-law for referring to his Constables as 'laughable fakes'.

He parked by the front steps.

Yuri was already inside, leaning against a rosewood bookcase, smoking a cigarette. He seemed dishevelled in an open white shirt. 'Thought we'd make a fabulous detour,' Yuri said, tapping ash into the burning grate.

'I'm jolly glad you did,' the Duke said.

'I think you've met Mr Zetao.'

He shook hands with the diminutive architect, who had a sketch pad under his arm and a look of fierce energy.

'Your groundsman led us round. He's quite the dish.'

The Duke flinched at the remark before they went on to talk about the extension. Mr Zetao did not have good English, but his language flowered when he spoke about concepts, structures, materials and so on, as if he'd learned English from architectural magazines.

Two hours passed. Yuri offered several absurd statements. He made abusive remarks about his father, and then promised to fund the entire extension. To Tony, he seemed pretty much out of control, but so be it. 'This is the sort of thing that would never interest my father's friends,' Yuri said. 'They are barbarians who know nothing of art. This house is a masterpiece – but they kill art, all of them.'

The Duke was amused but unquestioning. The Russians were the mad dogs of Europe, having none of the Germans' innate finesse. The French he found bloodthirsty and arrogant to a ludicrous degree, but Germany was order, with a passion for human progress that nothing could repress or obliterate.

Yuri said he could raise the funds immediately from the sale of a number of pictures. 'I'm thrilled,' the Duke said.

'And these are loans,' Yuri said. 'The terms are consistent. I believe in original causes, and you'll remember your friends.'

'Of course,' the Duke said. 'We are dealing with you directly?'

Yuri looked at him with force. 'Yes,' he said. 'I think you will find, Your Grace, that my father is now somewhat tarnished.'

That did it, and they nodded in agreement.

'And I'll pay this man's fees,' Yuri added. He turned to Mr Zetao, who was saying he was keen to *evolve* the project.

The Duke gave a single clap of his hands, pleased the filthy part was done, and keen now to be bluff. 'All architects should be cut in half,' he offered, 'and so should their fees.'

Mr Zetao appeared to grasp nothing of the insult as he bowed.

Yuri was enjoying himself. He laughed and lit another cigarette.

'I don't suppose one can find a whisky around here?' he said. The Duke pulled a velvet rope and ordered him a Talisker. Walking to a Georgian sofa table, he picked up a silver frame. It showed his wife and her mother with the poet Ted Hughes. 'I admit to being a tad concerned,' he said, 'about your family's, I mean your company's, relationship with certain businessmen. I'm thinking of this fellow awaiting trial, William Byre.'

Yuri rubbed his nose and sniffed.

'He is a very English sort of failure, Your Grace. He was my father's idea of someone with whom to do business. I'm afraid, if you read the newspapers, you will see the man is worse than Harvey Weinstein.'

'I don't know who that is.'

'Let's simply say that Sir William is a busted flush. He has a bad record with women, which is the worst sort of bad record to have at the moment. He is also a reprobate when it comes to paying back his debts.'

'It all seems rather tawdry . . .'

'Which is why we are finished with him. Even my father sees that such a man cannot be welcomed into our circle again.'

The Duke turned to the fireplace.

'Capital,' he said. 'We must be pure as pure can be.'

'I hear you're at Windsor tomorrow.'

'Yes,' the Duke said. 'Charity never ends.'

'You're telling me.'

That evening, the Duke and his wife had a kitchen supper. He brought a glass of wine to the table and they sat down to a cottage pie and an apple cobbler. The clock was ticking over the range and the pie was slightly burned, which they hardly noticed, Tony liking 'rations' and Candy hating food in general.

'I spoke to Elizabeth today,' she said. 'Something of a bonanza on the news front.'

'Oh, really?'

'Angus is now exclusively with the sustainable chutney woman.'

'Excellent,' he said. 'She might slow that family down a bit. And bring cash. They've been gadding about in the limelight for years.'

'That's not quite fair, Snaffles,' she said. 'Campbell's in the public eye. He's a thinker for hire, and rather good at it. They say that when Campbell is judging a prize or sitting on a committee, everything scoots along.'

'He's everywhere, causing a riot. Did you see the state of him at that frightful art show? He was talking even more bosh than usual. And he's in with these youngsters too. I don't know how Elizabeth can tolerate it.'

'I thought you liked his talk at the museum.'

'It was a great wheeze. All the left-wing boffins getting their knickers in a twist. Excellent stuff, but hardly dignified.'

He took his glass upstairs with him. They had separate bedrooms. They would huddle together from time to time, and in that way their marriage was conventional, but she was too light a sleeper and couldn't bear his snoring. He donned a dressing gown and dawdled into her room to borrow a comb. She was in her bathroom. He plucked it from the dressing table, spotting some books by the mirror. *Self-Approval*, one of them was called. Another had to do with the Bhagavad Gita.

Back in his bedroom, a text appeared on his old Nokia. He didn't like it. The journalist. 'You have ignored all my calls. Your office has done the same. Final fact-checking is now in progress on a major investigation we have been conducting on several fronts. If I hear nothing by the a.m., we shall simply report that you were unavailable for comment.'

441

On the wall of his den was a framed picture of HMS *Hermes*, and on top of his bureau were several group shots, cheek-by-jowl on the bureau around a sand-coloured beret, of young special forces officers he'd commanded. He sat by the window and looked down through the trees to Rhinduie and the Beauly Firth. He thought of the merry men of D Squadron, 22 SAS, under the cold stars of the South Atlantic. It was true to say that seventy-four days in 1982 had defined his life and he'd never again felt so alive or so necessary. Tasting the wine, he stared out and the dark water of the Beauly became a raging sea again, churning before him, with Harriers over-head and in the distance an illuminated ship that felt like home.

They accepted a lift to Northolt the next day. Candy didn't like to take flights from businessmen, but the young Russian had been insistent, and quite charming. Afterwards, as the car he'd provided slipped onto the A40, she put a hand over her husband's. She felt the vehicle was slightly vulgar, a Bentley with white leather interior, but quite amusing. Mr Bykov had evaporated into London, having kissed her hand rather affectedly, and shown during their short flight from Inverness that he was really a latter-day Diaghilev, an impresario with his talk of artworks and his streaky hair. 'I love people, Your Grace,' he'd said, 'and I find the more variety one reaches for, the nicer the time. The old guard doesn't understand this.'

Candy had thought it better not to respond. She was careful around her husband, but privately she agreed with what the young man said.

She and Tony were speeding past pylons. 'I do worry about Mummy,' she said. 'Kenzie called me this morning to say—'

'Don't tell me. The Countess is running off again?'

'Yes. She suddenly leaped at the chance of the Bahamas.'

'Good for her.'

He was looking out of the window on his side and she felt he was more than usually distracted.

'Don't be mean, Tony. She's not at all well. She was perfectly comfortable in Chester Street and now she's haring off to that ghastly cruise ship.'

'She likes it there, Nighty. Ships can be like that.'

'Kenzie said Mummy had an infection. It goes badly with the cognitive problem. But that silly Tite Street doctor said it was okay for her to board a plane to Nassau. She has to change in Miami and spend the night.'

'Well, shouldn't people have adventures when they're old?'

'For goodness' sake, Tony. You're impossible! Mummy is sick and on her way to bloody America and you think it's hilarious.'

'I didn't say it was hilarious. I said it was an adventure. And if your mother wants to end her days on a floating shopping mall, that's up to her. She's not doing anybody any harm and she can dream about her blessed elephants.'

Candy was feeling quite weepy. It wouldn't do, for an old woman to go off like that, when she's probably without the right pills and whatnot. She looked out of the window and saw a run of grey buildings with chimney pots. Maybe it was nerves, Candy thought. Even after all this time, she always felt nervous seeing the Queen. She felt sorry for Her Majesty, another elderly lady who must be tired of her duties. 'Kenzie says Mummy only likes to speak to Campbell. She wants him to go out there.'

'I'm sure he will,' Tony said. 'He lives on a flying carpet, that fellow. I've never understood her fascination with him. He comes from a housing estate or something. I suppose she likes the ill-conditioned mind . . .'

Candy wasn't listening. She was quiet for a moment, before saying, 'Apparently, Mummy spent £10,000 on her ticket.'

She looked up and saw a plane clambering into the sky. Maybe that was Mummy and she'd never see her again, a sign-off into *satori*. People on planes have a special power when it comes to being happy and remote.

The polo season had ended, but the Cup was for charity. It would be the final social wingding before winter. As they drove towards the Royal Box, she saw that everyone appeared to have a dog. The Mountbatten girls were in their flowery dresses and fur boleros – how cute they were, chihuahuas yapping at the heels of their Jimmy Choos. And then came the viscounts; their hair was also like fur, abundant and standing on end. Maybe they were all social media stars nowadays, Candy mused – influencers – living their uppity little lives but not really finding their central selves.

'I'm terribly parched,' the Duke said when the car stopped. 'Let's get in there, Nighty, and find a glass of something.'

Unfortunately, a PR person caught them on the way. She'd been waiting for them and said there were an inordinate number of photographers. She consulted an iPad and immediately started issuing times and cues, but Candy saw the Duke was in no mood, so she followed him into the lower balcony while waving the PR away. 'Please give him a few minutes to settle in,' she said.

'Jolly good,' the Duke said when they were inside the enclosure, stroking his tummy and preparing himself for social duties.

The event was being sponsored by a Japanese investment firm, so the Duke wasted no time in performing the first of his duties, speaking a few words to the head of the company, a smiling man with precision-cut grey hair who presented his wife as if she were a piece of ornamental glass. There were Argentinians outside and a delegation of players from Sandringham, whom Tony knew well. Candy saw him raise a jocular fist in their direction as they rode up and down. The box was full of dignitaries and minor royals. 'Mustn't let the side down,' Tony whispered as they turned to the polished faces. Candy broke off, in their jointly practised way, so that she could share the burden of receiving. 'Hello!' she said to a royal Greek friend of Princess Eugenie's, who would soon be off to St Moritz. The girl said she'd managed to get out of Fashion Week in Namibia.

'Namibia? I didn't realise they even had that,' Candy said.

'Oh God, yes. It's like totally the craziest thing. My agent called me and I nearly had a heart attack.'

After further conversation, Candy discovered the Greek princess was also a vegan blogger and her boyfriend was into ice diving.

Candy tried not to look bemused. She could see Tony was distracted again. He was giving his ear to the PR girl, who was using her hands a lot.

They sat down to lunch. Candy ignored the beef carpaccio with balsamic reduction. Then she played with the halibut, breaking it up with a fork. The woman next to Candy, a former Estonian gym instructor who was married to one of the Japanese businessmen, told her, with a few sniffles, that she had been struggling to get pregnant and was worried she might never have children. Candy consoled her as best she could, without mentioning the fact, or even hinting, that she herself was medically incapable of conceiving a child. The Mountbatten sorority continued giggling. A man with an unlit cigar explained to everyone that polo would have died had it not been for Lord Cowdray and the late Prince Philip, who opened this club.

She kept snatching glimpses of Tony. He seemed alarmed.

They were herded towards several rows of chairs. The idea was that they would watch the final few chukkas. Candy picked up her handbag, on impulse, and took out her phone. It said there were forty-two missed messages. The Queen was coming down from the upper balcony, so she couldn't read them – she couldn't be seen by the photographers to be staring at her phone – but she looked at the message still sitting on her screen. 'Did you know he was a Nazi sympathiser?' it said. The message was from an unknown number.

'Oh my actual God,' the Rothschild girl in front of her was saying. 'That's Yoshiki. He's, like, the biggest pop star in Japan.'

The Duke was standing beside his wife and perspiring. She tried to soothe him with a finger on his wrist, to no avail. She knew something dreadful was happening, but they were trapped in the Royal Box at the Guards Polo Club, the press in front of them and two dozen dignitaries on either side. The band began to play and the Queen walked down the red carpet in one of her lime-green ensembles with a matching hat. She paused beside Tony. Her Majesty leaned in and allowed him, the old family friend, to kiss her cheek. Her expression was like a mask of privacy and coerced enjoyment. She walked down to the front row and stood at her seat, next to Yoshiki, both their faces powdered white.

'What is it?' Candy whispered to her husband.

'I'm fucked, Nighty,' he said. 'They've come for me.'

She tried to compose her features. The photographers, she now realised, were done with the Queen and were focusing entirely on him.

As the match played out, the Duke left the enclosure and was led to a room at the back by the publicity manager from Great Veterans, the ex-servicemen's charity. The Duke had recently taken over from the Queen as patron, and this was his first big event, the handing over of the reins from Her Majesty and a major boost to the charity's coffers, thanks to the Japanese investors. When they got to the room, the PR opened her laptop and showed him a video.

'Is it bad?' he asked her.

She hesitated. She was young.

'Do you want an honest answer?'

'Of course.'

'It couldn't be worse.'

He could hear clapping and cheering outside. The Queen must be presenting the Cup. The video was on the website of the *Commentator*.

He could see himself in an establishment in Portsmouth, a club run by fans of Britain's military and naval forces. He could remember being there. He was holding a bottle of beer and talking to several middle-aged men. One of them was holding up a Nazi armband and another could be seen wearing a black T-shirt that said, 'Adolf Hitler. European Tour, 1939–45'. Much laughter. The camera turned to a man holding up a board of anti-Muslim badges – one of them read

'Combat 18', the other 'Blood & Honour'. The camera was on the Duke's face as he asked if the merchandise was for sale.

'We want to support our real heroes,' one of the men said.

'One hundred per cent,' said his friend. 'We support ex-army.'

'I'm all for it,' the Duke said to them. 'It's about time, let me tell you, that we stood up to be counted in this country.'

'Too right!'

He went on to list the foreigners, the immigrants who planted bombs and the thugs who knifed people in the street. 'Everyone seems to have forgotten,' he said, 'that we are closer to the people of Germany in 1932 than we are to any of these so-called refugees arriving in our country. Hitler overdid it, but he had ideas we can jolly well learn from.'

'Spot on,' a man said. 'That's what we're saying.'

In the room at Windsor, the Duke was aghast. He could remember saying such things, but very much in a private way. Not like this. He thought his heart might stop and he leaned on the young woman's shoulder.

'Are you all right, sir?' she said.

'Give me a moment. It's on a website?'

'It's gone viral.'

'I'm not entirely sure what that means.'

'It's already on every news show,' she said. 'Every website. I've been on to the people at Buckingham Palace in the last ten minutes. They are getting calls from everywhere, from the *New York Times* to . . . God knows. You name it.'

She raised her hand to her head.

'This is a nightmare,' he said.

'I know, sir. The Press Association has released a photograph of you kissing the Queen's cheek forty minutes ago.'

'I had no idea,' he said.

'Didn't you? Apparently the journalist has been trying to put these allegations to you for days.'

'I really had no idea.'

'You can read the reports in the car,' she said coldly, handing him printouts.

She didn't hide her anger. She told him she'd be liaising with the palace in an attempt to separate the charity from this mess.

He felt unable to wait for Candy. He needed space to think. As his car drove away there were obnoxious flashes in front of the vehicle.

He looked at the headlines in his hands. *The Times*'s website was calling it a royal scandal. 'Jesus Christ,' he said in the back of the car, 'they've gone ape.' He stared into the white leather of the Bentley. Then he looked at the allegations again, took out his Nokia and made a call to Yuri Bykov.

'I'm under attack,' he said to the young businessman.

'Well, a lot has happened in the last three hours,' Yuri said. 'You appear to be under attack from your own fair self.'

'What do you mean?'

'It's a double whammy, Tony. On the one hand, you're caught on camera suggesting Hitler might be an excellent role model in current affairs—'

'That's not what I meant.'

'And . . . on the other, someone in your foundation has leaked documents about your financial dealings with my father.'

'What the blazes are you talking about?'

'Tara Hastings in the *Commentator*. An old acquaintance, good at her job. She got hold of these pretty frightening documents, messages between you and my father, making it clear you accepted several undisclosed loans.'

'Jesus Christ.'

'Our deal's off, Anthony. *Everything's* off.'

In that moment, the Duke realised that physical danger had never worried him, but reputational danger had worried him all his life.

'Don't be ridiculous. We have lawyers,' he said. 'Teams of them. These difficulties can be worked around.'

'These documents are the real deal,' Yuri said. 'I think you're finished.'

'Good God, man. Have you lost your reason?'

Yuri was flash and theatrical, and perhaps he wasn't aware of how these things were managed.

'You're a proven racist,' Yuri said. 'And for a significant amount of time you've been cleaning money for my father and his friends.'

The Duke was out of his skin. What world was this? 'You and I sat down together only yesterday. What's this bosh you're talking?'

'When a person is over, they're over.'

'I shall speak to your father.'

'Knock yourself out, dear.'

'Listen, you fucking creep—'

'You know, sir, it's bred in the bone. I learned that at Oxford. But you really do overestimate your influence. I am not my father's biggest fan, as you know, but you are not so important to him as you think. You were briefly useful to me as a way of annoying him. You bark like a seal, we throw you a fish. The Queen's cousin in Kensington Palace is infinitely more important. Or he was. The Russian president gave him the Order of Friendship. Royals for hire. I hate to break it to you, Your Grace, but in that busy market-place you are nothing much.'

'You absolute imbecile. You people have no idea how this country works.'

'*Au contraire*, sir. I think we do. You spent some time yesterday wishing to separate yourself from men such as William Byre.'

'Wait a bloody minute—'

'You're really no better. No better at all.'

'Stop right there. This is absurd! It was me that got you your set at Albany. I used influence on your behalf. It was me—'

'I really must go, Tony. I have Lord Scullion on the line. Goodbye.'

And with that he ended the call.

449

# 36 The Differences

The next day, at home, Elizabeth told Campbell her sister was back in Suffolk, distraught. 'What on earth is happening to the world?' Elizabeth said, sitting down on the sofa and resting her laptop on a cushion. It was a few minutes before 10 p.m. 'Candy had no idea Tony even knew people like that. And it turns out they were running anti-Muslim campaigns up and down the country. Ex-servicemen, many of them.'

'It's a racist country we're living in, darling.'

'Yes, okay. But Nazis?'

Elizabeth didn't usually get involved in dramas, but she couldn't ignore this. After staring at her screen, she said, 'This story in the *Commentator*. Don't the kids know this girl? Tara.'

'They all know each other,' Campbell said.

She began to read from the screen. '"According to sources, the Duke of Kendal had forged a deep friendship with Aleksandr Bykov – a major Russian industrialist and friend of the Russian president – whose property in the United States has been seized and his businesses put under scrutiny as a result of sanctions. Via offshore accounts in Cyprus and the Isle of Man, Bykov is alleged to have squirrelled tens of millions of dollars in Kendal's foundations, restoration projects and artworks, in exchange for influence with British institutions and access to members of the Establishment."'

'I want nothing to do with it,' Campbell said. 'Tony's had it coming for years.'

'And that's *it*, is it?' Elizabeth said.

He felt it was all part of a necessary cleansing. He would do what

451

he could for his wife and her sister, but he couldn't feel sorry for the Duke of Kendal.

'The world is coming to get these people,' he said.

'You could make an attempt not to gloat, Campbell.'

'But I'm not gloating. It makes me feel sick.'

He knew his own sister might be one of the sources. It had her fingerprints on it, and she was close to the parliamentary committee. Since the day Tara Hastings had come to see him, Campbell had worried that she knew about every aspect of his hidden life and associations. She'd even turned up at that Gagosian party during Frieze. He didn't imagine Moira knew how dangerous it was to him, to people beyond the obvious targets of these investigations; or perhaps she felt it was time her brother faced up to the world he inhabited.

'She certainly has a bee in her bonnet, this journalist,' Elizabeth said, 'and quite rightly, I'm sure. First it was William.'

'Hating William has destroyed me,' he said, quietly.

'And this isn't a picnic with Candy, either! But we're not getting *involved* in any of this, Campbell. We are surrounded by it.'

'I have no interest in it,' he said. He wasn't being cool; he was scared, and he felt again that profound lack of faith in his own decency. Milo, a living riposte, was his only hope when it came to all this corruption. But there'd been fewer meetings recently, and the correspondence, he worried, was drying up.

'You don't have any *interest*?' she said.

She'd meant something different.

She went on. 'William Byre was a time bomb in your life, Campbell, and in his own. And my sister's husband is a fucking reprobate, and I want to protect her.'

'Okay, Elizabeth!'

'And I want to protect my children. And my husband. And myself. Do you understand? I don't want any more shit. Something is happening to you, Campbell. And your propensity for thinking you're taking a stand for freedom or proving yourself victorious in every fucking social situation you enter is baffling. Get off your moral high horse and start looking at your own choices.'

He stared at the painting above the fireplace. It's not that the past is more simple or more serene, with a better nature, but it can appear so, if only for minutes at a time, and that treasured Joan Eardley picture – the slashes of red, the pin-point blues – described a world of uncomplicated closeness, a young brother and sister huddled together by a sweetshop in Glasgow, close to where Campbell had grown up. In that moment, unseasonably, he had a vision of the Christmas tree from his childhood, covered in the glass baubles that his mother said had been her only inheritance.

'Okay, I get it. What is Candy going to do?' he asked.

'I think we have to go to Suffolk in the morning.'

He knew better than to object. He would go to support his wife.

'We can't leave her on her own,' she went on. 'Apparently, he's gone to Albany and won't take calls from anyone. There's press every-where. And she has nobody up there, nobody but the farmworkers.'

'And her mindfuckness guru.'

'A fat lot of good he'll be. I need you there with me.'

'Of course,' he said. 'I've got a lecture and a seminar tomorrow via Zoom, so I can do it from there.'

Upstairs, he packed a bag. He saw a bill from the Frieze Art Fair and put it in his pocket. For one of his online seminars he would need a few books and his notes on the third season of *Homeland*. He also picked up a volume that Milo had left in his office pigeon hole weeks ago – *Abolishing the Police*. 'I don't want to be part of society as it currently is,' Milo had written on the title page. 'And I won't be. That's all.'

Recently, Campbell had begun to notice how his spirit would sometimes fade in the young man's presence, Milo's very expression upbraiding him, the experience all the more disturbing for being so addictive. But he hadn't seen him since Frieze. Campbell had been drunk that night and he couldn't quite remember how the party ended, but he recalled Milo suddenly disappearing. At first, it didn't worry him because he wanted a break, but there was something odd in the way the young man had left that book. Campbell didn't see until he opened it again – another scribble in Milo's handwriting, this time at the back. 'The sun shines differently on black skin,' he'd written with a peculiar finality. 'We absorb the heat, and you'll never understand that.'

He stuck the book in his Suffolk bag. He wasn't sure how much central coordination there ever was in group action. Wasn't it merely people doing their own thing in the same direction? Moira didn't know Milo, and Tara Hastings didn't really know Campbell, but they had each been chasing something, and he felt himself to be a confused force that night at the start of winter, spinning – he admitted – on nostalgic energy and financial panic, and experiencing an overwhelming need to walk through the flames and be cleansed. He started writing a thank-you note to the boy and told himself he would drop it off at the girlfriend's hairdressing salon before leaving town.

Surrey often smelled of expensive cologne. There were parts of Moscow that were that way too, much like the shopping malls of Jeddah, a wonderful blend of smoky wood, warm leather and roses. In the back of a moving Bentley earlier that day, Aleksandr sniffed his hands while calling a CEO in Silicon Valley. He wanted to offer the man's company a major opportunity in Ukraine, a cyber operation in Odesa. 'I figure we could disrupt that market,' the CEO said.

After the call, Aleksandr looked at his texts. Several, often abusive, were from Yuri, the last one suggesting a meeting in London. There was a sale that Yuri knew his father was attending.

Aleksandr ignored all the messages.

Arriving at Christie's, he made his way inside and was shown immediately to a private room. An expert on the American artist KAWS immediately came up to shake hands. Aleksandr felt jangly:

he was never comfortable with art dealers, curators or salespeople who had direct access to him. 'What is that word?' he asked.

'KAWS? It doesn't mean anything. The artist's real name is Brian.'

Aleksandr's head was down. 'I'm interested in this large fibreglass. The grieving Mickey Mouse, or whatever it is.'

'Yes, a very fine piece, sir.'

'Could we take it out of the sale? You know, we could agree on a price now and then it's over?'

'I'm afraid we can't do that, sir. The auction is about to begin. We have expressions of interest from all over the world, and—'

'Twenty million. Right now. Dollars.'

'That's a remarkably generous offer, sir. But I'm afraid—'

'You don't want to sell it right now for twenty million?'

The salesman blushed and asked him to wait. He walked across the room and collared a grey-haired gentleman wearing a green tie. In a moment, the two men approached and the older one bowed his head and shook his hand. 'Mr Bykov,' he said. 'Welcome to Christie's, sir. I am sorry—'

'I offer you $20 million for the sad mouse.'

'One of our colleagues will happily bid on your behalf.'

'I don't want competition. I will pay it now.'

'We simply can't, Mr Bykov. If you don't succeed today, we will happily begin negotiations with the artist for something—'

'Only the sad mouse. This one.'

Aleksandr believed in his own style of dealership. Everything could be done on a handshake. All this stuff about fairness irritated him.

His phone buzzed. Yuri. 'I'm in the car. Come out.'

Aleksandr sighed heavily and raised a hand to the men from Christie's. He signalled to his bodyguard that she should stay where she was.

'I will be only one minute.'

His son stood smoking with his back against the rear of a white Aston Martin.

'Hello, Pater.' The Romanian henchman was standing at the driver's door. He nodded to Aleksandr, holding his eye for a moment. In the older Bykov's opinion, a Romanian could always live a double life.

'Where are my Impressionists?' Yuri asked. 'The ones that were lodged with my Belgian business partner at his apartment.'

'What are you talking about?'

'His apartment was robbed by your people.'

Aleksandr stared right through him.

'Monsieur *Lantier*,' the Romanian said. Yuri turned and glared at him: he had spoken out of turn.

'I need cigarettes,' Yuri said to him. 'From Davidoff. The shop is down there, corner of St James's Street.'

The Romanian spun his keys and stared.

'Gold-tipped,' Yuri added.

The Romanian departed, and Aleksandr took a step forward. 'Stay away from me. I will not discuss Lantier or the friends you made in order to embarrass me.'

'Mr Lantier had assets of mine.'

'I know nothing about him.'

'He made your friends angry?'

'Both of you did. You are street criminals. You are hooligans who take drugs in nightclubs. You trade in slave workers.'

His son stayed composed, nonchalant, but Aleksandr believed he was bleeding inside. Nothing breeds fear like success, he said to himself.

'You were born with a sickness for destroying yourself, Yuri. You should not have spoken that way to the Duke of Kendal. He is an idiot, of course, but he was my idiot, and was cultivated over a long time. If you had more experience you would know that these men come back, they *revive*.'

'That man is done.'

'No, Yuri. He is merely wounded, as you are. But the Duke has lawyers and royal cousins and traditions and estates. You have only me.'

456

'I have much more. I have freedom.'

Aleksandr was feeling for a certain English word. *Debauched.* His son looked like that. He was high on something and sick with illusions. 'Ah, Yurko. You are swimming in a sea of sharks and you are losing blood. You have had your game. Now it must stop. You must leave London and stop these criminal associations.'

'If you could only hear yourself, Pops.'

'Pops. Even your words are disgusting. You must go. You must end these activities that could bring such harm to us. I demand it.'

'Oh, Father,' Yuri said, throwing down his last cigarette. 'You and your cold war. You've never had a real fight on your hands, have you?'

That same afternoon, Milo and Gosia had gone for a walk in Hyde Park. He waited outside the Serpentine Gallery when Gosia went in to use the bathroom. From his inside pocket he drew out a crumpled letter.

> Dear Milo,
> Thank you for the book, but I don't know that it's really for me. It's a taunt, I imagine. I realise you've ghosted me, as they say. I just wanted to tell you something 'afore ye go', as the old whisky advert used to say. Your behaviour demonstrates why the world feels so angry now – because people like you are busy swapping out core identity for group identity, imagining that anybody who isn't you must essentially be part of what William Cobbett called 'the Thing'. I have spent my whole life, like most people, alone, but I guess you will not see that in your singularity. I wish you well in your thoughts and conquests.
> All the best,
> Campbell

Milo folded it away as she emerged from the gallery. She might have recognised the letter but she didn't say anything. He took her

457

hand and they walked in a westerly direction over the park, emerging into the bustle of High Street Kensington. He'd told her he needed extra equipment for the work he was doing, so they went to a computer shop in one of the side streets and bought a Pegasus32 external hard drive. 'I want to show you something,' he said. The road was on an incline heading towards Holland Park. Eventually, he stopped and pointed to a large white house on the other side of the street.

'That's where he lives – Anthony Crofts.'

'The Duke?' she said.

'That's right. His house . . . Correction: *one of* his houses.'

It looked like the shutters inside were closed. Nobody home.

'All my focus is on him now,' he said. 'We've got ourselves a little something with those videos . . .'

'I'm nervous, baby.'

He held her face in his hands and kissed her. Then he looked over at the black door and the bare cherry tree standing in the front garden.

'We've got this corrupt fucker by the balls,' he said. 'We're finding our place, and we're going to *rinse* this guy.'

The street was so replete with money, so private and respectable, that Milo wondered how many of the owners were scammers. 'I don't mind playing their game,' he said, 'if there's something brand new at the other end.'

She sighed.

'So the professor's out of the picture?'

Milo's focus went towards the roundabout. He needed a beat to work out the best thing to say about Campbell Flynn.

'It wasn't personal, but you've got to cut ties. It's all about the endgame – the out. The only thing that matters is what the professor has led us to.'

'And what is that?' she asked.

'Escape.'

# 37 Stevenston

Moira hadn't known the Glasgow of her mother and father, but it existed in songs and photographs, the tenements of their youth. Her dad had grown up in Rottenrow and recognised the children who were painted there, the weans with ragged school jumpers, messy hair and squints, the street life crowded in their eyes. That morning, Moira had felt the need to come off the motorway, and she drove up to the Garngad, getting out of the car to look down at the Royal Infirmary and the cathedral. To her left, she saw that the Rosemount Street flats, their childhood home, had disappeared. She thought of the old causes: motherhood, housekeeping, appearances. Only Campbell had a scholarship, so every other penny went into Hutchesons' Grammar, every penny their father hadn't drunk, and, when it all worked out, the children left Glasgow for England. Through her work, Moira had reclaimed home in a manner that her brother never really had, and she believed he was haunted by it all, referring always to the flat in Roystonhill as a scene of pain. He joked about it, and he'd gone far, but the whirring, fake fireplace was still there – his native sun. He'd never owned a home that could compete with the way Roystonhill owned him.

She took a few pictures with her phone. It was a memorable day: cold on the ears and warming to the heart. She sent the pictures to Campbell's phone, and he rang her pretty much immediately. 'You heading to Ayrshire?'

'Aye,' she said. 'It's a beautiful day.'

She didn't admit she was going to see Mrs Gowans. She knew it troubled him terribly, the whole Byre thing.

'The papers are having a carnival over this Tony scandal,' he said. She could hear him pausing, thinking, avoiding.

'Maybe you need a rest, Campbell. Like, some years are year zero, and you've had too much on your plate recently.'

He told her that UCL wouldn't be renewing his contract.

'Really? Why?'

'My scores on Rate My Professors have gone through the floor. Like, multiple low stars. We don't know if it's the Byre thing or . . . And my research assistant, Milo, I think he's backing away from me. Maybe my reputation's shot.'

'But you were always popular with the students.'

'Nothing's been right since that article in *The Atlantic*. I mean, nowadays people want to murder you for thinking your own thoughts.'

Moira switched the phone to her other ear, so she could warm her hand in her pocket. 'You won't like me for saying this,' she said, 'but I think you've been playing a major part in your own difficulties.'

He had a talent for selective reasoning. Campbell could see things beautifully, but only the things he wanted to see.

'I think I'm done with it anyway,' he said. 'I'm done with a lot of things, to tell you the truth. I'm sure the kid's busy or something.'

She didn't ask him what he meant. She would later wonder why she hadn't. But then, it had always been Campbell's way to surprise everybody.

'In the meantime, we're up in Suffolk. I need to be with Elizabeth while she's supporting her sister.'

'Don't forget to support *this* sister,' Moira said.

At her constituency office in Garnock she worked through the lunch hour, mostly answering emails. Calls had come in from both the *Herald* and the *Scotsman*, plus *Reporting Scotland* and *Newsnight*, asking for a response to the news about her brother's relative the Duke of Kendal, who, under legal advice, was contesting the accusations that he'd been involved in Russian money laundering, suggesting the monies paid were legitimate investments. He was also denying his part in the right-wing video, saying he had no recollection of ever having met the individuals concerned.

'No comment,' Moira said.

By four o'clock, the sky was inky. When people say darkness falls, they could be thinking of what happens in Ayrshire at that time of year, when the dark drops out of the sky at teatime, the street lamps smartly blinking to life like they've arrived for work. Moira felt it was cold in that Scottish way: cold as a legacy; cold inside the stones and inside the memory. She drove past Hawkhill Cemetery in Stevenston and took the first right at the garage, then began looking out for the turnings to get to Boyd Orr Street. The office had phoned ahead to Mrs Gowans, who had agreed to the visit from her local MP. All this horror had come into her life and Moira got the feeling, from the moment she met her, that Mrs Gowans had been preparing for something like that all her days.

'You found it all right?' she said to Moira as they came down the heavily carpeted hall to arrive at her yellow kitchen. Moira put a bag of groceries on the draining board. It was something her own background had taught her: never arrive at a person's door – a working-class person's door, she meant – without milk, teabags and a tin of biscuits. 'You didnae have to do that,' the woman said.

'It's a thing of my mother's,' Moira replied. 'From the war, I think. Never assume a person is ready for visitors. Bring a cake.'

'I ken what you mean. My mither was the exact same.'

Her face was pale and she had red hair. She smoked long cigarettes. Richmond Greens.

'It's my only vice,' she said.

In the living room everything was white, silver or grey, with spray-painted bamboo twists sprouting out of white pots on the mantelpiece. The cushions were either silky or furry and several had sewn hearts or the word 'Love' spelled out in sequins. The carpet was white in every room and the general softness of materials appeared only to underscore the hardness of the woman's life.

'Your home is spotless,' Moira said.

'Do you want me to turn the radiators up?'

'No, I'm good.'

'I only use the heating for a few hours these days,' she said.

Mrs Gowans was only about forty, but seemed older. She said she'd never met an MP before – 'Never had any need' – and told Moira she worked part-time in the change booth of one of the amusement arcades in Saltcoats.

'And you have working tax credit? Housing benefit?'

'Aye. It all helps.'

'But you manage all right?'

'No' bad. Put it this way – I don't go to the food bank.'

'Right.'

'Plenty do.'

There were several framed photographs on the windowsill. She assumed the ones of a baby and a toddler were Vicky.

'She was my only one,' Mrs Gowans said. 'And one was enough. Victoria was never what you would call a greetie wean.'

'She didn't cry much?'

'Naw. She was always that calm. You could bathe our Victoria and dress her and comb her hair and she wouldn't budge. And then they grow up and they start hanging about with the wrong ones. That's where it starts.'

'She was rebellious?'

'Oh God, aye. She was a handful. It was boys, then it was drugs, then it was stealing, and off to London and God knows what else.'

'I'm sorry, Mrs Gowans.'

'Call me Mary. The papers have been phoning, and they go, "Mrs Gowans . . ." and I say, "Call me Mary. We don't put on airs."'

'It was a journalist that exposed this man, William Byre, who is supposed—'

'Aye, Sir William. He rang me as well, from that prison he's in. He said his assistant found my number and he rang me.'

She sounded proud. Moira was outraged, but she tried to hold back.

'He phoned me out of the blue. I asked him what on earth had happened. Victoria always spoke that well of him – told me he was a "sir" and all that. And this was him on the phone. He said he'd had a nightmare going on with his businesses and trouble with his wife.'

'Okay,' Moira said.

'He didn't seem a bad man or anything. But then, Victoria died on her own. They said there would be money coming to me, because of the flat. It was in her name, apparently. But I don't know if I would want that.'

'Mrs Gowans—'

'I mean, he seemed a decent enough person. And she'd been into these things before. Drugs, I mean. Trying different things.'

'Mary.'

She looked up. Her green eyes were full of tears. And Moira tried to imagine what it must be like to have a child taken from you.

'I have to tell you something. I happen to know him. He was at university with my brother and they remained friends. I never liked him. He *isn't* sympathetic.'

'But I think he was, to Victoria. And I think he maybe couldn't see how lost she was, you know? She was always lost.'

'I don't know what to tell you. He isn't a good man.'

'Do you think he'll go down for all these things?'

'They have a way of getting off, these people,' Moira said. 'It's one of the differences that makes me unhappy. I believe he abused your daughter. He—'

'Don't say it, don't say that word.'

Mrs Gowans put her cigarette down in the ashtray. There was complete silence, then she wiped her eyes with the sleeve of her jumper and stared at the silver blinds.

'I know it's daft, right,' she said, 'but I thought she'd be Lady Gowans. Or Lady . . . his name. I just thought it would happen.'

Wiping her eyes, the girl's mother rubbed away the easy fixes that allow people to paint themselves as perfect. 'I probably didn't do very well myself,' she said. 'The truth is that Victoria deserved much better.'

She sipped her tea like it was reliable.

'I didn't know he was your brother's friend,' she said. 'It's a small world, though. It's really nice of you to come and talk to me yourself, to spend the time.'

They spoke about Vicky's funeral, whether Mrs Gowans would need help with the costs, things like that.

'Can I show you her room?'

They held on to the white painted banister. 'She used to come down to my work after school,' Mrs Gowans said. 'She was obsessed – and I mean *obsessed* – with the coin rivers, you know the machines where you drop in a coin? She would stand with her hands on the glass, totally amazed by the whole thing. I would give her candyfloss or a can of ginger and she'd be that happy.'

They went into the box bedroom at the top. It had white, fluffy rugs and a dressing table covered in stickers. On one wall it was Miley Cyrus, Taylor Swift and Natasha Bedingfield posters, with graffiti scrawled on them; the other wall was patchier, more like a giant pinboard, with an Obama flag standing out.

'She wasn't very political,' Mrs Gowans said. 'Not like you are. She liked him when she was young.'

Moira sat down. It felt like a museum, probably much colder than it used to be. On the table was a pencil with its pointy end sunk in a sharpener.

'She always wanted to go,' the woman said.

'To London?'

'It was her dream. To maybe make a difference, like working with young people or maybe starting her own wee business one day. Maybe meet somebody who would take care of her. Better care.'

A firework went off in the street.

'I don't think I'll ever be able to empty it,' she said. 'That would really be the end, and this is Victoria's room.'

Moira thought it was time to go, but Mrs Gowans insisted she stay for a drink. She didn't get much company and it was cold outside. In the kitchen, she poured two large glasses of Captain Morgan's Spiced Rum, adding Coke and ice.

'Goodness,' Moira said.

Mrs Gowans opened the back door to let the smoke out. The cold was rushing in, with a burning smell. Guy Fawkes Night. You could see a spray of colours behind the buildings opposite. They decided to put their coats on and go and sit on the wee square of patio at the back door, so they could see the fireworks. Mrs Gowans said Victoria had buried her pet guinea pig under the tree in the corner of the garden. 'She couldn't bear anything dying. She wanted life. She wanted the bright lights and all that sort of thing.'

Moira had been on the go all day. The fireworks went over the buildings, whizz-bangs and glittering gold.

'It was our lot they were hoping to blow up,' she said.

'What's that?'

'The Houses of Parliament. Guy Fawkes.'

'Aye, well,' Mrs Gowans said obscurely. 'What's for us will no' go by us.' She told Moira she could remember the bang that used to come in the afternoon from the old Nobel factory nearby at Ardeer. Gone now. Even the chimneys. 'I keep getting up in the morning and looking outside and thinking the world will be like it used to be, but it never is, is it? Some people would say that's a good thing – I'm sure you would, Mrs Flynn – but some of us just want our wee things around us and nothing more.'

'I know what you mean. I really do.'

Mary took her time and looked into the other houses. She smoked her cigarette. 'You know something, I think it could snow,' she said.

\* \* \*

465

Sailing from Larne to Cairnryan that evening, Gerry the truck driver could see the rock called Ailsa Craig. He was always giving information to the other drivers about its geology, the fact that the granite from those cliffs was used to make the best curling stones in the world. 'No danger. You can google the fuck out of it if you think I'm talking shite,' he said.

'I believe you, O'Dade,' one of them said. 'You told me before.'

He'd had trouble again with the border police. Turned out the chickens he was tipping in Ballymena were in Spanish cages, and they had to work out if the cages were part of the sale or not before they would let him through. Stefan wanted him back in Kent the next night for a trip to Northern France. If he got a move on and made good progress down to Preston with the cakes going to Morrisons, he could floor it on the M6 and get to Kent by the middle of the day.

'I saw Keyser Söze's daughter,' Charlo said in a quick call.

'Feng's kid? Wha'? In London?'

'Up in Kent. At the grow-houses. I think that's who it was. I mean, maybe *she's* Feng. Maybe they're all Feng, for fuck's sake.'

'Ah, mate. It's a mad world, so it is.'

Later on, they exchanged WhatsApp messages.

'Are you interested in moving the samphire?'

'No way Charlo. Not 4 me, m8. They're growing double already and selling it straight to London gangs and whatevs.'

'Eyeball you at Thurrock early doors? I'm dropping ambassadors first thing and I think you're on the crossing tomoz night. I'll buzz you at Moto.'

O'Dade was soon gunning down the A75.

Fireworks over the wee towns. Bonfires.

He stopped to use the bog at Dumfries and bought two Red Bulls and a packet of crisps. He had customised the seat in his cab and had retrofitted Apple CarPlay – it was magic, having the tunes at full blast. He didn't need the satnav for half of these jobs: he knew the routes. The cab was home to him, his living room, his bedroom, his games room and kitchen; his yoke was his life, and it could've been anything he was pulling, but it was better if it was clean. A few more months, that was all.

# 38 Finding Your Voice

Lloyds had been in Deptford the night of the trouble, same as Travis, but nobody was arresting him or Big Pharma. 'Travis had a knife out, bruv,' Pharma said. 'That's the difference. That's why T got bagged, you feel me? CCTV snapped him with a blade.'

They were by the skate ramps at Paradise Park. Lloyds's hoodie, under a heavy black puffa, said 'EA7'. He was good at keeping out the cold, managing the weather, so long as he still looked good. He had a couple of new rings and he wanted to show them off. 'Things blew up, fam. That's the story.'

'It was a conversation.'

'Yeah, I know,' Lloyds said. 'But the kid got stabbed nine times in the back and once in the heart.'

Pharma said it still didn't feel real. It felt to him like *Buffy* or *Lost* or one of the old-school telly programmes. The Deptford Cartel and their allies were baying for blood now. They were gliding up and down King's Cross looking for members of the Cally to jump. Someone got slashed at the Esso station. Revenge. 'Like a TV show,' he said, 'except you want this shit to get cancelled.'

Lloyds's second phone rang. The Ghost Line. He kept it for weed customers and he arranged a drop-off right there. Big Pharma was rocking from side to side to whatever the sound was in his head.

'Travis might go to prison,' Lloyds said.

'How can they know him all dressed in black? How can they pick him out? He just stood there, like anonymous.'

'But with a blade out, Bigs, like he was ready.'

'Travis wanted peace, cuz.'

'Whatever,' Lloyds said. He regretted the whole thing. But he still thought he could be the CEO, helping Travis on remand, getting videos recorded inside, merchandise, deals. Meanwhile, the weed business was growing so fast, good, regular money, working with these Poles, getting into new markets.

'It's all good, Bigs,' he said. 'We're making cash.'

He was Lloyds on the street. When he wasn't hustling, when he was at home, he was Jeremiah, and he told girls to call him that. He had his own place now, by the railway bridge on the Cally. Three of his own brothers were in jail, proper nutters, he said, all of them addicts or dealers, loved by their mother and crazy for gold before they were sixteen. He wanted a different life, the boss-man life, and he was getting started. His dad always warned him against Travis and the drugs, told him all the time that Milo was a better model, the kind of boy who didn't wait around for trouble to start. But Lloyds went at it from both ends.

'Is mumzy still dressing you, bro?' he said to Big Pharma as they left the park and walked down to Liverpool Road.

'What d'you mean?'

'You got creases in the front of your jeans.'

'Rah, man! I told her to stop doing that!'

A red Mercedes-Benz SLC stopped at the lights and the guy had the passenger window down and the car stereo booming. Lloyds picked up his phone. He pressed Shazam to capture the tune blaring out, a new thing from Polo G.

'Chicago, baby,' he said as they walked on.

Big Pharma had stuff to do, going back to a house in Paradise Park for a re-up on supplies. Lloyds knew his friend had opened up a sideline in dealing powder. He didn't say anything. You were a gang for most things but an individual once in a while. 'I'm gonna bounce,' Pharma said. He sang a few lines in his big, beautiful voice as he walked away, a tune by Lupe Fiasco. Lloyds kept turning to him, walking backwards. 'Gonna call Travis in his pen later,' he said.

'Tell my guy T he's a don, yeah?'

'I'll tell him that. I will.'

As Pharma carried on down Liverpool Road, the Mercedes returned. The window was still down, but this time a hand reached out with a gun and fired at him four times. As Lloyds turned to look, his friend flew off his feet with the blast. The street became a smear: a blur of red car revving away, smoke and scattered leaves, Devan falling backwards to the pavement and lying there with his eyes wide open.

William often lay in his cell at Belmarsh and thought about grand dinners he'd had in the past, and it seemed probable, in his undefeated mind, that he would have them again before long. He fancied he could hear the Thames rolling past, the open waters going to the North Sea, carrying his hopes downriver. He tried to recall verses he had studied about the capital city, and repeated them stretched out on the lower bunk of his cell, amid the shouts and the banging doors. It sent him off to sleep, or back to the old life, the snatches of Edmund Spenser he'd learned at Peterhouse, preparing for life in the invisible hands of the market.

> At length they all to merry London came,
> To merry London, my most kindly nurse,
> That to me gave this life's first native source;
> *Something . . .*
> An house of ancient fame.
> *Something . . . something . . .* whereas those bricky towers,
> The which on Thames' broad aged back do ride,
> Where now the studious lawyers have their bowers.

He wasn't in isolation, but he was on his own. The whole place smelled of piss and deodorant, but he'd managed to get a TV and regular deliveries of a few groceries. Bananas on the windowsill, books on the desk. It wasn't supposed to be this way. He saw Vicky's eyes in the middle of the night.

After exercise that morning, his mail was delivered to his cell. He opened a book from Amazon, *The Gladiator Mindset: Ten Steps to Achieve the Impossible* by the British swimmer Adam Peaty, and he set aside several letters. He was quick to free his copy of the *Spectator* from its polythene and study the cover. There she was: 'Antonia Byre: Flee Your Toxic Inheritance', in bright red letters. He'd been following his wife's progress from right-wing banshee to MeToo panjandrum with sad interest, and it was amusing to see her swapping her usual bile for an absorption in common suffering, which she now claimed to have been prevented from sharing with her readers for thirty years. Often, when she wasn't revelling in her new-found camaraderie with the sisterhood, she was writing about her personal ravages at the hands of Evans syndrome, a (for her) entirely new condition, which caused extreme anaemia, paleness, light-headedness and frequent bruising. Bruising! She had already begun to speak of stem cell transplantation and was founding a charity.

Sitting on his bed, he read the letters. One of them offered him Christian renewal and another one offered him a wife. Both had been written with malfunctioning pens, and the proposal, hot from Taunton in Somerset, came with a pressed flower, a carnation. The final envelope, he knew as soon as he saw it, was from Campbell. His handwriting had remained the same since the postcards he'd sent from Paris as a student. Back then, it was always a card from a museum, scrawled with boasts about last night's fun, and his writing always had the same old Catholic dash and promise. The letter was written on Club notepaper, a line through the Pall Mall address and 'Suffolk' written in. It was as if Campbell had finally convinced himself that his own moral outlook was the *sine qua non*.

Dear Will –

In my opinion, our children will always be children, and we never were children, <u>never</u> in our lives, it wasn't allowed. Elizabeth often tells me my adulthood is a revenge fantasy on my disappointed parents. We had a challenge, you and me, and I feel for you in your predicament and I send you love. I've been luckier. I had a daughter, and she may be spoiled, too, but she knows about life. Kenzie's virtue grows in tandem with her experience, which is all one can really hope for.

At a certain point, you need to look outside your family, the first unit of government, and see the society you have helped to make. In that sense, we have all done badly. I'm sorry, Will. Our values are polluted and our minds enslaved. And there <u>you</u> are, once one of the funniest men I knew, fallen to the very bottom. There is no justice, and there will be no freedom in the world until <u>all of it goes</u>, no decency, either, and I write this late at night by the fire and hope it exerts some grip.

I will pay back any money I owe, any loans. It was disgusting what you did and I fear it has permanently darkened my mind. I have always paid for everything myself and this won't change. There are plans afoot, and I am learning new tricks in the Bitcoin world, so I will soon have a clean slate and owe nobody. Nothing turns out as you expect in this life, but we must be part of the remedy. Our friendship is dead. These days are not built for older men. But there is surely something redeemable in all of it, as we set things straight, meet our debts at last, as we interrogate our language, accept the new reality and allow ourselves to question all the dogmas that maintained our privilege, kept us in charge and made us abusive. The game is up and we are free, William, we are young again.

Sincerely,
Campbell

There it is, William said to himself. A pathetic letter. Campbell was delusional, all his life, thinking he was ahead of everyone, thinking he was unimpeachable. He looked at pictures, but the big picture, and his part in it, escapes him.

In the workshop that day, William considered the abomination of that letter and the destruction of self it represented. His old friend had never understood anything about business, conquest, victory or control. He was a daisy chain, a clever enough entertainer in a world of paintings and museums, but riddled with the kind of opportunism he hated. That is true of most liberals, William said to himself, which is why they can't cope with power, why their political parties are a mess: they can't grasp their true nature, their real aspirations and the feeling – the certainty! – that what they want for themselves will be more than what they want for other people. It kills them. That's why they concentrate so much on feelings and injuries, on naming, on correctness, because they don't have the stomach for the inequality they depend on. And now, in the North of England, just as in Kansas or Illinois, people vote against their own interests, because they detest a culture that sees them as needy, they hate the caring elites who like to tell them what is good for them. In the modern world, William told himself, people don't mind being exploited so long as they can choose it themselves.

That day's workshop was part of a 'Be Your Own Boss' Enterprise Exchange. A young black guy was tapping on the bench at the back. He always had his earphones in, and was paranoid. He said he should be in solitary because there were gangs in the prison who would harm him. He said all this to the project officer. Again, it was a thing at Belmarsh; they wanted you to do activities, and there was a lot of mixing, which William hated. A bald, middle-aged Eastern European guy came in and said very little. He sat away from everyone, like he wanted privacy and was passing through England.

'Nonce,' one of the inmates said.

William was struck hard on the side of the head. He didn't know who it was, but he heard the alarm going and heard shouting and saw a flash of white shirts. The shouting seemed to go on for a long time and it echoed horribly. He was conscious enough to fight back, a kind of instinct to push them away and not go down, but then there was another thud on the side of his head, and he woke up in the Contingency Suite.

'H1-03,' he heard an officer say. 'Surname: Byre.'

'Be your own boss,' he said to himself. Looking up, he could see glass bricks on the ceiling and shadows above the bricks, the moving feet of people and muffled noises up there in another world. Distinct, like his mother's singing, he could hear phrases from Campbell's letter roaming through his mind.

'We never were children – never in our lives.'

'These days are not built for older men.'

'William, we are young again.'

He must have passed out, then a kind of fog took over. It was dark when he opened his eyes and someone was standing over him, bald, he thought. The man stuffed a sponge into his mouth and covered his face with a pillow.

# 39 Remembrance Day

At Albany a few days later, the Duke was in the downstairs kitchen watching a small TV. At 11 a.m., the Remembrance Day parade began and the presenters dwelled on Her Majesty's absence. He knew it was the beginning of the end; she wouldn't miss the Cenotaph unless she had to. Somehow the worry ceded to other worries, this state of disappointment. In normal times, he would have marched down Whitehall with the Great Veterans, but they'd ditched him. He understood. It would take a while for normal business to resume, even normal charity business. Holding a celery smoothie, he stood in front of the television to observe the two-minute silence. Then, as the Last Post sounded, he bent down and picked up a lipstick from the floor and put it in a drawer. He told himself that from now on he would stop it with these girls. He would improve. Eat healthier, stretch – as Candy said he must – and fight to restore his good name after all this nonsense.

There was a tattered flag framed on the stairs. A collector had found it in a shoebox at auction and had pieced it together, a Union standard covered in battle honours, seven foot by seven foot, which had been carried into battle at Waterloo by the Coldstream Guards 15th Light Company. He stood in front of it. It had all the rips and all the grime of that day and of the two hundred years since. The Duke's view of life and his philosophy of human nature resolved in the end into a vision of national character. That's all that mattered, really. That's all that remained to you in the brutal siege of growing old. The flag had cost him more than £200,000 and he felt it was the very best of his treasures. He had restored it to his family, to his name and to the glory of England, without whose values and trophies everything was lost and the future a surrounding darkness.

The bell rang and he opened the door to his lawyer, Mr Skene of Skene & Cooper, accompanied by his young assistant.

'Oh,' the Duke said.

'Meeting today? Did we get it wrong?' Skene asked.

'No, of course. By all means,' he said, ushering them in.

Skene resembled a rather etiolated undertaker, and, indeed, that was an apt description, the Duke thought. More than all the lawyers in Holborn put together, he knew exactly where the bodies were buried, and who put them there. He had been defending English aristocrats and their peccadillos for forty years, and the Duke's father, and several uncles, had sworn by his delicacy. As a breed, they formed a slick, grey, poker-faced stratum of English life, the lawyers with their heavy suits and their overcoats, the boys from Carter-Ruck, the men from Quinn Emanuel, the ladies from Schillings and Mishcon de Reya. One of the Duke's young friends in Parliament had recently called them amoral, which was quite right, he felt, their having done much work for the basest of the internationals, yet these lawyers were as English as toasted teacakes, and the young peer had probably not yet found himself in a jam. Skene's junior tripped into the room wheeling a suitcase of papers. He shook hands like a boy and his tie was too pink, but the Duke smiled equably and took them to the drawing room. Skene's eyes were so wet that his client was tempted to hand him a napkin. 'I'm afraid,' he said, clicking his fingers towards his junior clerk, 'we have what I would call a development.'

The younger man handed him a document.

'Read it to me,' the Duke said. 'I don't have my spectacles.'

'I shan't read it. I'll give you the gist.' Skene coughed unnecessarily. 'A certain party, we don't know who they are, but they appear legitimate, that's to say, they appear to have certain knowledge, and in that sense—'

'Yes,' said the Duke impatiently.

'They may be the source of the original video material.'

'I see. Go on.'

'We have had an approach. They might represent some sort of organisation. They say they have more material.'

The Duke looked at Skene with military fortitude. The lawyer would, in the old manner, have made a maddening but effective aide-de-camp; he fulfilled the requirements of a confidential secretary. 'To wit, they make a proposal,' he said, 'that if a certain sum is paid to them, a sum that they say is intended to be forwarded to a good cause, then the material will disappear.'

'So I'm being blackmailed?'

'In a manner of speaking, yes.'

'And what other manner of speaking could there be, Mr Skene? I am misrepresented by these hideous people and I am judged a cad. If I want to avoid any more of these revelations, I'm expected to pay up. What is that if not blackmail?'

'That, in effect, is quite right, of course.'

'How much do they want?'

The lawyer put out his hand for another paper. 'The party asks for £2 million, Your Grace.'

'Well, they're mad.'

'Quite so, sir, in effect.'

Skene began to outline what he felt was a second possibility. They had retained the services of a deeply trusted public relations firm, Prestons, who were already pursuing various strategies of damage limitation. Their advice was to refuse payment. 'They concur with our original statement and question the validity of these videos *tout court.*'

'Go on.'

'The word they use is "deepfake". They say you were never at the meeting described and did not actually say the words. They believe the video was, as it were, manufactured, which I understand is now feasible.'

'So I was never there.'

'You may have met these veterans in the course of your charity work. You may have stopped with them or passed through their premises—'

'But I did not say those words and—'

'Precisely. In effect, the words were manufactured using actors . . .'

The lawyer looked down at the document.

'. . . grafted together using old video material and images of you. The practice is well known in the world of celebrities, I believe.'

'And Prestons will pursue this line with the press and so on?'

'Indeed, sir. They'll say this is what happened.'

The Duke did not feel obliged to question it. He did not pay Skene to think well of him, and he was sure he did not. The gentleman was old, his pinstripes faded, and strands of grey hair clung to his pate. He had seen too much and gave the impression that he would be glad to retire to Hampshire quite soon.

'And the other matter?'

Skene looked up. 'Of the Russian investments, sir?'

'That's right.'

'There is no issue here, no proof of impropriety. I believe, sir, that there is scarcely an arts organisation in the UK, scarcely a foundation or a British political party that has not enjoyed such investments. The idea that these payments from Russian individuals are made in an effort to launder money in the UK is not a matter over which the beneficiaries can be held accountable. That is a matter for the Russians themselves. The loans and gifts came from legitimate British businesses, the main one in this case based on the Isle of Man, and the sums are properly accounted. The fact that one of these individuals, Mr Aleksandr Bykov, is facing international sanctions does not exclude the possibility of him and others investing as businessmen in London. Therefore, I conclude, in effect, you are in no danger from this connection, and I suggest we undertake legal action against any media outlet or individual who seeks to slander you in this regard.'

This was heartening. 'So we may dismiss it?'

'Indeed. As may a number of colleges at Oxford and Cambridge. As can the Royal Opera House and several newspapers.'

'Good.'

'I should say, however, that your alleged friendship with Aleksandr Bykov – and this is the view of Prestons also – may be unhelpful in a wider sense. As you are aware, he is being investigated, we believe, for money laundering, but also for taking part in extortion and racketeering, and for illegally wiretapping a British government official. There are also allegations that he has used the services of a Russian organised crime group who carried out the murder of a Belgian businessman. Bykov's house in Surrey was raided this morning by the Security Service. The gentleman may not be in London for much longer.'

The Duke walked to a corner desk, upon whose scratched surface he tapped a pen. The desk had belonged to his father and to his father before him. Albany had provided respite and security for all of the dukes in their pursuit of a private life. He looked into the pier glass, aware of the laughter and gossip that had passed before its silvered surface, and Skene's voice faded in and out as he considered his position more generally.

'A more immediate worry, Your Grace, comes, if I may say so, from your association with the younger Bykov. His associations are of an even lowlier kind.'

'Yes. He was astonishingly rude to me. Go on.'

'He is a playboy, sir, and feckless.'

'Well, indeed.'

'He is rumoured to be involved in the funding of a growing network of drug suppliers in this country, as well as, it is said, the network of migrant workers operating within it. This is extremely dangerous, politically, and could in effect prove much more damaging than any . . . other allegations.'

And there was young Bykov behaving as if Kendal was now very bad for *his* brand.

'That young man is *persona non grata*,' the Duke said. 'We had early discussions about him investing in a new wing at Segdoune Grange. The discussions came to nothing. I shall have no further dealings with him.'

'His world appears entirely unsavoury, sir.'

Turning from the mirror, the Duke felt he possessed the room again. England is a place where one can always be sure of one's foundation. Mr Skene had papers for him to sign and then he offered the gentlemen a sherry. All the while, he was thinking of the other videos his attackers might have, the more harmful ones.

'Would you kindly wait outside, young man?' the Duke said.

When the clerk had gone, he looked at Skene. He seemed tired in ways that indicated a tired spirit, and his eyes were sorrowful. 'Lord Haxby,' the lawyer said, 'wishes to speak with you about how best to deal with the Bykovs.'

'But I thought he worked with them?'

'A man like that works with everyone.'

The Duke nodded. But it was not for this that he had ordered his lawyer's junior from the room. He wished to enact something.

'Yes, sir?'

'With the video thing,' he said, 'I think we should do both. I propose we both deny it and pay the people off.'

'As you wish, sir. The payment is demanded in cryptocurrency.'

'Well, that is someone else's department. My office will supply the money to your firm and it can be held in escrow.'

'Of course.'

'And I take it there is no guarantee they will not simply take the money and use the material anyway?'

'That is unquestionably a risk, sir.'

'In which case, the denial acts as a safety net.'

'Yes. The material is fake. The payment can never be connected to you or to our firm. That, I learn, is the nature of such currencies.'

'Belt and braces, Skene.'

'In effect, yes.'

When they had gone, he poured himself a glass of port. His hands were shaking. It was the first time in his life that he actually saw his hands shake. It hadn't happened even on the long march with D Squadron over Pebble Island.

Campbell was at Thornhill Square, preparing to leave for Suffolk again after a meeting with the BBC, when the call came from someone on the news desk at *The Times*. William was dead. 'Please, no,' Campbell said quietly, ending the call abruptly. He walked down the stairs, stunned, and when he got to the hall he had to rush and vomit in the sink. He sat on the kitchen sofa for an hour with a tumbler of whisky, eventually finding his tears and sobbing in silence. When all the events of the year were over, Campbell would judge this to have been the decisive moment. 'People can say what they like about William,' he said to Elizabeth when he rang her, 'and he was terrible, but nobody who didn't see him when he was twenty can say they know everything about him. They don't. They only know the part that went wrong.'

'I understand,' she said.

'His comic engine turned all day and half the night.'

'Campbell, just order a car to bring you back to Suffolk,' she said. 'I'm here at Hinderclay House with Candy.'

He couldn't telephone Antonia because he wasn't sure what he would say. How could this happen? A trapdoor suddenly appeared in Campbell's mind, swinging on its hinges, telling him that any man can fall into nothingness. Sobbing into his hands, Campbell wondered if he was one of those who had killed William. His old friend was dead, and Campbell, chasing one whisky with another, entered a state of morbid depletion, feeling that a self he'd never fully revealed was standing with William in that cell.

He didn't get a car to Suffolk, he took the train from King's Cross to Cambridge, where he walked from the station to the Eagle. As usual, it was busy, but Campbell stood in the RAF bar and had several drinks while staring up at the smoky graffiti on the ceiling, old legends written long ago with lighters and lipstick. Friendship had been a movement with him, a cause, a belief system, a source of comfort, a religion. He took out his phone and sent a text to Milo, but nothing came back.

He was drunk enough to act sober when he arrived by taxi at Hinderclay House two hours later. Elizabeth hugged him, but bristled, he thought, at the state of him, or the larger state of him. Candy came into the hall and said she was sorry to hear about his friend, then launched into her own woes, which he leaped into as a form of relief. She talked about staff scrapes at the farm shop, her disappointment at the TV crew returning to America, her irritation at local inertia over her wellness spa, and then there was the issue of her husband being a national hate figure.

'I wouldn't mind a bit,' Candy said, leading them into the library, 'but we're offering these jolly wonderful treatments at the minute.'

'Such as?' Elizabeth said.

'The Winter Snail Slime Facial.'

'Is that actually a thing?' Elizabeth asked.

'Yes. From Elicina. It's said to be the best treatment in the world for dry skin. And the Saké Bath, which our guru discovered in Southern Japan. The amino acids in the saké are simply wonderful for plumping up tired skin.'

'And the good people of Suffolk aren't taking this up? I mean, aren't they sick of crabbing at Walberswick?'

'You're mocking me, Lizzie,' Candy said. 'And it's not fair. We've put heaps of bloody hard work into this place and it's a frightful bore—'

'Oh, Candy.'

'No, stop it. People queue for hours to see that unspeakable hole in the ground at Sutton Hoo. Or they rush in droves to buy William Morris oven gloves and poached pears at that hideous place near Yoxford.'

Campbell walked over to the drinks table. He had a tendency to stagger when he'd drunk this much, but he was fighting to hold it together. He looked down. It was the greatest thing, unimaginable in his youth, the megalopolis of bottles. The Grey Goose was like a steeple amid a terrace of whiskies and gins. Dubonnet. St-Germain. And there, labels out, like sentries in their level rows, were tins of mixers. 'You know how many Martinis they poured at the Rivoli Bar in the Ritz last year?' he said, lifting a bottle of Chivas Regal and tipping himself a decent measure. 'I have the figure. It's 12,200, at twenty quid a pop.'

When he turned, he saw Elizabeth's expression. She didn't like him in what she called his Burlington Bertie mode; she knew he was suffering, but she said he embarrassed himself when he spoke all monied.

'Stop. Judging. Me,' he mouthed in her direction.

'You're over there talking about expensive drinks,' she said, 'meanwhile there are 1.7 million children in England who depend on free school meals. And this government has to be pushed to provide them. What *fun*, Campbell. I'm surprised it doesn't trouble your busy social conscience.'

'Stop judging me, Lizzie,' he now said out loud.

She was still angry with him over the British Museum fandango, and he could see the William thing had shocked her out of her wits too. Everything that was happening with her family and now with him was disturbing to her. She was fierce that night.

He told her so. Almost skittishly, he said that she looked worried.

'Let me be clear,' she replied. 'It's *you* that worries me. I've been worried since Iceland.'

'I'm fine, darling.'

'No, you're not. You're a wreck. I'll ask you again: are we in trouble?'

'What do you mean, *trouble*?'

'Are we facing financial difficulties?'

'I'm dealing with a few things. Nothing to worry about.'

'I don't know what happened to the money from that book.'

'Don't fight, you two,' Candy said. 'I simply couldn't bear it.'

Elizabeth went upstairs and he felt lousy, lost. The death of William had finished him, he was convinced, in ways that he knew might take years to unfold. His friend had died in a prison cell and there was nothing he could do.

A car roared up and the Duke walked in. Campbell gripped his glass.

At dinner in the kitchen, the atmosphere was tense, if not morose, then it improved when Elizabeth, who'd descended, put her hand down by her side at the table so that she could stroke Campbell's. A housekeeper named Toby was tossing a chicken around on the Aga. Feeling his wife's hand, Campbell was reviving when Anthony began speaking about 'that crook Byre's comeuppance'.

'That's extremely mean, Snaffles,' Candy said, like a child. 'You know perfectly well he was Campbell's friend.'

'Why don't you fuck off?' Campbell said to him. 'If he was a crook then we're all crooks, and you *certainly* are.'

Anthony straightened up and Campbell twisted his napkin. The host was red in the face when he smiled, stung, fake-garrulous.

'Well,' he said, pouring a full glass. 'There can never be any doubt about whose side you are on. For the first time in thirty-eight years, I was unable to parade on Whitehall today with the veterans whom I represent. But I don't suppose you think about that, do you? I don't suppose you see the difference between your own wife's brother-in-law and some thief who ran a brace of sweatshops.'

'There is a difference,' Campbell said. 'William wore his wicked nature pretty much on his sleeve, Anthony. Always did. He had a bad character. Whereas you and the gallant Lords present your chests with strips of medals, as if the country's disasters were always the work of others. William paid heavily for his evil.'

'You really are quite silly.'

'I truly do think,' Candy said all chirpily, 'it's one of the reasons women dislike men. They always have to show you their medals.'

'Can we *not* do this?' Elizabeth said, looking from Anthony to Campbell. 'You have both had a stressful time.'

Campbell stroked her hand.

'He hasn't had a stressful time, darling,' he said. 'Not a bit of it. He's suffered a bout of awkwardness. That's what it's like with his sort. He's suffered an *embarrassment*. And nothing will change because the institutions upon which he relies are built to protect him. Neither he nor the prime minister nor any of their exhaustingly immoral little lackeys will take responsibility for what they did, and their money is untouched and their self-regard is unimpeded. They are shameless, these men. These leaders. They are unruinable, because they are built on ruins already, of solid granite.'

'Very good, Campbell,' the Duke said, tapping two fingers of one hand against two fingers of the other, like applause.

'I'm not sure that's absolutely true of Prince Andrew,' Candy offered. 'He seems pretty well stuffed.'

'It's terribly boring, all this,' the Duke said. 'And I don't want to go on, but one of my spies tells me you've been talking to the press.'

Campbell was shocked. 'I speak to the press only about my work.'

'Yes. The *Commentator* has a few details. Family matters, also. All wrong, of course. Doesn't your dead friend's wife write for that thing? And your sister was spotted having tea with one of their hacks on the terrace in Parliament.'

'You really are ridiculous. Moira is an MP. She sees people all the time. Your problems don't come from us, Anthony. Rest assured.'

'You imagine, on the other hand,' Anthony said, 'that all your dramas are rather prestigious.'

'Excuse me?'

'You people in the arts. Heaps of fun, I'm sure. But the stakes are so low. You don't represent anything, not even yourself.'

'And there it is,' Campbell said, throwing down his napkin. 'The English problem. You rank your vices above other people's virtues.'

'You haven't a clue, dear boy. You give yourself such high marks, but everyone who knows you knows you are out of your depth.'

Campbell wanted to spew his guts up. He felt vengeful, like a child. 'I'm glad the papers are exposing you,' he said. 'I hope they never stop.'

'Low company tends to keep low company.'

'How dare you, you fucking idiot.'

'*Stop*,' Elizabeth said. She looked at Campbell with her eyes of care and reason, the eyes he'd first met at college thirty years ago and hoped would always see for him. He'd always said he would see for her too – but he wasn't, was he? Reading her face for answers, he saw only the clear distance he had created. Yet she was still beside him, calm, waiting for him to return.

'You've made good use of this family,' Anthony continued.

A telephone was ringing in the hall. The Duke continued to witter on about loyalty, and Campbell retired from the conversation.

'Ma'am,' the housekeeper said. He held a roaming house-phone and was pointing it at Candy. 'I think you ought to take this.'

'Not now, Toby.'

'I think so, Your Grace. It's about your mother.'

# 40 Closing Ranks

The old world was well represented at the funeral, which took place at the end of November. Elizabeth was pleased there was a formidable gathering of friends from her mother's childhood. In the end, it's what had mattered most to the Countess, her time abroad and at boarding school during the war. When the mourners gathered at the Church of the Immaculate Conception in Farm Street (the venue Emily had stipulated), you could see immediately that she'd led an interesting life. The Rawalpindians, a pair of beautiful, grey-haired ladies in stupendous saris whom her mother often met for lunch, were standing outside after the service, taking off their masks. 'We once met her father, the Egg,' one of them said. 'He came over from India when Emily and David got married.'

'I never knew him,' Elizabeth said. 'Isn't it amazing to think of the people one never knew, including our closest relations?'

All manner of Wipps-Coopers had arrived from the country. Elizabeth couldn't really remember half of them, her father's cousins, but it seemed as if they'd come to Mayfair to say goodbye one last time to the Earl, via his wife, an English custom Elizabeth would probably have found offensive if it wasn't so nice. She fanned herself with an order of service and accepted compliments about the choice of readings and music. 'It was mainly Mummy,' she said. 'She had written it all down for us. Every tune and every poem. Never was the word "order" more meaningfully deployed.'

'But Campbell's eulogy,' a cousin said. 'Hilarious. All that stuff about Hemingway and that ship she lived on.'

Elizabeth was used to her husband being praised. She had long since neutralised any resentment about it; in fact, she quite depended on it. 'Well, he knew her best in a way. He knew her as she wanted to be known.'

The cousin put a hand to her heart. 'Her singing the old school song through the agonies of childbirth! And the insult from Naipaul – what was it he called her?'

'The Madame de Staël of Belgravia.'

'Killingly funny.'

The cousin obviously didn't like the Countess, and Elizabeth wondered if her mother was disapproved of more than anybody had realised. She had thought something similar when Campbell was giving the eulogy, wondering whether he had liked her as much as he'd always said, the speech having a subtle sting.

Candy had a sort of luminosity that day. She joined them under the tree in the churchyard and began ushering people over to the Connaught. 'You scrub up rather well,' she said to Angus when he came and took his mother's arm. 'And you read that poem beautifully. Kind of a harsh choice, though, wasn't it?'

'It was for her Uncle Freddie,' Elizabeth said. 'He died at the Battle of Loos. And they found that poem in his friend's kitbag.'

Taxis were arriving and departing. It seemed to Elizabeth that the photographers over the road wouldn't normally have come. They were there for Tony, no doubt, but they flashed a few times as she and Angus approached the doors of the Connaught, Angus giving them a small wave.

'Where's my daughter?' she said, stepping into the foyer.

The answer was before her. Kenzie, in a blue tuxedo, was standing at the entrance to the Jean-Georges restaurant. She had read 'The Owl and the Pussycat' with such simplicity it had made Elizabeth cry. She'd lost her as they walked out of the church – Emily had left her body to science, so there was no casket to follow – and Elizabeth really needed a touch of Kenzie's éclat to face the wake. Elizabeth rubbed her hands with sanitiser and walked towards her. They kissed, and Kenzie, so remarkably quiet, so competent, took Elizabeth's hand as they walked into the restaurant, where the mourners stood with drinks.

'It happens to be true!' a woman called Anna was saying. 'I'm talking about, I think, 1941. Our school was evacuated from unsafe Ramsgate to safe Herefordshire, into a stately home belonging to somebody called Major Wegg-Prosser. He was scooting off to America for the war and was a very ardent Catholic, so he wanted to leave his house to the nuns, so we – by which I mean me, Emily and the others – got the train from Paddington and the prospect of the journey was simply too, too marvellous.'

'You had a lovely time,' Baroness Lillie said to her.

Elizabeth knew the loud and rather bearlike Anna was a major donor to the World Wide Fund for Nature. It was she, rather hilariously, who had first got her mother involved, thereby robbing them of their inheritance in favour of elephants.

'Hereford was lovely. And excellent things happened. Emily went for a pee one night and passed out on the cold Pugin floor. She had very low blood pressure and was always fainting in the chapel and so on. Anyway, the nuns found her in the morning and she had double pneumonia. Nearly expired, poor thing.'

'Hello, Anna,' Elizabeth said.

'Darling, I'm terribly sorry about your dear old mum. She was v. funny.'

'She was, wasn't she.'

The smell of incense stayed with her all day. After a while, listening to people's stories about her mother, she was quietly overtaken with a sadness she couldn't share. It was partly, she felt, that her mother had always been a person for other people, not so much for her, and it was too late now to make it right.

Triangular sandwiches were going round. 'My word, what exactly is this, would you say?' Baroness Lillie was holding it up to the light.

'Tandoori turkey, I believe,' Candy said. 'With caramelised apple. Where's Anthony? He'll tell us. The apples are ours. We had two boxes of Cripps Pink brought from Suffolk yesterday by FedEx. Mummy would have been amazed.'

Campbell did what he could for Emily. He put the notice in *The Times* and gave the eulogy because Lizzie asked him to. He tended to get such tasks, being the writer. Emily had always been amusing, and yet, in the end, she was no traitor to her class, and it was only her riches that made her independent.

He could see Moira by the windows, talking to a person from Unicef. Kenzie was in a corner with the younger ones. Campbell was avoiding groups and he was also avoiding the Duke, whom he could hear behind him, booming at some poor clergyman about changes to the Military Tattoo at Edinburgh. Campbell quickly moved out of the room and across the corridor, hoping for a ten-minute breather in the Champagne Room. He sat down at one of the prissy little tables, staring up at a frosted, oval skylight, the unreal light of winter gathering over his many Londons. The waiter took his order, and soon brought the Connaught's version of a Vieux Carré – rum, rye, vermouth, Benedictine, bitters – turning his troubled mind into a smoke-filled room.

'A spot of me time?' the voice said. Campbell looked up. For a second the person before him seemed like an apparition, but the speaker was real enough in his own way – Jake Hart-Davies. He was thinner. His dimples were now like quote marks around the wise things he said.

'A good turnout for the Countess,' he went on.

'She was like you, Jake. She spent her life building an audience.'

He grinned like people loved him. 'And quite an audience,' he said. 'Very distinguished.'

Hart-Davies didn't attempt to sit down, but he adopted a stance and put a hand in his suit pocket, as if he was preparing to be photographed by Helmut Newton.

'You made a bad mistake, Jake.'

'I did. But, you know . . . the world loves a corrected person. The future belongs to those who know how to apologise.'

'So long as it doesn't happen again.'

'It won't. I see the times. I'm getting offers again. Men are lost.'

'Are we?'

He snapped his fingers. 'Wasn't it you who wrote that?'

In the gloaming of the bar, while Jake began to offload about his recovery and his gratitude at being 'humbled', Campbell wondered at the whole business of celebrity. The young man before him was fatally ill with the need to be thought special. To be famous was to have an ailment that could eat the body and the mind, a vice pretending at virtue then killing you before you'd had the chance to be good to anyone.

'So, I'm getting to know myself,' Jake said.

'Wonderful. *Know Thyself*, a hot new Netflix series starring Jake Hart-Davies, co-presented by Queen Latifah.'

The actor didn't laugh, he just nodded approvingly. He spoke of work in the pipeline, for Discovery and Audible, plus a low-budget horror and a catwalk assignment for Ashley-Jo's forthcoming menswear collection.

'It's called "Grey",' he said.

'A little something for everyone. No possibility of offending. And yet the true offences run much, much deeper, don't they?'

Jake wasn't ready for this. It was in his nature to expect applause even for the action of desiring applause. But it wasn't coming, so he folded his arms and made a serious face with his pouty lips and his puppy eyes. 'I don't think you helped me enough,' he said, with a lowered voice. 'You definitely didn't, man. You handed me the book and I was left out there to hang with all these big ideas.'

'What am I, your *daddy* too, Jake? You took the job. You fucked it up. You'll now make a ten-part series about your moral recovery. You'll finally write a book. It'll be terrible. Your fan base will grow because they love you when you're sorry. It'll be so cute, the way you happened to say a bunch of ghastly things you didn't mean. You'll come out as gay before too long. That'll be a big moment. You'll tour the daytime shows as a bright beacon of self-acceptance, surrounded by hallelujahs. And, one day, someone'll cast you as a man losing his looks who has a big lesson to learn, and you'll run with it from here to eternity, and you'll win your Oscar, and you'll cry at the Dolby Theatre, seeing it as God's message to the world that you really were a wonderful human being all along.'

'Wow. You *really* don't know me.'

When he returned to the wake, Campbell tried to avoid anybody who might expect him to be sanguine or reassuring, and was met with Antonia Byre. Perhaps he was too much attuned to the theatrical properties of these people, but Antonia seemed an absurdity in that moment, standing like Miss Havisham in black cashmere. Her face was dismantled with make-up, and she appeared – as harsh and opinionated people often do – to revel in the opportunity for mawkish grief. She was apparently now a permanent mourner, and wore her new garments aggressively, deploying their expensiveness as a form of defence.

Her voice was small, and she leaned on an ebony-topped cane.

'Hello, Campbell,' she said.

He had no words. They were all in his mind.

She didn't miss a beat.

'My dear,' she said. 'You must be devastated about darling Emily. I know how much she loved you.'

'She was a stylish person, I'll give her that.'

'*You'll give her that?* Did something happen?'

Campbell realised that his dislike of Antonia had made him careless. He had no intention of handing her such a gift, so he quickly corrected the impression he had given. 'I simply meant she was not given to clichés about life or death, she was too complex for that.'

'I see. Yes, I understand.'

494

'But we were very close. Naturally.'

She made the inhalations that approximate to tears. 'It's been a ghastly year,' she said. It occurred to him she could have been speaking about the weather.

'I see you are now an international tribune for abused women.'

'Don't be cruel, Campbell,' she said.

'You speak now for all the wretched of the earth? Well, God bless you, Antonia, and good luck – you are a shameless person.'

A little of her dark lustre vanished into pique. 'And you, Campbell, who encouraged my late predatory husband for all those years, who travelled on his coat-tails, perhaps you too have a memoir to write about your impeccable value system.'

He cleared his throat. He couldn't exactly breathe.

'I see Zak is doing brilliantly.'

'Yes,' she said. He was now 'very dear to me'. In the past two months, his profile had wonderfully increased. With a new determination, it seemed, he'd gone from hugging trees to influencing government policy. She predicted he would soon enter politics in his own right.

'He already has,' Campbell said. 'We all underestimated Zak. He's defining some of the new essentials for living, I think.'

'He's been a terrific comfort to me, believe it or not.'

God only knows, she'd struck so many poses as a journalist that she couldn't recognise the difference between opinion and morality. She'd already forgotten the brief spell, between their lunch at the Delaunay and William's death, when she defended men against opportunistic accusers, minutes before 'facing' her own 'toxic inheritance'. She'd forgotten the extent to which she had vilified her son and made him miserable. Campbell pitied her in her black robes, and hoped she might find solace in her talent for forgetting. He wished he could. While she spoke about her hopes for her newly discovered son, it occurred to Campbell that she'd probably been depressed all her life, squandering everything in shows of 'strength' which concealed all the things about herself that she couldn't bear. 'He needs me,' she said of her son, 'and I have books to write and a history of male violence to overcome.'

'Genius,' Campbell said as he turned. 'Pure genius. I wish you luck and I will never see you again.'

# 41 Jakub

Up in Mrs Krupa's flat three weeks later, a statue of Our Lady of Sorrows shone on the nightstand, next to her wedding photograph. A small Christmas tree was propped on a chest of drawers, and behind it, outside the window, you could see the petrol station on Caledonian Road. She went to the kitchen and poured a vodka. Memory was mixed with the present. She always viewed her late parents and grandparents as an aspect of winter, their sorrows like snow around the heart. Lifting her glass, she went back to her chair. 'I don't love my son,' she said out loud. 'I have never loved him, a sin against God.' She had struggled with it all year and the struggle was taxing. He was transporting people. In 1943, Catholics were taken, a fact her husband never forgot. He and Cecylia had brought such stories with them across Europe.

She often rang her young man, Jakub. Sharp like a black-and-white photograph, and easy-going like her brothers. He was kind to people, she'd noticed that, and he wanted to build a life in England, as she and Andrzej had, and to bring his brother too. It wouldn't be plain sailing at first: you have to suffer, she knew, to gain the freedom to do better for your family. But the people of her home-town were made of strong material. Perhaps he would provoke a sense of national pride in her son.

'Hello, Mrs Krupa,' Jakub answered his phone.

'You don't mind if I telephone you?'

'Em, no. It is nice to talk.'

'Well,' she said, 'I know you are far from home. When I first came to England I knew nobody. Forty years ago.'

'Thank you, Mrs Krupa,' he said.

'You were working today?'

'Yes. And my English I practise all day.'

'With the other gardeners?'

She knew it was a ludicrous thing to say, that her son was not really employing the young man that way, but Mrs Krupa believed illusions could become reality; that believing hard would put the truth in place. She was a Catholic: His miracles could bring Jakub to where he should be in life.

'Yes, I work with a lot of different people.' He hesitated. 'We use different languages. I am trying a few words of French too.'

'You will meet a lovely wife there. You will meet in Kent.'

'I don't think so.'

'Why not? You are very handsome. Believe me, there are Polish girls.' Now it was her turn to hesitate. 'Be careful which one you choose. They are not all the same. But to marry and have children, this is the way to happiness. The thing is to build a success and then go home. I always wanted to go back.'

'But you didn't?'

'I stayed for the children. But one day . . .'

He said he wanted to return for Christmas. He hadn't yet asked Bozydar for the time off, and the journey was complicated now.

'Białystok?'

'Yes.'

He told her he felt bad mentioning it to her. He said she'd helped him enough since he came to England. 'I'm not as good as you think.'

'Nonsense. You're perfect,' she said.

Mrs Krupa spoke about her work with the nuns in Shepherd's Bush. They were delivering food parcels to the poor at Christmas. 'The London people don't always want to be helped,' she said.

'Everyone wants to be helped,' Jakub said in Polish. 'When Robert is here, we are going to be free and do things differently. We will build a large kitchen, Mrs Krupa, and you can come and have dinner with us.'

'That's something we can think about.'

She said goodbye to Jakub. They would speak again tomorrow.

She was still in her sitting room at midnight.

Bozydar arrived at that late hour, red-eyed and tired but excited, holding a box of chocolates that he'd picked up at a garage. 'They have all sorts in Essex,' he said. 'You could practically buy all your Christmas presents at Moto.'

'Don't be silly,' she said. 'You go to Hamleys for Ben.'

She made him a cup of cherry tea. 'Ah, shit, Mum,' he said. 'This is like cough medicine. Can I not have a proper drink?'

'You've been spending too much time with these Irishmen. Nobody but a heathen wants a drink at this time of the night.'

He looked overweight. People never ate properly. They ran around with their phones and their credit cards, and they never sat down to a proper meal.

'Business is booming,' he said.

She took a necessary breath. 'Look after your own. Okay for these Irishmen, these Romanians, Bozydar, but you are a Polish man.'

'Mum—'

'Listen to me. I have enough of this with your sister. I don't want much, but I want you to remember where you're from.'

'I'm from London.'

'No, that is wrong. You are Polish. Your people are from Białystok. And that young man you took on—'

'Here we go.'

'That young man—'

'Yes, I get it. He works like a horse. He looks out for the workers. He looks like a catalogue model.'

'He is one of our own, Bozydar.'

He pushed the tea away. 'I don't think you know the guy,' he said. 'He's only a geezer who's on his way somewhere. The world is full of them. He came to London. We're using his brain, he's running a bit of *business* for us.'

She didn't want to know. She didn't ask.

'To see how *good* he really is,' Bozydar added, pressing something unwelcome on his mother, a warning about idealising this boy.

'Let him go home for Christmas,' she said.

'You what?'

'He wants to go home and bring his brother here. You must allow it.'

'His brother . . . Eh, okay.'

'Let it happen.'

'It's not easy now, getting people back. They can't just use their passports and jump on a flight, and we have to . . . bring them over. It's . . .'

'But let this young man go and bring his brother. That's all I am asking from you, Bozydar, and I *don't* ask . . .'

She looked at him, willing him not to upset her.


Jakub went over to the allotment with a mug of tea every time he had a break. Someone in the past had planted gooseberries, which he pruned back. He removed yellow leaves from a row of winter cabbages and then placed fleece over them for protection. Although it had snowed the night before, the snow was melting as it touched the ground, which was good news for the plants. At about five o'clock, he came out and dug two holes for the pear trees he'd bought at the garden centre in Whitstable. It was good soil. He sat back with a roll-up cigarette, thinking of the future.

Robert had sent him a link to Harry Styles. Jakub played the song on his new phone as he smoked and watched the sky darken. 'Nice nail varnish. Nice shirt.' That's what Robert had written in English, before a love heart.

'You might meet him in England, if you still want to come,' Jakub texted.

'London. London!' he texted back.

He could see his boyfriend's eyes. They would be ready for the next thing, the next part of life, the goal of prosperity. Jakub had always been practical. It was Jakub who learned to drive, who got the jobs, who saved the money, who went first.

He knew Bozydar was coming to the house that evening and it was all going to be good. Mrs Krupa would make the call. Christmas in Białystok. He would kiss the altar of the Sanctuary of the Blessed Bolesława for her. And in January, they would be two Polish boys in London. Jakub shivered. He'd always had a gift for overcoming despair and using what he had.

When Bozydar arrived, he smelled of beer. He and O'Dade had been to Broadstairs and Ramsgate and they'd stopped at a pub in Herne Bay. Out of the truck, Boz carried rolls of the brown paper they used for packaging. He ignored Jakub on the allotment and went straight into the house. They'd been busy in there all day drying and weighing product meant for Birmingham. Everything was done. Bozydar emerged from the first house, having checked the stuff being dispatched, before going into the next house to give instructions to the Vietnamese. Jakub thought it was bizarre the way he spoke to them, as if they were from another planet, like he had no concept of his own foreignness.

'We all wish to live on an island,' Jakub said to the marshes.

He picked up his mug and went into the kitchen as Bozydar came through the door.

'What's that?' Boz said, pointing to the mug.

'Tea,' Jakub said.

Boz was sneering. 'I thought it might be soup from my mother. She must be sending you beetroot soup by now.'

Jakub said nothing.

'How does it feel to be the favourite?'

He was slurring his words, his face was red. He leaned in close to Jakub and almost touched him with his forehead. 'The golden boy.'

'She likes to help people,' Jakub said.

'Does she? Is that what Mrs Krupa does? She helps people. I never knew that, Jakub. Isn't that fucking terrific?'

Bozydar rested his forehead on Jakub's, then quickly kissed his cheek, as if the effort to hate him was too much. 'You know I disgust her?'

He stood back.

'I know she wants the best for you.'

Bozydar sniggered. 'You must have your own mother somewhere?'

'In Białystok.'

'But where? Why shouldn't I know about *your* mother?'

'In Fryderyka Chopina. Near the university, the Faculty of Law.'

Bozydar stood up straight. 'Near the Faculty of Law,' he said, chuckling. He put his hand in his pocket and pulled something out.

'These houses are running like a dream,' he said. 'You're a leader. My mother knows fuck all about you, but she's a good business-woman, strong instincts.'

'I don't think she knows what we do here.'

'She knows,' Bozydar replied. 'But her life is all pretend.'

He tapped the side of his head.

He flicked on the kettle and put the item from his pocket next to it.

It was Jakub's passport.

'Well done. You've got your Christmas holiday. But that passport is no use for getting back, do you understand? They'll send you packing. They'll see you lived here illegally and skipped on your tourist visa. This passport is only good for EU travel.'

'I understand,' Jakub said.

'You can get buses to Poland. O'Dade is here and he will take you early tomorrow to Dover and across to Calais, yeah? He's delivering soft drinks.'

'That's fantastic,' Jakub said.

'I want you back here by 26 January. One of the drivers will trans-port you back across.' He tore a sheaf of £50 notes from a roll and tossed them on the worktop.

'She tells me you're bringing somebody. Fine. There's a job for him. You can both live here, and that's the end of the discussion.'

'Thank you, Boz.'

'You've got friends in high places, and we've got big plans here next year.'

Jakub took the money and stepped back. It wasn't enough to pay for the illegal crossing.

'No cost,' Bozydar said. 'You're a key worker, man.'

# 42 Yuletides

'Y ou can make a project of yourself, if you must, but not of your husband. People who baby their spouses, or their grown children, are doomed.'

To Elizabeth, this was a crucial belief. She stated it to her analyst that cold morning in December, with sleet falling on Primrose Hill. Something was coming to a head with Campbell. For some people, she'd said, it's as if only the ruination of their happiness will prove that they once were happy. She was covering the same ground with her analyst – increasingly their core subject. Campbell was displaced. A sort of financial panic had led to the writing of that ridiculous book, and maybe also to his bond with that troublesome student; something self-destructive lay there.

'And when you say "lay there" . . . ?'

'Well, precisely.'

'You're worried about sex?' the analyst asked.

'Not like that,' Elizabeth said. 'If anything, the sex has improved since he started worrying about who he is.'

'Then what do you think is wrong with him?'

'Everything and nothing,' Elizabeth said. 'It's inbuilt. How often do we stop in the middle of our lives and genuinely ask: "What's happening?" He has a fear of losing. He wanted life to be like an artwork, and it never quite is. He used to smile with me about such failures, but now he doesn't, and there's something newly *alone* about him. What can I say? Failure is the final stage of maturity with some people, isn't it? The last flowering, the imago, and I really think it makes Campbell feel alive to be so at risk.'

'And distant from you?'

'I think so, yes. There's power in that. But . . . you know. I'm not going anywhere. I'll be standing here when he climbs off whatever carousel he's on.'

'You make him sound like a child.'

'I think he is a child. A person waiting for his mother. But also he's my husband, a gifted man who struggles to fuse the different parts of his life.'

'Is he broken?'

Elizabeth paused and looked down at a running dog and child in the park, having the time of their lives in the winter sun.

'He's fighting for something he can't really be part of – youth, yes; enlightenment, maybe – and it kills him to think he might be part of the problem. And now this young man has vanished, the one who was working for him and feeding him stuff.'

'Vanished? And how is Campbell reacting?'

'He seems desolate.'

'You seem dismayed.'

'I think I am,' she said. 'At first, I was amused by these new preoccupations; I made a joke about there being nothing more old-fashioned than keeping up to date. And he still won't talk about money.'

'You feel he has secrets?'

'I feel he has terrors. He shouts in his sleep . . .'

'Like what?'

'Like Captain Ahab,' Elizabeth said. 'Every other night. I mean, a howl. A shout from the place where nothing is heard.'

'But *you* hear it.'

Elizabeth waited for the 274 bus. She enjoyed taking the bus to and from therapy, considered it part of the therapy. She told herself that she must be stronger than him and accept with grace that she was no longer young. She wouldn't be a hypocrite. She meant to settle into her talent, do something really good. She was by herself more than she had been, but she didn't mind, so long as she and Campbell had a meaningful union in which each of them might feel emboldened by the other's contentment. Yet, often now, when she turned round, he wasn't there and she looked in vain for the person he was.

When she got back to Thornhill Square, he was on the doorstep, signing for a delivery of boxes. 'What's all this?' she asked.

'Vintage Christmas decorations,' he said. 'I bought them at the Criterion auction. Genuine 1950s baubles.'

'Random,' Elizabeth said. 'We've got hoards of decorations.'

'I wanted authentic ones.'

By 4 p.m., the square was dim and the houses amber. It was the glow of everything being fine the week before Christmas. Except it wasn't fine. People were worrying about the new variant while the prime minister made it up as he went along. Yet the lights were glowing at number 68 and Elizabeth had friends coming for dinner. She was poring over Jane Grigson's *Good Things* in the deep Rectory Red of their kitchen, following a slightly elaborate recipe for a sixteenth-century sweet pie from the North of England.

'That smells delicious,' Campbell said, coming up behind her and putting his arms around her waist. 'Elizabethan pie.'

He was wearing a dark suit, which made the blue in his eyes stand out. She loved the feel of his arms. She had always said he was the best-smelling man in London, now with this scent of leather and white flowers. 'What's this one?'

'Cuir de Russie,' he said.

He playfully undid the ties on the back of her apron and turned her round for a proper kiss as he stroked her neck. He was happy. She said that to herself, even though she considered his happiness to be more reached-for than felt.

The week before Christmas Eve, every year since she was two, he'd taken Kenzie for afternoon tea at the Ritz. The first time, twenty-odd years ago, she was wearing a tutu, a plastic tiara and a pair of wellies. It was their own small ritual of memory now, and Elizabeth was happy to acknowledge it was exclusively theirs. Kenzie said that Christmas began every year at the Ritz, and she marked out all her changes, in age, hairstyle and appearance, from photographs taken in the Palm Court. She'd had her first cucumber sandwich there, her first cup of hot chocolate, her first glass of champagne, and it clearly filled Campbell's heart to the brim when the appointment came around each year.

'It makes me feel I got one or two things right with the children,' he said, holding his wife against the Aga.

'You made their lives, darling. Don't forget that.'

'And you have a night of shrinks and lawyers,' he said. 'All hell!'

He stole a bit of candied fruit from the cutting board. Wandering to the striped armchair with a Daunt's bag, he removed the books.

'What are you reading?' she asked.

'I've got this Delhi trip next month,' he said. 'Thought I'd read a few novels.' But what she saw was a book of essays, *The Elephant Paradigm*.

The doorbell rang and it rang for too long. Elizabeth moved to get it, but Campbell stayed her with his right hand, a perturbed look on his face. She poked her head into the hall as he opened the front door. There was a rush of cold. Mrs Voyles stood there in two coats and a beanie. 'I see you've got all your lights on,' she said, 'when other people are struggling to pay their bills and the planet is burned to a crisp.'

'What can I do for you?' Campbell said.

'My heating's off. The boiler I mean.'

'I warned you, Mrs Voyles. I said if you didn't let the workmen in to fix it, they would shut off your supply.'

'I get pneumonia. I have bronchiectasis. It was minus zero last night, and the councillor says it's against the law.'

Elizabeth stepped into the hall.

'It's evil, what you're doing,' she heard Campbell say.

'Let me,' Elizabeth said. 'I'm calling the emergency gasman.' She walked down the hall and saw that their tenant was trembling. 'It's going to be all right, Mrs Voyles. Please don't worry. I have a number for a 24-hour service. Would you like to come in and sit down, until I can get someone here to look at it?'

Campbell didn't move and he didn't speak.

'I'm going back to my own place!' the woman shouted. 'You and your fairy lights. I don't want anything to do with it. A person could freeze to death and you wouldn't care. The system is wrong, I'm telling you.'

'If you hold on a bit, we'll have it fixed,' Elizabeth said. 'Perhaps you have a friend who could stop by with—'

'You can't palm me off on people. I'm not being shunted around on your say-so.'

'I'm terribly sorry. If you can be patient—'

'Forty years I've been here! People coming and going. Used to be nice! They wouldn't leave a person without any heating—'

'We tried, Mrs Voyles.'

Elizabeth went to get the house phone and Campbell slammed the door.

'*Campbell!*' Elizabeth said, returning to the hall. 'You really mustn't close the door in her face like that.'

She went off and called the reliable plumber in Camden Town, and he said he would come over after dinner.

After the call, she saw Campbell on the stairs. He was standing at the long window on the landing and seemed to be staring out at the crane lights. In his dark suit he was a perfect silhouette. 'Don't worry, darling,' she said, rubbing his arm as she stood next to him on the stairs. 'I'll sort her out. You mustn't give it too much thought.'

He didn't flinch.

'Come now,' she added. 'This is your special evening with Kenzie. Don't let any of this nonsense spoil it.'

He seemed desperately far away as he looked at her. But he got his coat and his gloves and appeared to have snapped out of it by the time his Uber came.

When he'd gone, Elizabeth fetched an electric air heater from her study. She opened the front door and, with something of a struggle, managed to get it down the steps to Mrs Voyles's gate, which had a shining new padlock. 'Hello! Hello there! Could you please unchain the gate? I have a heater I can bring down to you.'

There was no answer.

Her grandmother's house in Chester Street had always been a state of mind to Kenzie, and as a child she had loved it there, among the Indian cushions and ikat lampshades. Now that it was hers, she had no intention of changing anything, not the walnut desks, the etchings of Morocco by Sir John Lavery and James McBey, the beautiful vases and the fire that glowed in the evening. Kenzie hadn't quite realised it until she moved in, but she'd always felt a bit endangered. 'That seems sensible,' Granny had said, 'because we all are, in a way.'

'Are what?' Kenzie asked.

'Endangered. Like we're running out of luck.'

Kenzie looked at herself in the dressing table mirror, took an atomiser filled with Shalimar and spritzed her neck.

She entered the cab wearing a vintage grey silk jumpsuit under a hot-pink jacket. Sandals in winter. Pink toenails. The fact that there would be no more romance with Ashley-Jo was now settled in Kenzie's mind. It wasn't the Battle of Waterloo, she thought, passing Apsley House, and she would always be happy to catch sight of A.J. fixing the world, one tweet at a time. But Kenzie was on a different flight path. The heat generated by most of her friends was now too much for her, and she looked for a cooler hand, one day, in hers, or else a life of quiet sufficiency and the bravery to go it alone. The cab rolled up Piccadilly: every night a new beginning. She got out at Dover Street and walked over to the Ritz with a complete sense of ease and independence. She saw her father standing on the steps, wearing one of his suits with a red tie of classic elegance. Daddy was a person of reliability and she paused for a second to watch his worried face lit by the street lights. It was sleeting and she suddenly saw it was mad to be wearing sandals.

She'd always known her father loved her: it shone out of him.

They hugged on the steps like old, fond bears. Kenzie felt special when they walked inside the Ritz at Christmas, and no catwalk, no party, no first night or premiere could ever match it, walking to the Palm Court, another year older. As a child, she used to play under the tree and she wanted to live there, her daddy's shiny shoes visible at the edge and staying put, until it was time for tea. He had wanted her to know luxury, but to know it as luxury, not as anything ordinary, and it worked. He always took her hand and squeezed it as they passed the Rivoli Bar and heard the piano.

The Palm Court had been refreshed during the closure and the waiters were buzzing about in red waistcoats and black tails. 'My favourite place,' she said. They sat down and surveyed the people at the other tables. Kenzie noticed that most of the patrons were now what her grandmother would have called foreigners.

'Cucumber sandwiches?' her father said.

She smiled at him. It was her cue. 'Why such reckless extravagance in one so young?' she said, quoting their favourite line.

*The Importance of Being Earnest.*

'A trivial comedy for serious people,' he added.

He'd got her into Oscar Wilde at the age of twelve. First the stories, then, in 2008, while everyone was talking about the financial crisis, they sat in the stalls at the Vaudeville Theatre in the Strand, with Kenzie wondering what the jokes meant, but admiring from a distance the actress playing Cecily. She realised, much later, that Daddy had probably worked out she was gay and had made Wilde a kind of touchstone, a brilliant, funny, constant helper with the task of accepting oneself.

'Two glasses of Pommery,' he said once again.

The teacups were tinkling and the waiters were brisk. When the sandwiches came, they each dived for the cucumber ones, as per joke.

'Cheers,' he said, bumping flutes, then sandwiches. It's like it had never occurred to him that being a father, being *her* father, wasn't the most wonderful privilege a person could have.

'Happy Christmas, Daddy.'

'The best sentence in the language,' he said, his eyes filling up.

'What are you like?' she said.

'I'm sentimental as a bag of sherbet, Kenzie. Getting worse every year. By the time I'm sixty, I'll have turned into my mother. She cried as if crying were a national sport. Poor Maw. She gave us the gift of her tears.'

'What was wrong with her, do you think?'

'I can only tell you she was in a state of distress for forty years. She couldn't lift the phone without weeping. Her life had gone wrong. There wasn't anything about it that she didn't find hugely distressing.'

'But she loved you and Auntie Moira, right?'

'"I watched yous, when nobody else cared,"' he said, impersonating his mother, then he sighed.

Kenzie noticed how much trouble he'd taken to make himself presentable, and how his eyes glittered.

'She tried,' he said. 'She and my father had no interests, apart from getting your Auntie Moira and me out of that block of flats.'

'He drove for a living?'

'He was a joiner. He fell off the scaffolding at work, in 1981, then he drove a minicab to get us through school. We went to a private school, though we lived in a council flat in Roystonhill. I wore office garb on Fridays, like a dress code for school, and when I put on my suit my dad would beam, as if all their trouble was worth it. My father had known real poverty and his ambition was to ensure we never did.'

'But he died young.'

'That's right. Of disappointment. The family illness.'

'Auntie Moira told me . . . there was some sort of public incident, a scandal or something involving them?'

He took a sip from his glass and nodded.

'He had a drink problem. Together they stole a coat.'

'Wait, what? A coat?'

'From a department store. My mother was looking for big things to feel, and that's the hallmark of melodrama, and he pushed her into it.'

'Jesus,' she said.

'It's not the stealing that bothers me,' he said, 'it's the thirst for shame and theatrics. Nothing in real life was ever enough for them. Nothing in *our* lives.'

For a second, he fidgeted with the knot of his tie. 'Your friend Oscar Wilde knew all about it,' he said. 'Lord Wotton says it in *The Picture of Dorian Gray*. "Crime belongs exclusively to the lower orders," he says. "Crime is to them what art is to us, simply a method of procuring extraordinary sensations."'

His eyes glowed with regret. Kenzie told him so, and said the sadness seemed to dislocate him visibly.

'Not only the sadness,' he said. 'The fear.'

She would remember that. She took his hand and changed the subject, skills she had learned from her pain-shifting mother. Kenzie had always had a gift for idealising her father and it wasn't something she intended to apologise for.

They started on the cakes. The meringue thing, the eclair. To Kenzie, it was the sweetest anything had tasted all year, or ever could. She told him she had given up Twitter, Instagram, Snapchat, TikTok and Ashley-Jo.

'In that order?' he said.

'Don't gloat. I know you didn't much like A.J.'

'I didn't mind them,' he said, obviously lying. (Polite people do that. They say the thing they ought to say before indirectly asserting the truth.) 'A.J. sticks up for people but has no sense of subtlety whatsoever. They don't care for other people's complexity, only their own, which is something of a disease with your generation.'

'You're too hard on Ashley-Jo, and more like them than you know. Both of you worrying about being correct.'

'I'm *evolving*, darling, as all people must. For instance, it's my duty to point out the way race is exploited by corporations.'

'Gosh, Daddy . . .'

'I'm not kidding. Look at that.' A waiter in white gloves was passing with a bottle of Coca-Cola on a silver tray.

'Take that beverage. The company is fuelling a diabetes crisis among black Americans and they won't address it. But they'll spend a few million of their vast profits on "diversity consultants" to signal their virtue and maintain their image. They'll tell employees to "be less white" and they'll "lean in" to the new wisdom, but they won't actually alter their product or their terms of employment. They'll put a black actor in an advertisement and call it a revolution. This is how the corporate world deals with a moral problem, by totally insulting it. And we all imagine something crucial is being addressed. It's not. It never is. And the workers get more exploited and the consumer gets sicker, but we all feel the world's a better place because the company gave a day's work to a black actor.'

'Wow.' Kenzie waited, then she spoke slowly. 'And have you changed your life, Daddy?'

He pursed his lips and leaned back. It was probably the sort of question he dreaded and he wasn't going to find an answer.

'It's Christmas,' he said.

There were so many things her father wouldn't talk about. He wouldn't say anything that might diminish all his efforts at success. He was the public thinker, but Kenzie knew it was her mother who had always held the family together. Mum had a tremendous, patient way of living, deploying her intelligence so that she could go on loving the people she loved. After Iceland, she had FaceTimed Kenzie and told her that her father might occasionally be haunted by a 'false self'.

'What's *that*?' Kenzie had asked.

'A person you're not, but who feels essential. In other words, a made-up self that a person can use as a shield to protect their true self.'

'But why would you do that?'

'I'm glad you have to ask,' her mother said. 'A child needs reassurance, and if he doesn't get it then a false self can take over. He grows up feeling there can be no real openness, because the true self isn't good enough.'

'And that's Daddy?'

'Possibly. It's just the case with some people as they grow older. Increasingly, there's a lifetime burning in every moment.'

Kenzie put the memory of that conversation away after biting into a raspberry-filled macaroon.

'What's all this with your researcher, what's his name – Milo?' she asked across the white tablecloth, and he flushed.

'What do you mean?'

'His friend getting arrested for some gang killing.'

He looked stunned. 'Go on.'

Kenzie dabbed the corner of her mouth with the napkin.

'Yeah, they're all talking about it.'

'A friend of *Milo's*?'

'From the Cally. Ashley-Jo hung out with them a few times.'

He nodded once and poured from the teapot. He seemed disconcerted but immediately in charge of his arguments and his manner.

'I can't speak for Milo,' he said, in a kind of decided voice. 'But I liked him because he avoided being a cliché.'

'Past tense too?'

He ignored her.

'Not everybody can do that,' he continued. 'But Milo did. We want stories where *everybody* is against type, but such stories have no reality.'

She liked that her father could speak to her. Not every parent could. He told her the friendship with Milo was a thing he'd needed.

'The validation?'

'Something like that,' he said.

He was silent for a moment, then he told her Milo's texts had stopped. He said he'd dropped a letter in at the salon where Milo's girlfriend worked, but there had been no response. 'It's like I did something wrong.'

'Mummy thinks the boy was just playing with you.'

He acknowledged what she said with a steady nod.

'Sometimes we need a holiday from ourselves,' he said.

Kenzie wiped another crumb off her lip with the napkin. 'It would be nice to live like a plant,' she said. 'Feeling the seasons. Growing silently.'

'That's how I see you, Kenzie,' he said. 'Like a perfect rose in Regent's Park. Your mother and I are so proud of you.'

She told him she was at the Oxford Weaving Studio and was colouring her own yarn with natural dyes, collected from the garden at Chester Street.

'You know what I love about you?'

She stuck out her tongue.

'Everything. But one thing in particular. Many people in your . . . age group . . . they choose to define themselves by hipster negatives, but you don't.'

'That's because I'm not cool enough.'

'You have a gift for coexistence. To my mind, it's the most essential thing to have when you're young.'

'Why?'

'Because it reveals your appetite for life. These kids who go on as if a person born thirty years before them is a different species, it's so stupid.'

'Ah,' she said, 'that's why you've always been friends with people like Granny. You don't do numbers on them.'

'How could we do numbers, if you think about it? Do you know how old time is and what an insanely tiny window we all occupy?'

'Let's google it,' she said.

She was laughing already as she took out her phone. 'Okay.' She keyed in the question 'How old is time?' and read out the first result. '"According to the standard big bang theory of cosmology, time began together with the universe approximately fourteen billion years ago."'

'I like "approximately",' he said. 'To make the universe comprehensible to millennials, do you think that means "fourteen billion years, give or take thirty"?'

'Oh, shush,' she said, replacing her teacup and reading the next sentence. '"While we experience time as psychologically real, time is *not* fundamentally real."'

'So, there you go,' he said. 'That's one of the reasons I love you. Because you get *that*.'

Carol singers appeared. She noticed the women were all wearing beautiful scarves over their black dresses. They started with 'Have Yourself a Merry Little Christmas'. She looked at her father, his hand on his cup, and he sighed heavily then coughed into his napkin. It occurred to her he was alone in a very significant way.

She decided to give it one more go. 'Sky had a big party in New York last week,' she said, 'to celebrate the fifth anniversary of *Aethon's Curse*. You know, that TV show Jake Hart-Davies was in.'

His eyes flickered. He smiled that capable smile. 'Really?'

'I didn't go, obviously. But apparently he has turned quite penitent.'

'Oh yes,' Campbell said. 'I'll bet he is. He nearly got cancelled out of existence.'

'People fancy him too much to cancel him,' she said. 'I mean, he had the nerve to walk into this party with Yuri Bykov.'

'They only get stronger.'

She took a breath, as if ready to embark on new territory. 'Why did you ever go near that guy?' she said. 'Didn't you realise actors are, like, the number one fruitcakes of all time?'

'We're all actors,' he said.

She told him that Bykov had commissioned a special Fabergé egg to mark the anniversary and given it to the actor. This encrusted, meaningless Fabergé thing, it was a symbol of everything she hated. It was made of 18-carat white gold and diamond panes with a huge ruby from Mozambique. Somebody said it cost $2 million, but looked like something from a shopping mall.

'Did your brother order two?'

'Don't be silly about Angus,' she said.

But she didn't go further. It wasn't right to talk to him about subjects that made him unhappy. He'd receded into his armour. He was probably thinking about his old friend William Byre and the shock of all that. Staring at the piano player and the carol singers, he muttered the words and tapped the table with a silver teaspoon.

Snow was falling on the Branicki Palace on Christmas Eve. It was −7°C in Białystok and the air seemed frozen with memory. Jakub was in a group with Robert and Robert's best friend Stanisław and Stan's boyfriend Grzegorz, and they had walked around the market stalls in Kościuszko Square before having a snowball fight in the park. Later, they all went to Plan B, a bar upstairs in a yellow building close to the Cathedral of St Nicholas the Wonderworker. They were downing shots. Jakub hadn't been thinking much about England, not since he reached Poland the day before, but now Robert was wearing the sweatshirt he'd bought him in London, a tiny Union Jack on the left breast. He had a waxed moustache, he wore a red woollen fisherman's hat and his eyes were sea green. Robert thought fashion was everything, and Jakub kept looking at his neck, his pink mouth, his smooth, strong jawline, wanting to kiss him.

Stanisław hosted a rock music podcast and Grzegorz worked in the city's English bookshop. Robert had met them at a Pride march in Warsaw. There had been anti-gay protesters by the road with banners. Jakub was much quieter than the others. More Catholic. He was the same age, but there was something essentially private in his sexuality. It's what drew him to other places, the idea that you could start again.

'Nationalism and intolerance grow together,' Grzegorz said that night.

'Not everywhere,' Jakub said.

'You're wrong, *kumpel*. Name me a place where it's not true.'

'Scotland,' he said. 'The Republic of Ireland.'

'There! He gives two examples!' Robert said.

'Time will tell,' replied Grzegorz, swigging a beer.

Jakub didn't feel like telling them about Mrs Krupa, about him not being out in England. He didn't feel very truthful.

Except for him, all the boys had tattoos. Robert had angel wings across his back and an homage to Lil Nas X. Stan had flowers on his shoulder like Lady Gaga's and Grzegorz had stars behind his ears. He had a friend from Warsaw, Aga, who now owned a boutique near the Sherlock Holmes pub in Białystok. She was a tattoo artist and wanted to be in London too. She arrived after their second round of drinks. Aga had pink hair in bunches, and she asked for a Jägerbomb and shared a bag of MDMA.

They went on to a pub called Glam and sat with a bunch of guys who were in a martial arts collective called Queer Fight Team. Jakub felt he belonged, for a while, doing shots and dabbing at the girl's powder, feeling high and sexy. He kissed Robert on the dance floor, and later, with the lights revolving and the beat of the music deep in his body, he thought about England. He told Aga it wasn't easy and you had to be willing to do bad jobs. 'Once they get to know you,' he said, 'you get better work and a place to live. London is so expensive. If you're willing to travel out of the city, you will find good people and gain experience.'

As he said this, he realised he was sounding like Bozydar.

'I mean, if that's your choice,' he said.

Poles love sharing misery, and Aga was down on Białystok. They made the best of it, they made their own scene, but she wanted Trafalgar Square. She'd seen people dancing there on TikTok and wished she had gone earlier, when it was easy.

'How is it you get back?' she asked, shouting over the music. 'You're taking him with you, and you have a place over there?'

'Yes. It's getting better all the time,' he said. 'So close. So real.' Jakub felt his adulthood had really begun. He'd stopped reading fantasy books. He'd begun to think about solid ground and real maps. He and Robert had talked about how difficult it would be to get established, but it was going to be worth it.

He danced in his seat and someone brought shots of red vodka. Tomasz, one of the martial arts guys, introduced a girl, and she and Aga were soon kissing. Jakub could see the studs in their tongues as their faces blended together. 'You're a really beautiful guy,' Tomasz said to Jakub, but Jakub told him he was already with someone, and they clinked glasses instead.

'Man, I'm exhausted,' Jakub said. 'Even with MD.'

Robert's rented room was in a block of flats near the Podlasie Philharmonic. The Queer Fight Team, Aga and the girl, they all walked there, singing through the snow. At the edge of Park Planty, they built a snow queen, a lumpy, grinning figure with breasts and a dick, which had them all laughing, stupid and drunk. They walked for five more minutes, and the others, carrying bottles, ran up the road, while Jakub stood on his own for a moment, listening to the sound of the wolves in the Akcent Zoo.

They were natural friends. It wasn't just sexuality, but a sense they all shared of international possibilities. Jakub had a traditional capacity for work, for silent endurance and biding his time, but he felt close to Robert's friends because they all understood the world as a borderless place. They saw limitations but they didn't accept them. When Jakub reached the flat, they had already put on a film by Sion Sono called *Tokyo Vampire Hotel*, which one of the girls said was a feminist exploration of desire for the post-virus generation.

'Nothing is ever over,' Jakub said.

Aga contradicted him. '*Tout est fini tout le temps*,' she said.

They whooped at the action. It became a party. The tattoo girl laid out pills and others came, a trans boy wearing a T-shirt saying 'Love Does Not Exclude'. After about two hours, when everyone was high or dancing or kissing in the kitchen, the screen still showing beautiful vampires in love or in death or somewhere in between, Jakub drank a glass of water and walked through to the bedroom.

'Everyone is travelling from old problems,' Robert whispered to him, closing the door with his foot and pulling off Jakub's shirt.

'Including us.'

'It will be better. England is us.'

He couldn't bear to tell him it might not be.

He lay down on the bed. As Robert kissed his stomach he looked towards the window in the corner, the flakes of snow falling.

## 32 The Old Man

# 43 The Old Bailey

Big Pharma's mother insisted that his funeral be kept small. She wasn't having any of it – the stupid cars and the over-the-top flowers, the brothers rocking up wearing the gear and banging shoulders and all that. 'London killed my boy,' she said. The police investigation exposed the background to the whole thing, and Lloyds was arrested and charged with being part of the group that killed Sluggz. His phone was found to have pinged at the location in Deptford that night, same as Travis's, though – according to the boys – Lloyds wasn't anywhere near the passageway when the knifing happened.

Early in the new year, 5 January, the trial started. At ten in the morning, Milo walked towards the Old Bailey. He stopped at an estate agent's office. Somebody told him you could leave your phone there for £2. Phones weren't allowed in the public gallery. The estate agent wore a loose tie and a scowl. 'Bet you do big business in here,' Milo said. 'Man handing in their phones. More than selling flats?'

'Nearly,' the guy said, passing him a ticket.

Milo sat near the front of the public gallery. When he looked down, he saw the legal teams milling about and Travis in the dock with a policeman next to him. No sign of Lloyds.

'Please be upstanding in court,' the usher eventually said. The judge sat down and addressed Lloyds's barrister.

'Mr Whitney, I understand you have submissions to make on behalf of your client, Mr Jeremiah Beckford?'

'I do, My Lady.' The barrister pressed down his wig. 'It would appear that Mr Beckford has elected today not to appear before the court.'

'And does he give a reason?'

'Your Ladyship may recall that Mr Beckford has been complaining of feeling unwell. Today he has mentioned hearing voices—'

'Voices?'

'Indeed.'

'Well, Mr Whitney, I must ask you to remind your client that these are serious legal proceedings. Mr Beckford is charged with being party to a murder. I'm sure you've explained to him that this is his opportunity to defend himself.'

'Indeed, ma'am.'

'There will be no benefit to him in malingering.'

'I have made that point myself, My Lady.'

'Looking at the dock, I see that we have Travis Babb. Mr Babb, you may sit down. If anything that is being said in court is unclear to you, it is very important that you ask for clarification. The jury here is the judge of the evidence in this case, and I am the judge of the law. Do you understand?'

Travis leaned his head and shoulders forward. It was a gesture Milo had seen a thousand times, all the way back to primary school.

The first witness was a taxi driver who had been called to a pickup in Deptford that night. Travis was denying he had been near the alley where the murder took place, and so was Lloyds, via his lawyers. The defence was that Travis had chased after the victim but had stopped short of the passageway where he was stabbed. Lloyds and Pharma were even further back, waiting by the car they had used to drive down from King's Cross for the meet, but the prosecution was still going for joint enterprise.

'And you are a driver for Data Cars?' Mr Gregory, the prosecutor, asked.

'That's right. Eight years,' Mr Hadap said. He didn't like being in the witness box, you could tell.

'And on the evening in question, you received a call, did you not, to pick up passengers at Garvey House in Bronze Street, SE8, at nearly 1.30 a.m.?'

'That's right. It was a cash job. Booked by a guy called Darius.'

Mr Gregory remarked that Darius had since disappeared, and was not a witness in this case, then he nodded to the court clerk. 'I now invite the jury to watch the dashcam footage from that pickup.' The video started playing.

It showed a cab rocking up under the street lights in front of a block of flats. Two men with their hoods up came towards the cab and got in the back. One of them wound the window down and shouted, then you could hear banging. The car was being attacked with a hammer and immediately it zoomed away. The boys in the back were shouting at the driver to stop the car, and one of them said, 'Shank, shank, shank.'

'Okay, please stop it there,' Mr Gregory said. 'Now, Mr Hadap, can you confirm that this is the pickup in question?'

'Yes. It was the man Darius who ordered the cab, but the boys in the cab were two other ones, going to Brixton.'

Mr Gregory instructed the court clerk to continue playing the dashcam footage. The camera was pointing in the direction of travel, but you could hear the voices of these two young men shouting at the driver to stop the car.

'Now, Mr Hadap, would you kindly help us here. The men jumped out of your cab, yes? They ran back in the direction of the man with the hammer, yes? Did you see the man who attacked the vehicle?'

'He was wearing a hoodie. All of them were.'

'He was attacking the car with a hammer? He was reaching towards one of the men in the back seat, is that correct?'

'Yes.'

'And he chased after the car when you drove off, is that so?'

'Yes, that's right. Then when I stopped, the boys in the back of my car went running back towards him.'

The footage showed the cab driver had also got out of the car. He saw Sluggz being chased into Candlestick Pass and stabbed multiple times.

525

'And tell me, Mr Hadap,' the prosecutor said, 'did you see at that time any other men, perhaps standing to one side as the attack took place?'

'Yeah. One boy was standing right next to the passage. He was lit by a street light. He didn't join in the attack. He was standing there.'

'And could you identify that man?'

'Like I said, his head was covered.'

'And was he carrying anything?'

'Yeah. He had a knife in his hand.'

'So, he was standing close to the attack, by the passageway, and he was carrying a bladed article, you say?'

'Yeah. Like a kitchen knife.'

Milo felt a rising panic. The prosecutor requested CCTV footage from the lamp post that overlooked Candlestick Pass. It was played several times, and, finally, in slow motion, it showed a figure running into the alley and, it seemed, accidentally dropping a hammer. He turned as three men came running after him – including the two men from the taxicab, both shouting – and you could see a fourth man, who stood at the opening of the alley. 'We are calling that man Male 4,' the prosecutor said. 'And I put it to you that the other three men in the passageway are members of a Brixton gang called the Hit Squad.'

Over the following days of the proceedings, Milo checked out the court furnishings and everyone's faces. He wished he could reach down to Travis. He hated seeing his friend sitting there, looking so stressed. Travis's people lived in bad circumstances and each of them was bothered by the police all their lives. The authorities don't see his culture, they call his talent criminal and they stop and search him, calling him antisocial. Then he does something stupid and justice must be served. It hurt to think about it.

A witness from a building overlooking the passageway said she'd seen three boys stabbing the victim.

The prosecutor made an unhappy smile, like he regretted having to ask. 'Miss Onuzo, can you tell me—?'

'That's all I saw.'

'I understand,' he said, 'but was there another individual there?'

'Yes. He was wearing dark clothes.'

'And was he holding anything?'

'Yes. He was holding a blade or something.'

'And would you say, Miss Onuzo, that he was part of the gang attacking the victim?'

'Definitely. He was with them.'

'No further questions.'

A week later, they were still probing the phone evidence. Detective Inspector Bagley was questioned about the log of all the calls that had pinged the cell site in Deptford that night, attaching particular numbers to 'persons of interest', including Travis and Lloyds. Apart from the victim, all the others had ditched their pay-as-you-go handsets, but the police had examined their texts and locations. He said a number ending 5050 was Travis's. And one ending 9426 was Lloyds's. DI Bagley emphasised that the handsets could not be recovered but said he could show the phones being used in the King's Cross area for most of each day, with excursions to Kent and Nottingham, and then, on the night in question, in Deptford. He made the point that many of the same locations and times were shared by a third phone number, which they believed had belonged to Mr Devan Swaby, a recently deceased friend of the accused.

Acting for the defence, Mr Copeland went on to say there was no proof that the phone associated with the number 5050 was ever in Travis's possession.

'Is it not the case,' the defence barrister asked Bagley, 'that most communication between these young men is by WhatsApp or Signal?'

'Yes, it would appear so, but—'

'And therefore, would you not say, untraceable?'

'We can link the location of the mobile phone to what was recorded by CCTV in each of the locations.'

'Yes. But you cannot then identify the holder of the phone, can you? You cannot, for instance, say with any certainty that this was the phone belonging to Male 4, can you? Nor can you infer from this evidence that Male 4 is my client?'

'From this evidence, no.'

'Thank you. No further questions, My Lady.'

A CCTV camera in a parade of shops on Caledonian Road showed, on the night of the murder, three youths, all with their hoods up, coming up the road, one of them swinging what appeared to be car keys. They stopped at Ritson House, bumped shoulders and one of them went inside. Milo's heart lurched. The boys: he knew it was them, and it made him tearful to see Big Pharma alive.

'The 5050 number was sited here at this time,' Bagley said, responding to a series of questions from Mr Gregory, the prosecutor.

'And do you believe the man entering that building is the owner of this phone?'

'Yes, I do.'

He appeared to study the police officer. 'Could you say if any of the people living at that address are related to the man in the dock, Travis Babb?'

'Yes. His mother lives at number 4.'

'And the so-called "burner" phone that you believe was Mr Babb's was sited in that area at that exact time?'

'Yes. It was 3.13 a.m.'

'And it is the same phone that was in the area of Deptford where the victim was killed?'

'Yes.'

'And matches with the timings on all the CCTV footage along the way?'

'That's right.'

Another three witnesses appeared. One was an expert in studying drill music for criminal content. He said the music put out by the Cally Active was full of references to beefs with gangs in South

London. In disguise as Ghost 24, Travis Babb was accused of celebrating violence.

'It's not *like that*,' Travis shouted. 'I went to fix it.'

'Mr Babb, if you have a point to make, I demand that you please relay it through your legal counsel,' the judge said to him.

The drill expert was a thirty-something academic with dreadlocks and a bright waistcoat. Mr Gregory asked him if the Cally Active gang recorded tracks about specific events.

'You mean acts of violence?'

'Yes. *Specific* acts.'

Gregory checked his notes.

'I'm referring to the murder of a sixteen-year-old male named Damon Taylor, who went under the street name 0044.'

'Yes,' the expert said. '0044 is named in several of the songs recorded by the Cally Active group.'

'And this young man was a friend of the accused?'

'I believe so, yes.'

'I won't detain you much longer,' Gregory said. 'Just this: when examining the lyrics of these songs put out by the accused and his friends . . . is it possible to infer from the content that they were in a battle with the Deptford gang, and in particular with the man they call Sluggz – Sebastian Legland?'

'Yes, sir. The lyrics refer to that individual by name.' He quoted from two songs and a video was shown to the jury.

'I didn't do *anything*,' Travis shouted from the dock.

The defence barrister tried his best to convey that it was all fantasy. The videos were merely display and the lyrics were a form of verbal combat.

'Many of the people who perform these songs end up dead,' Mr Gregory interjected, 'or end up killing.'

'I put it to you that many do not, sir,' the defence barrister said. 'In fact, most do not. In a similar way that most youths who watch horror films do not then commit similar atrocities.'

Milo saw that Travis was moving his lips. It was something he always did in an argument, readying himself to speak. Finally, it tripped out.

'This is a white court,' he shouted. 'White officers, white barristers. White judge.'

'Mr Babb!' the judge said. 'I am bound to warn you that this is a court of law. It is not a political rally or a public meeting. You will not shout out in court. You may give answers in evidence during examination. Do you understand?'

He didn't move. Then he tapped his chest and looked up. 'I didn't do nothing,' he said.

'I mean it, Mr Babb. There will be no speeches from the dock. Is that clear? You are showing contempt for these proceedings and I will not have it.'

During the recess, Milo turned round in his seat. Every person in the rows behind him was black. Taking them in, it occurred to him, instinctively, that one of them could be the person who shot Big Pharma. He considered it likely, but it disturbed him – the desire to know, an urge to do something about it. He tried to banish the thought: boy for boy, tit for tat. He looked past their dulled eyes, and then he saw another face, at the very back. Professor Flynn's. He looked different. Stressed. The man who had hired Milo to help him with his 'alternative life'. He'd lost weight and his cheeks were hollow; he was greyer. Neither of them nodded or spoke: they simply stared, then Milo turned away. He knew he had done enough to show the professor who he was. He was finished with him now. He stared forward, then dipped his eyes into the well of the court. They had both lost friends.

'Now, PC Shaw,' the prosecutor said, when the next witness had taken the oath. 'In your own words, would you tell the jury about an incident that occurred in Eltham High Street on 19 August last year?'

'We received a radio communication relating to a blue Corsa and we intercepted it at a set of traffic lights on the High Street.'

Mr Gregory QC tapped his bottom lip. 'Again, in your own words, would you be kind enough to tell us what happened next?'

'Well, we jammed the Corsa in – one squad car at the front and a van at the back. And as I approached the vehicle, I saw a bladed article being dropped out of the window on the passenger side.'

'A knife, you mean?'

'Yes. It fell to the ground.'

'And how would you characterise that knife, Mr Shaw?'

'It was typical. Like a kitchen knife. The sort of thing a lot of them carry.'

'Them?'

'Young men, I mean. Gang members.'

'And what did you do then?'

'I radioed to my colleagues that there was a weapon at the scene.'

Mr Gregory looked up towards the video officer. 'I think we can see the footage of this, yes?'

The judge turned to the jury. 'For clarity,' she said, 'the footage you are about to see was recorded on a camera worn by the witness.'

There was Big Pharma at the wheel of the car, Travis in the passenger seat.

'I didn't do shit,' Travis said in the video. He stepped out of the car and was cuffed. You could see him in his ripped jeans as the fed walked him away from the car. Watching Travis being interviewed by the side of the road, time began to run backwards for Milo. He knew what was coming.

'Would you kindly rewind the video?' Mr Gregory said.

It was wound back and frozen on the image of Milo's friends sitting by the road.

'Now,' continued the prosecutor, facing the jury, 'if you accept the testimony of the officer in charge of phone evidence, then the defendant was present in Deptford on the night of the murder. If you also accept that Mr Babb had expressed his hatred of the victim in rap videos available on YouTube, and if you accept, having seen it a moment ago, that Mr Babb was wont to travel in the company of bladed articles, then you might still be asking for that missing link, the one piece of evidence that puts Mr Babb at the scene of the crime at the time of Mr Legland's murder. Could we please watch the body-cam footage again?'

It played, then Mr Gregory asked that it be stopped. He walked closer to the screen and pointed to the frozen image. 'We see the accused, Mr Babb, clearly here. He is sitting at the roadside with his friend Devan Swaby, who later died in a shooting incident in Islington. I would like to draw your attention to what the accused is wearing . . .'

He pointed to Travis's trainers. Milo felt he was down a well. The court room blurred and became liquid before his eyes.

Soon, the witness was replaced by a female DCI from the Met's homicide unit, one of the officers who had prepared the case.

'Detective Chief Inspector Wilkins,' Mr Gregory said. 'These trainers, could you describe them for us, please?'

'They are distinctive,' she said. 'Black with white flashes and red flashes coming up from the sole. A white symbol of Michael Jordan beside the heel.'

'And do they have a name?'

'They are Air Jordans. Special edition Max Aura 3s.'

'Clearly identifiable in this image, worn by the accused – Max Aura 3s. And what can you tell me about these shoes, DCI Wilkins?'

'They were released in August, right before these crimes were committed. And this particular version of the shoe is very rare.'

Travis looked up at the public gallery. He saw Milo, a whole life-time of regret coming into his face. Travis shook his head, as if to say, don't sweat it, bro, it was always going to end this way.

'No,' Milo said silently, in anguish.

'Please remain where you are,' Mr Gregory said to the witness. 'Video officer, would you kindly play the CCTV in Caledonian Road from the night of the murder, the images grabbed, I believe, at 3.12 a.m.'

The images came up. 'DCI Wilkins, there are, we can see, three individuals at the street door of what we know to be the address of the defendant's mother, is that correct?'

'Yes.'

'And one of them is about to go inside. Let's play the video . . . stop.'

'Yes. One of them is stepping inside.'

'And what, Detective Chief Inspector, is he wearing on his feet?'

'I believe they are a pair of Air Jordans. Limited edition Max Aura 3s.'

'Perhaps the video officer would zoom in. Good. Can you see the trainers clearly, DCI Wilkins?'

'Yes. They are unmistakeable.'

'If the video officer would kindly go to the CCTV footage we have already seen many times, overlooking Candlestick Pass at the time of the murder . . .'

He turned to the jury with a calculated smile. The image appeared on the screen and Milo saw several members of the jury lean forward to look at their own monitors. The victim runs into the alley and drops the hammer. Then three men follow him, wielding long knives. They can be seen glinting under the lights of the alley. 'Stop there,' Mr Gregory said. 'Can you see a man standing beside the men who are stabbing the victim?'

'Yes,' DCI Wilkins said. 'Near the railway arches, right by the assailants.'

'Right by the assailants, you say.' He turned again. 'Video officer, would you be so kind as to zoom in on the figure.'

The image came up.

'We have been calling this figure Male 4. He is right by the assailants, who are as yet unknown to us. What is in his hand?'

'I believe he has produced a knife.'

'And what is he wearing on his feet?'

She turned to the accused. 'Air Jordans. Max Aura 3s. Limited edition.'

The air went out of the room. Travis stared ahead, as if the light of the court and the light of the world were too much for him.

Milo glanced behind him: his professor was gone.

'Could I direct the jury, My Lady, to evidence bundle 2, tab 8?' He gave the judge and jury a few moments. 'You will see in paragraph four a description of what Travis Babb was wearing at the time of his arrest. He was taken from a derelict apartment in Caledonian Road, King's Cross, to Highbury police station. A full description and photographs of what he was wearing at the time of his arrest are given here. Would you care to read it aloud to the court, Detective Chief Inspector?'

'The suspect wore a Dsquared2 puffer jacket with red insignia. Under that he wore a black T-shirt bearing a skull, by Alexander McQueen. He wore ripped black jeans and a pair of Air Jordan Max Aura 3 trainers, size 11.'

'Is it your submission, DCI Wilkins, that these shoes are the ones worn by Travis Babb during his apprehension in Eltham High Street on 19 August last year? Are they the same shoes seen at the door of his mother's flat in Caledonian Road on the night of the murder, which are clearly visible on the CCTV recording? And the same shoes as those worn by Male 4 at the scene of the murder of Sebastian "Sluggz" Legland in Candlestick Pass, Deptford, in the early hours of Thursday 26 August? That is to say, in your view of the evidence, do the trainers worn by the accused at the time of his arrest match the trainers recorded in each of these videos, including the one where he is holding a bladed article and is part of the gang that carried out the murder of this young man?'

'Yes,' she said. 'The trainers were too new. They were too uncommon at the time of the killing.'

'They were on the feet of Travis Babb?'

'Yes. The evidence points to him.'

'It points to *him*. No further questions.'

# 44 Unreachable

London from the air is now a reflective landscape. So much glass, thought Campbell, as the plane banked over the city on 25 January. He recalled the grey and brown that had characterised the capital when he first saw it in the 1980s. In those days, flying into Heathrow from the east, following the Thames, you would look down from your seat and catch the top of the Lloyd's building and the dome of St Paul's, perhaps a thrust of green from Hyde Park, but generally it was a tundra of low-rise brickwork and steeples. Now you had the Shard and the London Eye, a notion of tourism, Olympic Games and foreign currency, fired in the city's great furnace of deregulation and glinting in the sun.

It was unexplained, his feeling weepy in aeroplanes. It usually happened at around thirty-five thousand feet, but Campbell had felt it today when he saw the British fields. He had been ill in Delhi, where he was taking part in forty-eight hours of panel events about 'Imperialism in Art' and 'White Contrition', before delivering a stand-alone lecture on Rembrandt's self-portraits. He'd felt unwell at the Oberoi Hotel, unloosened, unlocked, buzzing with all his London problems, then he took part in a final event with Rory Gunn, a novelist and writer for the *New York Review of Books*. Gunn, it turned out, had written a review of Campbell's *Life of Vermeer* in the paper's latest issue. The essay was two years late and its title was emblazoned above the paper's masthead, 'Vermeer's Veneer'. Gunn was having a moment and enjoyed reading from his review during their session. 'The biographers among us,' he said, leaning forward in his tight little armchair, 'might agree that Professor Flynn has encapsulated an emptiness at the centre of modern lives. His Vermeer is thinner than watercolours, a ghostly absence, yet an excitable throng has found the book to be culturally alive. His Johannes Vermeer, in fact, has no life, no self, and is unreachable. We have an artist's life in which no one is anyone and nothing is everything.'

'I'll leave it to Mr Gunn,' Campbell had replied, facing the audience, 'to judge on the non-existence of selfhood and the limits of the excitable throng. What interests me, in the Dutch painters, is the reflection of reality, plus the compositional method, a matter of almost infinite deliberation and refinement.'

'No disrespect,' Gunn said, 'but we've had decades of cultural operators who think their job is to numb people with vague messages about beauty and well-being. Professor Flynn takes his authority for granted, but he's not rigorous.'

As his Virgin flight banked over the Thames, there was a sudden glitter on the water and it transported him to the Scottish coast. Campbell recalled the only holiday he ever took with his mother and father, to the town of Oban. Their guesthouse was up a steep brae that wended round an Edwardian folly. He could still see the curls of yellow butter in the tartan breakfast room, and feel the air of boredom and efficient judgment as they paid their bill in £5 notes, then the sight of his father, when the landlady had left the room, lifting silver cutlery from the drawer and putting it into the pocket of his raincoat, before leaving and walking down the hill. 'I'm mortified,' his mother had said as they followed quickly at his back, but she said it with a faint smile. Campbell had come into company somehow with his parents' needs. Perhaps the stealing had been a sort of revenge on unfair conditions and the complacency of others, a taking back. It made more sense to him now, with the breath of debt and dissatisfaction constantly at his heels. The recognition was more numb than warm, but he now felt closer to his dad.

There was a time, a year before, when Campbell wasn't sleeping, and Elizabeth spoke to him about sleep disturbances in young people, kids who stay awake for unconscious reasons. She also spoke about fidgetiness, and said he was like a child in that way: he must always be doing something or recovering from something. And when he did sleep, he often hollered, like the darkness too was busy and dramatic. Maybe he was always looking for ways of mastering anxiety. It was her habit to give people phrases to live with, phrases to own, that they might find useful. She'd said it could describe his feelings about his parents. They'd stolen items as a way of replacing people that were lost to them.

'They were short of money,' he said.

'No, Campbell. I knew your mother. It wasn't the money. She lived as if her life was elsewhere. She couldn't love in real time.'

'Maybe. She wasn't sure what belonged to her.'

West London was always placid during the plane's approach. You felt you could live forever among these terraced streets and floodlit parks and never be unhappy. The plane juddered and descended, and he experienced the grind of something underfoot, the distant sound of automation as the wheels came down. Campbell was rigid, recalling 'Sunday Morning' by Wallace Stevens, the last lines about casual flocks of pigeons sinking down to darkness on extended wings. He felt a marked shift in himself: he had come home early from the festival because his mind was unloosening, and all the pressures of his life were now gathered in this downward thrust into London.

He took a taxi from Heathrow to Victoria, flicking through his news apps. 'Country Edges Closer to Normality,' *The Times* said. 'Covid Tests Phased Out'.

'Take it easy,' he said to himself. 'Nice and calm.'

He wasn't ready to go home. Elizabeth had warned him he was too fragile to be flying abroad, and she'd been proved right. He needed a beat before showing his face. Thoughts cascaded as he got out of the taxi in Lower Belgrave Street and headed for the Queen's Gallery. *Masterpieces from Buckingham Palace* was in its final weeks. For a moment, he imagined that he saw a throng of children in the foyer

– schoolkids with their pencils and drawing pads – and he recalled the art appreciation club he and Elizabeth had set up and paid for at Charles Booth Primary School. The foyer was empty today, but he imagined the echo of children's voices.

As Campbell walked down the Chambers Gallery, the blue walls settled his nerves. He had enjoyed serene days at the palace. And there it was, *The Music Lesson* (1662), that limpid study of delicate enlightenment. Last time he'd seen Vermeer's masterpiece, the painting had been choked for space in the palace's long gallery, where salmon wallpaper and glaring lights made a mess of it, but now he could see it at eye level, and it was like looking at the deepest part of his own life. He saw unknown colours. And he agreed with an article he'd read in the *New Criterion*, arguing that the low perspective in the painting suggests the viewpoint of a child. Campbell would go further: what the child sees is the bourgeois world, a dream of mercantile comfort, the safety of gorgeous cloth, ceramics and silver platters, musical instruments and coats. As he looked, he began to see the terror of Carl Friis's world of destruction, all the delicacy of Vermeer's imagination given over to a ravening disorder, flames blistering the paint, burning the black and white tiles and replacing them with his own face in an ash-grey mirror.

He had a question as he stood by the Rembrandts. In the future, after the Queen dies and the monarchy embarks on its steady course to being over for good, the family's soap stars washing it into normalcy, what will happen to the Royal Collection? In other nations, it would go to the state, which is where it should have been in the first place, but in England he imagined the sordid dukes making for the hills with Titians under their arms. He stood in front of *Self-Portrait in a Flat Cap* (1642) and realised that this operatic person was himself. The eyes in the portrait look straight at the viewer, who sees himself mirrored as he looks at the artist. It is selfhood, thought Campbell, that is the theatrical mystery and the glory in that amber light. Yet the painting unsteadied him. He recalled the master's self-portrait at the age of sixty-three that hangs in Room 22 at the National Gallery, a roomful of dark pictures that had once brightened his life with warnings.

He went into the next room. The green walls mocked him, his own mind's indulgences making common cause with the figurations on the walls. He examined Rubens's stunning self-portrait and saw only William Byre. Take away the moustache, leave the dark eyes and the sagging cheeks, keep the knowledge of man's estate, and it was his old, dead friend looking back at him again. Three pictures along, he swayed before Jan Both's *Landscape with St Philip Baptising the Eunuch*, and bristled at the sight of the stooped man of colour being blessed by the white man in robes. Another two down, he saw Van Dyck's 1638 painting of the poet Thomas Killigrew and Lord Crofts, and he felt he had to be going out of his wits to be seeing the Duke of Kendal here. The eyes were the same. The painter's name was Anthony. Campbell stepped back onto the floor's iron grille. The work was conspiring against him, like everything else.

'Is this a blagger I see before me?'

The voice. It had the easeful irony of the young and he thought it must be one of his children's friends. He turned.

'I joke, of course. Good day, Professor Flynn.'

Yuri Bykov. His hair yellow against the walls of the gallery, he stood in a long fur coat and slim trousers, his sneakers large and comical. Looking back, Campbell would recall the look of malfeasance, and the reek of vetiver and myrrh (Eau Sauvage, he reckoned) that came from the man's extended hand.

'How's your friend Jake?' Campbell asked.

'Sparkling with revival.'

'Glad to hear it, or something like that,' Campbell heard himself saying.

Yuri was built for moving on.

'Listen. You're the very chap I need,' Yuri returned, with a flutter of his hand. 'We're here on a mission.' It soon became clear who he meant by 'we' when a small Chinese man with red spectacles appeared at his side. 'This is my associate Sun Zetao,' Yuri said. 'The renowned architect from Beijing.'

'How do you do?' Campbell said.

He saw a stain of red paint on Mr Zetao's thumbnail.

'My Chinese friend here is well connected,' Yuri continued. 'He knows *all* the markets.'

When Zetao eventually spoke, he offered words so sphinx-like they made the other two pause: 'Art most excellent.'

It seemed to Campbell that the Russian was high or not quite there, desperate, fragmented. Another mirror-self. Or was Campbell simply projecting? There were marks on his face, like he'd been assaulted or burned with cigarettes. He began rambling about the Rembrandts and saying he believed there was a companion piece to the painting of Agatha Bas, a second portrait. It was hidden in a castle in the Scottish Borders and he had a good chance of freeing it, he said.

'It doesn't exist,' Campbell tried to say.

'*Au contraire*, Professor. I have a buyer.' He went on to point out that there were thirty-six Rembrandts in private hands. 'In New York recently,' he said, 'we saw a portrait of a young woman wearing a plumed cap. Magical!'

There was definitely bruising around Yuri's eye.

'An unfortunate rictus of a mouth and beady eyes under the cap,' he was saying. 'Reminded me rather of Catsy Wemyss, that hilarious daughter of Lord Elcho who dressed in mad Victorian costume all the time. She was a giddy little ferret. Did you ever meet? Charming girl, but extremely lost and rather brazen. Wonderful at parties. We once turned up at Naworth Castle, where the Earl and Countess of Carlisle made us all dress up. We were *sans tenue*, but Catsy raided the old chests and it turned into an absolute riot. It was like the old days, you see – all the senior bodies, who thought they were coming to play bridge or mahjong, and suddenly they're all rampaging out on the moors, running half-naked and dancing on Hadrian's Wall or whatever it's called, completely blotto. That was Catsy. Very *Vile*

*Bodies.* Her grandmother was engaged in a *collaboration horizontale* with Baron Hans Günther von Dincklage, the German intelligence officer. All quite hilarious actually.'

'I've never heard of her,' Campbell said wearily.

'The mirror image of Rembrandt's young woman. Unfortunately, she was crushed to death by a horsebox in Shropshire.'

'Who was?'

'Catsy. She hadn't much luck . . . You are working on Rembrandt now, I hear?'

'He may be unreachable.' Campbell paused. 'Rembrandt is the father; Vermeer the son. And some of us, I'm afraid, are eternal sons, if you know what I mean. Beyond a certain point, we see only ourselves when we look at our fathers.'

The young man began boasting again. Campbell felt he'd conjured him out of the oils, or from a territory beyond the frames, where value and blood were intermingled. He felt numb as he listened, but brutally infected with all the viruses and sicknesses of the world and mortified to be among these ectoplasms of London life. He wanted never to see them again, but this was a struggle now beyond him, so inscribed was he in their various scenes, and he did not have the resources – not the freedom, not the money – to divorce himself. In the mania of the moment in the Queen's Gallery, he was bound in a way to the vulgar particulars of that young Russian, whatever they were. He saw it confirmed in the young man's smile and in his gross familiarity.

Travis was going down for a long time. Milo knew that. Lying on his bed two weeks after the trial and looking at the posters and books around the walls, he realised what a rescue fantasy he had about his childhood friends. He lifted a large book he kept by the bed and he rested it on one of his pillows. *Charles Booth's London Poverty Maps.* He often studied them, and they'd become sad tokens, showing the conditions of his neighbourhood 133 years before, each street marked by a colour classification relative to the social condition of its inhabitants: orange for 'Wealthy', red for 'Middle Class', pink for 'Comfortable', blue for 'Poor', dark blue for 'Very Poor' and charcoal for the streets that the Victorians had designated 'Semi-Criminal'.

He reached for the magnifying glass. Thornhill Square was like all the squares and streets on that side of Caledonian Road, orange and red, while the streets on Milo's side were charcoal and blue. Sutterton Street, Nailour Street, Frederick Street: altered now with newer housing, yet just as they'd been in the nineteeth century. Tilting the magnifying glass, he saw the Caledonian Asylum, a block up from the prison, now the housing estate where Big Pharma had lived with his mum and dad. He lay back and considered that vanished institution, the effort of another era to break the cycle for lost children and change the direction of their lives.

Opening his laptop, and drawing on the new hard drive, he entered the confected homepage of an invented user, where he opened the email account of an alias and thereby picked up messages from the office of Mr Molly. The agent for the Duke's lawyer was now very familiar, speaking as if they were transacting ordinary business on behalf of shareholders or borrowers, and Milo responded in a clipped style to everything he had to say about their 'transaction'. The currency, Mr Molly wrote, was 'currently held in escrow' by a neighbouring legal firm, and it would be released, 'that's to say, deposited, in the manner we understand to be normal in such cases'. It made Milo smile to see this language find its way into the grey areas of the Net. 'Our only stipulation,' Mr Molly went on, 'is that, for security reasons, the payments will be made in four parts, with a certain amount of time lapsing between payments. This will enable us to monitor your response and ensure that our donation does not in any way blow back.'

Milo replied, 'That's cool.'

Then: 'We will take immediate steps if the payments fail.'

Milo cut and pasted the correct Bitcoin wallet address into the email and sent it off with the sense that this work was nearing completion. He felt raw and suddenly remote as the laptop powered off and he met his own face in the dark screen.

His mother had fallen ill on 3 November 2020. It was the day of the American election and she'd been talking to Milo about the candidates when she had to steady herself, coughing by the kettle. Her breathing grew more laboured over the following day and she was struggling. After she tested positive for Covid, they took her to the Royal Free in an ambulance. They were alarmed at how low her oxygen saturation was. Milo and his father couldn't go into the ward, but she was still talking on the phone, mainly about the election, saying an idiot in the next bed had made a racist remark about Kamala Harris and she had got up off her pillows to tell him that Harris was one of the brightest people in America.

He could hear she wasn't right. He told her to take it slow.

The doctors talked about a ventilator, but her oxygen level was steady and they were slow to give her steroids. Her weight was a worry. Ray and Milo were there all night in the waiting room in Hampstead, now and then getting chocolate from the machine and cups of water given to them by the nurses. The place was packed. Families weren't allowed near the wards and the staff tried to encourage them to go home.

'They're not sure what to do up there,' Ray said.

'They will give her the machine probably,' Milo said.

'It's bad. Her lungs are inflamed at the best of times, with the sarcoidosis.'

Ray stared out as if he'd always known catastrophe. His hand was shaking as he held the cup.

They got her on the phone at midnight. Visitors still weren't allowed, but a kind nurse put her on FaceTime and it was . . .

Milo had to search for his own breath. On the screen of the nurse's phone, as he huddled in the corridor with his dad, Zemi knew what was coming, and she spoke in her most serious voice. She kept pulling down her oxygen mask. 'The whole country is on life support,' she said.

'Take your time, Zemi,' his dad said. 'Don't speak too much.'

But she got the mask off and spoke clearly.

'The word "epidemic". In Greek, it means "upon the people".'

Always the teacher, Milo thought.

She put the mask back on. He spoke to her. He said everything in those minutes that he'd ever wanted to say to his mother.

She pulled the mask down again.

'My beautiful boy. Your mother is proud.'

'*Ema'ma,*' he said.

'Look, Mouse. I am Zemi Nigussie Mangasha, from Amhara Region.'

'*Ema.*'

'And from King's Cross, London.'

The nurse said she must put the mask back on.

'Take the oxygen. Save your breath.'

They lost the connection. An hour later, they FaceTimed again. The nurse said the doctor had prescribed remdesivir.

Zemi was sitting on the bed. She took the phone.

'They fired on my *ema* and *baba*, in 1973,' she said. 'The Derg. And the charity brought me to London. The Frasers were good people. Forest Gate. You never met them. And one day at a meeting I saw your father.'

'You're speaking too much, love,' his dad said.

'Listen.'

She wanted to get her story out.

When they lost the signal again, Milo went home to get a bag of her personal things. They could leave items at the locked door of the ward, photos, sweets, hairbrushes.

Then Milo and his father went to a café on South End Green. A doctor phoned to say her temperature had spiked to 103 and her oxygen saturation had dropped. 'We're putting her on a ventilator,' he said. 'She's going to the ICU.'

They spoke one more time before the machine.

'*Ema*,' was all Milo could say at first.

'Listen,' she rasped.

'Fight it,' he said. 'Fight it, Mama.'

'I love you, my boys. Take care of each other.'

'*Ema*.'

The nurse was saying they had to go. She told them to say goodbye and then she held the phone up to Zemi as she lay on a moving bed.

'I will see you in the Summerlands,' she said.

In the morning they turned her onto her front, and Ray and Milo sat in the waiting room of the Royal Free and prayed.

If you were Zemi, you were four times more likely to die; and if you were Zemi, the best treatment came more slowly, and you had known it all your life. To the politicians who flout their own rules, to the Establishment that backs them up, Milo swore revenge. To the liberals who think they do well by managing language, giving up nothing while they spell out the difference between one grain of sand and another, he swore exposure. Milo understood as the year went on that nothing for him could ever be the same. Society was revealed, and he would show these people, provide for his family, and then disappear.

Only his father knew about that night. Milo had run to the ICU and banged on the locked doors and shouted her name. His mother needed him and he would never forget that short distance between them, a door and a few corridors, a door he would be breaking down and corridors he would be wandering through all his life.

'Goodbye, *Ema*. I will be with you.'

Mourners weren't allowed at the November funeral. It was Milo and Ray and an office assistant from Charles Booth Primary, who'd insisted on coming, and brought the love of the whole school with her. At Kensal Green Cemetery, with peace all around and a few birds sounding louder than usual in the white sky, Ray gave vent to his broken heart, telling Zemi that she had made his life. To Milo, his father had never seemed more Irish than he did by the graveside that day; it was the one place, the last place, where he could be Zemi's husband. From the pocket of his suit he took a photograph of the three of them on Bottle Island, on the west coast of Scotland. Milo was only five or six. His father kissed the photograph and dropped it into the grave.

Milo read a poem by Seamus Heaney. He took a handful of earth – 'clabber', his dad had called it when he bent down – and it felt, as it fell, as if England too was running through his hands. The ground was cold, the light clear.

Milo closed the book of maps and got off his bed. He found a clean T-shirt and jeans.

He had a painful job to do. It was time to see Mrs Swaby, Big Pharma's mum.

When he got to the block, he didn't want to press the buzzer. He waited and then nipped in the main door behind an old lady carrying shopping bags. On the fourth floor, he immediately saw Pharma's dad on the walkway. He was smoking, dressed in a suit, and had a blue tattoo on the back of his hand. Milo remembered it from childhood: the image of Lee 'Scratch' Perry and the words 'The Black Ark'. Milo walked towards him. Mr Swaby put his finger to his lips.

'Nah, man,' he said. 'Can't do it.'

He brushed past Milo and continued towards the stairs, head down. Milo approached the open door and pushed with his hand. He called Mrs Swaby's name. She came into the hall wearing her church clothes. She was transfixed. She stared at him and began shaking her head, her eyes filling up, the Bible clasped to her chest.

'An educated man like you,' she said. 'I wanted the same thing for him. To be educated and . . . you did nothing for him.'

'Auntie—'

'You could have taken him away to that college!'

Her dress was covered in blue flowers, her hat was pink – and he recognised the incongruous coat, a Palm Angels padded track jacket, sky blue, her son's.

'You know I loved Devan,' Milo said, stepping further into the hall. He remembered a warm place. It was freezing now.

She held out her Bible in front of her.

'You *loved* him! He's dead, Milo. Oh, my Lord, my child is dead in the street and lying in his own blood. He was twenty-two years old. They come after him and he lies dead. You loved Devan. You say that – words are easy. You couldn't look after him, Milo? Why not get these boys off his back? You *best friends*?'

'I tried, Auntie.'

'Nobody tried. Nobody tried. Nobody.'

'Auntie—'

'I'm nobody's auntie any more! You hear me?' She raised her voice now. 'I made you boys my life and all my life. It was all I ever wanted. Cooking for Devan and his friends and wiping your faces – no, no!'

'I'm sorry, Mrs Swaby.'

'God bless your mother in heaven. She's the lucky one, God bless her soul in God's kingdom. My child is dead.'

'Let me sit down with you, Auntie . . .'

She waved her hand with its long nails in front of her face, then she dabbed her eyes with a tissue and hugged her Bible.

'I am *devastated*,' she said.

The word never ended.

It came from the deepest place, a place known only to mothers. That is what Milo thought as he retreated. She wiped her eyes in the hall mirror before stepping outside and locking the door. 'I know you're a good boy,' she said, turning. 'But my days are over. I can't say no more.'

A few weeks earlier, when Milo's father came back from having his regular pint at Kennedy's, he had taken Gosia into the kitchen. 'Zemi and me, we made our own wee society inside this flat,' he'd said. 'It was one long conversation.' And then he made his best pronouncement: 'Be with an interesting person. Milo's like that. Make life interesting. That's all there is. And do it in a new forum.'

Gosia loved that. 'We have a secret plan,' she said, 'for all of us.'

'Do you now?' There was a fondness in his voice, and a trace of humour, as if it was a joke and they might just be children playing.

She still sometimes worried that perhaps it was all beyond their reach, or that it had come too easily, too suddenly. But they'd begun to pack boxes now. Milo promised it was all going to work. The first portions of the money were already coming through. The Eilean Ròin Community had been alerted.

'And what did they say?' Gosia asked.

He showed her the email.

'They guarantee us a place if the funds arrive.'

They were committed now, and a week ago he had explained it all to his dad. Ray's tone had been the same as before, but with a new core of pride.

On her last day at the salon, Gosia said goodbye to her workmates and they blew kisses. She was out in Upper Street, feeling full of promise. Nobody knew. She understood Milo had some tougher goodbyes to say, but he'd manage. They were young, and the winter sun was everywhere as she walked to the bus stop tapping her stomach.

# 45 The Crossing

Charlo Sullivan fairly battered Facebook that week, looking to see what his ex-girlfriend was up to and what the score was back home. Sometimes, he posted pictures of himself in his truck, driving past one of the tourist spots in France or with thumbs up at a bierkeller, a way of showing everybody he was out there living the life. Charlo would get himself a new shirt at H&M and take a selfie at a club in Amsterdam, holding up a loud cocktail. There was a hashtag on Instagram: #irishfridgemen. They all posted pictures there, and he was lonely at night, parked up at a service station or in a lay-by near the port.

On Tuesday 25 January, he drove to a car park in Essex, where he hooked up his yoke to Gerry O'Dade's trailer, which was full of biscuits from a factory in Devon. He crossed at Dover and took the container to drop-offs in Dunkirk, Bruges and Lille, listening to Hits Radio as he drove along. A few times he caught his face in the mirror and said, 'You're looking well, lad.' He bedded down that night behind the Carrefour Sainte-Victoire, and texted with his pals back home in the Tullygally Tavern.

He was woken early next morning by the local guards tapping on the window and telling him he was parked illegally. Parking, paperwork: bane of his life. He moved to a lorry park on the other side of the town and read his messages. He'd tipped all the biscuits so his container was empty, and Stefan had sent him new co-ordinates. There had been a fuck-up on a previous haul – the French police had stopped a truck at Coquelles and released all the migrants – so there was a double load now. Charlo put the destination into the satnav, but he knew where he was driving to, the farm road behind the industrial estate outside Roclincourt. The red barn.

'Forty-one ambassadors,' Stefan messaged on WhatsApp.

Charlo sent back a thumbs-up.

It was a cracking day but with frost over the fields. Calls came from Stefan and Bozydar on the run down.

'Did you get more piss bags?' Stefan asked.

'Roger that. From the Carrefour in Lille.'

'You got enough?'

'No danger,' Charlo said. 'My cab's coming down with piss bags and energy drinks, so it is.'

Boz said taxis had been arranged. Several people were coming from Lille and others from Paris, and everybody would be at the industrial estate for 10.30 on the dot. He texted Charlo the barcode and the PIN for the boat leaving Zeebrugge at 4 p.m. that day.

Charlo sent him a row of thumbs and a disco guy.

He reached the red barn and came to a stop with a skoosh of air from the brake pads. He could already see faces peeking round from the side of the barn as he walked the length of the container – Vietnamese, he thought; that's what Stefan had told him to expect. He opened the back doors and they came running. They had rucksacks or plastic bags; he counted eighteen. He half closed the doors and had a smoke and a piss at the edge of a field while he waited for more. Two cabs came, then three people carriers. He counted them in, but two guys approached him. The taller one offered his hand.

'The Polish boys, right. How yez?'

He'd met him down in Kent. The shorter one was wearing a beanie and had a moustache. He smiled a lot.

'It's not easy, like,' Charlo said, 'for some of you lads coming back.'

He craned his neck to look inside the container.

'It's mad busy today,' he added. 'I wish I could bring yez up in the cab with me. It's a long journey, like, and it's a nice day. Yez'll do most of the journey without me. I'm just the one driving you to the port. But don't worry about anything: once you're there you're there, fellas.' He handed them piss bags and opened the doors.

'It's okay,' the Kent one said. 'Thank you.'

As he drove off, Charlo saw a small blue aircraft flying over the field at low altitude. He opened a can of Burn and headed for the Autoroute des Anglais. If he got stopped by the guards, he would say he never saw the load going in and thought he was pulling engine parts or something like that. As he drove north, he got lost in his music coming through CarPlay, his mind involved in the chase-and-catch freedom of the road, wondering whether he might spend the night in Ghent while he waited for his next job. He could try that nightclub with the barmaid who said he had nice eyes.

He followed the craic online. You did kind of forget what was in the back of your truck, whether it was biscuits or people or fuck knows what, he said to himself, his mind going back to Lurgan and the messages he wanted to answer. He paid more attention to his speed. He went 63, 67, 93 kilometres per hour, back to 73, 67 again; he could see the digital figure, the slowing down and the speeding up, the hours passing. At 1.20 p.m., he slowed down on the N31 and turned into a service station in Lissewege. He made a call to Boz, who told him O'Dade was all set to pick up the load at the other end. Charlo went into the Esso garage and bought a baguette and a bottle of water. He studied the magazines. Maybe he would get a haircut in Ghent and see a film at one of the cineplexes. A WhatsApp message came from Stefan. 'Remember to bang the side of the container before you get to the port,' he said.

'I know!'

Stefan always reminded him. The knock told them to gather in the middle of the container to beat the heat scanners down at the port.

About twelve minutes after leaving Lissewege, Charlo entered the docks at Zeebrugge and stopped at the checkpoint. He showed the guy his barcode and used the PIN. It was proper cold down there at the docks, a freeze coming off the North Sea. There was a sign on the window of the booth: 'Strictly No Tailgating'. Charlo's container would be travelling on the *Clementine* at 4 p.m. Due to arrive in Purfleet at midnight local time. 'Thanks very much, *merci*,' he said to the guy.

He drove onto the uncovered deck and reversed into his spot. Jumping down, he unhooked the container and knocked on the side again. The metal was freezing cold on his knuckles and he meant the knock as a farewell and a goodnight.

'You're on yer way, lads,' he said under his breath.

These people from Shepherd's Bush have no idea what an altar cloth is supposed to look like, Mrs Krupa said to herself during the evening Mass at St Andrew Bobola. She'd given them money for a new one and they'd commissioned something from a local artist, who had made a thing covered in human eyes that was ugly beyond belief. She'd expected something beautiful and inspiring, probably white, maybe with doves.

A man was to give a talk in the hall. Cecylia was looking forward to the catering afterwards. The subject, it seemed, was about the danger to peace in Europe posed by Russia's manoeuvres on the border with Ukraine. The speaker used to work for the Ministry of Foreign Affairs in Poland and was now some kind of official with the embassy in London. Cecylia was quite bored. 'It would appear that sovereignty is not what it used to be,' the man was saying, 'or not what it should be, and we are closer to war now than at any time in the last thirty years.'

She slipped out and got her bag. She put on her glasses and saw a message from Gosia, saying she would pick her up at nine o'clock.

She texted back. 'Stop and eat here. There is too much food.'

'Not for me, Mama.' Then a second text: 'But I need to speak to you.'

She put her phone and her glasses back in her bag, and returned for the end of the talk. The priests were so proud of these events.

'Have *chłodnik*,' she said when Gosia arrived. The girl was blowing on her hands.

'Mama, it's freezing outside. I'm not eating cold soup.'

'It has radishes and egg.'

'Only you would think that an added bonus.'

Life would've been different if Andrzej was still here. Children respect their fathers. 'Somebody made *królik*,' Cecylia said.

'Nothing. I feel slightly sick, to be honest.'

'Always sick. You don't eat properly, Gosia.'

Later, when they got to the car, Gosia leaned into the back seat and gave her mother a striped cotton scarf she'd bought in Islington. 'It's from Petit Bateau,' she said. Cecylia wrapped it around her neck and gave Gosia a kiss.

'That's a beautiful thing,' she said. 'These factories where your brother helps find jobs for the young men – they make beautiful things like this, careful stitching and lovely patterns.'

Gosia fell silent. 'I pray we're right babe,' Milo had said one day at his computer, 'and I pray that we're wrong. It's never as much fun as you'd think, naming the guilty parties.'

'I wonder why that is?' Gosia had said.

Milo had turned towards her with a kind of decisiveness.

'We're all guilty of something,' he said.

She pulled away from St Andrew Bobola's and the car fell quiet. Cecylia reached into her bag. Three missed calls. Unknown number.

'I don't like these calls that come from people I don't know.'

'It will just be scammers, Mum. Salespeople. Phishing old ladies.'

'Doing what?'

'Never mind.' She touched her mother's hand, smiling, concentrating on the road. They'd have a cup of tea when they got home, and a talk. There was a quote from Emily Dickinson on the air freshener in the car and it danced about as they rumbled over the Westway. 'Not knowing when the Dawn will come, I open every Door.'

Gerry O'Dade had spent most of the day waiting in his truck in Essex, texting his mates and bingeing on six episodes of *World War II in*

*Colour*. It was the only thing he had liked at school, Spitfires and all that, and he would make an effort to turn up for the history lessons after early mornings at the farm. He could still remember sitting in that class, his hands stained with dirt and bee stings, wanting the British to win and not being sure if that was the right thing to want. Sometimes, when he got bored in the truck, he'd go out and break the ice on the frozen puddles.

He was parked on Eastern Avenue, in that part of Essex called Grays, where the Thames deepens and opens into the sea. The street was quiet. You never got bothered there, waiting to pick up or set off, and there was a roadside pit stop for sandwiches by the Waterglade Industrial Park. Once it was dark, about halfway through 'The Liberation of Paris', he got out of his cab again to buy a coffee. Later on, looking for something to do, he drove round the Rainham Marshes to Coldharbour Lane, to check it was clear for the Purfleet drop-off.

He went for a nap about nine o'clock, setting the alarm on his phone for midnight. He woke up a few minutes before the alarm, put on a clean sweatshirt and headed to the port. Looking up, he saw the Queen Elizabeth II Bridge, the headlights following each other across the darkness like tracer fire in a foreign war. He was still thinking about the Battle of Britain and the blaze of glory as he stared at the bridge. But they were just bored, exhausted drivers.

'That'll be me soon,' he said out loud. 'Rolling home.'

The boat had arrived on time and it usually took an hour for the container to be craned out and connected to the truck. He got a few texts from Stefan: to confirm the pickup cars would be at Coldharbour Lane as usual, around 1.30; to remember the clean-out; to park the empty container in the reserved spot at Moto. Charlo would be over the next night and would pick it up to do a chickens job in Preston.

Gerry drove down to the booth and showed the release note on his phone. Trailer GOH193B arriving at Purfleet from Zeebrugge on the *Clementine*. Twenty-five pallets of wine. It was this part, the port, that always made O'Dade nervous. He tried to play it casual as the guy waved him through to the loading dock. Another job: not too many now, then he could take what he'd saved up and go. He flicked up his collar against the cold, seeing the serial number on the back door as his container came down through the air. It always made him think of *The Wizard of Oz*, the scene where the house comes spinning down in the hurricane and lands on top of the witch. He'd loved that film when he was a kid, the way the picture changed from black and white to colour when they arrived in the new world. He jumped out to connect up, and his phone buzzed. A message from Boz. 'Give them air quickly. Don't let them out.' He replied with a thumbs-up and pulled on his gloves. It was always the same drill. He felt confident now, the fear over, as he secured the yoke and climbed back into his cab.

He drove back to Eastern Avenue. He was humming that tune, the one they all sing when they link arms and jog up the yellow brick road. It was amazing how they managed these things, getting people over the borders, over the water. He rolled slowly under a street light and stopped to put on his hi-vis jacket. Climbing down from his cab, he banged on the side of the container to let them know he was opening up. He was still whistling the tune. You had to be careful all the time and check for people watching, so he looked around and paused to put his phone in his pocket. Then he opened the right-hand rear door and stepped aside.

A thick cloud of vapour poured out of the container and billowed in the air. In the yellow light, he could see them heaped all over the container floor, dozens and dozens of people. Froth around their mouths. Blood. All the images hit him at once: most of the bodies were semi-naked, many of them open-eyed. Wrapped in each other's arms and absolutely still. Young people. Women.

'Holy Jesus.'

He opened the other door. He could see bashes on the sides and on the roof, a red handprint on the door.

They'd always been fine, in the past. They'd always be standing there.

The terrible smell. All dead.

He bent down by the rear wheels and threw up. He wished he could vomit everything that was in him, his whole life. There was nothing under the street light but him and his truck and that terrible heap of bodies. When he looked again, using the torch on his phone, he examined the faces. They were all Vietnamese, except for two men slumped together near the doors. He looked closer and he gasped, sobbing and stuttering to himself, 'Oh, no, oh no.' The boy who worked at the grow-houses in Kent. He'd driven him a few times up and down to Leicester, the nice lad, full of questions and all that, oh Jesus Christ. His eyes open. His mouth. Gerry stood trembling as if the lad was looking at him – Jakub, clutching a phone, his head resting on the chest of the man next to him.

'Holy fuck.' He bent down to be sick again.

He closed the doors and stood in the road. He took out his phone and called Bozydar, who answered right away. He was drunk.

'What's going on?' he said.

'They're all feckan dead,' O'Dade said, weeping. 'D'ye hear me?'

'What the fuck are you talking about?'

'Every last one of them's dead, Krupa. They're all lying dead.'

'The ambassadors?'

'The passengers in the back – the migrants, yes.'

'What? Are you sure?'

'And my name's on the docket. So's yours.'

'Let me think,' Boz said.

'There was too feckan many of them, mate. Too many! I'm gonna say I don't know how they got in. I was there to pick up wine—'

'Shut up, Gerry. Let me—'

'Phone Stefan. I need to get away.'

O'Dade hung up and climbed back into his cab. He started the engine, drove out onto the main road but didn't know where to go. A

WhatsApp message came from Stefan Popa. 'Drivers waiting. Where are you?'

'It's fucked,' he texted back.

Stefan rang immediately on the other phone. 'What's wrong?'

'They're all lying dead, Stefan. There wasn't enough air. Fucking dead. There's like dozens in there. That boy, Jakub. Oh, Jesus. You put too many . . .'

Stefan was silent. Not a word.

'Should I abandon the container?' O'Dade asked.

'Not that,' Stefan said at last. 'You have to say you had no idea what was in there. None of us had any idea. They hitched a ride.'

'But where's the real load?'

Stefan said nothing. Then: 'Say it was stolen,' he mumbled. 'Say you don't know.'

'I'm the registered pickup driver. Charlo's the registered drop-off. And both our trucks are owned by Krupa, and you booked the tickets.'

Stefan was silent again.

'We won't see daylight,' O'Dade said.

He turned the wheel and drove back round to Eastern Avenue.

'Kill this phone,' Stefan said after a moment. 'This is the last you will ever hear from me.' He hung up and he too was like vapour. In that moment, in the dark silence of the avenue and under the terrible sodium lights, O'Dade realised he didn't know anything about Stefan Popa, or this Feng, who did or didn't exist. He never knew them. The paper trail and the phone trail might lead to them, but Gerry was the one with the dead bodies. He called Charlo and got no answer, then he sent him a WhatsApp. 'Everything is totally fucked man. That load you dropped at Zeeb, they're all dead mate.'

He got out of the cab and found a drain. He crouched down in front of it, phoning Charlo again and this time leaving a voicemail. 'Kill your work phone. Make sure the address book is zapped. All the best, lad.' He then took the SIM card out of his phone, bit it to pieces and threw them into the bushes behind him. He snapped the burner. Half of it went into the drain and the other half he threw over the fence into the grounds of a power station.

Boz called him on the remaining phone to ask if he was sure it was the Polish guy. And did he have his brother with him?

'Listen,' Gerry said. 'I don't know anything about anybody.' Boz said nothing. Then the line went dead.

It was the silence that frightened him most, standing in that street and wanting to reverse time, to go home to Ireland.

He walked to his truck and made his last call. His hands were so cold and shaking so badly that he could hardly hit the numbers. He spoke quietly into his phone and it was as if a lifetime's puzzle was resolved in the dark.

'Yes, caller, is the patient breathing?'

'They're all dead,' he said. 'Just send the police. Send everybody.'

# BOOK FIVE
## Realisation

# 46 Members

Sergei Magnitsky, the dead Russian whistleblower, said London was levitating on a sea of dirty money. The Duke of Kendal had never met the man, but would certainly now agree. Pursuant to a new understanding with the Crown, the Duke – known in Parliament as Lord Crofts, also styled the Earl of Sundrum, Baron Eye and Viscount Fitzroy of Kiltarlity – was preparing to correct any wrong impression that might have been given of over-involvement with foreign businessmen. On 28 January, he sat on a bench outside the chamber, scribbling. A dossier of information on the Russian menace had recently been forwarded to him by his friend Lord Haxby, who was similarly cutting his ties with Aleksandr Bykov and his companies. 'Let us simply say, Your Grace, that we are mending the record. The Russians are known to be massing on Ukraine's border, an invasion seems certain, and they have turned out to be a bad investment for Britain.' The Duke now intended to say something in the Lords in support of sanctions, and he used the time when the bishops were leading prayers to sit outside and make a few notes: 'The brokering of prime properties to offshore companies, the granting of golden visas to kleptocrats – all shamed the nation and violated our national interest.'

After the debate, he handed his notes to the door-keeper, who collected them for Hansard, then filed out with the elderly lords. He made his way down the Library Corridor towards the Peers' Dining Room, stopping in at the Pugin Room to see if his guest had arrived. The room was empty, and he saw that he had twenty minutes before she was due for lunch, so he went on to the dining room and took a copy of the *Daily Mail*. Breaking off a piece of bread roll and buttering it, his mind wandered to the time before Christmas, when he'd felt at the end of himself and sort of done for, in terms of his old life. But now he was giving up the set at Albany and moving all the furniture to Suffolk and Scotland. He would live frugally and stay the course. For a spell, he had noticed a degree of quiet condemnation in the eyes of the other peers. The coverage had been savage. But toleration is its own reward: one doesn't maintain tradition by giving in to weakness. He remembered rather vividly a training officer at Sandhurst once telling him to buck up. 'You're not really a man,' he said, 'until you're ready to forget everything about yourself that you used to rely on.' He didn't wait to be pushed. He'd resigned nearly all his chairmanships and patronages – no more British Legion, no more Highland Salmon Trust – and he promised to devote himself, with the support of his extended family, to husbanding his estates and running the investment trust.

There was a row of faces on the front page of the *Mail* – the people who had died in a migrant outrage in Essex. The Duke read the story and stopped here and there, at a picture or a quote, the details quickly sliding from his mind into a general pool of bad business. 'They all died in British waters,' it said. The Duke tutted. Unspeakable things happen every day, but you can't think about them all, he told himself. Over the page, it seemed the police had retrieved all the migrants' phones, looking for clues, and had translated all the voice messages. 'Sorry, Mum,' one of them said. 'My path abroad has not succeeded. I'm dying because I cannot breathe.' The Duke turned to the next page and read a story about the prime minister ordering civil servants to lead by example and get back to their desks now the virus had been sent packing. The spirit of the Blitz must rule. It was difficult coming back, Anthony thought to himself, but coming back is what we do, and what the country does, and must always do.

A Scottish peer stopped by his table. '*Tony*,' he said. 'I thought we would've seen you at Edinburgh Castle the other night.'

'Oh yes?'

'The Lochbervie Fencibles' Burns Supper. You're always welcome.'

'I'm keeping the old nose clean, Donald.'

'Wise. But not forever, I hope. You have a place.' The peer bent down and filled the Duke's ear with his whisky breath. 'One military man to another: they come for the best at the behest of the worst. Mark my words.'

'Ever the poet, my friend,' he said, smiling up at the departing Scot.

It had come all at once to Anthony, and now he saw, as clear as the water in his glass, that the time of the old guard was over. They were unreconstructed. Now, the young person expected fairness, equality, diversity. He had been thinking about offering a long article to the *Scotsman*, 'The Act of Reunion'. Putting down his spectacles, he saw crossing the dining room Lord Scullion, who nodded; no words required. The nod did it, confirming the quiet circling of wagons to which each was now committed.

'I think they've been scrubbing this place with antiseptic,' the Duke said to Moira Flynn when she arrived at the table for lunch. She was rubbing her hands as he stood up. 'As clean as the gills on an Arctic salmon.'

'No handshakes, no kissing,' she said.

She sat down and placed a napkin on her lap.

'Wine?' he asked.

'No, thank you. This isn't a social call, Anthony. And it's only for Campbell's sake that I've agreed to come here. You're insanely toxic.'

He made his lesson-learned face. 'I'm on the water too. Let me pour you some. I take it a glass of fizzy won't upset you?'

'I want to record this meeting,' she said. 'And I won't be eating much. I want to make it clear that I am here as a Member of Parliament.'

'By all means. I'm sure you're an MP when you're asleep, or gardening, that's to say, every minute of every day.'

He ordered and nudged the newspaper at his elbow. 'Sad story everywhere today. Yet this country can't be as bad as you say, or foreigners wouldn't be so keen to come here. The *Mail* says they were paying £12,000 each to get across.'

She placed her phone between them. 'They all borrowed the money,' she said. 'Many families remortgaged their homes to help their children find a better life. Most of them were from one of the poorest provinces in Vietnam.'

'Dreadful business.'

'In 2016, the area was ravaged by a huge environmental disaster. A dodgy steel mill owned by Formosa Plastics contaminated the coastal waters that the local population depended on for their livelihood. It killed off the local fishing industry and devastated tourism in the area. That was the cause. The young people started moving away in large numbers.'

'You can't blame them for finding England attractive.'

'You can't blame them, full stop. They were economic migrants.'

'They were killed by a criminal gang, Moira. It says here. I'm sure they captured the worst of them when they arrested those lorry drivers. Irish, I gather.'

Her look had always been accusing. He'd met her type in the army: they were always on a fault-finding mission, relationships be damned.

'Look,' he said, 'I'm sure it comforts you to feel it's England's fault every time somebody dies trying to get here, but we've been pretty hospitable to immigrants in the past.'

'We are in the last years of a failed system.'

'Look to Russia,' he blurted out, 'if you want to know about a failed system.'

And that somehow brought them round to their topic. Quite nicely, he thought. He was eager that this rather untidy affair be put to rest.

He told her he had been subjected to a serious scam. The video of him in the Nazi club was fabricated, because he was never there. 'They made it up,' he said, 'putting my head onto the video in some fashion and manipulating my voice.'

564

'Are you kidding me, Anthony? They posted receipts.'

'All fake, I'm afraid. Right down to the video. I'm not into neo-Nazis, for God's sake. I was a lieutenant colonel in the British Army.'

'I have no idea what you actually believe,' she said.

'I believe in the values of this country.'

'*Do you*, Anthony?'

He thought she looked exhausted. It must be tiring being her. He could give her a list of British values, but he saw it would all appear rather unfortunate, at the minute. He tried to smile with his eyes as he took a sip from his glass.

'We will prove it in court if we have to,' he said. 'I'm working with a public relations firm to iron out any misunderstandings that remain.'

'Were they the ones who told you to reverse your position on supporting sanctions, Anthony? Did they tell you to employ a few people of colour? Was it their suggestion that you get rid of your shagging pad at Albany?'

'I beg your pardon?' He tried not to glare. 'I'm sorry to disappoint you in your conspiracy theory view of existence. Candy and I made a number of changes that we felt were overdue, including personal ones.'

'You're too stupid to realise she's leaving you.'

'We're very much together. Nighty will be spending more time in Tibet and is busy with her various festivals and charities.'

'It's only a matter of time.'

He continued. He would always continue. 'With Hinderclay House and Segdoune Grange, Crofts Castle and our home in London, there is a great deal of work to be done, and I can assure you, Moira, that my wife and I are fully committed to it, and to each other.'

He had never hated anyone so much. Left-wing people always got everything so wrong and they never saw what was happening in their own corner. 'Perhaps you should look to your own family if you mean to be helpful,' he said.

She whispered at this point. 'What self-flattery to equate your family with mine. Campbell's flaws are ones he can answer to.'

'I don't think you know your brother, my dear.'

'Perhaps not, but I know *you*,' she said.

The food came and only he ate. It's odd how confidence comes, but the Duke was feeling more and more on solid ground. 'One thing,' he said. 'I believe it was your good self who leaked the information to that journalist about my small financial dealings with Aleksandr Bykov and his charitable trust.'

She looked down at her phone. 'I excused myself from the committee owing to a conflict of interest. That's all I will say.'

'It's all right, Moira. I know it was you. But, as with the other thing, there was a lot of fakery involved, you see, and my relationship with Mr Bykov was actually totally above board. We are allowed to receive investments, and it seems not all were declared – part of an administrative oversight, for which a member of my staff has been reprimanded. We will be working towards more transparency.'

'I see it was worth it – the PR people.' She sighed. 'You can say what you like, Anthony. You hitched your family's name to Russian gangsters, men who are increasingly beyond the pale of all legitimate governments. They bought your influence, they paid for your architects, you installed them in British life, where they brooked no opposition, where they laundered their money. While you were talking "foundations", they launched a cyberattack on Estonia in 2007; while you visited Bykov's yacht, they ordered the use of a nerve agent in Salisbury, committed human rights abuses and are now making plans to invade Ukraine. We will live with these sordid operations for the rest of our lives.'

'I hate to interrupt you.' He looked at his watch. 'Time's marching on. Do give my best to Campbell and Elizabeth. I hope your work doesn't prove too tiring.'

Her face flushed. 'Others will always take the fall for men like you,' she said. 'People will die, all over the world—'

'Such a pleasure, Moira,' he said, standing up. He picked up his paper and nodded to the waiter to make up his bill at the desk.

Back in the day, he was known as Three Suppers Scullion, adept at spreading his campaigning and fundraising appointments across the courses, taking a starter in Highgate, a main course in Notting Hill and a pudding in Westminster, stopping for whiskies at either end with donors and supporters. Passing the Cabinet War Rooms, he remembered those brilliant nights at the start of New Labour. Was it the third way or the third course, Robin Cook joked, that got them into power? Scullion had been with them the whole way, sparring with the Blairite fanboys, hiding information from Gordon Brown. Those years were unbeatable, fixing the globe from Number Ten, yet how it all fades away, he thought: the cars and the protection and the calls from foreign ministers, and you're left utterly changed by the higher air but required to breathe as an ordinary person, except nobody is ordinary once they've slept in the Lincoln Bedroom.

At the foot of St James's, he stopped for a moment by the Carlton Club, remembering his first truly compromising suppers there. He put his hands in his pockets against the cold. There was frost clinging to the front doors. It's the thing they don't tell you at politics school: there's no turning back once you've shaped your values to meet the new reality, and he accepted these things about himself. It didn't matter: he was who he was. He continued up the street and entered Brooks's, his club, feeling pleased that the Whig dislike of radicalism was very much to his taste, more now than ever. He found Aleksandr Bykov with his female attendant sitting in a corner of the dining room. She left as soon as Scullion appeared. He sat down in a red chair. The afternoon already felt like an emergency.

'You are late,' Aleksandr said, with a petulant look. There was no movement in his forehead but there was metal in his eyes.

'I'm sorry. Parliamentary affairs.'

Bykov explained that he had come to London discreetly to answer some questions to do with the 'bogus investigations'. They could prove nothing, but the mood had switched and he would now defend his friends and continue his business operations from the relative comfort of his compound in Moscow.

'Of course,' Scullion said. 'We must always accept change.'

Bykov nodded gravely.

'Real change is very rare,' he said. 'We must *appear* to accept it. I have confidence that I will see my house in Washington again.'

He poured two glasses of wine. It always amazed Scullion, the vanity of these men, altering the future because it was possible, aiming to command all the elements, even the elements that are truly beyond their control, such as time. He stared into Aleksandr's too shiny, pore-less face, the eyes and the mouth ridiculous on a man of almost sixty, and wondered what he saw when he looked in the mirror.

Aleksandr told him a bad morning had arrived for his associates. 'Your politicians are eager to support our fascistic neighbours,' he said. 'It makes me laugh how quickly they now oppose us. Mr Johnson gave us freedom. Mr Brown gave us passports. Mr Blair gave us a reason to be here. London has been our friend.'

'It was fruitful while it lasted.'

'London is over. Your efforts, and Lord Haxby's, to lift the sanctions against me are unfortunately at an end. There will only be more sanctions now.'

'It has been a pleasure working with you.'

'*For* me, Lord Scullion.'

The New Labour hero bridled at that. Yet he felt himself fill with diplomatic fervour and he knew how to end a friendship.

'I will protect you as best I can from a distance.'

'You will move on. That is your instinct, my friend.' Bykov poured himself another glass of wine and nodded. 'We have begun to move our assets. Our yacht set sail last night from Montenegro. It heads to the Middle East.'

'There is always another act, Aleksandr. A man should not merely be judged by his staying power but by his ability to escape.'

'You once told me that. It has extra meaning in Russian. "Escape your life." And this brings us to my son. I have offered him a hundred ways to get out of this disaster he has created. We asked him to go home, we promised him a new way of life, a new situation. He refuses.'

'He uses England as a stick to beat your friends. His sophistication is a weapon, he imagines. He is disorderly.'

'Yuri lives in those operas. Look, I will not insult him . . .'

Scullion squirmed imperceptibly in his chair. This was the meeting where Aleksandr would decide to remove his son from circulation, but he wouldn't insult him, of course not, even though his words would soon be eclipsed by dark actions.

'We cannot forget this business involving the Belgian, Lantier.'

'The art dealer,' Scullion said.

'It was all too much. My son and this man stole money from the most powerful men in my country. And now, this week's disasters.'

'You tried to warn him.'

'And so did you, several times. But we failed. And failure is not allowed in the world I inhabit. Do you understand?'

Scullion merely dipped his head. He believed that if he said nothing in response to this question then he would remain innocent.

'There *are* misdemeanours that can be forgotten—'

Scullion could now resume. 'Yes. Those of the late William Byre—'

'Of course,' Bykov said. 'He was nothing. We have his assets. In Saudi Arabia we are already in charge of the investments.'

'That's good.'

Scullion lowered his voice, by instinct. 'And the Duke?' he asked.

'We call it a gift. It is important that we support His Grace in restoring himself, as he must do. He is a relation of the Queen. My son set out to damage our relationship, and the Duke was foolish, also. But it is, shall I say, the difference between day and night, and the Duke owes us nothing.'

'Of course.'

'You, Lord Scullion, understand that the great art in human affairs is discretion. In our world, it is beyond price.'

Not ever quite beyond it, Scullion thought. Yet he was expert in subsuming his own needs to the needs of the moment, or the client.

'My son was educated at the University of Oxford, yet he knows nothing of history. Discretion and respect and the passage of time are what protect business.'

Scullion looked into the fire and, after a moment, produced from his pocket what he knew could be a death warrant. 'My person at the Home Office supplied me with a note that confirms what I heard.'

He passed it to Aleksandr and watched him read. Scullion could practically recite the contents:

'Essex Police have this morning issued warrants for the arrest of four men whom they suspect of being connected to the deaths of the forty-one migrants at Purfleet. Thirty-six hours ago they charged two lorry drivers. The migrants are believed to have been heading to jobs in London and Kent, working on cannabis farms. The further suspects in the case are Bozydar Krupa – a businessman from North London; Stefan Popa – an unknown foreign national; Yuri Bykov – an art dealer and son of the sanctioned Russian businessman Aleksandr Bykov; and an individual they call Feng, whose real name is Peter Fong.'

Aleksandr looked up and his eyes were pink.

'I'm sorry,' Scullion said. 'I'm afraid Yuri's hobbies appear to have caught up with him, and this is of a different order.'

'It is in the *open*,' Aleksandr said.

'Precisely. It is already a matter for the police.'

The Russian crumpled the paper and threw it on the fire.

'There is nothing we can do,' Lord Scullion said.

Aleksandr stared at the burning note. Eventually he turned.

'Nothing,' he said.

# 47 The Unknowns

Peter Fong never forgot that life is an illusion and death the awakening. You mustn't leave negative energy behind, or anything at all, and so, tonight, he recalled the Tao and murmured lines to himself above the shop. He had sent his daughters to Hong Kong because he knew the police would eventually come. He understood how he himself was a rumour that people would wish to make real, the smoke in the air which explains the fire. He spoke to his trusted contacts in Romania and Germany, in Vietnam and France, who all told him, there will be noise for a time but it will settle down: so disappear again.

I am too old to travel and the money is safe, he thought.

As soon as the Essex bodies were discovered, he'd destroyed his latest phones and all links to the grow-houses, spending the small hours erasing computer files. The man Stefan – if that was his name – had gone already to the airport, and good luck to him. The Pole from King's Cross had disappeared. There had never been any direct contact with the son of the Russian magnate; he'd simply been a source of funding. Peter erased the files for bet365, where he had spent so many nights and so much of his money, reaching for peace. He'd passed today in the single room above the shop, dazed and unable to sleep or gamble, staring at the dirty white curtains and thinking of his two girls and all they might do. He waited.

When the news finally came that his family's plane had landed, he broke his laptop into two pieces, paying the boy from the local restaurant who ran errands for him to drop it in the canal. In the early hours, his contact in charge of incineration at University College

Hospital came and took seven bags from outside the shop. There was now nothing in the upstairs room but the empty desk and a chair. As he left the room, he saw a mouse run around the edge of the skirting and he wished it well in its panic.

Downstairs, he reached the bottom step and looked up at the naked bulb. It had a cloud at its centre and he thought of his dead wife, existing in safety, of his dead uncle, his father's brother, whose shop this had been a long time ago. A good death may come. *Báisè de xíshì*, the white happy event. He turned the light off, felt resolved in the dark, and emerged into the shop with a sense of happiness.

Super Mega Ultra Wheel and Lucky Lady's Charm: he would miss the midnight games, the colours from his laptop still flashing in his mind.

*At the gambling table, there are no fathers and sons.*

In the old days, when he'd begun his working life in the betting shop, it was difficult to furnish people's dreams. Then the Internet came, this beautiful engine. In his mind, he could see all the stepping stones, from Hanoi to Beijing and from Beijing to Moscow or Budapest, and from there to Paris and the coast of England. So much *wishing*. So much *fortune*. A light from outside was sufficient to see.

Standing behind the counter, he saw that his uncle's jars, abandoned for years, were covered in grime. He took a piece of newspaper and wiped the middle two jars on the lower shelf. The first said 'Zicao (*Lithospermi Radix*)' and the second 'Quan Xie (*Scorpion*)'. He pulled the two jars onto the floor, where they smashed, and he imagined reanimated scorpions running over his feet. Then he prayed. For hours he prayed: for the people who had died, for the people he had done business with and those he had helped to realise their dreams of a new life. Sitting these last few years in the upstairs room on Gray's Inn Road, arranging travel and pickups, he had heard only hope in the migrants.

At 5 a.m. a light blinked off in the blue street. His meditation was done, and he looked around at the charts and the calendars. They were ancient. One of them said '1991'. Staring at it, he imagined bells tolling outside at St Pancras. It was too early for bells, but he heard them distinctly. He went into the back of the shop and dragged through a chair. He double-locked the front door, opened the letterbox and threw the keys onto the pavement. He took the petrol can from the counter and shook its contents all over the shop and through the old treatment rooms. He lit one of the candles he'd found in a broken drawer, then walked over to the curtains and set them alight. The flames rose immediately and dark smoke began chasing itself over the ceiling tiles. He was calm. He sat in the chair, closed his eyes and soon he began to see the sun.

Cecylia was at home in Orkney House, bathed in fresh guilt. It was all her fault. 'Eat something, Mama,' Gosia said. She pushed the plate away and huddled in her armchair, clutching her Catholic Mass Missal. Life would be her punishment. Her grandparents had died in a sealed container, all those years ago. She'd grown up with such stories, and she couldn't yet find it in herself to imagine what the people in these chambers felt, what they experienced during the last minutes of life.

'He tried to phone me from that ship,' Cecylia said, 'but it wouldn't connect. I didn't answer. He was trapped. He tried to phone me for help – three times he tried.'

'I know, Mama.'

'A handsome young Polish man, ready for life. And we killed him, Gosia. Your brother killed him and so did I.'

'Mama.'

'He wanted me to help him.'

They hadn't yet gone to the police. None of the newspapers mentioned Bozydar. But Gosia knew they would come soon. Anything she said to her mother, any news she gave her, was met with the comment that they'd all forgotten Christ.

That night, Cecylia began removing pictures from the walls and put them into suitcases. The next day, she spoke on the telephone to the priest from St Andrew Bobola and to one of the nuns, mostly talking in Polish and breaking off in tears. For hours she sat with the phone held in her lap. She only went out to the bank and to take her stuff to the charity shops.

Gosia realised she was removing her life from the flat. From London. And then, two days later, she turned to her daughter and told her never to come back.

'Mama—'

'There is no point in you coming here.'

Milo was standing in the hall. Cecylia didn't acknowledge him. 'It was a mistake to come to this country,' she went on.

'You're not yourself.'

'Don't patronise me, Gosia. This place is finished. I have divided your father's money between us.'

Gosia walked into the kitchen with Milo. There was frustration and guilt in her voice. 'This is your home,' she shouted back through to her mother.

Cecylia came to the door of the kitchen. She looked at Gosia and finally acknowledged Milo's presence, standing beside her daughter.

'This was never my home,' she said. 'Go with him. Don't come back.'

Gosia returned later that week, but every time there was less of the flat and less of her mother. Using a spare key, she had gone to Keystone Crescent in search of any sign of her brother. The house was a mess but no one was there. Among the jumble of IDs and papers, she found a few items on the kitchen table that Bozydar must have taken from the house in Kent where Jakub had been living, including a laminated card.

'Here, Mum,' she said later on. 'I knew you'd want to have this.'

The card had the young man's face on it and his name underneath, 'Jakub Padanowski. Temporary Member. Leicester Railwaymen's Club & Institute.'

Cecylia turned it over in her hands, and said that the young man and his brother would now be in heaven. It was cruel, but Gosia couldn't hold back: 'He wasn't his brother,' she said. 'The man was not related to him. He was his lover.'

Something vindictive appeared on her mother's face.

'God have mercy on you for your lies.'

'They were in love. Their friends from Białystok spoke on the news. Jakub was working here to prepare a life for them.'

'You are a liar.'

But Gosia knew her mother's penance would be boundless.

They were never friends, Yuri Bykov and Lord Scullion, yet the politician was kind enough to tip him off. He told him he was a person of interest in the migrant case and a warrant was being issued for his arrest. There might be one day's grace, and he should split. He said this face to face, the two standing beside the old County Hall, buses scudding past on Westminster Bridge and Big Ben shrouded in scaffolding. Tourists were out on the river, floating over the surface of London, seeing what they had come to see, the buildings, the history, while two anonymous men beneath the London Eye lived out the last moments of their concealed history.

Yuri took the Eurostar that afternoon, coasting through Kent with a Vuitton wheelie case up on the rack; kept packed and ready in his rooms at Albany, just in case he had to go on a sudden adventure like this. London was never *le monde*. He fell asleep thinking of heroes who have known life and have no more illusions, and he decided in his half-sleep that he would be, from now on, like the royals who always behave in public as if they are enjoying a glorious privacy, not the half-crown royalties but the future kings. The music tripped in his mind and he imagined a sumptuous painting in place of the train window, a work by Delacroix showing the convulsions of the people.

'*Monsieur, nous sommes arrivés à Paris.*'

'*Merci. Merci.*'

575

He found a taxi easily outside the Gare du Nord and made his way to the George Cinq in under fifteen minutes. The slender boy at the front desk said the Presidential Suite was ready, and offered to summon the manager to greet him, but Yuri said he was tired and had travelled a long way.

He entered the lift with his luggage. He was paranoid and maybe he was conjuring phantoms, but it seemed unmistakeable to him that the woman walking across the lobby towards the exit was one of his father's minders.

In his suite on the third floor, it was all cool whiteness. The sofas were white and so were the roses heaped in Chinese vases. Perhaps his father was here at the hotel, looking to meet with him and propose that they join forces to rebuild trust with Europe; a new plan, something that would reinstate Yuri with Aleksandr's old friends. He went out onto the balcony to survey the city and admire again the rooftops and skyline of Paris. In the spa, he swam ten lengths, thinking all the while about the freeport at Bern, about paintings he had stowed away and investments he had made, the second life that might begin. He dried himself off and returned to his suite in a dressing gown. He went to the pantry, drank a bottle of Evian, got dressed in silk shirt and jeans. Before he left, he chopped out a line of cocaine on the marble table and snorted it.

He began to feel frisky on the way to Les Souffleurs. As the taxi ran past the Quai des Tuileries and then the Louvre, he felt euphoric, different. The bar, with its distinctive coloured lamps, was crowded that night, as it often was. He drank several vodkas and spoke to the leather guys. It was all obscured, somehow. The lights. The warping pace of everything. He saw French hipsters everywhere, people dancing, cocktails being passed around or downed at the bar. Yuri was accustomed to being out of it and feeling lost, but in Les Souffleurs he was underwater – it happened so quickly. People were fading in and out. He went to the men's room and he saw a pink lavatory. His head was swimming and the music thumped. He got the fear when he heard a Russian voice and realised he might have been spiked.

A woman's voice. Stairs. Wet pavements and a sign for a *tabac* and a car door suddenly open and the vehicle moving away. Lying down, he turned at one point and was sure he saw a face he recognised again. There was the noise of a GPS in another language and the car was moving at speed and he saw flashes of light that seemed for a moment like a premiere or a great party in Mayfair. He opened his eyes for a second, more shattering lights, then fell into darkness as they entered a tunnel at the edge of Paris.

# 48 Body Maps

Sitting in the graveyard of St Pancras Old Church, Campbell was smoking a joint made from buds of Amnesia he'd bought on the Dark Net. It was nice stuff, and it placed him apart from himself in ways that felt good but discrediting. He kept each roll-up in the silver cigarette case Elizabeth had presented him for his fortieth birthday. He felt a twinge of pain and regret when he recalled the dinner she gave him at Rules. It felt like another life, when he was happy and easy, certain of himself.

It was a cold day in February. He blew smoke towards the gravestones while looking at the *Commentator* website. Details about the disappearance of Yuri Bykov. The story, inevitably, was by Tara Hastings, and there were sidebars about the 'flamboyant, dangerous playboy', memories of his time at Oxford, the parties, his friendships with celebrities. But the Tara Hastings story had all the meat: his father's controversies, Yuri's attraction to London's underworld, and the allegation, now confirmed, that he was connected to the Essex case and the importation of migrants. Campbell stared at it and was lost in the sprawling web of it all, his mind strung out on this terrible pattern of events.

'Only disconnect,' he said to himself.

He reclined his head and spread his arms over the back of the bench. The trees were excellent and the sky was the colour of bone. The dislodgement in himself that he'd felt since Delhi, the semivisible crack-up so long coming, was now deep. The question in his mind that week was how much further he could fall. He wondered how he'd ever come to know such people – and how much *had* he known them, the likes of William and the Bykovs? He puffed the joint; something would have to give, he knew, emptying his lungs into the trees and feeling a huge sense of loss – the spirit of his life, the self-knowledge – yet enjoying the brief resurgence that can come with the illusions of freedom.

He sat up and put away his phone. Fashion now seemed like a jollification from the very distant past, a time of triviality he could scarcely imagine. He was a different person, but he stood up and tried to prepare himself for the final piece of work he owed the people at Monastic, after which he could search for the Rembrandt book that used to be inside him. He left the churchyard and began walking to Kentish Town.

He thought of all the different names for *Vogue* that he'd collected over the years. Russian *Vogue* – *Rogue*. British *Vogue* – *Brogue*. French *Vogue* – *Frogue*. Today it was plain old American *Vogue*, interviewing Cassie Tom at Spring Studios, talking to her before the photoshoot about her work as the illustrious face of Monastic and her near-thirty-year career as a style leader, a muse to painters and a dog whistle for fashion nutters. 'Please make sure you also get her take on the new scent,' *Vogue*'s chief marketing officer and US influencer Chad Oppen had said to him from New York. He'd also sent a callsheet and the most effusive thanks Campbell had ever had before setting out to write a piece. 'It's a joy to have a real writer on board with this one. I know you'll simply adore the legend that is Cassie Tom. She makes our job worthwhile.' Chad had also supplied the name of the person who would 'wrangle' the model in London and make it all happen, copying in the beauty director and the model's manager, Christine.

'Fucked if I know,' Christine said at Spring Studios, Campbell having arrived and made the mistake of asking if the model was ready. 'I can tell you this: she hasn't left the Dorchester yet and she fired Henry Rasco this morning.'

'She fired Rasco?'

'Yeah, mate,' Christine said. 'He's only the biggest snapper since

Avedon. But Cassie insists the session should be shot by her lunatic squeeze.'

'Her *boyfriend's* doing it?'

'That's what I said. Silvio von Delinquo, or whatever he's called. The Italian stallion. The guy's like Instagram on smack. Rasco had already fixed syndication rights all over the world. Fuck the fucking fuck – like, *to fuck*. If she ever answers her phone and explains what's happening, you'll be the first to know.'

'The boyfriend, wow.'

'Yeah. I've seen more personality in a fucking Photo-Me booth.'

They stood around in the cold warehouse, rails of clothes at the ready, flasks of steaming tea, tables of accessories and a gaggle of assistants staring at their phone screens. Campbell felt pretty high, but the circumstances were making him feel higher, the white light all frosty, the talent invisible as he sat on a battered settee watching the technicians rechecking the lights. The stylist had the look of someone who had spent about three thousand years waiting for narcissistic models. She ironed a stocking with the serenity you'd expect of the Dalai Lama. The model's manager began accidentally copying Campbell in on her emails. 'Little Miss Face-Ache has roped in the posh totty she's fucking to do this *Vogue* shoot. Nightmare! Editor's going ape! But today is the only window we have and fuck the fucking fuck.'

'WHAT!!!!!' replied the marketing person at Monastic.

'Blow me hard!' said the guy at Procter & Gamble. 'Rasco is like the God of Cool and she's a mad cokehead from Cricklewood.'

'True shit. I'm supposed to be her manager. If I had $5 every time the bitch fucked up I'd be richer than Bezos.'

And so they continued: the emails from heaven.

'Has Cassie left the hotel yet? TMZ reports she was out in Mayfair last night with Silvio and got proper hammered at Loulou's.'

'Spoiled brat has glam team standing here holding their collective dick. Shoot date can't be moved. Hair due Brook Street at 4. It's fucking Fashion Week!'

'This is the last time,' the Monastic guy emailed. 'Spaced-out slapper is losing it and everybody's sick of her. Soz, Christine.'

'Don't mind me,' the manager emailed back. 'Say what you like. I'm fucking sick of her too and the Italian Job has finished me off.'

Procter came back. 'Rasco had agreed to syndicate in the five key markets that are crucial for the launch. Stupid fucking people!'

'Bullshit queen and piss poor forever.'

'Puffy as fuck tbh.'

'We could've had Rankin! Mario Sorrenti! Nathaniel Goldberg! Instead we get fucking dickhead wannabe man-child, who can't take shit!'

The emails suddenly stopped. Then, fifteen minutes later, an email just for him, courtesy of Liang from Monastic.

'Dear Professor Flynn!' it said. 'I'm sorry you were copied in on that email chain. People letting off steam at the minute!'

It had now been five hours. Campbell went to the bathroom and finished the joint.

'I'm off,' he said to Cassie Tom's unfaithful manager and the waiting glam team.

'What do you mean?'

'I'll email Chad in New York. It's not happening.'

'But she's here now. Cassie, I mean. She's feeling a bit tender but said she could maybe speak for fifteen minutes after the shoot.'

Campbell mobilised his derision. 'She's out of her tiny fucking mind. You all are. The cosmic joke is you think this crap matters.'

'But you matter,' the manager said. 'You're the *wordsmith*!'

'Oh piss off, darling.'

The manager was at work. 'But we need you.'

'I've got an appointment to meet my son. Get somebody else to interview your deluded fucking client who thinks she's Napoleon.'

The manager stood up. 'She's a pain in the arse, I know.'

Cassie Tom happened then to come out of a side room, looking for an ashtray. She stood in a white bathrobe.

'What's gaa-nn' oan?' she said, like Mick Jagger.

'Hello,' Campbell said. 'I know you're a noted scholar and pedant of the knicker, but I refuse to wait here a second longer.'

'You're facking funny,' the model said.

'It's *way* too late,' the freshly irate manager was saying. 'Mr Flynn, *it's way too late!*'

'It's always too late,' he said, over his shoulder.

He could hear the model laughing as he went down the metal stairs. The whole day had gone.

Angus had flown in from Ibiza. 'It was epic,' he said. 'Totally nuts.' He was speaking to the person at the concierge desk at Claridge's about his winter residency at Ushuaïa. Her cheekbones were insane. He'd once sorted her out with a VIP tab at the club in Sant Jordi, and, like, cars and shit, and he'd introduced her to Calvin Harris, so the girl was totally in debt. He told her he was down to DJ at Coachella and was producing an animated film.

'You *lie*, Angus Flynn!' she said.

'Nah, man. Swear. Keep it peeped.'

Girls like that always got his lingo up. It was normal. Everybody flirted. He looked at his phone. 'Listen,' he said, coming back to her gaze. 'Could you reserve me a table in the new bar through the back? *Dos personas* at six?'

'The Painter's Room. Consider it done.'

An envelope had been handed in for Angus, which she passed to him and he stuck in the pocket of his denim jacket.

He went up to the Mayfair Suite and dropped his bag. He got his laptop out and sat on the bed to sync a few things out of Dropbox. He was DJing during Ashley-Jo's show in the ballroom tonight and wanted to sort out lighting cues. He'd done most of the work on the plane over to London, but there were a few straggly ends.

The envelope had been left by Jake Hart-Davies. He was walking for Ashley-Jo and would be in the ballroom that afternoon for fittings. He said he'd love to meet Angus properly, 'with all that happened'. The message was much longer than it should have been, given the actor was writing to a person he didn't really know. But Angus reckoned that would be the measure of the guy: overfamiliar, keen to take up space. 'I am rehabilitated and finishing a book about empathy called *Leave Home, Love Someone*.'

Half an hour later, the suite's doorbell rang and Angus opened the door to the actor, who looked like he'd gone the entire spiritual wholesomeness route. He sat down on a yellow chair. Angus told him he looked different on TV.

'The best companion in life is your health,' Jake said, 'and I've really gotten into luxury air.'

'You *lie*,' Angus said.

'So true, man. There's smog choking up the earth. Viruses everywhere. So I've joined the revolution in clear oxygen, the spiritual dynamics of breathing properly. I want to make a podcast series called *Catching Your Breath*.'

'Where did you get all this?'

'Luxury air camp. Montana. You spend weeks in log cabins fitted out with deluxe air filtration systems. It's all about circulation.'

'Ventilation.'

'That's right. People have to stop and breathe.'

'So, we're not all breathing the same air, bud?'

'No. That's the task. You must find your own air.'

'Jesus, your skin is bright. I need to get me some of that.' Angus picked up his laptop and sat in the other chair, feet up on the glass table.

'I was at the Global Wellness Summit,' Jake continued. 'I was giving a speech about what I call the "Total Community".'

'What's that, then?'

Jake was studying the middle distance.

'We're all cut from the same fabric. We're all essentially the same person, and we struggle to deal with that.'

'We're not the same if we're breathing different air, dude.'

'Yeah. We're working on it. But, like, a whole chunk of CEOs and surgeons general and shit were there, and it's like you could *end* disease.'

Angus snapped his fingers. He was into it. 'Gone,' he said. 'Like all disease gone forever, man, and to fuck with that shit.'

'Exactly,' Jake said.

Angus picked up the remote. It was weird to feel so informal with a guy you basically wanted to punch, but Angus could do that. He found a list show on MTV about 1980s love songs and fiddled with the sound controls while his visitor brought him up to date with the work he was doing for poverty and decency. Jake said this would definitely be the last modelling gig he ever did – it was a favour to A.J.

'Yeah, man. Me too. The favour to A.J. They sort of went out with my sister, but now they're distant friends or whatever.'

'I don't think I know your sister.'

'Yeah, Kenzie. She's properly into a normal life. Hates parties. Nobody sees her. It's just, like, weaving and—'

'She must be a really angry person.'

That threw Angus. He felt the story was turning.

'I don't think she's angry,' he said. 'Quiet passion, man. Brilliant people are made of that and Kenzie is one of them.'

Jake, it seemed, did a screwface when anything wasn't about him. Angus was noticing: even conversations that weren't about him had to confirm *his* thinking or elevate your view of him. 'The Hackney hipsters are moving on,' Jake said, lifting an onyx dolphin. 'The whole post-Internet techno mood is over, and they want a slice of everyday reality or whatever. A.J. is moving their business to Nottingham. It's all graffiti murals and natural wine.'

'Okay.'

'Something about lace. Something about kitchen-sink drama. A.J. says London is an imperial centre with no working-class people left.'

'Well, that's bullshit,' Angus said. 'They need to get out more. It's amazing to have so many views about reality when you don't live in it.'

'Says the superstar DJ.'

'I live on a magic carpet, mate. I'm not moving to Sherwood Forest.'

'Ashley-Jo's a leader of the future,' Jake said, 'and a lot nicer and a lot more thoughtful than most people who carry that burden.'

It was quiet for a moment or two. The top half of the actor's face was odd: it seemed as if he'd opted for a sort of bandit eyelift, turning him from being a handsome man into being a slightly grotesque impersonation of one.

'Comms break,' Angus said.

They both checked their phones. Jake mentioned something about Angus's father having walked out on a *Vogue* job that afternoon.

'What, in London? Today?'

'Yeah. Text from the Monastic people. They had to bring in a journalist from *GQ* with, like, twenty minutes' notice.'

'Dad's coming here at six.'

'You bringing him to the show?'

'Yeah, if he wants. He might duck out of it.'

Angus wasn't going to say any more than he had to, not to this guy.

'He's always pushing the boundaries, your dad. A strong writer. But sick, I think. I mean, lost in this sickness we have now.'

'What does *that* mean?'

'Very tired and overexposed. He needs better air. Like, he should go to Montana.'

'And you're the advice guy now, yeah?'

'I don't—'

'You don't know my dad, mate.'

'I really like him, but—'

Angus put his glass down. 'No, listen to me. *You don't know him.* You took a little gig off the back of him, and it was meant to be fun, but you had to turn it into the fucking *Ring Cycle*. It was all about you—'

'Hold on—'

Angus looked right at him. The mad bastard had made an error, thinking he could sit there slagging off his dad. 'Your fuck-ups, mate. There's a lot more where they came from, know what I mean?'

'No, I don't know what you mean.'

He wanted to throw him out. He'd had enough of his dumb blue eyes, his intellectual cardigan or whatever. 'Where's your friend? Yuri.'

'I don't know. He's not answering my calls.'

'They're saying he was dragged back to Moscow. Or fucked up proper. He was your friend from college, dude. That's got to hurt.'

'I don't associate with violence.'

'Don't you?'

Angus stood up and turned off the television.

'You're a stupid cunt, man. You lived off Yuri's money. And you prick-teased the fuck out of him and then moved on.'

'That's not right.'

'That's what all your friends say.'

Another one of the actor's things: to look wounded. And to rise so demonstrably from it all, like a heavenly creature, revived and absolved.

'Get out of my fucking room, man. I don't know you.'

Angus was relieved when he'd gone. He knew he wasn't Kenzie and he wasn't his mother – he hadn't their emotional intelligence – but if his dad was a fuck-up, he was a fuck-up with good intentions. He was somebody, but people like Hart-Davies were just passing through and taking what they could. 'The Total Community,' he said to the marble floor as he turned on the shower. 'Twat.'

The Painter's Room was like a public loo designed by Gucci, and Campbell was sitting opposite the pink bar roving through his Ancestry app when Angus arrived. Angus had noticed it before, this little addiction: the powerful sense of a rough-grained background his dad set himself against. 'Glasgow. It's really a thing all that,' he said.

'It's my background as well.' He signalled the waiter and ordered two drinks. 'The old-fashioned they serve in here bangs, Dad.'

'Mmmm. Nutmeg,' his dad said five minutes later, holding it under his nose.

Campbell was looser, a hell of a lot looser than Reykjavík; as if he'd thrown something off, that's how it seemed. He made a joke about the *Vogue* job he'd abandoned.

'Yeah. Cassie Tom's on another level,' Angus said. 'She was probably off her face. You did well to walk out. You've got much better things to do with your time than stand about waiting on that madness.'

'I'm trying to fight my own corner.'

It felt the easiest they'd been with each other in years. Like there was nothing to prove, and into the new space came the need for a bigger statement. Angus realised it and hoped his father would start them off. He tried his best:

'I'm happy for you and Kenzie, it all came good.'

'You don't mean that, Dad. But thanks.'

'Well, I mean it in the way that I mean it. You and Kenzie are happy, and it's a compliment to your mother. She brought you up properly. Never mind about me. I'm still bringing myself up, to tell you the truth.'

'I'm sorry, man – about Iceland.'

'That was me,' Campbell said. He rattled his glass. It had a huge block of ice in it and he made a joke of it. 'Iceland, ice – it all melts,' he said, looking down, 'though this particular monstrosity is currently immovable.'

Angus noticed the way he was drinking. He reckoned he'd had a couple before Angus arrived, then two more as they sat together. 'Are you okay, Dad?'

'Never better,' was all he said.

Angus told him about Jake Hart-Davies. 'I couldn't believe the guy. He was at the Global Wellness Summit, making an absolute tit of himself.'

'Good luck to him.'

Then his dad went off on one – about the bid to kill all disease being a rich person's fantasy, 'far from the problems of everyday life. I've been struggling with ideas of privilege for a very long time. When I deal with paintings, for instance, things come up—'

'Money,' Angus added, guilelessly.

'Yes, son. That too.'

Angus knew better than to offer help, but he saw that his dad's hands were trembling.

'Look. I worry about you, Dad.'

He wasn't sure how that landed. Quickly, the old man had tears in his eyes. 'It's funny being a parent,' he said. 'We never know how much of it is our fault.'

'It's the same when you're the son.'

Campbell nodded. 'That's right,' he said. 'It's the same. Family is like that and . . . believe me, I still think about my parents. I meet my mother in my dreams. She's happy and optimistic, wearing a lovely coat.'

He finished his second or third or fourth drink and sat back in the shell-like armchair.

'I'm not sure I was really qualified for the job,' he said, 'being a parent. Too much grief for me inside the concept.'

'But Kenzie's right,' Angus said. 'You've been good at it.'

'It was always a campaign.'

'It doesn't matter. You and mum did the business. Those amazing holidays we had in Cornwall – us going down the beach with torches at midnight looking for little shards of pottery that would get washed up on the shore.'

'Lovely times.'

It had always been his mode with his father: to wait. But now he wanted to go on the front foot and somehow reach him. 'What do you want from life now, Dad?'

Campbell smiled. He'd come into a clearing in his thoughts. 'Ah.

The distinguished question. Well, it would be nice to be the thing observed, to be like the perfect painting, in other words.'

It was the strangest answer. But it had been a good hour, talking like grown-ups about the things that mattered, torches flashing in the dark.

Once Campbell had left the hotel, Angus went to the ballroom to set himself up and make sure the Wi-Fi was clean. He waved to Ashley-Jo, who immediately came over to kiss him and say thank you. 'I'm nervous,' they said. 'All the press and everything. I really hope the message gets through with the collection.'

'Of course it will,' Angus said.

'I wish Kenzie was here.'

'Me too,' he said, feeling complex about everybody's happiness.

'Still, I've got all my friends. I've got you and Jake and great humans to share this with.'

A tremendous buzz had built up around Ashley-Jo. Angus hoped they would be completed by success. He loved that idea.

'I'd better go backstage,' they said. 'We're still stitching! You plan to bust it open with "Work Bitch", yeah? Britney Spears, then mash it up—'

'It's all under control,' he said.

'Everything's ironic,' they said, skipping away. 'You're the best, Angus.'

Mirrors fringed the runway, under banners for London Fashion Week and Clearpay, the sponsors. The stage designer Es Devlin was telling a carpenter to tilt the mirrors, so that the audience would see itself reflected back during the show. 'It's a mental structure I've created,' she said, 'as well as a physical one, and I want the interplay of desires.' The show was called 'Grey'. It was to be a celebration of 'the colour where each finds the other'.

With two hours to go, Angus went back up to his suite. Maybe it was the whiskies, but he felt nettled when he caught the lingering scent of Hart-Davies there, the scent of fresh air or pure delusion or whatever it was. Angus began thinking about Yuri and all the other people he had known at school. Soon he found himself sitting on the edge of his bed, spooling through the photographs on his phone. He went into 'Years', looking for a set from way back, like five years ago, sent to him by an old buddy who'd known Yuri's crowd later, at university. There was one group shot and four of Jake Hart-Davies on his own. Angus stared at them.

'Beautiful,' he said out loud.

He emailed the pictures to his dad, along with the description his friend had written: 'Halloween 2017, Oxford University Classical Drama Society. Main pic, left to right: Yuri Bykov, Mike Haddington, Zachary Byre, Olivia Buchan-Hepburn, Clara Aberconway, Jake Hart-Davies.'

'All white,' Angus added. 'Except . . .'

He must have fallen asleep on the bed. His phone was buzzing when he woke up and the doorbell was ringing at the same time. When he opened it, a production assistant was standing wide-eyed with a headset and clipboard.

'Sorry to disturb you . . .'

'Shit. Are we ready to go?'

'Yeah, bud. It's showtime.'

'Sorry. I must've fallen asleep. Plane journeys. Em . . .' He frisked himself then went to get his jacket.

'Don't worry, these shows always start late,' the assistant said, as the two of them made their way downstairs to the ballroom.

Fashion Week this year was what they called a digital-physical hybrid, but Ashley-Jo had been so hugely hyped by the press, and by human rights groups online, by the influencers who really had *influence*, that the whole thing felt like the first media carnival of the post-Covid age. The place was full. Fashionistas, celebs. Carl Friis, tapping his heart, blew a kiss to Angus from the front row, and Angus kissed back. He threw a peace sign to a couple of French execs from LVMH, then caught sight of the online gossip king Bo Spencer, new fashion head at Google, who only had eyes for his phone.

Before getting down to work, he looked again at the crowd. Now everybody was staring at their devices, some covering their mouths. He saw the editor of British *Vogue* shaking his head. 'No fucking way.' There was a hum of panic. A stage manager was pulling at Angus's arm and saying, 'Good to go!'

He hit the keyboard on his laptop. The music started and the lights lowered, but it was a sea of phone-glow out there.

Britney's face appeared on a giant video screen.

*'Britney's back. And freedom smells good.'*

She spoke the words against vamping guitars. A beat kicked in, then Britney melted into an image of Solange.

'GREY,' it said in giant letters.

A model appeared in frayed eco-wear, then a second in space-warrior box jacket and velvet ski pants, then another. Angus fired up Twitter on his phone – and there they were, *trending*, those images of Jake Hart-Davies in blackface, released twenty-two minutes ago on the social media feeds of the *Commentator*, the subject wearing a T-shirt saying 'Uncle Jake'. Angus was stunned by his old man's speed and felt a complicated surge of love and connection. He'd given his father a weapon he was happy to use. Then Hart-Davies himself stepped out, his rigid face aware of nothing but itself, the actor striding down the runway and stopping before the mega-flash of the world's press.

# 49 IRL

Antonia Byre was playing with the thought that a sort of forgiveness lies at the core of every wife's heart, and every widow's too. She was sitting in the hair and make-up chair at 7 a.m., a young Mancunian spraying Elnett and being quite boring about his dog. She was in Salford Quays to appear on BBC *Breakfast*. A monitor was set up in the corner of the dressing room. 'Isn't it garish, that red sofa?' Antonia said to her own face in the mirror. 'I never got the point. Who wants to wake up to a loud sofa and a couple of orange faces?'

'Be nice,' the senior publicist said.

The hairdresser was giggling. 'I didn't laugh,' he said.

Antonia was always admired by camp men for being *outrageous*. 'I mean, blood-red sofa,' she said, 'and a bright yellow dress. At the crack of dawn!'

'It's all about respect,' the publicist said, checking his phone. He was anxious that the agreed wording would appear in the introduction.

'R-E-S-P-E-C-T,' the hairdresser mock-sang.

They'd arrived in Salford the night before and stayed at the Holiday Inn. The PR guy said he was old enough to remember when the canal was a canal, when there wasn't a piazza or a Museum of Conflict or a fucking Wagamama on the other side of the water. 'Well,' Antonia said, 'the world has moved on and you'd better move with it.'

When it was time, she was led from the green room, stepping over a nest of cables and walking across the floor to sit on the famous sofa. The presenters looked to Antonia like they'd recently been injected with moral authority. They hardly made eye contact and fiddled with their earpieces while tapping on a pair of laptops. A package called 'The Prince Andrew Problem' was playing out – an unfortunate, no doubt deliberate piece of throat clearing, Antonia assumed – and then she heard the floor manager counting down, leaving the last seconds to dead air. 'Rebecca Stirling reporting for us there,' said the presenter with the surfer's hairdo and the invisible lips. 'Now. Every day, seemingly, we are met with fresh news of sexual abuse in the workplace and accusations of business malpractice. And perhaps too seldom, in the public glare of these allegations, do we ask what effect they can have on the families of the accused.'

The canary-coloured sidekick took over.

'High-street tycoon Sir William Byre was stripped of his title last year after allegations emerged of financial fraud and offences against young women – his company owned over six hundred shops worldwide, as well as the Angelique clothing brand, before they entered administration. Tragically, while on remand at Her Majesty's Prison Belmarsh, William Byre was attacked and killed by a fellow prisoner.'

Antonia admired how she landed that, with a small tilt of the head and a thin smile, as if justice was her forte.

'Mr Byre denied all allegations, and his wife' – she hesitated – 'the newspaper columnist and social justice campaigner Antonia Byre' – she turned to her subject – 'has been picking up the pieces.' The cameras appeared to swoop around. 'Mrs Byre, thank you for joining us this morning, and I have to say straight off this must have been the most dreadful experience for you and your son.'

'Good morning, Penny,' Antonia said, rocking forward. 'Yes. It's a strange country we live in. And these are strange times. For thirty years, I thought my husband was guilty of nothing more than providing twenty-three thousand jobs in this country. We invested in Britain because we believed it to be one of the greatest countries in the world.'

'Yet—'

'My husband was selling leg warmers and, you know, scrunchies in Petticoat Lane when he was fifteen years old. And then it was the shops, the high-street outlets, the factories. Our lives had been about doing business and providing jobs for the people of this country.'

'And then it slips away,' Penny said.

'Yes. Human nature. Male weakness. My late husband lost everything before he lost his life, and our marriage was broken.'

'He had an affair,' Penny said, 'with a twenty-three-year-old woman named Victoria Gowans. She accused him of abuse, and she later died.'

'This is what we came to know,' Antonia said. 'And I have to say, it gives me a feeling of solidarity and fellow feeling with women all over this country, all over the world, who are abused or abandoned or lied to by powerful men. Let's make no bones about it, Penny. I loved my husband. I believed in him and I worked hard alongside him to build a life for our family. And what one is left with, at the end, is a terrible sense of disappointment. All women know that.'

Antonia looked to the camera and stroked an eyelash.

'This must have been terribly difficult for you?' the male presenter said.

'Heart-breaking,' she replied, shaking her head. 'What mother – and I speak as a mother – doesn't understand the loss of a child?'

'This young woman—'

'Yes, poor Vicky Gowans, a sex worker who was abused. It makes you reconsider not only your relationship with such a man, but your whole life. It will take a long time.'

Antonia went on to explain that she was also overcoming a rare immune disorder and starting a new charity for vulnerable children. 'We've learned a lot this past year, as a nation, I think, and as a family.'

'Your son, Zachary—'

'Oh, yes. I'm so proud of him. He's grown up a lot. And he'll soon be heading up a new company, Clean Rivers UK.'

'He's had his troubles too—'

'And haven't we all, truly?' Antonia said. 'The thing is, women know how to balance their lives, as mothers . . . we know how to forgive . . . forgiveness lies at the core of every woman's heart, through good times and bad, and it's a terrible thing in life – your viewers will understand this – when people refuse to move on.'

'And isn't this convenient for you?' said Penny. 'You haven't exactly been keen on women's issues in the past.'

It was the worst moment. Antonia wanted to claw at the woman and rip her ugly fucking dress. 'Actually, I would challenge you on that a little bit, Penny. I've always been in favour – and an example, I hope! – of strong women's voices, and not letting people close you down. I was in an abusive relationship, and my message to other women is simply this: you *can* survive. As I say in the book I'm writing—'

'Yes – the book.'

Antonia didn't flinch. 'A development of MeToo. A personal book. It is called *Disabused: The Essential Guide to Forgiving*.'

When it was over, she left MediaCityUK without waiting to see anyone from the show. The guy from Hanover PR was walking beside her as they made their way to the car. 'That was awesome,' he said. 'Honestly. You hit every note.'

'Seize back the power, even from tragedy,' Antonia said.

Campbell had been seething in Thornhill Square for weeks. Elizabeth was away in Suffolk again, writing her book, all of her other appointments on Zoom, and he smoked a ton of weed and felt fogged and paranoid. Apparently, Jake Hart-Davies had been cancelled good and proper for the blackface thing and wasn't coming back this time. For a moment, it was delicious – the quick and easy forwarding of those pictures to the *Commentator*. But it alloyed instantly with a guilt and shame that hung around and grew. He avoided calls from his son, as if he'd soured their last evening. He avoided the tax letters and summonses, all stuffed into the drawers of his desk. And he avoided his sister's calls after her last voice-mail: the mother of William's dead girlfriend had seen Antonia on BBC *Breakfast* and was sickened by it. 'Mrs Gowans said she went on national television and told barefaced lies about her daughter,' Moira had said. As if it was *his* fault. Late that night, he remembered a quote from Sallust that he and William used to bandy about in the Falstaff Club at Cambridge: '*Alieni appetens, sui profusus.* Greedy for what you don't have, extravagant with what you do.'

He texted the quote to Antonia then blocked her.

He didn't bother to text Milo any more.

Maybe my wife has left me, Campbell said to himself. He was in her study and looking down at the winter bareness of the ginkgo tree. It was two in the morning. He phoned her, speaking before she could say a word: 'I have volumes to write. And I want to travel abroad with you again, seeing lakes and gardens.'

'Stop smoking that stuff. I can smell it from here.'

'I'm working hard,' he said. 'I'm discovering things.'

'Go to bed, darling. Please.'

The next morning there was a note on the mat from Mrs Voyles. She addressed him as 'Slum Landlord' and reiterated the same mad demand: she wanted five hundred grand to give up her flat – and now there was a freshly deranged angle, 'or I shall expose you for what you are'. That afternoon, he heard her wrapping the chain around her gate. He waited until she was out of sight, then took a pair of ancient bolt cutters from the shed and broke the chain into pieces, dumping them in the bushes.

Later, he walked all the way into town to do a *Prospect* podcast. The office was somewhere down by St James's Park. The presenter, who greeted him at reception, was around forty and wore All Star trainers, skinny jeans and a plaid shirt. His hair seemed carefully disarranged and he had views on everything, especially the views of others. He told Campbell on the way to the recording studio that he was much more of a 'liquid presence' than the presenter had expected, less of an

Establishment figure, and though he shrugged it off, Campbell was fooled into being delighted.

'Everyday politics is defensive these days,' he said when they began recording, 'and often not the brave activism it pretends to be. If you meet a young person who is pursuing real action, rather than merely segregating people and policing vocabulary, it's a golden opportunity. They exist. I've met one! But using the world's problems to define yourself without really engaging in change is a form of narcissism.'

The presenter was strategically sweet. He said he loved the image of the struggling intellectual in a time of radical conformists. Campbell ignored him. 'But the worst, I suppose, are the furious white dudes with their laptops,' he said. 'He wants approval. Forgiveness. Victory. Protection. He wants all the comforts the universe has to offer and he wants better Wi-Fi. The worst of them, these men and women who stormed the Capitol, they want their madness to be *respected*, and, if it isn't, they want the Apocalypse to follow very quickly. Technology has destroyed all sense of reason.'

In a moment's dead air, the host chipped in, tensing. 'Speaking of reality,' he said, 'or reality TV, at least. The widow of a close personal friend of yours, William Byre, was on the BBC last week asking for the things you mentioned – forgiveness and victory.'

'I'd rather not talk about them.'

There was a glint in the podcaster's eye. 'But Byre's alleged offences go back years. Surely, you must have suspected him?'

'I had no clue that I knew such people.'

'Really? That wasn't your circle?'

Campbell stared into the microphone like it was a place of rest. 'Just because you live your life doesn't mean you understand it,' he said.

The presenter leaned in and began reading from a sheet tilted in front of him. 'I mean, it might sound basic, Campbell Flynn, but have you ever in any meaningful sense been an activist or a person on the

Left? Or was your soft socialism something like a lifestyle choice and an attempt to stay in touch with your roots?'

Campbell felt he had come full circle. The guy was using the arguments of Campbell's *Atlantic* essay against him.

'I'm flattered you know me so well,' he said, and his interrogator blushed, folding his sheet of questions.

'So, what are you writing now?'

'There's Rembrandt,' Campbell said. 'And a new book of essays about art and politics. I'm thinking of calling it *The Past Is Dead Forever.*'

'Cool,' the young man said. 'You've got it covered.'

In the minicab home he felt exhausted. He recalled something his father had once said to him when Campbell was barely out of school. 'Most people go through their whole lives and they never alter a single thing.'

'What are they supposed to do, Da?'

'They're supposed to live up to their potential,' the old man said, 'and leave the planet a tiny bit better than they found it.'

As they drove up Theobalds Road, Campbell felt the full force of all the pressures and criticism, the shame and the loss, all of it recombined just then. He caught sight of a ring of snowdrops around a roadside tree, and the feeling redoubled. Not for the first time that week, he put his face into his hands and cried.

She was gazing down at a canal boat and wishing she could float away and not have to talk to people any more. Rupert had been hanging around the news desks and she could tell he was on the brink of coming over. He'd been offered an associate editor job at the *Daily Mail* on the back of her well-sourced reporting.

'Morning, Tara,' he said, sitting his coffee mug on her desk. '*Ver tempore*. Springtime. And we've gone viral again. It was right to rush the Hart-Davies story.'

'Yes,' she said. 'It's always good to obliterate a person's career in as punctual a fashion as possible, don't you feel?'

He parked himself on the edge of her desk.

'Don't give me that.'

'I do my job, Rupert. I don't always love it. I knew Jake when he was a young, pretty, idealistic person.'

'When he was painting his face black and casting aspersions on slaves? I'm sure he was a very wholesome youth, darling.'

'He was stupid, like we're all stupid sometimes.'

She had a bit of residual whatever for Rupert, despite his way of talking and his ridiculous tie. There was a time when she felt she could share something of herself with him. 'It was Oxford, you know . . .'

'Come on, Tars. It's not *Brideshead Revisited*. The guy was bang out of order, not for the first time, either. He had his chances. He's a dangerous hypocrite and you provided a public service by getting the story out there.'

'*Everyone's* a contact,' she said.

They had differing attitudes to scoops. Rupert liked to tot them up; Tara felt she was a little less decent after each one. He stared right at her. 'You don't feel sorry for these bastards, do you?'

'I do a bit, yes. They weren't always that way.'

'Look,' he said. 'It's there in the Romans. Cicero, Tacitus. No sooner is a man civilised than he opens up to corruption. No sooner is he rich than he wants power; no sooner distinguished, than he wants slaves. It's a story as old as time, but with new approaches and new kinks in the tapestry.'

'New ways of being human. And inhuman.'

'Anyway,' he said, pressing on. 'You'll have the *Press Gazette* award in the bag for this year, and I'm proud of you.'

'Thanks, daddy-kins.'

'Six major splashes. And pretty much bang-on for accuracy, so far as the world can tell.'

'*Pretty much?*'

'Not a hundred per cent on the Kendal thing. He's coming up with a pretty ruddy defence. We have the lawyers' letters to prove it.'

'Rupert,' she said, 'he's one of the most clearly guilty since we started. But you know what – he's safe because he's safe.'

'Meaning?'

'He has the Firm behind him. Family connections. He has the money and the gall. He has the lawyers. People like that can shape reality. He *believes* it. He thinks he's above it. He already has you frightened. And that's how it works.'

'Well—'

'It's always about class. It's other people who go to prison.'

He took a slurp of his coffee. Bored. *Next.*

'And on the migrants story, the Chinese link.'

'It's huge,' she said. 'The drivers are facing forty-one counts of manslaughter each. Just Irish boys who used to smuggle vodka.'

'And this weirdo lynchpin guy?'

'I filed the story two minutes ago. His real name was Peter Fong. That old acupuncture place that burned down in Gray's Inn Road? His remains were found there.'

'Seriously?'

'I have police confirmation.'

'One day you'll be the best in the business, Tara. Come with me when I go. I'll double your salary and give you your own office in Kensington.'

'Not on your life, laughing boy.'

He didn't hear her. He was tapping a pencil on his nice teeth. 'I'm serious. Ukraine has transformed everything.'

She looked at him with disbelief.

'So you need mass graves before you believe it? You need refugees at the railway stations? These Russian gangsters have been at it for years.'

'They're not all like that.'

'Of course not.'

She was packing up her things. 'You know the Russians paid for Brexit, right? It was their money that made the Tories believe London was invincible.'

'That's too much, Tara.'

'Just think about it,' she said.

She switched off her desk lamp and closed her laptop, sliding it into a tote bag with her posh notebooks and her phone.

'It's always about complicity,' she added.

Going down the escalator, she felt she needed to clear her mind. She crossed the road and wandered for a bit, finding that the fountains in Granary Square had been turned back on to mark the end of winter. She sat down with a coffee at a table for two, watching the students pass by and looking up at Gasholder Park.

# 50 The Listeners

Milo got a mid-morning train from King's Cross on 1 March to see Travis. He was behind the door in Cambridgeshire, two months into a fifteen-year sentence, and the conversation on the phone was all about an upcoming appeal, a transfer from Whitemoor, items he wanted on his canteen list and the revival of Ghost 24. Travis was telling himself he was going to beat this whole thing, that he never did anything to hurt the kid in Deptford. 'I never harmed nobody in my life. That's the truth.'

Milo didn't have the guts to tell him he was dreaming.

England was green. He looked across the table at Gosia, knowing they would soon go and that today was a goodbye.

'A text from Mum,' Gosia said. 'She says it's windy today.'

The train rushed through the sunlight.

'She doing her church thing over there?'

'Every day. Every single day.'

She put away her phone and looked out, as if stories and remedies were being blown about in the world.

'I hate to say it, but I think Jakub was a bit freaked by my mother,' she said. 'Life can be so cruel. He was probably just a totally ordinary guy, but he was forced to act all perfect because that's what she wanted him to be.'

'She wanted a saint and she got one.'

'Catholicism,' she said, 'all that denial and guilt.'

'Sitting in Poland with that.'

'Poor Mama. But she'll be able to live with it all. She needs her agony.'

'Triple sad.'

At the prison, there was a bench by the car park, and Gosia insisted she would be happy sitting there with her book. She didn't want to go in. She felt awkward because of her brother and everything.

'You sure you'll be okay?'

'Take your time,' she said.

Ecological restoration, he thought. It was one of the phrases Gosia had used the first time they met and now it felt like a plan.

The visitors' room smelled of new carpets. It was filled with tri-angular tables with blue plastic seats, and Milo sat waiting. Travis came in with his rolling walk, his attitude intact, wearing a grey sweatshirt, joggers and plain white trainers. There was a new hard aspect about him and he wore plastic rosary beads around his neck. 'Hey, broski.' They bumped shoulders and touched fists above and below. With a grin on his face, Travis produced a Snickers bar from his other hand and gave it to Milo.

'Old times,' he said. 'I kept it for you, man.'

Milo sat looking at the brown wrapper and he smiled up. Travis said one of the older officers had told him it used to be called a Marathon.

'Yeah,' Milo said. 'I saw it on a programme. They changed the name.'

Travis nodded. 'Life's a marathon, not a sprint.'

Milo pocketed it and held the edge of the table. He didn't know where to start with Travis, or how to end.

'I'm busy in here,' his friend said. 'They got me down for a computer refurbishment thing, in C wing.'

'Is that, like, work?'

'Yeah. For IT schools, Africa or whatever. You're locked up from 6 p.m. every day and all you got in there is some tiny TV with, like, hardly any channels, and a guy's praying flat out on a mat, you get me?'

'Your cellmate?'

'Yeah, yeah, yeah. Shifa – he's cool, though, know what I mean? From Birmingham. His name means "cure".'

They fell silent for a moment. Travis was blinking his right eye, something he always did as a kid when he was nervous. He told Milo about the start, going into the cell, the induction. 'That night was mad. I mean, next level, bruv.' He said he was sitting in his cell and all he could hear was inmates shouting names. The prison officers let you have one phone call, but Travis didn't have any numbers. They were all in his phone and his phone was locked away somewhere. He couldn't have called Lloyds anyhow; he was in another prison.

'I ain't seen him,' Milo said.

'Nah, man. Swear down. No more moves for Jeremiah. Not for years. I hope he gets to see his nature programmes, though. Boy loves them.'

He was rasping, talking fast. Milo wished he was less hopped up. They had hard things to talk about and he wanted him calm.

'Have you spoken to your mum, Travis?'

The boy blinked and his eyes reddened. 'My mum's an addict, Milo. I don't think she even knows where I'm at.'

Travis told him more about that first night, admitted he'd asked for the Listener. He couldn't sleep and he didn't know what was gonna happen. 'So they have these people, the Listeners; they're like the Samaritans or whatever, and you can talk to them. There's at least five hundred guys in here and you don't know what's going on.'

'I bet.'

'A few of them, they say I should try to appeal.'

'You got the solicitor, right?'

'Yeah. But I *was* there, Milo. Carrying a shank. They killed Sluggz and I was there. In those Jordans, you know what I mean?'

The words hit Milo but he didn't respond.

Travis sucked his teeth and seemed to sink with it. 'They say if you aid or abet or counsel or procure the crime then you are guilty.'

'But you didn't plan to hurt him.'

'Maybe it's all part of the big man's plan.' He pointed to the ceiling then touched his chest and Milo saw there was a pain there that had been obscured by their friendship. They leaned into each other and let the silence breed. Milo fantasised for a second that he might breathe in his friend's spirit and take it out of there, take it to a new life and leave the old body to do the time.

Travis was lost to him and all that life was lost to him, and he could see the poor guy reading it in his eyes.

'It's all good, cuz,' Travis said. 'All good.'

Milo saw marks on his wrist, ink stains and blood scratches, like he'd torn at himself with a ballpoint pen.

'We'll try to get you out,' Milo said.

'Nah, bro. Can't happen. Man pays for what he does and what he doesn't do.'

More silence.

'How's your beautiful gyal?'

'I love her, man. We're going to start a new thing.'

Travis nodded and his smile grew. 'Like Zemi said. Like Auntie always said.'

'Back to the start, Travis. I'll write to you.'

He kissed Milo on the forehead, then kissed the cross around his neck.

'You go, brother. You got to flip the script.'

Milo felt the grief of the last eighteen months was breaking over him and holding him still.

'You can do that too, Travis,' he said desperately. 'Like, in the future.'

'Nah, man. I don't think so. I'd love to have been a sports teacher, though. Teaching football and that to young kids. Like Mr Panday.'

Milo leaned in again and embraced him. The officers craned at the door in case he was passing dope. He sat back, defeated. He could feel the warmth on his chest, the warmth of summers past, and the terrible gap.

Gosia read her book all the way back to London. It was about the islands. She propped it on her stomach, looking up a few times. With her eyes she commiserated with Milo about all the things that were impossible to say. She watched him go to the space between the carriages and put something in the litter bin there, but she didn't ask him what it was. 'Listen to this,' she read, when he sat back down. '"Every day we would see something new and wonderful. I remember a flock of about two thousand kittiwakes closely massed on the skerry of Lisgeir Mòr at the north end of Fianuis. They were a pretty enough sight like that, but when all of them suddenly took to the air and of necessity fanned out to give themselves flying room, it was a vision prodigal in its loveliness. It was a gigantic unfolding of resting life into brilliant animation."'

Milo smiled and shook his head. 'Mum used to say it was the genuine task in anybody's life, to find your country.'

'I can see her pencil markings in the book,' Gosia said.

'It's the thing she always talked about. She dreamed of it, her Highlands again, after her own long journey. But I never knew, really, if she meant *home* – like Ethiopia – or *there*,' he said, pointing to the book.

'Maybe she meant both, the old place and the new place,' Gosia said. 'She dreamed of a road that carried the old road with it, right back to the start.'

Her face was lit up when she said that, and Milo nodded.

'Like Caledonian Road,' he said.

They settled back to look at yellow fields. Milo checked the news on his phone and saw that Jake Hart-Davies's upcoming book on empathy had been cancelled. 'He came back the first time,' the entertainment columnist wrote, 'but now he'll be lucky to get a job bagging popcorn at the Sunniside Empire in Sunderland.'

Gosia put her earbuds in. Approaching King's Cross, she passed an ear to Milo. 'Listen to this.' A woman spoke. 'I don't know what it's going to take to make the world right. I do know that you should not be sitting waiting for it to happen, for somebody else to do it.'

'What's this?'

'She's called Joanne Bland from Selma, Alabama. She does historic tours.'

'She's right,' Milo said. 'And when things go wrong, they're your own mistakes. And maybe that's what freedom means.'

'Not the police. Not the banks.'

'And not the Duke of Kendal,' he said, smiling at her.

He gave her back the earbud and she looked at him, shaking her head. 'What an amazing year,' she said. 'Everything.'

Milo gave one of his shrugs, as if 'amazing' was a suburb of normality and he and Gosia had merely been witnesses.

'These criminals will go on, but every year there will be fewer, because people are beginning to *see them*, you get me?'

'And that was the project?'

'Nah,' he said. 'Man was just missing his mum.'

The middle classes collect items in order to be themselves, but if all your furniture and pictures are inherited, you have to do it with people, collecting and placing them exactly so, which is rather a rum job. This fact occurred to the Duke of Kendal as he stood in his hallway in Holland Park that week. He had never liked the place, it had too few staff and too many mirrors, and he believed he and Candy had felt a touch miserable there, which they never had in Suffolk, or he at Albany. Candy was still in Tibet with a delegation from the farm. She wanted 'a breather', she'd said. She was staying longer than the Duke would have wished. Nighty was a silly goose but not a bolter, he said to himself, and when she returned they would make a few improvements.

'Ready, Your Grace?'

'Give me a moment,' he said. He had a headache. The pain had been there since the day before, pulsing with his thoughts, a military tattoo of grievances.

The gentleman standing next to him was Mr Skene, the lawyer, examining a sheet of paper. 'Your shoes are alarmingly well polished, Skene,' the Duke said, trying in this moment of crisis to be bluff.

'Never knowingly underdressed, sir.' The lawyer pulled out a watch on a chain, as if to emphasise the point. 'We have a few more minutes.'

Around them buzzed a host of PR people. Over-caffeinated fools, each of them, the Duke said to himself, and then to Skene. 'In general, one must give oneself up to the idea that they are protecting one in a time of need.'

'Quite so,' Skene said, with emphasis.

'A time of great stupidity,' the Duke continued, 'when the world requires reassurance once the wrong impression has been given.'

'Indeed.'

The Duke couldn't see the quote marks any more. It was all him; he sounded innocent, he sounded plausible, and he believed it.

Mr Skene went over the main points again and said everything was 'secure'. That was the word he used, a word no other person would understand. The Duke gave a quick nod, feeling the kaleidoscope of dangers he had faced was now resolved in the grey of business. No mention was made of the millions to be handed over, and neither he nor his trusted lawyer speculated for even a second about what organisation, or what group of individuals, or what person, the money would go to. Skene's rigid mouth did all that was required, cementing the Duke's deniability.

A man whose name he could never remember, a partner at Prestons PR, came up and more or less bowed. 'The tone today, sir, is sombre and judicious, regretful but not in a personal way.'

'Thank you,' the Duke said dismissively.

'You are most welcome, Your Grace.'

The Duke turned to Skene. '"Regretful, but not in a personal way". That's about £10,000 a word, wouldn't you say, old boy?'

Paul Scullion appeared from the drawing room, wearing a suit that was too narrow in the leg and too bulked at the shoulder. He wore heavy shoes, and yet, even here, on the marble floor, he made no sound, much like the nimble bird that lands on snow without leaving a mark. Over breakfast earlier, Scullion had informed the Duke that Aleksandr Bykov was back in the Kremlin. The Ukraine business had overtaken everything and their own association with the Bykovs was small data, to be deleted. 'Our friends will trouble us no more.'

'One never thought of them as *friends*,' the Duke said.

He stood on the carpet before the front door. Turning once, he looked in the mirror, examined his tie and fixed his pocket handkerchief. He felt he must have a temperature and his lips were dry. He could hear the noise outside. In that moment, his mind departed for the coast, to Hove, where he used to lunch with the veterans. One is required to show guts against a cold front and a bashing sea. The man from Prestons opened the door and the Duke saw a throng of photographers all the way back to the gate, framed between the white pillars and overhung by branches of cherry blossom. He jutted his chin and stepped forward. The mob had never encountered such a gentleman.

'Good morning,' he said. 'I'd like to make a short statement.'

A number of them stood on ladders.

'The last several months have proved to be an ordeal for myself and more importantly for the people who work alongside me, and, especially, my family. In a single day last November, whilst serving at a charity event, I found myself under attack on two separate fronts, each of them ludicrous, and framed so as to present me in the worst possible light. The details are well known, and detestable. I have never espoused the views given to me in that video, and, as a former lieutenant colonel in the British Army, I find them repugnant. The videos, we believe, were made by individuals on the Internet engaged in what is called "deepfake" recordings, where previous images and broadcasts are edited together to tell a lie. The people behind this smear, who have never been identified, did it for reasons of extortion, and we have refused to pay them. The video may look like me, and sound like me, but it is most certainly not me. We have been the subject of a hoax, which has upset my family hugely. At the same time, we have been subject to false allegations as to my financial dealings. For charitable purposes, our foundations have, from time to time, accepted donations or investments from legitimate companies with representatives in the United Kingdom. In good faith, we allowed contributions towards the maintaining of national buildings, the purchasing of artworks or the development of important historic sites. Let me be clear, there was no quid pro quo involved, there were no favours done, there was no influence being bought. We support wholeheartedly sanctions against Russian criminals and call for a new inquiry into dirty cash, and we join the Foreign Affairs Select Committee in denouncing the past influence of these men on UK markets. We decry the recent movements of Russian troops against the people of Ukraine. Again, as a former serving officer of the British Armed Forces, I find it absurd that anyone could imagine my interests lie anywhere but with Britain's.'

He folded the piece of paper and waved his hand.

'I will defend my family against all fake news and all false allegations wherever they appear,' he said. 'And where possible, we will be taking legal action against individuals and organisations who promote this nonsense. Not everyone in England can defend themselves against this . . . this bile. But we will.'

There was a battery of questions but he ignored them all. He saw the bigger picture. He still believed the truth of what he'd read when he was in the army: the issue of individual personality is a hindrance, and one must take one's place in the established order.

'Also, today we are announcing a fresh direction for our various charitable and business enterprises. The Segdoune Foundation, as it is now called, will seek to expand its work in medical research and the arts, under our new chairman, Lord Scullion of Wrayton. We look forward to protecting Britain and promoting global innovation.'

The onslaught was so loud that the questions were barely distinguishable.

'Do you know the whereabouts—?'

'... ever wear a Nazi uniform?'

Mr Skene touched his arm and said there would be no further questions. The Duke felt a definite scratch in his throat and he coughed to clear it.

'Thank you. You've been very kind,' he said, and as he turned he heard the familiar voice of a man from *Newsnight*. 'Sir, we have evidence of Tory reliance on Russian money. Were you not part of that network . . . ?'

When he turned back to the open door, Anthony Crofts, the 10th Duke of Kendal, also Lord Crofts, the Earl of Sundrum, Baron Eye and Viscount Fitzroy of Kiltarlity, noticed the hall was dark and empty of people, yet somewhere in the distance he could see an illuminated ship in a squall of gale-force winds and rain. He could taste salt on his lips and feel the numb cold and perceive the enfolding dark as they fought their way back.

# 51 Needlepoint

It was a close, still spring evening, near midnight, when Mrs Voyles dumped two bags of rubbish on the doorstep at number 68 and pressed the bell. 'You people live like pigs,' she shouted in Campbell's face when he opened the door.

'What are you on about?'

She kicked the black bags. 'You have vermin hanging round. And then you try to stuff your rotten bags into my wheelie bin.'

He leaned right into her face. His head was all over the place. 'There's something really wrong with you, isn't there? There's something missing in your fucking brain.'

'Ah, now we see it. The Glaswegian. Good at shouting at women, are we?'

'Get away from my house.'

She didn't budge. 'Smells of drink and keeps a slum.'

She took her time over every syllable. He started to feel nauseous.

'I'm telling you. Get the fuck away from my house.'

'But it's not yours, is it, Professor Flynn? Not really. Because you haven't done the right thing and bought me out.'

'And I never will, do you hear me?'

She was staring at him but her hand was trembling. He realised he'd scared her. The power thrilled him, but some vestige of his better nature intervened. He suddenly wanted to change tack and reverse all this, ask her about her dancing career, her friends, her years in the area. But he realised it was impossible.

'And you so fair. Took the chain off my gate. Turned off my gas. Showing everybody how right you are, in the *Guardian* and all that.'

'Get off my doorstep. Please.'

'I've seen your sort before.'

He straightened up and put a single finger on her forehead. Cruel thoughts again unloosed as he pushed her away. The last thing he saw before closing the door was the red mark he'd left on her forehead and her shocked eyes. The square was empty. It was dark. He'd never in his life felt so solitary.

He took two Xanax, but didn't sleep. He drank four brandies, but all the lights in the street, the glow on the digital clock, the lit phone, every midnight reflection had gathered into a single, meaningful beat that filled his mind as he lay there.

He took another Xanax in the morning and brushed his teeth to Radio 4.

The *Today* programme was part of Campbell's dream life. People came on and played their parts like actors in a Jacobean drama. He felt he knew all the roles. 'In yesterday's Cabinet reshuffle,' he heard, 'Lord Haxby was appointed Secretary of State for the British Union. In this newly created post, the Conservative peer will lead the effort to make a success of Britain's exit from the EU, while at the same time "renewing the bonds" between the four territories of the United Kingdom. "In other words," *The Times*'s leader has it this morning, "the well-connected Northern Tory is now Minister for Breaking EU Protocols and Ensuring that Ireland Doesn't Unite and Scotland Doesn't Become Independent."'

'Who are these people?' Campbell said to the mirror.

'Lord Haxby joins us now . . .'

He turned off the radio. He tried to think about who he was, about who he had been, and all he could see was a blank page. He used to think he had values, but all of that had vanished now. High-minded values are merely low-minded prejudices dressed in the robes of office, and Campbell, the lively critic, the boy who'd read Lionel Trilling under the bedclothes with a torch, had lost the ground he had once hoped to make level, and was falling inwards as he climbed back up the stairs. This time last year, he'd wanted a fresh start, financial release, approval from the young – everything at once – but all he'd gained was a powerful sense that he was totally stranded in the middle of his own life. 'The liberal imagination,' he muttered, pausing on the third landing, 'what was that anyway?'

Smoking a joint in his study and looking at his computer, Campbell checked his Bitcoin. It had fallen sharply again. He began digging into the Dark Net, ordering more weed and sinking deep into his anxiety. He frittered away the morning following the pathways and reading the mad manifestos that perfumed the marketplace, shaking his head at the visions of power these people were selling and finding them, just fleetingly, sane. He reminded himself to pick up from his PO box in Barnby Street. New pills, fake notes. He went down to the kitchen and poured himself a large single malt with two ice cubes. At lunchtime, he was fully high and had a formal, closed feeling about himself.

Stepping out to go to the PO box, he saw that the word 'SLUM' had been painted on the pavement in thick black paint, or possibly tar. He stared at the letters, and Mrs Voyles's open gate. He covered his face with his hands when he saw the paintbrush lying against the railings. Something beyond rage took over. The morning's researches on the Internet coalesced suddenly into a pulsating theory that modern life is like a war on decent human effort, and that impositions – parking tickets, being held in a queue, thought-policing, sitting tenants – were conceived to drive you out of your mind. Striving for reason, he replayed an argument he'd had with Elizabeth on the phone a few days before, when she'd said she intended to come back to London to visit a 'wonderful' show of Louise Bourgeois at the Hayward called *The Woven Child*.

'For Christ's sake, Liz,' he said. 'Isn't Dürer still on at the National Gallery? Whistler at the Royal Academy?'

She paused, like she was working something out.

'You know what, darling? You're miserable and you won't deal with it, and you're turning our home into a psychic war zone.'

'Not me and you?' he'd said, feeling hurt. 'We're good.'

'No. You *and you*. You and your causes, you and the woman downstairs, you and William Byre, you and your parents. You and our son, you and . . . these bizarre *projects*. For the love of God, Campbell . . .'

The pause was loud. Elizabeth complained about his behaviour, his strangeness, and worst of all, his self-pity.

'I don't know what you mean,' he said. 'I'm dealing with a few important issues.'

'It's like living with someone with moral dementia!' she shouted. 'You have *no idea* what you sound like. You can't remember yourself. Everything you say is something in your own defence. What the fuck is wrong?'

'I'm sorry,' he said.

He'd been standing at the kitchen window during that exchange, swayed by the garden mood and the perfect sky, its Magritte clouds. Flakes were falling from the trees. An unseasonal drift. Reality dissolving.

'I've asked you before,' she'd said. 'Let's be totally straight. Are you worried about money?'

'I don't care about anything—'

'It all started when you sat down to write that silly book. Well, I don't know about "started". It probably started fifty-three years ago. But this last while—'

'I'm sorry.'

'Stop saying sorry. I'm not interested in apologies. I love our house, our life, but I can't work in London at the moment. You're not . . .'

'It's been a bad time for my health, Liz. I've been feeling—'

'You're smoking pot. You're drinking. Is that good for your health?'

He liked the tree snow. The unusualness.

'She was so lonely, my mother. So angry.'

'Jesus.'

Looking back at his house, he hated it. 'This fucking place,' he said to its white, painted bricks, its many windows. Putting a hand in his jacket pocket, he felt a foil of tramadol he'd stored there – pills from one of his secret vendors. He took two and would soon chase them with as much whisky as he could find. He felt he was wandering out towards an afternoon, an evening, a night and a dawn of absolution, a place of oblivious peace, where downstairs neighbours and lost values, money troubles and dead friends simply don't exist. What he craved was stillness, the uninterruptable serenity of a small room with a blessing of natural light, but he couldn't have that, so he ploughed into Caledonian Road and the coming dark.

It was always a topic for Elizabeth: the many ways to get there. Sometimes she drove via Royston and took the Thetford Road, twirling onto the motorway and gunning for the London imperative, and at other times, like this particular morning, she drove with a sense of country ease through all the villages, Wortham, Wattisfield, Hepworth and Stanton, watching the sun come up over the flat fields, before she joined the caravan of drivers on the M11 as they headed towards the Shard. It was true she'd got used to Zoom sessions in Suffolk and long days of writing and walking. Her idea of an exciting evening was a spontaneous trip to Dunwich for fish and chips, or a glass of wine at Walberswick.

Campbell wasn't a frequent phoner, but he would usually leave drops of information about himself throughout her day. He lived like a single man in many respects. But he still wasn't answering and it had been two days. Kenzie hadn't heard from him, either. As Elizabeth threaded her way through Walthamstow and up Seven Sisters Road, she tried his number again. No answer. It was around 9 a.m. when she arrived in Thornhill Square and saw the yellow ambulance, all the dread of her adult life collecting in her stomach at once.

'What happened?' she said, running from the car.

'It's not pretty.'

'Tell me!'

'Very violent attack, I'm afraid. Really roughed up.'

The paramedic was speaking into his phone. 'Elderly female. I'd say seventy years old.' He raised his index finger at Elizabeth, asking to be given a minute. 'Major concussion,' she heard him say. He half turned, as if trying to be discreet with the next detail, but Elizabeth heard him say that the victim's ear was badly torn. 'Yeah, entirely severed, I reckon.'

'Oh my God.'

She saw a man in a pale grey suit standing on the pavement, talking to a police officer. He was Mrs Voyles's friend, the estate agent.

'That's her neighbour . . . the owners, Mrs Flynn,' he said, pointing. 'They took the chain off her gate. Mrs V. warned them she was vulnerable to intruders.' Elizabeth was struggling to understand. A second policeman came up to her and asked who she was and if she lived in the main house.

'Yes. I'm Elizabeth Flynn. We're the landlords, I suppose you'd say. Has something happened to Mrs Voyles?'

'Please remain calm, madam,' the officer said.

'Where's my husband?'

'Have you been out, madam?'

'Yes, I've come from our house in Suffolk. Can someone please tell me what is happening here?'

'And is your husband not with you?'

'No, no – he must be inside the house.'

'We're getting no answer, madam.'

At that moment, two paramedics came up from the basement flat carrying a wheelchair with Mrs Voyles sitting in it, wearing an oxygen mask, her eyes slowly opening and closing. There was a heavy bandage around her head and it was already soaked with blood. 'Very basic down there,' one of the paramedics said to the policeman as they passed.

Mrs Voyles. An intruder.

Elizabeth had to suspend her worries about Campbell.

The officers asked her a few basic questions and she tried to answer them. It turned out she knew nothing about their tenant. She didn't know if she had any family. The policeman began to ask about their relationship, but Elizabeth said she was anxious to find her husband. He said he and another officer would return later and take statements. 'That would be fine. Poor Mrs Voyles, how frightful.'

She took out her keys.

In the hallway, she shouted his name. She could hear music upstairs and followed it. On the first landing, she found a catalogue for the Louise Bourgeois exhibition at the Hayward. She picked it up, the page showing an embroidered spiderweb. 'Campbell?' There was a burning smell and when she looked into the sitting room she saw the remnants of a fire in the grate. She bent down and saw among the ashes a part of what she knew was the cover of Campbell's *Vermeer*. She shouted his name again and hurried up the second flight of stairs.

In the bathroom, a bright red radio was playing Jazz FM and a whisky bottle stood on the closed loo seat. And then she found Campbell in his study, lying on the sofa and facing the wall, one arm hanging down. Her eyes took it in rapidly, the graffito in black marker on the wall above his head – 'Please don't abandon me.' A full glass of whisky on the carpet beside an ashtray filled with stubs. The fumes were overpowering. She gently pulled his head round and gave in to panic at the sight of his face.

'Campbell!'

He opened his eyes. They were pink and scandalised. He was unshaven.

'What are you doing?' she said.

He seemed in shock. He tried to stand up, staggered. 'I've got so much work to do. So many things on my desk.'

'For God's sake – what's going on, Campbell?'

The police returned two hours later. Campbell was wearing a clean
shirt and a cravat under a brown cardigan. He was showered and
shaved, but to Elizabeth he resembled an injured actor and he
could barely speak. As the policeman questioned him, there was to
Elizabeth's eye a crucifixion in her husband's face. They wanted to
know if he'd heard anything the night before.

'I can't remember a single thing,' he said quietly.

'We have evidence that two individuals were seen in the vicinity of
Mrs Voyles's flat at around three o'clock in the morning.'

'I didn't hear.'

'Loitering at the gate.'

'I must have been asleep.'

'When were you last outside your property, Professor Flynn?'

'The night before last. I was out on the day of the Ireland rugby
match and—'

'You were drinking?'

'I was picking up a few things . . . and . . . having a drink, yes.'

'In the evening?'

'In the daytime, then in the evening.'

'And where—'

'I was mainly in Caledonian Road. I went into town at one point.'

The officer was taking notes. Elizabeth felt the certainty of something dreadful. It made no sense at all, yet her dread felt grounded in
something totally real.

'Can you tell us the places you visited?'

He tried to name the different pubs. He knew he had ended up in
the Irish theme bar across from the British Library.

'O'Neill's?'

'Yes, that's right.'

'Until what time?'

'I think it was closing . . . I'm not actually sure.'

'And what happened then?'

Elizabeth had never seen him look this way. Not in thirty years of marriage. He was like someone staring past himself. 'I came home. I must have come home. I remember drinking and taking a bottle upstairs. That's all I can say.'

'And what did you do?'

'I went on my laptop.'

The police left, but she knew they'd be back. After they'd gone, Campbell said he thought he'd had the same day twice. Binged for two days. He couldn't recall the details, but things were coming back: the weed, the effects of the different pills. 'Oh God, Liz,' he said later that evening. 'Is this really happening?'

'Can you speak to me about it?' she asked.

He turned with a boy's tears in his eyes.

'It's what we live with,' he said. 'Whose fault is it? Who does the bad things? And this was me. I did this thing.'

She pulled his head onto her shoulder and rocked him.

'I can't believe it, but I made this happen. I'm *accountable*,' he said, sobbing in her arms. 'I don't know any more. I don't.'

That evening, she checked him into the Nightingale Hospital, suffering from depression and possible manic ideations.

Unreality had broken in. She sat at the kitchen table, blind with incomprehension. When Moira arrived in a taxi, she kissed Elizabeth in the hall, put down her bag and went straight to the kettle, shaking her head.

'He wasn't right,' she said. 'All year, he wasn't right.'

They spoke for two hours. They couldn't bear to address the topic directly: whether he'd done it himself or got someone to do it.

'There are sides of Campbell's life I know nothing about,' Elizabeth eventually said. 'I should have been more involved. He needed me.'

'He needed, and needs, more than he himself can understand,' Moira replied. 'And that's been the case since he was a boy, Liz. He was always Mr Capable.'

Elizabeth felt it was all to do with money.

'Finances?'

'Yes. My parents were the same. Never discussed it. They had arrangements to pay for things, and I always thought Campbell wanted—'

'To be in charge of it.'

'Precisely. It was part of his success. But I'm convinced he's somehow got us into real trouble. He was always spending. Daft about tax. Criminal, maybe. And he borrowed, heavily.'

'From where?'

'William Byre.'

'Oh God,' Moira said.

'I suppose I rigorously ignored it. I'm casting about, but maybe it's all related to Mrs Voyles – the money aspect. She wanted paying off – a lot of money, half a million – to move out of the basement, and somehow it got under his skin. As if it wasn't really—'

'About Mrs Voyles.'

'That's right. That's exactly right.'

Moira put her hand over Elizabeth's and rubbed her wedding ring.

'It will all be tangled up,' she said.

'More than we know, Moira. More than we know.'

'But now's not the time.'

Campbell was in the hospital for a week. Elizabeth visited twice. The police came again and took away his computer. Kenzie was in Bath and called to say she wanted to come home.

'Can you explain what happened?' she said.

'They think Daddy did something terrible, darling. So does he. But we don't know. Something on the Internet. He can't be sure, in his present state.'

'Oh, Mummy. Did that boy have anything to do with it – the student?'

'It appears not,' Elizabeth said. 'Though your father said something very odd. I asked him about Milo and he quoted your granny.

Something she said to him in Venice about a corrupt therapist, somebody who duped your grandfather. "He was mugged by a would-be healer" – something like that. That's what Campbell feels happened to him with that boy. I'm sorry, darling. It's awful and he isn't making sense.'

Angus called and told her he felt guilty. He said he'd known Dad wasn't right after they'd last met and that he hadn't done anything to help him. 'I'm in Sweden tonight,' he said. 'Should I cancel the gig and come home?'

'No,' Elizabeth said. 'Let's wait a bit.'

'Did he hire men to beat her up?' he asked.

'I don't know. Her ear was pretty much torn off.'

'Jesus fuck.'

'It isn't him,' she said. 'It isn't him.'


He returned to Thornhill Square on the Monday. He was turned inside out, but very quietly so, and his vulnerability contained an acceptance. He sat on the kitchen sofa with a pad in front of him and a glass of water, waiting to confess.

'I can't be sure about it,' he said. 'But . . . I imagined teaching Mrs Voyles a lesson. She wouldn't stop. I thought my laptop could manage it, in a perfect world. It doesn't make sense yet. Too many holes.'

Elizabeth put a hand to her chest. She felt there was so much riding on the phrase 'in a perfect world', and on that word 'imagined'.

'It was a fantasy,' she said.

'It was something I wanted, yes. To make her stop.'

'Take your time,' Elizabeth said.

'I must own it,' he replied.

The leaves of the ginkgo tree were golden again. Elizabeth was looking down at it and mulling over the particular meaning of 'blackout' when the first journalists arrived. Tipped off: the police must be coming soon. The reporters knocked on the front door and posted notes through the letterbox. They pretended to be friendly and understanding; one of them wrote, 'How does this happen to a civilised man?'

In the afternoon, a van drew up. At first, addled with fear, she thought it was the police, arriving mob-handed. But it was a delivery van. Two smartly overalled men. They explained they had 'a piece' purchased by a Professor Flynn. After they brought it in, Elizabeth signed the slip and then peeled back the bubble wrap to see inside. An extraordinary, delicate cabinet, studded with mother-of-pearl. Even to her eye, it was a significant antique, an embodiment of prosperity way beyond his means.

Her dismay rose to anger.

The remittance slip from the Oscar Graf Gallery was in an envelope taped to the side of the packaging. 'Glasgow Display Cabinet, 1901,' it said. '£78,000 including VAT.'

'Fuck. *Fuck!*'

Campbell was unmoved on the sitting-room sofa, staring at the mantelpiece. Elizabeth came down and gently shook him out of it. 'Tell me everything,' she said. He swallowed hard and squeezed her hand.

'Yes.' He stood up and led her to his study.

'This will come as a shock,' he said.

With a fastidious mixture of deliberation and sorrow, he sat her down in an armchair next to his desk and opened the bottom drawer, taking out Jiffy bag after Jiffy bag, wads of envelopes, some of them open and some still sealed. In each of them were blister packs of pills, baggies of powder or wraps. She could only identify the cannabis. From one envelope, she drew out a sheaf of £50 notes, their pinkness too garish.

'What is this?' she asked.

'The Dark Net,' he said. 'It's where it all started.'

Elizabeth turned over the envelopes. They were addressed to 'Andrew Samson' and came either via a PO box or were sent 'c/o Professor Campbell Flynn' at his university office in Gower Street.

624

'You've been taking all this stuff?'

He only nodded and opened another drawer. There were red letters from HMRC, some ripped in two. Elizabeth took them into her hands and saw figures in the tens of thousands and more. Some of the letters were from debt collection agencies and several were court summonses.

'Oh, Campbell.' She crumpled the letters into her lap. 'We could have dealt with this. We could have solved this together.'

'I know.'

'Why couldn't you speak to me?'

The pupils of his eyes were like full stops, as if he yearned for an ending. He still had the hospital scent, the antiseptic note on his skin. 'Lizzie,' he said.

He had lost everything. She could see from the statements that the effect was crippling, life-changing. She struggled to take it all in, and when she caught her breath, she asked him what had happened to his book advance.

'Gone,' he said.

'But how? You didn't use any of it to pay your taxes?'

He wiped his eyes and stared. 'If I had my laptop here, I could show you,' he said, 'but every penny went on Bitcoin.'

'You spent it on cryptocurrency?'

'All the book money. All the tax money. Everything that was put aside for VAT. Plus I cashed in two life insurance policies. I sold Emily's painting. Everything.'

She looked at his empty desk and all the paper on the floor.

'Okay, but the currency is still there?'

'It would be, and still valuable, even with the drop in price—'

'So, you can get it back?' she said. 'The Bitcoin?'

He shook his head. There was no colour left in his face.

'Not any more,' he said. He told her that on the night before Mrs Voyles was attacked, he believed that he had used one of the coins . . .

625

Elizabeth's body had gone cold. She almost wanted to throw herself at him and hold him, stop him from saying any more.

'. . . I can't really be sure, but after using some of it . . . having *conceived* and *commissioned* what happened . . . downstairs – I panicked. I panicked, Lizzie, and I burned the codes.'

'I don't know what that means.'

'Last year, I set up my Bitcoin wallet with Milo. For security, you invent a seed phrase, twelve random words, and these are the key that allows you to open your wallet and recover what you own.'

'Right,' she said. She could tell by his face. He had sunk himself.

'I wrote the twelve words in the back of a copy of *The Life of Vermeer*.'

'You wrote them in your book?'

'At the back, yes. Twelve words. For safekeeping. I knew I would always find the seed phrase there, at the back of the book sitting on the window ledge. But in the middle of my blackout . . .'

He was struggling with the force of it.

'Twelve words, Campbell? My God, you can remember *thousands*.'

'I believe I burned that copy of the book in the fireplace. They are gone.'

And suddenly, in his eyes, serenity.

Whatever dream he'd had for a long time was now at an end.

'Let's go and sit down,' she said.

In the sitting room, he began shivering.

She hesitated. She was almost relieved. 'Milo, your researcher—' She stroked his arm. 'You needn't cover for him, you know.'

Campbell looked at her with a kind of tolerance. He shook his head in an almost imperceptible way, as if for everyone.

'He had nothing to do with Mrs Voyles. A person can explain a box of matches to you, but it's not their fault when you use them to start a fire.'

She knew he was telling the truth, as he saw it.

'My issues had nothing to do with Milo. He simply showed me the things I asked to be shown, and a bit more.'

'So where is he now?'

He looked at his palms in turn, then rubbed his hands together, as if to give them companionship.

'Milo is done with this family. I suppose I was a kind of experiment. He took himself out of the picture and walked away. He left me to myself. Months ago. He has nothing to do with any of it, and it's all pretty clear, Liz, if they can access it. There will be data and transactions in the run-up to the attack on Mrs Voyles.'

'But how can you be sure if you don't remember?'

'I don't remember it blow-by-blow. But I know I wanted it, and I can see certain moments quite clearly. The wanting Mrs Voyles to stop. Wishing her ill. The burning of the book. I saw it weeks ago on the Dark Net, these men on Genesis Market. I saw that you could pay them in Bitcoin. To "talk to people".'

'This is a nightmare,' she said.

He was nodding next to her. 'Yes. Connections in a dream: you think something, then it happens.'

'In that state, your state, there's a question about how responsible you are.'

He wiped away a tear.

'Nah, Liz,' he said. 'The evidence will be there.'

They sat together a while longer, holding hands in the calm, exhausted terror of it all. She lifted her head.

'Who's Andrew Samson?'

The name on all those packages in his desk.

He nodded up at the painting above the fireplace, the Glasgow children in their school jumpers with their downcast, anxious eyes. 'It's the name of that boy,' he said. 'Joan Eardley's model for the kid in that picture.'

They had a final hour together before a different knock came at the door.

Campbell went down to the hall and put on his shoes.

The officers stepped inside. They read him his rights. He was being arrested on suspicion of having conspired in an assault which resulted in actual bodily harm. The older officer leaned in. 'There is evidence on your computer that digital currency may have been offered as payment to assault the victim. Do you understand?'

'It's what I suspected,' Campbell said.

Elizabeth was panicked. Her throat felt stopped with all the things she hadn't said, the warnings she hadn't heeded, the terrible unknowns.

'This is not right,' she said. 'At the time, my husband was in the middle of an alcohol and drug-related psychosis.' She said the words 'diminished responsibility'. The officer said this would be something to be taken up later.

As they put the handcuffs on him, Campbell turned to her. His eyes were as blue as the day they first met.

'It doesn't matter,' he said. 'It was me. I nearly killed the poor woman.'

# 52 Natural Light

One day in May, at the church of St Roch in Białystok, the coffins had at last arrived from England and a procession of young people came as the two boys were laid to rest in the avenue of graves called Franciszka z Asyżu. They had families, of course, though Jakub had seldom mentioned his to Mrs Krupa. His parents and his sisters led the cortège and their heartbreak was carried in silence. There was no brother. Cecylia stood back, but it was she who was left after the funeral to make sure that the graves were kept tidy. She came every day now, and as spring progressed she found she was busy. She kept a trowel and a fork in a flowerpot by the tree that grew over their plots. She thought of his smile. It wasn't Jakub closed in the dark, she said, it was only his remains, his and Robert's. She would tend to them both. It was too soon for them to have gravestones.

It was warm again. She gave money to the church and was now in a furnished apartment near where her grandmother had lived, keeping the house clean and sweeping the common areas. At Mass every morning, she prayed for her son. The police had found him and he would soon go on trial in London. He would be in jail for a long time and she might never see him again. It was settled: she would pray for Bozydar and ask for God's forgiveness, and she would meet him again, perhaps in another world, when Gosia's child was grown and Cecylia had gone to her rest. Each age will make its own evils, she said. Her own people had suffered, as well as so many others, yet St Jerzy Popiełuszko, one day soon to come, would rain blessings from the right hand of the Lord.

One Friday afternoon, as the wind was picking up, she caught a bus to a street near the university and found her way to the English bookshop. It stood under a block of flats by a main road. The place was busy, people coming and going with boxes. The young man appeared in the café. They had met at the funeral. Cecylia had been so grateful, in the terrible emotion of that day, to meet some of Jakub's friends. She told them only that she had known him for a time in London, and they accepted that and made a fuss of her, as if Mrs Krupa represented the new life that Jakub and Robert had wished for.

'Thank you for your postcard,' Grzegorz said.

She told him it was a treat to speak English. She asked about his days at the bookshop and the new work for the refugees.

'They have been coming across the border,' he said. 'We go to the train station. We are housing as many as we can.'

The young man seemed to have a liking for visitors. She nodded, feeling that everything he said was a necessary expression of their loss. When they'd drunk their coffee, she told him she had taken up enough of his time.

'Are you okay, Mrs Krupa? You don't have to go yet.'

'You remind me so much of him,' she said, wiping her eyes and taking a step back as if to organise herself for an important task.

'Thank you,' he said, taking her hand. 'Jakub was a quiet guy. He was employed as a local gardener. He went to England to get better work and he wanted to stay. He didn't tell us much about London, but I know you tried to help him.'

'May God have mercy,' she said. 'There's something I wanted to give you.' She put her hand into her bag. 'It's something his mother might want, or you, his friends.'

She brought out the card and put it in his hand. The Leicester Railwaymen's Club & Institute.

'Jakub Padanowski. Temporary Member,' Grzegorz read out. He turned the card over in his hands and tears filled his eyes. 'Is that England?'

'It used to be,' she said, and put a hand to his young face.

He had something for her too: the address in Fryderyka Chopina of Jakub's mother. Mrs Krupa put it quickly into the pocket of her coat.

'Go and see her,' Grzegorz said. 'Mothers together.'

When they said goodbye, Mrs Krupa embraced him, sobbing for a moment on his shoulder, then patting his arm, before abruptly turning away and becoming lost in the comforts of the crowd. She reached St Roch as the evening began. The sky was beautiful. She laid fresh flowers on the graves, lit candles in red jars and sat down on the bench opposite to smoke her Karelia Slims.

Gosia called infrequently, and the calls felt empty. She wasn't telling her mother anything about her life, not really. Cecylia felt it was part of her penance that she was now a departed voice in the world of her daughter, and had no right, perhaps, to know the truth of her life. She missed Ben, her grandson, and the very few calls his mother allowed were fleeting and sad, leaving Cecylia more alone than before, home in her city after a long absence, but dwelling in the absence. It was in the hands of the saints now, and she cried for all these young people, gone from her life.

'Hail Mary, full of grace, the Lord is with thee.'

She folded her phone into the pocket of her cardigan. The boys were buried side by side and their candles flickered in the breeze.

Milo was busy that final week. He worked late at the kitchen table, his laptop open and its blue light filling the room. It was a place of such memories for him, having dinner with Zemi and his dad, addressing prejudice and the injustices of history, as they saw it. But now it was nearly done, the plan achieved, the van packed. Just one or two important last tasks. Tomorrow he would be free and could wave goodbye to the flat, the road and the city too.

In the middle of the night, Gosia came down and stood by the table.

'What you doing, babe?' she asked.

He smiled and kissed her stomach.

'A wee bit of social work,' he said.

'Come to bed. There's nothing left to do. We did it.'

'Still buzzing. Just a bit of late-night justice,' he said.

She sleepily took a glass of water and went back upstairs.

He had reached the high point of his expertise. In his mind, it was a sort of miracle, the way all the houses he'd discovered in the tangled digital woods, with their long corridors and their hidden doors, had finally given up their keys. And how, like tonight, he could simultaneously open the locks to reveal the rooms inside. A year ago he couldn't have done it. Determination had brought him here, and luck. Hackers' years are like dog years, and he was an old man now in his T-shirt and shorts.

Helped by hackers in box bedrooms from Hong Kong to Calabasas, he adapted that night a Trojan they had been injecting into Airbnb and eBay, which hacked wealthy accounts and used the funds to book and pay for flats all over Ukraine, rooms nobody would visit, sitting empty and being paid for as the bombs fell. The bug also used unwitting funds to buy items on eBay that didn't exist, sending the money to charities. It was addictive, and Milo continued finessing the pathways and copying the bugs for hours. During breaks, he watched friends in Berlin perform multiple denial-of-service attacks on Russian hotels. They clogged websites with anti-war messages and turned off palace fountains. A top woman in Baltimore said they were working out how to scramble tank signals. There were dissidents too, smart kids from Perm and Kolpashevo and Nizhny Novgorod, disabling the present from within and bleeding toxins from the old systems.

'Might fail,' the Baltimorean said to Milo in a chat room.

'Samuel Beckett,' he wrote back.

She sent thumbs. They all sent thumbs.

At 4 a.m. he opened a new window on his computer and checked that the final payment had been sent to the GoFundMe account of the Eilean Ròin Community Buyout.

Now, he could turn to his final task. He took the bugs he'd been working on and prepared to inject them into a number of bank accounts in different territories, a move that was set to inaugurate a carnival of involuntary benevolence, the installed bots programmed to dial selected phone-in charities, breeding thousands of withdrawals from the bank accounts and emptying the coffers before anything could be done to stop it. Milo ran last checks, making sure his Trojans were veiled, and then he activated them, attaching an army of gremlins to the offshore accounts of the Duke of Kendal, Lord Scullion and the late William Byre. He set it off and then tied his beautiful construction with a bow. He hid the traces, and vanished the moment he closed his laptop.

When he did, he felt Zemi's presence all around him in the silence of the dark kitchen.

'I got there,' he said, wiping his eyes.

Daybreak came at last for the Mangashas.

He watched from his bedroom window as the dark thinned out on Caledonian Road, everything quiet except for the occasional siren, and he thought of Campbell Flynn. Madness. On remand at HMP Pentonville, not ten minutes from his house in Thornhill Square. Milo felt sorry for him: he had taught his professor the basics of the Dark Net and he had gone the way of his own mind, as people do. Milo had no idea that computer realisation would lead where it did – to his own route out, yes, but also to the professor's incarceration, that old woman savaged in a basement. But this was Britain, where the routines of civility and the habits of art are threaded with a history of brutality.

Milo had not been involved in Flynn's actions against his tenant, but he didn't want to risk any accusations now that he was on the cusp of escape. He picked up his phone from the bedside cabinet. Using his thumb to scroll down his address book, he found Professor Flynn's number, his email address, the department website, and with one deft finger he zapped them all. Zeroing in on the phone's memory cache, he dumped all the emails, everything from the professor, all the text messages and everything else, except one very important file concerning Flynn in his Notes app, which he locked with a password.

He could already taste the new air. Gosia was asleep, both arms curved around her belly, and his dad was snoring in the other room. He looked around the empty walls. But the slogans still hung in his mind.

'People are as free as they want to be.'

'You don't have a home until you leave it.'

He slipped downstairs and went outside. He made his way under the bridge and past the old swimming pool, going down the canal to York Way. And then he walked slowly back, thinking of Pharma and Lloyds and Travis, laughing and pushing their way down Copenhagen Street, the boys of yesterday. At Pharma's estate, looking up at the buildings, he imagined sea petrels over the roofs, a scene of light and air, as awaited them all on the Summer Isles. It was settled. The island and its sixteen houses could now be bought by a collective of travelling people, the last million pounds having gone to the GoFundMe account from a private source only hours ago. Milo smiled. He had a temporary cottage. He imagined a golden eagle high over Islington, and he pictured his young family running on a windy beach among the kittiwakes, in a place Zemi understood. It was a dream fighting for reality, a patch of the universe beyond postcodes or the delusions of personal ownership. A phrase had followed him all his life and now its meaning was clear: 'The only secret is to begin.' He would see what they could build, what he could become, in this new place. A partner, a father, a son and a neighbour. Walking on, he hoped for a garden and a small school, and he saw himself at the end of each day in a spotless room at the edge of the sea, alone in the evening in the light of his laptop, reaching out to the future.

Ray was standing by the van when he got back. 'I could murder a coffee,' he said, scratching his grey hair. 'You went on a victory lap?'

'Thinking about Mum. She should be with us today.'

'She'll be waiting up there for us, son. In a way.'

'In all the ways,' Milo said.

The world had made too little space for Zemi, but now Milo had filled it with her – her spirit, her values.

He passed Gosia on the stairs. She wore a floaty dress and sandals and had a bucket and spade she'd saved from her mum's to take with them. 'You're crazy,' Milo said. He stroked her arms and went up to the kitchen to get a drink of water. The cups were in the van, so he drank it from the tap, the last refreshing drink in the old place, and when he looked up he saw the poster pasted above the fridge, the only poster left, a looming ship and the words, 'NO to the Immigration Act of 1971'.

It was around eleven when they left. The last things Milo packed into his rucksack were his laptop and charger. He had a final look round the flat with his dad and was hit by the cold durability of the place, the sense of a life beyond them, beyond Zemi, the walls already crying out for fresh paint and a new kind of noise. 'Everything moves on,' Ray said. He dropped the keys through the letterbox and turned to his son. 'Too late now,' he said. 'What's this mad place called you're taking us to. Eilean Ròin?'

'That's right. Top of the world.'

'And what kind of place is it?'

'Nobody knows,' Milo said. 'We have to invent it.'

He opened the passenger door of the van, kissed Gosia, made sure her seatbelt wasn't tangled and that she had cushions.

They went around the back of Camden, towards the M1. Milo wanted to stop by Primrose Hill for the farewell view.

'Look at that,' he said, as they entered the park, 'the bluebells are mad. Sing us the one about the dusty bluebells.'

'They're late this year,' Ray said. 'We're into May.'

'Just sing us the song.'

'"Tipper-ipper-apper on your left shoulder . . ."'

Ray sang as if the city needed an education in the wonderful things he knew.

'"Follow me to Belfast City, Follow me to Belfast City, I'll be your master."'

When they reached the top, Milo walked forward, into the panorama. 'I won't lie,' he whispered, 'that view is something you won't see anywhere else.' He looked at the tall glass buildings crowding the city. To the right of the London Eye, the moon was a faint disc and it felt peaceful to see it. A flag was flying over the Palace of Westminster, and further away, beyond the Thames and all its secrets and all its bridges, he tried to imagine the streets of South London, the dark nights and the stories that never end. But there was a world beyond that too, out past the visible horizon, where he imagined the far regions of Europe, and flats in the embattled cities that would be empty tonight, though paid for in advance. He took a deep breath, and when he turned away he felt only the breeze and the warmth of the spiritual sun.

Elizabeth may have loved her husband without knowing him. She now asked herself if she had ever really recognised his solitary nature or the collection of fears that had grown so suddenly to fill his life. It was obvious to her that they couldn't stay in Thornhill Square, so she had put the house up for sale, finding a buyer within four days of it being advertised, after which she spent many days staring into the cold fireplace, wondering how it had all happened.

'So, Mrs Voyles will get her money,' Moira said.

'Yes,' Elizabeth replied. 'Apparently, she'll be renting a cottage in Wales. The guy we're selling to works in the City and didn't hesitate to buy her out.'

Mrs Voyles was out of the hospital and living in temporary housing.

'And the criminal injuries people?'

'Yes, she'll get compensation. And so she should.'

'Absolutely,' Moira replied.

But for both of them, it hurt.

They had gone for a walk in Camley Street, the nature park. It was a beautiful, warm King's Cross day at the end of May, with clouds like bales in the sky. They bought coffee and strolled on the wood-chipped paths. Elizabeth could hear the sound of tumbling water from a weir on the Regent's Canal and, on the other side, the Eurostar leaving St Pancras. Both women had been shattered by events, relying on each other for hope, comfort and information. Elizabeth kept rolling back in her mind through all the years of her marriage, looking for clues, the germ of his fury. It had all the signs of a psychotic break, and she tried to see it as the undoing of a decent man, a creative husband and kind father who was tied inside himself to private grief. She thought about the title of that book she'd dismissed, the ghostwritten one, *Why Men Weep in Their Cars*. Why hadn't she seen beyond the seeming joke of it, the bid for quick money, to the cry underneath?

For Moira, the facts had come as a shock. She'd known very little about the pot-smoking and the drinking, the new friends and the cryptocurrency – but of course she knew about William and the stuff with Elizabeth's brother-in-law, and she said she'd recognised that he was upset to be associated with all that. Walking through Camley Park, she told Elizabeth that he had very good legal representation. There would certainly be the question of diminished responsibility, a clean record, other factors.

'To his family, Campbell has always been a happy person,' Elizabeth said, 'until recently. A little alone, perhaps.'

Moira nodded, remembering old things.

'Idealism. It's an affliction, isn't it? You can hurt people with it. When he was young, I worried that anyone who loved art so much might find ordinary life hard, damaged by the constant need for ideal conditions.'

'But to bash in an old woman. To rip off her ear.'

'I know,' Moira said. 'It's unthinkable.'

Elizabeth said all the certainties that had sustained their lives for so long now lay about them in ruins, and she couldn't help feeling that it was all part of some long-awaited judgment.

'Don't say that. Things will get back to normal.'

'But that's just it, Moira. I don't want "normal". We thought we *were* normal. Turns out we were delusional even about our delusions. You're the politician. One day we might look back and say normal was the word we gave to our negligence.'

'You mean, as a society?'

'I mean *as people*.'

Elizabeth dabbed at her nose with a tissue.

'That Vermeer book, it was so full of emptiness,' Elizabeth said, 'and that other book, the anonymous one . . .'

'What do you mean?' Moira asked.

Elizabeth touched her forehead and seemed harassed by the mystery. 'Nobody knows anything about Vermeer's life. That's the point. If you asked whether he'd had a mistress or how he grew up, nobody knew. I encouraged Campbell to write that book because I thought he would grasp the condition.'

'Well, he did,' Moira said. 'It's a wonderful book.'

'Yes, but it's a terribly sad book, in a way. All Campbell understood was the emptiness. Turns out anyone can be a missing person.'

There were moorhens floating through the reeds at Camley Park. They stopped to look at them and watch the schoolchildren, a group with worksheets and pencils. Some of them were dipping nets into the water and pulling out pond life. 'Do you think that student came after Campbell? That he planned it?' Moira asked.

'I can't see how,' Elizabeth said. 'They found each other.'

'He came along at a time when Campbell . . .'

'Needed him.' Elizabeth frowned, reconsidering. 'Though what he actually needed was someone who might reconcile him.' She seemed at her saddest then, and she turned away.

'It's nobody's fault,' Moira said, reaching for her arm. 'Certainly not yours. Not the young man's, either. That would be too easy.'

'I was told he lost his mother. It turns out that Campbell and I met her once, doing charity stuff for the school she taught at.'

'Well,' Moira said after a moment, 'they had something in common. Maybe several things in common.'

Elizabeth said that whatever the sentence, she would bring him home to Suffolk afterwards.

'The press loves an orgy of execration,' she said, 'and we have given them enough cause, what with my brother-in-law . . .'

Moira shook her head, as if words failed her.

'You know he rang me last week?' Elizabeth resumed. 'Spoke about my sister as if she were some sort of escaped filly.'

'She left him? I told him she would.'

'She's on a permanent health retreat with that wellness guy from Suffolk, Fergus, and good luck to her. "You silenced Candy for years," I told him.'

'And what did he say to that?'

'Pure self-pity. "You'll be on to wife number two soon," I said, "and you'll have your heir and everything will go on as before." Except it won't, I said, because people have had enough and there are new energies in the world.'

Moira nodded in agreement, making a wreath of her own thoughts, and linked her arm with Elizabeth's as they walked on.

Children's voices. 'Tadpoles!' one of them shouted, then another: 'Legs, and tails!' Elizabeth pointed to the gasholder flats on the other side of the canal and said that William Byre's son used to live in one of them.

'He's become quite a force within the anti-pollution lobby,' Moira said.

'Good for Zak,' Elizabeth said. 'You've got to admire him.'

She thought of her own two, amid the excited voices. How quickly life was passing.

'Our mum – she was always staring at something we couldn't see,' Moira said. 'And it took years. But I think Campbell eventually saw what it was.'

'Oh, yes?'

'It was shame,' she said. 'It haunted her.'

She paused and clasped a leaf between her fingers.

'Let's walk slowly back,' Elizabeth said. And as she said it, she leaned in and the women embraced each other without speaking – as if, to each of them, the complications of men and other creatures were in sudden abeyance, waiting for solutions that would exist as soon as the past was over.

He didn't object to the stories. He always knew that when his life came tumbling down, it would occur in public. Disasters and triumphs occurred every day, every minute, happening to families, companies, communities and nations, and he had no one else to blame. By accident and by design, Campbell had found himself to be fuelled by the energies of a whole society, both the parts he was born into and the parts he adopted for himself. It all seemed rational, as he sat inside Pentonville prison, as though this particular road had been waiting for him all along, and the loss of himself was the expression of a higher freedom.

He was by himself for safety reasons, and perhaps out of pity for the older man who carried books and seldom came onto the landing. He wasn't expected to be detained for long, but he was considered a flight risk, so the court refused bail and ordered evaluations. Elizabeth arrived in the visitors' hall, a person of character, here to see her husband, whatever the conditions, and to Campbell it felt like they were young again, all the forbidding pressures of status suddenly blown away. He looked at her with love across the octagonal table. 'There's one good thing about humiliation,' he said. 'You're no longer afraid of what people will say.'

Down in the dining hall or up in the showers, the inmates hollered and joked, and he kept to his own table while asking no questions. He thought about numbers, the volume of traffic on the landing, the dispersal of prisoners, and read about the building. He sat in the corner of his cell reflecting on the meaning of observation. The prison was modelled on the idea of the panopticon as conceived by Jeremy Bentham and John Stuart Mill; every human being in the building could be seen from a central point, providing an equality of view. Campbell ruminated on the problem after lights out. It wasn't true, of course: nobody could really see him, but he was inside his perspective box, a place of illusions as well as facts.

Eventually, a letter came in the post. It was addressed to 'Campbell Flynn' and the envelope had been half opened then sealed again with a strip of tape. It was postmarked 'Ullapool' and contained a single piece of paper.

Dear Professor Flynn,
      I've heard a few things. Life won't improve by itself.
      Thanks for the books, the drinks, the conversations, whatever.
      Remember: 'There's nothing like the hand of the people for making a new world from what is demolished.' I won't see you again but I'll think of you.
      Please pay your taxes. Here are your 12 words:
      Townhead, Housecoat, Rabbit, Tulips, Peterhouse, Eagle, Lollipop, Needle, Bookshelves, Elizabeth, Hallway, Celestial.
      Peace,
      Milo

Campbell remained at the window, steeped in light. He held the letter with both hands and stared at the page as he read it over and over again.